Christopher Ransom was born and went to university in Colorado, but moved to New York and then LA with his wife to pursue various careers such as selling ads for media magazines and screenwriting. They then bought a 140-year-old birthing house in Wisconsin, where he wrote this, his first novel.

The Birthing House

CHRISTOPHER RANSOM

SPHERE

First published in Great Britain as a paperback original in 2008 by Sphere

A CIP catalogue record for this book
is available from the British Library.

ISBN 978-0-7515-4171-7

Typeset in Caslon by M Rules
Printed and bound in Great Britain by
Clays Ltd, St Ives plc

Papers used by Sphere are natural recyclable
products made from wood grown in sustainable forests and certified
in accordance with the rules of the Forest Stewardship Council.

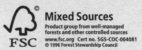

Mixed Sources
Product group from well-managed
forests and other controlled sources
www.fsc.org   Cert no. SGS-COC-004081
© 1996 Forest Stewardship Council

FSC

Sphere
An imprint of
Little, Brown Book Group
100 Victoria Embankment
London EC4Y 0DY

An Hachette Livre UK Company
www.hachettelivre.co.uk

www.littlebrown.co.uk

This tale, concerning mothers and wives
and the men who drive them to darkness,
is for the two strongest women I know . . .

Sandra Ransom

Who told me every day that I could

&

Pia Gandt

Who was there every day while I did

Death borders upon our birth, and our cradle
stands in the grave.

Joseph Hall, English bishop and satirist

1

Conrad Harrison found the last home he would ever know by driving the wrong way out of Chicago with a ghost in his car. When he crossed the Wisconsin line he was lost, too tired to care, and what traveled with him remained invisible and unknown. The wide green medians and fields of plowed fertile soil were relaxing. The road was black and smooth, free of those brain-jarring seams found on concrete highways. The spring thunder and rain moved over him from the side, pummeling the rented gray Dodge in bursts as brief and intense as a car wash. He could have gone on this way until he reached Canada, but an hour or two later there was some traffic and the sign for the Perkins in Janesville, so he exited.

He might have been tired and lost, but he was suddenly hungry, ravenous. Filled with the kind of animal appetite that shuts out all else and goes to work like it needs to prove something. He ordered the country fried steak with three over easy, and when the girl came to take the plate away he said, You know what? Let's do it again.

In between dinners, he picked up the paper the last

guest had left in the booth. He liked to read the classifieds, to see what scraps people were offering, what hope they sought. He fell into the local real estate listings. The photo was black and white, all grainy and pixelated newsprint.

140 yr old Victorian in Black Earth. 4 bdr, 2 bath on 1 acre. 3500 sq. feet. Front parlor, library, orig. woodwork, maple floors, fireplace. Cornish stone foundation. Det 2-car garage. Historic turn-of-the-century birthing house restored to mint. Perfect for family! $225,000. Seller motivated. Call Roddy @ 608-574-8911.

Now lightheaded from all the hash browns and gravy, he swallowed the last of his third cup of coffee and carried his meal ticket to the front counter. He paid with cash and left the girl a twenty for no real reason other than he felt, for the first time in his life, burdened by money. He juggled the page he'd torn from the *Wisconsin State Journal* and powered up his mobile. There were no messages, or maybe they had not come through the regional carrier's towers yet. Or maybe Jo was too busy to call.

The man who answered was polite. Sure, he could show the house as early as nine o'clock tomorrow morning. And did he know how to get to Black Earth?

Conrad said he was pretty sure he'd remember the directions, all the while thinking, What a name for a town. Don't worry, Dad. I'm not far behind.

So maybe he knew there was a ghost traveling with him after all.

2

From the front it appeared modest, a simple vanilla bean Victorian on a street of pleasant others. But later, when he would find himself walking the long slope of backyard alone at night, Conrad Harrison would come to see that its humble if charming façade masked ingenious depths and a height that seemed to grow at night, like Jack's beanstalk. The needle-helmeted dormers, covered front porch, chocolate pillars and squat front door brought to mind a fairy-tale house made for trolls or elves, not city people.

It was not love at first sight, but she made his heart beat faster.

Conrad tried to mask his excitement, if only because that was what you were supposed to do when considering a major purchase. He tried for a moment to imagine Jo's reaction if she were standing here beside him. It looked like the kind of house she was always talking about. Something old, something to redecorate when she was ready to settle down. But she wasn't here beside him now and the realization that he didn't much care what she thought gave him a deviant thrill. The house was like another woman in that way. Looking was just looking, and there was no harm in looking unless looking turned to touching. Or buying.

'Got kids?' Roderick 'call me Roddy' Tabor said, smiling like a man in a milk commercial. Instead of a dairy moustache, Roddy had a badass seventies cop 'stache and wooly sideburns, sans irony. The realtor was tall, very slim and balding. The brown suit and wide, brown tie were priceless. Conrad liked the realtor the minute he'd spotted him behind the desk at the crummy, wood-paneled real estate office down on Decatur Street. Roddy had grown up in Chicago, and they'd talked about city life vs country life for all of the ten or fifteen minutes it took to walk from 'downtown' Black Earth up the broken sidewalk hill to 818 Heritage Street. 'Perfect place to raise some kids. Property taxes are steep, but the schools here are top-notch.'

Conrad cleared his throat. 'No. No kids. Just the two dogs. Both rescues from a shelter in Los Angeles. But they're like our children.' Conrad thought about mentioning the other pets he liked to keep from time to time, the animals that weren't really pets at all, but didn't. You never knew how people were going to react.

'Sure. Young couple. What's the hurry, right?' Roddy turned the key. 'Oh, door's unlocked. Pretty common 'round here.'

Conrad stepped past the realtor and laid his eyes on the first of several living rooms. Actually, he knew they weren't all living rooms. In these Victorians it was

4

parlor-this and sitting room-that. Whatever you called them, they amounted to a lot of space to spread out, play cards, eat, watch TV and entertain friends. They would need new friends.

'I don't go for the song and dance myself,' Roddy said, dropping the keys on the ceramic tile and oak mantle. 'Figure adults know what they like when they see it. Holler if you have any questions.'

'Will do.'

Roddy ambled into the kitchen, helped himself to a glass of water, and stepped out back for a smoke.

Conrad found himself in the dining room, paced off the long maple floorboards, ran his fingers over the pin-striped wallpaper. Not a crack in the plaster walls or a splintering window sill in sight. The doorframes were straight. In the kitchen, the original wooden shelves and pantry drawers were nicked black in many places, aged smooth and full of character. The trim was a clean, buttery shade of toffee. The lines of the house were immaculate. The house felt solid.

But confusing.

Conrad started in the front parlor, then exited through the French doors that opened into the main foyer, making a U-turn back into the dining room and living room. From there he backtracked and took a left into the family room and deeper into the kitchen. Once inside the kitchen, he forgot where the living room was, even though it was just on the other side of the wall. He went up the rear stairs from the kitchen, over one landing, through the library, and down the front stairs (which, despite the beauty of the black maple banister, seemed somehow formal and forbidding, though he couldn't say why), winding through the main floor clueless as to what he had already seen and what was new.

'You'll get used to it,' Roddy said, startling him. 'Ever seen a house with servants' stairs?'

'No, not really.' Conrad followed Roddy through the family room.

Roddy pointed to the faded hinge patterns on the doorframe at the base of the stairs and mouth of the kitchen. 'See that?'

'There was a door.'

'Yep. And another one here.' Roddy tapped the door-frame at the kitchen's front entrance. 'This way, you have two doors here, the help stays in the kitchen, out of sight from the proper company while you're warming your feet by the fire. When dinner has been served and the good doctor is sipping his brandy, the maidens duck up the servants' stairs here—'

Before Conrad could pursue the doctor reference, Roddy dashed up the servants' stairs. Conrad followed at a less eager pace. When he hit the landing, Roddy made a sweeping gesture into the smallest bedroom.

'Goodnight, you princes of Maine, you kings of New England,' Roddy said. 'And *voilà*. Servants are out of sight for the night. Let the party continue.'

'*Cider House Rules*. Nice.'

'That's right,' Roddy beamed. 'You're a movie guy.'

'Not really.' Conrad had mentioned Los Angeles and the screenwriting thing, as if that still mattered to him or ever had. 'I was in sales. Did some consulting from home. We had friends in the business. The writing was just something to do.'

'Oh? You cash in your chips?'

'Ha, yeah, no.' He'd never admit as much in Los Angeles, but out here, standing next to this stranger, Conrad decided to skip the embellishment for a change. 'A guy I knew used to hire me for cheap rewrites, but I never sold any material. Nothing original. I was laid off from a software firm. Been working in a bookstore until my wife gets another promotion. I don't really know what I'm doing, actually.'

Was Conrad imagining it, or did Roddy's smile slacken a bit on that one? Maybe not too smart, mentioning the layoff – probably just raised a red flag on the financing.

'Uh-huh, and what does your wife do?'

Conrad hesitated. 'You know, Roddy, I don't know what she does any more. I mean, I know she works for a company that sells pharmaceuticals, or consults with pharmaceutical companies. Or medical supplies. I think she's something between a sales manager and a project manager. She travels a lot, that I do know.'

'Sounds promising.' The realtor seemed sorry he'd asked.

The bedroom was perhaps eight feet by six, with two small windows. Small enough for a child's twin bed and a trunk full of clothes, no more. It seemed cruel.

Conrad nodded. 'Where's the master?'

They continued through the library and around the black maple banister in a sort of zigzagging shuffle that led into a T-shaped hall branching to three bedrooms. The master was just a regular bedroom, not much larger than the other two spare rooms, but three times the size of Tiny Tim's room in the back.

'This is the master,' Conrad said, failing to conceal his disappointment.

'Old houses, my friend,' Roddy said. 'Back then people didn't use their bedroom for a whole lot. Not like now where you got your flat screen, your Jacuzzi, your orbital whattya call it, one of them gerbil wheels.'

'Not very LA,' Conrad offered.

'Bingo.'

'Besides,' Conrad said, taking over the pitch. 'We have a library. What do we need a TV for?'

'There you go. I'll give you some time up here, then we should grab some lunch before the saloon closes.'

'No problem. I'll be down in a few.'

'We're gonna feed you some fine Wisconsin cuisine, Mr Harrison.' Roddy clomped down the front stairs.

Conrad poked his nose into the first of the remaining two bedrooms. Unremarkable, but a perfect size for Jo's office, with a small window overlooking the rolling back-yard.

He turned to the bedroom nearest the master. The knob wiggled loosely but he had to knee the wooden door from the frame to pop it free. Before it could swing all the way in, a short girl-woman with white hair scurried out, bumping his shoulder as she slipped by. Before he could get a bead on her, she swooped around the banister and trotted down the front stairs.

'Whoa, hey.' Conrad tasted a wash of adrenaline like a nine-volt battery pressed to his tongue.

'Sorry 'bout that,' she said in a flat, nasal tone, her face lowered even as she hit the foyer and exited through the front door.

White jeans or painter's pants. A blue pocket tee over a pudgy midriff. Small feet shod with chunky black skate shoes bearing a single pink stripe. Didn't get a look at her face, but her arm skin was white with white hairs standing up in a line to her wrist – he'd noticed that much. The scent of vanilla filled his nostrils, reminded him of a birthday cake shaped and decorated as a snowman, the one his mother had baked for his third birthday.

'It's okay,' he said to the empty foyer.

Another buyer? A lingering daughter sent to pick up the rest of her things after the move? But she hadn't been carrying anything on the way out, had she? No box of sweaters. No lamp or framed art left behind by the movers. Huh. Must be just one of those chance encounters made possible by a house between occupants.

He turned back to the bedroom she'd just exited. It was decent size, maybe fourteen by sixteen. Two windows with bright red shades and black beaded tassels like something out of a western whorehouse. Deep pile the color of moist moss, didn't match. No furniture. But the same scent of vanilla was here, stronger, with something herbal hanging beneath it. From the girl, or just the smell of the house? He felt a pang of regret like walking in on someone in the bathroom. Like if he'd been here a minute earlier he would have caught her in the middle of . . . what?

Conrad backed out of the room and left the door open. He wondered if Roddy had seen her go. He'd ask about her later, after he'd studied the library.

The library. The house had a library.

'Hell, yeah,' he said, entering a patch of sun pouring through a street-facing picture window. But even while he ran his fingers over the ornately carved fronts of the pine shelves, his mind returned to the girl. She reminded him of someone, but he couldn't put his finger on whom. That didn't make sense, though, did it? He hadn't really seen her face. Maybe the shape of her body, something about the way she'd trotted down the stairs. Like a girl trying to get out before her parents could call her back and remind her of her curfew.

The house was nice, if somewhat anti-climactic. What makes this house a birthing house? What makes any house a birthing house, besides the fact that probably a lot of babies had been born under her roof? It didn't feel like some sort of makeshift hospital ward or shelter where you'd have one large room with a bunch of beds, their occupants coughing on top of each other. It was just a house. So what if a doctor used to live here. Birth was life, life was good. Right?

Children. The relentless question childless married couples are bombarded with pretty much non-stop after age thirty.

Is that what this was about? The way Roddy looked at you when he realized you were eyeballing a four-bedroom house with nothing but a wife and a couple of pound mutts in tow. If not to start a family, what exactly are you hoping to do here? Do you really want to move to the middle of nowhere? Sure, Los Angeles is crowded, traffic makes you homicidal, the air is a fucking smokestack, you never use the ocean, and Jo's job is shit. But at least there's stuff to do there. Movies, hiking, gallery parties, the best tacos in the world. Women. Ungodly women everywhere you turned. Enough to make you groan just walking down the street. A city was a space to live tightly, then stretch out your career, your lunches. A place to play around, get involved with strangers, make deals behind your employer's back, hide.

It was killing them, the City of Angels. He knew it was only a matter of time. It was too easy to watch five years of your life go by. People thirty, forty years old still living in apartments and driving leased BMWs, trying to hit something big. Too many casual friendships, too much need. Maybe just too many choices.

Jo's parents were retired – mom in Phoenix, the old man splitting time between Roxbury and London. She wasn't any closer to them emotionally than geographically. Flying back to Connecticut for Christmas every year had become every other year, and then every third or fourth. Jo was a Wi-Fi wife, always working from home, hotels, airports. She was too busy for family. What did she care where they lived?

Conrad's family was Jo and the dogs. Simpler now.

This was doable.

The house was warm. The smell was in him. Conrad's

blood churned and his pulse escalated. The library seemed somehow familiar and foreign, a place he'd come back to after a decade of forgetting. A draft brought the clean, wild scents of nettle and lavender, overpowering the vanilla scent from the girl – *forget about the girl, there was no girl* – and he was not aware of the erection forming under his black Lucky Brand dungarees, only of the titillating possibility of a new environment, of new hope. Maybe even a whole new life.

Call Jo, talk things over. Stay a few days, kick around the town.

He dialed her mobile, got only silence. He looked at his phone. There were no signal bars. Maybe the house or the big tree out front. Or maybe the whole town was a black spot.

Didn't matter. That was just fear trying to slow him down. And there was another, deeper voice drowning out the fear. He did not recognize it, and it did not have a name, though in time both of those things would change. It came from the house as much as it came from his head or his heart. It was buried beneath years of stone, and it had been buried on purpose.

This is a new beginning, it said. *This is your only hope. To save the family. It is our birthing house, and we deserve to be born.*

He had no idea what the words meant, but they felt true.

When he turned, Roddy was standing at the library's rear entrance.

Conrad nodded. 'We'll take it.'

'You wanna call your wife, talk it over?'

'She trusts me,' he said. 'And this feels like home.'

'Boy, I guess she must. You have some financing arranged? I can throw you a name if you want someone local. Real honest guy down at Farmer's—'

'Not necessary.' Conrad pulled out his wallet, removed and unfolded the little slip of paper. 'No loans, Roddy. Just point me to a bank, give me a couple days to clear this.'

Conrad held the check out, displaying the insurance company's logo in some sort of hope that he wouldn't have to explain the rest.

Roddy took a step closer and frowned. 'Jesus, son. That's a big check.'

'Is it?' Conrad guessed five hundred thousand dollars was a lot. Not specific, though. Not a sum calculated by tables and software. This was the kind of round figure that suggested payoff. Considering the source it seemed insignificant.

'Your last house burn down or something?'

Conrad looked at Roddy. He hadn't told anybody since he'd gotten the call a week ago. Jo had been in Atlanta. He told her what had happened, of course, but he hadn't known how it would end. She offered to go with him, cancel her trip. He said no, he'd be fine. The man from Builder's Trust Nationwide had been there at St Anthony's, anxious to close the matter and avoid litigation, which Conrad had no interest in pursuing. He hadn't even recognized the man in the bed until the very end, when it was like watching the man fall asleep the

13

way he had more than twenty years ago. Even recognizing that didn't change anything.

'Construction accident,' Conrad said.

Roddy reared back and looked Conrad over as if he'd missed something obvious, perhaps a limp or a facial tic that would bespeak brain trauma.

'My father was an electrician.'

'Oh. Oh, jeez.' Roddy was nodding. Then he stopped and ran one palm over his mouth. Conrad could see him putting it together. Living in Los Angeles. Insurance money. Got lost on the way back from Chicago. Erratic behavior, jumping into a new deal. When he spoke again, the realtor's voice was quiet. 'Was it . . . recent?'

'Seven days ago.'

Roddy visibly twitched at that. 'I'm very sorry, Conrad. You must be—'

'Don't worry about it.' Conrad crossed the room and patted Roddy on the shoulder as he went by, suddenly wishing to be out of the library, out of town, back on the road.

Roddy caught his arm and held him back. The big realtor's grip was gentle, but it stopped Conrad and made him look up.

'Hey. Nothing would make me happier than to sell you a house today. But I wouldn't be doing my job unless I asked. I can sit on the property. You want to maybe take some time on this?'

'I appreciate that.' Conrad looked out the picture window facing the street and the enormous tree blocking the view. 'Dad traveled a lot for work. Sometimes out of state. Then one time he didn't come back. Haven't seen him since I was six.' He turned back to Roddy. 'Hey, what say we just pretend I won the lottery or something, huh?'

Roddy did not respond.

The moment stretched out and Conrad imagined Roddy suddenly grabbing him by the arm and paddling him over one knee. He burst into uneasy titters. That seemed to help. Roddy grinned and offered his hand. Conrad shook it and held it longer than usual.

'This is a fine town full of nice people, Conrad. You and your wife are gonna make a good life here.'

'Thanks, Roddy. Thank you for your help.' Shit. Now Conrad did feel like crying, but that was just gratitude, not grief. He swallowed it down.

'You hungry?'

'Starving. You?'

Roddy slapped his belly. 'My man, I love to eat.'

They went to a lunch of the locally renowned Cornish pasty stuffed with cubed beef, potatoes, onions, and rutabaga. The miners' dish was hard and salty, even with the cocktail sauce you were supposed to splash all over it. But Conrad was so hungry after knocking back the first three bottles of Spotted Cow he gobbled his lunch down and forgot to ask Roddy about the doctor, the girl or any other player concerning the history of the birthing house.

3

With its tiled roof, yellow stucco façade and rainbow of bricks that went up over the porch, the house Joanna Harrison had rented three years earlier should have been easy to love. It was a 1940s bungalow on a quiet street in Culver City, three blocks from industrial compounds, three blocks from the Sony lot and only one block from Washington Boulevard's diners, art galleries and coffee shops. Conrad's windfall notwithstanding, they'd be priced out of the rent in another six months and forget about qualifying for the mortgage – they'd already tried, but the landlord was asking $670,000 and 20 per cent cash down. She'd decorated the house as if they had bought it, but to Conrad it had never felt like home. Just another temporary stop until they found the next thing.

In the backyard was a tall avocado tree that never produced edible fruit. He could always see them up there, ripening in the sun, until one day they dried out and fell, too young and hard or desiccated beyond consumption. He knew it was the landlord's job, but he took the tree's ill health personally. He felt he should be up on a ladder, pruning or doing something more so that it might yield real fruit, but he never got around to learning exactly what.

It was just past 9 a.m. on a Tuesday when he dropped off the rental and the taxi delivered him from LAX. Her silver Volvo wagon was sitting in the driveway. So, sick or just running late, Jo was home. Good. Maybe she'd take the entire day off. He could make her her favorite omelet (red peppers and Swiss, with a dash of olive oil) and they could roll around in bed all day, open the windows and fuck the stress away the way they used to cure their hangovers.

He moved through the living room and saw the wine bottles on the coffee table. Cigarette butts mashed into the congealed cheese on the pizza box. Candles burned down. Allison must have come over, Jo's divorced friend with the augmented breasts and the little travel agency over in the Marina specializing in Japan. They liked to get into the wine and talk about their relationships, a once or twice a month habit Conrad dreaded not so much for the mess they always left but because he didn't think Jo had much to learn from a woman who needed plastic tits to feel wanted.

Alice and Luther *click-click-clicked* in from the bedroom, all sleepy and stiff-jointed, yawning their greetings while their tails wagged with no real enthusiasm. Alice was the brindle, her coat like that of a chocolate tiger. Luther was splotched black and white like a cow. Fifty pounds apiece, rescue muscle turned chubby and about as scary as your average golden retriever. He bent and petted them and murmured in their ears.

17

He shuffled into the bedroom. Jo was sleeping on top of the spread, wearing his favorite vintage Sebadoh tee and her black lace panties, her bare feet a little dirty, her mouth open.

Ah, beautiful wife. Even in her morning state. She was a heavy sleeper, a heavy lot of things. Worker, drinker, emoter, lover. During periods of stress, she was always moist. Her eyes, nose, mouth and loins watered up with her moods. She had irritable bowel syndrome from the work anxiety and rushed dietary choices. If she didn't have a cold, she had allergies. If she wasn't seething, she was lusting, and not always for sex, not always for him. In truth, she frightened him. He liked this about her; felt she kept him from becoming a snail in the great lawn of Los Angeles. If he was the snail, she was the nautilus. Curled around herself on the bed, even now, waiting for him to crawl inside.

There was a click of door and creak of hinge in the hall behind him. Conrad turned and saw his friend, their friend, Jake Adams, standing there in those great shredded surfer-boy jeans Jake always seemed to wear, unbuttoned at the navel. Jake was an actor who'd been bumming around Los Angeles for a decade, taking bit parts in indies and the occasional episode of one failing sitcom or another, always treading water and never really making it. He was not wearing shoes, socks or shirt, and Conrad thought of telling him *No Service*.

'Whoa, hey, 'Rad,' Jake said, scratching his unshaven neck.

Jo sat up as if he'd yelled her name.

Conrad looked at Jo and then back at Jake. His next thought was, *If this motherfucker came on my Sebadoh, I'll break his head open.*

Jake wiped one corner of his mouth and bit his pinky nail. Jake's lips were chapped raw. His eyes were red, alert.

Are we up to coke now, Jo?

'Go.'

Jake pointed and leaned toward the bedroom as if asking permission to retrieve the rest of his clothes, but Conrad just shook his head, once. Jake blew air from his cheeks and then padded through the living room. Conrad kept his nose turned up and eyes closed until he heard the front door shut, and it was almost inaudible when it did.

When he turned back to Jo she was staring at him, flushed, her lower lip quivering.

'It's over,' he said.

The color drained away. She didn't know the lyrics, but she knew the tune.

He patted around for it, reached into his pocket. He handed her the MLS printout Roddy had given him. There were six photos, in color. The house from the front, the sprawling backyard, the front parlor, master, full bath and library.

She unfolded the paper, turned it sideways. She looked up, her whole face a question mark.

'I signed the papers two days ago. Offer accepted.'

She was trying to understand what was left for her to negotiate, to explain.

'My father bought that for us.'

Her expression crumpled and she coughed. He almost asked her if she was okay, but she started to cry and he was glad for that.

'I called you.' A heaving breath. 'You should have let me come.' A ghastly inhalation. 'Conrad, I'm so-so-so—'

'No. No going back. Not so much as one fucking minute. Start packing if you want to come. Otherwise leave the dogs and get out.'

He went to the kitchen and grabbed a trash bag from under the sink. His fingers ripped through the plastic and he shook it open like a parachute. He grabbed the nearest thing – the toaster, fuck the toaster, they hadn't made toast in years – and threw it in the bag so that it clanged deafeningly on the floor. You had to start by throwing a lot out. It made the packing go faster, the move a clean getaway.

4

They were in the house a week before it came for him.

Joanna Harrison was dozing on the couch in the TV room while her husband stood on the deck, breathing through a sweet clove cigarette that burned his throat and floated a candy cloud above his empty thoughts. The cigarette was the kind found on the back covers of men's magazines, the smoke of wannabes. What Conrad wanted to be this night was content, and, for a few more minutes of this vanishing sunset hour, he was.

Content equally with himself and his lot: a full acre of sloping lawn, century-old maple and black walnut trees, and a garden as large as a swimming pool, its aged gray gate roped with grape vines. Raspberry and clover grew thick in the shade of the shaggy pines still moist with the day's sweet rain.

He heard running water and looked through the window into the kitchen. Her blurry, sleepy-slouched shape hovered for a moment, probably filling a glass to take to bed. He waved to her. She either did not see him or was too tired to wave back. The shape faded . . . back into the house.

21

He wanted to follow her, but he waited. Let her brush and floss, finish with a shot of the orange Listerine before she turned back the freshly laundered Egyptian cotton. You can't rush these things. These are delicate times. Eyes closed, he could almost see her stretched out in one of her tank tops and cotton boy-cut underwear, a big girl-woman reading another marketing book he always said were made for people on planes. She must be happy here. Otherwise, she would be cleaning and planning and avoiding bedtime.

Summer had arrived early. The house was muggy. He wondered if she would be warm enough to go without covers, but cool enough to allow his touch.

He had been shocked to discover that he wanted her more now. He was still madder than hell about the entire stupid scene and all its implications, its mysteries. But he knew the balance of things and how he'd not been holding up his share of them was half the problem. Maybe more than half. She'd almost slipped away. Even before that nasty little homecoming it had been months, and since the fresh start (that was how he thought of it, but never named it as such, not aloud) he'd been watching for signs. If Luther and Alice were in their crates, that was one sign. If she had showered that was yet another, though never a binding one. None of the signs were binding, which added suspense to the marriage and kept his hopes in a perpetual swing from boyish curiosity on one side to blood-stewing resentment on the other.

He walked up the deck steps to the wooden walkway,

into the mudroom. He climbed stairs (the servants' stairs off the kitchen, not the front stairs with the black maple banister, which for some reason he had been avoiding since the move) and felt the weight of the day in his bones.

By the time he finished brushing his teeth he was tired the way only people who have unpacked 90 per cent of their possessions in a single day can be tired. His mind was empty, his muscles what his mom said his father used to call labor-fucked, the old man's way of suggesting that work is its own reward.

I'm sorry, Dad –

Work. He knew his hands still worked for her. He thought she liked his hands better than just about every other part of him. He no longer relied on his appearance as the catalyst, didn't know many men married more than a few years who did. He knew he wasn't a Jake. At thirty he was what divorced female bartenders had from time to time called cute, no longer handsome, if he ever had been. He felt remarkably average. He had acquired a belly, but the move had already burned that down from a 36 to a 34. With the yard work he'd be down to a 32 – his high-school Levi's size – by the end of June. Jo always said she liked his laugh lines, the spokes radiating from what his mother used to call his wily eyes. Wily used to be enough, but now he was just grateful for a second chance. He could live with average – so long as he could still seduce her.

Conrad wound his way through the back hall, making

the S-turn through the library, into the front hallway. The creaking floorboards were a new sound, allowing him to birth one final clear thought for the day.

This is a healing place. This is home.

Conrad waded into the moonlight pooling on the new queen-sized bed – another purchase, this one more deserved – he'd made without her input. The ceiling fan was whirring, the dogs were curled into their crates on the floor, and Jo was waiting for him on top of the new sheets. She was without a top, wearing only loose fitting boxers (his), which were somehow better than if she were naked. That she had gone halfway without prematurely forfeiting the under garment was a gesture that made him feel understood. The arc of her hips rose off the bed like the fender of a Jaguar and his blood awakened.

With his blood, his hopes.

No longer content, Conrad stretched out, not caring what funny tent shape his penis made as it unfolded like a miniature welcome banner. He rolled to one side, facing her. She smelled of earth and lavender and something otherwise herbal – new scents for her in this new place. Her belly was nearly flat except for the smallest of rolls just above the waistband, and he loved this, too. He called it her little *chile relleno* and she would slap him, but it didn't bother her, not really. Her hips were womanly wide, but with her height she remained sleek, especially when prone, like now. She stood a little over six feet to his five-nine. His fingers grazed her fine brown navel hairs. Her eyes gleamed under heavy lids, glassy and black as mountain ponds at midnight.

It was a beginning, and he was a man who loved beginnings more than middles or endings.

'Come,' Jo said. Or maybe *Con*, half of his name.

'Hm?'

'. . . not ready.'

'Not what?' His hand found the elastic rim of her waistband, then moved into the open front of his boxer shorts on her.

'. . . about behbee,' she murmured.

'What, Baby?'

Not baby. Upper case, Baby. A nickname he used.

'. . . owin me the behbee . . . be-ah-eye,' she mumbled, which sounded like *was going to be all right*.

'Of course,' he said, like it was his idea too. He had no idea.

'. . . bee woul' go a father.'

We should go farther.

He pushed one, then two fingers lower to her mound, but her legs were crossed and he swerved off course, touching only her thigh. Just her thigh, but soft was soft and his excitement ratcheted up another notch.

'—not ready,' she squeaked, rolling away.

Shit. Might not have been sleeping before, but was now. Snoring, too. Weird, he thought. Had she done this before? With the eyes open and the talking?

Should he let her sleep or try one more time?

Yes . . . no. He kissed her goodnight and rolled on his back, allowing the fan to push warm summer air over his fading, obedient hard-on. His mind dropped into that lower gear, the one that is not yet sleep but somehow dreaming already.

In the half-dream he was in the house, beside her, finding the wetness and sliding in not for the first time but as if they had been moving this way for minutes or an hour. He was all corded muscle and arched away, feeling her soak him in her own undulations. The movement was soothing, almost non-sexual, like being rocked in a crib.

Her grip on him strengthened and clenched, pushing back with legs and ass, drawing his ejaculate out in a sudden burst that ended too quickly, leaving him weak and sleepy all over again.

Drifting . . .

Until the dream, the same one or some new post-coital version, was split by the sound of crying. His body twitched itself awake, and he knew these were not Jo's tears. This was the noise a newborn makes after sucking in its first violent breath as it enters this violent world. It was a sound that had skipped mewling and launched straight into wailing, and it was coming from behind a wall or far away.

Faintly, under the baby's hacking shriek, there arose another sound. This one *did* sound like a woman, and he imagined the infant's mother, or the midwife, perhaps. This older cry in the dark was a trailing scream, as if something was pulling her away from her child and down a long corridor that narrowed to nothing.

Panicked, he rolled over to shake Jo – *why hasn't she woken up and grabbed me?* – and felt the cool stirring of air as she lifted off the bed. He could see only blackness, and with the drone of the fan he could not hear her feet padding on the wood floor. A flash of her silhouette in the doorway left a retinal echo, but the room was too dark to grasp any details. If he saw her at all, she was gone now.

To the bathroom, he thought. There she goes, carrying my seed. The semi-sleep-molestation and abrupt ending made him wince with guilt, but he did not seek her out in the ensuing silence. Exhausted from the day of unpacking (and tossed dream sex), Conrad decided the crying was but a fragment of the dream, a lingering audible planted by her words.

'. . . the behbee, the behbee . . .'

The crying returned once, quieter and farther away, until like a passing thunderstorm it faded to nothing.

He hovered on the edge of sleep.

Something's wrong.

He sat up and rubbed his eyes. She had not returned.

'Jo?'

She did not answer.

'Jo,' he said, louder. 'Baby, you okay?'

His eyes adjusted to the dark. The dogs were standing at the master bedroom door facing the hall, whining, tails stiff like the hairs on their shoulders. Conrad flattened his body and counted to ten. It's rational, he told himself. When something so unexplainable and real (the dogs made it real) as a crying baby in your childless home wakes you, it is normal to ignore it and go back to sleep. So back he went, as deep as a man can go, until he forgot all about the crying sounds and her cold departure, her absolute absence. He did not think again about the sleep-slouched shape he'd glimpsed through the window, fading into the house.

Even when, in the morning, waking to a half-empty bed, he padded downstairs and found her where he'd left her before he stepped out for a smoke at dusk, sleeping on the sofa.

Alone.

5

Well, not really alone. The dogs looked up at him but did not abandon their mistress. Jo was curled around a body pillow, arms above her head, eyes open but unmoving.

'Morning, kids,' he said. 'Morning, Mommy.'

Jo blinked and her mantis arms folded down. 'Coffee?'

After waiting for the pot to fill, Conrad brought her a cup the way she liked it – strong, with milk and a heap of non-dairy creamer. Had to have it both ways, did his wife.

She sat up and accepted the mug, leering at him over the steaming brew. 'Are you mad at me?'

'Why would I be?' He was thinking he should have made iced tea.

'I fell asleep on the couch.'

Conrad shrugged. 'Waiting makes it better, right?'

'We've been waiting a long time. You must be going out of your mind.'

'Yeah, it's funny. I think the move sort of tapped me out. All this work. It's good for us. I feel good.'

Jo sipped her coffee, unable or unwilling to pursue the

29

topic of what was good for them now. He guessed she was going to do the safe thing and wait for him to bring it up, and that was fine. He could postpone that forever.

'So.' He heard a wet lapping sound and looked at the dogs. Luther was licking the small flap of skin where his balls used to be. 'What's on deck today?'

'I thought I'd do the unthinkable and go to Wal-Mart. We need trashcans, sponges. House stuff.'

'I have a little project going in the garage. Mind if I stay here?'

'Oh, yeah. I keep forgetting we have a garage.'

'The doors don't work. It's a mess.'

'Are you turning over a new leaf, becoming a handyman?'

'Not really,' he said. 'It's kind of a surprise, something I wanted to do with a little of the money left over. So don't go in there for a few days, 'kay?'

'Ooh, a surprise.' Jo studied him a bit, then lost interest. 'When I get back I think I'll tackle the garden, get my hands dirty.'

'Save some energy for me.' He offered a lame and hopeful smile.

'Not so tapped out, after all.' She slapped him on the ass and went up to change.

He had knocked down all but two book boxes forming the massive pyramid in the library when the phone rang. Her voice echoed up the servants' stairs, excited.

'Oh, hi! Yes, we're great. Everything is just beautiful.' A long pause ensued. Jo punctuated the beats with a series of 'Uh-huhs'. His stomach lurched when he heard her say, 'Donna! Sudden is right.' And then in a lower voice, 'Of course I'm interested.'

Donna was Donna Tangelo, Jo's headhunter. Calling from LA, already.

Conrad folded up more boxes and continued his eavesdropping for another five minutes.

'Yes, Donna, we'll talk it over and I'll call you back tomorrow, I promise. Thanks for thinking of me.'

Before he could ask what the hell that was all about, Jo bounded up the stairs and announced, 'I'm hopping in the shower, honey.'

He flexed his mouth for another thirty seconds, turned away from the closed bathroom door and went to the kitchen for a beer to celebrate the completion of the unpacking. It was the time a cold beer tasted best, especially a Coors Light on a hot day.

Upstairs the shower stopped hissing. He thought about her up there, covered with nothing more than water droplets in the humid afternoon. She would apply lotion to every inch of her skin and then dress quickly, throwing her hair into a ponytail before it could dry. The window to spontaneous post-shower sex narrowed with the age of the marriage. He did not want to lose her to another job that made her a basket of stress, but running up there with a boner wasn't going to change that.

Ah well, there was the cold beer.

They were eating pizza over the little two-top, a rusted wrought-iron thing they had purchased at the Rose Bowl

31

Flea Market for twenty dollars and decided to call quaint. After a month of pretending school was out for the summer, the prospect of yet more change lent the meal a first-date feel. He was alarmed by how difficult it was to read his wife as she set her pizza slice down, eyeing him cautiously.

And they're off!

'So, you think I should take it?'

'It's very flattering.' He could tell she wanted to take it, so he spoke slowly, carefully. 'Maybe a little soon? Like maybe you want to keep your options open before you jump back in?'

'Yeah, no, I love it here, sweetie,' she said. 'I really do.'

'So?'

'Well, if I took this, we wouldn't have to touch our new little nest egg.'

'So it's purely a money thing?' The old sales routine: ask questions, put them in a box. Yes or no. Shut down and close.

'No, but there's less than we thought,' she said, her face tightening. 'Of my share, anyway. I took what you gave me and paid off the rest of our debts.'

Conrad set his pizza slice down on the paper plate and patted his lips with a paper towel. 'And?'

Up until the insurance from the accident, Conrad's income from the bookstore and various dubious writing assignments had been so small Jo had handled all of their finances except for pocket money and a few small bills: DirectTV, his cell phone, the lone credit card in his name only with its laughable $700 credit limit. After he paid cash for the new house, he'd given Jo half of the remaining two hundred and change to pay off her MBA ($43,000) and told her to 'Set up some IRAs or something.'

'And we have to be careful now.'

Then she explained exactly how fragile their new little nest egg was.

Another twelve thousand went to her father, who'd loaned them the moving and deposit money on the LA property. Somehow Conrad had managed to forget about this. Another four thousand for the movers to get out. It had only cost sixteen hundred to move from Denver to Los Angeles, but that had been metro to metro. LA to the middle of Buttfuck, Egypt, or at least Black Earth, Wisconsin, cost a lot more because 'there aren't a lot of Cheeseheads heading west,' she said, and Conrad laughed. In pain.

'There were other debts,' she said.

'*Other* other debts?' He really had no idea. He'd always assumed the bulk of their lifestyle, furnishings and vacations had come straight from Jo's income, which had been north of eighty thousand last time he'd asked.

'The credit cards were pretty bad.' She winced.

'How bad?'

'Thirty-four thousand.'

He winced back. 'We had thirty-four thousand dollars in credit card debt?' He could not keep his voice from rising. 'For what?'

She sighed. 'Conrad, I was pretty much paying for

everything. Rent was twenty-two hundred alone. Utilities, the cars.'

'I sold my Maxima a year ago.'

'I know, honey, but you were upside down on the equity by almost three thousand.'

'Still, thirty-four thousand? Jo, Baby, c'mon! Maybe ten thousand went to furniture and stuff, but—'

'I wanted to have nice things, okay? I wasn't working my ass off to live in an empty house. Your TV was two thousand.'

'Jesus! If I had known—'

'Conrad, stop. I wanted to get you something special for your birthday. Don't be difficult.'

'Is that—' He tilted his beer and suckled. 'Shit.'

'Need another beer, honey?'

'Yes, please.'

She fetched him one. She knew this was harder for him than it was for her.

'Thanks, Baby.'

'Where were we?'

'I was about to ask, is that all?'

She patted his hand. 'And I was about to say in a hesitant tone, well, not exactly. I took a pay cut a year ago.'

'A year ago.'

Jesus, wasn't this something you talked about with your husband, even when you kept separate checkbooks?

'David sat me down and asked me if I liked my job. I lied and said yes.' David Donaldson was the VP of Sales at her former company, PrimaPro Pharmaceuticals. Jo'd called it mind-destroyingly boring work for a merciless boss, but it paid well. Or had paid well. 'He said I was talented and worked hard, but he couldn't really afford a director of marketing and another for sales, that whole bullshit spiel. "We're a sales firm, not a marketing firm." Like it was my fault he hired me before the class action bullshit tanked the stock.'

'Jo, why didn't you tell me?'

'Oh, you didn't really want to hear about it. I don't blame you.'

'I did too want to hear about it.'

'Conrad Harrison. You'd just gotten laid off. I was scared. And you were never home. Nights at the bookstore while I worked days. We hardly ever saw each other. That was the deal we made until something better came up. I understood that. Now we have to pay for it. Can we leave it at that?'

He stared at her, unsure who was to blame.

'We carved that whole life out and it wasn't easy to cut back. I loved that house. I wanted to buy it—'

'We never could have afforded it. Or did you really want to stay in LA for another five years?' He loaded that question to the hilt.

'No. *No*. This is a great house. I'm just trying to adapt. Think about the next move. My next move. Job, I mean.'

Conrad sighed. 'I'm sorry. Cutting your salary down. You shouldn't have had to deal with that blow by yourself. That must have been horrible.'

'It wasn't. But I might've gone shopping a few times to ease the pain.'

Her forced laughter made him sad. They had lost control of a lot more than their finances in the past year. They had lost even the normal day-to-day verbal tennis ball going back and forth across the net. The financial shit was the same as the thing with That Fucker Jake. And not so different from Conrad's thing. The thing with the girl, Rachel. Not that he'd done anything, but still. It had been close. Bad choices they wouldn't have made if they'd kept each other in the loop. The money was like that – it came from the same place, anyway. Worst of all, here they were talking in a healthy way and it sucked, yes, but it was honest. He didn't want it to end. He wanted to sit here in their new old kitchen until they were discussing holes in their Medicare coverage.

And it was pretty clear that, since his father's death, money was not the real issue. She needed something to do, he'd rushed her, and now here they were.

'I just want you to be happy,' he said.

'It's eight weeks,' she said. 'And the next training class starts day after tomorrow.'

He wouldn't taste another beer this good until she came home.

Jo did not cry as they said their goodbyes inside the Dane County Airport. Surrender had been reached; neither husband nor wife had the energy to continue the debate. Conrad shuffled aside to make room for three generations huddled around a tall girl in a University of Wisconsin sweatshirt, the whole fam-damly seeing off their pride and joy for the summer.

36

Conrad squeezed Jo's hand. 'I can stay a while.'

'You're sweet,' she said, releasing his grip. 'I trusted you about moving here. Trust me on this one, for a little while?'

Trust was still a loaded word – he could make a list of loaded words now – and he let the comment slide. He kissed her scar for comfort. The thin line ran from the left arch of her top lip to the exact middle-bottom of her nose, one of childhood's accidental fissures he'd always found sexy, the snarl of a *femme fatale*.

He passed another Perkins and looped around Madison on the Beltline at a steady sixty miles per, stealing glimpses of the Capitol dome at the top of State Street. Then he was winding his way on to Highway 151, which split off Madison and went south to Black Earth and then another fifty miles to Iowa. Suburbs gave way to box stores and furniture outlets.

After that, farmland. The familiar rolling greens. Dense mini-forests gathered around the streams. The silent sweet manure field of nothingness, tranquil as the sea. Just as it had been when he discovered it the first time, it was a lonely patch of country, but soothing, almost hypnotic. Made him glad they'd left California.

Conrad saw the sign for *Black Earth, Pop. 2713*, and switched off the cruise control. Riding the business loop, he passed a farm equipment dealership and a graveyard full of enormous granite headstones. Apparently, these small towns liked to keep their dead front and center, on Main Street if possible. Would they live here long enough to raise a family, a family that would bury him in yonder graveyard? How soon would it come? Another thirty years, or forty? Fifty was not out of the question, but even that seemed too short a time. Look at Dad. One day you're working and joking around with the boys with your hand on the box and ZAP – you're fucking fried, end of story. No more time to apologize to your son.

He nosed the Volvo alongside the curb and stared through the windshield, up at his house. Again, that nagging question:

If not for to have children, what are we here for?

He sat in the Volvo and listened to the tick of the engine and creak of the upholstery. The idea that she might not come back pressed down on him like a seatbelt possessed. Perversely, his mind tightened the belt further by reminding him of the last one who'd left him.

Holly.

Why was he thinking about her now? Holly was more than twelve years ago. What could a high school romance hold to his life now? To Jo? To this beautiful new home?

Don't think about Holly. She's old news.

Her tears. She cried for what we did.

'Enough of this shit.' He exited the car, bidding Holly to stay buried.

He was on the porch with one hand on the door when the man started yelling.

'Harrison! Conrad Harrison!'

For a second, Conrad was sure the voice belonged to his father, that the whole thing had been a strange dream

38

and now he really was dead and the old man was coming to lead him away for good. He turned around slowly.

But it was only Leon Laski, the former owner of 818 Heritage Street. They'd not met, mainly because Laski had groused about the closing dates and Roddy had kept them out of it. 'Believe me, it's better this way,' Roddy had said. 'You don't want to meet the S-O-B.'

Too late – here came the S-O-B, barreling up the sidewalk and across Conrad's lawn. In his hands, a heavy wooden soda crate, stiff-armed away from his body as if it were full of dirty diapers.

'Excuse me?'

Laski dropped the crate on the porch. 'This all belongs to you now.'

'Is that right?' Conrad said, a skeptical grandfather.

Laski was shorter than Conrad by six inches, but he was clearly the larger man. He had the hard-packed muscle, ruddy cheeks and battered hands only middle-aged mechanics and sailors seem to acquire. His gray-blond beard and scraggily locks were more frayed rope than actual hair. He wore blue workman's pants and a plain brown shirt with a name patch that read LEON stitched to the tit.

'Wife packed her up on accident . . . crazy bitch.' Laski's accent was aggressively northern Wisconsin.

The dogs went off like fireworks.

'Quiet down,' Conrad yelled at the door, though he was glad he had Alice and Luther if things turned nasty. 'Sorry, dogs aren't used to the place yet. I'm Conrad Harrison.'

'Ya say.' Laski ignored the proffered mitt, removed a moist, splintered toothpick from behind his ear, and began to gnaw at it like a beaver, his tongue darting over his callused thumb and forefinger as if they were next. 'Anycase, don't need more'n I already got to unpack, so dare ya go.'

'Fine. Thanks, I think.' The crate was covered with a sheet of black felt tucked into the sides, obscuring the contents. 'Something for the house?'

'Could say that, ya sure could.'

'Uh-huh. Well, looks like you cleaned out pretty good. I'll call Roddy if I find anything.'

Laski whistled through his toothpick. The end flapped wetly like a ruined party favor. 'Cleaned out all right, all right, but I wouldn't call it pretty anything. You two woulda taken another week getting your shit together, we'd a lost the deal on the new farm. But you go ahead and tell 'at big buck Roddy anything you want. I got what I need. We're clear.'

Conrad managed to smile. 'Anything else I can do for you today, Leon? No? Good.' He grabbed the crate and turned for the door.

Laski spoke in a low, slithering voice. 'You got kids, boy?'

'What was that?'

'I hear dem mutts tearing up your floors in dare, but I don't see no kids. Appears you don't got none yet, but what I mean is, you plan on having any?'

'No, we – why would you ask that?'

'Just curious.' Laski pointed one thick finger at

40

Conrad's front door. 'You have yourself a nice life in 'at old house.'

Before Conrad could reply, Laski wheeled on his dirty boots and knuckled down the walk, flicking his toothpick in a high arc as he disappeared around the corner, his vehicle out of sight or non-existent.

Conrad slipped inside and summoned his courage to open the crate.

6

Alice and Luther pogoed at him as if he'd abandoned them for weeks instead of hours. He set the crate on the coffee table and rolled around with them, letting them slobber on his face. There wasn't a pill on the market that cured mild depression – or just a shitty day – as fast as these two dogs.

Then he quit stalling and went to the crate. The covering was indeed felt, but thick as a shroud. As he lifted one corner he was overcome by an irrational thought: what if it's a trap? Like the kind used to catch badgers or snap my hand off at the wrist? But that was ridiculous. Nothing more than his imagination blowing off steam.

Wedged inside the crate was a large portfolio or scrapbook. It was heavy. Maybe five, six pounds. Why in the hell would Laski think this belonged to him?

Conrad examined the cracked spine and yellowed paper edges. It wasn't a book. It was an album, but photo albums had ten, maybe twenty cardboard pages. This thing had fifty or more, some thin, others not.

The first page had pinpoints of black mold in the crease, but he could see the rest well enough. It was a charcoal sketch. Bare land, the lines done over and over, mostly grass and a few shrubs and a single sapling with no leaves. The plot of land stretched back over a rolling slope, narrowing on the page to give depth to the short horizon. Deeper, 'over' the rise of the land he could just make out two slashes of the artist's pen. At first he thought it might be another tree, but no, upon closer inspection, his nose almost touching the musty paper, he could see the clean lines, one shorter and horizontal over the taller vertical.

A cross.

And why not? Black Earth, like a lot of Middle America, was full of devout Christians and probably had been more so a century ago.

But why did the rest of the sketch seem familiar?

'Hey – shit.'

He backed out the front door and up the cracked sidewalk to the street. He looked at the book and then back up at his house. His house and the lot. Standing next to him, almost exactly one third of the distance from the western property line, was a tree that topped out at least twenty feet higher than Conrad's roof, its trunk as thick as three men. The house was two and a half stories with the attic – the tree was pushing fifty feet. He looked back at the drawing, then back up at the tree. The huge tree stood where the sapling in the drawing stood, and the slope of the land in the sketch matched Conrad's yard.

'How 'bout that,' Conrad said, smiling for the first time all day. It wasn't quite like discovering buried treasure, but it still gave him a child's satisfaction. If the MLS printout had been accurate, this tree was, like his house, over one hundred and forty years old. 'The house's birthday tree.'

The next page wasn't a sketch. Pasted to the stiff yellow paper was a photo of unusual size, roughly seven inches high and nine inches wide. The light looked rusty, the photo developed in sepia. The framing and scale matched the sketch, but that was where the similarities ended.

The people gathered in front of the completed house looked cold, arms crossed, angry that they had been called out for this impromptu Kodak moment. All were women, late teens to geriatric and everything in between, garbed in the frumpy black dresses and white bonnets of maids or nurses. *Little Midwife on the Prairie*. Maybe a family . . . no. They all wore such dour expressions and pale countenances, he was unable to imagine them as anything other than employees. He didn't think more than a few of the women were relations; their size, shape and facial features were too diverse to be of the same stock.

Relations, stock.

My God, he thought, I'm musing in the vernacular of their time just looking at them, and it feels right. No, it feels *proper*. And what is, what was, the purpose of this gathering? If they were marking some special day, why the pug chins and hunched backs? The tired boredom in their sunken black eyes? Some of them were looking away from the lens, as if someone or something on the street had captured their attention. Or maybe they had simply refused to look into the camera. This made more sense because they were looking in different directions, not focused on any one point of interest. The women had no shape except bulky, even the one with the breasts.

'No, they were bosoms back then,' Conrad said to the book. 'Bosoms or teats, depending on the company you ladies kept.'

Another woman, this one in her twenties or thirties (it was hard to tell; for all he knew women had aged twice as fast at the turn of the century), was holding her skirts above the ground as if preparing to step over a puddle. Another stood ramrod straight with a broom clutched in her thick fists.

Wrapping up his inspection, Conrad found only two common details uniting these women. They all wore black boots that rose above the ankles, mannish in their thick soles and metal eyelets and pointed toes. The other was that none was smiling. Not all were sour or angry. It was simply that happiness, even a forced smile, seemed a foreign thing to them.

His thoughts turned to the unseen photographer. Would he have been their employer, the owner of the house? A doctor? Or a hired man, a local with the equipment and a knack for taking pictures? Conrad guessed the latter, for it was clear even to his untrained eye that, grim as its subjects were, the photo itself was quite good. Nothing you'd want to hang on your staircase wall (it might give someone cause to fall down the stairs), but a strong piece of work nonetheless. In its own droll way, it was almost lovely.

Who said the owner was a man? Maybe the house had been full of women, and only women.

Midwives, wet nurses.

Mothers, daughters, granddaughters.

What if some of them are still here?

He went over them again one by one, his nose close enough to the warped paper that he caught the scent of a sun-dried milk carton.

Roaming, searching . . .

His eyes locked on the one he had missed, the one standing behind the first row, elevated in her stance on the porch step so that only her face was visible between the shoulders of the other women. He saw her clearly then, recognized her open mouth, the teeth exposed as if preparing to bite.

No. Not possible.

But there she was, hollow-eyed and waxen like the others. The tall raven-haired woman in the photo stared back at him with something akin to hatred, and he recognized her, of course he recognized her, for hers was a face he had come to know intimately. She of the compressed lightning bolt of a scar, the lovely fissure running from under her nose to her lip.

An involuntary cry escaped his throat as he ran into the house, leaving splayed on the sidewalk the album containing a century-old photo of his wife.

7

Conrad stood in the front sitting room, looking out the window to the album on the ground. Twenty minutes had elapsed since he'd fled the scene. What if the neighbors had seen that little show? What were they thinking of the nice young couple from California now, 'Rad?

He must have been mistaken.

Feeling foolish, he put his hand on the doorknob and stopped. If he went back for the album, he would have to bring it back inside the house or throw it away in one of the new Rubbermaid cans out front. Either way, he knew he would have to look one more time. How could he not? His wife was in there, with teeth that wanted to bite.

Even if it turned out to be a coincidence, a striking resemblance and nothing more, he did not want to see that woman again. She had those black eyes. That starved look only women who've suffered and absorbed evil can project. And if it was a coincidence, what did that say about his state of mind, his wife gone only a few hours?

Just before he turned the knob there was a quick, pitter-pat rapping at his door. Conrad's heart jumped. A woman was standing on his porch, a shadow shifting behind the gauze curtain Jo had installed last week.

Christ! Who the fuck was this? Was she coming out of the photo to ask for her supper?

'Conrad, everything all right?' The voice was country-sweet and tinged with humor. Ah, yes – Gail Grum, his new next-door neighbor. Conrad and Jo had met Gail and her humongous husband three minutes after staggering out of the car, foggy from the drive from California. He remembered feeling overwhelmed by Gail's politeness. 'You left your book on the sidewalk, do you want me to put it on the porch?'

Conrad opened the door and smiled. 'Sorry about that. Phone was ringing. Thank you, Gail.'

He accepted the album and tucked it under one arm while she plowed on.

'I hate to bother you – I'm sure you're still unpacking. Do you two need anything to help you get settled in?'

'Oh, no, you're not a Hobbit – bother, I mean. Sorry.'

He didn't mean to say it. Most people would have found it rude. Gail laughed like he'd told a terrific joke.

'A Hobbit! Maybe I am!'

Gail was five feet tall when standing on a phone book, a fifty-year-old in better shape than Conrad at seventeen. Her smile was warm and toothy. As she spoke her hands never stopped moving, waving like three fawning members of a welcome committee. He found it impossible to be abrupt with her. She was wearing the same gear as when they'd first met four weeks ago: a tank top that revealed her strong, tanned arms, green cargo shorts with a pair of cotton gloves hanging from one pocket, and yellow rubber gardening clogs with no socks.

The dogs broke out and clobbered Gail with affection. 'Okay, Luther, Alice, stop that.'

Gail only encouraged them. 'Look at them go. Upsy-daisy! Oh, how sweet! They're beautiful. Oh, they must be so happy in their new home! Joanna said you rescued them – they must love you soooo much.'

It was this immediate taking to his dogs that warmed Conrad to Gail Grum. 'I'm sorry, you're just standing there. Would you like to come in? I have iced tea.'

Gail flapped her hands. 'Oh, no. Listen, I saw you run inside and I just wanted to make sure everything was all right.'

'I was up late unpacking and didn't sleep well, been a mess all morning, and . . .' he trailed off, taken by the motherly look in her eyes. She wasn't just listening to him; she was hanging on every word. Without meaning to, he blurted it out. 'Jo left me.'

'Oh no!'

'Oh, not like that,' he said. 'She took a job. She's in Detroit for eight weeks of something they call intensive consultative sales training.'

'But you just got here. Eight weeks? What are you going to do? I'd just go crazy if John left me!'

'Ah, yeah, well,' he said. 'It's a great job. Just kind of sudden.'

He stood there in the doorway for another ten minutes, filling Gail in on all the details. He told her how he was already looking forward to Jo's first trip home at the three-week break, and added, 'but hey, at least I have the dogs'.

'We're having the Bartholomews over for roast beef, even though it's summer, I know, we like our hearty meals, ha-ha-ha. Have you met the Bartholomews, across the street?'

'I haven't met anybody.'

'Oh, you have to come over, Conrad. It'll be so much fun!'

'That sounds great, but don't wait for me. I might have to finish this . . . thing.' He didn't have a thing, but he wanted an out. 'You're very kind.'

She slapped his hands. 'I'm not kind. This is what we do. You don't know it yet, but you now live next to some of the best people you'll ever know. Anytime after seven is fine. See you tonight, Conrad!'

Conrad watched her goofy garden clogs flapping across the yard. When she had popped back into her house, he closed the door and dropped the album on the coffee table.

It's not that I'm afraid of it, he told himself, heading up the stairs to check his email. *It's simply that there is no possible way the woman in the photo could be my wife and I've got better things to do than stare at a bunch of memories that belong to someone else. So fuck that, okay?*

Right.

It was after seven when the phone rang. That made it past eight in Detroit, but she was still all kinds of excited from her big first day, which irritated him.

'Is Detroit everything you dreamed it would be?'

50

'Actually, it's nice. The offices are in Troy, not really Detroit, and it's pleasant in a Midwest corporate way. Sort of like the Long Beach of Detroit, without the ocean. My suite is a dump, but kinda cozy.'

'The Residence thing?'

'It's like going back to school. Everyone eats at the buffet in the clubhouse every night and there's a sand volleyball court and a pool. I met a nice girl named Shirley. She's twenty-three, two kids. She was crying all day because she misses them so much. But then I was thinking, well, if little Shirley from Akron can make it here, then I can definitely make it, right?'

'Of course, Baby. You're brilliant. You'll do fine.'

But what about me? What am I going to do?

'What have you been up to?'

'I've been invited to dinner.'

'Really?' The way she perked up, he knew she had been hoping for this.

'Gail came by earlier.'

'Oh, sweetie, please go. I don't want them thinking we're rude.'

'Well, she knows you're gone, so she can't think you're rude. But I told her I was tired, and I am.' He was inching toward the album on the coffee table.

'We need to get off on the right foot.'

'I can see them rolling out the Pictionary now.'

Jo sighed. 'Conrad.'

'I know.'

They said goodbye. Then, before he could chicken out, he flipped the cover open and stared at the photo of the women in black. It was night and the lighting was dim in the living room. He had to squint to make out their faces. At first he couldn't find her and he was sure he had imagined the whole thing. His eyes darted and then he locked on her, saw her teeth and her scar—

'Fuck you!' Conrad threw the album across the room. He-had not imagined seeing her the first time. He had not imagined seeing her now.

It was Jo.

The dogs darted to the couch, swerving wide of his path. He felt like an asshole for losing it like that. But he couldn't ignore her now whether he tossed the album in the garbage or set it on fire and danced on the ashes.

What if there are more? What if she's in a whole bunch of them? What will you do then, 'Rad? What if she's on every page staring back at you with those glossy black eyes, smiling into the camera so close you can see into her soul?

No, impossible. With six billion people on the planet (not even counting the dead) there had to be an explanation. It simply could not be his wife.

And he was not crazy. Lonely, yes. Recovering from a very stressful exit from the City of Angels, yes. But not insane. He needed to investigate the house's history, these women, but where would he begin? Who else besides Leon Laski would know about the house? People who lived here. People who—

'The neighbors.'

He hopped off the couch and ran upstairs to get ready for dinner. A few laughs, some human company. Jo would be pleased with the effort.

8

The House of Grum was another Victorian, barn-red with crème and robin's egg trim, pillars slim as dancers, with bursts of filigree on top. The front porch was narrow, wrapping around and widening on one side. Inside, the décor was somewhere between antiquarian and mid-twentieth-century frugal farmer's wife. The dinner table would seat twelve, but tonight was attended by only two couples – Gail and John Grum, and the neighbors, Steve and Bailey Bartholomew – plus Conrad. Both couples were comfortably attired in Lands' End (worldwide headquarters was just two towns over, people kept telling him): cargo shorts, untucked shirts with button-down collars, slip-on shoes. Canvas shades of ecru, loden, heather abound.

This is us in ten years, Conrad thought. But if this was the Game of Life, he was missing his pink peg. If Jo were here, she would do all the talking, knowing what to reveal and what to hold back. As it stood, he felt like a fraud and kept waiting for one of them to call him out on it. What do you do? Is it true you paid cash for that house? What the hell are you doing in Wisconsin, Conrad?

Hiding? Or running?

But they didn't call him on anything. Instead, they fed him and watched him like the polite stranger he was, and spoke kindly, even when he began to pry.

'So what's the story with the guy used to live in my new house,' Conrad said, pushing his roast beef aside to dig into Gail's peach cobbler.

'What about Leon Laski is it you want to know?' Gail Grum said, a spoonful of vanilla ice cream hovering under her nose.

'Oh, I dunno,' he lied, reminding himself these people might very well still be friends with the man who once owned his house. 'He came by earlier today and, well, it was weird. Some issues with the closing, I guess.'

Gail pulled the spoon from her mouth slowly. 'Leon can be a touch abrasive at times, but they're good people.'

Big John Grum turned to his wife, 'How long were dey in dare? Ten, twelve years?' At six-six and pushing two hundred and fifty pounds, Big John towered over his little garden gnome of a wife. He was a carpenter and a mason, with the hands to show for it. The gentle giant was also a haggard giant.

'Oh, nooo. More like sixteen,' Gail corrected.

Big John shook his head. 'Leon's just upset he's overextended himself on that farmette. He was probably all in a rush to get the money out of your deal, and now that you're here he doesn't know where to put his family. Don't even have plumbing's what I hear. Be another three months yet.'

'Poor Leon's going to be shitting in the woods all

54

summer long,' Steve Bartholomew added. Steve had the tidy presence of a financial manager, but his voice filled the room. He strode around with his belly out, red in the face, his gray-flecked black hair shorn military tight enough that Conrad could see the shiny sunburn on his scalp. As with many men of his disposition, Steve's wife was his opposite. Bailey Bartholomew was so quiet she seemed to disappear, popping back into the conversation only to temper her husband.

'In the woods, huh?' Conrad said. 'Do we have poison ivy around these parts?'

'Yes, we do!' Gail said, laughing with the others.

Steve drained half his wine and fixed on Conrad. 'A man raises his family in a house, I don't care how well he does in the transaction – and that house was worth a lot less when Leon bought it – it's never easy leaving your home.'

'Of course not,' Conrad said, feigning sympathy. 'I'm sure Leon's a decent guy.'

Gail touched Conrad's arm. 'Greer – that's his wife – was probably just worried about the kids. Four is a lot to carry around, with or without plumbing.'

'Three,' Steve corrected. 'But she's preggo again.'

'Actually, Steve,' Big John put in. 'Wasn't it two plus the pregnancy?'

'Oh, that's right,' Gail said. 'I can't keep track.'

Steve scoffed. 'Don't even try. It's like ten little Indians over there.'

'Okay, everybody,' Big John said, heading to the back porch for a post-meal smoke.

A mutually regrettable silence ensued.

'How old are his kids?' Conrad waited, but suddenly no one wanted to crunch the numbers. All eyes around the table had drifted away or downward.

Steve nudged Conrad in the ribs. 'Our Leon's a regular Johnny Appleseed. Shoots more bullseyes than Robin Hood.'

'Steeeeve!' Bailey wailed. 'You are terrible.'

Steve winked at Conrad – *aren't I a piece of work?* – and Conrad smiled, realizing he liked Steve and his cruel humor. Suddenly Conrad imagined spending long summer evenings on his porch with Steve, the two of them getting red in the face over the state of the world. He realized he was making a new friend, or could be.

Bailey turned to Conrad. 'They lost their first two. Years ago. So sad. Gail, did Greer ever—'

'No one knows,' Gail said. 'Could have been something rare. Just . . . one of those things.'

'They should have called the doctors sooner,' Steve said. 'There's just no excuse.'

When no one added to that, Conrad decided to let the topic go for now. But two kids 'lost'? Something bad had happened, oh yes.

'I'll kill you, you asshole!' the girl screamed. 'How dare you fucking touch me. No, no! Come back here, Eddie! Eddie, you piece of shit!'

Her voice was an octave shy of a shriek and it was coming from outside. A car door slammed, the engine revved to the moon and tires barked.

Conrad jerked in his chair, certain the car was coming through the walls.

The front door banged open and a teen girl crying her eyes out barged in, colliding with her mother. Everyone turned to witness the drama.

'Liebschen!' Gail grabbed her daughter by the elbow.

'Don't touch me!' The girl clawed back like it was her mother that had been hitting her, if hitting was part of it. Conrad glimpsed tears and blood near her mouth, but not much, and it was hard to be sure with the long hair tangled over her features.

Before Gail could corral all five feet nothing of her daughter's whirling madness, the girl turned on them, aware she was making a scene. Face gone red, blue corduroy jacket flapping, exposing the bulges, her awkwardly large breasts like twin summits over the earth orb that was her belly peeking from under her skin-tight tee. Her entire life on display, daughter Grum glared across the table and locked on Conrad with eyes as large and green as turtles.

'Who the fuck is that?' she said. 'What's he looking at?'

All he thought was, *Damn, that girl's pregnant.*

And she was the one hiding in my house the day I toured it with Roddy.

'Nadia, out.' Gail pointed like a hunter for her setter.

Conrad felt a snap of embarrassment for her, followed by shame, like he was on some jury deliberating her guilt. All that was missing was the big red P on her chest. He turned away quickly and saw Steve shut his mouth, wisely offering no comment while Gail wrestled her into the adjacent room, applying a mantra. 'Nadia, calm down, Nadia, calm down . . .'

He owed her one, in a way. The girl had taken the attention off of him. He felt relieved and run over. She had that effect on him from the first. Even in her tears, her corded neck mottled with angry red patches, her white hair flying, little Nadia Grum was, to a wounding degree, gorgeous.

His birthing house was a sauna. Hoping to cool down and stave off the inevitable wine hangover, Conrad took a beer from the fridge and returned to the album. The whole notion that his wife was trapped in there now seemed absurd. He plopped down on the couch and flipped the pages idly, skipping the first photo of the women, the ones he had begun to think of as the Heritage Street Gals. He didn't really want to know if Jo was still with them, waiting for him to look again into her dead black eyes.

The next few pages were sketches of the house under construction and he skimmed them without much interest. Then the book seemed to fall open to a gatefold containing another photo. The perspective was from garden level, inside and looking out one of the basement windows. The photo was a close-up and it required some effort for him to make out its true subject. Around the window frame were the nubs of the natural rock foundation. In one small gap in the mortar was a large brown spider – Conrad, who knew something about reptiles, amphibians and arachnids, guessed it was a brown recluse – perched with the weight of its thorax tilted back, one needle-like foreleg extended. A woman testing the temperature in a body of water. Her web had been spun out in every direction, and desiccated insect carcasses remained stuck within the spokes. Her fat body – no, wait. It wasn't her body bulging this way. It was her egg sac the photographer had been after.

She was nearly bursting.

Conrad stared at the spider, imagining her offspring. Hundreds of tiny brown spiders scurrying beneath him, crawling in the foundation, in the walls, in the soil all around, descendants of this old girl.

The spider connected his thoughts to the Heritage Street Gals and, without reflection, to talk of the Laskis' lost children and even the pregnant Nadia Grum. And then his mouth went dry.

The album was all about the house. A history he wanted no part of.

There were fifty or more pages remaining.

Head pounding, Conrad carried the album to the fireplace, rolled three balls of newspaper into the grate, wedged the album in and set the entire works ablaze.

9

The routine was comfort. The routine was habit. The routine was boring.

The routine lasted two weeks.

He kept telling himself if he could stay positive until Jo's first planned visit home, all would be reconciled, or at least renegotiated.

He was wrong.

Hot, jobless, wifeless, he roamed in a fugue from one hour to the next. The days passed so slowly Conrad found himself staring at the kitchen clock (a plastic hen happily handing eggs to a farmer), wishing for a gun to blast it to pieces.

And he was trying, at least in the beginning. Conrad forced himself to rise and shower before eight, to dress as if he had a job. Clean-shaven, freshly polo-ed and khakied, his navy and lemon-striped Adidas kicks (his one concession to acting the man of leisure) laced neatly, he would walk the two blocks to the Kwik-Trip and pick up the *Wisconsin State Journal*, a watery coffee and maybe a banana or plain cake donut for breakfast. After reading the paper during his meditative and open-door toilet time, Conrad would walk the dogs around town. He became familiar with the houses, many of them old like theirs. Most were smaller. Some were twice as large, but these looked tired, thirsty for paint. He told himself 818 Heritage Street was the best in the entire town. That it was a special place.

After walking the dogs, Conrad would work the yard, pruning here and there, never making much of a dent in the wild grapevines and pine trees. It had been a wet spring, and so far June had delivered heat in the morning, rain almost every afternoon and sometimes again at night. The result was a gardener's dream climate of steamy, lush growth. He would weed the gardens until his back spasmed and his arms trembled. By noon he always found himself back inside the house, panting, guzzling iced tea, spitting and wheezing from the humidity or some allergy he could not classify.

To combat the afternoon malaise, he took to drinking iced tea by the gallon. It poured through him while he wasted hours checking email, surfing the web, reading scandalous DrudgeReport and PerezHilton headlines: This Little Starlet Went to Rehab, This Little Starlet Forgot to Wear Panties When She Pumped Gas. This Little Terrorist Had Roast Beef, This Little Husband Had None.

Left to fend for himself, he cooked four-course meals and shared them with the dogs. He looked out the windows and tried to time his trips to the mailbox with the neighbors' comings and goings. Steve Bartholomew worked from home – architecting databases with co-workers in Bangladesh – and always asked about Jo, which only angered Conrad. He talked with Gail Grum when he saw her in one of her six or seven gardens that grew in her backyard and between their homes. Sometimes Big John would wave to his junior neighbor as he unloaded diamond-blade saws and scrap rock from his truck at the end of stone-dusty days.

He thought about Holly, his one that got away. Every guy had one. Eventually you forgot her and moved on, and he had, but she was coming back. He fought the indulgence, however, and in her place turned his imaginings on Nadia Grum. The expectant girl next door. A little blonde ball of blustery ignorance. Did she live at home? Did she have bruises from her fight with what's his name, the boyfriend? Teddy? Davie? What did she do with her days? Was she a student? A dropout? Was Teddy preparing to be the father?

Was he still fucking her?

He spoke with Jo every night. Their conversations were short and depressing. She was always too tired to discuss the job and her routine in any detail. As they talked, Conrad would lie on the couch and imagine her lying on the bed in her pajamas in her suite, both of them flicking channels as the conversation dwindled to static sighs and half-hearted miss-yous, neither willing to admit they were stuck in a rut, separated by a lot more than Lake Michigan. He mentioned how excited he was to have her home for the weekend, floated the idea of a special night out in Madison – drinks on Monona Terrace, some live music, maybe.

'Ugh,' she said. 'All I can think about is sleeping in my own bed, cuddling with the dogs and taking a long, hot bath. The tub in my room is tiny and I just want to sleep for days.'

'Yeah, you sound tense,' he said, angling for the common thread. He imagined her long body folded up in the suite's tub, a washcloth draped over her eyes. 'We could always, you know . . . like we did that one time.'

She didn't remember 'that one time', back when they did all kinds of things. Undaunted, he hinted around it three or four times. She yawned. Finally he just said: 'Here's an idea. You're alone there. I'm alone here. Pour yourself a glass of wine, let's get crazy and have a hot and dirty conversation.'

He could hear her tense up and he immediately regretted the suggestion.

'No, not happening,' she said. 'Sorry.'

Maybe she was just tired. And maybe he was being too sensitive, sounding weak, which she always despised. Either way, her answer felt cruel.

'I wish you'd never gone.'

'Conrad, please. We chose this.'

'But I didn't go away. You did.'

'Don't be mad.'

'I'm not mad.' *I'm fucking horny. Seventeen years old revved up and ready to go fifteen rounds!* 'It's been a long time.'

'I'll make it up to you, honey. No pouting.'

63

'Yeah, yeah.'

'Call me tomorrow.'

'I will.'

'I love you.'

'Love you, too.'

It didn't add up. Shouldn't she be the one trying to make it up to him? Shouldn't she be writhing at his feet for the way he forgave her? For the house he'd bought for her? For getting her out of the rut, no questions asked?

He couldn't recall the last time they'd had sex, but he remembered their last night together in this house all too well. He'd had the chance and somehow he'd blown it.

It had been late and they were in bed. They had been tired from chores, but it was a shared pain and therefore good.

Jo had leaned against his shoulder and whispered, 'I love it here.'

He'd been cranky on purpose. 'What kind of training makes you leave home for eight weeks?'

'Think of it like, I dunno, the down payment on your own business. As soon as I'm done, I can telecommute—'

'—from anywhere in the world,' he finished for her. 'Is that what Donna said? Are you still selling me, now?'

'Maybe I am selling you. But if I do this, you can take all the time you need to figure out what you're going to do next. And I don't care, I really don't. Take as long as you want.'

'I thought this would be different. I thought it would be a relief for you.'

'What's to relieve?'

'I never liked being the man who depends on his wife. I'm supposed to be supporting you, and now I am.'

'I don't want you to support me.' She had said as much before and this always bitched him up. He had married a smart, capable woman, but he couldn't help feeling useless for the past couple of years. Maybe it was a man thing, not just a Conrad thing, but that didn't change the basic truth of it. 'It's six figures. One-fifty plus a bonus, to be precise.'

'Yeah. That's a lotta lettuce, Baby. But will you be happy?'

'With one-fifty? How can I not be?'

'Jo—'

'That's not what I meant. But this is a good thing. You know I never wanted to be the stay-at-home mommy. I have to do something.'

'Is that all this is about? Career fulfillment? Or is there something else going on?'

'Like what?'

'Jo. Okay.' He chose his next words like a man on a game show who's just realized this one's for the trip to Maui. 'We never went into it. You might have thought I was avoiding it, or just too mad to deal. But I want you to know. I . . . I understand what happened.'

'What does that mean?' She wasn't looking at him. Just whispering, but he could feel her tighten under his hand.

'It means it happens. People who aren't full seek sustenance elsewhere.'

The minute that followed was a long, silent one.

'Maybe this job is my way of filling myself up,' she said.

'Is it?' *Yes, maybe I am willing to allow you that much. For a little while. And by the way, what am I filling myself up with?* 'If you're sure you want it, then you should go for it.'

She pushed him on to his back and began kissing his neck, his chest, pushing his shirt up. 'I'm not sure. I'm never sure about anything.'

'You're not?'

'No one is.'

'Oh.'

'It is kind of scary, but exciting, too.' She nibbled at his waist.

'You don't get scared.'

'Yes, I do.'

She was waiting for him to put her fears to rest, to explain what was eating him up. But he hadn't been able to find the words, not when she was preparing to leave. She rested her head on his stomach. He was immediately aroused. She noticed and popped him free. The unexpected movement and sheer heat of her tongue made him groan. A minute into it, she'd paused and looked up, speaking in a voice as faint as a radio transmission from Iowa.

'I need you to know something,' she said.

'Whuh?'

'What you walked in on. It wasn't what you thought. I admit it was very close, and wrong. But it wasn't sex.'

Amazing. A little three-letter word. Timed right, it was a sledgehammer.

'Please, don't,' he said.

Her grip remained firm but the stroking had ceased. Her eyebrows arched and she bored into him.

'Look at me,' she said. He sat up on his elbows. 'I've never been unfaithful, Conrad.'

He did not accept her words, but neither did he disbelieve them. They just hung there between them. He wanted to throw her off and throw her out. He wanted to roll her over and fuck her until she wept.

He fell back and covered his eyes.

She started to cry and he hated her for that. His balls were ready to explode and he hurt worse than that in worse places. But no, he wasn't going to comfort her. That Fucker Jake had been there. Whatever had or had not happened in the house, Jo had fallen asleep in her panties and his Sebadoh and That Fucker Jake had been there.

She pulled herself up and rested against his shoulder, releasing him when she felt him softening. Even if he wasn't so sure about the past, he believed she was being faithful now. What were dropping bad habits and moving away to start a new life together if not faith that your marriage would work out?

'I guess we're both a little freaked out here,' he said.

'I'll make it up to you next time, okay?'

What if there is no next time? a nasty little voice shot back.

'I just want you to want this as much as I do,' he said. Meaning, in that male way, the sex and the love and the marriage and the house. They were inseparable to him.

'I do.'

It seemed a trade he'd failed to make – his comforting words for her sexual favor. A small thing, perhaps. A lost opportunity on both fronts.

And so, 976-wife rejecting his person-to-person potty mouth, Conrad's frustration deepened until he caved in and embarked on one last running attempt to get the job done by himself, if only to prove that he still could (and so that he might last more than thirty seconds when she returned). His tall and beautiful Jo was out of town, but there was a high-speed pipe and a portal of infinite titillation at his fingertips.

The overture to the main event arrived courtesy of Visa and a mega site that humbly billed itself as ShavedPussyEmpire.com. He searched in vain for something less Chesterish but the tamer domains like NiceYoungGirlsYourParentsWouldApproveOf.com and ArtfullyDepictedNakedLadies.com had been blown out of the water early in an Internet porn arms race toward mutually repulsed destruction.

Knowing this, he hesitantly Googled 'free sex movies' and got the universe of porn, none of it free. Settling upon a site that appeared somewhat legit (ho ho), he linked around until he had eliminated the most ghastly fetishes and entered, 'The World's #1 Destination for Shaved Pussy!' After failing to become aroused by the thirty-second free sample clips, he fumbled his credit card and tried to shoo the dogs out of the office, but the door wouldn't stay latched. Luther kept nosing in, and there was simply no way he was going to perform an act of onanism with his dogs staring at him.

He finally shouted loud enough to stop their scratching at the door and logged in, only to find himself staring at so many hairless girls in pigtails and academy plaid performing such unnatural acts of faked arousal, the 'director's' distracting and often mean-spirited verbal cues lobbed at the coke-addled nubiles, that he was overwhelmed (okay, nudged) by guilt and couldn't bring himself beyond a plumpie, let alone to climax.

After five minutes of frustrated tugging, he angrily logged off, waddled to the bathroom (the door latched, hallelujah), his pants sliding down around his knees and launched into act two, standing over (no, not the sink, you filthy pig) the bathtub, eyes closed, visions of Jo riding him reverse cowgirl style with the lights on (she had done it once and only once, on the living-room couch, pretending not to remember when he'd made the request several times since, which only made it more precious) dancing in his brain.

As he ramped up to the third act reveal, his mind performed a sort of miraculous shuffle function, a libido iPod playing every song in its pitiful six-soul library of ex-girlfriends, adding several *Hustler* Honey of the Months that had been burned into his memory from the teen years when you only had the one magazine and protected it like fire for the tribe, the iPenis playing them all at the same time at full volume, parading every girl and woman Conrad had ever bedded or seen naked before his mind's lubricated eye like a carnival wheel, round and round she goes and where he comes nobody knows, all of the breasts and hips and hair and necks and asses and lips and moans and grunts shuffling again and again until Jo slew them all and claimed her rightful spot on his lap, the ultimate authority who knows what her man needs to finish the job, the Tarot card that read simply The Wife, riding him with such hip-flexing force and the gleaming crystal reality that can only come from memory, never fantasy, that for a minute he forgot he was bent over the tub and alone in this strange small town in this huge strange house, a man with a past he desperately wanted to forget, and he lost himself in the backs of her thighs and the dimples and fine black hairs above her ass above him, her wetness wetting the length of him and he felt huge, enormous yet fully enveloped, just so fucking *owned* by this animal called woman, this being called Joanna, this entity that was physically larger and infinitely more complex than he would ever be and he slipped out ready to burst and she grabbed him and planted him back inside without missing a single stroke, she was so tuned-in, and best of all he was giving her this moment too, sending her fears away by making her come and she slowed, crunching down on him, squeezing him in contractions, her voice heavy, almost male in its animal need until she came and he came with her, there inside her and here, now, in the bathroom, his fantasy and lonely reality coalescing so forcefully he felt her

70

anger and weight clap into his body and her face – *her* face, the *other* face, the sepia woman in the photo staring at him from inside his head, her crooked smile exposing her sharp teeth – and he fought her back too late, crying out in repulsed terror as he began to ejaculate—

And an invisible lead weight slammed into his neck, dropping him to his knees, stopping the blood flow to his brain and sounding an alarm of pain that stretched from his shoulder to his forehead.

Pants around his knees, his orgasm interrupted but still surging, purging him of his life force, his seed, Conrad lost consciousness on the bathroom floor.

HOLLY

Once upon a time there was a boy, and this boy, he had something inside him. Hunger, curiosity, need. Older things without names. Things that got a hold of him at an age younger than most. Things that need to find a way out, things that need a home.

She arrived in a pink sweater and blue jeans faded almost white. She had bad new wave hair, thirty bracelets on one arm, and she carried a purple Mad Balls lunchbox instead of a purse. She was a true child of the eighties. Her sweater, her cheeks, and her lippy smile (when she did smile) were all shades of pink. She was a drug called Girl. Just staring at her released endorphins and filled him with light.

I know what you're thinking. It's not that. Girl was not his first sexual encounter. But she was his first love. She was the girl no one could get to, which is what made him try harder. But he could not win her attentions. He was too young, too plain.

He studied her and made plans and two more years passed. Eventually she noticed him, the quiet kid who stared at her like she was made of golden candy. She knew who he was, of course. They had some classes together, but different circles of friends, and she was a circle of one. Holly Bauerman. There isn't anything in a name. But she was Holy. This was the time in which he wore her down with one simple act of courtship: staring.

He stared at Holly Bauerman in class, in the halls, and wherever he saw her around town, at parties and in the clothing store where she worked. She found him creepy at first, and then became curious. Once, on a Monday night, he spray-painted her name in ten-foot letters on the street in front of her house. No one knew it was him. But she knew.

She resisted, but what else has the power to melt us than the adoring eyes of another? If you have ever been adored this way, and by adore I mean with the perfect mixture of fear and craving, then you know. It is not something one can give to oneself. Only another's eyes have the power to show us how beautiful we can be. When his longing became obvious and overwhelming, her disgust turned to disinterest to a thing she missed when it was withheld, until finally the watching became a form of ego food she could no longer live without. She went to the Last Day of School Picnic alone and he was there.

'Hello, Holly,' he said. 'Happy last day of school.'

'What do you want from me?' A kind of tough, quiet panic entered her voice. She stood there in her plaid shorts, her pink tee shirt and plastic bracelets, her lunch-box-purse swinging like a second grader.

'If I don't see you all summer,' he said, 'then what's the point?'

'There is no point. Point of what?'

'The best days of my life have been the first day of school,' he said. 'I just wish I had more than four of them.'

She didn't have to think back to know that this was true.

'So are you going to give me your summer, or should I get it over with and kill myself?'

She laughed, but later confessed it was the most romantic thing anyone had said to her. They spent the summer together. Once they started talking, she relaxed. He became a clown, a little brother she could abuse, a friend to cheer her up, a reliable jester in her not-so-funny world. The world that had given her things like divorce, eating disorders, rival cliques, a dented and rusting Volkswagen Rabbit – this world he washed away. Puppy love brought them together, but what bound them was divorce. They had that brokenness in common and he thanked his parents for that much, for making him into something resembling her. His new wave girl morphing into a little prep-hippie before his eyes.

The summer was slow and warm and full of nights sitting on the hood of her car at Flagstaff Mountain, looking over the town. They pretended they were in a 1950s movie and he bought her milkshakes. She showed him how to dip the fries in the shake. They stayed away from parties. It was better just to walk in the park, go to the movies, or stay at home and talk on the phone. One day they talked on the phone from ten in the morning until midnight.

She made him take long hikes with her. She told him how she loved wild flowers, herbs, iced tea. She brewed her own special concoctions on the deck in glass gallon jars. She said it was a healing art, preparing this sun tea. She said that tea was purifying, good for the soul. He had never felt so clean as when he was with her. She collected herbs from the mountains and brewed special batches for him and he believed her. Later, when she grew bold toward the end of that endless summer, she leaned back in one of her mother's chaises longues and poured iced tea down her chest and let him lap at her swimsuit. She filled her mouth and kissed him while he drank from her, a bird to her fountain statue.

Then school came, and it was news. People did not agree that it was a good fit. He was too strange. Wasn't he that kid who played with snakes? But they didn't care. They were in their own world and they laughed at everything. At the teachers, other kids. At their parents. At policemen who pulled them over for speeding. At people who cared, at people who tried.

Their physical courtship lasted six months and he was patient. They kissed for hours, sometimes all night. It became serious before the sex and after, deadly serious. They lost all shyness in bed and talked through every step of it. She taught him how to touch her and for how long until it worked better than it was supposed to work at age sixteen.

In the last semester of their senior year they were seventeen and, though they did not know it, afraid. They had been together for nearly two years and become one of those inseparable couples that cause teachers to cluck their tongues and parents to lie awake wondering how can it possibly be so serious at this age, having forgotten in their middle age that love at seventeen is deadly serious because nothing else matters, it is the first and purest and . . . because it's love at seventeen.

So the boy set out to become a man, at precisely the time when his tribe was most unwilling to let the girl become a woman.

10

When he regained his senses he had no idea how much time had passed. Daylight had faded somewhat. His shoulder throbbed and the bathroom seemed to be tilting in every direction at once. He raised himself on shaking legs and began to pull his pants up. What just happened here? How much time had he lost? Minutes . . . or hours? The last thing he recalled was experiencing a too realistic vision of Jo and the first strand of a mighty orgasm.

He patted the front of his boxer shorts and pants, then up higher to his tee shirt. He bent over, which made his headache sing, and scanned the floor, the tub, the sink. Where the hell did it go? He longed for an ultra-violet light, one of those scanners they used on *CSI*, the better to locate his discharged DNA.

Conrad cupped his package, shifting things around. He was sore in the way that suggested he had, in fact, climaxed. He felt it in the muscles of his loins, the need to urinate. But his chafed, limp penis was clean and dry. He held his hands up in front of his face, turning them in the light. For a moment he caught the scent of lavender, of summer spices. But it was faint, and then gone.

So, let's get this straight. It was so good I blacked out, but didn't come? Then why do my neck and shoulders feel like I've been playing catch with an anvil?

Someone knocked him down, there was no other explanation. And not the dogs. Couldn't have been the dogs. The door was still latched.

Someone knocked me down . . . and cleaned me up? Or was I out so long it dried, becoming invisible?

Hey, who knows, maybe the house swallowed it up!

'Jesus Christ.'

Swearing off masturbation for at least another week, Conrad undressed, climbed in the shower and let the cold water run. At age thirty, he was tired of his sex drive, frightened of where it was leading him.

Conrad was walking the dogs when he saw the car come to a stop at the four-way intersection, and by then she was attempting to escape. The boyfriend – Teddy, Eddie, something always unsteady – braked hard. The passenger door swung all the way out and rebounded into her shin.

'Ow, you asshole!'

It was early in the afternoon, eighty-eight degrees, and no one came out when she started yelling. Eddie grabbed at her shirt to keep her from fleeing and Nadia's palm cracked against her boyfriend's cheek, causing him to blurt, 'Aw, fuck!'

'Aw, fuck, is right,' Conrad said to the dogs, stepping off the curb. 'Here we go.'

There were two types of kids here, he'd noticed. The

almost unbelievably plain second- and third-generation farm kids and do-gooders who'd yet to be exposed to even the imagined horrors of teen angst. Coming from what appeared to be a loving home and despite the company she kept, Nadia seemed like this type.

The other type was Eddie's type. They used to be called townies, but now . . . whatever they were called, Eddie's car was not helping his case. It was one of those compact models Pontiac made for about three years. Teal-green with purple pinstriping down the side – just a little sexiness to make the buyer feel like this mass-produced hunk of shit would help him express something. The mortarboard tassel dangling from the rearview mirror suggested the best days of Eddie's life were behind him, and the thumping bass emanating from the sub-panel in the back was a white trash-y, effete disco – *uhn-tiss, uhn-tiss, uhn-tiss* – that nearly drowned out the yowling hole that was the muffler. The entire package had to be violating at least three noise ordinances.

At least until Eddie and his cruiser stalled out and began to roll down Heritage Street in reverse, when everything became quiet.

Conrad cleared his throat. 'Nadia?'

'What?' she said, tearing herself from Eddie's clutches.

'Sorry to bother you. You know where we can go swimming?'

Eddie peered over her shoulder. The boy's lacquered buzz cut and wispy thin sideburns reflected sunlight and made his acne gleam.

Conrad smiled. *You see me, you little fuck? Good, 'cause I'm on my way.* Alice and Luther crossed leashes and started whining to go for a ride.

Nadia blinked at him. 'You want to go swimming?'

'My dogs are just about to croak from this heat; thought we'd find a watering hole.' Luther and Alice pawed at the door. 'Conrad, your new neighbor? It's Nadia, right?'

Eddie continued to project his best thousand-yard stare through the windshield. It was nine hundred and ninety feet short. Conrad winked at Nadia – *work with me, girl.* Nadia smirked – she got it.

'They look like they could use a swim,' Nadia said. 'Hey, hot doggies, what's up?'

'By the way.' Conrad nudged the door open so the dogs could play their part. 'I'm Conrad Harrison, you must be Teddie, right?'

'Eddie,' Eddie said, scowling at Conrad's out-stretched hand. Nadia was cooing at Luther and Alice as they nosed into her lap.

'These two are Luther and Alice, my sweet little baby bulls.' Conrad felt a pang of guilt for using them this way, adding to the stereotype he and Jo had tried to prove undeserved ever since adopting the mutts. 'Oh, don't worry, though. Terrier mixes are no different than any other species of dog. In fact, they're a lot like people. Most are good, some are bad, and it all depends on who raises them.'

'Shit, I gotta go, Nads, get those dogs outta my car.'

'Sorry, Eddie. Let me just – hey, where was that

watering hole, did you say?' Conrad made a show of trying to pull them out, leaning over Nadia. 'Darn it, they don't want to come out. Come on, Alice, let's get out of the nice man's car.'

'Here, let me.' Nadia hauled herself out and unwound Alice's leash from her legs.

Conrad pulled Luther from the front seat. 'There we go, all clear. Sorry.'

'Tssh,' Eddie said and turned to his girlfriend. 'We going or what?'

'Hold on.' Nadia turned to Conrad. 'You still need to know how to get to Governor Dodge?'

'The what?'

'The lake up the state park. Dogs are allowed.'

'Oh, yeah. Cool.' He stood there in the street, nodding at her.

'Tell you what,' she said, glancing back at Eddie, who was revving his engine. 'Why don't I draw you a map?'

'That'd be helpful.'

'Eddie, why don't you—'

Eddie squealed the tires and blew the stop sign near the Kwik-Trip, cranked his music and floored it around the corner.

Nadia watched the spot where Eddie had just been, then nodded and snapped her fingers.

'Thanks for that.'

'Oh, no, it wasn't—'

'Yes, it was. I needed rescuing and you rescued me.'

'If that's true, then I'm glad I was walking by. I should get them home. You going this way?'

'I live next door, don't I?'

'So, you do live at home?'

'Where else would I live?'

'I don't know. None of my business, actually.'
Dumbfuck.

She walked beside him as the dogs careened, sniffing every inch of the sidewalk. He noticed her small feet, the retro Eastland mocs she wore with no socks, the laces done up in that preppy pretzel thing like two little boat fenders hanging over the sides – shoes Holly used to wear. She wore simple blue canvas shorts and her calves were muscled, a soccer player's legs. A plain white tee on top, snug over the soccer ball of her belly. He guessed she was five or six months along, but he was afraid to ask. The rest of her was shorter than he remembered. Compared to his nearly Amazonian wife, this was like walking a girl home from school. It felt like he was already courting her, and that couldn't be right, no matter how much benefit of the doubt he gave himself.

Nadia said, 'Oh, and don't tell my parents, okay?'

'About?'

'About Eddie,' she said.

He kept his eyes on the sidewalk. 'Of course.'

What else could she have meant, 'Rad?

'Hey, by the way,' she said. 'What's with the red light?'

'The red – oh, in the garage. Must seem pretty weird, huh? New neighbors and there's a spooky red glow emanating from the garage.'

'I wasn't spying.'

'No, I know. It's kind of neat, actually. Or at least I think so. Do you want to see them?'

'Them?'

'Yeah,' he said, tromping faster as the dogs pulled him through their little Eden of a backyard. 'I pretty much guarantee you haven't seen these before. Come on.'

Nadia followed him to the detached garage where the red light glowed night and day.

'There's nothing dangerous in here, you have my word. But before we go in, do you have any phobias?'

Nadia stepped back, crossed her arms and pursed her lips.

Conrad nodded. 'I guess I better just spit it out. I have snakes. Non-venomous, harmless snakes. In cages.'

This was the moment when they either turned and fled or got all bright-eyed and brave.

'Snakes. You have snakes, like for pets?'

'Ah, not so much pets as a hobby. Snakes aren't really pets, because they don't like or dislike people. Well, some of them are afraid of people, but most of them are indifferent.'

'Yikes.'

'If it's not your thing, we don't have to—'

'Show me.'

'You sure?'

She nodded quickly, tensed but excited.

'I knew you would be brave.'

They stepped inside. Conrad dropped the leashes and deactivated the ADT system as the dogs went on a sniffing spree along the indoor-outdoor carpet. The six hanging fixtures housed twin four-foot Vita-Life bulbs and the space was full of purple-tinted white light. A portable swamp cooler for dangerously hot days sat in the corner. The old workbench was clean, with towels, water bowls, plastic hide-ins and cleaning products stacked neatly to one side. Along the front of the bench hung three stainless-steel gaff hooks that looked like dental instruments made for an ogre.

Nadia noticed none of these things. Her attention was fixed on the fiberglass cages on the rolling iron racks against the south wall. The cages were four by two by two feet each, three to a tier, two tiers wide for a total of six. The front panels were sliding glass doors with keyed locks. Without the aid of a human hand, nothing was getting in or out of these cages.

In the corner of each cage and rigged to a series of digital thermostats, a lamp holding a one hundred and fifty watt infrared bulb glowed, ensuring that the thermometers read 86.5 degrees, twenty-four hours a day, year round.

'They can't get out. Have a closer look.' He waved her on.

Nadia stepped forward cautiously, looking back at him with huge eyes. 'Oh-my-gosh, this is so crazy. If my mom saw these she would die!'

'Yes, let's not surprise her then, shall we?'

Nadia stepped closer to the only cage with some activity. Inside, perhaps eighteen inches from the girl's face, his largest female was peering over a natural wooden branch siliconed to the wall. Half of her nearly six feet

stretched up, her head raised as if in prayer to the invisible sun. She moved like a levitating wand, the muscles
along her neck and mid-body holding her steady, exposing the cream-colored belly and vertical slashes that
swept up and back like tiger stripes before fading into
the iridescent black velvet scales that covered the rest of
her fist-thick girth.

'That's Shadow, my largest female.'

Shadow's forked tongue waved lazily, testing the air as
she moved closer to the heat-radiating patch of fuzziness
that was the girl.

'Holy shit!' Nadia put a hand over her mouth. 'Is she
going to bite me?'

'No, she's just checking out the action. Snakes have
very poor vision, so what she's seeing now is just your
general shape. They don't have ears, so when you see
her tongue moving like that she's tasting the air, so to
speak, sensing vibrations.'

'So she can hear my voice?'

'She might feel it. And in the wild, they sense vibra-
tion on the ground, approaching animals.'

'What are they, boa constrictors?'

'They are a type of constrictor, but not boas. A very
rare species called Boelen's, or black pythons. They're
found only in the mountains of Papua New Guinea.'

'Where's that?'

'Near Australia, at the end of the Indonesian Archi-
pelago. They're heavily protected and somewhat illegal
to export from their native country, and very illegal to
import into the US.'

'What'd you do? Smuggle them?'

'One of the curators at the San Antonio Zoo is a friend of mine. Dr Hobarth sold me these wild-caught specimens at a reduced rate, off the books, so I could try to reproduce them. Captive-bred babies are more stable, free of the parasites you get with wild caught animals.'

'People buy these? How much?'

'Wild caught, not much. Too hard to keep. But assuming the babies are healthy and eating, which is the hardest part, to get them eating once they hatch, they'll go for eight to ten grand per head.'

Nadia gaped at him. 'Ten thousand dollars? For a snake?'

'And each female may produce six to twelve eggs. I'd have to split the proceeds with the zoo, of course.'

'That's ... that's a lot of money,' she said. 'Why snakes? Is this like your job or something?'

'It used to be. When I turned sixteen, my first job was working in a tropical fish and reptile store – Dr Hobarth owned the shop while he was finishing his Ph.D. By the time I got out of high school, I had thirty-five or forty snakes in my bedroom. King snakes, milk snakes, rat snakes, boas, pythons, a couple of iguanas and a monitor lizard. My mother was very patient with me. I used to do shows for elementary schools, give talks at the Humane Society. I reproduced some of them, sold the babies for a few hundred dollars here and there. Sold off most of my collection to pay for college. I always wanted to keep Boelen's, but I could never afford them. Then I sort of came into a little money, and here they are. They are my favorite species.'

'How do they . . . you know . . . ?' Nadia blushed.

'What?' He knew but he wanted to hear her say it.

'Do it.'

'Snakes aren't all that different from people. Once their primal needs are met – food, shelter, the right climate – they just hook up. It's survival, so they aren't too picky, as long as they are healthy. They cross paths, the decision is practically made for them. The actual physical part is a little different. With snakes, the boys have two.'

'Shut up!' Nadia said. 'Two? That's so gross!'

'Yeah, well, you do with what Mother Nature gives you, I guess.'

'Then what?'

'Then they wrap their tails around each other in a twist. Sometimes the male uses his mouth to hold the female by the neck. They sit like that for a few hours or a few days. Then they separate and move on.'

'What does your wife think?'

'She's not afraid of them, but I think she sees them as some juvenile part of me that won't grow up, you know? Like I should be too old for this kind of creepy-crawly kid stuff. Maybe she's right.'

'She won't be complaining when you buy her a new car with the money from the little kiddy snakes, right?'

'No, she won't. Do you want to hold one?'

'Do they have poison?'

'No, pythons are not venomous. They constrict their prey before swallowing them whole.'

'Is she going to constrict me?'

'No, she is very tame and she would never try to eat you because you're much too large.'

'What does she eat?'

'Rodents, birds.'

'Like rats?'

'Or chickens. But I've got them on rats now.'

'Ew! Where do you get rats?'

'Pet stores.'

'Isn't that kind of mean?'

'Everybody's got to eat.'

She watched the snake. 'Are they slimy?'

'No, those are the amphibians. Snakes are smooth, not slimy.'

'She is sort of beautiful.'

'Here.' Conrad unlocked the door. Shadow did not flinch, even when he picked her up, supporting her body like a garden hose draped over his forearms. He went slowly, more for Nadia's benefit than the snake's.

Nadia screwed up her courage as the serpent stretched out and raised her head, her tongue flickering gently, moving toward his face. The snake rested her neck against his shoulder and began slithering over his back while her tail hung semi-loose over his arms and waist.

'I can't believe I'm doing this.' Nadia set her hand on the snake's back and did not recoil at the first touch. 'She's so smooth. Like velvet.'

'Boelen's have exceptionally smooth scales, very delicate skin. See the iridescence there, the way it makes little rainbows in the light?'

88

'Yeah.'

'Boelen's survive in the higher elevations because her black scales absorb heat.'

'What's that on her lips?'

Shadow had come around his other shoulder. On her top lip, the vertical scales were thicker, the black grill of a sleek new car.

'Those are called pits. She senses heat with them. For hunting.'

Nadia let the snake slither forth, feeling the muscled length settle on her arms. Conrad stepped from under the snake's body and allowed the full weight to hang on her.

'Oh my God. She's amazing.'

'Yes, she is.' He could see that she was proud of her bravery.

'Thank you for showing me this, Conrad. This is really, really cool.'

'My pleasure.'

She was like the camp kids that came to the Humane Society. They started the hour crying and cowering in the corner. By the end they were fighting each other to be next in line while their parents stood stiffly at the back of the room, eyes accusing him. Except with Nadia there wasn't much fear to begin with.

'Hey, Conrad. What are those?'

'What?'

'There, in the box thingy.' She pointed. 'The white stuff? Is that her poop?'

'Uh, maybe.' Snakes defecated white calcified urates,

89

like hardened marshmallows. 'Those are kinda big to be – hey, wait.'

He froze, trying to process what he was seeing.

'What is it?'

'My God.'

'What's wrong?' She had seen something in his eyes.

'Those are eggs.'

'And they're not supposed to be?'

'They can't . . . she's never—' He checked the locks on all the cages, opened Shadow's cage and searched under her hide-in, the water bowl, the paper substrate. Foolishly looking for what he knew wasn't there, a sign that another of the animals had gotten inside with her. 'She can't have eggs, not now.'

'Why not?'

'Because Shadow has never, never once been with a male. Hobarth documented everything meticulously. And she's not even mature. I wasn't planning on putting her with the others until next spring and, even then, that was a dream. I figured two years, but this, uh-uh. There's no way.'

'They don't just lay eggs like chickens or something?'

'No, they need to be fertilized. They must mate to become gravid. No mate, no eggs.'

'One of the others got to her, you think?'

'No. Not a chance. And if they did, what, they locked themselves back in? No. The crazy thing is, I was just thinking how she looked too slim.'

'It's a good thing, though, right? She's not sick?'

'No, she seems healthy,' he said, returning to the eggs.

90

Eight or nine white orbs the size of a cue ball, all but two stuck together in a moist clutch. He was wide-eyed, giddy and a little frightened.

'That's like, what? A hundred thousand dollars?'

'Nadia, it's much more than that,' he said, stars in his eyes. 'This is a virgin birth.'

'Okay,' she said. She didn't understand he meant it literally.

'This is a miracle.' His eyes were full of a hunger that made her step back.

'Really? Wow. I . . . I guess I should be getting home.' She headed for the door. 'Thanks for everything.'

'No problem. Sorry, I'm a little out of it. I need to call someone. Dr Hobarth's going to freak.'

'Okay,' she said. 'Good luck.'

'Yes,' he said. 'You must be some kind of luck.'

He was still laughing when she shut the door behind her.

An untouched female. Nine Boelen's eggs.

'Holy shit.'

11

His hand was on the phone when he realized she still didn't know he'd bought the snakes. She would argue that he was being silly and juvenile. But this wasn't the same as the organic juice pyramid scheme, or the Pre-Paid Legal side business, or any other half-assed endeavor he'd thrown his hat in with over the past five years waiting for his real life to begin. These were different. They were an investment, one he knew would soon pay large dividends. She would understand. Once she laid her eyes on the off-spring. But even with the good news about the eggs, he had to catch her in the right mood.

He set the phone down and it rang immediately, star-tling him to fumble the receiver.

'Hello?'

'Conrad!' A one-word accusation. 'Where have you been?'

He heard her crying and was seized by the idea that she knew he had walked Nadia home and lured her into the garage.

'I was in the yard. What's wrong, Jo?'

'I'm not, I'm not feeling so good. I'm having a hard

time staying in class. I keep telling myself it's just nerves but it won't go away. I keep thinking about it.'

'About what?'

'About what? Everything. This, us! I'm living in a hotel in a random city, I don't know anybody. You have *no idea* what this is like.'

'I'm sorry, Jo. Calm down. I do know what it's like. I'm living in a city where I don't know anyone, either.'

'It's not the same. You're home! You have the dogs.'

'They miss you. We do. A lot.'

She was still on the verge of shouting. 'Have you even thought about this? One week we're living in Los Angeles and now, what, we just decide to move to the middle of nowhere? I don't think this is what we thought it would be.'

'What did you think—? No, skip that,' he said. 'I know what we said it would be. What is it now?'

'I think you need to do some serious thinking.'

Some serious thinking! 'About?'

'About everything.' Her voice had resumed a normal pitch. This frightened him, that she could be nearly hysterical one minute and then go Dr Phil the next. 'For starters, why did we have to leave Los Angeles? No, don't answer me now. I want you to think about it because this is really important, are you listening?'

'Yes.' *Talk, don't talk. What do you want me to do, woman?*

'This isn't like us, it's too fast, the whole thing. It's like we woke up different people. I know you've been through a lot with your father dying, but I'm sorry. There's more to it. You're not being truthful with me. I know something … else … happened to you. Something bad. You've always been aloof, but you're different now. Darker. And I'm sorry if that sounds paranoid. But I'm not sorry because it's how I feel, so don't try to blame me.'

This, more than anything about his wife, made his blood jump. The way she dumped everything on him and, whether he deserved it or not, backed it all up by telling him that he could not, dared not, dispute it because this was the way she *felt*. He equated this sort of haired-out logic with fundamentalists who burned books because they were offended and pissed off at the world. She felt bad; it was his responsibility to change until she felt better.

'—and then there's your career. Because I can take care of myself, but I don't want to take care of you, too. And you shouldn't want me to.'

Wasn't that what married people were supposed to do, take care of each other? And, Christ, he'd just inherited five hundred thousand dollars. What the fuck was this about?

'I'm solvent now. We're ahead of the game here, Jo.'

'It's not about the money, Conrad. You have to do something real.'

'Something real? Like what? Selling more software I don't even understand? Like traveling around the country so much neither one of us is home to so much as feed the dogs, let alone a kid?'

'What has that got to do with anything?' It was an actual screech now. 'You don't think I will make a good mother?'

'No. Yes, of course you will. I'm just saying we're both still in transition here. I'm going to find something else. Just have some patience.' *And stop acting like you have it all figured out because obviously you do not.*

'Are you going to figure it out?'

'Yes—'

'Because I can't take another diversion.'

'Now wait a goddamned—'

'That's not what I meant. I'm sorry.'

He was fuming. A diversion? They'd moved to Los Angeles for her goddamn career, not his. And the staying home all the time. She said it was nice knowing he was home. She'd even started to call him Mr Mom, for fuck's sakes.

'If you thought the past few years were a diversion, you should have spoken up,' he said. 'Instead, you waited for me, and I changed. I was the one who pushed us to move. Before I came home to find That Fucker Jake standing in the hallway with his dong in his hand. Jesus!'

'Conrad, I don't want to fight.'

'You don't – hey, that's actually funny.'

'I can't. Not here.'

'Then don't.'

'Okay.'

'Okay.'

'But you should know . . .' she said in a condescending tone.

'What?'

'I'm not coming home this weekend.' This wasn't

lobbing one over to see how it would play. This was something she knew from the minute she called.

'Why not?' He made his voice cold.

'I don't feel like it.'

'You don't feel like it.'

'No.'

'Fine, then do whatever the fuck you feel like with whoever the fuck you feel like and leave me the fuck alone!'

There was a small tea saucer lying on the kitchen table, next to the cordless phone cradle. When the phone went down like a torpedo, it nicked the saucer and shattered the porcelain into a thousand white slivers, one of which embedded itself in the cheek meat just below his left eye. There was a ringing sound from the shattering and for a second he thought it was her calling back. He reached for the phone, heard silence and threw the phone at the wall and kicked the chair up in the air where it did a neat little somersault and landed almost perfectly straight again.

His breathing came in ragged gulps like he'd been punched in the balls.

And it was a lovely summer day.

She doesn't feel like coming home? And why should she? She's got Shirley from Akron to keep her company.

'Fuck Shirley, fuck Shirley's baby, and fuck you Jo, fucking Oscar-The-Grouch-cheating-ass-bitch.'

Easy. Deep breaths. He would go to Wal-Mart and buy a new phone, and maybe sign up for whatever shit-poke regional coverage worked out here, because his

Verizon mobile still wasn't working in this house and he just wanted to put the stupid thing in the garbage disposal. Later. Right now he needed to calm down and figure out what to do with the next two weeks until his wife deigned to visit him in their new home. He needed to think about his freak-ass snake eggs, and the fucking hundred year-old photo album full of ugly fucking women he burned because he was too afraid to turn the page.

He poured himself an oceanic glass of iced tea and drank it in one go. God, he could never remember being so thirsty. The summer air was so thick you could drink by wagging your tongue in front of your face. He refilled, walked upstairs and thought about Los Angeles. Rachel, the girl from the bookstore. Oh, he should have given it to her upside down and from behind when he had the chance. He went to the bathroom and tweezed the saucer shrapnel from his face, squeezed the cut like a pimple, swabbed it with witch hazel.

Luther and Alice followed him from a safe distance. They were staring at him and he stared back, all three of them panting. He opened all the windows in the library and the master bedroom. He finished the second glass of iced tea. Properly brewed iced tea with no lemon or sugar was better than most water. He wished he had brought the whole pitcher with him so he could fucking bathe in it.

Conrad fell into bed with his dogs beside him, pulled one pillow over his eyes and thought about showering in a golden waterfall of iced tea, some Edenic setting with sprigs of mint growing from rocky walls, drinking and drowning in the pure wash of it. Ice cubes floating around his balls in the basin, tea seeping into his pores until his skin was stained brown, tea-swamped and purified. With his belly full of the stuff, Conrad drifted and cooled and soon fell into the deluded reprieve of an angry, deviant nap.

Later, he woke in darkness to the sound of the dogs stirring from their crate beds, the *click-click-click*ing of their nails on the hardwood floor. Abruptly they stopped. And he sat there waiting for the dogs to jump on to the bed.

'Come on, Alice,' he said, realizing he was about to pee the bed. Too much iced tea.

Silence.

When the clicking started again, the sound was different. Instead of going *click-click-click* in timed groups, now he heard them individually. Not the dogs, the clicks.

Click . . . silence . . . *click* . . . silence . . . *click*. He smiled at the image of Alice tiptoeing, stepping on a single claw at a time, but the smile vanished as the next *click* drew closer and he realized there was no weight behind the sound. This was not the sound of a dog at all. It was something else.

He found the lamp, twisted the knob, and crunched his eyes shut until his pupils adjusted to the flood of light. He blinked at the foot of the bed, waiting for the next click to offer a clue as to the dogs' whereabouts.

But it's not one of the dogs, and I think you know that now, don't you?

Conrad leaned over. Nothing on the hardwood floor.

Click.

There – on the other side of the bed. It was in the room, whatever it was.

'This is ridiculous,' he said to the room. Before he could talk himself out of it, he jackknifed belly down over the covers to see into the blind spot on Jo's side.

Between the dog crates and the bed was a two-foot path of wood floor. A pair of Jo's panties collecting dust sat crumpled in one corner, the lavender Victoria's Secret ones he liked on her. Down this little wooden path, at the foot of the bed, there appeared to be twin Popsicle sticks jutting out from the post of the bed frame. For some unknowable reason, the flat sticks made him think of crude shoes, what you would see if you were to encounter a clown hiding behind a tree. As soon as this image came to him, as if reading his mind one of the feet jerked up perhaps two inches and stepped forward, and the rest of the doll pivoted around the post and tilted its head . . . up at him.

His heartbeat became violent even as his limbs and back seemed to fill with concrete. Blood rushed into his face, neck and scalp, making everything itch.

'Oh, for the love . . .' he moaned.

Less than twelve inches tall, the home-made doll looked like a finger puppet or some poor child's art project. The legs were thin sticks attached to the flat feet and the cloth stitched over the body was of faded pink flowers on white, frayed and yellowed with age. Just below the neckline the thing appeared jolly and fat, the stuffing wrapped inside coarse cotton, bulging in obscene contrast to the stick legs. The doll had no neck, but it had a head.

It did not have a face.

Under the dry and stiff black hair that sprouted from the crown, where there should have been button eyes and a cute cross-stitch of a nose there was only a blank pad. Most queer of all, while the little rag had the hair and dress of a female, he sensed the other sex in its posture. It felt mean and hard, a little male troll that would speak in a clipped, ugly voice if it had one. He really hoped it did not speak. A few seconds passed. He was starting to doubt that he had actually seen it move when the doll took another step – *click!* – and then another after that one, moving with renewed purpose, as if had just found what it was looking for.

But that's crazy, because it has no eyes.

Conrad was splayed crooked on the bed, immobilized as the absurd stick figure doll, no wider than a Scarecrow Barbie, came at him in rapid steps – *click-click-click-CLICK-CLICK-CLICK!* – and raised its pipe cleaner arms to attack.

It wants to put my eyes out, his mind cried, *damned if it doesn't!*

Conrad's bladder wrenched in pain as the thing trotted alongside the bed. He flung himself away and tangled himself in the bedding as he scrambled off the other side. His right foot hit the floor and he had the crazy, self-preserving presence of mind to yank his bare foot back up in case the thing had taken a shortcut and was now coming at him from under the bed.

What if it jumps up on to the bed? What then?

How can it jump? It's only a pile of sticks, no taller than a number two pencil. Hey, it fucking walked, didn't it? No, at the end there it had started to run.

Get the fuck out of here!

His feet hovering over the floor, Conrad glanced over his shoulder – nope, not coming over the bed – and then back to the floor. He couldn't see the doll now, but he could hear it. *Click-click-click* . . . pause. It was pacing, maybe coming around the other side, taking the scenic route for Chrissake, but coming just the same.

Blood humming through his veins, eyes wide and snapping left to right, Conrad planted his feet, shot off the bed, and bee-lined for the open door. Approaching the threshold he (*Don't look back! No, fuck you, I have to!*) glanced down just in time to see the doll marching stiffly after him, swaying left and right, and the moment stretched into a vacuum of pre-car-crash clarity that seemed to last five minutes.

He saw the doorframe floating toward him; behind him the doll high-stepping like a Nutcracker reject. He saw the arms reaching up, but not *after* him this time, no, instead arcing out and back down until the tiny home-made fingers dug into the wiry black hair and proceeded to yank it out in clumps, shaking its dead growth at him with that blank pad of a face somehow conveying pure, untainted hatred.

Conrad's shoulder slammed into the doorframe,

pinwheeling him sideways and down. His forehead bounced off the black maple banister (another two steps of uninterrupted momentum and he might have crashed through the banister, head first down to the foyer) and he hit the hallway floor shoulder first, hipbone next, jaw last, the culminating sound like billiard balls after the sledgehammer break.

The panic and pain mixed into a blinding cocktail and he used his last bolt of strength to roll sideways. He was eye-level with the doll, the room darkening as he hovered on the edge of consciousness. His vision blurred, the doll becoming two dolls coming for his eyes until he could almost feel their tendril fingers crawling into his skin like insect bites. Pain flared behind his eyeballs, and then he could only squeeze his eyes shut and tremble.

When some time passed and he felt no stabbing and heard no more clicking sounds, he opened his eyes and blinked. There was no sign of the doll. The room was quiet. Empty. He got to his feet and circled the bed, weak through the knees and unsure of what, if anything, he had really seen.

There was a clicking in the hall. He tensed for it.

Alice came around the corner and looked up at him. She was sleepy. She had slept through the whole thing. Probably woke up when he hit the floor.

Conrad rubbed his head as he traipsed through the library and into the bathroom. As if timed with his bladder's release, his heart pounded in slow, heavy thumps that faded only when he had flushed.

He took three Advil and lay back down on the bed.

102

His head began to pound in earnest, and he knew it needed some ice. He was still thinking about going downstairs to fetch some when he drifted back to sleep.

The next morning Conrad showered, drank four glasses of iced tea, and went to the office. After poking around on Google for forty-five minutes, he read the following excerpt from an article titled, 'Before There Was Teddy: The Evolution of Manikins, Poppets and Other Teaching Icons', originally published by *ON FOOT*, Ohio State University's journal of anthropology.

> Not every culture approves of your average toy store doll. Some older customs prevent children from playing with manufactured dolls bearing a human likeness. The Amish, for instance, have long forbidden girls to play with human-resembling caricatures. Many dolls found in the Amish household would not have the same features as, say, Barbie or Ken. Imagine, I suppose, a thing made of cloth and other natural materials. Certainly one would not find dolls with eyes, a three dimensional nose, artificial hair, etc. Such a doll would not have much of a face at all.
>
> The guiding principal here is similar to their disapproval of being photographed, one of biblical origin. Exodus 20:4–6. 'You shall not make for yourself a carved image, or any likeness of anything that is in heaven above, or that is in the earth beneath . . .'

12

If Jo had been home she would have talked some sense into him, told him he was having nightmares, convinced him to go see someone. But she wasn't home and he didn't know when she would be back. He still felt guilty for screaming and hanging up on her, but he was also still hurt by her refusal to come home. What had she said? 'Because I don't feel like it.' Now that was cruel, wasn't it? Unless . . .

What else had she said? 'I'm not feeling so good.' Was it possible, in his quick jump to self-pity, he might have mistaken her words? What if all she really meant was, I'm too sick to fly? I feel like shit?

'So I'm the asshole.'

After completing a short walk around the block, Conrad let the dogs inside, unhooked the leashes and went for the phone. Then he remembered he was supposed to go to Wal-Mart to replace the one he'd busted all to hell.

We came to start our new lives together, he would tell her. *Baby, I love you more than anything and whatever happened out there I won't take no for an answer. You need to come home soon.*

Before something bad happens.

*

As soon as Conrad had driven the fifteen miles, exited Highway 151, and passed the last dairy farm, he was confronted by the mini-city that was Wal-Mart. The parking lot was vast, hot and full of American nameplates. He'd heard the state's residents bemoaning the retail giant's destructive effect on their small towns on National Public Radio, which, he'd noticed, regularly named the chain as a sponsor. But when Pringles were seventy-eight cents a yard and cordless phones started at $9.23, why shop anywhere else?

'Vote with your dollars, assholes,' he mumbled, yanking a cart from the fossilized greeter. 'Sorry, not you.'

After grabbing the cheapest phone on the shelf, he roamed the DVD new releases, saw nothing worth $13.88. He lost track of time and came back to himself browsing, for no real reason, an aisle of bath towels. He put two ugly green ones in his cart.

Standing in the checkout lane, Conrad fell into a glazed, tabloid-induced stupor until a frog-voiced woman exclaimed, 'How about that, childrens? It's the nice man who moved into our house.'

Conrad turned to see a gaunt woman in her thirties or fifties with gray-streaked black hair and leathery skin pulled so tight around the bulge of her pregnant belly it seemed to drag the corners of her mouth into a pouting brat's frown. She was wearing a large halter-smock and dirty jean shorts. He knew at once she was Leon's Laski's wife, and that he should be polite, but he couldn't stop staring at the tangle of grimy tykes crawling around her legs, swinging from her arms and slapping at her knobby knees.

'I'm Greer Laski, and you're Conrad, right?'

'Oh, hello, Mrs Laski . . .'

There were three of them, ages three to eight (not counting the one in the oven) but it was difficult to tell with their arms raking gum and candy to the floor, the Whiffle ball bat knocking alternately at the cart and a smaller sibling's head. They all had the same genderless cropped haircuts of a cult, and two of them wore identical grass-stained Spiderman pajamas. One fixed him with a drooling, open-mouthed and one-eyed stare, the other eye hidden behind a metal mesh patch hanging by a single strand of dirty medical tape. When she spoke, Mrs Laski's voice came in an accented, babbling run. But what kind of accent? It was more than the usual Wisconsinese his neighbors let slip. This sounded like some unique crossbreeding of shine-drunk Appalachian, Elmer Fudd and Jodi Foster in *Nell*.

'These are Anna Maybelle, Davey and Louis . . .' (massaging her distended belly) '. . . this one's a surprise. How are you settling in? Gosh, we loved that house, we sure do miss it, don't we kids, say hello to Mr Harrison.'

She pronounced it *Miss-tawh Hay-wiss-un*.

'Yes, we're doing fine.' Conrad tried to maintain the veneer of politeness while swiping his check card in the machine.

'Do you want any cash back?' the cashier said.

'No, thank you.'

'Press no.'

He did, then turned back to (what kind of name is Greer?) Mrs Laski. 'How is your new place?'

'Oh, it's hard, ya know. It's really hard, Conrad.' *Rea-wee hawd*. 'With the kids and the movers and ya know how Leon having trouble with crew and his back since the move, but we're doin' okay, aren't we kids, honey stop playing with those batteries, no, Anna Maybelle, no new cereal this week.'

'Okay, then.' Conrad edged out of the line with his single bag in hand.

But Mrs Laski thwarted the getaway by grabbing his shirtsleeve. 'I don't care what anyone says, Conrad, that house is a perfectly good place to raise a family. God watched out for us in our old home just like he's watching out for you now, m'kay? Oh, h'okay, Mommy has to press the button, kids, hold on a second.'

Ah. God is watching us all.

'Yeah, about that, Mrs Laski. Is there something I don't know about our house, your old place? Leon gave me that book and if there is some significance . . . ?'

Mrs Laski's eyes shot up from her pocket book and held him with a hard stare, but it lasted only a second before she was smiling again. 'Leon should have never left that with you. It's a lotta history, ya know, Conrad.' A lot of *hiss-tow-wee*. 'He doesn't like to talk about it, but it's not like we're ashamed of it.'

With her bags in her cart, Mrs Laski dragged the train out of the line and followed Conrad toward the front doors. He knew he could outrun them, but not without appearing insane. One of the kids was now literally

107

clinging to her leg, sitting on her foot so that the woman had to walk in a loping gait. Conrad did an involuntary and quite rude double-take when he saw that one of the boy's hands was – *oh dear God* – missing three fingers and gnarled into a ball of flesh, twin nails growing out of what should have been the first knuckles. On the back of the 'hand' was an Idaho of lumpen black fur.

'You can have it back, it's no big deal to me either way,' Conrad said over his shoulder, forgetting he had already torched the album. He shuffled faster past stacks of bulk water softener. Guilt wasn't even a factor now. They were so loud and grubby, it made him feel sick to be in their company.

'Oh, no no, too late for that. The book stays with the house.'

The house? You can have the house!

He realized, tallying it as a group, each child was malformed in some way. *Jesus Christ, is she his wife or his sister?*

'I'm sorry,' he said, feeling sweat leak down his ribs.

'There wasn't no devil at work in there. Lots of lil 'uns made their way into this world thanks to those women.'

'I'm not sure—'

'My family's not cursed. Accidents happen everywhere. We were happy there for a long, long time.'

'Never mind, it's not—'

'Those women were there for each other in hard times. And we all come upon hard times, don't we, from time to time?'

Conrad finally understood, and knew that he had known all along. The women were the lost women and their midwives, broken souls who came to heal . . . and got stuck bearing children . . . like the Laski kids.

'God always gave us more children, and He wouldn't do that in no home that was cursed.'

Something from dinner with the Grums came back to him. Gail and Big John and Steve arguing about how many children the Laskis had.

It's like ten little Indians over there, Steve had said.

Could have been something rare, Gail had said. *Just one of those things*.

'I'm sorry for your loss,' Conrad said, watching the flicker of dark martyrdom in her eyes.

But she recovered quickly. 'No regrets, Conrad.' *No ree-gwetts*. 'And who would trust a hospital any more these days, right? Those places are full of diseases.' Mrs Laski was giggling. 'A hospital! That would be ridiculous!'

Roddy's reference to the doctor. The sketched cross in the yard.

Conrad wanted to slap her face and tell her this wasn't funny. He realized the only things stopping him were the children, staring up at him as if he had joined their traveling circus.

'I have to be—'

'Do you and your wife have any kids yet, Conrad?'

'I'm sorry, I have to get home.' He did not look back as he fled to his car.

'Say goodbye, kids, say bye bye mistah hay-wiss-son!'

Ten little Indians. Some made it out, some did not.

All of them born in his birthing house.

*

The phone had not been docked long enough to hold a charge, but that turned out not to matter. Their conversation was short.

'What's wrong?' He could tell she was crying, again or still. 'I'm sorry I yelled at you, Baby. That was shitty of me. I just miss you.'

She sniffed. 'I went to the doctor today.'

'Okay.' The house was hot. So hot and humid it made him sway and plop down into one of the chairs at the two top. 'What kind of doctor?'

'It wasn't a surprise. I've known for a while.'

'A while?'

'I'm pregnant.'

13

She was right – it wasn't much of surprise. The rest of the conversation had been a blur. He hoped he'd said at least some of the right things. She had been too tired to go into it. They agreed to keep it a secret for a few more weeks. There was always a chance she would miscarry, and he was ashamed to feel a sliver of hope that she would. No sooner had he thought that than a wild shot of pride and longing he had never imagined filled his heart. He wanted to be a father. This was it. Time to become a man. Do it right, better than Dad.

But that longing was fleeting, too. Something other than Jo's new condition and Mrs Laski's traveling circus was eating him. Something about the timing of her pregnancy did not make sense.

He could see it only one of three ways. Jo was lying and not pregnant, which she would never do. That sort of emotional manipulation was beyond even her. The other possibility was, under the stress of the move and all the shit that had gone on leading up to it, he had forgotten having sex with his wife. That did not seem likely, because men don't forget, ever. The last possibility was that she was pregnant with Jake-the-out-of-work-actor-fuck-buddy's baby.

She claimed they hadn't had sex. But what if they had? What if she had been lying just to gloss it over and move on? He hadn't really wanted to know one way or another before. But now he did. Oh yes, now he needed to know everything.

Oh, this is bad. This is fucked up. How do you ask her if the child is really yours? Without detonating a nuke?

Answer: you don't.

Then, with the out-of-control force of a nightmare, the rest of it clicked into place. Something far worse than deceit or infidelity.

What if he was not the father because there was no father?

What if it was the same with her as with the Boelen's? What if it was something in this new environment? Everywhere he turned he was confronted with pregnancy, eggs, children: he had become surrounded by burgeoning life. There should be nothing frightening about that. It could all be a coincidence.

Unless the house made things this way. Unless everyone who lived here was touched by it.

Unless the house was hungry for more.

14

'It's not only impossible,' Dr Alexis Hobarth said. 'It's fucking impossible. Those animals have been separated, in my care and my care alone, for the past three years.'

'I'm sitting on nine apparently healthy Boelen's eggs, Alex.'

Dr Hobarth was something of a jet-setting playboy in the reptile community. He'd returned Conrad's call while attending the annual National Herpetological Symposium in DC, where he was to deliver a paper on a new subspecies of water monitor his team had discovered on a remote island in Indonesia. So far Conrad had explained the situation with the eggs, but kept his fears about his wife to himself.

'So,' the doctor said, amused, 'what are you doing in Wisconsin, anyway? Are you out of your mind or do you just crave cheese?'

'Alex, it's not important why I'm here. What's important is I have nine eggs in my garage. You told me yourself there was zero chance of fertilization before they reached sexual maturity, at some four years of age and six or seven feet in length. Not only that, she's been eating like a horse since she arrived. You know a gravid female doesn't eat, I don't care how good a keeper you are, and I'm not that good.'

'You have photos?'

'Of the eggs?'

'Yes.'

'No, I don't, as a matter of fact. But I will be happy to email you photos later today.'

'Where are the eggs now?'

'In the garage.'

'You left them with the female?' Hobarth's voice registered concern.

'I'm not an idiot, Alex. They're in vermiculite, sealed in tamper-proof acrylic shoeboxes, holding steady at eighty-eight degrees. Humidity here is high, so I haven't bothered misting them.'

'All right. What do you want me to say?'

'How about, wow, that's a miracle?'

'A miracle? Conrad, please. If anything it's parthenogenesis.'

'What's that?'

'The animal kingdom's version of your virgin birth.'

'I'm not a biologist, Alex.'

'Cases involving insects and plants are well documented. Less so with vertebrates, but it happens with some species of fish, amphibians, and, yes, even reptiles. Every now and then you read about it happening at one of the zoos. A tiger shark couple years back. A komodo dragon just a few months ago. But hold on. Don't get excited. It is possible for a female to lay eggs without the benefit of fertilization, but it is extremely rare with reptiles, and almost impossible to prove because most of our stock comes from the wild, where the female's mating history remains unaccounted for. Even with semi-captives such as our Boelen's, it's dicey because most keepers do not document thoroughly enough to disprove the animals in question have never been put with the opposite sex. But I am not most keepers. I'm the fucking Curator of fucking Herpetology at the fucking San Antonio Zoo.'

'But it's possible? This partho thing, it's a real thing, not some Ripley's Believe It or Not hoax?'

'It's real, but it doesn't make any sense for your animals, or the Boelen's in particular.'

'Why not?'

'Because parthenogenesis occurs only in all or predominately female populations. As with honeybees, when you have a queen and her many drones. Parthenogenesis occurs only when the queen bee, the only female in the hive, dies before reproducing another queen. The male drones panic, or their genetic make-up panics, knowing their future is lost without her. In her place they begin to reproduce, but it is all in vain. They will only bring more males into the hive, and eventually these drones will die, too.'

'How do you know that isn't exactly what happened?'

'Because it's all in the environment, Conrad. Parthenogenesis occurs when environmental conditions are near perfect, when the balance of females to males is less than ideal, or all male. On top that, the Boelen's is such a delicate creature, even in the wild, it's a wonder they reproduce at all. It is why they almost never breed in captivity, let alone accomplish something as rare as this kind of virgin birth. The odds of this happening in a small population of males and females . . . in your, what, your garage? Preposterous, my friend.'

'But, Alex, how would she know there are males in her population? For all she knows, she is alone in the world.'

'Oh, so what you're telling me is, you've never put these animals in a bucket for a soak, never put them in the same bag for transport, never once shared cages, never once left one of them to crawl over another?'

'Not long enough to get their freak on.'

'Conrad, they don't have to get anything on – they just have to understand, to sense that reproduction with the opposite sex is possible. It's like us guys in a bar. We don't even have to be in the bar, or a whorehouse. We can look through the window, smell the perfume wafting out the door. This stuff is in the air. We've known for some time that snakes track pheromones emitted at mating time. Believe me, the snakes know who is or isn't next door, especially when they haven't closed the deal since last spring.'

'Shit,' Conrad said.

'Speaking of, how's your rack these days, chum? Things between you and the missus going all right since the move? You sound a little backed up.'

Conrad ignored the swipe. 'Have I ever lied to you?'

'Well, there's a simple way to prove all this one way or another.'

'Yeah, what's that?'

'Hatch the eggs. We can fingerprint the DNA on the hatchlings. If there's paternal contribution, we'll find it.'

'You can do that now?'

'It's not cheap, but you hatch these Boelen's, the zoo will pay for it.'

'I guess that's something,' Conrad said, dissatisfied but out of ideas.

'You've got eggs? Fine, take care of them. Keep me posted on their development. When they hatch, I'll see that we're published and we'll go to Costa Rica to celebrate.'

Conrad heard chatter in the background and the doctor cleared his throat.

'I'll let you get back to your talk, Alex. Good luck with that monitor paper. Maybe they'll name the thing after you.'

'That is my intention. We've an excellent shot at *Varanus salvator hobarthi*, as is only proper considering I discovered the little beasties.'

'You deserve it, Alex. Sorry I bothered you.'

'Conrad?'

'Yeah?'

'I don't care how it happened. You hatch those eggs, it's a hell of an accomplishment.'

'Thanks, Alex.'

'Dr Hobarth to you, knucklehead.'

Conrad slipped the cordless into his pocket and stared at the eggs in the box. The black, volcanic-looking vermiculite soil was slightly moist and sticky, the eggs

117

leathery, free of fungus, healthy. No sign of movement within, even when he shone a flashlight over the smooth, opaque surface. He wasn't really expecting to see much – it would be another hundred days before they hatched.

If they hatched. Man, that would be something.

He thought about Jo and the life she carried inside of her now. He tried to feel the same welling of pride, but it wasn't the same. Compared to the delicate Boelen's, adding one more child to the six billion souls ravaging the planet seemed trivial. Or maybe it was a proximity thing. The eggs were here, now, under his watchful eye. Jo was in another state, pulling herself away from him with every passing day.

He hoped that when she came home he would feel that the life within her was his creation, too.

15

By the time Conrad finished their evening walk, he could smell the ozone in the air and the humidity was like a fist of moist cotton balls in his chest. Fat drops fell on his skin, warm as bathwater. Just before he made it home he saw movement out of the corner of his eye and turned to see Gail Grum waving him over.

'One second!' Conrad let the dogs in and darted across the Grums' lawn.

'You made it just in time.' She was laughing when he joined her under the covered porch, where she had established a narrow wicker living room. Gail had to raise her voice above the din of the rain. 'What would you like to drink? I have beer or iced tea.'

'Iced tea. Please.'

When Gail returned with his tea and a Sierra Nevada for herself, another arc of lightning illuminated the gray afternoon haze.

'How's the job hunt?'

'I'm still gainfully unemployed.'

'Oh, goodie. Now that I know you're free you can't say

no. Nadia told me how you rescued her from that awful Eddie the other day. Very smooth, Conrad.'

The gist: Gail and Big John were embarking on a road trip through Kentucky and Tennessee. Bourbon distilleries, horseback rides, something involving a canoe. She showed him B&B brochures. The stated purpose was to visit a sister, but Conrad gathered the real motive here was to re-ignite the dying cinders of their middle-aged sex life. One of the stops was named Lovers Last Ranch, for God's sake. Pay Per View, massages, balcony spas . . . yes, Gail had good reason to be excited. She was already out the door, practically vibrating with visions of saddling Big John up for one last ride into the sunset.

'The catch is,' she said, sipping the beer.

The catch was Nadia. She had been 'acting up' all last year. Her freshman 'adventures' at UW Madison had led her down some 'wrong paths' with 'poor choices' in friends and this summer she had 'relapsed' several times.

'Drugs?' Conrad asked, cutting through the quotation marks.

'Not that I know of. But, you know,' Gail frowned, 'Eddie is sort of like a drug, so maybe you could say that.'

'Young love can be that way,' he added, ready to play sage to the hand-wringing parent.

'You know she's pregnant,' Gail said.

'It appears so.'

'Obviously we wouldn't be leaving during this time, but Nadia's very determined to do this all on her own. She insists we go, and John really needs this vacation.'

'Sure, she seems capable.'

Gail finished with her vision of his role for the next ten days, fourteen if they got carried away. Conrad would 'feel free to stay at home', which made sense seeing as how he lived next door, ha ha. But Nadia was not to be trusted with the house. 'One friend at a time . . . no Eddie, no parties, no loud music.' It was to be a strictly pizza and Netflix affair. In addition to keeping one eye on Nadia, Conrad would need to mow the lawn, to water all the plants, check the mail.

'Sure,' he said. 'I need the exercise.'

'Actually, we also need our gutters cleaned. John's worried all this rain's going to start seeping into the basement.'

'I can do that.'

'The important thing is to be present at regular intervals. We'll pay you, of course.'

'I'm home all the time. I wouldn't hear of it.'

Gail touched his arm. 'Just a few hundred dollars. John would insist.'

'Then I won't argue.'

He didn't need the money, of course. But at least he would be assuming some sort of responsibility. Helping the neighbors. Maybe a chance to learn something about the house through Nadia.

Nadia. Pretty little pregnant Nadia.

It depressed him that his new neighbors saw him as closer to their own level of maturity than Nadia's. It suggested he was an adult, which he knew he was, on paper. He just hadn't realized other adults saw him this way, too. He felt too young to be a father, too old to be Nadia's friend.

Stop whining. Have some fun. You're still 'Rad, man!

'I'll be honest, Conrad,' Gail said, the beer having its way with her. 'We like you. And we just don't know anyone else we can trust. Steve and Bailey offered, but if we had someone our age poking around, Nadia would fly off the handle. I think she relates to you. Maybe you can be the cool older brother she never had.'

The older brother. Nice.

'When do you leave?'

'Tomorrow.'

'Whoa – watch out, Kentucky!'

'It's like fate.' Gail leaned in close enough that he could smell the garden and her sweet, beery breath. 'Do you believe in fate, Conrad?'

'I used to believe it was all in my hands. That we made our own choices and there was nothing else.'

Gail nodded. 'And now?'

'I try to keep an open mind.'

Jo again, back on the horn. 'That's great. It's perfect for you, honey.'

'Really? You're not disappointed?'

'Why would I be?'

'I just thought maybe you'd want me to be out looking for a real job. There are sales jobs in Madison, temp work.'

'Is that what you want to do? Sell advertising?'

'No.'

'So our new neighbors offered you some easy work. Maybe it happened for a reason.'

'Like fate?'

122

'Sure,' she said. So far she hadn't mentioned the pregnancy. He knew they weren't ready to go into it, maybe not until she came home.

'So the job is good? You're confident this is the right thing?'

'What? Oh, it's good. It's fine. It's not really the kind of job I can see myself in for the next five years.' She snorted, implying the ridiculous.

'Sweetie?'

'Yes?'

'Why do I feel like you've made some decision and haven't told me?'

'Like what?'

'Jo.'

'What?'

'You're so "whatever", like you had another brilliant breakthrough.'

She sighed and he heard the bed squeak like she'd just given up and plopped down to dig in for the inevitable.

'I'm not going to turn this into a whole production,' she said.

'I just don't want you coming to some big decision without me. Don't tell me today it's Detroit and tomorrow it's Amsterdam or—'

Somewhere in the room, a door shut. He heard a faint 'Oh, hey, is this a . . . time?' in the background. The voice sounded neutral, possibly male. There was a muffling sound and he heard his wife say, 'Gimme one second.'

'Who's that?' Conrad said.

The phone unmuffled. 'You know what I think,

honey? I think you need to remember I'm just not really there right now.'

'No shit, sweetie.'

'And we might as well get it over with. I'm not going to be there for another five weeks.'

Stay cool, boss. 'Heh heh. Yeah. Please tell me that was a joke.'

'There's a lot going on, for both of us. The move, the house, the job, and your father even though you weren't close and I still think you need to see someone about that, but it's your choice, so okay, and there's everything else. And it's too hard to do it all at once.'

'So . . . ?'

'So, I'm saying, we're not going to do it, not now. We're just not.'

Anger, like whiskey in his belly, flaring out.

'Conrad?'

'I'm coming out,' he said.

'What?'

'To see you.'

'Conrad, no.'

'Why the hell not?'

'Because I don't want you to.'

'Why not?'

'I don't want to say it.'

'Say it, or so help me I will drive there tonight.'

'I can't stand you right now.'

'Nice, Jo. Real nice.'

'I need space.'

'What does that mean?'

She wasn't crying. Not even close. She sounded like a woman he had never met.

'I'm not coming home and I don't want you to come here because I don't want to see you. Do you understand?'

'Ever? What the fuck? Jesus, who's in your room, Johnny Depp? Does he have, a what, a fucking earring, too?'

She didn't say anything for fifteen seconds. Was she trying to make him suffer? Make him go off?

So be it.

'You don't want to see me ever again. You're leaving me, the dogs, the house? And what is this, "I can't do this right now" shit? Are you thinking about having an abortion?'

He'd never even thought of that until just this second and now it was like a neon sign in his brain – SHE'S GOING TO KILL YOUR BABY – while he stood here in a fucking birthing house. If she did not answer soon he would start screaming and not stop until someone jammed a needle in his arm.

'You bitch—' he started, and then she did scream. No, it was yelling. Like his father speaking at some terrible hoarse volume, controlled and therefore twice as scary.

'You fucking asshole! Are you out of your mind? I'm pregnant with your child! I just moved across the country with you because you decided to buy a house without even asking me! I'm in training for eight weeks, I miss my home, I miss my dogs and, yes, until tonight, I missed you. I can't deal with work and being pregnant and your insecure bullshit about one stupid night that I passed out after talking – TALKING – to your friend. So, no, not now, do you understand?'

'I'm sorry,' he croaked.

'I'll be home in five weeks and then we can worry about whether or not we have the baby, but right now I am trying to follow through on a commitment and I NEED TO GET THROUGH THIS ALONE!'

The same sexless voice said, 'Do you want me to go?'

'No,' she said.

'Who's that—'

'Night, Conrad.' She hung up on him.

So arrived the night that Conrad Harrison learned, to his utter amazement, that there are certain times you don't want to see a young woman's breasts.

As Big John showed him the plants to be watered, the windows to shut when you ran the a/c, and the ladder and tools for the gutter repairs, Conrad felt something was eating the big man – something other than the hope his wife was packing in her Samsonite. Like, for instance, leaving his obviously troubled and not at all unattractive pregnant daughter with an older male he hadn't had time to get to know over bocce and a six-pack.

Conrad did his best to ask questions and nod his head with a vigor that suggested he was memorizing all this just fine, thank you, no need to write it down. The truth was, all of Big John's directions were going in one ear and out the other. He was still obsessing about Jo. Someone had been in her room.

'I want to be clear on the roof access here.' They stopped at the end of the second-floor hall facing the street. Conrad was staring off into space when Big John slapped him on the shoulder. 'You still with me, bud?'

'Yeah, sorry, John. Been a long day.'

'You got that right. Now, when you go out to clean the gutters over the porch, do not attempt to use the ladder from the yard. Because it is *not* long enough, and you will fall and break your neck and then Gail will never let me hear the end of it.'

'Right. No ladder.'

'I don't expect you to do the top gutter – there's only one and I'm pretty sure it's clean – but if you do get a wild hair up your ass, bring the small ladder up here, use the ladder into the attic, open the front-attic window. Using a broom you ought to be able to reach anything on that last stretch of roof, but I repeat. Do *not* crawl outside of the attic. That little patch needs new shingles. Unless you want to do a Greg Louganis into Gail's ferns, stay inside, got it?'

'Of course,' Conrad said.

There was an unlatching sound as the bathroom door opened. Nadia exited wearing a navy blue towel around her waist like a man in a locker room. Her damp blonde hair clung in sticky whorls to her frost-white and drip-drying back. The curves of her wagging hips held the towel low, revealing the dimple above her butt cleavage as she crossed the hall to the linen closet.

Conrad sucked air through his teeth.

She didn't see them standing in the hall until her father barked, 'Nadia, for goodness' sake!'

Nadia did a half-pirouette, covering her breasts with one arm as she looked over her shoulder and scowled, her eyes darting to Conrad and back.

'Daddy, you scared the crap out of me,' she yelped, slipping through her bedroom door at the end of the hall.

Conrad looked away . . . too late. Before the dewy daughter had made her escape, he'd glimpsed one heavy breast squeezed up in the hook of her arm. True, all he spied within the fold was pale flesh (by chance the nipple had been sheltered), but the exposure of the stretch-marked topography of her pregnant belly and milk-laden (*bosom, they were called bosoms or teats back then!*), breasts set off an uncomfortable male charge between father and neighbor.

'She thinks she's still living in her damn dorm room,' Big John said.

Conrad kept his eyes averted. He didn't want Big John thinking he was a willing participant in this impromptu peep show.

'They got steers and heifers sharing showers up the school. Can you imagine what that's like?'

'Oh, yeah, they do that now, I guess,' Conrad said, legs literally shaking.

'Well, that's pretty much the whole shootin' match, anyway. Let's go see what Gail's gone and zapped for ya.'

As they moved down the hall, the soapy smell of the girl rode out on a wave of shower steam and settled upon his neck, mingling with the beads of sweat, and he

128

entered the kitchen with a cluster of stubborn girl molecules working its way into his pores.

Gail handed him a plate of angel hair pasta with home-made pesto that burned his sinuses. Conrad ate standing over the kitchen counter while Gail wrote down the emergency phone numbers. He saw Steve Bartholomew's name and another he did not recognize. As he was leaving, Gail gave him at least three more hugs and thanked him.

'No, thank you,' he said, light-headed from the meal, the girl.

'What for, putting you to work?'

'For making me feel at home.'

'Aw.' Gail tilted her head in sympathy. He hadn't meant for it to come out that way. 'You miss her.'

'I don't know what I was thinking letting her go.'

Nadia Grum.

MySpace. Her space.

Pink and black frames, looping cursive text for font. Blank spots popped to life while cell phone snapshots of the girl next door looking younger and not yet pregnant filled the screen: with her friends in the woods, standing on a car, on the football field, in her bedroom, sitting on the bed, a bandana on her brow. Hugging various girlfriends, their faces plastered with clown make-up. Nothing gratuitous, nothing revealing, but he was transfixed. The candor with which she displayed herself and the details of her life made him feel like a creep. He learned more about his neighbor in fifteen minutes than he learned about high-school classmates he had known for three years. No wonder parents the world over were terrified.

In a box decorated with flowers and hearts, guitars and guns, her profile:

Name	Nadia Helen Grum
Birthday	1 October 1986
Birthplace	Black Earth, WI
Current location	same
Eyes	blue
Hair	blonde
Height	5′ 0″
Weight	120
Zodiac sign	Libra
Status	single
Heritage	Slovakian, Irish, American
Shoes you wore today	my Old Navy flip-flops
Weakness	cheese pizza
Fears	being stuck in a rut
Goal for the year	G.T.F.O.O.H.
McDonald's or Burger King	ugh, neither!
Single or group dates	how about neither, again?
Coffee or cappuccino	coffee
Do you smoke?	not any more, I swear!
Have you been in love?	no
Are you in love now?	see above
Do you want to get married?	what's the point?
Do you believe in yourself?	I better, I must
Pets?	none (we miss you, Jasper!)
Hobbies?	dancing, shooting hoops, shopping

Favorite TV?	*Veronica Mars, Entourage*
Favorite books?	*On the Road*, anything by Salinger
How often do you drink?	not enough
Do drugs?	not any more
Dates in the past month?	0
Are you a virgin?	what do you think?
What place would you like to visit?	Seattle
What are you looking for?	truth
Qualities?	dependable, opinionated, fun
Ideal man's style?	I'll settle for sloppy if he's clean
What is your greatest regret?	next question, please
You would like to be remembered?	fondly

Her cliché answers and trumped-up confidence were empty calories, leaving him hungry for more. The most pressing questions – *Who is the father of your baby? How has the pregnancy changed your life? What are you going to do now?* – would have to wait.

Question: *Have you ever been in love?*

Answer: *No*.

He returned again and again to one photo. She was sitting in a slat-backed wooden chair at a small desk in someone's bedroom, her hair pleasantly ruffled as if it had been wet and then slept on. She wore masculine black reading glasses and she was looking up in surprise, her eyes wide and her mouth hanging open, as if the photographer had crept up and caught her in a private act.

HOLLY

If every love needs a home, then theirs was each other. And if every couple needs a home to shelter their love, Holly's mother's house was their sanctuary. Holly's father lived on the other side of town, and he was busy rebuilding his life, building a new brood. Holly was allowed to choose where she lived, and her mother played cool to keep her daughter in her camp. Soon our boy was spending all his time with Holly – including nights, weekends and even the taboo school nights – and together they lived as a new family.

His mother was tired after work and relieved to have him on someone else's watch. Better for her son to be at Holly's than running with boys who didn't have girlfriends and spent their time wrecking cars, stealing CDs and burning cats. He always told his mother the truth – I'm going to Holly's – and then forgot to call home to say he was staying. Nobody seemed to mind.

In her mother's home snuggled up against the foothills of the Rocky Mountains there was a finished basement made up like an apartment for a real adult (kitchenette,

132

living room, full bath, spare room and Holly's cocoon-like bedroom). They lived like a real couple and forgot about school until the alarm went off and they had to commute, sore and feeding each other fruit and listening to The Smiths on the way to class.

The sex had evolved things, but the basement house below the real house was the thing that made it real.

They took baths, cooked five course meals, watched movies and became like newlyweds. They dressed alike in shirts and jeans purchased with Holly's mother's credit card. They ate magic mushrooms, smoked good pot, sipped wine. They ate grilled shark, large salads and entertained cleansing fruit diets together. They had small parties with close, chosen friends from school, but they never lasted, the friendships. There wasn't room for anyone else. People grew bored of them, spiteful of their closeness, and drifted away.

Holly always had fresh money in her account. But when they got bored they shoplifted clothing, bedding, lunch, seafood dinners. They walked out on hundred-dollar meals and no one cared enough to stop them. They grew daring in their dalliances, monstrous in their self-absorption, reckless in their search for new thrills.

His grades went down as far as they could go. Hers dropped too, though not enough to alarm her parents. Holly was better at school and talked of college and how they might go to the same one. He did not dwell on the future. Now was all that mattered; it was all he could see. Things were perfect, and he knew she felt the same way.

College, no college. He would drive a truck or major in physics or both if that was required to keep them together.

That their separation was already imminent was his denial. That she could thwart it without planning was Holly's.

Sometimes they saw Holly's mom's face on the realtor signs. Holly's mother had the combinations to key boxes to the best homes on the market. They went with her mother to a Sunday afternoon showing and hid in the bathroom. They noticed how the other couples were not much older than they were. They decided it would be more fun to have the whole house to themselves. In her mother's home office they found the filing cabinet and the real estate listings and the combinations.

They took the list of combinations and went to the house that Friday after school. They parked down the street and walked around to make sure no one was inside. They entered before the sun went down. They did not leave until early Sunday morning.

The house was well stocked with fruit, fresh pasta and pre-made sauces, gourmet meats and cheeses and wine. Friday night was a fit of giggles and exploring the house, crashing early in front of the TV. Saturday they slept late, watched movies, made up stories about the owners. The sex was on hold as if they were saving for this night. In the evening, he cooked while Holly turned on the stereo and set the table.

It started gradually, over dinner.

'More wine?' he asked, pouring for her.

'Thank you, darling,' she said with all the proper weight.

'How's your pasta?'

'It's great.' She picked up her fork for the first time.

'Really? Because you're not eating any.'

She set her fork down. He saw that her hands were shaking. It made him nervous that she was nervous.

'We don't have to stay,' he said. 'We could pretend it never happened, go to a movie.'

'What? No, Connie.' She was the only one who ever called him that, before or since. 'If someone comes home we can always say my mom sent us to house-sit.'

'You think they'll believe that?' He had been listening for a garage door clunking to life or the rattle of keys and lock.

Holly smiled. 'So we went to the wrong house. What are they going to do? Arrest us?'

'Maybe. Maybe worse.'

'They're sixty-five.'

'How do you know?'

'I checked them out. He's a retired doctor. She's a teacher, kindergarten. Half-days. The kids are out of college and out of state.'

'You're like a detective now.'

She shrugged and sipped more wine.

'What is it, then? My cooking?'

'I'm sorry. I'm just . . . kinda freaking out,' she said. 'About what's going to happen next year.'

He suddenly saw the whole thing collapsing.

Tonight was too much, they'd gone as far as they could go. She had decided to call the whole thing off before she went away to college, before it got too close and too bad.

'Are you having doubts about me, about us?'

'Connie! No. Don't look at me that way.' She ran around and wedged herself between the table and his lap. 'We're perfect,' she said, kissing his neck. 'I just want this to be special. So we never forget.'

'Of course it's special. It's always special.'

'But tonight is different. I want it to be just us.'

'Who else is there?'

'No one, silly. But later, I don't want . . . you don't have to, you know, use anything between us.'

He thought about that. Since the beginning he had used condoms. They were smart enough to know that, as often as they 'got beastly' (her term), 97 per cent effective was 3 per cent very likely.

'Really?' he said, not really understanding.

She put her mouth around his ear. 'I want to feel everything. I want you to feel everything.' She pulled her mouth off and smacked him loudly on the cheek. 'It's the natural way to fly, sweetie.'

'Want me to clear the table? It's a nice table.'

'It's not big enough.' She was already walking away. 'Finish your dinner and don't come back here for at least twenty minutes.'

'Where's here again?' he said.

'The big room down the hall. Promise to wait?'

'I promise.'

She went down the long hall past the slate foyer and disappeared into the master suite.

He had always been an imaginative son, and now he imagined all manner of sport and pastime awaiting him in this new space. But he could not see that by following his love into this house he had also set in motion its inevitable murder.

16

Untold hours after falling asleep on top of the covers with Luther and Alice curled at his feet, *Match Point* playing quietly on the bedroom DVD-TV rig, Conrad woke alone to the sound of a baby crying. It was the same choking, newborn *ack-ack-ayyyych* sound from weeks ago, and he knew it was not the movie he'd left on because now there was only the eerie blue screen with the DVD format logo.

He turned on the lamp and looked to their crate beds on the floor, but the dogs weren't there, either. The baby's crying quieted to a tired, tapering sigh and then stopped. Or left. He did not think it was coming from the street or a house next door; it had trailed off the other way, toward the rear of the house.

In its place he heard a scratching, the sound of a garden rake pulling on a thick lawn. There were three methodical scratches and then a pause, three or four more and another pause. The sounds were coming to him from the hall.

If it's another doll I'll just stomp the fucker to pieces, he thought, walking out of the master bedroom. One of the dogs whined. He couldn't tell which, but they usually roamed in tandem. The scratching came again, from the spare bedroom adjacent to the master, the one Nadia'd been in the day he toured the house.

Feeling relieved but still on edge, Conrad shuffled down the dark hall, wishing he'd remembered to buy some nightlights at Wal-Mart.

The door was closed. Conrad pictured his dogs in the room, doggishly wondering how the door had closed behind them. Or maybe they were standing at the window, tails erect, the fur on their napes stiff and bristling at something that had startled them from outside.

Conrad opened the door and patted around for the light switch. He could see their outlines. They were hunched over the floor at the center of the room, backs arched, snouts pressed to the carpet, digging as if he were not even there.

Whatever it was, it had been compelling enough for them to nose the futon aside to get to the floor – he could see its bulky frame in shadow off to one side.

His hand found the switch plate and swept up. Golden light shot through the dusty glass bowl full of dead flies and other winged insects. The dogs looked up at him in surprise, their eyes dilated black orbs, then returned in unison to their buried treasure.

Conrad squinted. The carpet and padding had been peeled back like the skin of an animal, exposing floorboards like ribs.

'Luther! Alice, quit that!' And they did, but they didn't look happy about it.

The hole was jagged from their labors – they had cleared a respectable three-foot circle before he had stopped them. The boards were not the same color as the rest of the floorboards in the library and the hall. These planks were an unnatural shade of chocolate, marbled like steaks. The plum color ran against the grain and was deeper in some places, lighter in others. Near the border of the hole he saw a patch of lighter wood, the natural color of pine.

Then he understood. He wasn't looking at painted wood.

He was looking at a stain.

It looked as though someone had spilled a bucket of brown paint and never bothered to clean it up. No, not paint either. Spilled paint dries in thick, opaque blotches. He could just make out the wood grain beneath the blotches.

A delicate breeze passed through the window he'd opened days ago in a stubborn attempt to cool the house without turning on the a/c. The wind brought with it a smell he could not immediately place. It was musky, like blood only stronger – the scent of a woman's menstruation.

His mind leaped to a shameful memory, to a teen Conrad who had on a whim inspected his girlfriend's panties while she, Holly, was in the shower. He had seen them lying next to her dresser, underneath the jeans she had been wearing less than twenty minutes before. Mistaking them for the same pair she'd been wearing when the rumpus began, he had picked them up and felt the stiffness of the fabric. Not really conscious of his need to know, he had pressed his nose to the brown stain in the crotch and sniffed, then cast them aside with a strange mixture of guilt, sympathy and revulsion. It had lasted less than a second, but the smell remained hidden in whatever part of the male brain that records such things, storing it for some potential future biological imperative. This scent filling the air now wasn't Holly's, but it was from the same place. The same essence.

It felt like a warning.

Or evidence.

He knelt between the dogs and stopped his nose six inches from contact. It had not been such a bad smell then, in Holly's bedroom; just another aspect of her he still found fascinating. But here, in such quantity, in his house, marking the floor like a long forgotten murder scene, the scent sparked in his imagination and

(*Greer Laski and her mutant children all of them deformed born here in the birthing house*)

made him gag.

Conrad reeled to his feet and turned away. He coughed, putting a hand on the door to steady himself. When the worst had passed, he rubbed his tee shirt over his face. He was sweating and it suddenly felt twenty degrees hotter in here, even with the summer breeze.

Wanting nothing more than to be out of the room and away from the stain, maybe as far as the couch downstairs for the rest of the night, Conrad opened his mouth to command the dogs out . . . but no words came. His throat locked up and held his breath hostage, silencing

141

him while the baby cried out, louder than before, much too loud, and his chest suffered an invisible blow that sent shockwaves through his heart and lungs. He was sure the baby's coughing panic was coming from his own mouth – it sounded that close.

The dogs jumped back and began barking savagely up at the ceiling. Conrad's spine tingled from his neck to his tailbone. His stomach somersaulted and he swayed on his feet. While the dogs continued gnashing at the air between the three of them, the room jumped another ten degrees in the span of perhaps three seconds and Conrad broke into a hot, slippery sweat. Red blotches in the corners of his eyes, pinholes of black dancing in the air, darkness closing in.

The baby wailed and he was certain that if he did not leave this room, soon, he would die.

But he could not move. His legs and lower back cramped, hunching him into a ball. The futon in the corner snapped open and began to shake, a vague image of a table overlapping the futon and its frame. In flashes he saw the shadow of a long body, the raven-haired sepia woman who was but wasn't Jo, stripped naked and bathed in sweat as he was. Her body shone in the light, and her mouth was open wide, her scar pinched in a crooked snarl as her head thrashed from side to side. Her teeth chopped at the air as if unseen hands were wrestling her down. Her belly was enormous, a shining white globe rivered with blue veins. Below the navel he glimpsed the glistening pelt of her mound and it was with another kind of shame he felt his arousal quicken.

Her hips thrust and bucked but she could not escape the invisible hands that pinned her to the table. She slid around its black leather surface and he tried to scream.

Pulses of light scorched his retinas and his jaw popped, trying to pull air into his burning lungs. He could not see the baby, but it was here, crying like it was being jabbed by cold hands and colder metal instruments. Invisible blades jabbed into his ribs, against his temples and shoulders as Conrad and the baby tried to survive some unknowable assault.

The woman on the table howled in agony, sending a mist of spittle up at her invisible assailants before she was slammed down one final time. Having lost the battle for good, she faced him and that is when he realized she had no face. Above her lips peeled over her teeth there was only a formless white slate of flesh.

The barking *ack-ack-ACK* ratcheted up into a primal howl and it hurt his ears, bored into his brains. Luther and Alice were full-on fighting now, gnashing at each other's throats in anger and confusion.

'Help! Help!' Conrad choked, losing consciousness as one of the dogs turned on him. There was a dull moment when something punctured Conrad's hand, and his mind's eye saw a freshly sharpened pencil stabbing clean through the soft meat between his thumb and forefinger. Then the wound lit up his brain, sending a signal flare of white-hot pain that cleared his vision in an instant. Conrad jerked his hand but it was stuck in something wet, and for a horrible second he was sure the floor had opened up and bit him. He saw a drop of blood, fat and heavy as paraffin in a lava lamp, floating in the air. Luther shook his head from side to side and only then did Conrad realize his dog had bitten him, was still biting him, clamped down on his hand bones and did not want to let go.

Conrad's throat clicked loose and he yelled. Luther cowered on his hindquarters as if a bolt of lightning had just gone off in the front yard. Conrad's hand slipped free and Jackson Pollacked the floor as he drew it back and wrapped it in his sweat-soaked tee shirt. And then the faceless thrashing woman was gone and the table was just a futon and he was here with the dogs, his knees buckling as he fell to the shredded carpet.

'Out! Get out!' This time they obeyed, bolting down the hall. He stood trembling with his hand curled inside the bloody shirt. The pungency that had been in his mouth and down his throat had been replaced by the sweet scent of fresh mowed grass.

He elbowed the light off, pulled the door shut with his good hand and backed away, the sweat all over his body cooling rapidly. He was shivering and very thirsty. He nearly went to fetch his beloved iced tea, but the pain in his hand became real and he hurried to the bathroom before he could bleed to death, freeing the woman on the table to come back for him.

17

Black Earth counted fewer than twenty-eight hundred souls among its population, leaving approximately one tavern, bar, pub, supper club or other drinking establishment for every one hundred or so people. Take away the minors, the recovered, the immobile elders and the infirm, and it should not have been too difficult to find the red-faced Laski.

Conrad started at the top of Main Street and hit them all, seeking the older crowds, the blue-collar guys who came in at five and left a stack of cash for the bartender to chip away at until it was gone.

'You know Leon Laski?' he would ask the bartenders. Most said yes, but he wasn't a regular. 'Tell him Conrad Harrison is looking for him.'

'Whatever you say,' they would say.

Conrad moved on.

On the second afternoon he was at the Decatur Room nursing his fourth Bud longneck, feeling the cool bottle against the hole in his hand – it wasn't really a hole any more; it was, in fact, healing rather quickly – when the former owner of 818 Heritage Street walked in. Same work pants and long sleeves as before, plaster-white dust or paint speckles dotting his hands, neck and ears.

Laski took a Miller from the bartender, an attractive skunk blonde who would not have been out of place at a Def Leppard concert circa 1988. He shared a laugh with a mechanical old man at the bar, then glanced over his shoulder and looked directly at Conrad.

Conrad nodded without smiling.

Laski sighed, wiped his brow with his forearm and ambled to the corner table like he'd rather not. When it was clear Conrad was not going to be the first to speak, Laski set his beer down, magically produced another broken toothpick from his ear and hooked his thumbs through his belt loops.

'You look like a cowboy's been line-dancing with the wrong heifers,' Laski said, chinning at Conrad's hand. 'Trouble on the home front?'

'I spoke to my lawyer today,' Conrad lied.

Laski's smile faltered. 'Oh, can't be all that bad. Maybe we got off on the wrong foot. M'wife . . . she's not been herself lately. Said you was real nice to her the other day over'ta Wally World.'

Conrad smiled unkindly. 'I met the kids. They seem nice.'

Laski took a stool. 'You just gonna sit dare with a red ass or tell me what's on your mind?'

'Take a wild guess.'

Laski leaned in close. 'Your wife pregnant yet?'

Conrad tried not to give it away, but Laski saw what he needed to.

'Probably, what, about six weeks? Right after you moved in it woulda happened, so yeah, about six, maybe eight weeks. Only she just told you, right?' It was pretty goddamned specific to come out of the blue like that. But not impossible to guess. Young couple moves from the city into a four-bedroom house. 'You're trying to remember when was the last time you slipped her the Slim Jim. Because when it happens, it comes fast. All of the sudden you're gonna be a daddy. It's terrifying.'

Conrad finished his beer. Laski sipped, pretending to watch the Brewers on the TV above the bar.

'Okay, Laski. You want to play this game? Let's play this game. I hear things. I see things. Crying sounds. Something is tearing the place apart, opening the floor. You sonofabitch – you bring me this album with a baby tree, a photo full of ugly women, spiders. You want to tell me something? Tell me what happened in my house. I hear there's a lot of *hiss-tow-wee*.'

He didn't remember seeing Laski order them, but two more beers arrived. Conrad swiped one from the table and guzzled.

'Baby tree. That's funny.'

'What?'

'You know, like the placenta tree. Baby tree. Funny way to put it.'

'Placenta? What the fuck does that mean?'

'Old wives' superstition. Not important.'

'Jesus Christ.' Conrad thought about leaving then. He really didn't want to know more. But he had to. 'What happened in the house, Laski?'

'You think it's haunted?' Laski's eyes never left the TV.

'Without question.'

Laski nodded. 'What else?'

Don't tell him about the doll. You want him to think you're fucking nuts?

'I woke up in the middle of the night and heard this clicking sound. Fuck, it was—'

Laski cut him off, trying to make light. 'Hey, you think your house is haunted. Wait till you got a family. That's the real horror show.'

'Fuck you, Laski.'

'Aw, don't be like that. You think your house is haunted? Why? Because it's old? I got news for you, kid. A haunting is just history roused from her sleep. Any house can be haunted, even a new one. Know why? Because what makes 'em haunted ain't just in the walls and the floors and the dark rooms at night. It's in us. All the pity and rage and sadness and hot blood we carry around. The house might be where it lives, but the human heart is the key. We run the risk of letting the fair maiden out for one more dance every time we hang our hat.'

'So it's me? You think I'm nuts?'

'I didn't say that. I said what makes 'em haunted ain't *just* in the walls.'

'You think I'm crazy? Bullshit – I wasn't hallucinating the sound of a baby crying any more than I hallucinated my dogs finding a bloodstain under the carpet. We can go back right now—' Conrad was off his stool.

'Sit down.'

'You lying old fuck.' Conrad slapped the table. 'You knew all about it.'

Patrons turned to see what was what.

Laski waved them off. 'Sit down. There, we're just talking now. You're right about the history. It was a birthing house. But haunted? Now let's think about that for a moment. What does that mean? Like in one of those places where the shit gets handed down. Andyville, what was it called?'

'Amityville? Jesus!'

'No, no, listen. This Amityville was, what? Possessed? Some guy murdered his wife and kids up in dare? The Devil? What was the deal on that job?'

'Both, I think. No, it was the son killed his family first. The next one was the husband.'

'Right, so why come I lived dare twenty-six years and never seen boo?'

Conrad had no answer for that.

'You got to keep it together, Conrad. Play by the rules. Use your head.'

'I'm telling you—'

'But let's talk about murder, like one of these movies where the guy chops his wife and kids to bits and leaves a trail of black heart evil all over the house. It's like a coat of paint, this evil. Okay, so dare's dat den. And who cares where it came from. Satan, mankind, don't matter. It happens to good people, because even good people got problems. And problems is what your haunted house feeds on, son. Just like a one of them payday loan stores.

So it goes, and sometimes it goes to murder. But if all that evil came from some murderin', what is the opposite of all that?'

'Of murder?'

'Yes, what is the polar opposite of murder?'

'Life.'

'Close. Murder is removing life from this world.' Laski was a professor now. 'Bringing life into this world is . . . ?'

'Birth.'

'Birth. Now let's say dare's a house. A house where not one murder was committed, but birth was committed, and frequently. Hundreds of babies entering the world through this house. Women come and go. Women are drawn to it. Women from all walks of life, from next door, from the next town over, hell, some of them from out of state. And the folks who live dare too, the family. Young ones and old ones. Women on top of women. You got pregnant mothers and children and runaways and strays. Dey come to this house. Why? Because it has magical vibes? Because God has blessed this house?'

'That's what your wife thinks.'

'Excuse me, but fuck m'wife. She's crazier'na badger with a sticka corn up its ass.'

They finished their beers. Conrad had arrived at drunk, and Laski was close behind. The man had begun to philosophize.

Conrad flagged the waitress. 'She said God has blessed this house. It doesn't feel like God blessed this house.'

'And fuck God, too,' Laski said. 'This is about the women.'

'The women in the photo?'

'Some of them. Some others.'

'What happened to them? Something bad happened?'

'Not necessarily. Women give birth and die in hospitals, too, and in greater numbers. A soul for a soul, if ya like. But that's not why dey come. Dey come 'cause the man who lives dare's a doctor. And this is all happening in a time when the nearest hospital, the only real hospital in the northern part of the Midwest for hundreds of miles around, is in Chicago. Later, another one opens in Iowa City or Des Moines, M'waukee. But back den, if you lived in south-west Wisconsin, you had few options outside of the home. These women don't want the Father, Son and Holy Ghost. Dey want the miracle of modern medicine. Dey want their baby to have the best chance at a healthy life. Even the ones who believe God created the world in seven days, comes to life and death, or in this case birth, do dey put their faith in God? No, dey put dare faith in science. Or a midwife. Folk remedies, natural birth, modern medicine. It all comes down to getting the most knowledgeable person in the room when the nipper's slidin' downda chute.'

'This is insane. How can you sit there and tell me this?'

'Ain't telling you a thing a hundred cultures on this earth don't already believe. You're gonna believe what you wanna believe anyway. I can see dat.'

'I might also sue your ass off.'

'You ever see women around babies? Just makes 'em want more babies. Dey can't help it. Da cunnie is a grand mystery to men. What do we know?'

'Tell me what happened.'

'Life. Life's what happened. All this blood splashed on the floor and the walls and the wailing women and the sweat and the pain and the prayer. It's just birth. And what does all this birth do to a house? Your super-natural tales would suggest that death opens a door. And why not? It's a violent act, the spirit leaving the body and all that crap. But birth is violent, too, make no mistake about that. Bringing a new soul into this world makes a helluva racket. Some cultures, dey move the pregnant females away just before birth, or during them menses, figurin' if the evil spirits a comin', might swoop down now when she's got her legs open. I don't know shit about spirits, but I know the Indians got a special teepee for the women. Some folks, like them nutters up in Idaho what got shot in the back by dem Federalis, dey had a birthing shack. Dey were afraid of something besides the government, all right. I don't know about opening no doors, but if dare's doors to be opened, then birth must be one way to open them. Maybe all this ushering of babies into the world could do that.'

'Is that what you believe is happening?' Conrad said. 'The birthing house wants another baby? Are you telling me that's how you kept it . . . happy for the past twenty-six years? Having babies?'

'I'm just a family man,' Laski said, his shit-eating grin revealing yellow teeth.

'Right,' Conrad said. 'And your kids?'

'What about my kids?'

'They're all . . . each one has an abnormality. What happened to them?'

'Bad genes.' Laski went back to watching the game, like they were discussing Ford versus GM.

Bullshit. 'You had more, didn't you? More than the three I saw your wife with.'

'Who tol' you dat?'

'Is it true?'

'You got no idea what you're talking about. You've never been a father.'

'What happened to them? Did they die, or did someone . . . did some*thing* . . . murder them?'

'You know . . .' Laski stood and hooked his beer into his arm, shelling a peanut. 'We were happy dare, once. Good times, bad times. Not so different from any life in any other house.'

'Then why'd you leave?'

Laski turned to Conrad, weighing his response. 'My wife, she didn't wanna sell. But we got her for a song. I figured the market was ripe.'

'Fuck you, Laski. What the fuck did you tell me all that for if not to tell me something? You want to confess? Because if something happens to my wife—'

'Yeah, what you gonna do? Move back to California?'

Suddenly the argument was over. Conrad wanted to

crawl across the table and smash his bottle over Laski's head.

'My wife is pregnant. I don't know what to do, Leon. I need help.'

Laski looked Conrad in the eye and nodded very slowly, imparting his last and only real piece of advice. 'Listen to the woman of the house. Be a man, but keep your pecker in your pocket unless you're planning on putting it to righteous use. And listen to the woman of the house.'

18

Conrad stood leaning over the bathroom sink with a tube of ointment in his good hand. The problem was, they were both good hands now. The dog bite that had started as a hole requiring sutures was now but a faint red dot, the surrounding tissue pink, clean and dry as paper.

It's healed, he thought. *Damned if it hasn't healed itself up in two days.*

He turned again to the bathroom window facing the backyard, not admitting to himself that he was hoping to see Nadia Grum. He thought he'd seen her there each night since her parents left town, standing still or pacing by the fence. He thought she might be sleepwalking, but eventually she seemed to snap out of it before darting back behind her house.

Twenty minutes later he was dozing on his feet, his face pleasantly cooling against the window, when he saw movement, a shape. It took him another half a minute for his eyes to adjust and see the woman standing in his backyard. Not on the Grum side; this time she had crossed over. She looked up at him and tiredly raised one hand, then turned away slowly.

He lost her for a moment, but she reappeared, walking the flagstone path toward the detached garage at the rear of the property. No, not Nadia. Nadia was blonde as a cocker spaniel, and even in the darkness he could see that this woman had black hair. He might have tried pretending she was Nadia if she had been wearing jeans and a sweatshirt, or even a white nightgown that implied sleepwalking. But the woman who was now headed toward the overgrown vegetable garden at the end of the property wasn't wearing street clothes or pajamas. She was wearing a black dress, the kind that billowed under the waist and fit snuggly above it.

She's crazy, he thought. *One of the locals gone off the radar. She needs help before she wanders into the garden and steps on a rusted rake.*

Conrad trotted down the stairs, leaving a path of lights on as he went. The stove clock read 4.13 a.m. The dogs scrambled out of bed to join him in this new adventure.

But by the time he made it outside and to the edge of the garden, she was gone. He tried to imagine a woman in a long dress scrambling over the six-foot fence bordering the entire back half of the property, but it wasn't working. The late-night numbness lifted all at once and Conrad became frightened all over again. He padded up the flagstone path in bare feet, detouring to the Grum residence on his way home.

He knocked and waited. And knocked and waited.

One last rapping tattoo on the door and then he would

give up before someone called the cops. Twenty seconds passed. As he passed their front bay window, he saw a curtain drop and blonde hair on the retreat.

'Nadia?' he whisper-shouted. 'It's just me. Conrad.'

He was still standing there feeling like a peeping Tom when the front door opened. She pushed the screen door with one hand, subconsciously caressing the orb of her belly with the other, leaning out as if she didn't trust the porch with her bare feet. She was squinty-eyed with sleep.

'Hey, Nadia, sorry to bother. Were you just out back?'

'I was sleeping, Conrad.' She became alert mid-yawn. 'Why?'

'I, uh, just wanted to make sure you were okay.'

He noted the small blonde hairs stiffening on the gooseflesh of her upper thighs, just below the hemline of her boxer shorts.

'I'm supposed to be watching the place,' he said. 'Doing some chores—'

'They don't trust me to be alone.'

'Oh, no, it's not—'

'It's fine. I get it.'

He smiled at that. 'Yeah, good night, Nadia. Sorry again.'

As he retreated, she said, 'Conrad?'

'Yeah?'

'Think you could give me a ride tomorrow? Or today, I guess it is.'

'Sure.'

'To Madison?'

'What time?'

'Uhm, like ten? It won't take long, maybe just an hour there and back, maybe fifteen minutes there?'

'No problem.'

'I'll pay for the gas.'

'No, it's the least I can do after scaring you.'

'You didn't scare me.' She gave him a tired smile.

'You don't scare very easily, do you?'

'Not any more.'

He told himself opening the car door for her was more an acknowledgement of her condition than an act of chivalry. Her white hair and whiter skin were glowing in the sun, illuminating the blue veins in her cheek. She wore a knee-length pleated skirt and plaid Tommy wedges, and a snug, navy-colored long-sleeve top. The top slenderized her arms and made her look more pregnant than she had five hours before.

She carried a pink and white Puma sport bag that was either a large purse or small duffel, its contents as much a mystery as their destination.

'Morning,' he said.

'Hey,' she said, sinking into the Volvo.

In the car, her scent. Like she had spilled vanilla extract on her shirt. Made him think of ice cream. Milkshake girl. It was going to be a long ride.

'Thanks for doing this,' she said, doing her lipstick in the visor mirror.

'No problem.'

'Oh, do you know how to get there?'

'You'll have to tell me where we're going once we get near Madison.'

'Right.'

She offered no more details. He figured doctor's visit and wondered if she would want him to come in or wait in the car. Conrad merged from the town's business loop on to the entrance ramp to Highway 151. He locked the cruise control at seventy-two.

'So,' he said, testing the waters. 'I ran into your old neighbors at Wal-Mart the other day. Mrs Laski and her . . . kids. What's up with them, right?'

Nadia nodded without interest.

'Did you know them?'

'I used to sit for them.'

'Really? How was that?'

'I'm glad they moved.'

'Why do you say that?'

'Their kids were difficult.'

'Yeah, I can imagine. They had, what, three? Or more? Because your parents seemed confused—'

'Can we not talk about the Laskis, please?'

'Sure.' *Bingo*.

A small herd of alpacas grazed in a field. Conrad could swear one looked at him as they drove by.

A while later she said, 'Do you miss Los Angeles?'

'I miss the food. In-N-Out burgers. Chicken tacos at Baja Fresh. Not much else.'

'I thought LA was fun?'

'It was, for a while.'

'Why did you choose Wisconsin. You have family here?'

159

'No. It just seemed to be everything LA wasn't. It's quiet.'

Nadia blew air though her mouth. 'It is quiet.'

A minute passed.

'I don't know why I'm telling you this,' he said. 'But here. Okay, why we left Los Angeles. We're not doing so well, Jo and I. I went back to Chicago a couple months ago. My father died in an accident.'

'Oh, God.'

'No, it's not a big deal. Really.'

Nadia frowned.

'That's not what I mean. I'm sorry he died. But he was never around. He was a stranger to me. I just – anyway. I wish we would have had a chance to do it differently, but he made his choices. But when I got home, a friend of ours was there. With Jo.'

'Were they . . . ?'

'She says no. But I think yes.'

'So that must have sucked royal.'

'Yeah. But the thing is, I wasn't surprised. Or I was, but only for a minute. I kind of knew something was wrong. And I'm no saint myself.'

'What did you do?' Nadia's eyes were very wide. Like maybe she was thinking she'd rather not be in the car with him just now.

'I didn't do anything. Really. But I thought about it. There was a girl I worked with.'

'She was your friend, or you just worked with her?'

The cruise control was holding steady. He steered with the heel of one palm. There were no cars behind, in front, or beside them. The way the wagon pulled them along, it wasn't even driving. It was like being on a ride.

'I thought about it a lot. We came very close to doing something very stupid. But we didn't.'

'Uh-huh.'

'No, Nadia, really. I didn't. I could have. We hung out a little, went for some drinks after work. From the bookstore. We had dinner once and went back to her place, and I know she was interested in me, despite my situation.'

'Was she a total slut?'

'No. She was really normal, I think. I didn't stick around to find out.'

'Does your wife know?'

'I don't know. I don't think so.'

'But?'

'But she knows something.'

'Why didn't you tell her after you caught her and this other guy?'

'I just wanted it to go away. Do-over. Off-setting penalties.'

'What's that, football?'

'Yeah.'

'Nice.'

'I know. It sounds crazy now. But I gave her a choice. Either we stayed and fell apart or we moved and started over.'

'Starting over. Yeah. No, I bet she knows.'

This alarmed him. 'Why do you say that?'

'We're smarter than you think.'

'No, I have known for some time that my wife is smarter than me.'

They ticked off a couple more miles of farmland in a cocoon of comfortable anti-conversation before she said, 'Speaking of starting over, you're taking me to the airport.'

'What?'

'I'm going to stay with some friends in Seattle.'

He looked at the pink Puma bag on the floor. 'Does Mom know?'

'No, and you're not going to tell her, right?'

'Shouldn't I?'

Nadia leaned over, close enough for him to smell the smell of her under the vanilla. 'She would never blame you. She'll say it's typical.'

Conrad pulled off the highway and parked on the shoulder. He turned off the ignition.

'What's wrong?' Nadia sat against the door, facing him.

'You can't just leave,' he said.

'Why not?'

'Because it's not a good time.'

Her flirting confidence had gone sour. 'What's not a good time?'

'Now, before she comes back.' His hands trembled and Nadia's eyebrows formed a V as she leaned against the door. 'All this stuff is happening now. You can't leave.'

'But I am leaving. And why do you care?'

'It's about making things right. At home.'

'You don't even know me. Just because my parents hired you, I don't owe you shit.'

He was glad she asked because he was tired of waiting to say it out loud. 'I think you know. What's going on there.'

'Where?'

'My house. Whatever is in there . . . doesn't want you to leave.' A bolt of pain launched back from his left eyeball and sat there at the base of his skull, pulsing.

'Your house? What are you—'

'I need your help. Maybe together we can figure it out.'

'Figure what out?'

'History. The stuff with the house. If you help me, we could really do something about it.'

She forced a laugh. 'You're out of your mind, dude. I'm going to Seattle.'

He thought it over. 'No, that's not the story.'

Nadia put her hand on the door handle.

'Don't,' he said. 'Please. If you really want to leave, I'll take you to the airport. But think about it.'

'Think about *what*?'

'Nadia. Tell me the truth. Where were you when you got pregnant?'

She stared at him.

'Were you in my house?' He knew he sounded deranged, but he had to know. 'Like that day I bumped into you before we moved in? What were you doing in there?'

'I don't know what you're talking about.'

'Yes, you do.' He was staring at her pregnant belly.

'What makes you think it had anything to do with the house?'

'You saw the snakes. Those eggs. That wasn't an accident.'

'Oh my God, don't do this. Don't. What are you – no, don't even. I need to leave.'

'You grew up next door.' Her eyes were starting to well up. 'You're not afraid of me. You're afraid of the house, aren't you? Afraid of what's inside.'

Nadia started shaking. 'Fuck this.' She grabbed the door handle.

Conrad grabbed her by the shoulder and pulled her back. 'How many times did you babysit for the Laskis? Did Leon do something to you? Or did you see something in the house?'

Her lips moved but no words came out.

He softened his grip. 'Jesus, I knew it.'

'Was it Eddie, or Leon Laski? I can help—'

'I don't want your help!' Her voice hurt his ears.

'You want someone's help!' A fleck of spit landed on her neck. 'What the fuck is in Seattle if not someone who's gonna help you? You can't run away, Nadia. It doesn't work.'

Nadia's fist sprang forward and knocked him in the forehead. His head bounced off the driver's side window in a clock-clock. She looked as surprised as he felt.

'Ouch. That hurt, Nadia.' He laughed, reaching for her. 'Calm down.'

She cocked her fist again.

His hand went up. 'Wait, not again, Christ!' She relented. He wiped his eyes. 'How much money do you have on you?'

164

'Three-fifty.'

'That's not going to get you to Seattle. And if it does, you'll be broke by the time you leave the airport.'

'I told you, I have friends.'

'Oh, did you meet them on MySpace? Are they going to let you sleep on the futon?'

'Drive the car,' she said.

'A thousand dollars.' It just popped out. He hadn't even thought of it.

'You're sick, you know that?'

'I'll finish the chores your mom gave me. Before your folks get home, I'll pay you a thousand dollars. But you have to tell me your story.'

'What story?'

'Everything you know about what happened in the house. After that, you still want to go to Seattle, I'll give you a ride to the airport and I won't tell them anything. Deal?'

She was thinking about it. The money helped, but he didn't think it was all about the money.

'If Eddie finds out—'

'Right,' he said, starting the engine.

'Did you plan this?'

'No.'

'Is this what you did with that girl?'

'What? No. This has nothing to do with sex.'

'So you did have sex with her.'

'No. Nadia, for Christ's sake. I'm scared, okay? I don't know anybody here. My wife's gone. I don't know if she's ever coming back. I just need someone to sit there and tell me I'm not losing my mind. Haven't you ever needed some help like that? Just for a couple days?'

He could see that he had scored a minor point with that one.

'We're just going to talk, right?'

'Just talk.'

'I'm not going to fuck you for money.'

The fact that she could even summon the words in her state sent a nervous quiver running around his stomach. 'I know that, Nadia.'

The car made a U-turn over the grassy median and headed toward Black Earth.

19

Steve Bartholomew was watering his rose bushes and smoking a cigarette when they pulled up. The cigarette dangled like the hose, two limp extensions of the man: one trickling water, the other smoldering fire. Conrad waved obnoxiously.

'Morning, Steve!' *See how routine this is?*

Steve waved back, his hand slowing as Nadia got out of the car.

'Morning.' She waved without turning and headed toward her place.

Steve watched her for a few seconds and went back to his roses. The hose had one of those canisters attached to mix the blue powdered crystals with the water. Steve's roses were yellow and large.

'Nadia.' Conrad gestured toward his front door. 'Don't you want to meet Luther and Alice?'

'We're doing this now?'

'The sooner we're done, the sooner you can leave.'

She followed Conrad inside. He went to the kitchen while Nadia trailed behind, cooing at the dogs in the living room. The dogs fell in love with her, but they fell in love with everybody. Conrad poured two tall glasses of iced tea.

Nadia was standing next to the phone when it started ringing. 'Uhm, want me to get that?'

'Sure.' He hoped it was Jo. She could use a little wake-up, even if it cost him.

'Hello?' Nadia said, accepting a glass of iced tea. 'Yeah, he's here.'

He took the phone. 'Hello.'

'Let me guess,' his wife said. 'That's Nadia.'

'Yes, should I introduce you?'

'No.'

'Okay. How are you, Jo?'

'You haven't called.'

'I tried, but you weren't answering. Figured you didn't want to speak with me.'

'Is she standing right there?'

'Yes.'

'Do we have to talk in front of her?'

'I don't know, are we talking?'

She ignored the question. 'I've been ordering some stuff. Did you open them?'

'The boxes? No, not yet.'

'Can you put some stuff together, fix the house up?'

Nadia pointed the front door, mouthing *should I go?*

Conrad shook his head. 'What are you sending again?'

'Furniture, supplies. I want to use the guest room, the one closest to our bedroom. Oh, and rip up that hideous carpet. I want to strip the floors and refinish them.'

'In the guest room?' His headache had returned. A

pair of Chinese table tennis champions in his skull, going for the gold.

'Yes, in the baby's room.'

'The one next to our bedroom?'

'Why, do you think it should go somewhere else?'

'What?'

'God, are you even listening to me? You sound bad, are you getting sick?'

'No, I'm not, I'm fine.'

'Which one?'

'I'm fine. That's fine. We'll get some walkie-talkies so we can hear her from our bedroom.'

She paused, then spoke with a kindness he hadn't heard in weeks. 'What makes you think it's going to be a girl?'

The house. The house gave it to me, Jo. Don't you see? This is the house's project, not ours. We're just the vessels doing the meat work.

'I don't know. It just feels right.'

She cooed. 'Oh, that's so sweet. I'm kinda missing you.'

'Yeah?'

'I discovered something about being pregnant.'

'What's that?'

'In the morning I don't feel so hot, but at night?' She giggled, a dare.

'Yeah?'

'I usually fall asleep at like eight, like a short nap, and I have these dreams.' She made an unmistakable *mmm-mmhhh* sound.

'Are you—'

'And when I wake up, I feel like I just had the most incredible sex.'

'What, like—'

'Last night I had to change my clothes after.'

'Change your clothes.'

She giggled again. 'Think about it.'

He got it. 'You're killing me, Jo.'

'Must be the hormones. It's incredible. I wish you were here.'

'Me too.'

He could see her in the hotel room, her swollen belly, all sleepy and writhing in the sheets. Her hand slipping beneath the waist of her panties. He was wracked by a lust that made his knees buckle.

'Too bad Nadia's there. I should let you go.'

Nadia who? 'Wait!'

'Call me later,' his wife said.

'Definitely.'

By the time he had set the phone down his headache was gone. He stood over the sink and drank the iced tea until his erection went away. Why does she do this? He couldn't get her on the phone for a week and now she's got the cord wrapped between her legs? Was it because Nadia was here? Was she staking out turf from four hundred miles away?

He found Nadia in the living room, on the floor with the dogs.

'I'm hungry,' she said.

'Me too. What're you in the mood for?'

*

170

They were seated at opposite ends of the long dining-room table Jo's father had given them as a wedding present. Conrad had made sandwiches, then Nadia napped through a *Monk* marathon. When she woke up, she was hungry again and he cooked penne with Knorr parma rosa sauce. Now he was excited and frightened, and he forced himself to conceal both.

'I was only thirteen the first time it happened. I wasn't even doing it for the money. It was just something to do. Same as the older girls I looked up to. My parents insisted I ask for some money for my time. I think I got a dollar an hour.'

'How old were they?'

'Anna Maybelle was six. Davey was a little younger, maybe four or five.'

'So they'd be in their late teens by now?'

'I guess.'

'That can't be right. When I saw them at Wal-Mart, all the kids were young. I think they had the same names, too. Does she have more?'

'She had two then and she was pregnant with another. Then the twins. I don't know how many she has now.'

'Wait, she had three when I saw her. That's like five kids. And twins? Did they move away or something? The ones you were watching?'

'Moved away. They went away. I don't know why.'

'Nobody ever asked? Even with the names? What's that, like naming your dog Rover Two?'

'Maybe I was confused. Hard to say 'cause by the time my parents started to worry, the Laskis were already

171

sorta on their own. They didn't talk to anyone or go out much. I told you, this isn't going to solve anything.'

'Okay. You were thirteen.'

'Right. But I was also, you know, not your average thirteen-year-old. I was . . . like I am now or close enough.' Here she gestured at her breasts and hips as if to say, what I have now is what I had then. 'I guess my parents knew what happens to girls who are that developed and go babysitting.'

'What happens?'

'Either boys crawl through the window and stuff happens or the father who drives you home gets ideas and stuff happens. Either way something that isn't supposed to happen happens. They kept asking me to call every hour or so to check in. They knew Leon and Mrs Laski had a wedding up in Eau Claire. I was gonna be alone for eight hours at the least. I could tell my mom wanted to come and help me. But my dad said no, it would be good for me to handle them alone. And they were going to be right next door. So no big deal. I liked kids. Or I thought I did, until I started babysitting.

'Those kids. I knew they weren't right. Davey was so quiet, he never seemed to care if he was hungry or thirsty, so I had to ask him a lot if he needed anything. Anna Maybelle was different. All she wanted to do was play with her dolls.'

Conrad raised his hand. 'Dolls?'

'Yeah.'

'What kind?'

'That's what I'm telling you. Why, what's wrong?'

172

'Nothing. Go on.'

'These little home-made dolls. Now those gave me the creeps. They were made of wood. The Laskis didn't have a TV, either, so maybe that was all she had, but still. The dolls were old and dirty from years of playing. Whoever made them forgot to give them a face. But that wasn't so bad. What really bothered me was their hair. It was like human hair, but dry, brittle. I tried to play with Anna Maybelle, and it was hard, but what was I supposed to do? Let the girl sit there alone all night? What's wrong?'

Her words had turned him white. 'I'm fine. Don't stop now.'

She frowned at him. 'There must have been four or five of them. Anna Maybelle was busy changing their clothes around, which weren't much more than some beat up house-dress-looking things, also probably hand-made. You could see the stitches on them where someone, probably someone's grandma, had sewn them together. Scuzzy little white trash dolls is what they were. She called one Chessie, like Jessie. And I guess I sort of lost myself for a while then because time passed and I was still making this doll walk and talk and doing little voices, but I wasn't playing with her. Anna Maybelle. I was just babbling to myself and making strange noises and making up stories. How Chessie was going to the store and how Chessie was getting her hair done, because it needed some work. I think . . . I did that for a while, a long while. Because when I looked up both Anna Maybelle and Davey weren't playing any more.

They were just staring at me, their dumb mouths hanging open.

'Sorry, that's not very nice. But that's how they looked. For a minute it was like the dolls had become more real than the kids. Like the kids were made of wood and the dolls were . . . I was so lost in their voices it took me a few minutes to realize I was the only one talking. When I looked up, the kids weren't moving or saying anything. That just made me mad. Like they were trying to trick me by sitting perfectly still. I had to yell at them to stop staring off into space like that. Those poor kids. They must have thought I was losing it. When I looked up at the clock I thought maybe twenty minutes had gone by. But that was wrong, by a lot.'

'How long were you playing with them?'

'All night.'

'What do you mean, "all night"?'

'The whole night, Conrad. It was eleven thirty when I stopped. We had been in the living room, sitting on the floor since before seven. I know because I remember looking at the grandfather clock when it gonged right before we sat down and I remembered thinking, that thing is loud. But I never heard it again, not once I started playing with the dolls. I didn't hear anything the whole time. As soon as I realized it, my back hurt and I knew. I'd been sitting there all night. In fact, I would bet anything that they didn't move or say a word the whole time. When I imagined myself sitting there for hours, babbling like an idiot, like, yeah, okay, like I was one of them . . . like one of those retarded kids . . . it scared me.

174

I started crying and I blurted it out. "What's wrong with you? What are you doing?" They started crying. I tried to calm them down but they wouldn't come near me. Davey crawled away fast. Anna Maybelle stood up and actually ran away from me. I had to chase them upstairs.

'Then I smelled it. Going up the stairs. Both the kids had crapped their pants. I mean, sure, they weren't right, but they were well past potty training. It happened while I was playing with those ugly little wooden dolls. So I don't know how long, but they were sitting there in their own filth, for hours. I got upstairs and cleaned them up, but they wouldn't even look at me. I felt sick to my stomach that I had lost myself like that.'

'That sounds pretty bad. What did you do?'

'I put them to bed and waited for the Laskis to come home. I tried to convince myself it wasn't possible. But it was. I was hungry, too. Like I hadn't eaten for a week. And my mouth was dry. I was so thirsty. I was dying of thirst.'

She paused, watching him.

He was thinking about iced tea. 'That could have been panic. Don't people always need water when they are in shock or something?'

Nadia drank more water and they sat in silence.

'Is that it?' he asked. 'Did you go back?'

'No. I didn't want to babysit for them again anytime soon. I stayed in my room, went to school, and tried not to think about the dolls. And I did forget about them. But then, very slowly, something changed. I tried to stay away, but eventually I missed them. I had to go back.'

'You felt bad for what happened? You wanted to make it up to the kids?'

'No. I had forgotten all about the kids.'

'I don't understand.'

'I started hearing voices. The same ones I made up, but saying things I never said. They just came to me. They were all different and they weren't mine any more. They were their own voices.'

'The kids?'

'Not the kids. I wasn't missing the kids. After a few weeks, I missed the dolls.'

'What did they say?' But he didn't really want to know.

'Lots of things that didn't make sense. Most of it I forgot as soon as it happened, like waking up from a dream. But one thing I kept hearing in the girl doll's voice. Chessie, the one I played with, the one with the dead straw hair. I heard her in school, in the middle of the day, reading my algebra book. She called out to me in that high voice. *Come back. Mommy, come back. Doctor gonna kill baby you don't come home soon.*'

20

The following afternoon, Conrad finished mowing the Grums' lawn just before the rain started. He waved at her through the front window and pointed at his house. Nadia nodded and waved – *yeah yeah, I know*.

The afternoon gave way to dusk and she had not come back. He flipped through a couple of Jo's house magazines and debated the wiser of two options – go back to the Grums' and try to get her to open up on her home turf, or call his wife – until he drifted off. He was just about to slide over the cliff when someone started knocking on the door, pounding like they'd been there a while.

When he opened it, Nadia was headed back across the porch.

'Hey, I'm home. Sorry.'

She turned around slowly, clearly disappointed she had not been able to sneak away.

'Sorry. I nodded off. I was beginning to think you were avoiding me,' he said, leaving the door open.

'I need the money.' She followed him inside.

'Have you eaten dinner?'

'No. I'm starving.'

He was sensing a pattern. 'What are you in the mood for?'

'Something with cheese. I'm craving cheese.'

Dinner was a frozen pepperoni pizza and more iced tea. She said sorry, she got really grouchy when she was this hungry. They ate in silence.

When she sighed and leaned back in her chair, Conrad said, 'Better?'

Nadia burped. It was loud and abrupt, a thing she did without embarrassment or excuse. He remembered she was a teenager, or close enough. Before the meal he might have been a piece of furniture. Now that she was sated, she seemed interested in him again.

'How did you meet your wife?'

'Can we maybe talk about the house instead?'

'Who says we're not?'

'What's Jo got to do with the house?'

'You came here for a reason. I figured she was half the reason.'

He walked around and poured them each another glass of iced tea. Nadia was gulping the stuff down as fast as he was, and they were a little wired from it. Good – maybe it would keep her talking.

He set the pitcher between them. 'How's that one go – oh yeah. It's never a good thing when the new woman asks you about the last woman.'

She gulped, dribbling on her chin. 'What did you just say?'

'Something I read.'

'I'm not the new anything.'

'I know.'

She glared at him.

'Nadia, relax. I know.'

'Good.' The way she watched him, he reminded himself to watch his words. 'Was she your first love?'

'No.'

'Who was your first?'

Conrad sighed. 'My high-school sweetheart. That ended badly.'

'How bad?'

'How about, I still have nightmares about her, and she was twelve years ago.'

'Tsh. Get over it, dude.'

'You've never been in love.' It was a statement, not a question, but she took it as one.

'Nope.' Without hesitation. 'What, did you ask my mom about me?'

'No.' He grinned and looked away.

'What?'

'I saw your, uh, MySpace thing.'

'My wha— oh. Why?'

He shrugged. 'I was bored.'

'You're a total pervert!'

'Nadia, please.'

'Is that what you do when your wife's away? Surf the web for porn?'

'Porn? Did I miss something on your page?' He laughed.

'You're disgusting,' she said.

'I thought it was nice. I felt like I learned something about you.'

'Like what?'

'That you've never been in love.'

'Creepy . . .'

'So why did you put it up there, then? It's still called the World Wide Web, isn't it?'

'One of my friends made me do it. MySpace is so gay.'

'Why haven't you ever been in love?'

'"In love." God, you sound like my dad.'

'Hey, I don't know. What do kids call it these days?'

'I'm not a kid. And they don't call it anything. Now they just hook up.'

'So why haven't you ever been in love?'

'You can't force it.'

'Well, actually you can, but you shouldn't,' he said.

'What's that mean?'

'You asked about my wife . . . no, that's another long and not very interesting story.'

'Isn't that what we're doing? Telling stories?'

So it was going to be like this. She was not going to open up again until he gave something back. 'Okay. I guess I was still messed up over Holly. When I met Jo I didn't really understand how different we were. I was working in customer service at this software company. She was already in sales, making good money. I was sort of floundering after not finishing college. I was just happy someone wanted me. We started sleeping together. She didn't even want to call it dating at first. Then she got this job offer in Los Angeles, and suddenly it was tearsville, and why didn't I come with her? I didn't have much else going on. I was like . . . you know, I just figured this out after we moved here and Jo went away. I'm the housewife.'

Nadia pushed back her chair and waddled to the couch with the dogs, pulling Alice into her lap while Luther curled at her feet.

He followed her into the living room with the iced tea and struck a Vanna White pose, the pitcher held up next to his smiling face. 'See, I'm the housewife.'

'Housewife.' Nadia shivered a bit dramatically, smiling into her glass as she finished it. He set the pitcher down and sat on the couch opposite her, their bare feet facing each other over the coffee table. 'Why are you the housewife?'

'This is like the 1950s in reverse. You know, when men went to college to get a degree and women went to college to find a husband. I married a smart woman with ambition. The first one who batted her eyes at me. I don't even know what she sees in me now. She's always into her job. She can't relax. I thought I was doing something great here. Buying this house. We moved here, a month later she's out the door. I think I'm having a third-life crisis.'

'Third-life crisis?'

'Haven't you heard that yet? We don't wait until we're forty. Now it's after you've lived a third of your life.'

'I'm about to turn twenty – I wonder what I'm having,' Nadia said, sitting up as if she really wanted know.

'I think you're having a baby.'

They both laughed at that.

'Now she's the one in the big scary business world. What do I do? I cook, clean, ask her about her day. I sulk. My father left me some money, which can only make things worse. I could join the PTA at this point, but I don't have kids. Maybe I was meant to be the stay-at-home dad.'

'Would you really want to?'

'Sure, why not?'

'Most guys around here just wouldn't.'

Conrad drank more tea.

'So what are you going to do?'

'I've got nine Boelen's eggs in my garage.'

'Did you talk to your friend at the zoo?'

'He doesn't believe me.'

'There must be an explanation, right?'

Was she being coy, or was he really that far off base?

'Nadia.' He waited for her to look at him. He drained his glass and spoke very softly. 'Who's the father?'

Her expression was flat. 'What if there is no father?'

'What does that mean?'

'What if it was a miracle, like your snake eggs?'

'You really think so?'

'Please.' She got to her feet and walked to the door.

He followed her. 'Wait, come on. You can't just drop that on me.'

She stopped and faced him. 'Do you really believe it's haunted?'

If she was messing with him, he would seem a fool. If

she was testing him, trying to trust him, he needed to tread carefully.

'I don't know,' he said. 'That's why you're here, isn't it?'

'Maybe I'm just fucking with you. Trying to take your money.'

'You can have my money. All of it.'

Nadia shook her head. 'This was a bad idea.'

'What were you doing in the house that day?'

'What day?'

'You were in the upstairs room the day I first toured the house with my realtor.'

'No, I wasn't.'

'You don't remember bumping into me in the hall?'

'No.'

'Really? Because the way you looked at me when I was eating dinner at your parents' house, I thought you recognized me.'

'No, that was the first time I ever saw you.'

'Did something happen in the house? To you?'

'It was a mistake. You wouldn't understand.'

He rested one hand on her shoulder. 'Nadia? Hey. You're talking to the housewife, remember? I made a mistake. People make mistakes.'

She kept shaking her head, looking at the wall. He could see she had something to say, but she didn't want to say it tonight.

'My wife is pregnant,' he said.

'Congratulations.'

'Nadia.'

183

'Con-rad.' Sing-songy, avoiding it.

'I'm not the father.'

'Then I'm sorry. For both of you.' She turned for the door. 'I have to go.'

'The thing is, Nadia . . .'

She was on her way out.

'I wish I was.' His hand fell off her shoulder.

'Good night, Conrad.'

Fifteen minutes later he was in the office, shutting down the computer and heading for bed when the phone startled him.

'Hello.'

'Hey, asshole.'

'Jo?' Shit! He'd promised to call her.

'No, it's Nadia.' Panic and anger in her voice, heavy breathing. 'And this is so not funny.'

His antennae went up. 'What's wrong?'

'I'll call the police, you piece of shit.'

'Why?'

'Is this a game for you two?'

'Who? What game?'

'Who do you people think you are? Did you think I wouldn't figure it out sooner or later?'

'Nadia, slow down.' She was nearly hyperventilating. 'Is someone there? What's wrong?'

'Fucker. I trusted you!'

'Nadia, tell me what happened. Are you hurt?'

'You're such a shitty liar. I know she's there!'

'Who?'

'Your wife!'

'Jo? She's in Detroit.'

'Oh, really,' she scoffed.

'Yes, really.'

A pause on her end, a little hiccup of breath.

'Nadia? What makes you think my wife is here?'

'Your wife's not home?'

'No, I told you that.'

'Conrad?'

'Yes.'

'If your wife's in Detroit . . .'

'Uh-huh.'

'Then who is that woman standing at the window, staring at my house?'

21

He was in the office. Walking ten paces around the corner would not only give him a view of the library, it would put him in the center of the room. The house was dead quiet.

'Nadia?' His voice was quieted by extreme force of will. 'Tell me where you are. What do you see?'

'This is such bullshit.'

'I can't see. Tell me, please,' he whispered. The office door was open. If someone were in the library, it would be a short walk around the corner.

She was still crying, but that seemed to be tapering off some. 'She's right there. I can see her in the window. I'm – I'm not doing this!'

The line disconnected.

Conrad opened his mouth but the words caught in his throat.

Count to ten.

Listen.

He couldn't hear anything beyond his own pulse thumping in his ears. He turned toward the open door. He tried to see it before he went to see it. He knew that the library had two windows separating the wall-to-wall bookshelves. The largest window faced the street and was not visible from the Grum residence. The other window faced Nadia's house.

Go look. You must go look.

Where are the dogs?

She must be mistaken. What could she see that would look like a woman?

He had neither the courage to move nor wait in here all night. It occurred to him, too, that if there was someone here and she did come for him, he would be trapped in the office.

He pressed *69, wincing at the beep of each key. The phone rang three times.

'What?' She was annoyed.

He cupped his hand over the mouthpiece. 'Nadia, wait. I'm stuck in the office. Help me.'

'Was she listening to us the whole time? Were you hoping to drag me into some sick game between the two of you?' Nadia sniffed and blew her nose.

Her insistence turned his bowels to water.

'What does she look like?'

'I can see her shape right now. She's tall, with long, dark hair. She's wearing a black dress or long coat.'

'Now?'

'Yes, now!'

'Wait, this is important. Don't hang up.'

'Conrad, is that your wife? That's your wife, right? I won't tell anybody. I don't even know why you're doing this. Just tell me that's your wife.'

He could no longer speak. The line went dead. He closed his eyes, letting his imagination play a cruel game with his mind. The game was called, Which One of These Things Is More Frightening Than The Other? The idea that there was an honest to God ghost in his house, right now, and he was about to see her, his sepia-toned woman sneering from the photo? Or that his wife was home? That Jo had been here all night, watching them?

No, not Jo. It couldn't be Jo. He'd just talked to her earlier today – no, that was yesterday. She could be here. But she wouldn't.

He imagined the other turning away from the window, the one he'd seen in the yard, her scratchy black dress heavy upon her shoulders and wide hips, lurching toward the garage where the eggs – *and the babies, the buried babies, too* – were hidden where the cross used to be. She was pregnant. She had the same dark hair and height and posture as Jo. Her mouth a slanted line with graying lips, her nose – no, she didn't have a nose. The woman bucking on the table didn't have eyes or a nose or anything above the mouth. Would her hair be coarse like the mane of a horse? Like the doll's? He could almost hear her black boots scrape against the wooden floor and—

And then not seeing was worse than seeing, and he moved. The steps to the doorway were slow and enormous, but he made them, turning ninety degrees into the hall, peering into the library, until only the front half was visible. The front window. The shelves of books.

He felt her. Her presence in the room like a scratchy wool blanket draped over his shivering cold body. He could feel her in the room as surely as if she were standing behind him breathing on his neck. He knew this as fact, and now he absolutely had to go all the way.

He took three quick steps, the floorboards creaking as he entered the library. The blood pounded up through him, threatening to blot his vision as it had in the room with the dogs, and he held the phone out to ward off whatever was coming for him. He blinked rapidly, willing the red and black dots clouding his vision to go away.

She was upon him.

She was—

The library was empty.

He was blinking, his heart stuck in an elevator ten stories below its natural position. He smelled cloves and something earthen, a sweet spice in the air, but after a few deep breaths that was gone, too.

'She's not my wife,' he said to the room. 'She's someone else. Someone lost.'

Gone. She was gone. It felt wrong, a let-down. He had been hoping for a confirmation, even if it drove him mad. At least he would have known.

He walked to the window, where Nadia claimed to have seen her. He wanted to deny her space, blot her out. He pulled aside the flimsy silk curtain and looked out to the Grums'.

A bedroom window, lights off.

He almost dialed her again, but what would be the point? He would only wind up scaring her worse than he already had. They'd been talking about Jo. Bad things in the house. Scary stories that were bound to have an effect on a girl in her condition.

'Luther! Alice!' His voice was hoarse, but he heard the *whump-ump-ump-ump* as the dogs unloaded from the couch and came trotting to the front stairs and the softer padding as they ran up the deep pile carpet runner to greet him, and for a second he was certain it would not be them, it would be her, come back to finish him.

But it was only the dogs. He bent to pet them, to reassure them and himself. When he stood upright he was face to face with the window, and in its reflection, as if superimposed over his face, a pale woman with black hair stared back at him.

He had been wrong about her face, so very wrong because she had no face before, in the room a few nights ago, but now it seemed, yes, even now her face seemed to be forming itself into something very old and something new. The flat, fish-belly white patch under her hair wrinkled and contorted as he heard the swish of her black dress fanning out behind him. Cool air pulled all around him and her starved ovoid visage filled the glass in jarring increments like a poorly edited film. He glimpsed a line of black stubble high on her head where her brow was filling in even as her stilted footsteps drummed across the floor and she fell upon him, her cold calloused hands wrapping around his neck.

22

Conrad, Luther and Alice slept on the high-school football field three blocks away.

When he had felt her cold hands closing around his neck, he'd screamed like a child and fled the house. The dogs had gone nape-hair wild and barking after him. When they reached the field, the dogs ran in wide circles – it was playtime for them. He'd fallen to the grass and thought about what was ruined now – their fresh start, the new life. Maybe that had all been a false hope, perhaps it was never meant to be.

The sky was so much clearer here than in Los Angeles. Without the smog he could see all the constellations he did not know the names of. He knew that Jo was sleeping now, in Michigan. What he had seen in the house could not be his wife. A ghost, an echo, a reflection. Whatever she was, he had seen the impossible and it sickened him to think she was in the house, had maybe been there all along.

He missed Jo that night more than he could remember missing anyone since Holly, and he would have cried himself to sleep if he had not still been in some form of shock.

The night was warm and long, full of half-visions every time he nodded off on the grass with the dogs by his side. He dozed on the football field as the air cooled, and he became aware of the orange tint of his eyelids soon after.

He woke on the field and the dogs were gone.

When he had climbed the steps out of the stadium and made his way down the three blocks to Heritage Street and to his front porch, he found them beating their tails against the door.

They wanted to go home. They had no other choice.

After searching the house (feeling and finding nothing out of place) his fear was cut in half, and the thirty-minute hot shower washed most of the other half away. The yesterdays were becoming like dreams, their contents vanishing as quickly as he could forget them. He left messages with the front desk and on her cell, telling her only that he missed her.

He sat in the office thinking about a job. Thought about becoming a father. Wasn't that a job? There had been an article on Salary.com he'd seen a few months back. Some crack team of industry experts added up the hours and skills and decided stay-at-home moms were worth $131,000 a year. Stay-at-home moms had to be a nurse, a chef, a teacher, a driver, and a nanny all in one. Maybe all he had to do was wait for Jo to have the baby and – snap, just like that – overnight he'd be worth $131,000.

Right now house-sitting was not a job. But he had an obligation.

*

She answered the door, left it open and walked back into the kitchen while he followed her in.

'There was no one there,' he said. He knew she wouldn't come back if he told the truth. He might have imagined it, he told himself. 'I never saw anyone in the library.'

She ignored this, as well as his assertions that Jo was in Michigan and he was not playing games. What would be the point? He confessed that, yes, he had felt something, but that could have been the fear working on his imagination.

'Maybe there was a . . . presence in the house, but if so, that only proves what I've been telling you all along.'

'What's that?' she said, drinking a peach yogurt concoction from the plastic bottle.

'That I could really use your help.'

'I think I've been telling you all along I don't have any answers.'

Conrad nodded. 'What are you doing for dinner? I can cook something, unless you have plans.'

She set the yogurt down and burped. 'No, I don't have any plans.'

'You look like you're doing well. Do you need anything for the baby? The, what, the prenatal vitamins?'

'I don't need anything,' she said.

'Everything was fine when you were there, right? I know it got a little personal at the end there, but I thought we had kind of a nice time. Don't give up so easily, Nadia.'

'You think I'm crazy,' she said, flipping through a copy of *US Weekly* with a pregnant starlet on the cover.

'No, I don't.'

'You will.'

'No, I won't.'

'Sooner or later every guy calls me a psycho.'

'That's why you've never been in love?' She closed the magazine. 'You're not psycho, Nadia. I know psycho women, and you're not one of them.'

'Thanks.'

Jesus, could he say anything that didn't make this girl roll her eyes? 'Look, I won't bother you. I'll be making teriyaki bowls later.'

'Maybe,' she'd said. 'But probably not.'

He tried to stare her down but she would not budge. He went to his ace in the hole.

'Five hundred now,' he said, placing the bills on the table. 'Two thousand after.'

She looked at the money. 'After what?'

'After the rest of it. But no more breaks. We don't have much time.'

Nadia was stretched out across the love seat like it was a fainting couch. He hoped the food was a way in, like the money. She'd wolfed down two bowls of sticky rice, with broccoli and thinly sliced filet mignon he'd marinated and grilled for her. He'd eaten one bowl and then gone back to the iced tea. It calmed him to watch her eat.

Feeding her, feeding the baby.

'You really know how to cook,' she said. The dogs

huddled around and under her legs. It was what they did when Jo was here and he felt another pang of guilt that this neighbor girl, not their true mistress, was the one keeping them company.

'I'm glad you liked it. There's more if you get hungry again.'

He left the dishes in the kitchen and took a seat on the couch to her right. He was wearing his Sebadoh tee, camo shorts over bare feet. It was too hot for shoes, and he wondered if he looked younger than thirty.

She was wearing holey jeans and a faded green pocket tee shirt, his favorite look on most any girl. Her feet were bare and her toes had been painted iridescent pink, like little pearls. She'd done something home-made to her hair. It was shorter and choppy around the bottom. The bangs were pulled back on the center of her head, leaving the rest of her straight hair hanging squarely around her face. Her pregnancy had moved from a sometime distraction to a sort of Merlin ball that worked the opposite way: he fed by gazing at it, or wishing to gaze into it, to see the future. He looked at the bulge under her shirt and imagined a honeydew melon, a huge scoop of ice cream. Then, like she'd thought of it ten minutes ago and was ready to dump it on him, she told him another story.

'A few times after the time with the dolls, I was attacked in your house.'

'*Attacked* attacked? How? Where?'

'Upstairs. In the guest room.' She nodded up at the ceiling.

'What happened?'

As before, she looked away as she recounted it.

'I was alone, or just with the children. The Laskis were out at the VFW. I made brownies while they sat in front of the fireplace and played with those block things, those thick Leggos for dummies. I tried. I really did. But every time I got close to them, they would just stare off into outer space. So I pretended to be with them while I was on the phone with Eddie, then I put them to bed at eight like I was supposed to.'

'You knew Eddie back then?'

'I've been friends with Eddie since I can remember.'

'What kind of friends?'

'Eddie's not important now, not in this story.'

'Okay. So you put the kids to bed.'

'I even read them a story.'

'Which one?'

'*The Tale of Pigling Bland*, I think. One of those little antique books they had that smelled like mold. They didn't fall asleep after I'd read it twice, so finally I just got up and turned off the light and went into the next room to read.'

'What were you reading?'

'Does that matter?'

'I'm a book guy. Just curious.'

'*One Day in the Life of Ivan Denisovich*.'

'For school?'

'No.'

'That's a helluva a book for a thirteen-year-old.'

'Not really. The style is very simple. That was part of the point.'

'To capture the voice of the everyman,' he said.

'And to make the story accessible to every man,' she added.

'Jesus. I hadn't even thought of that, and I've read it twice. Did you get that when you were thirteen?'

'I don't know. And, no, it did not give me nightmares, if that's your next question. It wasn't the book.'

'And you're sure no one was here, just the kids?'

'Positive.'

'What time was this?'

'Maybe eight thirty. Does that matter?'

'I don't know.'

'Then shut up and let me finish.'

'Sorry.'

'I think I fell asleep. I mean, I must have, because one minute I was reading and the next minute I was waking up really fast. Like when you have a dream that you're falling and your stomach freaks out and then you wake up right before you hit.'

'I think I had that same dream in this house.'

She rolled her eyes. 'Everybody has that dream. It's like the most common dream you can have, next to flying. I looked it up.'

'Excuse me.' *Smarty pants.* 'Go on.'

She settled into the memory, zoning out with her hand stroking Alice behind the ears. 'So I'm falling, I wake up, and the room is blurry and kind of dark. I can see shapes in the room with me. There are at least three of them. They're big, like farmers. Big rough women in heavy coats or dresses. All in gray wool or black. They are standing in the corner, watching me. It's the *zeks*, I thought. From the book. But not like I really thought they had come from the book. It was just a name that popped into my head. I knew these were something else.'

'*Zeks*,' he said. 'The prisoners in the labor camp.'

'Right. The name just stuck in my head. I can't see their faces because everything is blurry but I can smell some chemicals and it makes me panic like I need to get out of the house and maybe that's why they're here, to get me out. I try to get up from the chair and ask them what's wrong but I can't move. The *zeks* are moving in a circle, surrounding me. And I guess this is when I realize it's me. Everything that's wrong here is me. I'm the thing they're staring at.

'They start to close in, tightening the circle. It looks like they're holding hands but I can't tell for sure. They seem to float toward me instead of walking. I can't hear or see their feet. I can't lift my head. The closer they get the more gray they are. Like animal skin beneath the fur. Finally, when they are almost on top of me, I can see their faces but there are no faces. Everything above the shirts is gray. Flat, like smooth stone. I'm so out of it I'm more curious than frightened, but something inside me is saying this is bad and getting worse. My body is trying to . . . my mind is understanding that my body wants to jerk away or get up but it's like my body is thinking of it, not my mind. My mind is just watching.

'When they lean over me and their arms are coming down at me I know they are touching me. I can't feel the

198

arms or hands but they are too close not to be touching me. I'm numb. Then I got scared. Because if they're doing something to me, shouldn't I be able to feel it?'

She paused and looked down at her hands as if wanting to make sure they were still attached to her arms. 'You're not going to believe me with the rest of this.'

'I believe you now. Why wouldn't I believe the rest?'

'The next part is where Eddie stops believing me. Like I'm telling him this for his entertainment or some shit and he gets to choose what parts he likes and what parts are stupid. But he doesn't get to choose. You don't get to choose.'

He nodded. 'I promise.'

'One of the *zeks* touches my forehead. Her hand is right above my eyes even though I can't move my head to look up. She stands beside me while the other two women are crouched in front of me. All I can see is the room in front of me at about waist level and a little bit above. The tops of the heads are smooth and gray like the rest of their heads and faces. Then they all jump back, because suddenly someone else *was* there. They all moved back and stood in the corner, like they were afraid of this other one.'

'What other one?'

'I don't know. I couldn't see. He was taller, thinner.'

'It was a man?'

'I don't know. I couldn't see him. He was wearing black like the others and his face was covered, like one of those women in the Middle East. Maybe it was a woman. I don't know – but she was big.'

199

'Jesus, do you think it was—'

'I don't know!'

'Okay. Calm down.'

Nadia rubbed her eyes before continuing. 'The other one was in charge. She, he. It took over. She leaned over in front of me and started pulling in bursts while her other hand is squeezing something, maybe pressing me down. And then, very faintly, for the first time I begin to feel something.

'I can feel something hard inside me, like my thighbone or my back, and it's being pulled like the handle of a stuck refrigerator door. I'm scared of what it might be and what they're doing. I think if there is something bad inside of me I want her to get it out. That doesn't make any sense, I know. But for some reason I still trusted them. A part of me feels the same way you do at the dentist. It's my fault I have a cavity. The dentist is the guy who's been working on your teeth for years. It's not pleasant, but you know he's right. You have to let him work. It was like that.

'Then two things happen at the same time. I hear a voice in my head and it's my voice but it's not me talking. It's telling me *no, don't let them do it, don't let them do it, you have to stop them*, and it's getting louder. It's me shouting at myself to stop whatever they are doing. The second thing that happens is I start to feel pain. It comes slowly like it's real far away. Like a train. I visualize it as a train and I can barely see the light on the front, but it's coming, and the light is the pain. The closer it comes the bigger and brighter the light becomes and the more it hurts and I know when it gets here it's going to be unbearable. I can't stop the train. I don't know why it's coming but it is.

'The one kneeling in front of me bobs her head like she sees something she likes and the me inside of me starts shouting *no stop stop stop get away get up and get away* and finally the pain wakes me up because it's so close now I can see the blackness behind the light and it feels like someone is burning me from the inside out, and it makes my body jerk and then I *have* to move. The more I move the more it hurts. And the more it hurts the more scared I am. She starts pulling again and I can feel the arms in front of me, and maybe something like hands inside of me. I'd never had anything inside of me, not *inside of me* . . . not then, and so I can't be sure, but I'm pretty sure she's inside me and she wants to take me apart in there. *You'll never be put back together again!* the voice screams at me. *Once it comes out you can never put it back in!*

'Then the worst thing happens. All three of the *zeks* in the corner snap their heads up all at once. For the first time I can see their eyes. Their eyes are marbles, black like a newborn's eyes. I'm still waiting for them to smother me or tear me apart when she rakes her arms down over me and the pain explodes inside me and the blood, so much blood, it's black like ink comes out and covers her arms and her face. The ones in the corner run from the room but she stays a minute longer, speaking in a voice that is either mumbled or in another language, I can't understand her, but it's a prayer she saying over me,

I think. And then she is gone. The pain is so bad the dark room is gone and everything is white and I can't think or see or move, it's obliterating me the pain is so incredible. It's beyond me, it's impossible to describe because I wasn't there any more and it felt clean. Like it was washing them all away, the *zeks* can't hurt me, and she can't be inside me any more because the pain and the white is too strong for them. And that's it. Then it was over.'

Conrad swallowed audibly. 'Did you wake up?'

'I was awake. I had been awake the whole time.'

'I don't get it.'

'It just ended. The white and the pain faded and when it was gone I was alone on the bed. I went to check on the kids. They were lying in bed with their eyes open, staring at the ceiling. They looked like they were dead.'

'Jesus, did they see them, too?'

'I don't know. They wouldn't talk. I asked them if they were okay, but they just sat there and I couldn't deal with it, so I turned out the light and went downstairs. The Laskis came in laughing. They were too drunk to walk and Mrs Laski left her purse at the place, so I said forget it, pay me later, and I left.'

'Did you tell anyone? Besides Eddie?'

'No. Not then. The next day Leon came over and gave me seven dollars, asked me how the kids were. I said they had a hard time falling asleep. I think he knew, though, because I was still kind of shaken up and he said something like, "I know it ain't easy putting them down,

but that's the way it goes around here, so thank you."
Something like that.'

'I'm not sure . . .' Conrad began, then stopped. She was like someone with an alibi and doesn't care who believes her because she was certain of the truth. 'Nadia. If you felt fine after, how can you say it was real?'

'Why are you making me do this?'

'Am I making you do anything, Nadia? Really? Because it seems to me you keep coming back, you keep telling me these things.'

'The *zeks* – those gray women – they were real. They took my baby away.'

'Who—'

'I'd never been with a man. But I knew I was pregnant. And someone else, those *zeks*, whatever they were, they were judging me. When they saw I was unfit, they decided they didn't want me to have the baby. So they took it.'

She was a scared kid. She was confused. She's still fucked up about it. Something had happened, but not this. She was wrong, had to be.

'I told you, you don't get to choose what to believe.'

'Then explain it to me, because I don't see how.'

'It took me a long time to understand. It was real, but it didn't happen to me. Not then. Not that night.'

He realized she was crying.

'I was seeing myself, later, like I am now. I saw myself pregnant, and now I am. I saw what would happen if I got pregnant . . .' she was near to sobbing '. . . and I didn't deserve this baby.'

'Oh, no, Nadia. No.' He went around the table and sat beside her, resisting the urge to hug her. He held her hand. 'Don't think that.'

She looked around the room. 'Now do you understand? Why I don't want to be here?'

'Nothing is going to hurt you here.'

'It doesn't matter. You couldn't stop it. If they want to take it, they will.'

'Did you tell your mother? Anybody?'

'Not my mom. Eddie didn't believe me.' She fell into his shoulder and cried. He didn't know what to say, so he held her there for a few minutes until she slowed down and caught her breath. 'What if I don't deserve it?' she said.

'Why wouldn't you deserve it?'

'Because I'm not married. I don't know how to take care of it.'

'That doesn't matter,' he said without hesitation. She wasn't teasing him now. This was real. He still didn't understand, but he was glad she let him in. 'Whatever it takes. I'll help you.'

23

He was back in high school, aware that he hadn't been there for years. He was the older self but also the boy he had been. He was wandering through the halls looking for her. He found her in the cafeteria, sitting on a crackled brown leather couch in the corner. The lunchroom had been half-transformed into someone's house, a house party. He waded through the other students, ignoring them as he pressed forward, thinking of what he would say to her. He knew he had to get it right. Had to say the right thing or else he would scare her away.

When he arrived she looked up at him. She had the same flawless young face, all wide glowing cheeks and semi-flat nose.

Holly. Holy Girl.

He wiped his hands on his jeans. He was a mess, the older version. Wanted to hide this version. She wasn't supposed to see him this way.

'Holly,' he said.

'Shhhsh. Don't say anything,' she said in a whisper. 'She'll hear us.'

Conrad thought of Jo, a stab of guilt pressing into his

belly. He turned around and the cafeteria behind him was a black wall. A terrifying black edifice. His fault it was here. He'd brought it with him, let her down. Had to save her. His heart slammed as Holly turned and her face changed—

He snapped awake in bed, in the house, blinking into the dark. He felt the blackness with him, in the room. He dared not sit up or move. If he did, it would come to the bed and devour him, end everything.

His eyes adjusted to the dark and still he saw only different shades of black against black. The curtains over the window. The open closet a funnel of black going blacker. The wooden sleigh bed curling like a wave at his feet. A blanket draped over the sleigh frame.

A shadow moved.

He did not move so much as his eyeballs.

At the foot of the bed, there was a body standing over him. She was tall. Not moving. She was watching something, looking down. Tall enough to be his wife.

Not real, he told himself.

Maybe she came home early.

Could not open his mouth to ask her anything. Impossible to act. The terror so great he thought he was dying while she loomed over him, staring down, willing his heart to stop.

Not real, he kept thinking. She's not real. Not real, not—

She moved.

Or maybe she had been moving all along. For he saw now that her arms were rocking back and forth, slowly.

Holding something in her arms, her head tilting forward, her face and eyes invisible while she looked down at the bundle in her arms.

'Behbee,' she whispered. Her voice hoarse, deep. 'Ohmmma save the behbeeee.'

It was a full minute later, another interminable minute of watching her arms rocking, when she turned. Her body moved stiffly with grief away from him, out of the bedroom.

No footsteps in the hall. He felt rather than heard her departure and only then did he breathe. The bed shook as the tremors rippled through him. He almost began to cry, but he was afraid to make a sound.

There is another woman in this house. She wants something, and she's growing bolder.

The next morning, Conrad found more packages on the porch. It was not the first batch, but it was the big one. He hauled them in with the others and opened them all, a summer Christmas he had been avoiding. All the invoices were made out to Joanna Harrison. The boxes disgorged drapes with zoo animals on them, rustic wooden shelving units that looked more like Lincoln Logs than furniture, and a designer trashcan designed to keep baby shit off your fingers when disposing of diapers. But it was this final item that kicked off the project and got him going full-tilt.

'Okay, kids,' he said to the dogs, opening a cold beer and thinking he was overdue for a good old-fashioned drunk. 'Let's do this.'

Using a painter's razor, he slit the plastic manifest and inspected the packing slip from the largest box. TOTAL: $2845. He sucked at his beer. The invoice was the yellow copy torn from a generic three-layer pad. At the top, the pressed ink stamp read

Karl Stobbe Carpentry
Wisconsin's Finest
Amish Carpentry & Woodcrafts

He arranged the contents in an exploded view across the living room floor, taking extra care to keep the dogs from running off with the sanded pegs and support beams.

There were no instructions, and Mr Karl Stobbe, fine craftsman that he was, had not left a phone number or web address on the invoice. Conrad knew the usual stereotypes about the Amish – most were in Pennsylvania but plenty had settled in Ohio and Wisconsin, too – living without telephones. Maybe Stobbe was the real deal. Conrad stared at the contents for almost half an hour before he packed it all up and carried the box upstairs.

He set the kit in the library, tuned the radio to NPR's classical station, and began ripping up the carpet. Avoiding the stain on the floor as best he could, he pulled staples from the wood and chipped away the dried, stuck padding. He dragged the mess to the garbage cans on the side of the house. He returned to the fridge for more beer three times – he was sweating the stuff out as fast as he could drink it – and lost himself in honest labor.

He swept the floor, scraped paint and then used Jo's Ryobi belt sander to strip the wood of blood and blood dust in an attempt to restore its natural color. He swept the floor again and when he saw that the stain was not going to go away without replacing some of the boards, he decided, to hell with it, let's keep the blood and spill some paint. He did not stop to eat and eventually he forgot about the beer.

When he ran out of paint he returned to the porch and unwrapped the pallet. She had ordered gallons of the stuff delivered from the local hardware store a week ago. Quality, custom-mixed latex in peach, lavender and sea green. A gender-neutral palette, very progressive. Finished with the floors, he started on the walls. He inhaled sweet fumes and remembered moving to new apartments with his mother. New beginnings. He was a man who loved beginnings. The way he left a job before giving it time really to learn something new and get promoted. The way he had started a new screenplay before finishing the old one. The way you met a girl and had no idea what comes next. The way he avoided cleaning up the old mess. Moving. Always a fresh start, never a permanent home.

He brought in the throw rug she had sent a week ago, the one with the sailboat braving indigo waves under gold stars and a smiling silver moon. It took Conrad the rest of the night to peg and glue the oak slats in place, set the natural fiber bed pad in the tiny fortress center to the room so that the moonlight would catch it the way

(the house showed him)

he saw it in his head, and sweep everything clean once again. He brought in the lamp she had chosen, an ivory-colored ceramic beast with lion's feet at the base and winged shoulders above, a safari motif on the shade. When everything was in its place, he sat on the floor and stared at the crib, alone in a transformed room the dogs still would not enter. In the dark with the lights off and the moon on the soft carpet, ashamed.

The crib was the thing. Even empty it changed everything. Made the future real, a thing to hold on to.

He fell asleep on the floor beside the crib and awoke hours later in his bed. She came to him before dawn, as if preparing the room had been an act of penance and she were his reward.

He was in high school again. Some event setting up and waiting to be played out. He felt like a king. His friends were all there with him, the best ones from the days when they were all kings. He was wearing his favorite pair of Adidas basketball shoes, the orange and blue Knicks colors, his Ewings. He felt unstoppable. A cool can of regular Budweiser in his hand. He was glad to be back with the Budweiser, the choice of kings and Beastie Boys back in 1989.

It was the buoyant feeling of prom night, of having an infinite life ahead of you and the right girl by your side. Then his friends were calling to him – let's get out of here, dude. But he wanted to stay. Holly standing over him, where they'd left off the night before.

Holly was neither as tall and formidable as Jo nor as short and full as Nadia. She had the build of a cyclist. Her legs were sculpted and thick through the thighs and calves, her ass as firm as two volleyballs. He smiled into her waist as she leaned against him. Her smell was familiar and somehow also new, the smell of jasmine blossoms and another herb, nettles perhaps. The little new age bohemian even then, before it had become fashionable to go natural in high school. He remembered her thing with iced tea.

She pressed her weight fully against his lap, pinning him to the couch. Her wheat-thick hair was soft against his cheeks and over his face. Her skin was cool and smooth. He heard himself whispering in her ear, 'missed you so much . . . missed you so much . . .' over and over, stuck in the lingo of the adolescent and unafraid to plead with her.

Under her rocking movement and warmth and sweet spicy scent, his body responded and he tried to lift her up but her thighs were iron-clad, holding him down. Her hand closed against his crotch and squeezed. Her hand was cool, her grip exquisite. Her breath childlike, scented with milk.

He raised his hands to touch her neck and breasts and hips, but his fingers kept slipping through her hair. She was all hair and gossamer cloth, a shifting wisp he could not grasp.

She leaned back and maneuvered him inside. He sighed in surprise at how she was wet but somehow cool, even down there. She warmed with him inside and fell heavily back down upon him as her hips pushed forward and back, rolling, the fullness of her bush – different, thicker than he remembered – scraping his waist and the tops of his thighs. The physical sensation brought him another level closer to consciousness and she fucked him this way for a minute longer. The whole experience was a reminder of some recurring dream he had come to expect but never taken this far.

But thinking it was a dream always killed the dream and so he tried to deny himself further awareness.

She rode him, bringing him closer in a hurry and then paused, adjusted herself on top of him, grunting in anger and all at once he was awake, at home, in his marital bed. Fear like electrified water shot through his legs and snapped his back straight, but her hands pinned his arms to his sides and her full breasts pressed against his chest. The fear amplified the sensations – good and bad – tenfold.

He tried to see her face but her head was down, monitoring the point where they met, a triangle of black that opened and closed with a wet slapping sound he found erotic and disgusting. She gained substance before his eyes. Her dark form shifted from the ethereal to the clumsy and mechanical, driven by something other than love or even lust.

He struggled beneath her. She yanked his wrists up and planted his palms against her breasts, which were heavy and sheathed in white lace. They were fuller than he remembered, and her entire front was wet, hot with her sweat. He thought her injured; he thought of accidents and blood.

She moaned, winding him tighter. His mind bounced between fear and escape for another thirty seconds while inside her the muscles contracted and pulled. Her walls closed in. To this tension she added a rocking movement, forward and back, repeating the dual motion until he lost control. The sensation conjured a rope with twelve knots at six-inch intervals pulling out of him from his legs and spine through his cock, each knot detonating white flashes of blinding pleasure in his reptilian brain. Only when she was climbing away from him like a spider in the dark did he hear himself screaming.

She scurried out the door with one last fretful moan and her feet padded staccato-like down the hall.

Footsteps. This time he heard her footsteps.

Or thought he did.

Conrad sprang forward and heard his lower lumbar pop in at least three places. He tried to stand and was greeted by pins and needles from the waist down. He fell back into bed, his penis still lost in its own delirious spasm. Muscles shot, cold and shivering wet with her residue, he felt like a freshly shucked oyster, soon to be eaten.

'Why are you doing this to me?' he shouted, trying to laugh after.

No one answered. He sat on the bed listening, turning it over in his head, until he had nearly convinced himself it was another bad dream or a hallucination.

In the morning he thought of Nadia. Nadia had been here before. She even said she did not remember being here the day he bumped into her while Roddy was downstairs having a smoke. But she was just a kid. Would she really come to him in the middle of the night? Not likely.

The only other possibility – that it had been Jo, that she was watching him, toying with him – was so ridiculous that he convinced himself all over again it was a dream. He was lonely, sex-deprived. He had been through a bad couple of months. He might be having a nervous breakdown. It wasn't real. It was only a—

It was like before. When he had woken up on the floor of the bathroom. The skin of his penis was chaffed, stinging and sore in the right places. What did that leave? A nocturnal emission? Fucking the pillows?

Probably. Yes, definitely.

But when he lifted the plastic cup of warmed-over tea from the nightstand to his nose, he could smell her. He remembered feeling the warm blood on her breasts. Then he saw the evidence. Not blood. In the morning light his fingers were chalky, dry, crackly white. He put two in his mouth without thinking and the texture was brittle, sweet. You don't remember, but you know.

A mother's milk.

24

'So what've you been up to?' he said, filling his coffee cup from the Bunn machine in the Grums' kitchen. The coffee was thick, as if it had been sitting all morning, the way he liked it. Nadia was sitting on one of the stools at the kitchen island, flipping through the paper, sipping from a Winnie-the-Pooh mug and pretending he wasn't there. 'You feeling all right? Nadia?'

'Sleeping a lot. I feel like shit.'

Her flannel shirt and shorts clung to her plump curves and he searched her body for something that would affirm his suspicions – a scar, a line, the coarser hairs at the tops of her thighs – something to jar his foggy memory of the flesh he had cupped and caressed some thirty-six hours before.

'Everything okay with the baby? Did you call your doctor?'

She winced but did not look up from her paper. 'I can handle it.'

'Your parents would want me to ask. When are they due back, anyway?'

'Four or five days.'

'I'm behind on my chores.'

'I got the mail,' Nadia said, the sarcasm blatant. She slipped off her stool and went around the corner to the living room.

Conrad sipped his coffee. This didn't fit. She was not acting in any way clever or seductive. If she was playing games and sneaking into his house at night, she was one messed up girl. He went into the living room. Nadia was tucked under an orange Ralph Lauren blanket. He could see the little man on the horse near her feet. She unpaused the DVR.

'What's on?'

'*March of the Penguins.*'

He looked at the TV. Hundreds of the fat little birds were huddled together while the frozen wind whipped around them. Close-ups of the birds squatting on their eggs on the ice. It looked impossible.

He said, 'If I was a penguin I would leave. Go to Mexico.'

'Don't be an ass. This is amazing.'

'What part is amazing?'

'All of it.'

He watched their fat bodies hunker down, a community under the dark wind. They appeared miserable.

'What part do you like best?' he said.

'They share responsibility. They take turns until the baby is hatched.'

'Is that the one—'

'Shut up.'

He shut up and watched the penguins tough it out.

Morgan Freeman explained how, when the mothers are away getting more food, the fathers take over and sit on the eggs. The fathers did their best, but sometimes they fucked up and the eggs rolled away and died. The mothers returned with food to feed the fathers, and they traded places. Sometimes, when one of the mothers returns and finds out her egg has died, she tries to steal another mother's egg. But the community won't let her. She is grief-stricken, inconsolable and ostracized.

'That's so sad,' Nadia said, sniffing.

He watched the broken egg on the ice, the little dead bird inside. 'What happens when the mother goes away and doesn't come back? What does the father do with the egg then? Find another mother, or just take care of it on his own?'

'I don't know,' she said, looking up at him with glassy eyes. 'What happens?'

He was still formulating his answer when the phone rang. She looked away, wiping her eyes. After three rings he said, 'What if it's Mom and Dad?'

'Knock yourself out.'

Conrad went to the kitchen. 'Grum residence.'

'Yeah, where's Nadia?' The guy on the other end sounded startled, out of breath. His was the panting of a wired, anxious little man.

'Who's calling?'

Nadia padded in and poured orange juice. The carton said NO PULP! 50% More Calcium!

'I said who's calling, please?'

'Chuh!' The spitting sound of incredulity. 'Who's this, the neighbor guy?'

'My name is Conrad.'

'Where is she?'

'If you tell me who's calling, I'll see if she's home.'

'Eddie. I know she's there.'

'Okay, Eddie, please hold.'

Conrad held the phone out. Nadia shook her head slowly.

Conrad experienced a ridiculous, eleventh-grade thrill. 'I'm sorry, Eddie, she is unavailable. Can I take a message?'

'She won't talk to me?'

'She's not available, Eddie. Would you like me to tell her you called, or is there some other message?'

Eddie breathed into the phone. 'Are you f-f-fucking her now?'

Conrad resisted the urge to laugh. The boy's emotionally induced stutter induced pity and he did not want to be cruel. Well, not in front of her.

'You know, Eddie, I realize at your age that must be the most important thing in the world. But girls don't like it when boys talk out of school. So what do you say, guy, think you can rise above it?'

Nadia frowned and Conrad made a 'chill, it's under control' wave of his hand.

'Oh, you f-f-fucker,' Eddie moaned. 'Y-y-you are! And if you aren't, you're t-t-tryin' to! You f-f-fuckin' asshole!'

Something banged in the background and Conrad pulled the phone away from his ear. 'Hey, hey. That kind of language is uncalled for. Now it's none of my business,

Eddie, but if you two aren't exactly best friends these days, this temper of yours might be part of the problem, you know what I'm sayin'? If she wants to talk with you, she'll call. Personally, I'll advise her not to, but she's a big girl. She can make up her own mind.'

Eddie's breathing filled the line before he cranked up again. 'PUT NADIA ON THE PHONE, YOU MOTHERFUCKER!' Sans stutter. 'I'LL FUCKING KILL YOU IF YOU DON'T PUT HER ON THE PHONE!'

Nadia reached for the phone, but Conrad waved her off. He wanted to own this little shit now. Reach through the phone and break his skinny red neck.

A repeated banging sound on Eddie's side.

'Eddie?' Conrad said. 'You want to stop pounding your fist into your trailer wall for a minute?' The pounding stopped. 'You're taking out your frustrations on your wall because it's that cheap wood paneling they put in doublewides like yours. That's right, I know where you live. You make a threat like that, normally it's none of my business. But the Grums hired me to watch out for their things while they're away and Nadia happens to be one of those things. So for a few more days, guess what, it is my business.'

'Asshole, asshole, asshole—'

'Now I want to give you a piece of advice. Are you listening? Eddie, are you listening?'

'Yes!'

'Good. Now, when you make a threat. The first thing you have to do is stay calm. Because when you sound like a hysterical little bitch, no one takes you seriously. The person you're yelling at thinks, no, this guy sounds like a girl, he's just blowing off steam, he ain't gonna do anything. Are you with me, Eddie?'

'Yes.'

'Rule number two. Make sure you know something about the person you're threatening. This is very important because the last thing you want to do is make a threat you can't deliver on. Now, I haven't exactly kept my fighting weight over the years, but I'm capable, Eddie. Last asshole who threatened me, in front of my wife? Well, I plumb went sideways, Eddie. Put his head through a window at Ruth's Chris in Westwood. Paramedics had to pull glass out of his neck. Why do you think I had to leave LA? The stress, Eddie.'

This was fiction, of course. But it seemed to be working. Eddie was silent. Nadia watched him with her arms crossed.

'B-b-bullshit.'

'Now see, you just skipped ahead to rule number three, Eddie. You gave yourself away by hesitating. And you never hesitate when you make a threat. It's too late – the other guy knows he's got you.'

'You can't threaten me! I'll call the cops!'

'Yes, you call the cops, Eddie. File a report if you like. Do whatever makes you feel like a man, Eddie, so long as you stay away from Nadia. Because here's what will happen. Are you listening? If you come around here again, if you drive by and maybe decide to poke your nose into the Grums' house or make any more threatening phone calls or do anything other than mind your own sad business, I will come to your house and I will beat you silly with a cinder block. I'll drop it on your chest, Eddie. I will leave you bleeding and alone, unable to jerk off with your two broken arms. Now, is that what you want?'

Eddie was crying. It couldn't be from this speech, either. There was a lot more behind it. Most likely a broken heart. Conrad's stomach lurched.

'Let me know you understand what I'm telling you, Eddie.'

'C-C-Can I please! S-S-s-speak with Nadia?'

Unbelievable. The kid had crossed over from stupid to pathetic and brought stupid with him along the way.

'Eddie, give it up. The girl is gone. Gone gone gone. Now please, for everyone's sake, go away.'

'She's a whore! Tell the whore that the father of her—'

Nadia reached for the phone and Conrad clicked off.

'Sorry, he had to go.'

She yanked the phone away. 'Asshole!'

'What? Are you telling me you still like this creep?'

'You don't know him!'

'What's to know?'

She stormed upstairs. Conrad stood in the kitchen and finished his coffee, staring at the IN USE light on the phone's cradle. The light was off. Unless she was using a cell, she did not call Eddie back.

Time to go. He'd done enough work for one day.

*

221

He went to Dick's and bought some groceries. More iced tea and one of those sun tea bottles to brew it on the deck. He paused in front of the newsstand and flipped through baby magazines. Threw three in the cart for Nadia. He paid for his groceries and drove around front to wait for them to be loaded – they had a number system and you just sat there while the kid in the apron filled your trunk. No tips allowed.

The front door was unlocked. He made a mental note to start locking it. He was halfway to the kitchen when he noticed the blood and shattered glass on the floor. The frames were broken, three of Jo's matching mirrors from the front living room destroyed. Leading out of the glass shards, the paw prints.

When had he last seen the dogs? Had he fed them this morning? He could not remember.

'Alice! Luther!'

He ran yelling their names as he searched the house, at once hoping and fearing that the perpetrator was still in the house.

25

His dogs were bleeding, and had been bleeding for some time judging by the paw prints and smudges and stripes of blood on the floors, walls and couch. He ran calling their names into the dining room and made a U-turn into the front parlor. The TV room. The kitchen.

No dogs.

Conrad's pulse went off the chart. If something has happened to my dogs, he thought, if someone hurt my first and only real babies, I will simply run amok.

He'd hung the mirrors high on the walls. No way the dogs jumped up and dragged them down – and why would they? Someone was here, broke them, and left the dogs to cut themselves. Or worse. Someone – *Eddie! That little fucking shit, Eddie!* – broke in and went fucking nuts and maybe there was a struggle. Maybe the dogs attacked him and he had pulled the mirrors down, scaring them before—

When he had checked the entire first floor, he circled back to the front stairway.

'Alice, Luther! Daddy's home!'

He stopped halfway up the stairs and listened. Was

that . . . ? Yes, familiar whining. He pounded up the stairs and lurched into the library bent over at a forty-five-degree angle, head turning like a cop in a police drama. The library was clear.

The upstairs felt wrong. You learned to sense where your dogs were at all times and the upstairs felt empty.

The master bedroom was also empty.

'Alice! Luther! Come on, babies!'

A sound like rocks falling on hollow walls – *whock-whock-whock!*

The basement.

Jesus, he hadn't even thought of the basement. He had been meaning to take the broom down and give the whole works a good spring-cleaning and refill the water softener system with salt pellets while he was at it, but, like most things he had been meaning to do, he had forgotten.

He took the front stairs two at a time, rounded the foyer and careened back into the kitchen, yanked the basement open and tripped over her.

Alice had been at the door, scraping her paws on the wooden steps and the door. His feet caught on her legs and he tripped, then skated down two more steps, his hand snapping the rail as he slammed down tailbone first, lost his wind, and slid down the six remaining stairs until his feet stopped against the foundation wall and sprawled him on the landing.

He saw more blood on the door above him and trailing from her as Alice came down after him.

She's on her feet, how bad can it be?

And where is Luther?

Alice's claws scratched his chest and legs as he stood and sucked in the first, pained breath, getting his wind back. He inspected her through watery eyes. He couldn't see a wound that required immediate attention, but she was shaking, her bristly brindle coat bunching up more in confusion than in pain. Maybe anger for being banished to the basement.

Then he saw her ear. The seam where the ear connected to her head was gaping pink and white tissue like a second, smaller mouth. Pat-pat-pat went the blood on the floor, but it wasn't flowing, so that was something.

'Okay, baby, calm down, calm down. Where's Luther?' Like she could tell him.

Conrad ducked under the ventilation ducts and wooden crossbeams in the basement proper, peeking around makeshift walls and unfinished rooms. There weren't many hiding places. He charged forward, knocking into the water heater and doorframes. The only closed room was Laski's abandoned workshop: a wall of pegboard, a plywood bench set upon four by fours, scraps of indoor-outdoor carpet. No blood.

There was another, deeper space left of the shop's entrance, with a separate light. Conrad flailed for the beaded string hanging below the bulb. *Cha-chink*.

Luther wasn't in here. There was still the backyard. On the way to the short wooden door that opened to the backyard, he stopped and pivoted, heading back to the one place he hadn't checked.

In the basement at the front of the house was a

smaller space, lower to the ground, where the furnace was tucked behind the stone support wall under the fireplace and chimney. At the very front of that, in the deepest recess where the foundation floor became a pile of dirt and cast aside rocks, the ground sloped up as if reaching toward some forgotten cellar door or coal chute.

Conrad crouched, shimmied forth, and found his dog.

Luther was huddled in the corner, hopping gecko-like from one front paw to the other as if the ground were too hot to stand on. He was staring at the wall, like the teacher had called him a bad boy and sent him to stand in the corner.

'Luther? Luther!'

When Luther turned, the dog's eyes were two pinpoints of gleaming white, his black and white cow spots shivering. The dog had been intent on something on the stone foundation wall. Now he looked confused, and Conrad's skin crawled. He took a step and Luther growled. It broke his heart and worried him all over, but he needed to get past the dog's fear and tend to the wounds, if there were any.

Conrad came in fast but steady, speaking in his gentlest voice, 'It's me, Luther, it's okay, good dog . . .'

Luther lashed out in a snapping bark that missed Conrad's hand (the one that had just finished healing) by inches. Conrad scooped up his dog and crouch-dragged him backward, and it was like dancing in a cave with a wet seal. Finally they were clear and Luther stopped fighting and then it was a half-blind spree up the stairs into the kitchen.

He spent half a roll of paper towels trying to staunch the flow before he realized the dogs, in their agitated state, were going to bleed out before he got them under control.

Compared to Alice, Luther looked as if he'd attempted to tightrope walk a fence barbed with concertina wire. Luther's legs and paws were cut in at least six places. The front of his chest just below the throat was a coin purse, and Alice's ear was still hanging halfway off her narrow marbled head like so much furry lunchmeat.

Conrad snatched the keys from the kitchen table, scooped Luther up and bolted for the car. He left the front door wide open and Alice did not need to be told to follow.

He opened the rear driver's side door with one hand and spilled Luther into the backseat; Alice brought up the rear. Then he was behind the wheel, weaving up the street, the blood spattering on the seats and doors and windows and up to the passenger visor as the dogs jumped from backseat to front and back again. He yelled at them to calm down as he blew through the first stop sign and floored it past the Kwik-Trip. He had gone a mile up the old Highway 151 business loop before he realized he didn't even know where the vet kept offices, or if the town even had one.

She answered the door dressed in jeans and a faded Abercrombie tee, and for once his eyes did not settle on her belly. Her face went pale when she saw the blood.

'My dogs are hurt. Can you take us to the vet?' For one agonizing moment he saw the hesitation, that moment of distrust even the best neighbors have before they decide to jump into the scene of impending tragedy. 'Please help me, Nadia.'

God love her, she nodded quickly and followed him.

'You drive while I try to get them under control.'

'Oh, shit!' She saw the inside of the car.

'Yeah. Come on, I don't know where the vet is.'

Nadia stared at the stick shift.

'It's just dog blood,' he said. 'Move!'

'I can't drive stick!'

'Just put in second and pop the clutch when I say go.'

The car rolled down hill a ways. 'Go!'

Nadia popped the clutch. The Volvo sputtered . . . then shot down Heritage Street. Conrad crawled in back and tried to still his pets. By the time they reached the small farmhouse on the outskirts of town – it didn't even have a sign, just a wooden figure of a horse next to the mailbox – Alice had her nose out the window like she was enjoying a Sunday drive. Luther was in Conrad's lap, heavy with a kind of gulping motion sickness, eyes droopy.

'Easy, boy. Easy.'

Fifteen minutes after his wife phoned from the front desk, Dr Michael Troxler came in from the field wearing a pair of muddy wellingtons and Oshkosh overalls over a bright madras shirt. He had a streak of mud on the wire-framed glasses standing over thick gray moustaches. Dr Troxler was at least seventy years old, reeked of manure and moved like an aging linebacker who could still open-field tackle an errant calf.

'What do we have here, young man?' Troxler bent to scratch Luther's head.

'My dogs are cut up,' Conrad said, fighting the urge to *scream hurry up you old goat-fucker*! 'I think she's got just the ear cut, but Luther here is gonna bleed to death if we don't do something soon.'

'Okey-doke. Folla me.'

The examining room smelled of alfalfa and medicine. Conrad shot Nadia an evil look – *are you kidding me?*

'He bite?' Troxler had his back to the table, sorting bottles and syringes until he found the right combo.

'No. He's a good dog.'

'Get him up on the table and hold him. I'm gonna stick him pretty good.'

Conrad didn't know what he'd expected, maybe some doggy version of *ER* with IVs, latex gloves and scrubs. But Troxler didn't even bother to wash his hands. He just pulled Luther's hackles up with one huge mitt and rammed a large needle into the fold.

'That's not gonna knock him out, but keep a watch on him cause he might feel like falling over. And we don't wanna drop ya, do we buddy?' Troxler patted Luther on the head.

Conrad swayed on his feet as Troxler used a thimble and needle large enough to hook marlin to thread black cord through the many holes and slashes in Luther's legs and undercarriage.

'This breed's rambunctious, got to use the thick stuff.'

When he'd finished with Luther, Troxler said 'Next', and wound his pointer finger in a loop. Conrad set Luther

229

on the barn-dirty floor and Nadia held Luther steady while Conrad heaved Alice up. Alice's turn came and went much faster, having just the one deep cut in her ear.

When he had finished with the sutures and was dabbing the outside of the wound with more gauze soaked in Betadine, the purple solution staining the doctor's thick fingers a morgue yellow, Troxler said, 'They fight like this often?'

Conrad became the defensive parent. 'They don't fight. I think they knocked some mirrors off the walls or something. There was a lot of broken glass when I came home.'

'They get into all kinds of mischief, don't they?'

'Yes. They do.'

'That'll do 'er.'

Despite his earlier misgivings, Conrad felt like hugging the lumbering veterinarian. Even without the usual shaving and sterilizing, all the bleeding had stopped. And the old man's calm through it all had helped.

Nadia led the dogs to the car while Conrad settled up with Mrs Troxler. At the front desk, he thanked the doctor profusely and offered to clean up the blood on the floor.

'Just get them critters home and make sure they drink some water when they come out of their stupor. The one lost some blood, and he's gonna be slow for a couple days. You bring 'em both back in ten days we'll pull the sutures out.'

Mrs Troxler was filling out an invoice. 'What's your name, young man?'

230

'Conrad Harrison. What do I owe you?' As she tallied the work he patted his pockets. 'Oh, hell. I was so worked up before we left the house, I didn't bring anything with me.'

'No trouble, dear. Bring it by anytime,' Mrs Troxler said. 'And tell your wife goodbye for us.'

'She's not—. Thank you. I will.'

When they were halfway to the house, Conrad said, 'Do you have any money?'

'Twenty bucks or so.' The car jerked as Nadia fought with the stick.

'Stop here.'

Nadia wheeled into the Kwik-Trip. 'What for?'

'I need a drink.'

Conrad was on the TV room floor, leaning against the wall, the remaining half of the Budweiser twelve-pack between his legs. He felt like he'd just passed some test and the beer might as well have been iced tea for all the buzz it gave him. Nadia was sitting crossways on the couch, the dogs sleeping soundly at her feet, as Troxler had promised. Nadia's suspicions and weariness of their ordeal seemed to have vanished. She was smiling more, talking him through it, helping him cool off.

'God, look at them,' he said. 'No idea it happened.'

'We saved them, didn't we?' Nadia said.

'Yeah, we did. I don't know what I would have done without you.'

'When you came to my house you looked like someone died.'

'I thought they were goners. Just fucked.'

'Oh, you're okay now, girl.' Nadia kissed Alice on the nose. 'You're not fucked.'

'I don't know what I . . . I wouldn't make it without them.'

'They're like your children, huh?'

'You have no idea how much.'

'I might,' she said. 'Some day soon, I just might.'

'Yeah, you might.' Conrad sighed, watching Luther. 'I'll tell you this. The woman from the rescue shelter found him tied to a street post on La Cienega when he was seven months old. Ribs like a xylophone, mange, broken leg. He was terrified of the endless honking taxis and banging trash trucks. You could tie a steak to the stop sign, he still wouldn't walk down a loud street.'

'Oh, Luther, you just can't stay out of trouble, can you?' Luther snored. 'So, you just found him at the pound?'

'No, no. It was a bit more than that. It took us six weeks to adopt him. This rescue group, Mighty Mutts. Run by a veterinarian, total non-profit. They don't mess around. They put us through a lot of waiting, came to our home, made us fill out a ton of forms. I kept calling, pleading my case. Jo was against it at first. She can't stand the hair on her clothes, if you can believe that. But I knew. I never wanted anything so bad as I wanted that dog. He's my boy.'

'Why'd it take so long?'

'The rescue people know. Dog bonds with his master. People will give up a dog like it's a hobby. A bag of garbage. You give him up it breaks his heart and he rarely gets over it. Lot of dogs walking around out there, nervous wrecks, all faith in life shattered. Some turn mean. But the ones that do get over it, they never forget. They love you like you have never been loved.'

Nadia watched him drink. He knew he was getting dopey-eyed, slurring a little.

'Luther never really got over his fear of walking, and he was destroying the house with the separation anxiety. People said medicate him, but that's not right. He was only a year old. We tried herbal supplements, more toys, a litter box, pads on the floor, short trips to the front porch, forcing him, letting him take his time. Jo said get rid of him. I told her she could leave anytime she wanted. Finally the rescue group said get another dog. Jo and I fought about that. A lot. We adopted Alice, who didn't have any fear. She helped Luther get over it in one day. He wouldn't leave her side, followed her right down the street.'

'So you saved two dogs' lives.'

'Best thing we ever did. Sometimes I think they are better than us.'

'You and your wife?'

'People. Better than people.'

They sat quietly for a minute. Nadia said, 'She couldn't have kids? Before, when you got the dogs?'

'I don't know that she ever wanted them.'

'But you did.'

'I never avoided it . . . I think it's better not to plan too much. You take what life gives you.'

'But eventually you need a plan,' she said.

'Like Seattle?'

'Hey now,' she said, scolding him. 'Unless you have a better one, Seattle it is.'

It came out light, but then she paused like she'd just realized what she'd said and she became very still. He'd never seen her look so scared.

'Nadia.' Conrad smiled and wagged his beer and set it down before rising from the floor. 'I want to show you something.'

Nadia followed him up the front stairs.

'Watch your step,' he said as much to himself as to Nadia. 'This banister is a hundred and forty years old.'

When they reached the guest room, he pushed the door open and pulled the switch on the safari lamp. Warm light filled the room, floating a halo over the crib.

'What do you think?' he said.

'Oh, Conrad. This is very nice. Did you do this by yourself?'

'Yes. You really like it?'

'It's more real than any room in the house.'

He liked that. 'Nadia?'

She turned and faced him in the doorway.

'We didn't . . . we were not together in any way. Not for months before we moved here, and we haven't been since. What she carries inside her, it did not come from me.'

'Come on. Don't say that.'

'It's the truth.'

'I'm sorry.'

'But I'm more worried about you,' he said, pulling at her shirt with two fingers. 'I told you I would help you.'

'Conrad. You're a nice guy. But I'm leaving soon.'

'You don't have to.'

'Yes, I do. And she's coming home, eventually.'

'There's another guy out there, in her room. I heard him. I don't think she is coming home. And maybe I don't want her to.'

Nadia shook her head slowly.

'Something is happening inside this house,' he said. 'And we are a part of it. Maybe fate. I don't care. I want to take care of you. I can't stop thinking about taking care of you.'

He leaned forward, his breath beery and loose. She stared up at him, unmoving. He kissed her on the mouth. Her lips hung open, undecided. Then her tongue pushed in first and he swooned, literally. She pushed him back against the wall, holding him up.

'You're kinda drunk,' she said.

'But I know what I know,' he said.

'And you're exhausted. Come on.'

She led him into the bedroom. She was so small in front of him. He could look right over her blonde hair and he wished he had the strength to lift her up and set her down on the bed, but he was too tanked to be gallant.

'Here.' She turned him sideways and he leaned over to kiss her again. She put one palm against his chest and pushed gently.

'My dogs.' He flopped on the bed, clothes and all. 'We can't leave them down there.'

235

'I'll watch them.'

'Promise?'

'Yes.' She turned off the light. 'I promise.'

'Nadia,' he said in the dark.

'What?'

'Don't leave me alone here. I won't make it without you.'

She lingered a minute, and he passed out before he could hear her walk away.

HOLLY

If you ask men when they are happiest, their first and rather unimaginative answer is usually something along the lines of, *right after I come*. And that is a peaceful time. All the fighting and working and wooing and pleading are past; the lucky man has been satisfied and done his best for her, and now the siren has him down. Time to drift and recharge and meet the world another day, which fills us up with more longing, anger and madness until we start all over again.

But remember I said happiest, not most peaceful. If someone were to ask me when I am happiest – have you guessed this by now? That our boy is me, that his story is my story? Of course you have, for you are a very bright girl who only happens to be a little lost, as he, as I, once was lost – I would answer, not at the end, when it has been done, but at the beginning. The moment when you know it is going to happen, and you have the whole event, in all its twists and turns and tests and mystery lying directly on the path ahead. And here I should add I am not speaking of sex, or not only of sex, though it was sex that taught me this. How I am most alive when I am standing on the precipice of the next beginning.

Consider the steamed lobster and melted butter and tenderloin and home-made bread are set before you by a kind waitress and you have not eaten all day. Consider iced tea with mint, its tall glass dewy with waiting for you to finish mowing the lawn on a hot July afternoon, that first bite as it washes over your scorched, panting tongue. The way the lighted Christmas tree looks when you come downstairs in padded feet to see all those gleaming boxes and ribbons and bows. The puppy whining in its crate that was put on this earth to be your best friend for the rest of his life, whether you prove him worthy or not. The smell of your crisp white Stan Smiths on the first day of school and how that fertile green emblem is going to telegraph to that one girl in the hallway exactly what you cannot find words to say, that you could have gotten any current style in the store but you are cool enough to have gone classic, old school, and this might be the year you become her boyfriend. That is what any good beginning does – takes you back to the moment when it was the first time, when it was all new, when you had nothing but new experiences in front of you and it was all magic.

Of all the beginnings, this night, in these strangers' home, though I could not know it then, I was standing on the precipice of the last and only true magic I would know until I found this house.

It was to be a miracle. What other miracles are there but beginnings? It is being born. And if birth is a miracle, it is a shame we cannot remember it. Because this I remember, and, in some ways, it was the moment I began to live.

Which is to say, also, that it was the beginning of my death.

When my twenty minutes were up, I made my way down the hall, passing family photographs I did not linger over. My mind was focused and relaxed, but I locked the front door just in case.

When I reached the door at the end of the hall I saw the orange flicker of light. Candles. I should tell you now, in case you're wondering what was so special about this night, that though we had made love and the other kind, that fast, quickie sex perhaps two or three hundred times, we had never made love in the light. Whatever position we found ourselves entangled in, however raw our hunger was expressed, as dirty as we spoke to each other (we had covered a lot of ground, as I said before), it had always taken place under cover of darkness. As a child of divorce and possibly some madness on her mother's side, Holly had suffered from anorexia before she came to our junior high school. I was told, though she didn't like to speak of it, that she had to be institutionalized for a period of four months. Since the first day I saw her in the halls when we were fourteen, she always had the body of a young woman: curves, breasts, thighs a bit chunky, though she would slap me to hear that now. Her butt was what you would call a bubble butt and the rest of her had a perfectly healthy weight and shape. I don't know if she ever accepted this new version of herself, but I know she trusted me when I told her I liked her body this way better than the other way, the one I could only imagine. If she still heard the voice in her mind that said, *You're too fat, lose some weight, because no one, especially Daddy, will love you this way until they are afraid of you*, she was not listening to that voice now, tonight, as I entered the bedroom.

I understood immediately that she had not been preparing herself with lotions, creams and lingerie for the past twenty minutes. Nor had she showered or primped. It was the candles, dozens of them or perhaps a hundred that had taken her twenty minutes to light. Had she delivered them earlier or found some stash in the house? I do not know. They were on the night tables, the headboard, the dressers, the leather trunk at the foot of the bed, the window sills. I say that like I was studying the décor, but that is absurd – my eyes went the only place they could go, directly to her.

She had stripped the bed and remade it with only one layer, a fresh fitted sheet of sky-blue Egyptian cotton, five-hundred-thread count. I know this because for months after I searched for the exact texture and weight of that sheet. She had two pillows behind her head, and all was bare.

She was stretched across it diagonally, so that she faced me upon entering, the tips of her toes pointing at me like two hands in prayer. She smiled at me with a slow, involuntary widening at the corners of her mouth, her lips spaced just so. One arm was up under her head, her hand buried somewhere in the thick fan of her hair, which hung loosely and combed out over her shoulders to the tops of her breasts. Her other arm was at her side, her hand resting flat on her belly somewhere between navel and the lowest rung of her ribcage. She was the color of honey. Her eyes, normally wide with daring, were now low and glistening like an addict's, so that she was looking down at me even though it was I who stood above her, moving closer to the foot of the bed as I removed my zippered sweatshirt, the tee shirt under, and kicked off my jeans.

Now is where you will ask me to skip ahead to the outcome, but I'm afraid I cannot do that. What seems like sparing you the details is to rob myself of the better understanding that comes with telling the thing the way it happened, and some details matter more than others. So cover your ears if you don't appreciate what I am about to say, but understand that to me, to the seventeen-year-old me and the man I have become, these seemingly tawdry details matter. They matter very much.

My Holy Girl, she let me look at her.

She consented to my inspection, so I stood there, now in my loose boxer shorts, the pink Oxford ones she had stolen for me at the outlet mall, and I studied her. It was not so easy as head to toe or toe to head or anything like that. I would watch her chest for signs of heartbeat until I saw it, the skin over her breastbone literally pulsing, perspiring. I remember sitting beside her looking down and noticing for the first time her tiny purple dots where the hair follicles on her calves had been traumatized from her last shave. I saw the curve of her toes, thick and characterless. The balls of muscle on the inside of her knees were shiny in the firelight of the room.

No doubt I said things that were juvenile and ill equipped. 'I can't believe how beautiful you are' and 'you're a goddess sent here for me' and 'don't move, just wait, I want to memorize you for all time' and all those things you will laugh at now, but I meant them, and they were true. When I said she was a goddess, I understood that she held a power over my soul, and that if she were to command me to end my life with her at that moment, I surely would have. I believed in her the way one comes to believe in any other god, a work of genius, a fact of life, that song. The horizons revolved around her soul and her soul was the sun. Holly Bauerman was love incarnate.

Her heart was strong and rapid, so different from her expression, which remained languid like her pose. I traced her breasts with the speed of a tortoise traversing a desert, I marveled at the pebbled brownness of areoles, the network of veins, the fine blonde hairs sprouting around them. I'd looked at them a hundred times before, but I had never *seen* them. At my touch she tensed and told me my fingers burned. As I traced her belly and hips I let my fingers rest on the stretch marks, those clues to her history like white tiger stripes in miniature.

I suppose this watching went on for hours, but it could have been minutes. Each moment was condensed and stretched out like a rubber band as time elasticized. When at last I could not resist I drew my two middle fingers from her calf behind her knee and up her thigh in a slow arc until they brushed against the lips of her sex (she called it her chi-chi, which at the time sounded to me like a toy poodle but now recalls something more accurate, the *chi*, or life force, in Eastern philosophy) and they came away instantly wet in a way that shocked me. She had remained so calm, I did not realize what had been going on inside of her. I looked down, of course I did, and watched my fingers exploring her, trying not to gasp as I saw not only the color and quantity of her desire but the markings we were making on the sheet. I confess that my adolescent mind did not understand fully what was happening at first. I worried for a moment she had lost control and truly wet the bed. She reacted to my touch by reaching out for me – *Enough is enough*, she said without so many words. *Come to me now*.

But I could not, yet. I needed to understand, to create, to wallow. I let my fingers roam back to that spot and around and inside and over her hips and thighs and back inside until she was covered in her own salty sweetness and on the verge of her first of this night's orgasms, and only then did I lose all thought and sit upright to allow her to pull my shorts off.

I felt clumsy on top of her and we slid against each other, searching for the right angles. The prospect of feeling all of her made it like the first time again. The heat of her soft belly flesh pressed against me as her hand encircled me and slid down, and in the confusion I assumed I was inside.

She was staring at me, wide-eyed with desperation

and patience. That she had planned this and wanted me without protection, that when she said she loved me like no one else and would always love me, filled me with the power and purpose of a righteous man.

'I want to be with you forever,' she said, whispering to me, watching me as I watched her. 'I want to love you forever. Can I love you forever? Will you promise me there will never be anyone else and that we can have each other and be like this forever?'

'Yes.'

'Do you love me?'

'More than anything. I love you.'

We spoke fast, repeating these declarations until they became vows.

I moved against her and slid into her and up against her and out again, over her triangle and to her navel. I was shaking all over and she cradled my head in the back of her hand, pulling me down, moving her hips up against me. Without guilt or thought I cried out in actual pain and shuddered as the pulses of my ejaculate made us comically wet and still we had not done the 'it' part of it.

'I'm sorry, I'm sorry . . .' I was mortified.

'Shush, no, it's beautiful,' she said, kissing me. 'This is only the beginning.'

I felt her hands reaching for me, or pulling on me to keep me up. This latter, if it was her intention, was not necessary. At seventeen and coming down from one of the most powerful climaxes of my life, I had lost nothing. In a way it was better, for now I could start again and do it for her.

'This is what I want,' she whispered. I waited for an explanation while her hand circled between us, on me and then elsewhere. 'I want you, I want all of you. Inside me. I want you forever. I want to have your baby.' Her eyes glowed as she said it again, making sure I understood the words she had never spoken, not even in jest. 'I want to have your baby.'

I lifted myself off of her so that perhaps twelve inches of space remained between our bodies and I watched as, eyes closed, her breath coming in gulps, she gathered the threads of my semen and applied them to her sex with a repetitive motion that was somehow repulsive and graceful. I did not understand. Just know that, whatever distortions you are tempted to assign my recollection, don't make the mistake of thinking she was putting on a show for my benefit. Though it was the most erotic act I have ever witnessed, it was also without thought, instinctual. Her hands moved as if she were not in control, efficiently cleaning up the mess like the sweep of that woman's hand in the paper towel commercial, only more primal, the way one imagines our ancestors weaving reeds. Each sweep of her palm gathered whatever fluid it could find, and then smoothed it over the cusp of her belly and further, down into the place God intended. She pressed her fingers into herself, rubbing herself until she was bucking against me.

I watched. I kissed her. I watched.

What did I know, at seventeen? She could have been performing some secret act only women learn when they have sought counsel to help them conceive. I certainly did not know that this was an act no woman, including my wife, would ever perform in my presence again. I knew only that this was it, the greatest proof my girl could offer that she loved me, that when she said forever she meant forever. Because, when you think about it, what is more risky to a teenaged girl than getting pregnant? What commitment is more long term than having your child, knowing she will likely be ostracized for it?

On another, more selfish side, my ego soared. What so many women understandably find repulsive – this thick, bleach-smelling substance – Holly was devouring to a place so much more dangerous than her mouth. I watched her hands do their work until her muscles clenched and pulled my seed deeper within her, and I understood the degree to which I had misjudged her love for me, how all-encompassing it had become, and that our future was sealed, that we would forever be us. I understood I would never, ever be alone again in this world.

Whatever you think happiness is, whatever you think it really means to be safe and secure and loved, I can tell you this. It is never more present in us than when we have coveted and loved and risked everything to claim another, and having done so found our equal, having reached the mutual understanding that we want the same thing, and that the thing we want is nothing. *Nothing*. Not money not fame not cars not houses not artistic greatness not even children, nothing except the person we are mated to, lost and found. This ecstatic mental state so perfectly in tune with our physical design is our home, the only real home we are given a chance to find in this life, the place we are lost, found, safe, forgiven, remade and forged into better men, the home we are forever trying to get back to, the one true birthing house.

When she had become almost frantic and I could bear observing her from a distance no more, I pulled her hands away and pushed myself inside her again, and this time I stayed.

We stayed this way for more than seven hours. I keep telling you it was not about the sex, but now it was the sex and nothing else. I know that I came inside her three more times, and she every time with me, pulling me deeper. The candles burned to their foundations before we drifted off to sleep.

Are you sleeping now? Is my voice soothing, or does it frighten you? If you want me stop, that is okay, too. Not every story needs to be heard to be understood. But I think you have heard this story before, or at the very least have felt it growing between us. That is why I'm telling you now – so that you will know everything about me, so that nothing will grow between us.

When you wake up, in the end, we will be together.

That is all that matters now.

26

It was a beginning, and he was a man who loved beginnings more than middles or endings.

He told himself he was being foolish. He told himself he was being a fucking idiot. He told himself that his wife was smart, beautiful, decent, forgiving, working to preserve their new hope in the ongoing experiment that was their marriage, and most of all that she was pregnant with his child.

Or a child.

But every child needs a home. He'd given Luther a home. Then Alice. It wasn't enough. He needed the other half. Wasn't that what the Bible said? Eve was the rib, and you missed her forever. Except, in this age of MBA wives and husbands who were good at cooking and cleaning and wringing their hands but not even handy enough to change a pipe under the sink, Conrad knew he was the rib. Jo, his host body, was her own strong woman and she was pulling away.

Nadia Grum was here. Half a family, waiting for the right man.

He had admitted that he wanted her. Wanted her, but

wanted what of her? Not sex, or not only sex, because he was if anything painfully aware of her condition and the preposterous nature of their situation. Sex was a distant thing if it was there at all. In its place, something unnamable, and more powerful.

Oh yes, he could see how a sane man might decide it was time to seek counsel in the form of one's doctor, one's wife, one's family. But Jo was his only family, and like a man running from the avalanche of emotional debt but not yet bankrupt of pride, he chose to leave Jo out of it. To call his wife and inform her of his experiences, his utter emotional fucked-uppedness, would be an Armageddon, what the marriage shrinks called a relationship-ending event. No, whatever the end turned out to be, he would determine the course on his own. He knew that seeking advice would not change his wishes. Because the real horror is that when you're busy ruining your life, self-awareness doesn't stop you.

Sweating out the beer in their new cotton sheets, thinking of her one story below, he could see all these things, but he was powerless to them. And to one more thing.

The house.

Something had happened here, maybe several somethings involving life and death and the things that slip through the cracks in between. Something had been born here and it lived here still. He did not have all the pieces, but he felt it. He felt the will of the place working on him every time he returned home and it was not going away. It was, in fact, getting stronger. It had broken the mirrors, out of anger. Angry that he was next door with her, or that they hadn't been here, where they were supposed to be, tending to business. He wanted to know it. He wanted to touch the ghost, if that's what it was, maybe even help it. Her. He was terrified, repulsed, and drawn to it as he was drawn to the girl and the destruction she would bring down. And never mind Dr Alexis Hobarth, the animal sage, and his scientific explanations for what was, in effect, a miracle birth. He wasn't religious, but he wanted to be faithful, to find something deserving of faith, even if it cost him his marriage. Maybe this house would offer such an article. And maybe this thing inside him, driving him, was but a quaint strain of madness. And if so, so what? Wasn't love like that? An excuse to go mad, just for a little while? Who didn't wish for that? A padded room to protect you while you flipped out, a chamber where your most vile stench will be expelled and ventilated, a darkened theater to project your dreams on to the willing patrons of your all-too-human freak show.

A house to call a home.

She slept on the couch that night, and stayed with him for the next sixty hours. The incident with the dogs had put them together and unlocked a hidden need to abandon reality, together. He supposed she was interested in more than money for a plane ticket. Maybe not a father for her unborn child, maybe not yet.

But if circumstances made it possible, the next days made it real. What was once a hidden thought, a phrase tinted with flirting, a lingering question, now became a tactile sensation, the electric of the boundary pushed.

There were no long conversations or weeping confessions. They did not make love physically.

Instead, theirs was a time of domestic gestures and offerings. The bump of the hip while he cooked over the stove. The looking out the window saying nothing, seeing how it felt to stand side by side. Once, when he had come down from a shower dressed in a clean shirt, she squinted and plucked lint from his shoulder. It was a small thing done like she'd done it a hundred times before, almost simian in its normalcy, but it was a statement. The female claiming a small right. After seeing the baby's room prepared that way in the warm light, she moved through the house no longer a guest, but a new resident.

They woke late the next morning. She was at the refrigerator, searching, grumpy.

He understood what to do. 'Stay here. I'll be right back.'

Into the bloody car to fetch real groceries. He spent three hundred dollars on good food and fell in love with feeding her. He prepared omelets with mushrooms and tomatoes, flipping them in the pan like a pro while she watched. Hash browns he'd shredded himself. Buttered toast. Fresh juice. What else did she like?

The stint as a prep cook in college came back. He cooked three meals a day. She would sit and watch him move around the kitchen. Never seen a man cook, she said, fascinated. He put things together she'd never eaten: Thai green curry and miso soup, green chile stew with warm tortillas, London broil with twice-baked potatoes and asparagus sautéed in olive oil. Salmon filets, sweet beets, mesclun greens with walnuts and Michigan cherries and crumbled blue cheese. Dozens of rolls and a loaf of home-made bread from the wedding present breadmaker. Cheesecake, pound cake, pecan pie and strawberry ice cream. Her appetite was astonishing. She ate for two, then three and sometimes four. She smiled the most after finishing a meal.

She helped him change the bandages around the dogs' legs. He could not be sure, but it seemed that the cuts were healing almost despite the sutures. The dogs no longer limped or slept all day. They acted like they had never been wounded. He was reminded of the quick healing in his hand, but he did not dwell on the idea that had struck him since he first moved in.

This is a healing place, and we are healing.

They lounged, watched movies, soap operas. He hadn't seen *Days of Our Lives* since high school, when Holly had forced him to watch it with her after school. Usually he would indulge her for half an hour, then get restless, horny, until Holly caved in and they had sex. Holly. They had been the craziest couple in high school – or the only real one. Watching TV with Nadia was different. It was a way to be together without doing anything. It was safe. Nadia said her feet hurt and he rubbed them from the other end of the couch until she fell asleep in the late afternoon.

The clock ceased to matter. They stayed up late,

woke early, napped. They played Scrabble through the afternoon thunderstorms and she surprised him by beating him two out of three.

She slept on the couch even when he offered her the upstairs bed, insisting he would behave and stay in another room. She refused. On the second day he came down to find her lying still like one of Laski's kids. He sat on the couch next to her and she sat up suddenly, startled, then pressed her mouth to his. He tasted her morning breath and she pulled his hair. They pushed against each other's mouths for fifteen minutes without anything else. He somehow knew to keep his hands down, and that was better. She moaned when they kissed, and he stopped, thinking her crying again. But she wasn't. Nervous, excited, don't want to talk about it. He couldn't remember if Jo had ever been so moved by a kiss. Nadia would kiss him that way for ten minutes, then push away. She would disappear into the bath for half an hour and resurface wearing his old tees and boxers. She came down one time in his Sebadoh and he thought that was perfect.

The dogs were warm to her, but he sensed they knew. He would catch them looking at him and he would think, *They know. They know she is not Jo and something is wrong with this picture.*

The second night he could not sleep and he went to her on the couch. She was sleeping. He sat next to her on the couch and watched her. He placed a hand on her swollen belly – she must be seven months now – and she woke to his touch. He did not pull his hand away and she left it there, looking up at him. I'm falling for this whole deal, he thought. The woman and everything inside her and what it will cost. When she sat up he said sorry, but she said it was okay, she just had to pee.

When she returned she held the blanket open for him and the morning passed in a cocoon of unmoving, unsleeping silence. Two bodies learning something before their brains could catch up.

He was dozing spoon-to-spoon when she said, 'I don't know why, but I feel safe with you.'

'You are.'

She sighed heavily with contentment, and he felt now was the time to ask.

'Nadia,' he whispered.

'Mh-hm.'

'Is that why you tried to run away? Because you weren't safe with Eddie?'

'Yes.'

'He is the father.'

'Yes.'

'Was it here? In this house?'

A minute passed before she answered. 'The Laskis moved out over a year ago. The house was empty last fall and winter. Eddie and I . . . we had nowhere else to go. I'd spent so much time here growing up, it felt almost normal, like I deserved to be here. We spent the afternoons hiding out in the rooms, drinking wine, smoking cigarettes. For a while we were both happy, but kinda out of control. But then it happened, and my parents would not allow us to see each other again. Eddie was always wild, but he got mean after that. How did you know?'

'It just makes sense. The house wants life.'

'Does it? Because sometimes I feel like it doesn't want me here.'

'Why would you think that?'

'I dunno. Maybe because I've always been an intruder.'

'No.'

'It's true. First I was the babysitter. Mrs Laski was always suspicious of me, and I saw the way Mr Laski looked at me.'

'You are beautiful enough to halt birds in flight. Can you blame them?'

'Then I was with Eddie, when no one owned the house, and I became pregnant. I was never really frightened here, not during those afternoons, but I always knew I was breaking the rules. I always felt like I was angering her somehow.'

He did not think to clarify whether if by 'her' Nadia meant Mrs Laski, the house itself or someone else.

'I thought about getting rid of it. Eddie asked me to. But I kept putting it off and putting it off. And then one day I didn't care what anybody else wanted. It was like the time I was baby-sitting, when the *zeks* came for me. I'd already lost it once, and I couldn't go through that again. This baby is my baby, but now I am an intruder again.'

'You're not. I invited you in.'

'But I am not the woman of the house.'

255

'Is that something you heard from Laski?'

'I don't remember. It just feels that way.'

'Well, it's my house now. And I want you to stay.'

He kissed her neck, fell asleep in her hair.

On the third morning he woke to find her in the kitchen banging around, looking for a pot. He made her peaches and cream oatmeal and he could tell something was gnawing at her.

'What's on your mind, Ms Grum?'

'I'm antsy,' she said. 'I need to get out and do something.'

'Yeah, sure.' He nodded and looked outside. It was sunny, with a light breeze coming through the front screen door. 'You wanna go for a walk?'

'Actually,' she said with a shining fear in her eye. 'I think I need to go home. Just for a few hours.'

He didn't ask for what. He went to her and kissed her. This seemed to calm her momentarily. She gave in, sucked at his tongue for a minute, then giggled and ducked away from him. Back to grumpy.

'You shouldn't be doing that.'

'Why not?'

'Because it's getting too easy.'

'Too easy?'

'Comfortable. We'll forget ourselves.'

'That's a good thing.'

'Not if we get caught.'

'I'm not afraid,' he said. 'Let's get caught.'

'No one knows, Conrad.'

He smiled. There was something to know.

'Are you for real? Is this – are you sure you want this?'

'Not a few hours,' he said. 'One.'

'Promise you won't change your mind?'

He kissed her. She started to cry and he heard himself speaking before he'd even made the decision.

'I'll call Jo. I'll tell her—'

'No!'

'—the truth.'

'No.'

'Nadia. We have nothing to be ashamed of. This stuff happens. If we're honest about what we want, they will understand. Not right away, but I'm not afraid.'

She smiled through her tears.

'Come right back.'

But he was afraid, and he did feel guilty.

He sat for a while at the kitchen two-top with the phone in his hand. It seemed so natural when she was here, but now, trying to shape his . . . no, not plan, it wasn't even a plan yet . . . desires into a thing his wife would understand, he was terrified. There would be no understanding, only screaming.

Rage, accusations, pain.

Get it over with. Come clean. Because this situation here, right now, is untenable.

He dialed Jo's room. No one answered. He dialed her mobile, got voicemail. She could be out. She could be ignoring his calls. She could be with That Fucker Jake. She could be studying.

257

'God damn you, Jo. God damn you for leaving me,' he said. 'If your father had died, I would never have left you. Never. Just remember this was your choice. Leaving me alone here in this house was your choice.'

The robotic woman asked him if he wanted to replay his message, or rerecord it. He clicked off and dropped the phone.

His hands were shaking. He went to the cupboard and removed a bottle of Jim Beam. He drank it straight and warm from a plastic tumbler, punishing himself and blotting her out for a little while longer.

He slept late and woke to the sound of knocking. He got out of bed and felt every stair on the way down. His emotions were blunted. He had found himself drunk so quickly he had never got round to calling Nadia to see why she hadn't come back. He vaguely recalled wishing she never would, then crying because she hadn't. His father had made an appearance at some point, and after that it was just black. Now his synapses felt as if they had been coated with maple syrup and then set on fire. When he opened the front door in his boxers and morning half-wood, she was just standing there wet-faced.

'What's wrong?'

'I didn't mean to,' she said. She was holding a small red cell phone away from her body like it was a bloody knife.

'Didn't mean to?'

'Promise you'll help me.'

He pulled her in and shut the door. She grabbed him and squeezed hard, her belly pushing into his waist like the head of a ten-year-old between them.

She looked up, her chin digging into his chest. 'Eddie's dead,' she said. 'I think I killed him.'

27

'He probably deserved it,' he blurted before clapping his mouth shut.

'I didn't mean to, I didn't mean to . . .' She kept saying it and she didn't sound defensive so much as stunned. She was hiccupping and shaking all over.

Conrad moved her into the living room. 'I'm sorry. Here, it's fine it's fine sit down. I'll be right back.'

He went to the kitchen and poured her a coffee left over from the previous morning's pot, added a wallop of Brennan's Irish Cream and speed dialed one minute on the microwave. He went over it in his head. It didn't take very long or help much. Conrad had been home for the past three days and nights, with her. She'd left for a night and now what? Now Eddie was dead? How? Was someone else involved? Nadia wouldn't kill Eddie, really, would she? She was pregnant, for God's sake, and she clearly had feelings for the boy.

Poor kid.

Nadia, not Eddie.

Well, maybe him, too, but maybe not. Maybe Eddie

had been asking for it. Maybe Eddie accidentally set his meth lab on fire and got stuck charring in the blaze.

She was sitting on the couch, her shoulders bunched up to her ears like she had just been rear-ended by a full-size SUV, her face still pale from the impact.

'Here. Go slowly and take deep breaths until you're ready to tell me.'

She accepted the mug and just stared at it. It looked like an oil slick with the Irish in it.

'I don't know whuh-whuh-what happened. I left my cell phone at home, otherwise I would of-huh-huh heard sooner.'

'Heard what?'

'The phone. He called like thirty times. But he didn't say anything. Until last night. He left a mess—oh, God. No, I can't . . .' She was crying again.

'Okay. Hold on. Breathe. That's it. Breathe.' She recovered a bit. 'He left a message. On that?' He was pointing at her cell phone.

'He's been going crazy this whole time. For weeks. He had this . . . this *plan* for us. He promised to take care of us.'

'What did the message say?'

'I can't listen to it again.' She dropped the cell phone.

Conrad picked it up, flipped it open. 'How do I listen?'

'It's in my address book, under voicemail.'

Conrad opened her address book, scrolled down through a dozen names, selected voicemail and pressed call.

A voice said, 'Please enter your password.'

'What's your password?'

'Two-one-two-one.'

He entered the numbers. The voice said she had one saved message. He pressed one.

At first there was only heavy breathing, but he recognized it as Eddie's near hyperventilation. Same as from the last time they had spoken. Something slammed loudly and Conrad pulled his ear away for a moment. Then Eddie started screaming.

'God damn you, how can you do this to me? To the fucking baby! Why are you hiding from me? You want me to leave you alone? I'm not good enough? Is that it, you fucking whore bitch! Fuck you, fuck you, fuck you—'

Conrad shook his head. The kid was having an absolute tantrum. Nadia turned away and gagged. Conrad reached out for her, but she jerked away.

'—fuck you, fine, fucking fine, if this is what you want, you got it, bitch,' Eddie's voicemail continued. 'You made this mess, you clean it up. I'm leaving this whole shitty deal, right now. You ready? You ready, Nadia? Suck on this!'

There was a deafening bang. Conrad was pretty sure it was a gunshot. Then a clatter, as if the phone had been dropped. After ten seconds of silence, coming from some distance away from the phone, there was only a low moaning sound. It was sickening, something that could not be faked, and it went on and on. Finally the time allotted for messages expired.

Conrad closed the phone. 'Jesus.'

'I killed him,' Nadia said.

'No, you didn't. We don't even know for sure if—'

'He shot himself! I know he's dead!'

'Nadia—'

'I knew he was going to do this! Don't you see? I could have gone over sooner. I could have talked to him. He was going crazy for three days!'

'It's not your fault.'

'You don't understand, you can't . . . Eddie's fragile. I almost asked you to come with me, but I thought that would only make him worse.'

Conrad held her by the arms, gently but firmly.

'Nadia. Calm down. What did the police say?'

She reared back. 'The police?'

'Nine-one-one?'

'I didn't call the police! Are you crazy?'

'Who did you call?'

'Nobody. He's still there.'

'Where?'

'At his house!'

She hung her head in her hands and cried, chugging hard. Anger rose up inside him. They were supposed to be sorting things out and making a plan, not dealing with Eddie's problems. Now she was a wreck. Eddie was dead. I'm in over my head here, he thought. Way over.

'Nadia, we have to call the police.'

'No!'

'No?'

'You have to go there with me!'

'No. What good could that possibly—'

'Maybe he's not dead.'

'Explain that.'

'What if he's just hurt? Maybe he's alive and needs help!'

'If you're worried about that, if you thought he was alive, why didn't you call for help?'

She squeezed her eyes shut and then opened them, grabbed the coffee and threw it at the wall. The mug shattered above the TV and dripped down to the floor.

'I'm asking for help now!' She got up and ran for the door.

He caught her on the porch, held her by the arm. 'Nadia, wait. Stop. Just stop.' Conrad looked across the street and thought he saw a shape in the Bartholomews' window. 'Don't make a scene of this or you are on your own, do you hear me? I will go with you and we are calling the police when we get there, so you better get your story straight. Can you do that? Can you be calm now?'

She nodded.

'Stay here. I'll get dressed.'

He ran upstairs and pulled on a pair of shorts. His flip-flops. Brush the teeth – fuck it, later. When he came back she was standing beside the Volvo. Steve Bartholomew stepped out his front door and crossed his lawn, heading directly toward them.

'Get in the car,' Conrad said under his breath. 'Morning, Steve!'

They slipped in and Steve raised one hand to wave them back. The car was still splashed with dusty dog blood. Conrad turned the motor over, stomped on the juice and made the Volvo work. In the rearview mirror, Steve was standing on the sidewalk, hands on his hips.

'Where's Eddie live?'

'You said you knew.'

'On the phone? Nadia, I was bluffing. Wait. He actually lives in a trailer?'

'Yes.'

'Oh.'

Lucky guess, huh, 'Rad?

Eddie lived in Dewey, a forlorn hamlet of starter homes some seven miles south of Black Earth. They took 151 toward Dubuque and followed county road XX east until they came to the only stop sign. Next to that, *Welcome to Dewey, Pop. 784.*

'There some sort of state law says if a town can support just one business it's got to be a Kwik-Trip?'

Nadia ignored his attempt at levity. A small stone Lutheran church stood catty-corner. A post office. 'Where now?'

'Go straight.'

They passed an abandoned tin car wash and they were heading out of town again.

'Turn left up there.' She pointed to a fork in the road that led them past a babyshit-brown entrance gate proclaiming Valley Village Court, *Where Wisconsin Families Settle Down!*

They entered the trailer park proper and Conrad let the Volvo troll. There was a slight dip in the road, but he did not see anything resembling a valley or a village, just a shotgun smattering of turtle boxes no person should ever call home. Nadia pointed to a reddish-brown unit with a blackface jockey statue in the yard and a mailbox marked 64 *The Kellogs*.

'Eddie Kellog?'

'Park here,' she said.

'I'm guessing no relation to the cereal dynasty?'

Nadia shot him a nasty look and he turned off the car. She reached for the door and he held her back.

'Hold on. What are we walking into?' She stared at him. 'Nadia, his parents? Where are they?'

'His mom lives at his aunt's house in Iowa City.'

'He lives alone?'

'For now, yes.'

'Where's Dad?'

'He lives in Milwaukee.'

'Neighbors, friends? Anyone else who might pop by while we're in there staring at the body?'

When he said 'body' she bit the heel of her hand.

'You sure? Eddie has no friends? Because I see a lot of cars.'

'No one here likes him.'

'Let's go.'

They stepped out into the hot sunlight. Going to be another scorcher – not a good day to decompose. He hoped it wasn't going to be bad. Conrad had never seen a dead body before – his father didn't count, because Conrad had fled the hospital room after that last breath, signed the papers and never looked back. He needed to remain calm, keep an eye on Nadia. She might break down again – and, if so, fine. He could deal with her. But they could not afford for both of them to lose their shit. They reached the porch.

'Should we knock?' Conrad whispered.

'Won't do any good.' She opened the door for him and he entered.

The lights were on. Eddie's home was ... decent. Brushed cotton sofa and matching armchair, a large television and handsome black audio appliances stacked beneath. The breakfast nook looked like granite, a bowl of tangerines on top. Short pearl carpet, very clean. It all looked like someone had poured their home equity into the interior instead of just moving to a better town, a better life.

'Is it always this clean?'

She nodded. 'Eddie's a bit of a neatnik.'

Conrad moved down the hall. He smelled fresh laundry and looked inside a closet with shuttered doors. A stack of white tees and black cargo pants were folded on top of the over-and-under laundry unit.

'Did Eddie have a job at The Gap?' he said.

'What?'

'Never mind. This the bedroom?'

She nodded and he guessed she wasn't going to leave her post in the kitchen.

Conrad grabbed the knob, realized he was leaving prints and wiped it with the hem of his tee shirt. He took another breath, gripped the knob through his shirt and opened the door.

More white carpeting, cheap IKEA-type furniture, a desk with a black Dell PC on top. The monitor was a flatscreen and large. Next to the desk: simple pine bookcases lined with junior college textbooks and *Ultimate Fighting* DVDs, first-person shooter games, a new Xbox console tucked inside a storage unit below the desk. The bedding was all black and military crisp. Conrad saw no blood or sign of a struggle. If Eddie was here, the kid was folded into the closet.

This whole deal was starting to feel like a set-up.

Conrad backed out of the room and looked at Nadia. She was hugging herself, pacing a square into the kitchen floor.

'Are you sure he was calling from home? Nadia?'

She looked up. 'He's not . . . ?'

Conrad shook his head.

She stomped down the hall. She pointed to the bed and a small animal noise rose up within her as she lunged forward and ripped the bedding off revealing clean white sheets.

'Well?'

'The blood . . . he shot himself. You heard the message! This is impossible. Someone took him away.'

'How do you know he wasn't trying to trap you?'

'He wouldn't do that. Someone knows. Someone cleaned it all up!'

She went to the bathroom, looking behind the door.

'What makes you think he was in bed?' Conrad said.

For all he knew, they were both playing with him. But why? What could he possibly have that they wanted?

'He always called me from bed. There's nowhere else to go in here.'

She came back. 'Did you check the closet?'

Conrad went to the closet. Somewhere outside a screen door creaked and latched. He listened for footsteps coming up the walk. He heard none. He stared at the cheap aluminum closet doors with their fake shutters and waited for a sound, a clue. Maybe Eddie was going to jump out and brain him with a sawed-off baseball bat. He felt strangely calm. You could sense when you were trespassing in front of a watchful eye. This clean little home felt empty. Conrad's hand worked with its own curious will, the metal door folded out. Aside from clothes hanging in color-coordinated groups, the closet was empty.

No, it wasn't.

There was a suitcase on the floor, a big one, open and full of folded clothes, like the laundry in the hall. A *Time Out – Seattle* city guide. Planning to follow her to Seattle?

He heard a click.

Time to get her talking, she's been lying to you, boss.

Conrad stood. 'Nadia—'

Eddie was taller than he remembered. His hair was better, recently cut, neat over the ears. He had her in a chokehold. A blue-black gun with a wooden grip was pressed to her abdomen and shaking, stabbing at the outermost bulge of her belly. The boy was shaking, too, eyes roadmap red. A large square Band Aid was stuck to one side of his forehead, a maroon bullseye.

Jesus, he's a lousy shot.

'Where's your big money now, fuckface?'

The kid was as quiet as . . . something pretty quiet, Conrad thought, trying to come up with a casual response to the situation.

'Hi, Eddie.'

'You're in my house, fuckface,' Eddie said.

Was this the kid's only name for unwanted guests? Couldn't he do any better . . .

'I'm sorry, Eddie, don't worry about him—' Nadia started to say.

'Shut up!'

Conrad tried to breathe deeply without showing it. Jesus, it was hot in here. 'What money, Eddie?'

'I thought you could help us,' Nadia said. She was trying to signal him with her eyes. 'He can help us, Eddie.'

'Absolutely, Eddie, just hold on a sec,' Conrad said.

'You hold on, asshole, you just hold on.' A little too cool for Conrad's liking. The stutter was taking a time out, apparently. 'You think you can buy it?'

'What?' Conrad heard the words, but he did not understand.

'You can't buy it. I won't let you take my baby.'

Nadia yelped. Eddie was jabbing her with the gun. Jabbing her right in the – wait a minute. Was she in on this? Had she tried to trick him?

'Eddie, don't!' Nadia was being too loud. She was—

The gun.

The gun was everything. Look away. Show no fear.

Conrad forced himself to look into the kid's eyes, but

270

his eyes kept going back to her. Nadia was as white as the carpet. Her cheek twitched violently. Eddie's mouth hung open like he was being held hostage, too. Saliva dripped from his lower lip and fell past the gun, hitting the floor with a soft *pat*.

The gun . . .

Conrad reached out. 'Eddie, we were worried—'

The gun exploded.

28

When the gun went off in the hot confines of the trailer's hall, Nadia fell to the floor in a limp heap. Eddie's snarl froze and then he just looked surprised. Conrad flinched from the pop, covered his head and yelled, 'Don't!'

When he opened his eyes she was bleeding from just below her equatorial center, maybe Tanzania on the globe of her belly. Eddie was staring at her like some fourth party had pulled the trigger, like he was the other victim.

'I-I-I'm sorry,' Eddie said.

'You little fuck,' Conrad said.

The kid's remorse evaporated as soon as Conrad stepped forward and reached for the gun. Eddie went ape shit, screaming into the bathroom. Conrad shoved very hard and the trigger-happy suitor fired another shot into the wall before tripping over the toilet and slamming against the half-open sliding shower door, which rattled at an astonishing volume but did not shatter. Eddie's gun hand slapped the wall, Eddie slipped and Conrad leaped on top, his senses on full alert. He punched down, missed. Aimed for the neck, punched down, missed. Sweat-greased and hyped through the roof, Eddie slid beneath Conrad, spun out and yanked the towel rack out of the wall as he rebounded up and dashed past Conrad, careening off the wall and directly into the door, closing them both into the bathroom. He fumbled at the knob, but already Conrad had a ball of Eddie's shirt in one fist. Conrad yanked Eddie back and turned to the side. Eddie pivoted wildly, lost his balance, whirled past like they were swing dancing. Eddie's feet tripped on the edge of the tub and he began to go face first between the sliding shower door and the back-splash, directly into the tub. Conrad was still holding his shirt like a bronc rider and for one long second Eddie hovered over the tub, bent forward, the horse halting before going over the edge of a cliff. Conrad realized he was losing his balance, too, and he did not want to land on top of Eddie in the tub with a gun between them. He jerked his arm back once, bringing Eddie nearly vertical again, then kicked him in the ass as hard as he could, releasing the shirt at the last minute. Eddie's spine arched with whiplash and his hands flew out on instinct, trying to brace his fall. His right hand – the one holding the gun – hit the soap cradle, bent inward at the wrist, and the gun bucked. The shot went high on the right side of Eddie's forehead and exited his ear, spraying maroon and gray sludge over the grout and the bottle of Pert Plus to his left.

Conrad flinched back over the sink and covered his face. His ankle twisted and his knees gave out. He sat there on the shag throw rug, staring at Eddie's twitching legs until they stopped. Another minute seemed to pass before he realized what had happened. He stood up. Eddie was face down, his neck askew. Something shiny and white dangled from his ear . . . and it was the rest of his ear. Conrad was only slightly relieved he did not have to look into the boy's eyes.

His first coherent thought was, *Thank God it wasn't me.* His second was, *It's his fault. I didn't shoot him.*

And last but not least, *It happened in the shower. Easier to clean up.*

He was reaching for a towel when he remembered Nadia.

Jesus Shitting Christ she's pregnant and shot.

He turned away, closed the bathroom door, and crouched next to her in the hall. Nadia's foot pedaled the air and banged against the wall of the trailer a couple times, found purchase, and pushed her shoulders against the opposite wall until she was stuck and partially folded, her eyes rolling back and around, searching while her mouth puckered and emitted 'nnnya-nnnyaa-nnnyaa' sounds.

Conrad pulled her shoulders off the wall until she was lying flat on her back. It seemed important to get her straight. Her shirt was red from the waistline up to her breasts and sopping wet. His vision became foggy. Eyes watering up as if the wind were blowing invisible particles into them.

'I'm here, girl. Okay, we're going to be fine . . .'

He didn't know this would be fine. He ran back to the bathroom and – *don't look! don't look at that problem in the*

274

shower, not yet, not now! – grabbed two yellow and white striped beach towels off the rack, spun to the sink. Was he supposed to wet one first? No – soak up the blood. The medicine cabinet was open and he saw a tin of Band Aids and some Preparation H.

He crouched and pressed a towel into her abdomen. Nadia screamed and kicked.

'Hold still, hold still!' He sounded too loud, so he repeated it softer until she blinked and saw him, twisting against the pain, trying to get away. She beat her head against the floor and clenched her teeth, staring through him, and he knew she was angry on top of the pain. Was he to blame for this, after all? Probably, in some way.

Three gunshots. Someone must've heard. The police will be here soon.

He felt the towel dampening beneath his hand and lifted it to make sure he was pressing in the right spot. Her shirt was up, revealing white skin gone grainy and smeared. He couldn't see the wound's exact location yet. There was too much blood. He inspected her hips. Jesus Christ, where was it?

'Be still. Nadia, be still!' The blood was pooling in her belly button. 'Oh God . . .'

Nadia was whimpering. So much for the hope she was in shock. Shock would be a blessing. 'Burns, it burns,' she whimpered.

He put his finger to her navel and she screamed, jerking toward him. When she came up, his finger slipped under the flap of skin at the ring of her belly button until he was certain he was poking her in the guts.

Nadia howled and stretched herself taut as a piano wire. He snatched his hand away and fresh blood poured out.

'I know, I know! Stop moving!' Amazingly, she swung her hand around and clutched his forearm, her grip fierce. That was something, wasn't it?

'Easy, easy, I have to stop it.'

She gritted her teeth.

Conrad wadded the end of the second towel to a conical point and pushed it in. She opened her mouth to unleash another scream and nothing came out. Her circuits overloaded as her face went ash-gray and her breath locked up. She blinked through tears for a long silent spell. When it broke, the hot gust of her sour breath poured over him without a sound. Then she started panting, everything on autopilot.

Now she was in shock.

He had pushed the towel under the flap of skin. It went sideways, a tear in her outer fabric. He lifted the towel again and fresh blood flowed once more, but not before he saw that the core of her navel was intact. The bullet had not gone in. It had gone across shallowly, sideways through her belly flesh, entering at the navel and exiting three inches closer to her hip. It was possible that the curvature of her belly had prevented Eddie from getting a direct shot, and in doing so saved the child. Her skin under the blood was stained gray with either gunpowder or the first bruising. Underneath the ripped exit wound he saw yellow fatty tissue made pink with her blood.

No sirens. What are you waiting for, asshole?

The saner voice in his head screamed at him to call an ambulance and get the girl to a hospital. Yet he hesitated. This wasn't his fault, but there would be many questions. What made Eddie go off? What had you two been doing before this happened? How could you let this happen to our daughter? Our grandchild? Gail and John would rush home. Nadia would make the news. Jo would never return, or kill him when she did.

They would blame him. Tell the truth – you shot Eddie, didn't you? You wanted him out of the picture. Well, now he's out of the picture!

'Oh fuck, oh fuck . . .' Panic was setting in.

Wait. The phone. Eddie killed himself. His suicide note was on Nadia's phone!

Fine. Let Eddie be Eddie. But Nadia needs an ambulance – now.

But still he hesitated. Needed to get his story straight. He couldn't think it through, and the longer he sat there the more frightened he became. He just wanted to go home. The sane voice was losing the battle, being drowned out with each passing second by another voice, the one that had been there as his hand healed from the dog bite and been there still as the dogs themselves healed.

This is a healing place.

Was this what it wanted? The house and the things connected to the house? To make life out of life?

He imagined it was so.

*

277

He parked behind the garage and carried her up the backyard, over the deck, into the house. He had to set her down in the kitchen to catch his breath and she almost fell down, but he caught her. After more screaming and coughing, he got her up the stairs and into bed, carrying her like a bride. It took another twenty minutes to stop the bleeding, and he held the towel on her, offering her water she could not swallow without coughing and shaking and reopening the wound.

He went through the motions of doctors he'd seen on TV, in films. He cleaned and semi-sealed the borders of the bullet-torn flesh with Neosporin before applying butterfly bandages from the first aid kit they'd moved from Los Angeles. He cleaned, dabbed and staunched it with more ointment and clean gauze, taping her waist all the way around with more of Luther's flex-bandage. It held. Outside, the wound was the shape of a question mark. Whatever the damage on the inside, it would have to take care of itself.

Finally, half an hour later, her breathing slowed and she whimpered one last time before dozing off. She was tougher than he would have guessed, maybe tough enough to have made it in Seattle. A granite slab of guilt pressed down on him. That he had pushed Eddie to do this to her; that she was here at all.

He held her hand and thought about the baby inside. The life between them they had discussed only in vague questions and long silent stares now seemed enormous, everything. A bullet had grazed its soft thin shell and what was inside was now a little hero.

This is a healing place. If she does not get better in a day or two, I will take her to a doctor.

He didn't think anyone had seen them come home.

The afternoon and evening passed. Conrad awoke just before dawn with a pounding headache, convinced this was the day the Grums were coming home. He counted back, ticking off days that had become a frightening blur, until he realized Nadia's parents were not due for two or three more days. Perhaps.

He did not call to alert them to Nadia's condition, and she had not asked him to before the double-dose of Tylenol PM took her under for the night. He'd also slipped her two of Alice and Luther's Baytril tablets, a broad-spectrum antibiotic he knew from working with Dr Hobarth to be mild and safe for human consumption. She did not question the pills – she was just out.

The Doctor. You're playing Doctor.

He did not answer the phone when it had rang just before midnight. He doubted Jo would call so late. He had no idea what he would have said to his wife, and did not have the energy to pretend everything was fine.

Early the next morning there was a knock at the door. By the time he'd gotten up and pulled the curtain aside, they had gone. If they had found Eddie, the police would have come in a car, or three. He saw no police cars. Another UPS shipment from Jo? He did not see or hear a truck. Still, he remained at the window, waiting for Steve Bartholomew or the mailman or someone to reappear in his front yard, looking up at the second story, pointing an accusing finger. No one materialized and he did not linger.

Through the morning Nadia was in and out of it, but stable. The wound had reddened, puffed, cracked and seeped blood, and he changed her bandages. The bleeding had stopped. He brought her orange juice. Nadia swallowed more Baytril but did not speak. She fell into a long afternoon nap. He stretched out and lay beside her, careful not to disturb her.

Twenty-four hours had passed since Eddie went Eddie on them.

The second time the doorbell rang, he was awake and assumed his post at the window. It was nearly dark. No cop cars. Just as he dropped the curtain aside, he saw a figure step back in the yard and look up. Conrad could not make out a face. Might be Steve Bartholomew, their trusty neighbor. He dimly recalled how just a few weeks ago he'd thought Steve was the kind of man with whom he might strike up an easy friendship. Maybe be more than just neighbors, borrowing each other's tools and drinking beer during the annual neighborhood water-balloon fight in the street on the Fourth of July. But that window of opportunity had passed.

The figure on his lawn paced like a tiger in the zoo, peering into the front parlor windows, searching for an opening. The tiger planted his hands on his hips.

Conrad whispered into the curtain. 'Go home or pounce, buddy.'

The figure disappeared and Conrad lost the line of

sight through the thick leaves of his one-hundred-and-forty-year-old maple tree. He relaxed.

Dong-dong-dong! The doorbell.

'Fuck.'

Nadia stirred in the bed. 'What's going on?' She squinted at him in the dark, her hair matted, eyes crusty with sleep. 'Are my parents home?'

'Nothing, it's fine. Stay there.'

The doorbell rang again, setting the dogs off.

Conrad slipped out of the bedroom. He left the lights off as he padded to the door – no use backlighting himself before he knew who was there. He stopped and grabbed a knife from the block on the kitchen counter. It could be the police. He left the knife in the kitchen and headed for the door.

29

Conrad flipped the porch light on, casting their visitor in a yellow spotlight. The guy had his back to the front door, but it was obvious from the buzzed flat-top and hunter-gatherer posture it was Steve Bartholomew.

'Hey, Steve, what's up?' Conrad stepped out and pulled the door shut before the dogs could escape and Steve could move in.

Steve turned. 'Conrad. Did I wake you up?'

'Yeah, as a matter of fact.'

'Oh, are you sick?' Conrad realized he hadn't showered in some forty-eight hours.

'My dogs are beat up, Steve-O,' he said, going on the offensive. 'I came home to smashed mirrors and bleeding dogs, and it wasn't easy finding a vet in this little conclave of ours, so I apologize if I haven't been exactly out and about.'

Steve frowned. 'Your dogs?'

'You saw Nadia and I leave the other day, right? She helped me get them to the vet. Thirty-six stitches in Luther's legs. Alice almost lost an ear.'

'What happened?'

'I have no idea, Steve. Dogs can be dogs.'

'How's your wife? She come home yet?'

'No, she hasn't.'

'I'm sorry. Sounds like you got them fixed up. Speaking of fix up, how's your little job next door going?'

For a minute Conrad was so sure Steve knew about Nadia he forgot about the work he was supposed to be doing at the Grum residence.

'Yeah, how 'bout that?' he said, stalling for time. Did that mean the Grums had called Steve, maybe poking around after they couldn't reach Nadia at home? Or had he seen something suspicious? 'Seems like every time I get around to pulling the ladder out it rains.'

'Anything I can help you with? We're expecting John and Gail, what, tomorrow?'

'Day after or the next. And no thanks. I'll manage.' Conrad yawned. *Beat it, Steve-O.*

'Hope John and Gail had a good time. They deserve a break. These kids'll wear you out.' Steve grinned without pleasure. 'I know Jesse's keeping me awake more nights than not.'

'Jesse's your daughter?'

'Yes.'

'You said she's up at UW Madison?'

'Virginia Tech. School's fine, but these kids. These kids.'

'How's that?' Conrad didn't know if this was going somewhere or just small talk.

'I didn't like the boys she was hanging around with here in town. Wastrels, the lot of them. Only now, she's calling her mother every night. "Mommy, Josh is being a jerk. Mommy, Josh said it's normal to see other girls in college." You see where this is going.'

'Actually, I'm not sure—'

'I ever get my hands on this sapling Josh who's been sticking it to my daughter? He even thinks about coming to my house for one of his booty calls? I'll drive him down to the limestone quarry and only one of us is coming back.'

Conrad flinched. Steve was suddenly too close and smiling too widely.

'So, where's Nadia hiding?'

It came out so quickly that Conrad heard, where you hiding Nadia? But of course that was silly. If Steve really—

'She's not at your place, is she?' Steve glanced over Conrad's shoulder.

Conrad scoffed. 'No. Maybe she's out with friends?'

'What about Eddie? He been around?'

'She said he was calling her, trying to put the band back together. But I didn't get the impression they were exactly hot and heavy these days. I tried, but she told me to mind my own business, Steve.'

'Her parents are not going to be happy, Conrad.'

'She's twenty. It's not like she's a minor. Can't ground her, can they?'

Easy, 'Rad. This whole show is dry kindling and you're throwing lit matches.

'She's nineteen, and pregnant,' Steve said. 'And you obviously don't have children.'

'Nope, not yet.'

'Uh-huh. Well, if you ever want to, you might do well to tell Nadia to get her ass home before Big John returns. I've seen the man bend rebar with his bare hands.'

'Jesus.'

'Imagine what he'd do to your neck.'

'Eddie's neck,' Conrad corrected.

Steve nodded. *I know, and you know I know.*

'Good luck with your chores, Mr Harrison.'

'Night, Steve-O.'

Conrad went to the liquor cabinet and poured three fingers of warm silver rum. It tasted like rubbing alcohol and burned for five minutes while he checked the doors front and back, locking everything twice.

The night of Steve's visit, she began to feed herself and he watched her from the reading chair he had pulled into the room. He knew the big talk had arrived, and he waited for her to go first. Her voice was strong and clear, almost professional.

'I feel much better now. But I think I should see how bad it is.' She reached for the bandage.

'No, no, don't. It's superficial, but it needs more time to close up.' He patted her hand. 'I was very worried about you. You're lucky Eddie was a bad shot.'

'Did you call my parents?'

'No. Should I have?'

She licked her lips. 'Where's Eddie?'

'You don't remember?'

She just stared at him. He considered what to tell her.

If she knew the truth, she would probably panic and ask him to call the police. And she might never forgive him.

'It was bad, Nadia. I wasn't thinking straight. I was worried about you.'

'Did he run away?'

'No.'

'What happened?'

'There was a fight. He had the gun in his hand. I didn't . . .' He couldn't finish.

'Is he dead?'

'Yes.'

'You just left him there?' She didn't sound angry, just stunned.

'I had to take care of you first. I should have called an ambulance, but I didn't want it to . . . we were there, but it was Eddie's fault.'

She was crying soundlessly.

'Tell me what to do,' he said. 'I'll do whatever you want me to do.'

Nadia closed her eyes.

'He left his suicide note on your phone, Nadia. He shot himself in the head on your voicemail. You thought he was dead.' She squeezed her eyes together. 'We tried to help. Now he is. Dead. I'm sorry.'

After a long while, as if trying it out, she said, 'We were never there.'

'I think that is the best way. Don't you?'

'Will you leave me alone now?'

'I don't think—'

'I need to be alone.'

He stood in the baby's room and listened to her crying through the wall.

Later the same night, after she woke up and he fetched her another glass of water, she seemed to have improved physically but lost something mentally. She was drained, sinking into this quicksand he had accumulated for her.

'Do you have a plan?' she said.

'I'm working on it.'

'Someone's going to find him, if they haven't already.'

'You said he lives alone,' Conrad said. 'Right?'

'How long has he . . .' She could not finish.

'A day and a half,' Conrad said. 'If they found him, they'd be here by now. We need to get our story straight.'

'Our story? Are we going to jail? Are they going to take my baby?'

'Hey, hey. Easy. I would never allow that.'

She was crying again, without even changing her expression. This frightened him more than if she had been sobbing.

'Nadia, we can do this. If you still want me, I will see it through to the end.'

'Your wife is pregnant. Don't act like a hero when all you want is to throw your life away, too.' She coughed. 'My parents are coming home in two days and then this shit is going to be the next local scandal. If you want to help me, it's time to make it real.'

'I'm trying,' he said. 'I will.'

'Maybe I'm being punished. Do you think I'm one of

them, too? One of the women who runs away but keeps coming back?'

'Like the women in the photo?' he said.

'Like the women with nowhere else to go.'

'No.' But it had crossed his mind.

'Do you think if we stay –' she coughed '– it can be different this time?'

'Yes.'

'What about Eddie?'

'Eddie let you down. I will never let you down.'

He held her, and watched her cry until she fell asleep.

When he woke later he had no idea if it was the same night or the next night, but it was still very much night. The room was pitch-black. Nadia was sitting up in bed, staring at the wall. She was speaking to someone. Repeating something.

'. . . a young girl's heart', he heard her say.

Conrad turned on a lamp. 'What? Nadia?'

Nothing in her expression had changed, but her eyes were different. Flat. Dead. And when she spoke, her voice came out the same way, as if under someone or something else's influence. The voice was jilted, old and sore.

'Thread through a needle cannot mend a young girl's heart.'

30

Conrad moved around the bed to be in front of her, to see if she could see him. She stared right through him. She was flesh and bones – alive, but not aware.

'What does that mean, Nadia?'

'Thread through a needle cannot mend a young girl's heart.'

She had not blinked. Her eyes were watery, their pupils big as nickels.

'Nadia, can you hear me?'

She did not respond.

'What happened? Is there someone here in the house?'

Nothing.

'Is there something in the house?'

He moved from the bed to the chair, afraid to be close to her.

'Nadia, what thread through a needle? What's that?'

Her head rotated slowly, stiffly, her chin tucked and her eyes averted. It was not her voice that answered. Her words came awkwardly, her sentences strung out.

'Try take ohmma bay-bay way.'

'Who?' He went rigid in his chair. 'Who took all your baby away?'

'Man.'

'Man? What man?' He heard Roddy's voice in his head, the reference to 'the good doctor'. 'Do you mean the doctor? The doctor who lived here?'

'Was no docca no mine what he say.'

'Who was he?'

'First he take all-ma mothers and women runsaway. Then she growed up and he took the insides away. Then he bury'm others and took 'em behbee away.'

Conrad saw sketches of the house, the unsmiling women on the porch. His scalp began to crawl. He sat up straight and seriously considered bolting from the room, the house. But he couldn't just leave her here.

'Who are you? Where's Nadia?'

'Runsaway.'

'Nadia ran away?'

'Nah-dee run . . . away.'

'I don't understand. Nadia, are you Nadia, or are you telling Nadia to run away?'

'All-ma.'

'All ma? All mothers? Are you someone's mother?'

'All-ma not runsaway. All-ma *stay*.'

Then he understood. Not all-ma. Alma. A name. Someone named Alma was speaking through Nadia. Where had he heard this before? Something from the past week. Then he knew. The woman in the room. She had been rocking her arms. *Ohhmma take care of behbee* . . .

Oh. Holy. Fuck. This was not right.

'You are Alma? Alma, what about Nadia?'

'Nah-dee not fit. Nah-dee betray.'

'What? Why – how did Nadia betray Alma?'

'All-mommas give a life . . . if she wan haff a life.'

'Why?'

'To haff a life she must gif a life. Life . . . circle begins and end on-on-on same ssss-sphere. In betwee the juuur-nee from one side t'other, circle provides. For we each owes a life.'

'No.' He did not like the sound of that, or any of it. She sounded like Greer Laski, like an idiot child. 'Nadia must stay. Alma *cannot* stay.'

'Once long time house full of womans and behbees. But long time now circle . . . circle of this houses belong only t'Alma.'

'This house belongs to me,' he said. 'And I don't want you to stay, Alma. I want Nadia to stay.' But he was too shaken to say this with any real force or conviction.

'Alma not runsaway.' Her lips were trembling, sneering. 'Alma stay.'

'Why?'

'Alma tur . . .'

'What?'

'Alma turn.'

'Alma turn for what?'

Alma – Nadia – looked up at him, her lips pulled back in a sickening and false grin. 'Docca no! Alma behbee no take away,' she said. 'Docca never never never taken Alma behbee away!'

Her eyes were black, murderous. Her hand lifted

slowly from her side and hovered in the air between them. He leaned back. She reached out until her fingertips began to tickle his throat.

Conrad slapped her face. It had been building inside and then his hand just moved. Immediately Nadia and the thing inside her recoiled, started blinking and coughing, and then she was crying. Softly, then louder, then softly.

'Nadia? Nadia, wake up. Wake up, wake up—'

'Chessie behbee mine,' the girl croaked in Alma's voice. Then her voice changed through her next words, reverting to Nadia's softer tone. 'No one, no, I won't let them take my baby away.'

'I know, it's okay, Nadia, we're okay,' he said. Nadia was back, shivering all over, cold when he put his hands on her arms. Maybe it was a nightmare. Maybe she had been talking in her sleep. But he didn't believe that. He had an idea who Alma was. He'd seen her before. Touched her . . .

He held her until her breathing slowed and she slumped over, going limp in his arms. He rested her back on the pillows. He was too stunned to think through their situation, and eventually he gave up the fight and fell asleep.

It was not restful or lasting.

'Conrad. Conrad, wake up!' She was hissing like an old woman.

'Uhn . . . hm.'

'Someone's here.'

'Uh-uh.' He had been so far down, where there are no dreams at all. He just wanted to sleep forever. 'Is jus' Steve . . . took care him.'

She shook him hard. 'Conrad! Someone was here.'

He came around again. 'At the door?'

'No.' Nadia clutched the skin over his ribs, pinching into him. 'She was here. Not sixty seconds ago. In the room. Standing at the foot of the bed.'

'Nadia, don't.' Now he was awake. He sat up and faced her in the dark and saw the whites of her eyes. She made a tiny whining sound, like Alice when she was waiting to be let out into the backyard. 'You were dreaming. I didn't hear anything.'

'No. Conrad, no.' He could feel the dry heat of her breath on his ear. 'Same as the one in the window. She was tall, with dark black hair. She was wearing black clothes and her skin was white. When she moved – oh, God. She just stood there staring at me. I could – oh, Jesus, I heard her neck cracking in the dark.'

Conrad swallowed. 'How long?'

'She was there when I opened my eyes. I've been frozen waiting for her to leave for almost an hour.'

'Did you see her leave?'

'Yes.'

'Did you hear her leave?'

'No.'

'If you didn't hear her . . . her footsteps . . . she's not real, is she?'

Nadia pointed to the foot of the bed. 'There.'

He could not see past the frame where their feet had

piled up the blankets, kicking them off in the heat. He sat forward on his knees, one hand lingering on the girl as he focused on the shape. A low, guttural sound rose from the end of the bed, followed by two, then three faint *clicks* on the wood floor.

'No—' Conrad lunged forward. 'Leave us alone!'

Nadia turned the switch on the lamp and screamed.

The dark shape lunged up, then scrabbled back, growling. Conrad fell on to his stomach. Alice barked at the two of them, as startled as they were. Nadia scrambled out of bed and fell to the floor. Alice panicked and fled the room.

'Stop it!' Conrad said. 'It's just Alice.' The adrenaline washed away, leaving a tired anger behind. 'Fuck.'

'I can't take this.' Her knees were tucked into her chest, one leg sideways. Sitting in the corner, she appeared at that moment like an ugly, misbehaving child and he barely suppressed the urge to smack her again for scaring him.

'God damn it, Nadia.'

'I saw her.'

'You had a bad dream.' He forced himself to lower his voice, lest he raise Steve Bartholomew again. 'You thought you saw something, and you did. My dog, Alice, who is now scared shitless on top of being cut to hell. So please. Before the police decide to lock us both up.'

But Nadia was still shaking her head. 'No. There was a woman.'

Conrad stared at her, telling himself that there must be another explanation, even though he knew it was a lie.

'I'm sorry. Get back in bed. I need to check your bandages.'

'You don't believe me?'

'It doesn't matter—'

'Then what the fuck is that?' Her arm shot out, pointing.

'What? I don't—'

He walked to the doorway.

It was lying on the floor, center to the doorframe as if it had been delivered. Of course he recognized it; it had come from his kitchen. He picked up the knife. It was the long serrated one, the thin blade that came to an almost needle-like point made for cutting fish. Tied to the handle was a thin yellow ribbon laced through a scrap of yellow paper.

On the yellow paper, in a fine and femininely looped script, four words in black ink . . .

other mother must go

31

'It's your wife,' Nadia said. 'She came home. I need to leave.'

He was still holding the knife, reading the four words over and over. Jo's handwriting? He didn't think so, but it still made him feel sick just holding it. He set the knife on the dresser, wishing for it to disappear. Nadia had gotten to her feet and was bent over in pain. He knew that if she had the strength she would have bolted.

'Don't do that.' He rushed to her side and tried to maneuver her back into bed. 'Not in the middle of the night. Let's think about this.'

'I need to go home.' But she sat down, winced, and leaned back into the bank of pillows he was arranging for her.

'It's not Jo,' he said. 'Why would Jo do this?'

'What do you mean, why? Because she's trying to send us a message? Because she's crazy? How should I know, she's your wife!'

'No, no. Jo is not the kind of woman to play tricks. I'm not saying she doesn't have a temper. And, yes, if she saw us here, if she came home and found us . . . convalescing together, she would be upset. She would be very fucking upset.'

'Oh my God. Are you trying to make me lose my shit? This is so wrong. Please take me home.'

'I'm just saying, Jo wouldn't be creeping around at night, watching us. She would be screaming her head off. And the dogs. No way would she be able to get within half a block of the house without the dogs going wild. They haven't seen her in a month. No. Uh-uh. It's not Jo. This is something else.'

Nadia gathered herself up, trying to maintain. 'When was the last time you talked to her?'

'Just yester—' It seemed like yesterday, but the last time they had actually spoken was at least three . . . no, at least four or five days ago, before the incident with the dogs and the mirrors.

'Jesus,' he said, rubbing his eyes. 'I can't believe this.'

'What?'

'I don't remember the last time I talked to my wife.'

'So, there you go. Michigan is like twelve hours by car and an hour by plane. She could have come home, maybe seen something strange and decided to wait and see. She could be watching us right now, Conrad!'

'Don't panic,' he said. 'You're going to hurt yourself.'

'Don't tell me what to do,' she said, hiccupping.

'Nadia, it's not Jo. Where would she be staying? The Dairyland Motel up the street? This isn't some murder mystery with stakeouts and the jealous wife. That's crazy.'

'Are you sure? Because it sort of feels like it.'

'I know her. Trust me.'

'Maybe you're not telling me everything.'

'Nadia, for all I know you put the knife there.'

'What? Why would I do that? How would I even——'

'You were talking in your sleep. Completely out of it.'

He dared not tell her about the 'conversation' he had with Alma. For one, he was trying not to believe it had actually happened. For another, telling Nadia she had been invaded by a spirit that wanted her to 'give a life to have a life' would only confirm her worst nightmares and send her jumping out the window.

'So, what are you saying? You think I'm a total psycho now?'

'No. Just . . . maybe we don't know everything we're doing here.'

'How do I know you weren't the one who brought the knife back? And how would I know where you keep your knives, anyway?

Conrad frowned, not at all appreciating having the tables turned. 'You think I'm part of this? I'm trying to help you, not scare you away.' He grabbed the knife off the dresser. 'For all we know, Laski's wife's gone off the deep end and come back to scare both of us. Now, she was fucking nuts.'

'Mrs Laski is not a tall woman with black hair. Your wife is.'

He had no response for that. He headed for the door.

'Where are you going?'

'To search the house.'

'No way. You cannot leave me here.'

'Nadia, I specifically remember locking the doors, twice. If someone broke in, I'll know.'

'What if she didn't break in?' she said.

'What do you mean?'

'Just what I said. What if it's . . . her?'

He knew, but he didn't want the girl to believe it, too. 'I didn't see anyone in the library.'

She watched him. 'You're lying. You've seen her, too.'

'If it was her, then you don't have to worry.'

'Why not?'

'I have to say it now? Okay, because she's a ghost.'

'A ghost,' Nadia said.

'Sure, why not? And who cares, because what can a ghost do?'

'I don't know,' Nadia said. 'This one seems to have written a note and dropped a knife on the floor.'

She said this almost flippantly, but the notion rocked him. Alma had taken control of Nadia long enough to speak in her tongue. Could she have come back and sent the girl to fetch the knife? To write a note? Warning herself – Nadia, the other mother – to go away?

If they stayed another night, would Alma command Nadia to take her own life? Or his?

He rubbed his eyes, hard. 'I have to check the house.'

'You better come back soon.'

'I will. I promise, no one's going to hurt you.'

He moved around the stairs, through the library. 'Alice, Luther,' he called. 'Come on, doggies.'

The sound of their nails clicking on the wooden floor echoed softly up the butler stairs. He paused in the back hall, listening. Somewhere a door creaked. He thought that must have been Nadia, deciding she would be safer with the bedroom door closed.

All three doors were locked.

The dogs were on the couch. Alice raised her head when he entered the room, giving him that *Are you going to feed me now?* look. Luther yawned and stretched his back, producing a disturbingly human-sounding fart. If they were still in the living room, what was with the clicking? Had they walked into the kitchen, then gone back to the couch?

He left the dogs and set the knife down on the kitchen table, glancing at the note one last time. He went to the fridge and poured a tall glass of iced tea, letting it drip down the hollow of his throat while he stood over the sink.

The knife was just about the worst kind of unsettling. He did not believe Jo had gone that far off the rails. But another part of him, the part that had read enough detective novels to question motive, wondered if it wasn't possible. The enraged wife thing was an obvious angle. The problem was, it didn't feel like Jo.

What if it was you?

What if you've lost your mind for this girl and the stress and killing that kid and all the loneliness has finally driven you to the point where you know not what you do in your sleep? How about that, 'Rad?

300

This possibility bit into him like a viper, poisoning all confidence that he was doing the right thing by trying to manage the situation alone.

What have I done? What am I about to do?

No, you wouldn't be standing here thinking about it if you were that far gone.

But you do need help. Quit fucking around and call someone.

He needed to talk to Jo. He picked up the phone and tried to develop an explanation, a cover story to hide the panic.

Just tell her –

'Aw, shit.' He sat down hard on one of the chairs at the two-top. All at once he was out of gas. As long as he covered his tracks, there would be no relief. The whole secrecy routine was eating his guts. He needed to end this before someone else got hurt.

He made himself the same promise all over again. If she answered, he would tell her everything. Ask for her help. Be honest. Let her panic and scream at him if that's what it took, but he would come clean.

'You put your fate in her hands and cut Nadia loose and start over. With or without Jo, you start over like a man.'

He dialed before he could change his mind. The line buzzed. Four, five times. Conrad's knee did a little jig and he tried to smother it with his free hand. Seven, eight. The oven clock read 2.12 a.m.

A throat rattled wetly. 'Har-ugh. Uh-huh?' The guy sounded like he'd been drinking Jack and cokes all night.

'Ah,' Conrad searched for the words. Was it the same guy as before? That voice had been softer. It didn't seem like the same guy, but . . .

'Hello?' the guy said forcefully, waking up.

'I'm sorry,' Conrad said. 'I'm looking for my wife.'

'What?'

'My wife. Joanna Harrison.'

'Nope.'

'What do you mean, "nope"? She's not there?'

'Nope.'

'Where is she?'

'Why would I care?'

'This is room three-four-one-eight?'

'I guess so.'

'Who are you?'

'I'm tired,' the guy said. 'Look. I just moved in. Your wife was, what, here on training?'

'Yes. This is her room.'

'Not any more.'

'Did you know her? You one of her friends? Classmates?'

'Don't think so. They told me some woman from the last class left for a condition. Medical purposes, whatever.'

'Medical purposes? What the fuck does that mean?

'I don't know.'

'She's gone? She left training?'

'Look, I didn't get a name. I just started the new round of classes. And I have to be up in three hours, so good luck, ace.'

The phone sounded like the guy was trying to bury it under the mattress.

'Wait!' Conrad said.

'Yeah?'

'You see her leave? She leave anything behind? Come on, I'm her husband. Help me out here.'

'They just said this woman had to leave training early. It happens.'

'Who said that? What's this medical shit?'

'Davidson, the training instructor. There's a few of them, so I don't know if she was in the same group. Hey, it could have been a rumor. I don't know. I asked if she got fired or couldn't take the pressure or what. They said no, she had a medical thing. Hey, you think they were just saying that? You get that with a lot of these sales things. Fucking corporate. I really don't wanna do eight weeks if the program is shit. I'm here to make money, you know what I'm saying.'

It wasn't really a question, and Conrad wasn't really paying attention. He was too busy imagining bad things. Jo in a hospital somewhere, for Christ knows what. Or she's on her way home. Or already here. Watching.

'Fuck. Oh, fuck.'

'Hey, take it easy, bro. You want me to call someone, have the company get in touch with you?'

'Yeah, you think?' Conrad hung up.

He dialed her cell. Her voice crisp and professional, asking him to leave a message.

'Jo? Sweetie? It's me. Where are you? I'm sorry I yelled. Why won't you pick up? Some guy answered in

303

your room. Please, please call me as soon as you get this. I'll keep trying. Why haven't you called me back? I love you.'

He clicked off and lunged out of his chair to check the windows—

He never made it.

Before he had taken two steps, he noticed that the door to the basement was ajar, a faint glow emanating from below. He knew damn well he had closed the door and turned off the overhead shop lights after finding Luther down there.

'Conrad!' Nadia said, startling him from upstairs. 'Who are you talking to?'

'No one. Stay there. I'll be right up!'

He grabbed a flashlight from the junk drawer and tromped down the stairs. By the time he remembered this was the sort of expedition you'd want to take with two dogs by your side, it was too late.

In the basement he found what he was looking for all along.

The air was moist with the scents of lime and mold. The basement was something between a crawlspace and a real basement. And yet there were signs the space had not been written off as uninhabitable. If one used one's imagination, as Conrad did now, wagging the flashlight around, one could see where a man (doctor) with a load of guests (patients) might find the cooler, peaceful depths of the house suitable for short periods of recuperation (torture).

It might have been a place to heal.

Or a temporary morgue.

The non-perimeter walls were covered with cheap walnut paneling, most of it bulging with moisture and splitting at the seams. The carpet was newer, but the cement beneath it might have been easier to clean, to disinfect. And what of this, the trough-like groove in the cement floor running out of the south-east room into the center drain? Was that routine flood protection, a gutter for water from a burst pipe or heavy rain? Or was it something else? Like, say, a place to wash the really bad ones down?

Conrad pulled the chain on the bulb hanging in the basement's main 'room', and turned three hundred and sixty-five degrees, wiping cobwebs real and imagined from his face as he went.

He tried the shop first. This room had the newer electrics and a wall switch and the fluorescent bulbs were on. He felt better having the extra light behind him while he worked up the courage to check the last room, the place where he'd found Luther sliced up and cowering. The shop was empty.

He aimed the flashlight at the boiler room, swinging it in wide arcs over the stone walls and the sloping dirt mound under his front porch. The flashlight's beam narrowed with each step, leaving more darkness in its wake. One of those dull *whumping* boiler noises would have been enough to send him running in a blind panic, but all was quiet.

Had the dog been interested in this spot on the floor,

or the wall? Enough to cut himself to ribbons trying to get in? Conrad looked for blood or teeth marks – anything that would confirm a dog's persistent interest. The image of Luther gnashing his teeth on solid rock conjured the same kind of eerie screech you hear when the class asshole rakes his fingernails across the chalkboard, and Conrad cringed, stepping away.

The thought wasn't out of his head for two seconds when he heard another sound, equally electrifying.

'*Aaayyy-ay-ay-aaaaack!*' Just as before, the baby's cry wormed its way into his head and fried his nerves. It paused, hitching in fits and starts, and then rose again in that same choking, raspy cry. The shop lights went out, leaving him with only the flashlight to illuminate his way.

Oh Baby, oh Baby, what the fuck is happening in this place?

It was an awful sound, but something in the urgency took hold of him and this time he heard it for what it had been all along – a cry for help.

'Okay, okay, it's okay,' he babbled, moving out of the corner. 'You want help? Okay, are you hungry? Are you hurt?'

His hand shot out and flipped the switch. The lights flickered once and fell dark. In this half-second that lit the room like a distant lightning flash and left retinal echoes even as the room was plunged back into pitch-blackness, he saw a shape darting from the corner of his eye. He tried to track its movement, but it was gone. Two steps later his kneecap rammed into one of the workbench's legs and he bit down on his lip to keep from shouting.

The anger came back with the pain and he brought the flashlight up quickly. But now the infant's wail had been muted, perhaps by his clumsy and clattering response. His breath became ragged, the beam moving in erratic swaths before it slowed and fell at last on the swaddled bundle resting on the workbench. A tremor ran the length of the beam even as it shrank, the diameter of its spotlight closing down until it was shining from less than eighteen inches above this tiny package. He held the beam still and everything under its cone became the world.

He was aware that something larger than his own fear was at work here, and that he was powerless to stop himself, forced to watch the rest happen as if to someone else.

Under the beam a dirty hand appeared and patted the soft fabric grayed with the indifferent passage of time. The beam swept from one end to the other until it found an opening and the dirty hand peeled back the layers with the grace of a florist stripping petals from a dried rose. With nothing left to stop its progress, the beam shone deeper, revealing the face of a doll burnished and painted with all the color and detail of a proud toy-maker whose principal calling is to animate what can never be. All the maker's love was evident in the way the thin strands of hair had been combed and made glossy over the tiny painted brows and suggestion of a nose. The beam stilled over this creation and for a lingering moment the illusion achieved its goal; its beholder regarded the doll with some reluctant swell of his heart and returned the smile. And then his heart broke. The only hope for a lasting art vanished as all life's likeness fell away, revealing black holes where once were eyes, tiny blackened nubs of teeth, and the decaying, bird-like ribs, spine and pelvis of a newborn.

32

If it was a sin to keep a woman not his wife in the marriage bed, then it was also a sin to leave the child in that dark forgotten corner of the basement.

As he climbed the stairs with the bundle in his arms, that which weighed no more than the balsa model airplanes he and Dad had labored over on those endless summer nights of which you can never grasp the fleeting nature until you have grown sad beyond your years, he thought of death. Not only how it seemed to prefer the young and unprotected, but how you can see it every day all around you and never understand it until you are holding it in your arms.

How death was final, yes. But also how something lived on, trying to communicate with the living. How, too, it was all the sickening secrets revealing themselves, finding depths you did not know you possessed, giving birth to some new you both loathed and welcomed.

Someone wanted him to know her secret. In delivering hers, she had forced his own to the surface. He had been chosen to share it because she knew, somehow, that her secret was safe with him. That he would understand. That she might rouse his empathy to an act of faith.

He placed the bundle the only respectful place he knew, a place it would be safe until the rest of it had played out. Setting the swaddling on the natural fiber pad inside the crib, he pulled the blanket over the older, rotted cloth. He would return when she had made clear the rest of her wishes.

He left the safari lamp on, fearing he would not again be able to make the approach in the dark, and shut the door.

He had to deal with Nadia first. Something here was testing them. Something had brought them together, and he would need her to go all the way with him. Their survival required a different confession.

He went to her and rested his tired body next to hers on the bed.

'Did you see anything?' she said, breaking the ringing silence in his ears.

He nodded.

'Was someone here?'

'Someone was here,' he said, closing his eyes. 'We don't have much time.'

'Conrad. I want to go home.'

'I know.'

'Can we go now? Why can't we go now?'

'Listen,' he said, inching close to her on the bed, taking one of her dry hands in his. 'I have never told anyone what I am about to tell you. I think you need to see how we got here. Me to this house. You in this room, with me.'

If she could see his face, she would not have been able to stay, the pain be damned. He was grinning like a child fascinated by some enormous and just-grasped scheme: the sound of his mother's car arriving in the driveway at midnight, the orbit of the planets, conception at the cellular level.

'What happened?'

He leaned over and kissed the exposed white space just below the wound.

'Conrad?'

'Her name was Holly. You remind me of her. Sometimes, when you are with me, it's like she never went away, Nadia. And that's strange, I guess, but it's beautiful, too.'

His heart filled with something beyond blood as he remembered her face, her eyes full of hope and trust.

'No one knows what we did, Holly and me. No one knows anything about it.'

Nadia's grip tightened around his fingers. 'Did you hurt her?'

'What we did was, we made a baby.'

HOLLY

That night in the house we had entered as children and left as something else; we exchanged much more than cells and fluids and the physical particles that transmit. We created a third entity that depended on the two of us, a spirit that was made of the part of myself I had willingly abandoned inside her, and she in me. Having given this, we were never whole again, together or apart. This is something else I say without the benefit of sarcasm. There are days when I wish we had died there before it ended, but end it did.

Eventually we dressed, packed up the candles, remade the bed and cleaned our dinner plates. We folded our single blue sheet and took it with us out the door, locking everything up the way we had found it. The sheet was Holly's idea, after I suggested we wash it.

'No,' she said with territorial authority. 'They can't have this one. This one we keep.'

Later we would refer to it as 'our night' or 'the night' but we never discussed what had passed between us.

We both knew she was pregnant.

We never talked about what we had wished for. The

words, the promises, the vows. They were there. But we could not square them with the rest of our seventeen-year-old lives. The secret we carried was about to blow up and we had no way of knowing how much destruction it would leave behind. We wanted to prepare, I think, but we didn't know how or where to begin.

Like everything else that had been our secret – the long walks at night, the shoplifting, the drugs, the sleep-overs – we wanted the conception of our child to remain ours and ours alone. To tell our parents, our friends, would somehow diminish it.

Of course we were terrified.

Looking back, I still believe that if some twist of fate had dropped a million dollars in our laps, killed off our parents or in some other catastrophic way destroyed the rest of the world for us, we would have made it. We would have emerged stunned but ultimately glad, free to live out the secret life we had made together.

How did it finally end?

I thought that would be the hard part. But now that the rest has been told I find that everything that came before was the pain. Seeing myself with her has always been the hard part. The end is easy. The end, unlike Holly and the five years I knew her and loved her, is not alive. The end is easy because it has no life, no soul. It is easy to tell because it is death.

When Holly's mother found out her daughter was pregnant and that we wanted to have the baby and make a go of the life we had imagined together, she was almost freakishly supportive. But there was the other half. Holly begged her mother not to, but eventually Mrs Bauerman had to tell Mr Bauerman.

Mr Bauerman had more money and therefore more power, and he did not take it well. He sent Holly away.

To a private school? A town? Another country?

I searched for two years. When I would not stay away from her father's house, he had me arrested. I wrote letters, talked with lawyers and worked on Mrs Bauerman until I was a weeping, vengeful menace that even she had to turn her back on. The family moved to be with her, or so her friends told me.

Eventually my mother wore me down. She said she would support me as long as it took, but I had to let go.

The reason I quit was pretty simple, actually.

I realized, reading some book or another at three in the morning on my mother's threadbare sofa, that if Holly really wanted to see me, she would have found a way to write or call. She had done neither. I knew that whatever she had gone through to get to the point where she didn't want to see me or talk to me had also killed her. Everything between us had been real. But whatever forces her father had marshaled, whatever people or doctors or hospitals he brought in to dissolve her wishes and render her speechless, whatever world she lived in now, well, they were stronger.

I was just a kid. I tried to be a man, but in the end I was just a kid.

You think of them living somewhere with some other guy. Maybe he is an executive, or owns his own company. You see them standing on a porch, holding hands.

Your love is now a woman and your unborn child is now a son. He's ten. He rides a skateboard. He needs a haircut. You think you will be upset by this, but you are wrong. Seeing this would make you happy, because then you would know.

I never knew where she went, or if she kept my child. That is the sucking black hole of it. I never knew. I let go, but you never let go.

I moved, worked, tried college a few times, and then my mother died. I never saw my father, but someone told me later that he had been there, at her funeral. He went back to his life and the last time I saw him he was burned and dying of a stroke in Chicago.

He was a coward. He failed. He ran away. I never ran away. I won't ever run away. Because if the world can take my child and my family, is it not possible that same world can deliver me another?

This is why I chose this house. This is why I am here. Now I have found you, Nadia. I have been dying since that night. But I'm here to take care of you.

This is a beginning.

I understand why you are crying, but you should stop that now, Nadia. And trying to pull away. Now that you know my story, you must understand why I will never, never let you leave.

33

He waited in the silent room for her response, a judgment. Now that it had been told, a stab of regret went
through him. What had he done? What must she think of
him now? Telling her had been like going back there
with Holly, a little bit. Okay, a lot. He could not really be
sure what he had said and what he had seen only in his
head. When another minute of silence passed, he suspected she had fallen asleep. Then a violent, full-body
twitch seemed to confirm this, but no. She was awake.
Whatever she'd heard, she'd heard enough.

'Conrad, I'm sorry.'

'What for?'

'For you.' Her voice had changed yet again. Or maybe
he had been hearing Holly's high voice and forgotten
Nadia's flatter tone. 'But I don't think we should do this.
I want . . . I need to talk to my mom.' She hitched a few
times. He could hear the tears running down her cheeks,
patting the pillow.

He coughed. 'Aren't we a little past parents now?'

'We can talk to them. They're going to find out,
anyway.' She paused, and he let his silence tell her what

he thought about that idea. 'I'm hurt. Maybe when things calm down—'

'The baby is home, where he should be. And as long as we take care of the baby we'll be safe.'

'But—'

'We need to make amends and do it right this time, Nadia. There is no other way.'

He counted seventeen heartbeats before she said, 'What did you find downstairs?'

'We're being tested. But we're going to be good now.'

'Tell me. I know you saw something. It's making you confused.'

He grabbed her hand and squeezed. 'We're healing. This is a new life between us. This life. And this life between us.' He rested his other hand at the top of her belly to see that she understood. She stared at him, eyes glassy. 'I just want to be a good father. Will you let me?'

She rolled over on her side, her back to him.

He slid under the blanket and pressed against her. His left arm fell over her hip, his fingers spread in a fan, the palm resting on her soft belly above the wound. She tensed.

'I'll take care of you,' he said.

Her breathing slowed.

'You can choose,' he whispered in her ear. 'Who is the father of your child.'

She did not answer and he had to fight the sleep pulling him down.

'Tell me.'

'You.'

Later, early in the morning, Conrad dreamed of three gray women cloaked in black. They bowed their heads when they entered the room, following orders from another, darker presence that lorded over the proceedings. In the dream he felt the bed shift as the *zeks* carried her away to a place he was not allowed. He tried to scream but his muscles were frozen by her cool shape enveloping and pressing him to the bed until it was safe to let go.

When he woke just past noon the room was bright and Nadia was gone.

34

'When was the last time you spoke to her?' Gail Grum was placing souvenir bottles of barbecue sauce on the table in a neat little row, already sensing the need to restore order.

He made a face of recollection, and his face was convincing, because he did not know. Conrad had spent yesterday – the long day that followed the morning Nadia had vanished – catching up on chores, cleaning the gutters he had neglected for the past ten days. He had called Jo half a dozen times, but still she was not answering. He thought of calling the police, but that would open a line of questions he was not prepared to answer. Having Nadia or Jo by his side would give him someone to lean on when the questions came down – inviting more on his own was unthinkable. He waited for the phone to ring all night, and he could not remember sleeping. He had been frantically washing dishes and sweeping the floor when he realized the sun was rising. He had seen their car arrive just after noon, and went to greet them with the news.

Now, sitting in the kitchen with Gail while Big John

unpacked the car, Conrad was not as nervous as he had imagined he would be. He was concerned, even frightened. But he had no answers, and acted as such.

'Last time I spoke with her? Hard to say, Gail. I think . . . today's Wednesday?'

'It's Friday, Conrad. Are you all right? You look like hell.'

Did she suspect him of something? Or was this just part of the deal when you've come home to find your daughter missing?

'Oh, I guess I'm not, Gail. I meant to call, but I didn't want to worry you.' Gail tensed. 'It's Jo. She's left the training grounds. They don't know where she is. A man mentioned health issues.'

'Jesus!' Gail put one shaky hand to her cheek. 'She's missing?'

'She could be home any day now. Or not. We, uhm, we've been fighting.'

'Have you called someone? Friends? Family?'

'I appreciate your concern, Gail. But let me worry about that. I don't want to burden you two on top of this other thing.'

'Other thing?'

'Nadia. I didn't really think she's missing, you know. I mean, she was still talking to Eddie. I heard her on the phone a few times. She didn't share her plans with me.'

'Nadia doesn't make plans. That's the whole problem.'

'She's a smart kid, though. Tough. We had some nice conversations.'

Gail frowned. 'Conrad. I'm sorry. I'm still a little lagged from the trip. But is there something you're not telling me?'

'What do you mean?'

'Did she go to a friend's and ask you not to tell us? I understand – I encouraged her to talk to you, in fact. But it's not like her not to call or leave a note, even when we're fighting.'

'As I said, I was a bit wrapped up in my own problems. But that's not the whole truth, Gail. Nadia told me she was planning on running away. She asked me to drive her to the airport.'

'Running – the airport!' Gail had forgotten about the barbecue sauce.

'I know, hold on. I talked her out of it at the time. But she said she wanted to go to Seattle.'

'Who does she know in Seattle?'

'I was going to ask you. I thought maybe you had family there.'

Gail dropped into a chair at the kitchen table and dropped her face into her hands. 'Our family. Is in *Wisconsin*!'

'What's wrong?'

Conrad jumped at the father's voice. Big John Grum was standing at the kitchen's entrance.

'Nadia's run away again,' Gail said, bursting into tears. 'Welcome home.'

'I'm sorry.' Conrad placed the check for four hundred dollars on the table. 'I didn't do enough to deserve this. Let me know if I can help.'

Gail was still staring at the check when Big John patted Conrad on the back and walked him out.

He was headed for the grocery store with visions of iced tea waterfalls in his head when a new thought nearly drove him off the road.

There is a dead baby in my house.

Inside, he ran past the dogs, up the stairs and into the guest room. Sickened by the thought of the lifeless, skeletal form – and by the spell that had caused him to leave it there – he flung the door open and latched on to the rails of the newly assembled crib.

The crib was empty.

He forgot about going to the store, about food, about sustaining the illusion of normalcy. He simply walked down the stairs and fell on to the couch. His heart beat faster and harder. He considered the angles, finding no solace. Either he was imagining things or the house was haunted – and those could be two extensions of the same phenomenon. Whether the house contained spirits, other environmental conditions acting upon his perceptions, or his mind was simply playing tricks on him was at this point a discussion for academics. People who were not involved. They boiled down to the same thing – he could no longer trust his eyes, ears or thoughts. Not while under this roof.

Still, he tried. The answer was in here somewhere. He was missing something, something vital. A ghost was something perceived. He needed evidence.

Time was running out. He could run. Just put the

dogs in the car and drive away. Withdraw his inheritance and disappear to Canada. Would she follow him to a cabin in the woods? Would she emerge from his nightmares under any roof, not just this one?

No, he had to stay because he had to know. And because one of them would need a father.

If the tiny skeleton had been real (as real as the knife, the note) and his house was not haunted, then someone had been here. Someone could be here still, alive. Fucking with him. Jo? Whoever did this had to be insane, a broken soul gone way, way over to the other side of everyday criminal behavior. The sounds, the visions of the woman in the house, the absolute inhumanity required to exhume and deliver a dead child into another man's home? That wasn't Jo. He did not believe his wife insane.

I got news for you, kid, Leon Laski had said. *A haunting is just history roused from her sleep. Any house can be haunted, even a new one. Know why? Because what makes 'em haunted ain't just in the walls and the floors and the dark rooms at night. It's in us. All the pity and rage and sadness and hot blood we carry around. The house might be where it lives, but the human heart is the key. We run the risk of letting the fair maiden out for one more dance every time we hang our hat.*

So it's me? You think I'm nuts? Conrad had responded.

I didn't say that. I said what makes 'em haunted ain't just in the walls. Which led him back where he started. As much as he wanted to, he no longer understood his own motivations, and that was a circular thought best left unexamined.

Listen to the woman of the house. Be a man, but keep your pecker in your pocket unless you're planning on putting it to righteous use. And listen to the woman of the house.

Maybe he was losing his mind. And maybe before losing his mind the void in his marriage and the lust in his heart had set the rest of it in motion. He'd been caught trying to put his pecker to use. The events of the past few weeks had been a lot of things, but none of them were righteous.

Suppose Laski's fair maiden *was* real. Had he meant the woman of this house? Alma? Was he to stay and learn what she wanted? She had obviously come back for her child, or a child. Was he to remain and do her bidding, to deliver her another? Was that righteous?

Or had Laski been selling a simpler wisdom, some marriage survival tip about deferring to the wife? Maybe in this version Jo was the fair maiden. Mrs Laski had spoken of this blessed house, and how God always provided her with more children – despite their lost ones. Was Leon Laski blind to the rest? Or did he just know the secret to keeping the ghosts at bay? Refrain from original sin and do right by your creator, except when your wife starts cooing for another child to keep her warm on those cold winter nights?

Maybe the fair maiden was both. Maybe Jo and Alma were two sides of the same coin. Maybe Alma was using Jo to show him a version of herself he would recognize, and one day embrace.

He was willing to be righteous, to embrace the woman of the house.

But first she had to come back.

He waited for all of the women to come back, but mostly he waited for her.

He moved to the bedroom, then the library. This was the place he had first seen her. This was the nexus of the house, the seat of her longing.

He sat. He waited through the evening and into the night.

His back ached. His legs were stiff. He was dizzy from lack of food. He wanted a glass of iced tea, it seemed, more than he had ever wanted anything in his life. But he dared not go for it. That would require a trip to the kitchen, and anything could happen while he was away. She might show herself.

Worse, despite his thirst, he needed to take a piss. As soon as the thought was there, it would not go away. He needed to go now.

He glanced at the window where her reflection had been, and stole away from the library. It was only a few short steps to the bathroom, and he flicked the light on as he entered. He sighed over the bowl, and flushed. He turned back to the door, but the window facing the back-yard caught his eye, and he stopped.

How many nights had it been since he'd seen his fair maiden out back, walking that path to the garden? The night he'd run outside, and wound up on Nadia's porch? He could not remember, but by the time he stopped trying he was already there, at the window, looking out. He cupped his hands around his eyes, but the yard was dark and he couldn't see with the glare from the light. He backed up and flicked the switch off, then moved back to the window.

His nose touched the cool glass. He squinted.

After what could have been no more than thirty seconds, his eyes adjusted to the night and he began to make out shapes. The walnut tree. The bushy pines off to the left. The slope of grass riding down like an ocean swell. The garage, with only the faint red glow. His snakes! Christ – he hadn't checked the Boelen's or the eggs for days now. But he could not go out there tonight. He needed to be here for her. First thing tomorrow, then. His eyes walked back up the path and were almost to the deck directly below when he saw movement. A shape.

It was tall, rigid, halfway down the path. His eyes dilated. It leaned forward, pitching itself at an odd angle as a young tree bows to the wind. It took a step. Then another. It was moving slowly, almost plodding along, leaning forward the way a mule goes strapped to the plow in deep soil.

She was dragging something on the ground.

A burst of clicking ratcheted up the stairs and Conrad whirled away from the window, his top teeth biting over his bottom lip, drawing blood.

Alice and Luther were standing on the carpeted landing, staring at him.

'Jesus Christ,' he said, exhaling. They were hungry. They had heard him flush and decided he was awake. 'God damned dogs.'

He turned back to the window, but after a full minute of squinting and standing on his toes to peer down, there was no sign it. Of her.

I was imagining it.

He returned to the library and sat. The dogs stepped around him, whining and sniffing for food. He patted them reassuringly and sat down.

'Soon. Soon.'

Scenting the foul spirit he carried, they gave him one last confused look and returned to the kitchen. He heard them scratching at the door, knocking open cabinets for something to satisfy their empty bellies, and his own growled in sympathy. After several minutes, they *click-click-clicked* their way back to the living room to lie in waiting on the couch. His eyelids grew heavy and he fought to stay awake.

He drifted off and fell to his side, curled fetal on the floor. Hours – or perhaps just very long minutes – passed. He doze-dreamed of the dogs feeding. Heard their frenzy as the bag was ripped. The tinkling of the kibbles spilling, impossibly, into their bowls. Were they feeding, or was someone feeding them? There was a long silence. He lost track once more, and slept on.

It was still dark when he woke again, this time to the sound of water running. He listened with his eyes closed, trying to trace the flow through the pipes, to understand from where the water was flowing, and to what end. The flow stopped. The sound of dripping – *plop plop plop* – continued for a few seconds and then ceased. The woman was crying. Soft sobs that ebbed and flowed over the course of minutes that stretched on and on. Definitely not the child this time. This was a mother grieving as only a mother can.

She was in another room. She had come for him, and she wanted him to come to her, to find her. She wanted him to understand.

In the hot night a controlled panic entered his bloodstream, propelling him to his feet. His legs were throbbing, and he grabbed a bookshelf to steady himself. The blood fell down and he almost blacked out.

Water. She was in the bathroom, then. He walked out of the library, into the rear hall toward the bathroom. His feet shuffled on the carpeted landing, swishing.

A dim glow was visible under the bathroom door, which was open a hand's width. Hadn't he left it wide open only hours before? He went to it and pressed his palm to the old wood. He pushed the door open.

The woman in the tub was sitting upright, hunched over. Her long black hair draped in strings over her shoulders and breasts, on to her knees. She was not moving. Her hands and arms were dirty and he saw the maroon crusts around the shores of her fingernails. She was no longer crying, and he saw no intake of breath.

The bath was shallow, its water a pink cloud.

She lifted her head and stared at him.

Her eyes were also black and deeply set in a pale countenance. The mouth appeared as a seam, the scar above running from her top lip to her thin nose, then opened, revealing small teeth. She was dreadfully beautiful. The eyebrows were thicker, grown nearly together and her eyes were devoid of color or emotion. He could feel her weight, her bone structure, her hardened flesh in his mind as surely as if he were holding her in his arms.

His words were hushed. 'What do you want?'

'There's no one here. It's just me.' Her voice was raw. 'There's no one here.'

He moved closer, weightless with fear. He knelt beside her, looked into her eyes, the dark circles around them. Her metallic scent enveloped him.

'What have you done?'

Her eyes were full of death. This lifeless creature could not be his wife.

'Our baby is dead. I'm waiting for it to come out.'

35

But of course it was Jo. At last she had returned.

He waited in the bedroom for her to finish her . . . bath. He sat on the bed and tried to figure when, exactly, she had come home. At first he had assumed she arrived an hour or so ago, come in, fed the dogs, then gone straight to the tub. But that just didn't feel right.

The bath drained and the shower started. The dogs waited for their mistress outside the door, ignoring him as she rinsed and scrubbed and rinsed. He could hear her sobs through the spray. He had never seen her this upset. He knew he was responsible for half of it.

'Where were you?' she had asked in the tub, in that dead voice, staring at him with colossal disappointment.

'The house. The house is haunted,' he said.

She blinked at him. 'Get out.'

He stared at her hands. The dried blood under her nails. 'I don't understand what—'

'Leave me alone.'

He left her, shaken by the change in her eyes, her body.

He was sitting on the bed trying to understand what

was so different when he felt rather than heard her return. He stood and turned around. She was standing in the doorway, staring at him with that same faraway look on her face.

'Oh, Jo, Baby,' he said. He walked up and tried to hug her, but she jolted at his touch and blinked furiously.

'I've been in hell all week,' she said, moving away. He saw the bulge of the pad in her panties just before she drew her pajamas up to her waist and let the elastic snap. She pulled back the covers. She hesitated, smelling the sheets.

'I'm sorry. I let the dogs sleep with me. Haven't changed the bedding since you left.'

He stood there useless as she stripped the bed and went to the linen closet. While she was away, he replayed that answer in his head – *I've been in hell all week*. Did that mean she had started to miscarry a week ago? Did it really take that long? Or by 'hell' did she mean her general state of mind while not being able to reach her husband? Something about the timing felt wrong.

It's your wife, Nadia had said. *She came home. I need to leave.*

Was it possible Jo had been here?

No. Not for three days. He'd searched the house.

But one day earlier? He'd seen someone in the yard.

Jo came back carrying fresh sheets and Conrad studied her. Something more was off. She was no longer wounded, just tired.

'What?' she looked confused, suspicious.

'Are you sure we shouldn't be at the hospital right now?'

'I've been to the hospital.' She moved around him, tucking everything in. 'You would have known that if you'd answered the phone.'

'I was worried about you. I wanted to help—'

'Help? You're in no shape to help anyone.'

'But tell me again. When did you come home?'

'After I left the hospital.'

'When did you fly home? Did you rent a car?'

'I . . .' Her eyes glazed over. She thought about it too long. 'When I left the hospital.'

Conrad's scalp began to crawl. *She's talking like a goddamned robot again.*

'What did the doctor say?'

When he said 'doctor' she flinched, and not subtly. He took a step toward the bed.

'Jo? What did the doctor say?'

She flinched again. She stared at him, unsmiling.

'He wasn't much of a docca,' she said.

'A what? Did you say—'

Jo blinked, rubbed her eyes. 'Don't come to bed until you're clean.' She looked away, then abruptly crawled into bed and turned off the lamp.

Conrad could not bring himself to stand there looking at her in the dark.

But there are few states of mind a hot shower cannot improve, and as the water washed away his stale sweat and he dug into his scalp to clean under his fingernails, a frisson passed from his stomach to his toes, forcing a comical sigh from his mouth. She had been through a miscarriage. She was bound to be a little off kilter. What was important was she was home. There would be a talk. Perhaps a reckoning. She had been through something awful. Like Nadia. But now Nadia was gone and this was better. It was proper.

But what about the baby? Was it really gone?

He returned to the bedroom and watched her sleeping, thinking of the first night they had finished unpacking. How he'd been so content, so confident their new life together had finally begun. What if the past six weeks were just an interlude? What if this was the real beginning?

He sank into the clean sheets, offering a prayer as he slipped into darkness.

Please don't take her, too.

His first thought upon waking was, *Mother's home.*

No. Mother was long gone, and father, too. Jo. Jo was home.

But not in bed. The smell of frying bacon permeated the entire upper floor, with coffee underneath.

It was after eleven. He could not remember his last meal. His stomach growled as he pulled his shorts over his underwear. It would be horrible at first, but they would talk through it. They would talk and talk until the air was clear between them and then they would discuss the next steps. Maybe he would look for a job. She could stay home and heal. They could try again. He brushed and rinsed his mouth, dug a tee shirt out of the dryer. He slipped into his brick-red sandals (the ones he would never be able to wear again because they reminded him

333

of the blood) and trotted down the servants' stairs to join her in the kitchen.

The bacon was black and smoking in the pan. The kitchen smelled like death and his stomach clenched.

'Jo?' He kept his voice at a normal pitch and busied himself by shutting off the stove and wiping up the grease spatters all around the pan. She liked her bacon crispy, but this was pushing it. 'Jo? Where are you, Baby?'

Predictably, the dogs came running in. He dropped some of the charred stuff into their radar range and they snatched it out the air and swallowed without chewing. He looked out the window over the sink. She wasn't in the backyard. He saw the garage. What had he seen last night, from the bathroom window? A shadow? A tree bowing to the wind? After finding Jo in the tub, it seemed insignificant. Luther sprang from the floor and shoved Conrad in the back.

'Where is she, huh? Where's Mommy?' he said, throwing the dogs more shriveled black carbon. He tossed the pan into the bin. He unhooked the trash bag and carried it to the front door and stopped, the bag swinging in his hand.

He glanced out the front window. Jo was standing next to the mailbox. Talking to Steve Bartholomew, good ol' Steve-O. Well well. She stood stiffly with her arms crossed over her chest, hair pulled back. Tee shirt, pink sweat pants, no shoes. Like she went out for the mail and got waylaid by the curious neighbor. The bacon had been burning; she had been out there longer than she had expected.

Steve-O was doing all the talking and Jo was just staring at him, looking as stiff and tired as she had before bed. Steve-O looked grave, but that might not mean anything. He always looked pissed off unless he was guffawing at his own jokes and pouring wine down his throat. *Maybe she's just tired. Doesn't mean Steve-O's giving her a minute-by-minute surveillance report.* Steve jerked a thumb toward the Grum house.

Conrad's heart stopped and then beat double-time, sending a branch of pain into his shoulder. Gail Grum was with them, standing to Steve-O's right and slightly behind him. The skin around her eyes was visibly red from twenty-five feet away.

'Here we go.' The trash bag was slippery in his palm, the plastic sliding through his fingers as he yanked the door open and stepped out.

All three turned to look at him.

'Morning,' he said, pacing off the path from the porch to the trash cans on the side of the house.

'Conrad,' Steve said.

'Morning?' Gail said, looking sharply at Jo.

His wife didn't say anything. She just sort of squint-smiled at him.

Conrad dropped the trash in and replaced the lid. He stopped halfway up the walk and looked at Jo. 'Do you want me to shut off the stove, sweetie?'

She did not respond for half a minute.

'Jo? The bacon?'

She jumped. 'Oh, yes, please.'

Shit, she is a wreck.

Steve and Gail waited, watching him like they wanted him to go back inside so they could finish their chat.

He walked across the lawn to join them, completing their square. 'No word yet from Nadia, huh?'

'No.' Gail looked worse up close. Her hair was uncombed and her usually gleaming smile had been supplanted by a tight, lipless grimace.

'This business,' Steve-O said. 'It's not sounding too good, Conrad.'

Jo shifted her weight and looked at him like she was merely an observer, not yet fully a member of the drama. Even though she knew nothing, she seemed too . . . not relaxed, that was too generous a word . . . but unconcerned.

Suddenly Gail dropped her fist from her mouth and made a small, eeking sound. 'I have to tell you, Conrad, I have a bad feeling about this. I've spoken to the police!'

'Okay,' he said, hoping it came off as calm. 'That's wise. What did they say?'

'Eddie is dead, Conrad.'

'What?' Conrad said, genuinely shocked. Not by the fact, but by the knowledge. It was out. Now things were going to get really fucking hairy. *Watch your step, 'Rad.* 'How?'

Steve shot Gail a look before elaborating. 'Dale Stuart, his floor manager at Menard's, called yesterday when Eddie hadn't shown up two days in a row for work.'

'What happened? What about Nadia?'

'Eddie's wounds are indicating a possible suicide,

though the police aren't revealing much yet. As for Nadia, Big John went with Sheriff Testwuide. They're looking for her now. In four counties.'

The air inside the square absorbed the charges coming from each, becoming electric. None of them had all the pieces, but each of them suspected something was off. If he let it continue this way, waiting for them to add up their suspicions, they would turn it all on him in one great zap.

'Jesus. That's awful. What can I do?'

'What did she say, Conrad?' Gail was as close to blasting off. 'She must have said something! I know you know something!'

'Conrad?' Jo prompted, suddenly coming to life for the first time. 'Do you know something about Nadia leaving town? Did she say something about leaving this, who is it, this Eddie?'

Why was she chiming in now? Where was she getting this bit about Nadia leaving town? He stared at her. He did not think he had mentioned Nadia trying to leave town – not to Jo. He frowned at his wife. Jo nodded, just a little marriage nod, the kind so small only a spouse can recognize it. *Go on, tell them about Eddie*, the nod said.

If you say so.

Conrad looked back to Gail. 'Did Nadia leave her cell phone at your house, at home, I mean?'

'Her cell phone,' Gail repeated, blinking. 'I don't know. Why?'

'There was a message from Eddie,' Conrad said. 'He

was screaming. He said he was going to kill himself. We heard a shot.'

'Oh, my God . . .' Gail tottered back on her heels. Steve took her by the arm and bore down on Conrad.

'A shot!' Steve said. 'When was this? Are you sure?'

'Oh my,' Jo said, which really wasn't something she had ever said before.

'It was three days ago,' he said. 'And I'm sure because Nadia played it for me. Eddie had been calling her all the time, screaming and crying and begging her not to leave, telling her to get out of his life, threatening to hurt her if she left without him.'

Gail moaned again.

Steve made a fist. 'Jesus! Why didn't you mention this the other day, Conrad? Why didn't you call for help?'

'I was trying to help her, Steve. I told her we should call the police, and she panicked. She said Eddie liked to play with guns and she didn't want to get him into more trouble, because she was his only friend. She said he pulled shit like this all the time, trying to scare her, manipulate her. I told her she was crazy and she better stay the hell away from him. I made her promise, in fact, not to talk to him.'

'Not good enough, Harrison. You're an adult. You don't play around with guns. You call the fucking police!'

'God damn it, Steve, I tried! Nadia said she was going to run away. She said if I called the police or you, or you, Gail, she would leave town and never come back. We argued. She cried about it. I thought we had reached a deal. She promised to stay away from Eddie and not go anywhere without me, and I promised to back off.' Jesus, he was really feeling it now! Could even feel Jo beside him, nodding, encouraging him – yes yes, more more! 'Maybe you shouldn't have left your pregnant daughter alone, Gail. I'm very sorry, but obviously you – none of us – had any idea what a fucking basket case this father of her child turned out to be.'

'You lied,' Steve said. His voice was quiet.

'She must have run away, Steve,' Conrad said. 'Nadia was with me. We heard the shot. He couldn't have hurt her . . .'

Gail was sobbing.

Steve was staring at Conrad like he wanted to throttle him.

'Oh, I don't feel so well,' Jo said.

They all looked at her. She really was pale. She staggered back, just like Gail had a moment ago. She turned around in a slow circle and vomited into the grass. It was mostly orange juice.

Gail looked up at the sky and wailed. 'What is happening to me?'

'Oh, for Chrissakes go home,' Steve said, disgusted. 'Take care of your wife.'

'I'm sorry,' Conrad said.

'And stay by the phone, pal,' Steve said over his shoulder, walking Gail back to her house. 'The police are going to have questions, very soon. Count on it!'

Conrad followed Jo, who was trotting into the house.

*

339

Jo was in the downstairs bathroom, vomiting again. He knocked and spoke through the door.

'Jo, can you let me in? Do you need a doctor?'

'No,' she said, choking. 'No doctor.'

He backed away from the bathroom door and walked back into the kitchen. He was still shaking when he reached the refrigerator and popped his first beer. The beer went down like he'd just held it over the drain until the foam dribbled out.

'Fucking Nadia,' he said, looking out the window to the backyard.

'What was that?' Jo said, coming up behind him.

He turned, surprised by the change in her voice. She had her hair back in a band, her face splashed wet and pinker, more like herself. She was patting her brow with a hand towel. The sick woman from the lawn party had been replaced.

'Is this normal?' he said.

'Normal?'

'You look better, if that's possible.'

'I feel like I just woke up. What's all the fuss about with Nadia?'

'She was just a dumb kid.' He dropped the empty into the sink and popped another.

'Conrad. We need to talk.'

'No shit.' He turned to face his wife. She was scaring him, and he didn't like that. He was pretty sure she was hiding something, too.

'Did something happen between you and that girl?'

'Tell me about the baby, Jo.'

'You weren't there. You have no idea what I went through.'

'You left me. You told me to stay home.'

'That's not fair. You're hiding something. If our neighbors can see it, how obvious do you think it is to me?'

'You're not going to tell me what happened to our child?'

'Not until you tell me what went on in this house.'

'What went on in this house,' he repeated, tasting the words. 'Yes, that's one way to phrase it. Another way is, what is still going on in this house? Still another is, what has always been going on this house, what is going to happen next in this house?'

'Was that a threat? I don't fucking believe you.'

'You should believe me.'

'Don't even speak until you're ready to be honest with me. And then you better tuck yourself in, mister, because we are in for a very long haul with this little experiment.'

She was angry. So very angry. But beneath that he saw fear, too. Good. Let her be afraid, a little. She deserved it. Coming home and giving him this shit.

'You are a piece of work, you know that. I found this house for us. I gave this "little experiment" everything from day one, and what do you do? You move out of state, for what? For some job. For some money. You treat me like a walking hard-on while you're away. You disappear, I can't reach you, some douche bag in your room, hanging around like the gay sidekick on a bad sitcom. Did you convert him? Or was it Jake? Did you let him fuck you, Jo? You know what? I hope you did. I hope someone got laid while you were away, because it wasn't me, and it seems to me like you really could have used a good fuck in the past three months.'

Patches of red crawled out of her shirt and up her neck. She wheezed, holding the back of the chair like she was going to keel over.

'Right,' he said, going for his third beer.

'How. Fucking. Dare. You!'

'You already said that, Jo.' He had seen this conversation play out before in his head so many times it was almost a memory.

Her lips quivered. 'Who are you that you have so much black rage inside you?'

'Hey, Baby,' he said, affecting a sort of jive-ass tone. Rollo on *Sanford and Son.* 'You knew what kind of cat I was when we got hitched.' He thrust his hips back and forth, fucking the air between them.

She slapped him across the mouth, lit up his whole face. He tasted blood.

'I am two seconds away from calling the police on you,' she said. 'What did you do to that girl?'

'I told her to get a life.'

'What did you do to that girl?'

'I told her to get the fuck out of Dodge.'

'What did you do to that girl!'

He sighed. His wife was standing ramrod straight, tears running down her cheeks.

'Just tell me the truth,' she said, her voice hoarse. 'I might hate you, but I'll at least respect you for it.'

'Tell me,' he said, a nasty smile curling his lips. 'Did you lose it, or did you throw it away? Or was it Jake's? You know, I'm glad you lost it. Now I don't have to raise the little fuck and wonder every day if he's mine or if he belongs to the talentless asshole who fucked my wife while I was burying my father.'

Something in her broke. The fight was gone. His tall wife was sitting on the floor, head buried in her knees, sobbing. He knew that if he wanted to, for the first time in their history, he could punish her. He could win. He could reach in and grab her emotions like apples from a tub of cold water and take them out one by one and smash them on the sidewalk. But she was already crushed.

After a time she said, 'I've never been unfaithful to you. Never. Jake was too drunk to drive. He never even made a pass at me, you fucking asshole.'

She sobbed, and in her sobs he found her ugly. He pitied her then.

'Joanna,' he said, his voice soothing, eerily normal. 'I'm sorry. This has been the worst three months of my life. I want you to understand, okay?'

She looked up. Her face was turning gray again.

'The truth is. I tried like hell to seduce her. I did. I was not myself, but that's no excuse. How I got here, it's . . . leaving Los Angeles was something we both wanted and needed, but something else triggered it. Maybe my father dying. I don't know. When I was seventeen my girlfriend Holly got pregnant. I loved her in ways you will never let me love you. I wanted her to

343

have the baby. She did too. We were going to make it. We almost made it. But her father. Jesus, our fathers. It's always our fathers. I'm tired of blaming him. It's my turn now, isn't it?'

Jo wasn't crying. She was just staring at the wall, stunned.

'She disappeared. I could have a son walking around out there in Portland, or Austin, or Denver. Or a daughter. I would have loved either one, but I never found out. Then I met you. And we have been drifting for so long, Jo. I don't think you wanted to have a child. But it's all I ever wanted. It's all I want. I thought this house would change things. It was supposed to be our new start. I should have told you about Holly. But remember what you said about your cut in salary, how I really didn't want to know? Well, this was like that. You didn't want to know. I thought as long as we made a new life of our own, it didn't matter. It was past. If you had been here right after we moved. I don't know. I'd like to think I would have been happy with you. I would really like to believe that everything would have . . . *healed itself* . . . if you had never left. Can you understand that?'

Jo swallowed, raising herself on coltish legs. 'I'm, uhm, glad you're finally talking to me, Conrad. But I think . . . I really need you to tell me now. What did you do with Nadia?'

'It's not Nadia. I mean, you can't understand what this house does to you, Jo. Leon Laski. He knows. He tried to tell me. These women keep coming back. It was a birthing house, Baby. It wants to be one again. If you stay, you will have another child. That's what it wants. That's what we want, isn't it?'

'Wait, are you telling me you tried to get into Nadia's pants because the house wanted you to?'

The anger was gone. He was excited. It felt so good to tell the truth. Now he just had to make her see.

'Baby, that's a very small piece of something much larger. Listen, do you think it's a coincidence you got pregnant so soon after we moved here? Huh? No, of course not. It happened in this house. And I know what you're thinking, but listen. The women in the photo – shit, you haven't seen the photo! Why did I burn—it doesn't matter. It's a healing place. You should have seen my hand. And the dogs! The dogs were all cut up from the broken mirrors. She was here, the woman in the house is trying to get out—'

'What mirrors?' Jo shouted. 'The dogs are fine, Conrad. Please stop saying these things. You—'

'No, I know, they're fine now. Listen. This is how it works. God, why didn't I see this before? You were pregnant . . . then you left . . . and then you lost the baby. Don't you see? Here, look—'

'Stop!'

'What?'

'Can't you hear yourself?'

'No, listen, this is going to work. I'm ready to be a father.'

'No, you're not.'

'But I am.'

'Conrad, listen to me.'

345

'I'm—'

'I was pregnant before we left Los Angeles!'

He gaped at her.

'I knew right before we left. When you came home and saw Jake there, I knew what you were thinking. But you just shut down. I wanted you to have time to grieve, but not like that. I thought it would be too much. You weren't ready. I wanted to be sure we could get through this. The way you were holding your father's money over my head, buying this house. It wasn't like you. We were supposed to do all these things together. Everything together.'

'You were pregnant before?'

'Yes.'

'But you didn't tell me?'

'I'm not pregnant now. You need to see somebody, Conrad. Oh, I knew—'

'But the snakes.'

'What snakes?'

'The Boelen's pythons. Shadow dropped nine eggs.'

'You bought more snakes? Why?'

'Because they are beautiful. I wanted to invest in something, and I had the money to do something I had always wanted to do.'

'This was your surprise project in the garage?'

'Yes.'

'Why didn't you just tell me?'

'You thought they were stupid. You told me to grow up. But I knew. I knew they would help us one day.'

'I'm not sure how keeping snakes helps us.'

'She laid nine eggs, Jo. A virgin birth. The house wants life.'

'Stop saying that.'

'It's true.'

'Maybe so.' Jo's face had taken on a vacant stare, after seeing his fervor. Her words became disconnected. 'But I don't like all these secrets. I think I should go.'

She turned her back to him.

'None of this would have happened if you stayed here,' he said. 'Don't you see that?'

'It wouldn't have changed anything.'

'It's okay, Baby. It's past. You're home now. We can do it again.'

She walked to the kitchen entrance. 'The neighbors are waiting for their daughter to return.'

'Jo, wait. She said she wanted to run away. I admitted I tried to seduce her. But I didn't, and I don't want her now. I want a family. I want you. Why would I confess all this and lie about the rest?'

'I don't know who you are or who we've become.'

'I'm the father of your child.'

'There is no child.' She disappeared around the corner, into the living room. 'There is no child.'

But she didn't sound certain of that, either.

36

He was hungry.

After days of feeding that girl soup and sitting in the library waiting for the walls to open up, he was salivating, ravenous, his thoughts honed to a single goal: food. He searched the cupboards and in the empty spaces he conjured grilled T-bones smothered in sautéed mushrooms and peppercorn sauce, bowls of creamed spinach, piles of hot garlic cheese biscuits, salad drowning in Italian dressing and chocolate ice cream by the bucket.

He grabbed the car keys and looped around into the TV room.

'I'm going to the store. Do you want anything?'

Jo was sitting on the couch, petting Alice, staring at the TV. The TV was off.

'The store,' she said.

'Look, we're not thinking clearly. You've been through a lot. I haven't eaten a decent meal in days. So here's what we're going to do. I'm going to make you a lunch you'll never forget. We'll eat, we'll rest. Then we'll talk. I promise, we'll do whatever you think is right.'

'What will I do?' She said this to the blank TV.

'We just need to eat first. You look pale, Baby.'

He turned and headed for the door.

'Tell me about the snakes again,' she said.

He stopped, came back.

'The snakes? I'm blind with hunger, Baby.'

'Where are you keeping them?'

'I told you they're in the garage. I'll show you the eggs later, after we eat. I don't want you disturbing them now. If the temperature drops even a few degrees, it can damage the embryos. And then it's bye-bye ninety grand.'

'Oh.'

'I'll be right back.'

He drove fast and the store was only half a mile away. Inside, he filled the shopping cart with seventy-nine dollars' worth of food, yanking steaks from the cooler like a bear pawing salmon from a stream. He dumped potatoes into the child seat without a bag. They fell to the floor and he grabbed more, throwing asparagus and cauliflower in with them. Bananas. She needed potassium. He raced to the other end of the store. Three kinds of cheese. Milk. Frozen corn, peas, okra. Okra? Fuck, why not okra? A Mrs Smith's blueberry pie, Breyer's vanilla bean. He was in the checkout line when he remembered the wine. Once they had some food in them, the wine would grease the wheels for the rest

'One second,' he told the kid in the apron punching the register.

The liquor aisle was ten feet away. He searched labels and tried to remember what kind she liked. White, he knew that much, but there was no such thing as white wine. There was Pinot Grigio, Chardonnay, Sauvignon Blanc. He had always bought whatever was on sale, but now he wanted to get it right. For her. All the labels had kangaroos and dogs and moose on them. What the fuck was going on here? Had some genius in marketing realized we see ourselves as cute little cartoon animals like kids with cereal boxes? He reached for something with a koala bear on it and changed his mind, tipping the bottle off the shelf. His arm shot out and the koala bear smashed on the floor, sending a geyser of sour juice up his leg.

'Fuck!' He jumped back, crunching glass under his red sandals. Gashed his big toe. 'Jesus Christ.'

'It's no problem,' the kid in the apron said, coming round to help. 'Just watch your step so you don't cut yourself.'

'I'm sorry,' Conrad said. 'I'm just trying to find the right one.'

Something in his eyes made the kid stop and look at him.

'I'm sorry. My wife is not well. Can you help me?'

'Sure, yeah, it's no problem. What are you looking for?'

'White wine. Just any white wine. But a good one.'

'Maybe this one? It's pretty popular.' The kid pointed to a large bottle with a gorilla on the label. The price tag said $14.99.

'Sure, that's fine. Great.' Conrad reached for the broken glass.

'Just leave it.'

'You sure?'

'It's not a problem.'

'I appreciate it. My wife just got home from a long trip. I'm kind of in a hurry, you know?'

Not much time now. She could be ovulating.

'Sure. Totally.'

He almost turned the car around when he realized he had forgotten the charcoal briquettes – then he remembered they owned a gas grill.

He made it home twenty minutes after he'd left. He felt like he was walking on air. His stomach had shriveled into a tennis-ball-sized knot. It was going to take another fifty minutes to prepare the meal, but it would be worth the wait. She would appreciate it.

He was halfway across the front porch when the door opened and Jo popped out, her rental car keys in one hand and a small backpack in the other. It was her old forest-green L.L. Bean from grad school, the one she used to pack an extra bra and panties in when she stayed the night at his crummy little apartment. Panties in the pack. God, she had been beautiful. And wild, too. Now she looked pale, haggard.

'Where you going?' he said, standing five feet in front of her.

She jumped slightly. 'Oh, you're back.'

'I have food.' He held out the bags for her to see. 'Some steaks, wine. You need to eat, Baby.'

'No, right, that sounds good.' She looked over his shoulder, up the street.

'Where are you going?' He thought of all the acceptable

351

answers: to return the rental, to refill my prescription, to lend Gail a cup of sugar.

'Oh, I just don't feel like myself.'

'Obviously.' He looked at her hand holding the strap slung over her shoulder. 'What do you need? Do you need a *doctor*?'

Again, on that one word she flinched.

'No!' She blinked, and he waited. Then, in a calmer but still pleading voice she said, 'I'm not myself, Conrad. Ever since I came home I don't feel like myself. Please . . .'

He took a step closer.

'We should work this out together, Jo. Until they find Nadia. It's dangerous out there.'

'I never felt like myself here,' she said absently. 'That's why I went away.'

Conrad waited.

She continued to present her case. 'I'm not mad at you any more, honest. I'd just feel better if I got some rest. I can't sleep here.'

'Oh, you're not mad. Okay. Good. 'Cause when I saw you come out with your bag over your shoulder, I thought . . . I know I dumped a lot of this crap on you. You must have come home and thought I'd lost my shit here without you.'

She was breathing hard, and worse, trying to not to.

He stepped back and cocked his head to one side. 'I understand, Jo.'

'What?' She tried to smile.

'I understand how you feel. But the bag gave you away.'

She stopped smiling. Her eyes went to his hands, to the bags he was holding.

'That's your overnight bag. You aren't planning on ever coming back, are you?'

'Conrad. Please.'

He saw her think it through, weighing her odds. 'Nope. Not this way. Maybe out the back, but out here you don't stand a chance.'

She slumped, letting her backpack fall from her shoulder.

He reset the groceries in his grip and took another step forward.

She ducked, clutched the strap, swinging wide and up. The sound of nylon against his head was a dull *whap*, but he felt like he'd been hit with a sack of grain.

'Ah, sonofabitch—' He staggered into the siding.

Jo darted forward, all six feet of her waist-high. He kicked his leg out and surprised both of them by connecting with her neck. It was like kicking an iron pole, felt like he broke three toes. Jo fell down, coughing, then she was on her hands and knees scrabbling about on the porch like one of the dogs in a way he might have found funny if some last remaining sane part of him did not recognize she was still his wife.

'Stop it,' he hissed, disgusted. 'Do you want the neighbors to see this?'

'Stay away from me,' she coughed, pulling herself up, rubbing her throat. 'Stay away from me, you piece of shit.'

'You're not leaving,' he said, idly swinging the bag with the wine bottle. 'Just turn around and go back inside so we can talk.'

She looked past him again, looking for a way around. Then all the fight was gone and she was just standing there.

'I didn't mean to hurt you,' he said. 'I'm sorry.'

She nodded, rubbing her neck. 'Fine. You win.'

She took a breath, looked next door and kicked for his balls. She missed, but connected with his thigh and wheeled, darting back into the house, knocking the door open as she blew into the kitchen.

He dropped the groceries on the floor and missed her shirt by inches as she fled out the back door. He pounded down the wooden steps to the yard, glancing wild-eyed over the fence to see if Gail and Big John were getting an eyeful, and took the deck in three giant strides.

She was making a beeline for the –

(birthing shack)

– garage. He realized that in all the years he had never seen her run. It was something to watch, all that woman pumping her arms like a track star. She didn't look back.

She can't make the fence, he thought gleefully, *and the garage is locked. She's fenced in!*

'Jo, don't!' he yelled, closing the distance.

She was twenty feet from the garage. Closing. Long legs, thighs shuddering like a thoroughbred. Fifteen feet. Ten feet from a nasty surprise – the door was locked. He saw the rest, how it would play out. It was like it was scripted. As if he had made it all up and now it had come to life. He could see the beats forming on paper the way he used to write them.

The WIFE, an attractive brunette in her
early 30s SLAMS into the warehouse door,
YANKING to no avail. Her HUSBAND,
disheveled in a handsome, dopey way,
gives chase.

She WHEELS, her eyes as black and large
as a doe's, then back to the door,
KICKING as if her life depended on it.
Which of course it does.

                    HUSBAND
          Baby, stop, just please stop!

                    WIFE
                 (shrieking)
            Stay away from me!

CLOSE ON: her SHAKING hand, clutching the
doorknob. It won't budge.

                    HUSBAND
          (deranged; paying homage)
        The dingo ate ma' bayyyyyy-beee!

The door would not open. She would be forced to turn
and fight him on the lawn. The scene would end badly.
How could it not? That was the rule of conflict, the stuff
of good drama.

But this wasn't scripted and, instead of finding the

door locked, she hit it hard with one shoulder and banged it open.

He jogged across the rest of the lawn, mindful of that first step before the door. No way was she strong enough to break the padlock.

Someone must have left it unlocked. And it wasn't me.

The garage was dark inside – not even red. What happened to the heat lamps? He heard fumbling sounds, a shovel falling to the floor as he pounced over the two steps down and he was inside, landing on the carpet. The sliding garage doors were shut and he could see her moving past the cages, searching for the handle.

They were trapped.

He found the light switch. The overhead Vita-Lites flickered and cold white filled the room.

Jo turned, chest heaving, hair in her face.

'This is stupid. I'm not going to hurt you,' he said.

Jo's eyes shot to something on the other side of the cages. Her face contorted and the room was silent.

'Jo?'

Her scream erupted, an inhuman sound. He looked around, her screams fanning out as he tried to understand what, besides her stupid husband, was upsetting her so. She sounded like she was being impaled.

He saw the cages. He saw the snakes, black and sleek. One stretched out across the branches he'd built into the walls of its home. Another, lower, coiled like a fire hose, its head resting at the center of the nest it had made of its own body.

He saw the incubator smashed on the floor, the black

vermiculite soil spread out in wet clumps, the leathery eggs destroyed, their slug-like contents oozed and congealed on the floor.

Somebody had sabotaged the eggs.

Oh, fuckers. Murderous motherfucking whores!

Jo was still screaming.

He turned away from Shadow's ruined clutch. His eyes roamed across the cages and higher, to the corner of the garage where the hooks had been bolted into the wooden ceiling beams, the rubber hooks for hanging bicycles.

A yard of cord came down stretched taut. There the hands were bound by the same black rope. The arms, stretched until the shoulders had dislocated, were bruised all the way down and into the milk-white skin of her naked torso. Can't see shouldn't see don't want to see the face cover your eyes don't let her see you with the black eyes. Her breasts were full, engorged. Not black eyes. Black around her head. She was blindfolded, and later, when he had time to process such things, he would realize that had been an act of mercy.

Nadia's belly bulged, and the gash ran from under her breastplate to the pubis. Her intestines were strewn about, leaving what he could only assume to be her womb, ovaries and the rest of her organs spread between her knees, the tops of which touched the blood-soaked floor. Her legs were tucked behind her, the feet like the hands, bound and swollen purple.

He was walking in it. He saw his red sandals merge with the blood congealed and so thick the skin broke

357

like the top of a Jell-O mold. To one side lay one of the stainless-steel gaffs for handling the serpents. It was caked with blood and more of her grue.

Our Eden.

Nadia's mouth hung open, her teeth exposed. His mind short-circuited and he knew that he needed to stop the screaming but he could not move. It wasn't only that she was here and cut this way. A deeper part of him was not surprised to find her here at all. It was more the problem of how could it *be*, her insides all torn out like that, strung in this tableau pose, when she had seemed so alive just a short while ago and now he could still hear her screaming, screaming for the baby that had been so callously removed before its due date.

37

As her screams wound down and became whimpers and then one long chain of suffering breaths, he used the garden shears to cut the rope. The body slumped cruelly on to its face. He used the dirty plastic tarp to cover her naked back and buttocks. He knew that she deserved better, but there wasn't time for any of that now. Whatever fate had befallen Nadia Grum was irreversible.

His wife was here. Alive.

Jo was on her feet, swaying. Her face was wet with tears and mucus. Her eyes were wide from shock and red, her skin gaunt. Her entire body was under siege, the cords in her neck like cables on a suspension bridge as the earth quaked and threatened to tear her asunder. Her teeth were literally clacking. He understood the next few minutes – maybe seconds – would determine the rest of their lives and possibly end one or both of them.

He took a step toward her with his palms up, and she jerked back, slamming into the metal garage door with a nerve-jangling clatter. He stopped, but left his hands up high. He did not realize he was crying until he spoke.

'Jo, I did not do this. Please, don't run away. I swear to

you, on the lives of our dogs, on my mother's soul. I did not hurt this girl. This is the first time I have seen her since she was alive in our house two days ago. I am begging you to believe me one last time. I did not hurt this girl. I did not do this.'

He was not sure she could even hear him. The way her eyes were roving around, he suspected she might be hearing him but not seeing him.

'Joanna? Joanna Harrison. Joanna Keene,' he said, using her maiden name. 'I did not do this. A monster did this. I'm not a monster.'

But did he know that for sure? The past weeks were a blur of nightmares and strange changes. Someone had brought the knife into the bedroom. Nadia had been talking in another woman's voice. Alma's voice. But she couldn't have done this to herself – this required brute strength. Was it possible Alma had taken him over, moved him to act upon her cruel justice?

No, he would not accept that. He stepped forward, reaching for her.

'Stay away from me. You stay away!'

He kept his hands at his sides. She began to shuffle sideways but could not bring herself to abandon the hard surface of the metal door against her back. She moved on shaking legs, inching across the garage, her eyes hot and accusing.

'I won't hurt you. Please don't go. I won't ever make you do anything again, but please listen to me before you run away.'

She had reached the end of the wall and found herself

in another corner. Rushing past him on either side would require passing within arm's reach. It appeared to be a risk she was not ready to take.

'Someone else was here. The mirrors. She came in and broke them like she didn't want to be seen. She left a knife outside the bedroom door, Jo. She wanted Nadia to run away. She said it was her turn to be a mother. Alma! She said her name was Alma. I've seen her. She keeps coming back for the babies. I don't understand what's happening here, but you have to believe me, Jo. I didn't do this. I didn't do this!'

Her eyes locked on him. 'K-K-killed her. You killed her. You're s-s-sick, a sick man. Don't move or I will tell on you. I will tell them what you did.'

She snatched a scrap of fence lumber from the floor. A plank of treated green pine perhaps three feet long and sharp at one end.

His legs buckled and he sat down hard on the floor. *Show no aggression, only compliance. It's your only chance.*

'See? I'm not. I won't do anything.'

She lunged from the corner and stabbed the wood at him as she ran by him, up the steps, out the door.

She's going, she ran away, she's going now, she's gone gone gone forever now – forever –

– unless you stop her.

No. Let her go. It didn't work.

And you're going to be in Hell eternal unless you make it work.

He was out of plans, but he went after her just the same.

38

When he stepped into the backyard the sky had turned from blue to a darkening gray slate. He walked until he could no longer stand his thoughts – *what is she doing, who is she calling, where will she go* – and then broke into a run.

He had crossed the deck and hooked around the back porch, halting when he saw movement down low. For an insane second, and they were all insane now, he thought the house was swallowing her alive. Her feet were kicking and shoving against the porch boards as her body was pulled through the dog door.

Then he understood that she had no other way in but to crawl through. He could hear the dogs barking inside, but it was a hollow sound, buried behind the walls.

He ran forward as her bare feet disappeared and the little plastic flap's magnet snicked into place. He tried the knob and indeed it was locked.

The gate. Why hadn't she used the gate to let herself out so she could run to the car, drive to the nearest police station or hospital? Was she going for the dogs, or a weapon?

He yanked the bolt on the gate and the wood

screeched as it swung inward. He ran past the garbage cans around the side of the house. He slowed in case the neighbors had one eye out the window. He was relieved to find no one in the front yard, no patrol cars arriving with strobing lights to take him way.

The insulation. You insulated the garage to keep the snakes warm. No wonder everything was normal on the block; they couldn't hear her scream. Yes, and you couldn't hear Nadia screaming either, could you? How convenient. You were the one who ordered the garage insulated, just before you lured the girl next door into your twisted fantasy.

Stop it! Stop that shit right now!

He came through the front door. The dogs were barking from the basement. Jo was bent over the kitchen sink, retching herself empty. Again. He closed the door behind him and she turned around, snatching the same long serrated knife from the counter. The note that said 'other mother must go' was gone. Her face was pale, her mouth dripping water and a yellow trail of bile. Some of it stuck in clumps in her once beautiful hair.

See what you have done? Turned your beautiful wife into a monster.

'Jo, stop this. Someone's going to get hurt.'

She stabbed the knife out like a spear. 'Don't fucking move!'

'I'm not!' He stopped behind the threshold. 'Your fingerprints are all over it now.'

Her expression changed. Some new wave of disgust that he would try to implicate her. She lashed out with the knife twice more, but she was too far back to cut him.

'What are you doing? Will you at least tell me that?'

'Stay away from me!'

The dogs whined from the basement.

'You had to crawl through the dog door, Jo. Do you think I actually remembered to lock up before I chased you into the yard? And who put the dogs in the basement? Don't be crazy. Someone was here. They could be here now.'

She opened the basement door. The dogs scrambled out, and he knelt before they could get a handle on the menace building between mistress and master. They might sense danger, smell blood and take up sides. If they did, he had no doubt whose they would choose. Between his six-foot wife and the hundred pounds of street mutt, he wouldn't live to see his way into a jail cell.

He reached for them. 'Alice, Luther, it's okay now, come here—'

'Don't touch them!'

The dogs jumped and pushed off her like she was holding Snausages instead of a knife.

'God damn it, put that down, you're going to cut them,' he said, stepping in.

She came at him with the knife waist-high, jousting. He sucked in his breath and leaned back on his heels. The knife swooped at his chest and the blade glanced off the doorframe. He fell forward and she brought it back. He thought she was breaking for the stairs, but her arm went forward once more and she put the blade into his belly as if she were trying to stop his fall. She jerked back and the knife was standing out of him like diving board.

'See!' she said, staring at the knife in him.

The pain going in was like a punch, and then it was hot, searing him. Conrad hissed, glancing down. It was off to one side, but it was in more than halfway. There was very little blood.

'Okay, it's okay,' he said, reaching for the knife. But when he touched the handle the burning shot through his guts and made it impossible to move.

'Oh my God,' she said.

'Baby, I can't . . . walk.'

Her face was a mask of horror and shock, and then neither. She remained still, a dead calm descending over her, into her. Her features slackened, became blank. She wasn't crying, he noticed. Not even breathing hard now.

The dogs whined, sniffing something new, and then backed away, growling at her. Conrad stared at his dogs, their dogs. They had never been afraid of her before.

Jo's eyes had gone cold, dead-black as they had been in the tub. As they were in the photo from a century past. He remembered the figure in the backyard, dragging something on the ground. He remembered how confused she had been about coming home, how out of it she had been until after she left house to talk with the neighbors. The change that had come over her then, as if something was leaving her. She had vomited in the yard. How she'd come out of the bathroom a changed woman. Ever since she had come home, this duality had been inside her. One woman fighting the other. The red crusts under her fingernails were not from her miscarriage. Now, too late, he finally understood what had happened to Nadia.

Jo had come home, and Alma had found a new home.

'Jo. . .?' He coughed, and the tightening of his abdominals seared him all over again. 'Aw, no, Jo . . .'

She walked forward in three halting steps, her movements stilted. Her hand was steady and she placed it on the handle.

'Comes,' she said, her voice grown much older and much colder. 'Comes the time Nah-dee join the red hair of fire.'

'You didn't,' he said. 'Please say you—'

'Alma turn.'

'Jo . . .'

'Alma git rid Connie's lil' whore . . . now Connie be righteous father.'

She was smiling. Mother of God, this monster inside of his wife was smiling. He waited, pleading with her, searching for the woman he had known.

She looked into his eyes, into his soul.

He inhaled long and slow for one last attempt to reach her. The pain was glorious. Her face was inches from his mouth.

'Joanna come back!'

'Noooo . . .' Alma's voice cracked, and he could swear then that she was still there, fighting this thing inside of her until the one that wanted to keep him alive lost the battle to the one that wished him dead.

And that was his mistake, because Alma did not wish him dead.

Alma wanted a father for her behbee.

'I won't tell—' he began.

Jo blinked. His wife saw him for the monster she thought he was.

'Murderer,' she said and twisted the knife once, ruining something inside, then yanked it free. Blood poured, wetting his pants.

He screamed but no sound escaped his lips.

'Oh my,' his wife whispered, backing away from him. She was still holding the knife as her eyes rolled back in her head and she turned away and stumbled up the butler stairs. The dogs followed close on her heels.

'Don't leave,' he said, dribbling pink spittle.

The pain was enormous, a star. He was on fire from his knees to his throat. Urine leaked out, hot against his leg. He didn't want to die here. Not like this. Not at all. Not alone. He wanted to be with her. He knew he'd been bad, but she could help him die. She could do that. And though it blinded him, when he focused and bit through his cheek, he found that he could move after all.

He began to climb the stairs. He could hear her stomping through the library. With the dogs in tow, thudding on the floorboards.

She screamed. Once hard and sharp, followed by a second scream that went off like an air raid siren.

He was halfway up when the second scream froze him on the landing. Even in his dizzy, searing state he was certain the first scream had not been his wife's. Jo's was the second, the one that was still going in a great winding wail.

The first scream belonged to someone else.

'Aw, no,' he moaned. 'Nah, nah . . .'

The dogs began barking furiously and he lunged up, taking the six remaining stairs in two steps, snapping the handrail free of the wall as he hit the second floor and tripped, sprawling in his blood.

Claws scrabbling on wood. Jo struggling, fighting Alma. More barking.

A hoarse, animal voice. 'Get out of my house!'

'Leave me alone!' his wife shrieked.

'Alma save the behbeeeee!' she screamed.

The thump and crash of dead weight hitting the floor.

He was on his feet again, halfway down the hall. He could see across the library into the slit of the other doorframe where she danced, into the hall where the black maple banister curled all the way around.

The dogs have gone into a bloodlust. They're attacking her.

He loped, his guts boiling. Seconds stretched into minutes.

'Jo! I'm coming.'

His shoulder hit a shelf, knocking books to the floor.

Through the doorframe on the other side he saw a flash of gray skin. The curl of black cloth. The dogs jumping, gnashing. Jo's pink sweatpants kicking out. The whole mass twisting, flashing out of view.

Falling . . .

'Jo!'

He made it across the library but the dogs were

368

pulling and pushing her in a frenzy. He had time to see the knife on the floor and her arm yanked back –

'Justin Gundry Justin Gundry,' the darker voice screamed.

– as she slipped from between the dogs and he lunged, his fingers missing her shirt by inches as she fell over. He reached out but his hips connected with the banister and stopped him from going down with her.

He was stuck watching, their eyes meeting for the last time as she arced back, her long body bowing as she tilted head first, sliding down in some gymnast's move gone awry. For the next few feet she seemed to hover like that, sliding down in perfect balance, the banister pressed into the small of her back like a fulcrum while her body made up its mind which way to go. Gravity chose for her. Her upper body was where all the weight lived and it sunk first.

The dogs raced after her down the stairs, but even they could not stop her momentum as she back-flipped head first over the banister and dropped the remaining ten feet on to the wood floor. He heard her neck. It was the sound of a sapling birch cracking in winter. Her body folded over itself and she came to rest looking up at him.

The dogs went to her immediately, whining and licking her arms and neck and face.

He stood motionless at the top of the stairs, then fell to his knees, peering through the spindles under the elbow of the banister. He watched the stain spread through the crotch of her pink sweatpants, her body releasing what it no longer needed.

But for the sound of the dogs lapping at her skin, the house was quiet.

'I'm comee, Baby,' he said, his speech slurred. 'I'm onna be with you.'

He was light, floating down the stairway to meet her. Would she be cold? Would she tell him what to do when he got there?

He watched through the spindles under the banister, looking back and low now as he descended, until, tilting his head sideways, he could just make out the top of her head, her hair fanned out behind her.

The final slide down to the floor was painful, but the pain kept him awake a while longer. When he reached the foyer he collapsed, and the pain sharpened as if the blade were still in him, twisting and carving out the important parts, burning him in a fever that left him wet and chilled until all he could think of was that witch in that movie, melting.

Now he lay in the foyer, looking up at the stairway, counting spindles under the banister until he forgot how to count. Now he lay here thinking of his father. Now he lay here waiting to die.

His dogs came around once, sniffing him, whining, and then ran off. Time passed. He hadn't seen them for a long time. He hoped they would be able to escape. Find a new home.

The bleeding worsened for a spell and then slowed to a trickle. He wanted to die next to her. But even this was not enough to carry him further. He was stuck on the floor, and his head fell sideways so that she would be the last thing he would see. He reached a hand out. He wanted to touch her before she became cold.

'Jo . . . Baby.' He could feel the words but not hear the sound of them.

He stared at her. The fact of her death brought its full weight on him, and he would have endured this pain burning him inside every day for a hundred years if doing so would bring her back. He was shivering. He shut his eyes for a moment, then opened them one more time.

Jo's hair moved over the floor.

He blinked, forcing his eyes to stay open.

Her body tensed almost imperceptibly. He watched, fascinated, certain that he had imagined it. A minute passed. Then her spine jerked, arching her off the floor, and her neck began to crack as her head swiveled. She rolled to one side and took hold of her leg, pulling it like a dead weight log across the floor.

She sat up.

Oh, thank God. Jo . . .

She grunted, and got to her knees. She fixed upon him with her black eyes and smiled. Her teeth were red and broken and she was drooling blood on to her shirt. When she stood above him another of her bones popped. Her lip was split open along her ancient scar, and her mouth curled inward with her first inhalation, twitching like an epileptic's. When she coughed her blood rained down on him. He was still trying to scream when she leaned over, scooped him up like a doll, and began to climb the stairs.

39

He was nothing.

He was a blank slate of consciousness. The night was full upon him and he could no longer see or hear. A freezing cold enveloped him, seeped into every fiber, every pore, until his bones became ice. Something responding to his need was entering his body now, and she had a need of her own. His deadened perceptions were being fed, ignited by the smallest sparks of memory. He tried to name his thoughts with words but clasped only sliding images both fundamental and meaningless. At last he succumbed and let her thoughts flow into him. They wrapped around the tent poles of his imagination and stalled the heavy canvas of enshrouding death to stage a play, filling the tent with objects and performers to weave the history he had been hiding from since the night he burned the album.

The first objects came in a blur, things between words and images.

Candle.

Sky.   Stone.

Garden.

Wet.

Gray.

                                              Doll.

                    Mother.

Doctor.

It's as if someone has screamed this particular word in
his mind, and in doing so left an exploding pain behind
his eyes. His eyes open now, seeing a world unlike this
one and yet eerily familiar, for it is at once artificial and
historic, a private vision granted in sepia. While he is still
not sure where or when he is – or even *who* he is – he
understands, slowly but with gathering force, that she
has made it this way for him. She is constructing a way
for him to share her mind, transporting him back through
time a century or more, using a muted palate and jumping, impossible Super 8 home movie-like segments to
help him to bear witness.

He is in one of the smaller bedrooms of the birthing
house, standing before a mirror. He knows he is here, but
he does not see himself in the mirror. The reflection staring
back at him belongs to a girl. She is four or five years old,
thin, with blonde hair the gold of honey, a yellow ribbon
laced through the gold in a bow. She is wearing a black
dress that falls to her ankles, and small pointed leather
shoes. She watches him, confused. She is saddened by
something just beyond the reach of their shared thoughts.

Then he understands. His eyes are now her eyes. He
is with her, a guest or a prisoner, he does not yet know.

Behind him – behind her – there is a heavy knock on
a wooden door.

'Come now, Alma.' The voice is deep.

At this intrusion, the girl in the mirror startles and turns, her hard shoes clocking on the wood floors as she runs from the room. The floors of the house tilt beneath him and the front stairs become a blur as the vertigo returns. He loses sight.

The Doctor. Again this word that is more than a word, a formidable presence that cloaks her every thought like a god. It is all he hears in the blackness, and perhaps it *is* the blackness. He feels as if he is holding his breath for a long time.

When the sun sends streaks of peach and gold over his eyes, he opens them again and sees a large hand holding her hand, feels its heavy grip.

The Doctor's hand.

The Doctor is pulling her along the worn path in the backyard. Conrad, what is left of Conrad and what has now become child Alma, is filled with her emotions – fear, hope, the oblique sadness. They are walking over the wet green grass of the magical place, the once forested land the Doctor calls in his tall strong voice *Our Eden*, where the slope of the land rides like the ocean swell down lower to the garden and, off to one side, the place he thinks of as his garage but which she knows only as the forbidden place.

Speaking either to herself or to him, her voice comes to him again.

That is where he takes the Others like Mother when they are near their time.

His instinct is to speak, but no sooner does the

thought emerge than her much stronger thoughts clamp down on him from inside.

No. Do not speak. Mind what he say, and mind what he do.
He falls deeper into her, becoming only a spectator.

They have stopped near the iron-gated garden where the raspberry branches and grape vines curl and form a lush green wall, and the Doctor's hand releases her hand as he removes his black hat and places it against his broad chest, nodding at her with his sad gray eyes. He is hard-faced, with rosy cheeks and a rough black beard. There are red lines in his eyes and tight creases around his brow and grim mouth, and she is reminded that he harbors an intensity that can change from love to wrath in a blink of those sad gray eyes. She is hoping to do it right, always hoping to do it right for him. The April rain has come and the air is cool, cooling and wetting her dress as she kneels at his side while he says the words he says here. She can hear his heavy breath hitching through the words. She feels ashamed that she is not crying too, but she cannot bring the tears to flow as he invites her to the prayer he gives over the small cross planted before them:

> *Aye, Lord above us the fallen*
> *Accept our humble offerings and bless us*
> *In His wisdom and the sacrificial blood*
> *Of our fallen family*
> *We shall bear this burden of the innocents*
> *Lost*
> *And give thanks for the life He brings*
> *To our blessed house*

Our place of commune and husbandry
To rehabilitate and shepherd the mothers
Daughters of Eve, the All Mother, all
Though we welcome them into our blessed shelter
And warm them by our hearth in their time of need
Forgive us, Dear Lord, our humanly trespass
Know thy heart remains true though these hands
Sworn to heal and serve
Remain yet frail and prone to the sin of temptation
We are committed to His path
Forever and ever
Amen

He realizes he can do more than see; he also feels what she feels. His chest aches for her, with her now, as her throat tightens and her little voice emits this one word, understanding at last who has been buried here. It is not another lil'un from one of the Other Mothers.

– Mother

Alma's cry pierces the morning. She is trying to pull away from the Doctor, but he will not release her small hand.

– Do not cry for Mother, Alma

The Doctor's voice cracks but does not break.

– Be still

Alma is sobbing and swatting at the Doctor as he shushes her repeatedly, and unspools his lesson.

– This is our burden. This is our light and our darkness and our duty. To have a life we must give a life, for life is a circle that begins and ends along the same sphere. In between the journey from one side to the other, the circle provides, and for that we each of us owe a life. The wool that keeps you warm at night is of the sheep, the roof over our home of the forest, the blood in your veins of your mother. On top of the circle is our Lord, and He commands us to take when we are in need, to give when our time has come. Mother's time has come, and she is home now, Alma.

Alma does not understand the circle now, but the time is coming when she will understand all.

The world cuts. He sees only blackness.

Then, as if she has blinked, as if the camera shutter has been reopened, they are back in the house and the Doctor – Mother called him Dr Justin Gundry – is calling her name from the front parlor where he sits near the hearth. The angles of the room jog as Alma comes, allowing his embrace, for that is all that remains to warm her since the end of the cold cold winter when Mother went away. Alma knows Mother was the biggest and most beautiful woman in the house and the Doctor's favorite. Alma knows this because she saw the love in his eyes and the gifts he brought Mother when he returned from his travels to and fro a place he calls Redruth, the place he learned his first calling as a mason, where he learned to build a house on a God-proper stone foundation with his healing hands. Alma calls him Docca Gunree, but only sometimes, for her words are few and seldom heard. Docca Gunree has built a fire and now he offers her the doll Mother made for her.

Playing with the doll is a way to bring Mother back, for a little while.

But already Docca Gunree is rising and Alma pretends not to notice as he puts away his glass and takes her hand and leads her down into the basement. Here among the stone foundations and the cool floor are the beds. Alma is crying, but one quick jerk of her hand is enough to silence her. She crawls as bidden into one of the cots he has arranged next to the empty basinets. Docca Gunree pats her head and pushes the doll into her arms before turning back to climb the stairs. Alma makes the connection once again with the doll, recalling how playing with the doll is like singing the song Mother sang for her, back when Mother rocked Alma in her arms and said what a big strong girl Alma was going to be some day. Back when Mother promised she would watch over Alma, always.

Mother is here now in spirit, warming her from inside, even though Alma knows Mother has gone away. Mother reminds Alma that she is a very brave girl and that one day Alma shall have a room of her own. Alma dreams of Mother's voice in all its clarity and sweetness, and when Mother sings it is better than any feeling Alma knows.

Sleep the dream sleep o' sweet child
Mother is here
when the sun she rises and when she sets
Mother is your home, the only home Alma needs
remember Mother lives forever, forever in Alma's heart
remember every day, o' sweet child

no tears for me does child Alma shed
thread through a needle cannot mend a young girl's
heart
Mother is here o' sweet child Alma even when
thread through a needle cannot mend a young girl's
heart

When next she opens her eyes, the basement of the house is full of Other Mothers who are not Mother, coming and going before Alma can learn their names. The women of the house, sturdy pale women in black dresses and boots and caps or bonnets, are growing in number, too, but they are always busy tending the lil'uns in the basinets while Docca Gunree works long days and late into the night to perform the Lord's work. At night, Alma can hear Docca Gunree's voice through the floor and the hearth-stone walls warmed by the fire all the way down to her bed. Sometimes the women of the house talk of the day with him, and sometimes, Alma knows, he talks only to himself and the spirits he carries inside.

– More of the menfolk lost in battle
– Filling the house faster than we can take them
– They call it the Great War
– Some of them don't wish to see them behbees, rather to leave 'em behind
– This is a healing place, we shall continue the Lord's work
– 'Tisn't time in the day for me to take care of any of them, let alone dote on her

379

– But Justin, Dr Gundry, have you considered, sir

– What will I do? What can I do? I promised her mother

– She must learn to take care of herself if she wishes to remain in this house

Comes the night Alma wakes to screams. A commotion tramples above her head, shaking the floors and echoing down through the rock foundation. It is the middle of the night and the basement is so dark as to be black, but Alma knows the way and she scampers from her bed, up the stairs, passing the lil'uns in their basinets who have begun to cry.

Upstairs she becomes entangled in a procession of the women of the house led by Docca Gunree, who is pushing a new Other Mother Alma does not recognize in a wooden chair with wheels. The Other Mother in the chair is thin and her eyes are ringed with black. She is the one screaming and in her lap is a blanket soaked in blood. The procession flows through the front parlor, into the kitchen, and out the back door to the yard, down the worn path to the forbidden place. Alma follows unnoticed until they reach the door and then she is shut out.

She takes up her position by the window, trying once again to peer inside to see how Docca Gunree makes behbees from the Other Mothers. The night grows long and Alma grows frightened by the screams that do not end. When woman of the house Martha Marsten finally rips the door open and crying flees back to the house, Alma chases after her.

Inside, Martha collapses into a chair beside the fire and clutches Alma to her bosom and sobs into her hair.

– He says it has turned, the healing power has turned, but it is him what's turned, turned to the drink and playing God

Alma tries to comfort Martha but she is scared, trembling.

– His hands, I saw his hands, so much blood on his hands, heaven help us, Alma

Later, when the women of the house return, the Other Mother does not come with them, nor her child, and Alma never sees her again. She understands the Other Mother and her lil'un have gone to be with Mother, that now they are also doing the Lord's work.

When Docca Gunree returns, the women of the house step away from him and disappear into the corners, leaving him to drink beside the fire. When his tired grey eyes fall on Alma it is as if he has never seen her before. He tilts his head and blinks. Slowly, a recognition fills his eyes and he sneers at her, showing Alma a naked hatred she has not seen on any face.

– You carry the eyes of your mother

Alma's eyes brighten at the mention of Mother.

– She understood sometimes a woman must give a life to have a life

Alma is too frightened to speak or move.

– Your mother gave a life to have a life, for you to have a brother

This is the first Alma has heard of a brother.

– But these are cold times and the Lord cannot always provide for so many mouths

Alma thinks of the women feeding the lil'uns in their basinets.

– He took your mother away from us, and he had to be sent away

Alma blinks at Docca Gunree.

– It is inviting evil to keep the lil'uns who bring death upon their arrival

Alma does not understand, but she is more frightened than ever by the strange light in Docca Gunree's eyes. She turns and walks slowly down the stairs to the basement, crawling into her cool cot, pulling the single wool blanket over her shivering body.

When she awakens later he is standing over her bed. He is a huge figure dressed in black, his suspenders dangling at his sides, his enormous head leaning over her, his body swaying. Alma can smell the medicine coming from his open mouth from more than four feet away. She closes her eyes and pretends to sleep as he looks her over.

When he awakens next within her she is on the floor, deep in the basement, digging at the mortar around a rock the size of a small pig. She is using a steel trowel of some sort, patiently scraping at the chalky dust, humming as it falls away in a hissing cascade.

She is standing before the mirror again, in the guest room upstairs. But now the little girl is as tall and lithe as a willow, and her once golden hair has taken on the wash of brown that goes unnoticed until it is much too late. Her black dress is different, a handover from one of the other women of the house.

Mother has been gone four winters now, she says to no one.

She turns from the mirror and begins to wander, following the women of the house here and there, but when she attempts to help string clothes from the line over the path outside of the kitchen, woman of the house Big Helen shoos Alma away.

She wanders into the basement and looks over the lil'uns in basinets, counting how there are only three now out of twelve, and she knows that since the Great War has ended there are fewer and fewer Other Mothers and therefore less work to share. Alma knows that the women of the house wish her away now, and she must be careful not to upset the order lest he shoo her out of the house for good. She walks silently, in many ways already a ghost, into the deep corner of the basement and uses her thin but strong fingers to remove the piggy from the wall to open her lair.

Inside, she clutches her doll and dreams of Mother.

When she awakens next her body is sore all over from curling upon itself in the tiny space which grows smaller with each year. She is shivering and when she places a hand on the rock wall she knows the fire upstairs has gone out and that she has slept through supper again. She pushes the piggy loose and crawls out, her large feet cold upon the basement floor. She climbs the stairs in search of sustenance. In the kitchen she finds a pot of cold soup and a scrap of hard bread, which she breaks. Alma carries her bowl to the front parlor and prepares to load the fire, but a thump from upstairs startles her. She thinks perhaps the fire is still burning in the belly stove upstairs and she carries her bowl up, up and into the library.

The fire in the library is also cold. Alma hears the thumping sound again and forgets her soup and eats only one more bite of the hard bread before she turns to the room Mother made so pretty. Alma walks down the hall and around the black wooden banister at the front stairs for the patrons. Alma hears a woman in Mother's room and her heart jumps as a rabbit. Though she knows it cannot be possible, for a moment she dares hope it is Mother come home and that the weeping sounds are Mother crying tears of happiness.

Alma opens the door and sees three women of the house who have grown cold to her standing in the corner, heads bowed to the leather table in the center of the room with candles burning from every sill. The Other Mother on the table is tall and her lustrous black hair is strong, but she is not Mother. The Other Mother on the table is crying in soft rhythms and sweating all over her stripped bare body. Even though the winter is deep on the house, the room is very warm and full of the woman scents Alma knows from the house but stronger than ever before.

Docca Gunree is kneeling before the Other Mother in her time of need and his glasses are almost falling off his large red nose. His thick black hair and gray-streaked beard are oily and dripping from his labors as he speaks in mumbled commands. The Other Mother screams louder in three short peaks and then begins to howl. None of the women in the corner turn to see Alma, and Docca Gunree is concentrating so that he is unaware Alma has entered.

– the Lord has blessed Our Eden

Alma draws near, called to the table as if she might at last understand an important piece of Mother's history. Docca Gunree's face turns red as he pulls and shifts his black boots and becomes impatient the way Alma has seen Farmer Mitchell with the foals in spring in the field beyond Black Earth. The howl goes on for minutes and Alma must cover her ears it hurts so much until Docca Gunree jumps back and the streams of black spatter his arms and face. As if by magic the behbee is in his arms and the women of the house run from the room. Alma thinks of the doll the way the Other Mother's legs collapse. Docca Gunree pays them no mind as he takes the tiny behbee in his rough hands. Alma thinks the lil'un needs a bath so that he – Alma cannot see to know if he is a boy or a girl, but she knows he is a boy – can be swaddled and set in one of the basinets to await the women of the house come to feed him. Alma's heart hurts when he cries, which are somehow small and very loud in the hot room.

– forgive us dear Lord our humanly trespass

Alma sees the blue cord that runs from the lil'un's belly to the unseen dark between the Other Mother's legs and Alma follows it up and back down, marveling at the connection. Docca Gunree's other hand moves with the silver blade over the lil'un's small round belly and he cuts and cuts. Alma sees the cord and Docca Gunree shakes his head, fighting something inside of him Alma cannot see, and Docca Gunree curses, weeping as his large hand moves.

The world cuts. But the world does not cut away.

Already the cord is wrapped around the neck and Docca Gunree is pulling until the small crying sounds gurgle and stop. Alma does not know how she knows, but at last she knows about all the behbees Docca Gunree has made and how though he says sometimes a woman must give a life to have a life, *this is his choice, not His choice.*

Alma falls back on her bare feet and bumps against the wall.

Docca Gunree's face turns to her and his tears are flowing with the sweat and the black down his cheeks. His tongue pushes over his cracked lips. The Other Mother is not moving or screaming any longer and Docca Gunree's red eyes are seeing into Alma until he knows what she has seen, what she knows. She screams and runs back and around and down the front stairs and deeper into the house, into her secret hiding place grown cold. Alma pulls the piggy in place and flattens her body against the wool blanket and holds the doll Mother made for her close to her chest and closes her eyes as tight as she can. She is careful not to sing but she knows the words and Mother's sweet voice is here in the dark and her warm breath is on Alma's cheek. She pushes away the memory of Docca Gunree's face and the black and the little face and lips when he stopped and cut –

Sleep the dream sleep o' sweet child
Mother is here
when the sun she rises and when she sets
Mother is your home, the only home Alma needs
remember Mother lives forever, forever in Alma's heart
remember every day, o' sweet child
no tears for me does child Alma shed
thread through a needle cannot mend a young girl's
heart
Mother is here o' sweet child Alma even when
thread through a needle cannot mend a young girl's
heart

– and through the song Alma is with Mother and no longer frightened, even when his boots come thudding down the stairs and over the floor and the piggy is loose and the cold comes in and his hot wet hands are pulling her out. Even when he is tearing her dress on the piggy and lifting Alma high and throwing her down on the bed and screaming over her and pressing his wet lips and the salt penny blood and black beard against her young skin and his heavy hands are scratching are touching are shaking Alma for the first time in many months as he will again for many nights in the next six winters which are for Alma the longest seasons.

*

She is standing before the mirror. Alma. She stands bare before the tall glass and marvels at her body, the strange power she feels building within. Her legs are equine, rippling with sinew and whiter than snow. Her hips are as dinner plates, sliding beneath her flesh as she twists. Her breasts are heavy in her hands, and she traces the mysterious blue lines pulsing beneath the surface like rivers flowing to the wide rose circles, one larger than the other, each aching with a dull throb she encourages and fears. Beneath her waist is thick delta that has grown as luminously black as the strands falling below her shoulders. She places one palm over the cusp of her belly and closes her eyes. She thinks by now she should be able to feel the lil'un inside, but his pulse continues to elude her fingertips. All the things Dr Justin Gundry has done to her. Alma knows she has given a life, but she does not have a life. Not yet. Or perhaps, as she heard one of the last remaining women of the house comment late one evening last winter, the things he has done have already ruint her. Perhaps she cannot make life. Was a time this thought brought tears to her eyes, but that time has passed. Alma fears not this fate. She does not know her age, but she knows she is a woman. She knows that Mother was correct. Alma has grown big and strong, and at last she is prepared to take a life to have a life.

Downstairs the Other Mother with red hair of fire is singing her gayest song, as she has been singing for the past three months since her arrival, since Dr Justin Gundry gave her the lil'un. Dr Justin Gundry has grown old and feeble, but his spirits appear to lighten in this new Other Mother's presence. Though the Other Mother with red hair of fire sings, her voice is not sweet like Mother's. Alma knows the night is coming, and soon.

Alma is standing over the basinet where the lil'un with red hair sleeps. She awakens at the sight of her, her shining black infant's eyes searching in the dark. Alma extends a finger and she clutches it with a stubby but firm grip. She blinks up at her, and Alma loses herself in singing to her.

She is still singing when the Other Mother with red hair of fire enters with the oil lamp and begins shrieking.

– Away, away from my child, Justin make her go away

Alma is standing on the porch feeling the snow blow in. The Other Mother with red hair of fire is shouting but Alma cannot hear her words. She is staring at the Doctor, who cannot bring his red eyes to meet hers. At last he pulls his new bride inside and leaves Alma standing in the cold.

Alma is pacing in the woods, stomping through snow that covers her ankles as she rakes her hands through the winter air, clutching and snapping at branches. Her shrieks echo through the dell and no one is here to answer.

– mother mother mother mother mother

Inside her, he feels the color of her mounting rage and knows it is a blackness without end.

*

When Alma returns the house is silent, dark, sleeping. She moves through the front parlor, up the servants' stairs, into the library. She walks on soft bare feet and opens the door to the Doctor's quarters. He is sleeping deeply, the sour perfume of his medicine hanging in the air. Alma closes the door and retreats. She walks back around the black maple banister to the delivery room where some of the Other Mothers gave a life, that which has now become the nursery.

The Other Mother with red hair of fire is sitting in the rocking chair, head bowed, with her back to Alma. The lil'un coos in the night before returning to her feeding. The lil'un is still suckling when Alma brings the blade through her mother's throat.

In the basement, Alma removes the piggy and places the swaddling child in her lair, making a nest of the wool blanket, adding another to ensure her warmth until she is able to return.

– I shall call you Chesapeake, from the place Mother was born

The child with red hair stares up at Alma, reaching for her finger.

– Sleep the dream sleep, Chessie, until Mother returns

Alma's arms are burning. She has grown strong, but the Other Mother grows heavier with each step. The path to the forbidden place stretches out into the frozen night, and the snow is streaked red with each lumbering step.

She leans forward, pulling as a mule pulls the plow through deep soil. Inside the forbidden place is a table and Alma rests the body there. Above is a rope dangling from one of the beams. Alma loops the rope around the wrists and neck and pulls. She knows the ground is too hard for digging, but tomorrow she will have to dig no matter the weather. For she knows the secrets the Doctor keeps and what bones wait under the cross in the yard. For many years he has kept these hidden from the rest of their growing society outside of the house in Black Earth. Alma knows there are men of the law who would come if she sent word and the Doctor would hang for his crimes, as the red hair of fire now hangs for hers. But she knows too that exposure would bring the house from under them and Alma would be lost without a home for Chessie. Worse, the people of the growing society would perhaps spread their judgment and take her Chessie away.

She closes the door and washes her hands in the snow.

Inside she warms herself by the fire. Her hands are stiff, and she moves them over the flames. Her work this night is not finished.

Alma stands in the hall, in the doorway facing the sleeping Doctor.

– Comes the time

He is slow to stir and so she makes her voice stronger, undeniable.

– Justin Gundry comes the time to join Mother

Her voice, after so many seasons of silence, mutes

Doctor Justin Gundry with a fear he has not known, but already he is rising from his bed. He is on his feet quickly, then hesitating, unsteady. Alma is forced to bring the silver blade to use sooner than planned, but she is not yet concerned. He lunges. Alma has grown tall and strong but the old Doctor is stronger. In the struggle that ensues between the master quarters and the hall where the black maple banister curves all the way around, Alma is pushed back even as she employs a life of hatred and rock-hard strength to plunge the knife into his belly and up, up, under the breastplate. He gasps, spewing spittle in her face. She rolls him aside calling his name over and over to place her judgment and for Mother.

– Justin Gundry Justin Gundry Justin Gundry

Justin Gundry the mortally wounded falls, but not before clutching his orphaned child Alma to tumble with him. Together they descend to the main floor foyer and the sound of Alma's neck is as loud and small as a sapling birch in winter. He is on top of her, her hand still clutching the handle of the blade, the point of which the fall has driven into his spine. As he breathes his last, his gray eyes bore down and Alma releases the knife to take him by the throat. She crushes the bones under the flesh until his gray eyes run to black and rupture as he passes from this life into that which lies beyond.

In the deep of the house the child called Chesapeake cries out for its mother, for any mother, to mend her young heart.

Alma rolls the Doctor off her. She cannot feel beneath

her waist, but she can move her arms. She claws at the floor and begins to drag herself to her lil'un. Her cries echo all around her, and she cannot find the way down. She uses the last of her strength to lift her head, straining like a serpent there upon the floor, until the cords stand out and flex and the last splintered bone severs under the pressure and there is no more pain.

Alma's body abandons its functions even as her spirit, this indomitable inside of her, lashes out for the new life it has always desired, staining the floors and walls and stones as it joins the Other Mothers who have given a life to have a life.

Child Chesapeake's cries go unanswered. She perishes in the stone walls that hide their secrets until another Great War passes and the new people of faith come bearing hope for a new life. Only then are the Daughters of Eve, the All Mother, awakened, ready to usher in new Life and Its unending need into the birthing house.

The world cuts.

40

Time became once again a thing he could sense, and the room smelled of medicine. He was warm, floating in a womb of weightlessness, surrounded by dim sounds and occasionally rocked as in a crib. He regained physical sensations of soft cotton wrapping his naked body, but still he remained heavy with sleep.

He was too weak to rise but in the darkened room there was warm flesh and the pressure in his mouth. When the cool button slipped between his teeth at first he resisted, but his hunger was stronger and so he fed. During the feedings he experienced the last of the visions that weaved her history, and he came to understand that he had been feeding this way all through the long long night.

The last he remembered was the fight, and chasing his wife up the stairs so that he could apologize to her. There were flashes of her fall that came after, but nothing beyond the stairs. He knew that he was missing an important detail from the very end, but whenever he tried to remember his wife's face it escaped him. When the pain in his stomach flared up like an umbilicus of fire, she would come again, hovering over him, feeding him, filling him up as he had filled her during the lonely nights. He did not know how much he had healed, but he felt better after, full of her.

The pain was still a fire inside of him, but he was driven from bed by the need to know. He looked under the moist cloth around his waist and saw the purple-black thread where she had sewn him up. He was able to walk, slowly, and he moved down the stairs over the better portion of an hour. He shuffled around the main floor and checked every room. He looked behind the doors in the bathroom and the kitchen pantry and in the foyer. When the dogs began to follow him he stopped to feed them and nearly fainted bending over the bowls.

He went down the stairs into the basement. He shone the flashlight on the stone foundation walls and stood in the spot where Luther had been growling and bleeding. He stared at the foundation and traced the stones with his eyes until they fell upon the one that was loose. He was too weak to remove the stone to see what lay inside, but he need not bother. He already knew what secrets the little piggy kept.

If there had been any doubt, it vanished. Not doubt that he had lost his mind, for he knew that he had. He had fallen prey to loneliness and delusions brought on by guilt and the emotional, if not completely physical infidelity with Nadia. But if any doubt remained that Alma had been real, as real as his wife, this before him ended all such doubt.

A single loosened stone. He had not noticed it when

he searched before. But his dog Luther had noticed it, and knew something inside these stone walls was not right. He was for a moment, but only for a moment, relieved at the sight of it now. Because it allowed that he was not a murderer. He knew he had lost track of time – the time between Nadia leaving his bed and Jo discovering her in the garage – but he had never believed he was a true savage, a killer.

But he was guilty.

What had Laski said about hauntings?

It happens to good people, because even good people got problems. And problems is what your haunted house feeds on, son. Just like a one of them payday loan stores. So it goes, and sometimes it goes to murder.

Conrad knew that he was responsible. Alma may have performed the ritual removal of Nadia's unborn, but what had given birth to Alma? Had he not fed Alma as he had fed Nadia? As surely as the girl's pregnancy and hopes were fed by his domestic duties in the kitchen, so too was Alma fed by his yearning, his desire to be a father. From his first days under her roof, he had left the door open for her return.

She had always been here, but now she was loose, reclaiming her place among the living and breathing.

He had to do something about that.

He exited the basement through the wooden door to the yard. The night was cool and he walked slowly down the path toward Our Eden.

He stopped when he reached the grave. The dirt was fresh, bulging obscenely above the grass. A small cross made of sticks had been set on top, tied with string, just as the Doctor had taught her more than a century before.

He was about to start digging when self-preservation kicked in again.

The Grums. The police. They would have scoured Eddie's trailer. They could have evidence linking him to the crime scene by now.

No, the authorities would have been here, and he would have come back to life in a hospital, or a cell. The yard would look like the site of an archeological dig, and the neighbors would be lining up with torches to burn the house to the ground.

Not yet, but they would be here soon.

He said a prayer asking for her forgiveness and turned away from the dirt. He walked in agony back up the path, over the deck, and up the stairs into the house. As he focused on each step, wincing at the fire of his wounds reopening, some trunk in his mind unlocked itself and asked the final question.

For the first time since coming back to life, he wondered if his wife was here too or in some other place, with Nadia.

41

When he reached the kitchen he saw that the living room was blinking with red and white light. His skin crawled and his heart tripped. The blood began to pool at his waist, soaking the bandages anew. He moved forward, swaying, and clutched the mantle in the living room to keep from fainting. There were no sirens yet, but through the front window, through the gauzy curtains, he could see the cars parked in front of the Grums'. The lights on top were sliding in flat rows, greetings from an alien craft.

He closed his eyes.

They knew you were lying, and they are coming for you tonight.

Another siren squelched, and then a woman screamed from the front lawn.

I'm sorry, Gail. I'm so sorry.

Elsewhere his dogs began to moan, and he knew they were not upset about what was coming, but what was already here.

42

He turned away from the windows and the red lights. The dogs were standing in the foyer where Jo had come to rest, whining with their tails tucked low. He heard footsteps above and the dogs began to bay. With his neck arched back he could see directly up the stairway and under the black maple banister to the master bedroom hallway.

Her pale legs moved under a swishing dirty hemline, her bare foot turning away from the posts as she entered the bedroom.

'Stay,' he bid them, taking the stairs.

And, as he went up to meet the author of his resurrection, they did.

THREAD

As he climbed the stairs he felt like a dead man reborn.

He had come back, but as what? His skin felt porous and his feet light, as if he were already a ghost, all spirit ready to flee the flesh. But this notion was brief and with his next step obliterated by the stabbing pain in his torn belly and the warm blood that still trickled from his near-fatal wound. In a panic he reached for his chest and found his heart beating strong, audible in the silence of his ascent. He had survived, and now he wanted to live, no matter the cost. Beyond that, he knew only that the house was dark and he was finally going to meet her with clarity and purpose. He focused on the stairs one at a time, moving slowly, absorbed in every detail even as one fated moment slid away to make room for the next.

This is my house. These are my feet. See them climbing the stairs. See them carrying me to where at last my love will be revealed. For whatever she has become, she is the final product of my love. I will go to her, and I am going to her with a heart only she can mend.

Seven stairs, eight.

Nine.

Tonight I go to her. Tonight I go to be a man. To do man's work.

Oh yes, I'm still alive.

Here at the top of the stairs are the walls and the floor-boards stained with the tears of childbirth. Life has emerged through this house and life has passed out of it. There is a crack in the floor and it is the crack of the world, the house's hot canal, forever giving birth. From the home we are born and to the home we return. All that lies between is the hearth and the dying embers of the fire that once burned inside.

Tonight we will feel warm again, together. One last time.

When he entered the bedroom it was as if he had stepped back in time with Holly. They were intruders in a home they had claimed as their own, owners by the rights granted new love. Candles burned from night-stands and dressers and ledges and window sills. She had remembered their night, and made it so that he would remember. She wanted to please him. And so that even in the dark of night he could see her clearly. He stood on the threshold of the master bedroom and studied her as she lay in waiting on the bed. She was his Holy girl on the night she had conceived his lost child, weeping for what they had done. But he didn't want to go back to the pain and the loss, only forward.

With that wish, to his relief, Holly was gone.

In her place was Nadia, the curve of her milky white belly glowing, a shy smile on her lips. But he had never loved Nadia, not this way. Not with the depths of know-ledge and sorrow the house had unlocked in him. Their common history and shared suffering. He had never known love such as this, because his love was always shifting. You love one with an intensity that can kill, and then she goes away and another comes to take her place. You grow full of love and then lose it and you shrivel and die, and then you awaken. The heart has needs and the heart needs the body. You change, adapt, and find love again. It is survival. This one you wed and declare the one, the final, the ultimate. But she dies too, and yet you survive. Your love survives because your love needs a home.

Eventually there is the last love, and then only death.

Nadia was dead. As soon as he accepted that without deception, Nadia was no longer the woman on his bed.

In her place was a long form, the full six feet of her, the womanly sway of her curves. The second chance that could not be. His departed wife, Joanna. The candles flickered as a summer breeze lifted the curtains and she glowed in the dim light the way he had always dreamed her waiting for him in this house. The way he'd imagined her the night after the unpacking, when he'd thought he was bedding his wife and managed only to awaken a much older presence in the house. He let himself study her as long as it lasted, but summer was ending and what wind blew through the window was now cool as the breath of autumn. The imagination has power but the heart has more, and when his heart desired the final truth it was granted.

All his expectations slipped away and he saw her.

His woman in the back row, the one who scowled

because she was not like the others. Alma reborn, at first ethereal and later, after feeding on him, corporeal.

Daughter of Eve, the All Mother, cruel as Mother Nature Herself.

Alma.

Leon had done his best by her, but his best had not been enough to keep the fair maiden at bay. She had taken her toll on the Laski children – a maiming here, a stillborn there – and eventually driven his shattering clan from the house. If *Our Eden* had once been blessed with life, then its history of darkly human deeds had spawned Alma, and its healing power now came at a cost. A cost tallied not by God or nature but by the goddess who still resided here. She had waited until she could wait no more, until she found one who shared her pain, then gambled on his need, his tired lust. Perhaps God or Dr Hobarth's debunked theory of parthenogenesis had been responsible for Shadow's miracle clutch of python eggs. But God's had not been the vengeful hand at work in his wife's demise, in the gruesome termination of Nadia and her unborn. Alma, who had suffered God and man's wrath too long, had long grown tired of the miracle of life. Alma desired only the miracle of her life, a miracle that produced life for her.

He understood now that she would keep exacting her pound of flesh until she was given one to call her own. If fate had delivered him to her, his longing opened the door for her. Each taking new life from their darkest couplings. She had fed on him, then Nadia, and finally Jo. Alma had fed until she was finally strong enough to claim Jo and finish her work. Tonight she had offered him one last glimpse of the other mothers – Holly, Nadia, Jo – and one final choice.

The ghosts of women past, or the flesh of the ghost incarnate.

He chose Alma.

She was raven-haired and tall and her pose was stiff, her arms and legs resting in the parallel lines of a corpse on the autopsy table. Her skin was not gray – that had been a trick of the light. She was white. Startlingly so from lack of sun and loss of life and blood. Her back bowed proudly and her breasts were large and round, with wide rose tips. Her nipples were stiff and, though she made no attempt to cover herself, she was shivering. Her sex was full and black, the color of her love. With his eyes he traced the curve of her hips, the familiar lines of the woman she had been.

He knew this body well, this body she had taken. What was once illusion was now a cold and cruel reality. The skin and hair and the rest of her shell was Jo, but the spirit, everything that was the soul inside and staring back at him, was Alma. In this house she had lived for a century and he only a summer, but to each it remained the only home they'd ever known.

Husband and wife, until death do us part.

Outside these walls, the car doors began to slam and the voices became a chorus of shouts and orders barked. Their footsteps pounded over the porch boards, shaking the front of the house.

Conrad ignored them as his clothes fell to the floor in

a whisper. When he lay down beside her his heart beat stronger, and he was not surprised to feel his arousal quickening toward the familiar. He thought of murder and revenge and blood gushing between his fingers as they sank into her neck to end the thing that had taken Jo and Nadia and the other mother with the red hair of fire and her child, but Alma stalled all such dreams when she rolled to one side and pressed her cold shape against him. He saw stars under clenched eyelids until she pried his fingers loose from the bedding, and her touch was a welcome balm.

When he looked into her eyes and saw himself reflected in the black liquid pools, his fear began to ebb. She had saved him when he no longer deserved saving, when all others had abandoned him. She was offering him forgiveness.

He pulled her tightly against him, wishing to make her warm. To know that she was alive too. He wanted to stay with her forever. As if to prove her vitality and further allay his fears, her limbs stirred and claimed him, rolling him onto his back to sit astride his hips. Her lips were firm and he saw the fissure scar above as he kissed her there upon her healing. He tasted her cool tongue warming, warming even now, pushing into his mouth at the same moment that he pushed past her slick opening and deeper, to the end.

She pulled away before he could taste her breath, or know that she was breathing at all. But her chest expanded as she began to rock, wetting his lap, and their hearts began to beat in unison. He felt one last spike of the blackness, the fear and lust and hunger for violent revenge, certain that none of this would last and that he would die here, alone.

His thoughts swung between two choices, as they had for all men.

Love and death.

Life and murder.

An end and a beginning.

The front door burst open with a thunderous crash and the men were shouting his name, ordering him to come out, to reveal his sin. The voices fanned out through the house and the dogs sang as they set upon the interlopers.

She took his hands, folding them in prayer. She held him until her warmth spread through his fingers but he clung to the darkness, the grief, the anger.

His fingers crawled over her breasts and along her throat and she moaned, reading his intention as if reading his mind.

Without slowing she opened his palms and slid them down, lower, lower, placing them flat against her belly, showing him his work, holding his new world inside her body until he could feel what was to come, what he had never felt before, that which he had been searching for since it had been stolen from him years and years ago, when he was seventeen.

The men with guns beat a heavy drum up the stairs.

Any second now, in a sliver of time, a span within which life might blossom or be smothered, the law would fall on them and its weight and judgment would be mighty. Knowing this, he entertained visions of cold courtrooms and colder prison cells, of foster parents for the dogs and endless grief for the parents, of earth tilled for burial and graves wreathed with flowers, all of them strands of a future flowing from this human contest to go on.

But those were only visions, realities yet to be born. Until they cast him inexorably toward such a fate, he refused to allow them shelter. For at last his home was full, its hearth so very warm.

Inside her womb he felt the affirmation of his power to create, the other side of the darkness, his only purpose in this world, his final beginning.

The stirring within, its tiny beating heart.

Soon she would be a mother, and he a father.

Acknowledgments

If any first-time novelist and his first-born ever received a warmer welcome to the delivery room, this author is unaware of them. To my agent and friend Scott Miller, and the entire team at Trident Media Group, your faith changed my life. To my publisher, David Shelley, you are a gentleman whose passion continues to astonish. Thank you for introducing me to the UK, and for your interest in the house. Nikola, Thalia, Nathalie, the two Emmas, Richard, Simon and everyone else at Sphere – you are all multi-talented saints and I owe you many pints.

To the citizens of the real Black Earth, please forgive my geographical liberties and warped perceptions. I know this ain't your town, but the name was too appropriate to resist.

Love Potions

Christina Jones

ISIS
LARGE PRINT
Oxford

Published ishing Ltd.,
7 Centremead, Osney Mead, Oxford OX2 0ES
by arrangement with
Judy Piatkus (Publishers) Ltd.

The moral right of the author has been asserted

British Library Cataloguing in Publication Data
Jones, Christina, 1948–
    Love potions. – Large print ed.
    1. Aromatherapy – Fiction
    2. Aphrodisiacs – Fiction
    3. Love stories
    4. Large type books
    I. Title
    823.9'14 [F]

        ISBN 978-0-7531-7784-6 (hb)
        ISBN 978-0-7531-7785-3 (pb)

Printed and bound in Great Britain by
T. J. International Ltd., Padstow, Cornwall

For Nellie Williams
(aka Nellie Pritchard-Gordon) with many
thanks for absolutely everything but especially
for allowing me to *borrow* her gorgeous Milla
for this book.

CHAPTER
ONE

Okay, so finding a naked man in her bed wasn't *that* unusual. There had been one or two in the past — not at the same time, of course — but Sukie Ambrose had had her moments. Mind you, she had to admit, none of them had managed to look quite so spectacular at this early hour of a grey and chilly March Monday morning.

In fact the only thing wrong with this one, Sukie thought, staring at the lean, tanned torso rising and falling in sleep beneath her dark blue duvet; at the rumpled streaky ash blond hair which looked glorious against her navy pillows; at the superb cheekbones and the curve of long dark eyelashes, was that he was a complete stranger.

The initial terror which had kicked in as she'd switched on the light and found an unknown man sleeping soundly in her bedroom, was tempered by the sheer implausibility of the situation.

All right then, that — and the fact that he was truly beautiful.

Not that that made his presence any less scary, she told herself quickly. Some of the worst villains in history had been extremely attractive, hadn't they?

Surely some of those mass murderers of the grim and grimy past had been lady-killers in every sense of the word? And how often had she peered at some serial wrongdoer on the television news thinking guiltily that she'd have fancied him if she'd met him at a party?

So was he a villain? Someone on the run? A fugitive from justice? A crazed killer suddenly overcome by the need to catch up on his beauty sleep?

Sukie shook her head. Doubtful. Not that she'd known any crazed killers, but somehow snuggling under an anonymous duvet simply didn't seem to fit the Tarantino image.

Mentally downgrading the criminality a bit, perhaps he was a burglar? A housebreaker, taking advantage of both her and Milla being away from home for the weekend, and making the most of the facilities before making away with their belongings?

Sukie somehow doubted that too. The sleepy village of Bagley-cum-Russet with its one high-banked main road, cobweb of tiny lanes, and one pub and two shops, was surely never going to be top of any mobster's must-visit list, was it? And she hadn't noticed any sign of a forced entry when she'd opened the cottage's front door. And everything downstairs had seemed untouched and normal . . . but then, exhausted after her journey and simply glad to be home, she hadn't really been looking for indications that they'd been burgled, had she?

She could really, really do without this . . .

Blinking wearily, she stared at the sleeping form again. He was out like a light. Could he possibly be ill?

2

Maybe he'd wandered in from the winding village streets having suffered amnesia? Maybe he thought this was his home? Maybe he'd lived in Bagley at some time in the past and muddled up his cottages? No — Sukie discounted that one straight away. He was probably in his late twenties, as she was, and having been born and bred in Bagley-cum-Russet, she knew everyone who'd ever lived in the village.

He really was very, very pretty. And if he wasn't ill, and was far too clean and classy-looking to be anyone's stereotypical thug, why on earth was he in her bed? Unless . . .

What if he was a *squatter*?

That was it! One of that new breed of upmarket organised squatters reclaiming vacant properties as a protest against homelessness and materialism. Oh dear . . . Sukie felt more than a little sympathy with that particular cause, but could also feel a severe case of nimbyism coming on.

Sukie stared at him for a little longer. He really was sensational.

Should she wake him? Ring the police? Scream?

No, too late for screaming, and anyway she'd never been much of a drama queen. And the police would take ages to arrive and then there'd probably be forms to fill in and lots of questions and she was far too tired to even contemplate all that. Maybe she'd just sneak back out of the room, lock the door on the outside and wait for him to regain consciousness and ask questions later.

Dropping her holdall quietly to the bedroom floor and holding her breath while she wriggled the old-fashioned key from the lock, Sukie switched off the light and backed out of the room. Her hands were shaking as she locked the door from the outside. Damn ... Too noisy ... She paused, waiting for the explosion, but there was no angry shout from her bed. She pocketed the key in her jeans and listened again. Still no sound at all from behind the door. Clearly the intruder was exhausted.

Not as exhausted as she was though. Driving back to Berkshire from Newcastle through the night had seemed like a good idea at the time. Her three-day course — "Advanced Aromatherapy: Essential Oils and Infusions for the 21st Century" — had ended late the previous evening. The delegates had been invited for a night out on the town, sampling every hot venue the Quayside complex had to offer, with the additional tempting promise of spotting premiership footballers and reality TV stars at every turn.

But after three rigorous days of studying, attending lectures, practical sessions and a rather sneaky written exam, and having already spent three evenings of gallivanting with several like-minded beauticians to make the most of the Newcastle pubs and clubs after classes, all Sukie had wanted to do was go home to Bagley-cum-Russet and crawl into bed and sleep for a week.

Not possible now.

Of course she could sleep in Milla's bed as Milla wasn't due back until later today from her hen-party in

Dublin, but maybe this wasn't a great idea with a strange man in the cottage.

Oh, bugger . . .

Feeling bone tired and more irritated than frightened — after all the bedroom door was securely locked and the window, centuries old and much-painted over, opened only a few inches, so the interloper was safely imprisoned for now — Sukie tiptoed downstairs.

The sleeping man upstairs had put a bit of a dampener on the usual sense of euphoria Sukie normally felt on returning to the strangely named Pixies Laughter Cottage. It was her sanctuary, truly her home, a place she loved with all her heart.

She'd always hated having her cherished space invaded, and having it invaded by a naked stranger had thrown her completely. And, she thought with a weary grin, what on earth would her godmother have made of it all?

Cora, Sukie's maternal great-aunt and godmother, had lived all her higgledy-piggledy life in Pixies Laughter. Sukie had adored the elderly, eccentric Cora and spent an idyllic childhood with her in the low-beamed rooms, snuggled up in front of the log fire in the winter, playing wild games in the garden through long hot summers.

When Sukie's aspirational parents, living on the other side of the village in their up-to-the-minute stylised and clinically neat modern estate semi, had inherited the cottage they'd immediately planned to modernise it and sell it at some exorbitant sum to incomers.

5

Horrified at the thought of losing Cora's home, her happy memories and her childhood bolt hole, Sukie had begged, pleaded and eventually convinced her parents that she'd be the ideal owner for Pixies Laughter. After much wrangling a price had been agreed — nowhere near as high as the Ambroses would have managed to extort from strangers — and Sukie, having convinced the bank that she'd be a great mortgage risk, had moved in. The modernisations — central heating and a bathroom — had eaten into her savings and a further bank loan and more, and her parents had refused to help on the grounds that if Sukie wanted the cottage so badly she took it warts and all and paid dearly for the privilege. So a year previously she'd taken Milla in as a lodger to ease the financial burden.

The whole thing had caused a few ructions at the time, but feathers were now more or less smoothed down . . . However, Sukie's parents' visits to Pixies Laughter were few and far between despite only living less than a mile away, and Sukie's visits home to the minimalist semi were equally rare.

Sad, really, she thought now, as she ducked under the lowest beam at the foot of the stairs, that she hadn't immediately thought of ringing her parents for advice on the current situation. Apart from the fact that they'd be extremely annoyed at being woken up before dawn, they'd probably feel it was her fault somehow and would trot out trite and irritating lines like "you made your bed when you took the cottage on — if you've got a problem you've only yourself to blame".

6

Nah, she'd deal with sleeping beauty on her own and in her own time, Sukie thought, clattering across the uneven hall floor. The central heating was humming gently, and in the tiny brightly-lit kitchen, Sukie did what any girl would do under the circumstances. She put the kettle on.

She was just scrabbling in the dishwasher for a clean mug when the kitchen door opened.

She screamed and dropped the mug on the ancient quarry tiles. The bits skittered across the floor.

"What the hell are you doing here?" Milla, her cottage-mate, tall, slender and blonde, wearing a very skimpy T-shirt and a black thong, blinked from the doorway.

"I could ask you the same thing," Sukie snapped, rescuing the broken mug from under the table and wondering how come Milla always managed to look so perfectly groomed and glamorous even when she'd just woken up. "Why aren't you in Dublin? I didn't see your car in the lane."

"Caught an earlier flight. Still a bit tipsy. Didn't want to drive. Left the car at the airport and got a cab." Milla gave an elegant yawn. "Collecting it later. Why aren't you in Newcastle?"

"Couldn't stand the pace. And — there's a problem."

"What?" Milla flicked back her bone-straight silver hair and reached a slender hand into the dishwasher for two mugs. "What sort of problem?"

"We've got an intruder. Upstairs. In my bed."

7

Milla handed her mug to Sukie and laughed. "He's not an intruder. He's with me."

Sukie sighed heavily. She really should have guessed. Milla was always careless with her men. She'd once left one at a taxi rank in Reading while she nipped off to find a loo after a night out clubbing and completely forgotten about him. Rumour had it that the poor sap had still been standing there forlornly waiting as dawn broke.

"I should have guessed, I suppose. But couldn't you have labelled him or something? Like Paddington Bear: 'Milla's Man — Please Don't Touch'? Anything to indicate that he wasn't a threat? And why —" Sukie wearily spooned granules into the mugs, "— is he in my bed, not yours? And who is he?"

"Whoa! Far too many questions! Anyway, I've no idea about the last one —" Milla perched on the edge of one of the oddment kitchen chairs crossing her long perfectly shaped legs, "— which is the answer to why he's not in my bed. Even I'm not that shallow. I do like to be on least first name terms before I offer B&B. Thanks." She took the coffee. "No, honestly, we only met last night. At the airport: Waiting for a taxi. I didn't even see him on the plane. He'd been to Dublin with a stag-party. He was about as hung-over as me so he decided not to drive home either, and while we were chatting in the queue I discovered he came from Winterbrook so we shared a cab."

Sukie raised her eyebrows. The relief was short-lived. Even for Milla it seemed a bit unlikely, not to mention downright risky.

8

"And you didn't ask his name? What he does for a living? Like murder, rape, pillage? Chatting up blondes in taxi queues with the intention of relieving them of their worldly goods and their bank accounts and maybe their breathing?"

"Sukie, sweetheart." Milla shook her head. "You read far, far too many tabloids. He was just a fellow-traveller in need of a good turn."

Sukie slid onto the opposite chair. "Not good enough. Why is he here? Why didn't he stay in the cab and go on to Winterbrook? It's only a few miles away."

Milla smiled her sleepy-cat green-eyed smile. Sukie, who was of average height, curvy, with short, dark, spiky hair and blue eyes, sighed. She'd kill to look like Milla.

"He was sound asleep by the time we got here," Milla lit a cigarette. "Out cold. The taxi driver didn't want the hassle of unloading him single-handed at Winterbrook so he turfed us both out here. Poor bloke was almost asleep on his feet and I knew you wouldn't be back, so I gave him your room."

"Wasn't that a bit risky? You didn't even know him?"

Milla blew smoke towards the ceiling. "Like I said, he was practically comatose. And the cab driver legged it. I could hardly leave him outside in the lane, could I? So I woke him up, made him a cup of coffee which he didn't drink, pointed him towards your room and well, that's it really . . ." She stubbed out the cigarette. "And he is rather cute, isn't he?"

"Very." Sukie sipped her coffee. "And I should have realised he wasn't one of yours anyway. He's got a chin."

"Bitchy . . ." Milla stretched showing most of her slender toned midriff, then yawned again, still managing to make it look endearingly attractive. "I don't *always* date chinless wonders."

"Yeah you do. Well, when you're not dating city traders with sharp suits, sharper tongues and estuary accents."

"A girl has to maintain her standards," Milla shrugged. "You can't support my lifestyle on a labourer's wage packet, sweetie, as I keep pointing out to you."

Sukie winced. It still didn't solve the problem of the stranger upstairs in her bed and the fact that she had probably never felt so tired in her entire life.

"So — how were you and him going to get back to the airport to collect your cars? Oh no — don't look at me like that. I am not — not — driving you all the way to — good lord!"

A thundering crash from upstairs rocked the cottage to its centuries-old foundations.

"I think he's awake." Milla frowned at the ceiling. "Probably needs the loo. He doesn't sound very happy."

"No." Sukie bit her lip. "He wouldn't. I locked him in."

"You did *what?*" Milla shrieked with laughter. "Sukes, you're priceless! Then you'd better go and unlock him, hadn't you? And point him in the direction of the bathroom pretty damn quickly."

By the time Sukie reached the top of the narrow winding staircase, the man was pounding on her bedroom door. She unlocked it and stood back, screwing up her eyes in case he was stark naked.

He wasn't. Well not completely. He'd managed to pull on a pair of faded jeans, which did absolutely nothing to detract from the stunning rest of him.

"Thanks," he blinked at her through the long strands of ash blond hair. "Door seemed to have stuck and I walked straight into those bloody beams. Does this place belong to the seven dwarves or something? Er — sorry, but where's the loo? Please?"

"Bathroom's along the passage. End door. And mind the beams."

"Thanks." He gave a weary, bleary smile. "Er — do I know you?"

Sukie shook her head. "Nope. And I'm not Snow White either. But this is my cottage."

"Is it?" He looked confused. "Were you on the plane last night, then? I thought —"

"No, that was my taller, thinner, prettier, blonder friend."

"Oh, right — sorry — but I must . . ."

Sukie stood aside as he pounded along the passage.

"All okay?" Milla appeared at the top of the stairs. "Is he in the loo? Good — I'm going back to bed, Sukes. Catch you later . . ."

Sukie sighed as Milla slammed into her bedroom, then casting one last lingering look at the cosy invitation of her own bed, dragged a blanket from the airing cupboard and trudged wearily downstairs to catch up on her beauty sleep on the sofa.

CHAPTER
TWO

"And so you slept on the sofa and he'd gone when you woke up, had he?" Jennifer Blessing raised perfectly arched eyebrows at Sukie later that day in the peaches and cream draped splendour of Beauty's Blessings on Hazy Hassocks High Street. "And I bet Milla had disappeared too."

"Yep. Hopefully still living and breathing and not dragged over the quarry tiles to be buried in a shallow grave." Sukie, struggling untidily into her peach overall, nodded at her boss. "And I'm still fuzzy-headed from too little sleep, so can we possibly leave the rest of the cross-examination until later, please?"

"Cross-examination? You make me sound like a nosy old bag." Jennifer frowned but not very fiercely. Botox for Beginners had had a radical effect on her forehead. "I'm just a concerned employer, that's all."

Yeah, right, Sukie thought, feeling achy and scratchy and still irritated. She'd had a maximum four uncomfortable and restless hours on the sofa, and hadn't known whether to be pleased, concerned or annoyed that Pixies Laughter Cottage had been empty when she'd woken up.

Still, there'd been no signs of violence, and on the plus side it at least meant Milla and the nameless sex god had made other arrangements about collecting their cars from the airport, and someone — probably not Milla — had stripped her bed, remade it with fresh linen and even put her navy blue duvet cover, sheet and pillowcases into the washing machine.

If Mr Blond and Beautiful was a serial killer, he was a very domesticated one. Which meant, of course, that he could be married. Or seriously attached. Or maybe even . . .

"You did enjoy the aromatherapy course, though?" Jennifer interrupted Sukie's runaway train of thought. "I realise it pales into insignificance compared with coming home to find a naked man in your bed, but it cost a lot of money and —"

"It was great," Sukie yawned. "Oh, sorry. No, I loved it. Learned loads. Until this morning I was bursting with enthusiasm, couldn't wait to put it into practice and I will be again, promise. I just need to sleep for a week and wake up properly first."

"Good, lovely — I'm really pleased you got such a lot out of it." Jennifer batted her newly enhanced eyelashes. "Because you're a natural masseuse and I think offering this mobile service will really put us on the map. No other salons round here do home treatments, and those experimental ones we tried out round the villages last year went down well, didn't they?"

Sukie nodded. They had. Probably because they'd been free. The most unlikely people from Hazy

14

Hassocks, Bagley-cum-Russet and Fiddlesticks had volunteered for lip-filling and head massages and pedicures with the usual rural enthusiasm of getting something for nothing even if they didn't want it.

Jennifer patted her dark red hair in one of the peach-lit mirrors. "We'll go through the oils and fragrances you'll need later. My suppliers can get hold of any new stuff, then hopefully you'll be out on the road by next week. I've already had several enquiries after that splash in the *Winterbrook Advertiser*." She stopped patting and preening and peered at Sukie again. "Oh, sorry to keep on about work. You poor thing — you know I wasn't really expecting you to come in today anyway — and you do look awful . . ."

"Thanks."

"I'll make some more coffee, shall I? See if that helps?"

Doubting that anything would help apart from sleep, sleep and more sleep, Sukie nodded gratefully as Jennifer whispered away in her own slinky overall towards Beauty's Blessings' tiny kitchenette.

The cold March morning had lengthened into a cold grey afternoon, and not even the warm tones and even warmer scents wafting round the salon could lift Sukie's flagging spirits. Lamps glowed under peach shades, and Classic FM murmured tastefully in the background. Jennifer, Sukie knew, had poured her heart and soul, not to mention a fair whack of her husband Lance's hard-earned money, into the salon which was doing well, but somehow they both doubted if bucolic Berkshire was ever going to be quite ready for eyebrow threading, caviar facials, chocolate body wraps or even chemical derma-peels.

However, since Beauty's Blessings had opened the previous summer, the trade for basic facials and manicures had been steady, and thanks to a concerted leaflet-drop after Christmas, the massages and non-surgical face-lifts were becoming quite popular, but Jennifer was still keen to build the business further, hence the one-to-one home aromatherapy service.

This mobile expansion, Sukie realised, was mainly due to Mitzi, the first Mrs Blessing, having made such a stonking success of her Hubble Bubble Country Cooking outlet at the other end of Hazy Hassocks High Street. Jennifer, the second Mrs Blessing, was nothing if not violently competitive on all fronts.

Beauty's Blessings was housed in a flint and slate ex-cottage next door to Hazy Hassocks Dental Surgery, which had caused a bit of soul-searching for Jennifer as Mitzi's gorgeous, much younger, live-in dentist lover worked there, and this was originally considered a little close for comfort. However, although the location certainly hadn't been Jennifer's first choice, at the moment the relationship between the Mrs Blessings Mark One and Two was reasonably civilised, and as long as no one mentioned Mitzi's entrepreneurial skills on Jennifer's premises the two businesses blossomed in relative harmony.

A couple of hundred years ago Beauty's Blessings had probably housed a family of seventeen, and according to the more elderly residents it had had a chequered history once it had moved into commercialism. It had enjoyed life as a cobbler's early in the twentieth century, then in rapid succession an engraver's, a sweet shop, a dress shop, an estate agent's, a charity shop twice, followed by its most recent incarnation as a juice bar.

Sadly Hazy Hassocks simply hadn't known what to do with a juice bar and it had closed within six months.

As soon as Mitzi had opened, and made a success of, Hubble Bubble at the other end of the High Street, Jennifer had persuaded Lance to back her to fly solo too. Fortunately Lance ran a small building business so the extensive renovations on the defunct Juicy Lucy's hadn't been as costly as they might have been. Before Lance had been allowed to alter anything though, Jennifer had toured various Berkshire salons, attended trade fairs, consulted all the style magazines, checked with colourists, and ordered all the latest equipment, with the result that Beauty's Blessings now offered the most opulent and luxurious and up-to-date surroundings in the area.

Sukie lifted one of the filmy peach drapes and peered out of the window. Everywhere looked very grey and cheerlessly cold. Shoppers hurried past en route to Big Sava, heads down against the wind, their noses the only splash of colour in the uniform beigeness of their bobble-hat-to-bootee attire. Maybe it would snow, Sukie thought. She hoped so. Hazy Hassocks looked much prettier when it snowed.

Hazy Hassocks, with its winding sycamore-lined High Street filled with a mish-mash of shops and small businesses, was a large village a few miles away from Sukie's home in Bagley-cum-Russet. It was where the Bagleyites, and the Fiddlestickers from the neighbouring hamlet, did most of their shopping and socialising. Winterbrook, the nearest market town, offered larger supermarkets and banks and other municipal delights, while Reading was regarded as Up Town and reserved for shopping sprees of mega-proportions.

If the Romans had bothered themselves with this part of the county instead of concentrating their efforts on the Ridgeway, then the villages would all be within a few minutes' travelling distance of one another. As it was, the lanes twisted and turned back on themselves in convoluted loops, and while they looked only centimetres apart on the map, the reality was very different.

Jennifer had used the complex local geography to cash in on the beauty business. There were no rival rural establishments for miles.

"Thanks, Jennifer. You're an angel." Sukie took the coffee gratefully. "And as the junior here I should be making coffee. And sweeping up and washing the towels and —"

Jennifer laughed as much as her eye-lift would allow. "If the aromatherapy takes off we'll be able to employ a proper junior for those jobs. I was thinking of asking Winterbrook FE college if they'd like me to take some of their final year beauty students on day-release. And we won't have to pay them much because they'll be gaining invaluable practical experience here, of course."

Oh, of course. Jennifer could teach Shylock a trick or two. Child labour would be right up her street.

Wandering over to the desk, Sukie sipped her coffee, waiting for the caffeine to kick in, and studied the appointment book. It was reasonably full.

"Shall I go and see to Mrs Fellowes now? She must have been in the cubicle for hours."

Jennifer shook her head. Her mahogany bob didn't move. "I'm going to leave her for a few more minutes. The seaweed wrap is good — but not that good. Years of junk food and lager tops have taken their toll there I'm afraid. What she really needs is a body transplant . . . You can do Chelsea's nail extensions if you like. She's due in shortly for a complete revamp — I think she wants a hearts and flowers motif this time."

Sukie groaned. She was so tired, she wasn't sure she could cope with acrylic nails and mini-transfers and glue and clippers and emery boards, not to mention Chelsea's irrepressible non-stop gossiping, without probably doing her some irreversible harm. However, as arguing with Jennifer was never an option, with another yawn, she gathered together the necessary paraphernalia and staggered off to the nail-bar.

Ten minutes later she was half-heartedly buffing away at Chelsea's nails without, so far, having drawn blood.

". . . and then her mum and dad came home and took one look and — Sukie? Are you listening to me?"

"What? Yes, yes of course I am. Fascinating. Really. Try and keep your hand still — I need to get the

19

tweezers just right and these roses are fiddly — oh, sod it!"

Chelsea stared at the tiny rosebud transfer now raggedly adorning her wrist and giggled. "Mind not on the job, eh, Sukes? Not that I'm surprised . . . You look like you haven't slept for days — and who can blame you . . . Derry Kavanagh is enough to keep any girl awake."

"What? Who?" Sukie scraped the escapee rosebud from Chelsea's wrist and tried again. "What are you talking about?"

"Derry Kavanagh sneaking out of your front door at first light this morning?"

"Who the hell is — oh . . ."

Chelsea leaned forward. "Ah! The all-night passion ration hasn't affected your short-term memory permanently I'm pleased to see. I was just passing the cottage on my way to get the bus to work and almost bumped into him. Ooooh — it was lovely . . . And you're a dark horse — how come we didn't know you and Derry were an item."

So the sex-god had a name. Derry Kavanagh . . . Sukie nodded. Nice. Suited him.

"We aren't." She completed the next transfer on the white-tipped talon and sat back. "He wasn't sneaking out of my bed. Well, actually — no, what I mean is, he was with Milla. Not me."

"Oh." Chelsea looked crushed. "Really? I wouldn't have thought Derry Kavanagh was in her league. Not rich enough, not a fashion victim, not a flashy prat . . . Mind you, I suppose even Milla would forgo all those for a night with someone as lush as Derry. I know I would."

So would I, Sukie thought suddenly. Then pushed the thought away.

She shrugged and clamped Chelsea's stubby hands more firmly to the table for the final application. "There. All done. Er, — was Milla with him — Derry — this morning?"

"No," Chelsea chuckled. "Stoopid. If she'd been with him then I wouldn't have thought he was your latest, would I?" She held out her hands. "Lovely, thanks Sukie. Now I'll just need to keep them looking like this until Saturday night."

"Are you doing something special on Saturday?" Sukie followed Chelsea towards the reception desk.

In Beauty's Blessings' relaxation area Mrs Fellowes had been rescued from the seaweed wrap. Both she and Jennifer were flecked with dark green speckles and looked rather strained.

Chelsea frowned. "It's Fern's hen-night. In Fiddlesticks. At the Weasel and Bucket — bit of a busman's holiday for her seeing as she works there and practically owns the place, but still — surely you hadn't forgotten?"

Ah, yes — Fern's hen-night. Sukie slid Chelsea's credit card into the machine. Of course she'd forgotten.

Barmaid Fern, who was their age, was soon to marry ancient — well, he must be at least *fifty* — Timmy Pluckrose, landlord of the Weasel and Bucket. Rumour had it that their romance had blossomed the previous summer as the result of someone conjuring up an astral magic spell. Sukie didn't believe a word of it, but the

21

Fiddlestickers swore by their celestial celebrations, and who was she to argue with them?

And just how much did this illustrate the difference between her lifestyle and Milla's? Milla was invited on glamorous hen-nights: long weekends in Dublin, Ibiza and Barcelona — Sukie's invites stretched just as far as a couple of hours in the next village . . .

"I might not be able to make it." She handed Chelsea the card and receipt. "I'm not sure what I'm doing yet."

"Get away!" Chelsea laughed. "Your social diary isn't that full. And if you don't come we'll all know why you want to give Fiddlesticks a wide berth. An ex-boyfriend ring any bells? An ex by the name of Lewis Flanagan?"

Sukie groaned. She really didn't want to be reminded of that mad moment last year when she'd had the briefest romance on record with Lewis Flanagan. Lewis, who looked like some hippie rock god, had asked Sukie out once. They'd had a lovely evening — but Lewis, it was clear, was already mad about Amber, who had recently moved to Fiddlesticks. Under the circumstances, Sukie had known nothing would come of her relationship with Lewis, so they'd called it a day.

"Lewis wasn't my boyfriend," Sukie said quickly. "I only went out with him once. Months ago. We — weren't suited. And he's with Amber now and it's all ancient history . . ."

Well, it was. However much she'd fancied Lewis last summer, it wouldn't have worked out. Not when he was so clearly crazy about Amber. And anyway he wouldn't be at Fern's hen-night would he? Amber would though . . . And she liked Amber, honestly she did, but . . .

"Course it is." Chelsea pulled on her padded coat and grinned knowingly. "Whatever you say — but you'll have to be there — it'll be a laugh. We're all dressing up as fairies."

Oh God . . .

"And you'll be able to tell everyone about Derry and Milla, won't you?" Chelsea tugged her variegated hair from the collar of her coat. "There hasn't been any decent gossip for ages. And don't forget your present."

"Present? What present?"

"Fern's wedding shower present. Because we can't go to the wedding, and because they don't need *things*, we're all going to take her something girlie to the hen-night."

"Oh, right, okay." Sukie felt this was something she might just be able to cope with. She'd take Fern a selection of Beauty's Blessings' best skin products.

Chelsea grinned. "I've got her a 'grow your own man' kit from Herbie's Healthfoods. Timmy's a nice bloke but he's older than my dad! Right — think I've got everything. Big Sava's checkouts here I come. Thanks again for the nails — and see you tomorrow evening."

"Tomorrow?" Sukie fought another yawn. She really, really needed to sleep for a week. "I thought you said the hen-night was on Saturday?"

"It is, dumb-cluck." Chelsea swung her shoulder-bag in a swashbuckling arc. "Blimey — you really are fuddled, aren't you? Tomorrow — Tuesday? Hazy Hassocks village hall? Dance practice?"

Oh God times two zillion . . . Sukie groaned. Right now she was too tired to put one foot in front of the other. She'd never cope with *dancing* . . .

"I think I'll give that a miss, too . . ."

"You can't! You're giving me a lift. How am I going to get there without you?"

"It's the next village, not the Outer Hebrides. You could get the bus."

Chelsea pulled a face. "I don't think so. Even I draw the line at bussing it after dark. Don't you remember what happened to Sharon Midgely? Caught the bus at the Bagley crossroads, only going to Fiddlesticks, never seen again . . ."

"That," Sukie stifled another yawn, "was because she was dumping Mr Midgely for the bus driver and a life of sin in rural France. They found the bus abandoned at the Eurostar terminal if you remember."

"Yeah, well, okay — but if you don't go Topsy'll have your head on a stick." Chelsea pushed her hands into Winnie-the-Pooh mittens. "Death is the only excuse to miss a rehearsal as far as Topsy's concerned. You know what she's like about dancing —"

"Dancing?" Jennifer swept past them, peeling off her seaweed-encrusted latex gloves *en route* to the wash basins. "Lance and I adore dancing. We're learning to fox-trot."

Chelsea wrinkled her nose. "Not that sort of dancing, Jen. Our dancing. The can-can troupe. The one that Mitzi started — ouch!" She glared at Sukie.

24

"That hurt! What's wrong with mentioning Mitzi? Oh, yeah — right . . ."

Too late. Jennifer had marched off towards the gleaming basins, every inch of her slender back view radiating annoyance.

"Nice one, Chelsea," Sukie sighed. "Now she'll be stroppy for the rest of the afternoon. You know how ratty she gets when anyone mentions Mrs Blessing Mark One's ventures — especially in here."

A couple of years earlier, as well as Hubble Bubble, Mitzi had rejuvenated the Baby Boomers of Hazy Hassocks and surrounding villages by setting-up all manner of activities. The Bagley-cum-Russet can-can troupe had been one of her many triumphs. Six ladies of varying ages, including Chelsea who had replaced her middle-aged mum who was hamstrung after the first session, and varying degrees of expertise had been kicking and screaming with varying measures of success at local events for several months.

At Chelsea's insistence, Sukie had joined the troupe the previous autumn after another of the older originals had done herself irreparable damage during the splits. She'd thought at the time it would get her out a bit, would be more fun than gym membership, and might, just might, make her as toned at Milla.

All she'd achieved so far were calf muscles like a prop forward and more fishnet stockings and suspenders than an Ann Summers catalogue.

"See ya!" With an unrepentant grin, Chelsea clattered out of Beauty's Blessings into the chill bleakness of the High Street.

"Sukie!" Jennifer's voice echoed crossly from the depths of the cloakroom. "If you've finished chattering about nonsense, these u-bends are all blocked with gunge again! Bring your rubber gloves and the plunger!"

CHAPTER
THREE

"Don't move her!" Topsy screamed above the roar of Offenbach's finest. "Stand well back and give her some air! Leave her where she is, girls! She'll need intravenous fluids and a spinal board and possibly a neck brace!"

It was halfway through Tuesday evening, halfway through the Bagley-cum-Russet can-can dancers' rehearsal in Hazy Hassocks village hall. Valerie Pridmore had taken a tumble during a particularly energetic kick-and-twist manoeuvre.

The five still-upright members of the troupe stopped staring at Valerie, prone on the stage, and turned their attention to Topsy, excitedly tip-tapping her way from the murky depths of the hall, her eyes wide with vicarious pleasure.

"Stand clear!" Topsy yelled. "Wait for the crash trolley!"

No one took any notice. Everyone knew Topsy watched far, far too many medical soaps on telly. Topsy could have done *Mastermind* on *ER* or *Holby* and was word-perfect on the early editions of *Emergency Ward 10*.

Sukie, out of breath and aching, looked down anxiously at Valerie. "Are you okay? You haven't broken anything?"

"Bra strap," Valerie grimaced. "Nothing terminal, love. Just give me a sec to get my second wind . . ."

"Sukie — leave her!" Topsy, a hundred and ninety-seven if she was a day; small, shrivelled, her hair scraped back into a bun, and fitter than any of them, glared beadily like a bad-tempered tortoise as she reached the foot of the stage. She looked at Valerie and shivered pleasurably. "You'll probably need CPR, my girl."

"What I need," Valerie muttered from her crumpled heap, "is a safety pin and a double gin and tonic. Help me up, Sukie, there's a good girl. Ooooh, ouch . . ."

"I said don't touch her!" Topsy screeched over Orpheus reaching the seductive bit as she scrambled nimbly on to the stage. "She might need to get back into sinus rhythm."

"What I need to get into," Valerie puffed, "is a decent pub with —"

"No alcohol!" Topsy shrieked, snapping off the ancient sound system and leaving the gloomy village hall vibrating to silent echoes. "Nil by mouth!"

Sukie tried hard not to giggle, and hauled Valerie to her feet.

"Thanks love. Ooooh — blimey! I don't think I'll be high-kicking again anytime soon. I reckon I've pulled something."

"Wish I had," Chelsea muttered.

"Well . . ." Topsy stood, hands on hips, and stared at her raggle-taggle can-can troupe. "This is a pretty kettle of fish and no mistake. Can't you give her one of your massages, Sukie, and see if that helps? We can't be a dancer down at this stage — it'll ruin the routines."

Sukie tried not to smile. To be honest, she felt on a really bad day the Bagley can-canners could ruin the routines quite easily without any help at all. "Er — well, yes I could massage her leg, but not here. I haven't got any of my stuff and she'd need to be warmer anyway."

The can-canners might well have been sweating profusely from their recent efforts but the hall itself was sub-zero. Muscles were stiffening and perspiring bodies growing rapidly chilly.

"Let's get her home, then," Topsy said, clearly sulking at having been deprived of a fleet of paramedics and an emergency tracheotomy. "She'll need a comfrey rub."

"I could do with a comfy rub," Chelsea grinned, tugging at her sagging leggings. "But not from Sukie."

Leaning on Sukie and standing on one leg like a plump stork, Valerie shrugged. "Maybe my old man was right. Maybe I'm far too old for this game."

"Nonsense!" Topsy snapped. "When I taught ballet, my gels were as strong as oxen from cradle to grave. And look at Margot Fonteyn and Dame Nellie Melba — they were still dancing well into their autumn years. And this troupe was your idea, Valerie Pridmore. You were the one who told young Mitzi last year you wanted to be a Bluebell Girl, so don't go all Lib Dem on us now."

Sukie, despite shivering inside her baggy T-shirt and jogging bottoms, sniggered.

"It's no laughing matter." Topsy frowned. "We've got bookings coming up all summer — fêtes and galas and what-not — not to mention that wedding reception for young Fern and Timmy . . . We've rehearsed with six dancers. We can't rearrange the routines. We're going to need a replacement. Again."

"Bugger the replacement," Valerie sniffed, limping heavily and clutching her sagging bosom. "I'm getting me coat and going home. Anyone else?"

There was a whoop of assent. It was the most animated the can-canners had been all evening.

Pulling on thick jackets and gloves and scarves over their practise clothes, Sukie and Chelsea took charge of Valerie, while the remaining dancers, Betty, Roo and Trace, helped Topsy turn out the lights in the hope that there'd be no short-circuits during the night. Hazy Hassocks village hall was in dire need of re-wiring and re-heating. And probably demolishing. But as it was the only place for miles around that had the room for functions and activities, and Mitzi Blessing had practically sold her soul to the owners for the Baby Boomers to be able to use it at all, no one dared to suggest it should be closed for a refurb lest it never opened again.

"Did you cycle here?" Chelsea looked at Valerie as they emerged into a bitterly cold, black and blustery March night.

Valerie nodded.

"Leave the bike here then, and I'll give you a lift." Sukie shivered. "You'll never be able to pedal with that leg."

"I'll ride her bike home," Topsy said, emerging from the hall, tying a brown and grey paisley headscarf under her wrinkled chin which only accentuated the tortoise-look. "I walked over from Bagley."

Sukie sighed. Topsy walked everywhere. Quickly. It was so irritating to be outpaced on all levels by someone who was so old they instantly equated the name Victoria with Queen rather than Beckham.

Once Valerie was carefully ensconced in the back, and Chelsea'd strapped herself into the passenger seat, Sukie steered the car slowly through Hazy Hassocks' unlit rutted lanes and out on to the Bagley-cum-Russet road.

"Any more news on Milla and Derry Kavanagh?" Chelsea wriggled in anticipation. "Has he moved in yet?"

"No," Sukie shook her head. "Why would he? Milla likes to keep her options open — she'd never have a permanent residential fixture — and he definitely isn't her type. I haven't seen her — or him — since yesterday morning."

"She's probably moved in with him, then," Valerie said from behind her. "I know he wouldn't have to ask me twice. He's bloody gorgeous — only don't tell my old man I said so . . ."

Sukie frowned. Did everyone in the world know everything about Derry Kavanagh except her? How come she'd missed him? She really, really hoped that

Milla wouldn't go out with him. She couldn't face them being all lovey-dovey in Pixies Laughter's nooks and crannies. Not that she fancied Derry Kavanagh, of course. Definitely not. But even so . . .

"Milla was working late last night and left early this morning." she slowed down to avoid a couple of teenagers kissing passionately in the middle of the road and sounded the horn. "Move you silly little sods! Honestly — we were never like that!"

"Yeah, we were." Chelsea grinned. "After school . . . on the way home, remember? Along Twisty Lane? Oh, and especially after youth club. You used to drag Barry Lumsden off for a snog at every opportunity."

"I did not! Barry Lumsden was gross!"

"Good snogger though," Chelsea said wistfully. "Blimey, Sukes, that was all so long ago. We had loads of lads back then, didn't we? Spoilt for choice. And here we are now — rushing towards thirty and both blokeless . . ."

Sukie swerved round the still-entwined teenagers who gestured rudely. "Excuse me — I've had my moments . . ."

"Yeah, but not for a long time," Chelsea sighed. "And as you can't count the brief encounter with Lewis Flanagan, you haven't had a steady relationship for well over a year have you?"

"By choice. And you can't talk."

"I'm picky. Mr Right will have to be Mr Absolutely Perfect . . ."

Valerie giggled. "You youngsters are so funny. In my day you'd be considered on the shelf if you weren't

32

marching down the aisle on your twenty-first. You didn't play the field back then, you took what was on your doorstep. I was engaged while I was at school, married my old man on my eighteenth birthday, and had all my kids before I was twenty-five . . ."

Sukie and Chelsea exchanged horrified glances. The car jerked a bit.

"Ooops, sorry, Val. You okay? That didn't hurt your leg, did it?"

"No. I'm fine. Look, will you do me a massage though sometime, love?" Valerie leaned forward in the darkness. "One of your at home ones like you advertised?"

"Yes. Sure. Anytime — but it'll have to go through Jennifer's books. I've agreed not to freelance for the time being."

"Whatever." Valerie sank back into her seat with a stifled groan. "The sooner the better though, love. Before the weekend if poss. I need to be on my feet for work."

"Okay." Sukie nodded. Valerie was a dinner lady at Hazy Hassocks Mixed Infants. It wasn't a job you could do sitting down. "Jennifer says she'll have all the new oils and stuff from the suppliers this week — so as soon as it arrives I'll ring you and we can make an appointment — blimey!"

"What?" Chelsea peered into the darkness. "What's going on? Oh — how does she do that?"

They'd reached the centre of Bagley-cum-Russet, the bit where the two original villages melded at a zigzag junction marked by a Celtic cross. Topsy, leaning forwards over the handlebars of Valerie's bicycle, was just ahead of them.

Sukie grinned, and indicated left. "Jet-propelled, I reckon. After years of teaching ballet she must have legs like pistons. Right, Val — shall I drop you off at your bungalow first?"

"Can you take me to the pub, love? My old man's playing darts. I said I'd meet him there after rehearsals — and anyway, I really do need that drink."

"Me too." Chelsea nodded. "I'd rather go to the pub than be at home with my mum and dad arguing over the telly remote and my brothers fighting over the Game Boy and my sisters waging war over their mobiles and —"

Sukie laughed, executed a neat U-turn, and pulled up outside the pub.

"Coming in?" Chelsea asked as she undid her seat belt.

Sukie shook her head. "No thanks. I want a long hot bath. I'm all sweaty and disgusting — not to mention dressed like a bag-lady."

"Just about right for the Barmy Cow then, I'd say."

The pub, a tiny slate-roofed cottage with various bits tacked on in corrugated iron and white-pebbledash, was really called the Barley Mow, but after decades of Berkshire wind and rain sweeping from the Downs and a bit of help from the local yoof, the lettering on the faded sign was sadly defaced. Even the once-yellow illustration of a feathery stook had taken on a strangely bovine appearance.

It had been known as the Barmy Cow for as long as anyone could remember.

It was also not the sort of pub where people went by choice. Most Bagley-cum-Russet residents frequented it only when a trip to Fiddlesticks or Hazy Hassocks was out of the question, so the hard-core of Barmy Cow regulars were either ancient, barking, or both.

Sukie really felt she couldn't spend half an hour listening to the Berkeley Boys, the four ancient brothers who ran the Barmy Cow, yet again guffawing over jokes that had had whiskers in the nineteenth century.

"If you could just give me a hand to get inside before you go, love." Valerie peered piteously at the shuddery darkness from the back of the car. "I'd be ever so grateful."

"Of course . . ."

Heads down against the freezing wind, Chelsea and Sukie helped Valerie hop and hobble into the single low-beamed, fug-filled room of the Barmy Cow. It was all-over nicotine brown and smelled of warm beer and even warmer humanity. But at least, Sukie thought, her teeth chattering, it did have a real fire, even though grey ash spilled untidily on to the sludge-coloured carpet and occasional little puffs of acrid smoke belched out into the bar.

"Ay-oop!" Valerie's husband whooped from the direction of the dartboard. "Walking wounded alert! What've you done now, you daft bint? Told you you was too old 'n' fat for all that Folly Buggery business! Come over 'ere and let me kiss it better."

Valerie limped across the tiny bar-room to a ragged cheer from the disparate clientele, and was hugged expansively by her large, scruffy husband.

Chelsea exhaled slowly. "Oh, gross — still, I guess that's what passes for a romantic encounter in this place."

Sukie averted her eyes and nodded. "And I think after that I really do need a drink. Shall I see what the Boys are offering in lieu of WKD Blue?"

"Yeah, go on then — though I'm not holding out much hope. I'll see if I can find somewhere to sit."

The Berkeley Boys, all standing in a cramped shoulder-to-shoulder row behind the tiny dull and dusty bar, beamed at Sukie in unison. She smiled back politely, as always trying not to chuckle. The Boys, well over pensionable age and differing wildly in height and girth and facial features, always dressed identically. Sadly, tonight the outfit of choice included fair-isle tank-tops and paisley kipper ties.

Behind them, a portrait of their mother, the original landlady of the Barmy Cow, took up most of the space. The woefully inappropriately named Honour Berkeley, looking a bit like Ramsay MacDonald, still held court over the tiny pub years after her demise.

Cora, Sukie's godmother, had regaled her with stories of how the young and skittish Honour had left Bagley-cum-Russet to seek her fortune in London. Taking jobs as a chambermaid in various swish hotels, Honour had eventually returned to the village, her reputation in tatters, her finger devoid of a wedding ring, but with her head held high and the infant Boys in tow. It was rumoured that one of her gentlemen friends had bought the Barmy Cow for her, presumably to remove her — and him — from London and further scandal.

As a mark of her conquests, Honour had named each of her offspring after the hotels in which they were conceived.

Sukie scanned the crowded and disorganised shelves. There didn't seem to be anything even remotely drinkable on display. The Barmy Cow specialised — if that was the right word — in real ale for real drinkers; girlie drinks never featured strongly.

It looked, Sukie thought, squinting at the shelves of faded bottles, to be a choice between Cherry B or something called Pony.

"What would you like, my dear? Something feminine, I'll be bound? Can't see a pretty little thing like you with a pint glass somehow." Savoy leaned forward from the Berkeley Boys line-up. "Tell you what — Claridge found some Babycham in the kitchen yesterday. And we've got cherries left over from Christmas and some tooth picks somewhere. All the ladies love a Babycham, don't they?"

Sukie grinned at him. Maybe halfway through the last century they did. Oh, why not? "Okay. Thank you. Can you make it two, please?" Well, she wasn't going to suffer alone.

With an imperious click of his fingers Savoy had Dorchester and Hilton galvanised into action.

While bottles and glasses were dusted and cherries impaled, Sukie stared at herself in the flyblown mirror behind the bar. God — she looked a wreck: her spiky hair was in clumpy tufts, her make-up had all disappeared during the can-can routines, and her warm padded jacket, which had once been Cora's gardening coat, made her look like a rough sleeper. Still, at least there was no one remotely impressible in the Barmy Cow. In fact she looked quite band-boxy compared to the rest of the punters.

Putting an abrupt end to any misplaced thoughts of vanity, Dorchester and Hilton plonked two Babychams, heavily spiked with faded cherries, on the counter in front of her.

"We haven't got a set price for them," Dorchester beamed. "What do you reckon?"

Sukie looked down doubtfully. "A pound?"

"Each?"

"Well — no . . . Oh, go on then . . ."

Transaction completed, Sukie manoeuvred her way towards Chelsea.

"Don't ask." She pushed one of the glasses across the rickety sticky tabletop. "It was this or warm beer."

Chelsea took a tentative sip. Grimaced. Took a gulp. Grinned. "Bloody awful."

"Mmm." Sukie rolled some on her tongue and pulled a face. "Wonder why it's got bits in it?"

"Mine hasn't. Oooh look — your cocktail stick's disintegrated and all the cherries have fallen off and — why are you going purple?"

Suddenly unable to breathe, Sukie gave a panic-stricken choke. "I-think-I've-got-a-cherry-stuck-in-my-throat . . ."

"Not surprised." Chelsea bounced hers across the table. "They're as solid as ball bearings . . . Sukes? Are you okay?"

Shaking her head, gasping for breath, Sukie stumbled towards the door.

Chelsea downed the rest of her Babycham in one and rushed after Sukie into the bitterly cold car park. Yanking at the sleeve of the disgusting padded jacket until Sukie, still coughing and gasping, was standing beneath the illuminated Barmy Cow sign, Chelsea looked terrified.

"Okay, Sukes . . . Now I'm going to try and get it out. Stand there while I get behind you and press on your breastbone — or maybe it's your windpipe . . .? I've done this Heimlich thingy at first aid — now hang on while I just grab you and press and shove — press and shove . . ."

"Don't tell me!" An expensive voice echoed through the swirl of the wind. "Let me guess — it's some sort of lesbian chav mating ritual . . ."

As the cherry shot disgustingly out on to the car park, Sukie jerked away from Chelsea and stared at the long, low silver car, which had pulled up alongside the pub. She groaned. Milla, all immaculate power suit and glossy hair, was laughing from the driving seat.

"She got a cherry stuck," Chelsea snapped.

"I'm not even going to ask where or why — nothing surprises me any more," Milla chuckled, rolling up the electric window. "Oh, and as we're going into Reading tonight I'll probably be late home, Sukes, if at all. 'Bye. Have fun."

We? Just too late Sukie realised that Milla wasn't alone. Derry Kavanagh, his ash blond hair striking against a dark top, was in the passenger seat. Looking gorgeous. Looking at her. And laughing.

CHAPTER
FOUR

"Valerie Pridmore had to be carried up the path last night!" Marvin Benson's voice rang from the depths of the bungalow's dinette. "Nearly midnight it was. And that oafish husband of hers was laughing. Laughing — I ask you! I'm ashamed to say we live next door to the likes of them. They lower the whole tone of this Close. The woman's practically an alcoholic. Jocelyn! Are you listening to me? Did you hear what I said?"

In the kitchen, Joss Benson stared out of the window at the grey and drooping March garden. What a dismally disappointing month March was: too late for significant and lasting snowfalls to transform the visual boredom into a winter wonderland, and too early for sensual days filled with glorious sunshine and birdsong and hot flowers.

And how wonderful it would be to be carried home. Roaring drunk. Laughing.

Oh, lucky, lucky Valerie Pridmore . . .

"Jocelyn!"

Joss dragged herself back from fantasies of riotous drunkenness and laughter. There were far more important things to concentrate on. Things like Marvin's breakfast and getting him off to work, and because it was Wednesday morning, the bedrooms to clean, the floors to polish, the paths to sweep, and the recycling bins to be organised — and then her own work, of course.

Not that her own work was work, or even hers, as such, but —

"Jocelyn!" Marvin's voice had raised a tone and reached peevish. "It's seven forty-three!"

"And my breakfast needs to be on the table by seven forty-five if I'm to catch the eight forty-five," Joss mouthed in synchro as she picked up the tray. "Coming, Marv."

She backed into the dinette, smiling. Marvin hated the diminutive with a passion.

"I've told you before, don't call me Marv — and did you hear what I said about Valerie Pridmore?" Marvin arranged his boiled egg, toast, coffee pot, butter and marmalade into the pattern he'd used for the last thirty years of breakfasts. "And this toast is burnt."

Joss shrugged. "No it isn't. Just a bit more well done than usual. And yes, I heard what you said about Val. Were you spying on the Pridmores again last night?"

"I don't spy, Jocelyn. I merely observe. And this toast is definitely burnt."

Marvin seemed to spend an awful lot of time twitching the net curtains, watching the comings and goings in The Close. Especially when he had to get up for a late-night pee. He always said it was because of his role as Neighbourhood Watch co-ordinator; that he had to keep his finger on the Bagley-cum-Russet pulse so to speak.

Joss knew it was because he was nosy and small-minded and conservative and a killjoy.

She sat opposite him, as she always did, eating nothing, pouring a cup of coffee, trying not to let her irritation show. She really should have got used to Marvin's breakfast rituals by now: the scraping of the butter to every corner of the toast until the coverage was even, the aligning of his knife and spoon, the smoothing of the non-existent wrinkles in the tablecloth, the nodding of his head as he took his first mouthful of coffee.

Breakfasts were always silent affairs — apart from Marvin's crunching and gulping of course. It was the only time of the day Marvin didn't hold court. Joss welcomed the silence although the tinkle of the radio would be nice — or even a bit of breakfast telly in the background like the Pridmores had.

Oh — how wonderful it would be to be like Valerie Pridmore — noisy, disorganised, always cheerful, never knowing what was going to happen from one minute to the next. And madly in love — still — with her large, untidy, happy-go-lucky husband . . .

"Right, I'm off." Marvin said eventually, as he always did, dabbing, as he always did, at his moist lips with his napkin. "Make sure you finish those notes by this evening, won't you?"

Joss nodded, as she always did, and continued to nurse her coffee cup. They'd long given up the pretence of the goodbye peck. She only had five more minutes to go. Five minutes while Marvin collected his briefcase and his coat and his car keys and set out, as he always did, in his beige car to join the late-commuters at Reading station.

It was one of the perks, Marvin always said, of climbing the corporate ladder within the same company, man and boy. He was part of the highly-prized furniture. He had earned his position and his colleagues' respect through years of dedication and loyalty to the firm. And it meant he didn't have to be at his city desk until ten o'clock.

Joss had survived and supported the man and boy tribulations of Marvin's scramble up said ladder for the last thirty years, from lowly clerk-of-all-trades in the basement post room, to something huge in HR up on the glass-walled fifteenth floor. This had been Personnel in the old days, of course, and Joss really couldn't help thinking that HR sounded too much like something to do with hormone replacement therapy. And that there was a cruel irony in putting the intransigent Marvin in charge of sensitive employees' deepest problems and anxieties.

The front door snapped closed. The beige car purred into life and out of the drive.

Joss exhaled.

The routine chores took very little time, accompanied as they were, by mindlessly cheerful radio music. Needless to say, Marvin didn't like radio music. If Marvin switched the radio on at all it was for the more sombre programmes on Radio Four. Marvin liked to argue loudly with the presenters.

Joss, shivering as she returned to the kitchen from the back garden and the sorting of the recycling bins,

44

caught sight of her reflection in the window. Goodness! Her short fair hair was blown all anyhow, her unmade-up face looked pale and pasty, and her beige cotton trousers and sweater seemed to mould her into a thin pale toneless sausage.

I look like an uncooked chipolata, Joss thought sadly. Beige, pale, cold, uninteresting . . .

Still, she did match the rest of the bungalow. Currently, Marvin was an Ikea junkie. Marvin, a Sunday supplement style victim, had fallen in love with the clean lines and blond furniture and no clutter. Even at the beginning of their marriage Marvin had eschewed the then-popular dark, rich colours and painted the bungalow an all-over cream. The young Joss, simply happy to have her own home and a husband with ambitions and a car and job in London, had sighed a bit, and yearned silently for an orange and gold living-room, a raspberry pink bathroom, and a sultry bedroom in purple and turquoise, and then accepted the blandness.

Big mistake, she thought now as she whizzed the all-purpose mop across the all-purpose pale laminated floors. She really should have been more assertive earlier on. The acquiescence had become a habit. As had staying married to Marvin and everything else . . .

Only the bedrooms to do now. Well, only their bedroom really — the other two were never used. Not any more. They never had guests and the children, grown and flown, never came home to stay. Which was a blessing in a way. Joss sighed again. It was surely wicked and unnatural not to like your own children much? Not — she thought, as she straightened the cream linen duvets on her bed and Marvin's: a double bed with separate linen; a double bed in which they slept, side-by-side but a million miles apart — that they seemed to like her much, either.

Maybe that was harsh. They were affectionate in their distant way, and never forgot birthdays or Christmases, but they led such busy corporate lives with their busy upwardly mobile partners. Maybe if they had children . . . Joss shook her head. She doubted that either of her offspring would halt their careers to breed.

Ossie and Tilly had always been mini-Marvins — probably because he'd been the strong, dominant parent, while she'd been the cipher in the background, the one handing out love and cuddles and encouragement to a son and daughter who, from childhood, had never seemed to need any of them.

Too late to change things now, Joss thought, casting a final eye round the barren bedroom and closing the door. Far too bloody late.

"Yoo-hoo!" A cheerful shout from the kitchen interrupted her melancholy. "Joss?"

"Through here." Joss hurried across the now-gleaming hall towards the kitchen, grinning at the welcome sound of Valerie's cheery Berkshire growl. "Just coming — and why aren't you at work? Oh . . ."

"Done me leg in tripping the light fantastic," Valerie said happily. "Last night. So I thought you might to like to pop round for a cuppa and a natter?"

"Love to." Joss hurled the cleaning paraphernalia unto the kitchen cupboard. "Shall I bring biscuits?"

"Only if you've got them posh Marks and Sparks ones," Valerie chuckled over her shoulder as she hobbled towards the back door. "They're such a treat after our Big Sava specials."

This was Joss's one big vice; a secret that Marvin knew nothing about. Illicit coffee and gossip with Valerie Pridmore in the next-door bungalow. A deep friendship forged over the years between two women with nothing in common except their age and the proximity of their homes.

They'd got to the elbows-on-table-amongst-tea-mugs-and-biscuit-crumbs stage in Valerie's cluttered, warm and hectically-hued kitchen.

Joss now knew all about the disastrous fall while can-canning and the resultant visit to the Barmy Cow and the amazing effect several gins had when added to a handful of assorted painkillers supplied by the rest of the troupe. She really wished she had similar raucous stories to add, but as usual, there was nothing of interest going on in her life.

"I've got to get back to work soon as," Valerie said, pushing her mop of untidy dark hair away from her face. "I can't bear being at home all day. Don't know how you stand it."

"Oh, believe me, I've often thought about going back to work — but Marvin still won't hear of it. He says I have more than enough to do. Anyway, I'm probably unemployable now. I was a shorthand-typist before we married."

"Blimey!" Valerie spluttered bits of Marks and Spencer's best across the table. "You don't get them any more! It's all computers and things these days. You'd have to retrain. They do back-to-work courses at Winterbrook college."

"Yes, I've looked at them — but they're scary — even if Marvin agreed."

"Listen to yourself!" Valerie leaned across the table. "This is the twenty-first century! Your Marv doesn't have to agree or disagree. You've got your own bloody life!"

"Oh, I know . . . I don't want to make him sound like some Victorian ogre — but, well, we know where we are. The boundaries. He goes out to work, I stay at home and make things nice. We sort of rub along and it's comfortable and undemanding and —"

"Sodding boring?"

"Well . . ." Joss smiled. "Yes."

"Then do something about it."

"Too late. I've got no confidence at all. I'd be petrified in the workplace. I wanted to be at home when the children were small and I've just got used to it, I suppose," Joss gathered biscuit crumbs into a little pyramid. "It's my life, right back from being there when the children were young, and then even when they went to school Marvin preferring me to be a housewife, not wanting me to work . . ."

"Yeah, well, with his salary I suppose there was no financial need, was there? My old man's been in and out of work all our married life, love him. One of us had to knuckle down and bring home the bacon. Still, working at the school means I've always been here for the kids."

Joss nodded. Valerie had five children, all married, all living locally, all with at least two children of their own, all returning to the Pridmore's bungalow all the time with whoops of laughter and expansive hugs and kisses.

Marvin always closed the windows and tutted a lot when the Pridmores were visiting *en masse*. Joss simply ached with jealousy.

Anyway, she did sort of work: she had her typing to do — she typed Marvin's Neighbourhood Watch notes every Wednesday afternoon on her ancient portable typewriter with three carbons, and two mornings a week she collated the articles for the current month's *Bagley Bugle*.

The *Bagley Bugle* was the village news-sheet and Marvin was the editor — not that he did a lot of editing. Once Joss had checked through the pieces and discarded the more inflammatory ones, and proof-read the advertisements, and banked the cheques on Fridays — Marvin charged quite a lot, she thought, for local adverts — Marvin took the whole kit and caboodle off to London where his secretary, Anneka, used scanners and computers and laser printers and binders and all manner of hi-tech gadgetry to produce the six hundred and seventy-two monthly copies of the *Bagley Bugle*.

Maybe she'd suggest to Marvin that she had a word processor or a computer at home. Then Anneka needn't be involved and it would give Joss time to practise just in case she was ever brave enough to approach an employer.

"Young Sukie's going to give me a massage on me leg to get me up and running," Valerie's voice cut through this burgeoning media mini-plan. "You know, she's in the can-can troupe? Lives in Cora's cottage on the other side of Bagley? Works for Jennifer Blessing?"

"What?" Joss, lost in a world of screens and no Tippex, frowned. "Sukie? Oh yes. Pretty dark girl? Looks Irish? The cottage used to belong to that really weird elderly lady who talked to birds and animals . . . Was she called Cora? Yes, of course, I'd forgotten," Joss smiled. "We had several flyers about the mobile beauty therapy thing delivered — I thought the at-home massage sounded wonderful — but Marvin threw them all in the bin and said they were nonsense, of course."

"Of course," Valerie poured more tea. "Tell you what, if I arrange for Sukie to do my massage while your Marv's at work, why don't you come round and have a de-stressing one here? At the same time. He'd never know would he? And I'm sure Sukie'd be glad of the business as she's just trying to get this off the ground for Jennifer Blessing."

Joss grinned. Why not? What harm could it do? She'd pay for it out of her housekeeping by decanting Big Sava's cheap own-brand goodies into labelled jars in the cupboard. It was the way she'd financed her little treats for years. What Marvin didn't know couldn't possibly hurt him, could it? And a de-stressing massage would be another wonderful sinful secret luxury . . .

"Okay." Joss nodded, absent-mindedly reaching for the last biscuit. "You're on. Just let me know when — oh, looks like you've got another visitor."

Valerie squinted through the window. "Bugger, just when we've eaten all the biscuits — oh, it's okay. It's only Topsy. She'll have brought me bike back. She don't eat anything at all."

Topsy, still muffled in a mass of grey and brown, poked her elderly wrinkled face round the back door. "I've propped your bike up against the lean-to, Valerie. Oh, hello Joss — goodness me! Look at the pair of you. Sitting around scoffing carbohydrates and sugar — deadly combination. If you don't get an embolism your arteries'll be furred to buggery. You'll need Warfarin to get any blood through all that cholesterol — and probably a heart-by-pass, if not an angiogram."

"Thanks, Topsy." Val grinned. "Guaranteed to cheer us up, you are. And thanks for returning the bike. Lord knows when I'll be able to ride it again, though."

Topsy made a sort of snorting noise. "Don't know what we're going to do about replacing you in the line-up, neither. We took ages to get young Sukie in last year." She turned her brown-beady eyes to Joss. "You wouldn't be no good at a bit of kicking and screaming along to Offenbach I suppose?"

Joss shook her head quickly. "Two left feet, I'm afraid. Never even mastered the Valeta at school. And I'm far too old."

"Stuff and nonsense!" Topsy tightened her headscarf under her skinny wrinkled chin. "You're the same age as Valerie here and the majority of my gels, and as I always say, there's no such thing as too old. It's all in the mind. Still, I suppose I'll have to start advertising for a half-decent replacement, but she'll have to be a quick learner — we're already into the routines and rehearsals and —"

"Get Joss's Marv to put an advert in the *Bugle*," Valerie cut in. "It goes to every house in Bagley-cum-Russet. You might be able to find someone."

"Good idea — you never cease to amaze me Valerie Pridmore! There's a brain in there somewhere!" Topsy nodded towards Joss. "Can you do me a good rate for an advert as soon as possible, then?"

"I'll do better than that," Joss said quickly, fired by a sudden burst of enthusiasm. "I'll write an article about the can-can troupe — and say that you're looking for new blood. Well, not blood as such, but . . ."

It was probably the mention of blood, but Topsy gave one of her rare smiles. It crinkled her from forehead to chin making her face look like quarter pound of haslet. "Ah, I like it! An article . . . hmmm. That way there won't be a fee for an advert, will there? Good thinking my girl."

Joss beamed back. Marvin wouldn't like it. Marvin never liked it when she wrote pieces for the *Bugle*. Not that he knew they were hers now. He long since thought he'd put an end to all that nonsense. She'd become very adept with *noms-de-plume*. Again, what he didn't know wouldn't hurt him.

"And I can ask Sukie all about the can-can thing when she does our massages, can't I? It'll be like a proper investigative journalist gleaning all the snippets of insider gossip," Joss continued happily, having a vision of becoming Bagley's answer to Ephraim Hardcastle.

52

"Lovely." Topsy clapped her hands. "Oh! That reminds me! I've got to go and see young Sukie about them at-home massage things, as well. I need to put her straight on one or two things before she's let loose. I'm not sure she's got the full picture about what she's playing with. Not sure at all. There's a lot of folklore history in this village that she should be aware of before she starts rubbing lord knows what into people. Could all go very wrong if she ain't careful. Look what happened to young Mitzi Blessing when she first started concocting her Hubble Bubble recipes. Surprised no one died. Ah well, — no rest for the wicked . . . No, don't get up — I'll see meself out."

They watched Topsy's skinny, multi-wrapped figure stride off into The Close, then looked at one another.

"Barking," Valerie said fondly. "But good for her age."

"How old do you reckon she is?"

"Eighty-five or thereabouts — wonder what she meant about needing to speak to Sukie?"

Joss shrugged. "No idea. Probably something to do with magic and witchcraft and flower power . . . She and Cora were always cackling over herbs and nature's medicinal powers, weren't they?"

"Blimey, yes." Valerie wriggled more comfortably in her chair. "A pair of old hags and no mistake. Mind you, I suppose we shouldn't knock all that stuff. Whatever Topsy says, Mitzi Blessing's had a fair bit of success with her herbal cooking and folksy recipes, hasn't she?"

"But Mitzi Blessing is one of us," Joss said. "Normal. No one could ever say Topsy was that. Now, are you desperate to get on with anything or will you make a fresh pot of tea while I go and get the blueberry cheesecake I was saving for Marvin's supper?"

"Oooh, tough one," Valerie chuckled hauling herself up and hobbling towards the kettle. "You've got a wicked streak in you, Jocelyn Benson. You want to be careful — you're in danger of becoming a bit of a devil on the quiet."

CHAPTER
FIVE

"Quick! Before we have to open up, come and have a look at these." Jennifer Blessing beckoned Sukie towards a spare cubicle. "They've just arrived. Aren't they simply too lovely for words?"

At half-past eight on a grey, wet, cold Saturday Sukie felt that nothing could be *that* lovely — except maybe an extra hour in bed. She really wasn't a morning person, especially on Saturdays when it appeared the rest of the world was allowed to slumber. And the soporific, warm, sensuously-scented salon only served to enervate her further. Sleepily, she squinted at the peach leather cases displayed across the massage table in front of Jennifer.

In an instant her lethargy was forgotten as her fingers itched to touch and stroke.

Rows of pretty little faceted glass bottles with gorgeous multicoloured gemstone stoppers nestled in the folds of cream silk lining, and glowed like dozens of glittering jewels. Even the more prosaic pale apricot plastic containers of base oils and various synthetic essences seemed alluring in such a sumptuous setting. The essential oils, the essentials of her business, displayed like this, were just so pretty, and colourful and *girlie*.

Etched in italic gold on the tiny black labels, the names — juniper, eucalyptus, bergamot, lavender, clary sage, geranium — which she knew as well as her own, seemed to ring with a new magical mysticism.

"Oh, Jennifer — they're absolutely, absolutely —" she searched for a fulsome enough word. "Absolutely ravishing. Wonderful. Fabulous. Look at them . . . there's a really comprehensive stock here, something for everything I reckon, and they look so beautiful and — well — almost too pretty to use. Thank you so much."

"You're welcome, although of course it's as much for my benefit as yours. Probably more as I'll be taking a cut of the profits," Jennifer said with her usual candour. "But I agree, the suppliers have come up trumps this time. Look, they've even tooled 'Beauty's Blessings' in gold leaf on the cases. Very professional. I knew you'd love them."

"Oh, I do. Now I can't wait for Monday morning — which will be a first — to get started. And I've been thinking, I might even set up a massage table in the back parlour of Pixies Laughter. It's supposed to be our dining room but we never use it, and it might be nicer for people who don't want all my stuff spread all over their living rooms or who prefer a bit of privacy. What do you reckon?"

"That's not a bad idea — and if you take on the massages away from here it'll give me space to install that spray-tan booth I've always wanted. I'll check with the powers-that-be about inspection and home licensing and what have you for your cottage, although as you're a qualified practitioner I don't think you'll have a problem there to be honest — and add it to the next lot of adverts and — damn! Is that my phone?"

"No, mine." Sukie scrabbled in the pocket of her overall for her mobile. "Sorry, Jennifer — oh, it's a text from Topsy. She keeps trying to contact me about something which is apparently vitally important. We keep missing one another."

"Is it to do with the dancing?" Jennifer pouted her glossy lips.

"Don't think so. Something to do with my aromatherapy I think. She keeps saying I mustn't start my massages without talking to her first — or I'll be sorry."

"Crikey — sounds a bit strange. Although maybe she just wants a cut-price massage," Jennifer smiled. "If so, I think you ought to decline, kindly of course, and recommend a tannery — her skin looks like leather. No, sorry, cruel of me — but she is a weird old bat, isn't she?"

"Very. But an ace dancer even now. She must have been a veritable Ginger Rogers in her heyday. And, of course, a frustrated nurse on the quiet."

"Oh, I know!" Jennifer laughed. "She's mad on medical stuff, isn't she? She wanted to give the kiss of life to my Lance once when he choked on a pickled gherkin in the Faery Glen. Had his head yanked back against the wall and his tie off and her fingers down his throat before you could say Hamlet manoeuvre."

Sukie started to snigger at the malapropism then stopped quickly. Jennifer hailed from Essex. Sometimes there were language difficulties. And the memories of her own close-encounter with Heimlich were still very raw — and definitely no laughing matter.

She turned the snigger into a little cough. "Blimey. What did you do?"

"Wrestled her off before she throttled him. She clung on like a bloody limpet. I practically had to beat her off with a stick."

Sukie winced at the picture. Fortunately her phone chirruped again before she could say anything else.

"Topsy again? She's very persistent, I'll give her that." Jennifer applied a further coat of gloss to her high-shine lips. "And is it just me, or do you always find it sort of strange that old people have mobiles and *text*?"

Sukie nodded. Actually, she did. But Topsy seemed quite adept at it, using all the correct abbreviations. Maybe she'd chivvied some hoodied child from the Bath Road estate to give her lessons.

"She says she'll be waiting for me at Pixies Laughter when I get home at lunchtime." Sukie squinted at the hieroglyphics. "Says again it's imperative that I don't do anything until she's spoken to me."

"Poor old thing. Clearly going to give you some pearls of wisdom circa 1920. So sad when the mind starts to go and you cling to the past and can only see danger in change. Topsy probably thinks massage is seedy and you're going to turn Bagley-cum-Russet into a sort of rural Reeperbahn Strasse. She's probably got so little going on her life that everything becomes a matter of national security . . ." Jennifer giggled with as much animation as much as her recent non-surgical chin-lift would allow. "Right, well, as soon as you've finished making your assignations with the geriatric double-oh-seven, I suppose we better get ourselves ready to beautify Berkshire."

And still chuckling, Jennifer swished off to open up the salon for her always-busy Saturday morning trade.

Having texted an affirmative reply to Topsy, Sukie smiled a last soppy smile at the cases and their contents as she clicked the locks shut. The massage oils had totally lifted her spirits — which was just as well. They'd been lurking somewhere just south of despondent ever since Tuesday evening.

Of course it had been humiliating in the extreme for Milla and Derry to see her jigging around with her mouth wide open and Chelsea clinging to her back outside the Barmy Cow, but that was just Sod's Law. No, the worst thing was Derry, who she'd secretly turned into some perfect love god, laughing at her for doing so.

Face of an angel, heart of a bastard, feet of clay, Sukie had decided. He and Milla deserved one another. Definitely.

And she hadn't even been able to escape him. Milla had arrived home, fortunately alone, on Wednesday morning, refusing to answer questions, beaming from ear to ear and singing in the bathroom which clearly indicated a night of unbridled passion, and had been out with Derry every evening since.

It was so unfair.

And on each occasion when Derry had arrived at Pixies Laughter to collect Milla he'd looked gorgeous — Sukie wondered if he had a live-in stylist to advise him on the best clothes to wear with that stunning layered ice-blond hair and dark blue eyes — and smiled at her and said polite hellos in the nanosecond that Milla allowed them to be alone together, but had made no apology at all for laughing at her discomfort.

Ah, well . . . Fortunately today was going to be pretty hectic so there'd be no time to fester about the vagaries of beautiful men with no manners: work until midday, the mysterious meeting with Topsy, then the joys of dressing up like a fairy with Chelsea for what would probably be a truly dire hen-night.

She checked her appearance in one of the peach-lit mirrors and struck a self-deprecating pose. "Ooh, Sukie Ambrose, you lucky, lucky girl. Bet Paris Hilton'd kill for a social diary like yours."

Then she straightened her slinky overall, checked that her hair was at its spiky best and her eyes perfectly kohled, and prepared to join Jennifer to do battle with Beauty's Blessings' Saturday morning clientele.

By lunchtime the weather was still grey, cold and drizzly. With the peach leather cases ensconced in the boot of her nondescript hatchback, Sukie made short work of the journey between Hazy Hassocks and Bagley-cum-Russet.

Topsy, wearing a long grey mac and a fawn headscarf which made her merge with the murky surroundings, was waiting by the cottage gate. There was no sign of Milla's silver car or Derry's always-dirty jeep, which hopefully meant they weren't in the cottage.

"Sorry I'm a bit late," Sukie apologised, hefting the cases from the car. "Everyone seemed to want nail extensions or facials for their Saturday night out. No — I can manage these, thanks — go on indoors, it's so cold and you've probably been waiting ages and . . ."

"Stop babbling," Topsy said sharply. "And stop treating me like I'm an old lady. Age," she tapped the headscarf, "is all up here, my girl. And up here I'm still in my prime."

"Of course, yes sorry — go through into the living room." Chastened, Sukie motioned with her head as she piled the cases on to the hall table, praying that the living room was reasonably tidy and that Milla and Derry hadn't abandoned their cars and their inhibitions somewhere and weren't currently indulging in sexual athletics on the sofa. "Would you like a cup of tea?"

"No thank you," Topsy looked round the room, which was fortunately Milla and Derry-free, and agilely skirted the clutch of fat cushiony non-matching armchairs to stand in front of the black grate where gas-logs burned now rather than the real thing. "You've kept it much as Cora had it, then?"

"I didn't want to change it. I loved it. It's always been my home. Even when I'd had the central heating installed I put everything back as it was because that's how Cora always had it and . . . okay, I guess you don't want to talk to me about Cora, do you?"

"Actually I do. No — I'm not going to go all maudlin on you — and we're both busy people so I'll cut to the chase. I could have spoken to you at rehearsals — but this is a delicate subject and there are far too many wagging ears there."

Sukie was intrigued now. Was Topsy going to tell her some alleged dark secret about Cora? Had her scatty godmother, in Topsy's fertile imagination, been a Cold War double-agent, or a cross-dresser, or a secret dope peddler?

"You want to tell me something about Cora? But there's nothing I don't know about her."

"I think there probably is." Topsy released the headscarf. Her hair was scraped back into its bun and pressed tightly to her skull. She looked even more tortoise-like. "Me and Cora were friends from the cradle. We shared a good many things. Things that youngsters like you have probably never got wind of. As soon as Valerie Pridmore mentioned you were going to make a business of these flower power massages I knew I had to put you straight."

Sukie bit her lips. If she wasn't harping on about the latest lifesaving surgery as employed in the medical soaps, Topsy was inventing Bagley-cum-Russet folklore. Sukie had no doubt she was just about to find out that Cora had been a Grade A witch and spent her free time in levitation and flying too close to the moon. She sighed.

"And don't sigh, my girl. I've got hearing like a weasel I'll have you know. Now, look at this . . ." Topsy marched across to the window, her back straight as a ramrod under the mac. "What do you see out there?"

Sukie joined her in peering through the tiny leaded panes at the back garden. "A sort of dripping, damp, tangled mangle of weeds. It's on my to-do list for the summer but —"

"Not weeds," Topsy interrupted. "Raw materials."

"Sorry?"

"Raw materials. The raw materials for your craft. Cora's garden is, and always has been, a veritable storehouse of natural energy."

Sukie laughed, but kindly. "Topsy — is that honestly what this is all about? Cora's garden? All those strange old plants that used to be in my adventure playground which I've shamefully neglected and will restore to their former glory as soon as the weather warms up a bit?"

"Those plants," Topsy said sternly, "aren't there by accident. Don't think, young lady, with the usual arrogance of youth, that you're the first person in this cottage to work with infusions and oils."

"What? You mean — ? Cora . . .? No, you're wrong. I spent all my life with Cora. She never so much as used a sprig of lavender in the airing cupboard."

"And why, when she has a garden full of it, do you think that was?"

"I honestly don't know. But I do know that I have a whole case filled with synthetic oils and essences — I certainly won't need to wade around out there in all that weedy mess to find the perfect plant for my massages. Look, Topsy, I'm sure this is very interesting

63

but please don't try to involve Cora in some imagined practical magic rubbish."

"Rubbish?" The beady eyes glittered. "*Rubbish?* You can't have lived here all your life and not known that things — unexplained and inexplicable things — have happened here in Bagley and the surrounding villages. You know full-well that Mitzi Blessing didn't stumble on her Hubble Bubble kitchen-witch recipes by accident in Hazy Hassocks, or that those star-ceremonies in Fiddlesticks don't produce results that no earthly reasoning can explain?"

Sukie shook her head. "Herbal cooking might just make susceptible people believe that there's magic afoot if they want to believe it — and the Fiddlestickers are all crazy anyway and their star things are just an excuse for a party . . . But Bagley isn't like that."

"Yes it is." Topsy turned away from the window. "And it always has been. Maybe in your lifetime these powers have been left undisturbed, but way back, when me and Cora were gels together, and long, long before that even, Bagley-cum-Russet had more magic than Hazy Hassocks and Fiddlesticks put together. And Pixies Laughter Cottage was always at the root. Cora knew only too well about the power of her garden. She wouldn't have used her plants while you were around, that's for sure. In fact after all the trouble, she left it well alone. That's why she didn't as much as pick a sprig of rosemary for her lamb roast."

"Trouble? What trouble?"

"My lips are sealed." Topsy clamped her mouth shut to illustrate the point. It looked like a ruckled grey zipper. Then she opened it again. "Let's just say, Honour Berkeley wasn't the only woman in Bagley to rue the amount of time she spent in this garden. No, as soon as I knew you were going to be dabbling in perfumery and oils and rubs and balms here, I had to warn you what you might be unleashing."

Sukie tried really hard not to laugh. Topsy was clearly insane. It was all too Harry Potter meets Winnie the Witch to be true.

"No." Sukie frowned. "Sorry. I simply don't buy it. I don't want to be rude, but Honour Berkeley — if the Boys and the gossip are to be believed — was a whole generation ahead of you and Cora, and a bit of a flapper-slapper to boot, so how could you know anything about her? And what on earth does the cottage have to do with Honour Berkeley's — or anyone else's — *troubles*? I've never heard so much nonsense in my life. And honestly, Topsy, you — well, everyone knows about your dreams, the dancing or the medical profession that simply didn't happen for you — and so, well, maybe . . ."

She stopped and stared at Topsy. Topsy stared defiantly back.

Sukie shrugged, not wanting to hurt Topsy's feelings. "Look, the whole village knows that you have a very vivid imagination. It must be hard sometimes to remember what's real and what isn't. I don't blame you for making things up. But please don't drag Cora into your fantasies. Cora was —"

"Cora was a matchmaker."

CHAPTER
SIX

Sukie hooted with laughter. "A matchmaker? Oh, pul-lease! Come on, Topsy, pull the other one. Crikey, I've heard some nonsense in my time, but —"

"It's far from nonsense," Topsy said quietly. "Cora was the best in the business."

Actually, Sukie wasn't a hundred per cent certain what a matchmaker was. She vaguely remembered that old Barbra Streisand film, of course, but surely Cora had never been one of *those*?

Aware that Topsy was still watching her carefully, she knew she'd have to be very kind and gently disabuse Topsy of this latest fanciful notion before it, like the medical terminology and wanting to turn the entire village into Bluebell Girls, got completely out of hand.

Using the voice she used for Beauty's Blessings' clients when a facial hadn't quite cut the mustard, she smiled at Topsy. "Look, it's pretty chilly in here. Why don't we sit by the fire and talk about this — and are you quite sure you wouldn't like a cup of tea?"

"Don't treat me like some geriatric imbecile," Topsy snorted, her eyes narrowing. "I've still got all me marbles! This is for your own good. And while we're on the subject, there's another thing — have you never questioned why this cottage is called Pixies Laughter?"

"No — but why would I?" Sukie walked quickly across to the fireplace. "Because it always has been for the last two hundred years, I suppose. It's just an ancient version of Dunroamin', isn't it? I've never thought about it — although I do know my parents wanted to change the name to Rose Cottage when they inherited it because they thought Pixies Laughter was too twee for words. Thankfully they didn't get round to making the change — and I certainly won't — and what's that got to do with Cora being a matchmaker anyway? You're just confusing me now."

Topsy turned away from the window. "The cottage is called Pixies Laughter because that's exactly what happened here. According to local folklore, hundreds of years ago, probably before the hamlets of Bagley or Russet existed and certainly before they joined together as one village, this site was a hidden meadow, an enchanted place filled with magical plants, a place where illicit lovers met in secret and drank petal wine and where pixie's laughter could be heard on the night air . . ."

Sukie valiantly tried to disguise her sniggers as she bent down to switch on the gas logs. "Oh, of course! Silly me! Why didn't I think of that? This whole place is awash with sprites and elves all the time! Sometimes you can't even get into the bathroom because it's full of goblins!"

Topsy tutted at such levity. "This isn't a joke, Sukie. There are things that have happened here that no one could ever explain. Cora could hear the pixies' laughter. That's how she knew she had the power. She knew she was in tune with a magical world. You've never heard them, have you? The pixies laughing?"

"No!" Sukie frowned. Was Topsy actually safe to be allowed out alone? "Of course not. I don't believe in fairies . . ."

"I'm glad you haven't heard them. It probably means you're not blessed with the gift."

Sukie wasn't sure whether she was supposed to be pleased or disappointed by this. All she knew was that she really, really mustn't hurt Topsy's feelings. This poppy-cock was clearly very important to her. As real to her as her medical obsession and her frustrated dancing dreams. "Ah, well — we can't have everything, can we? I'll just have to learn to live with being out of tune with the little people. But do you think, seriously, if there was anything like that here — if Pixies Laughter was haunted in any way — that Cora would have allowed me to live here without warning me?"

Topsy hadn't moved from the window. "One it isn't haunted. And two, Cora didn't give the cottage to you, did she? She left it to your parents — who, if you'll forgive me saying, are the most unimaginative, stolid, uninspiring couple I've ever met. There was no danger of them being touched by the magic, or having the least curiosity about the cottage or its past. I'm sure Cora willed it to them, knowing that they'd probably sell it and that you'd never live here, never have to find out about its history."

"But my parents must have *known* the cottage was okay and that Cora wasn't a-a matchmaker . . ." Sukie sank into her favourite deep-cushioned armchair, still stumbling over the word. "They let her be my godmother, for heaven's sake. They wouldn't have done that if they'd thought she was a witch."

"Cora wasn't a damn witch! She was your mother's aunt. An aunt, I must say, who your mother shamefully ignored because she refused to conform. Asking her to be your godmother was simply paying lip-service to the family. They wouldn't have known anything about the matchmaking. I doubt if your parents knew, or cared, very much about Cora at all."

Sukie nodded. That much was probably true. Cora and her parents had always been light-years apart. It was however unpleasant to hear this from Topsy.

She really wished she could rush to her parents' defence. Or even wanted to.

Tempted at last by the warmth, Topsy crossed the room and held out wrinkled brown hands towards the fire. She watched the blue and red and yellow flames dancing. "All her life, all your mother has cared about has been her social climbing and the latest must haves. Heavens — I've never known a more self-obsessed person than your mother, even as a little girl. She should have married that awful pompous prig Marvin Benson." She stared at the fire for a moment longer, then smiled at Sukie. "Oh, did I tell you I asked his wife, Jocelyn, if she'd like to join the can-canners? She said no but she's going to do an interview with you about the troupe for the *Bagley Bugle*. Won't that be nice?"

"Sod the Bensons and the can-canners and the bloody *Bagley Bugle*," Sukie snapped. "Don't start back-pedalling now, Topsy. You started telling me this nonsense about Cora — so you just carry on. Go on. You were saying that Cora left Pixies Laughter to Mum and Dad because she knew they weren't into Saturday Night Satanism and therefore wouldn't have any sixth sense about sacrificial altars in the garden shed or recognising a ducking stool in the outside privy? Is that right?"

"Don't mock, Sukie, dear. Please don't mock. This is nothing to do with devil-worship or black magic or witchcraft. I know Cora really wanted you to live in this cottage because you loved it and she loved you very much — we discussed it a lot — but she knew it might be too dangerous. She always felt you were a little fey . . ."

"Fey? Bloody fey? I'm not fey! I'm not a bloody hobgoblin! This is real life! I'm an aromatherapist, working with synthetic oils and fragrances. I'm hardly likely to go ripping up clumps of nettles from the garden at dawn when I've got all those gorgeous little bottles of — what — what have I said now?"

"Nettles. Dawn. There you are you see, you automatically mentioned the most magical time of day for herbal-gathering and nettles in one breath. Nettles are one of the most potent ingredients of any love potion."

"Bollocks! I just said dawn because it's what fairy-tales are all about, and because nettles are the most boring plants ever and they grow everywhere and the garden is full of them and — and *what? Love potions?* What love potions?"

Topsy turned away from the gas logs and perched on the edge of one of the cushiony chairs opposite Sukie. "You really haven't been listening have you? Cora made love potions. Haven't I already explained?"

"You said she was a matchmaker. Even if I believed that bit, which I don't, I thought you meant she was a sort of pre-computer Dateline-dot-com or something. You know, got her mates together, sorted out which blokes they fancied, had a word in a few ears, that sort of thing. You mean she concocted mixtures from plants — like dandelion and burdock for beginners — and forced them down people's throats?"

Topsy sighed. "The drinking potions were her main stock in trade, yes, but Cora worked with infusions and oils as well — which is why I needed to tell you just in case —"

"I suddenly got the urge to go skipping round the garden pulling up weeds, boiling them, mashing them down, straining them into bottles and rubbing them into unsuspecting people? Yeah right — very likely when I have all the twenty-first century fragrances and essences and oils I need out there in those cases; oils and infusions which will help my clients and enrich their lives — not bloody poison them!"

Topsy said nothing. Just perched on the edge of the big fat chair still looking sad.

Sukie sighed. She really didn't need this. She had enough silly things to occupy her waking moments. She looked across the room, through the window at the darkening steel-grey sky and the scudding charcoal clouds, then back at Topsy. "Okay, so if she was so bloody good at being a matchmaker — how come she never married? And what about you? Did you get the late Mr Turvey to propose by chucking one of Cora's bottles over his head and chanting — *love divine, Algernon Turvey be mine* — or some such nonsense?"

Topsy winced. "That's rather insensitive of you, dear. But since you ask, then yes I used Cora's special skills — but it wasn't quite as blatant as your version. I wasn't in love with Algernon Turvey, but he was with me. He was never the love of my life — but I asked Cora to make him my husband . . ." Topsy smiled, clearly in some far-off place. "Look, dear, I can understand why you're angry and confused. I just wish I hadn't needed to tell you any of this — but I promised Cora, promised her, that I'd always keep an eye on you — and if there was any danger at all that you might find out about the flower magic —"

"Which I wouldn't have done if you hadn't told me, would I?"

"But you might have done. With your chosen trade and working from home . . . I couldn't risk it. I'd never forgive myself. Look, I've probably said enough for now. Just be careful, Sukie, that's all."

"No, it's not all. Tell me all of it. Everything." Sukie leaned back in her chair. "I still don't believe any of this

72

— but you can't stop now. So — go on — tell me the rest. Please, Topsy. I promise I won't mock."

Topsy stared deep into the fire. "There's not much to tell. Me and Cora, we were friends like you and young Chelsea — just as giggly and giddy. Hard for you to believe, I'm sure, but I haven't always been an old lady, and nothing much changes. When Cora and me and all the other village girls were your age and younger — and like you, had rampaging emotions and needed love, all the young men had gone to war. All of them. Well, most. There were some who weren't fit enough, or in reserved occupations, or pacifists — but the majority of boys our age, boys who we yearned for just as much as you youngsters do today, were suddenly taken away. Gone. To fight. And probably die. Gone to who knew where, for who knew how long . . . Imagine it, how you'd feel, if that happened today."

Sukie stared at the dancing flames of the gas logs. How would it be? Just awful . . . Too awful to contemplate if young men like Lewis Flanagan and Derry Kavanagh and all the other gorgeous boys were suddenly taken away from the village to fight and possibly die . . .

"So do you mean, once all the boys had gone to war, if the girls couldn't have their first choice, then Cora concocted something from weeds to make them fall in love with whoever was available? The old men or the invalids? Any port in a storm? That's disgusting . . ."

"It's very easy to be prim about it now, Sukie, but it wasn't like that at all. It was just that some girls, left alone in these villages, lonely, scared, bored — whatever

— needed love. There were other boys stationed near here, or visiting foreign servicemen, who were also desperately lonely and homesick and separated from the ones they loved. Goodness, you know how these things happen? Cora mixed potions for them because she had the gift. She saw it as a service for the lovelorn and lonely. Just as a short-term thing, of course, but some of the relationships developed into more than that."

"What was wrong with that? The war lasted years and years. I suppose the women at home would have had to move on, and if they found happiness with strangers . . ."

"All very well for the single girls, but when the local boys came back after the war there were some pretty serious liaisons in place. Do you understand? Married women, fiancées, madly in love with Other People? Not all down to Cora of course, but scores of desperate women, who had taken her elixirs to start with, begged her to make them fall in love with their men again — men who had been away for five or six years and who were virtual strangers. It all got a bit unpleasant in some cases. Cora never forgave herself for some of the more unfortunate pairings or marriage break-ups . . . it wasn't what she'd intended. That's what I meant by troubles — and that's why she stopped matchmaking."

Even if it had happened — which Sukie still doubted — it was all ancient history. Maybe just maybe, Cora had discovered some sort of herbal mind-altering plants . . . and maybe, just maybe, there were enough lonely and gullible women in the village to believe it would work. But that was then — this was now, real-time, and simply not relevant. It was, as so many of Topsy's stories were, simply a rural myth writ large.

"Okay, if I buy that much of the story, it still doesn't explain why Cora never managed to make her love potions work for herself or why you ended up with Non Turvey who you didn't love."

Topsy seemed to withdraw into the collar of her mac, like a tortoise disappearing into its shell. Her voice was very faint. "Cora and I were in love with two village lads . . . very much in love. When it was obvious that the war was about to start they were all fired up with patriotic zeal and enlisted. They said that way they'd get the pick of the fighting jobs rather than waiting for compulsory call-up and becoming cannon-fodder . . ."

Sukie started into the flames again. How strange to think Topsy and Cora had been like her and Chelsea . . . They'd done World War II at school. She knew all about it. It just hadn't seemed to have involved real people . . . Real girls in love with real boys . . .

"And what happened to them? The boys you loved?"

"Cora's boyfriend was blown to bits in the back of a Lancaster bomber, mine was killed in the Western Desert . . ."

Sukie swallowed. She wasn't sure where the Western Desert was but it didn't matter, she couldn't look at Topsy.

"Cora certainly wouldn't have looked at anyone else. Her heart was broken for ever." Topsy's voice was still quiet. "Me? I probably shouldn't have done it, but I

75

didn't want to be Miss Jean Millett for the rest of my life."

Jean Millett? Sukie frowned and opened her mouth then shut it again. Of course, Topsy must have been saddled with the nickname the minute she married Algernon. It was like her geography teacher; Miss Black one term, married to a Mr Crawley in the holidays, and forever after known to the entire school as Creepy.

Topsy plucked at the folds of her mac with skinny wizened fingers. "Non Turvey was a farm-hand. He didn't go to war. He had flat feet and a dicky ticker to boot. He was here and he was a man and he was young and he liked me. It probably sounds odd to you, but I really wanted to be married, so I asked Cora to make a potion for me to take . . ."

"And it worked?"

"Yes. We married and were happy enough until the dicky ticker did for him. I never stopped loving my first beau. And I knew I didn't love Non like he loved me, but Cora kept giving me top-ups, and me and Non bumbled along together for the next thirty odd years. And no I don't regret it. It was still better than being alone."

Sukie said nothing. For a moment she could see herself as Cora and Topsy and the other girls must have been back all those years ago. And she could understand how, without the freedoms and diversions of twenty-first century life, they must have been desperate enough to grab at anything. But even so . . .

Topsy leaned forward in the big fat chair. "Sukie, all I wanted to do was warn you that things can happen here. The gentle magical power of plants has been used for thousands of years — and especially plants grown in places like Pixies Laughter. Cora knew how to engage earth energies — no, don't laugh at me. I told her she should have let you know what went on here — but she said it wasn't necessary because you'd got your heart set on being a beautician and that this place would never be your home and that you'd never be tempted to use the garden . . . I think she thought that you'd be standing behind a counter in a department store with your face plastered in make up . . . She clearly had no idea that it would eventually involve these flower potions and massages or that you'd be living here."

Surely it was all far too bizarre to be true? But, what if it wasn't? What if Cora really did have some sort of gift? What if the tangled garden of Pixies Laughter really was a storehouse of *magic* plants? Sukie listened to the March wind buffeting round the cottage making the gas logs sing.

"So did Cora write all this down? All her potions? Did she have an ancient recipe book like the one Mitzi Blessing found for her herbal cookery?"

"No."

Sukie stared at Topsy. The denial had been too quick. Far, far too quick.

"I don't believe you. She did, didn't she? It's here somewhere, isn't it? Still in the cottage?"

"No," Topsy said again. "There was no book. Nothing written down."

"You know there was!" Sukie struggled from the depths of the fat cushions. "Topsy — you *know*! And you hoped that it would have been chucked out when mum and dad cleared the paperwork out of the cottage after Cora died — but you can't be sure, can you? There's still a lot of her stuff everywhere — so it could well be here, couldn't it?"

Topsy stood up in one graceful movement, straightened her mac and headed for the hallway. "There is no book. No papers. No recipes. Cora had it all in her head. Everything died with her. Sukie, I'm sorry if I've upset you with any of this — but I don't regret telling you. You have the information now. What you do with it is up to you. Now, if you'll excuse me, I really do have to go. I like to be snugged in early of a Saturday night ready for *Casualty* . . ."

From the window, Sukie watched Topsy stride down the garden path and disappear into the grey gathering March gloom.

The cottage suddenly seemed strangely silent. Lonely. Despite the cheery gas logs she shivered. She wished Milla was home. She wished Chelsea would turn up and fill the cottage with giggles and scurrilous gossip as they prepared for the hen-night. She wished she couldn't hear the soft sighing of the wind and the hiss of the rain. And she really wished it didn't sound quite so much like gentle, distant, high-pitched laughter.

CHAPTER
SEVEN

Saturday evening in the Bensons' bungalow was as ritualistic as the rest of the week. In fact the whole day was organised with almost military precision: in the morning Marvin washed the car or played nine holes of golf while Joss shopped — food shopping only — in Hazy Hassocks; lunch was at one on the dot and something light on toast; in the afternoon Marvin dozed in front of the sports channels, and Joss gardened if the weather was fine and read if it wasn't.

And then in the evening . . . Well, Saturday evenings were the worst of all.

Joss, sitting in front of the dressing table mirror, staring wistfully at her reflection, as always hoping that someone sensuous and wanton would smoulder back at her, wondered why no one had ever warned her that vowing "until death do us part" would mean that on Saturdays she really, really wished it would be sooner rather than later.

She and Marvin always "did something" on a Saturday evening. It was as much of a ritual as the rest of the day and far less enjoyable. If they went out it was never to dances or concerts or the theatre or the cinema, all of which Joss would have loved. Especially dancing. She wondered why she'd told Topsy Turvey that she couldn't dance — years of denial probably. Marvin loathed dancing and it simply seemed easier to say she was useless at it. She probably was now anyway. Use it or lose it, as everyone kept saying . . .

No, there was no Saturday night dancing because they always went out to eat. Usually to supper parties with Marvin's Rotary or cricket club chums, or at the Golf Club in Winterbrook, or to restaurants recommended by the Sunday supplements which served tiny, pretty meals which never, ever lived up to Joss's expectations or satisfied her apparently unfashionably healthy appetite.

Slowly, she fixed her pearl ear-studs: pale, safe jewellery to match her pale, safe face and cream silk sweater. So bland . . . What would Marvin say, she often wondered, if she shimmied downstairs with more make-up than Danny La Rue and a flamboyant outfit in scarlet and orange? What would Marvin say if she suggested they did something impromptu and daring? What would Marvin say if she told him how she hated Saturday evenings more than any other time of the week?

Occasionally on Saturday evenings they stayed in and invited people to dinner parties at the bungalow. These were the worst ones of all. If they could have invited people she knew and felt at home with it would have been fine, but Marvin had, over the years, actively discouraged Joss's friends from visiting The Close, and eventually even the more determined ones had drifted away.

80

So they entertained Marvin's cronies and Joss loathed the bitchy, snobbish small-talk with people she hardly knew and with whom she had nothing in common, and always felt under pressure to produce the latest designer meals which would pass muster with Marvin's pals and their squeaky-voiced well-bred wives.

Joss had always felt she was what was known as a good plain cook — well, good plain everything really — and longed to dish up hearty stews and pies and casseroles and steamed puddings. But Marvin wouldn't have any of that. No, she had to sweat over arty-farty cookery books and create drizzled things in stacks, and remember if pomegranate or blueberry was the latest culinary fad.

At least tonight wasn't going to be one of those, although where they were going remained, as ever, a mystery. Marvin made those decisions.

Standing up, straightening her neat taupe skirt, Joss wished that she was accompanying Valerie Pridmore and her husband to the Barmy Cow for a riotous night of drinking, darts, and laughter.

Marvin, of course, never set foot in the Barmy Cow; and, to be honest, it was a dive — but it was a dive filled with people who were happy with their lot, who enjoyed what they had and didn't spoil the here-and-now by yearning for the what-may-be. People who knew how to laugh and sing and have a damn good time. People like Valerie Pridmore and her husband who still made love . . .

Even the Berkeley Boys amused her. Marvin, who had never shed his ancestors' Victorian Values, would go all prim when they were mentioned and call them the Berkeley Bastards. Marvin, who knew foul language was the verbal currency of the underclasses, always felt he could use the world bastard in its correct context without the sky falling in.

"Jocelyn!" Marvin's voice rang through the bungalow. "Are you ready? It's nearly seven!"

Joss dragged her beige raincoat from the wardrobe — it was still grey and cold and drizzly outside — and slid her feet into her sensible low-heeled courts which she always wore because she always drove on Saturdays so that Marvin could drink, then walked across the hall into the living-room with her usual sense of death-row dread.

"Ready . . . Who are we eating with tonight?"

Marvin, polished and poised for the off, gave her a cursory glance. "That skirt looks a bit snug. You could do with losing a couple of pounds — oh, we're meeting Simon and Sonia. You like them, don't you?"

Joss, who always felt she'd like Simon and Sonia a lot more if they'd do something interesting like spontaneously combust, said nothing.

"Old Simon has got the needle because I beat him hollow at golf last week," Marvin guffawed, straightening his cricket club tie. "Sonia says I owe her a decent dinner because he's been unbearable to live with ever since."

Someone owes me about thirty years' worth of decent dinners then, Joss thought, as she removed the car keys from their hook by the front door. "And where are we eating?"

Please, please not somewhere minimalist and *nouveau* with food she didn't recognise.

Marvin pushed past her through the door and shivered in the damp onslaught. "Damn chilly tonight! Oh, a chap on the train the other morning said he'd had the best meal ever at a little local hostelry. Can't think why we've never tried it before."

Joss could. Little local hostelries were, according to Marvin, filled with feral yobs, chavs, scum and inbreds.

"Not far for you to drive tonight," Marvin sounded as though he was handing her the moon wrapped in silk. "We're going to Fiddlesticks. To the Weasel and Bucket."

"What the hell are you doing down there in that cupboard?" Chelsea shrieked at Sukie's rear view. "And why are you still in your dressing gown? Haven't you showered yet? It's nearly seven o'clock!"

"Ow!" Sukie, startled by Chelsea's sudden appearance, leapt up, cracking her head on the open drawer above her. "Ouch . . . that hurts . . . don't laugh . . . And how did you get in?"

"The front door was unlocked. I let myself in. Why the hell are you spring cleaning now?"

"I'm not spring cleaning . . . I'm — er — looking for something. And I showered ages ago and . . . and — good God!" Sukie blinked, focusing on Chelsea properly for the first time. "What on earth have you come as?"

"I'm a fairy." Chelsea, her painted face covered in silver glitter, pirouetted, waving a pink and silver flashing wand above her head. "Nice, innit?"

Sukie blinked some more. The brief pink net tutu barely covered Chelsea's brief pink knickers; the white satin bodice looked suspiciously like something from a porn shop; the pink fishnet tights and ballet pumps were — well — odd; but the most amazing thing was the fluffy flashing candyfloss pink tiara sitting atop Chelsea's variegated hair.

"You didn't walk through the village like that?" Sukie giggled. "Please tell me you didn't . . ."

"Nah, it's far too cold. Dad dropped me off. He'll be back to pick us up in fifteen minutes and take us to Fiddlesticks. We'll have to get a taxi back, mind. Er — I don't suppose the love god is here, is he?"

"Who?"

"Derry Kavanagh, of course." Chelsea frowned, her tiara winking and blinking. "I'd love to flash me wand at him."

"Sad." Sukie grinned. "So sad. And no he isn't here. Neither is Milla so he won't even be dropping in to collect her. You'll have to go and do your Fairy Vamp act on someone else tonight."

"Bugger," Chelsea said good-naturedly. "And as the pub is going to be filled with women it'll all go to waste. We could always hang around for a bit and see if Derry turns up I suppose . . ."

No we couldn't, Sukie thought. Derry Kavanagh had laughed at her once — he'd never get the chance to do it again. "Oh, I doubt if Milla will bring him back here anytime soon. She's probably got him shacked up in some five-star boudoir as we speak."

"Lucky cow," Chelsea sighed. "Oh well, in that case you'd better get a move on before my dad arrives. Yours is in one of these carrier bags."

"My what?"

"Outfit. Fairy stuff."

"I'm not dressing up."

"You bloody well are. We all are. It's what Fern wanted and it's her hen-night so you have to. Now go and do your slap and get dressed — and I'll look for whatever it was you've lost in that cupboard."

No, Sukie shook her head. No way was she dressing up — and definitely no way was she telling Chelsea that she'd spent the last hours driving herself crazy thinking about Topsy's ill-timed revelations and subsequently scouring Pixies Laughter for Cora's allegedly non-existent love potion recipes.

"I'm just wearing a pink T-shirt with my jeans and a bit of body glitter."

"You are not! Everyone's dressing up. And you're wearing this," Chelsea thrust a Big Sava carrier bag towards Sukie. "Same as me. Ronald made them specially."

"Would that be Ronald of Bagley-cum-Russet? Couturier to the stars?"

"Ronald from Hazy Hassocks," Chelsea sighed. "You know Ronnie? That odd one of Mitzi Blessing's Baby Boomers who Topsy got to make our can-can dresses. He's great on show-bizzy outfits. Loves the glitz and sequins. You can pay me later."

Sukie peered into the carrier bag. "And this is the same as yours, is it?"

"Exactly," Chelsea said proudly. "We'll look like twins."

"I'll look like a fat tart. And as my legs look like raw sausages at this time of year — pink fishnets will really look good on them."

"Duh!" Chelsea struck a pose, wand above her head. "And what does Topsy always say about fishnets? 'Make sure you're wearing a pair of tan tights or stockings underneath, gels, and the fishnets will work wonders on any legs.'"

Sukie giggled again. "Yeah, well maybe she was right about that — but I'm still not being seen in public in the rest of it."

"Of course you bloody are." Chelsea shoved Sukie towards the twisty staircase. "Go and get dressed — and you have remembered Fern's present, haven't you?"

"Yes, the bottles are on the hall table — if you grab them while I'm upstairs and put them with yours I won't forget them, but —" she squinted again at the fairy outfit, "— I'm really not sure about this . . ."

"Blimey, Sukes — it's no more revealing than the can-can dresses — they're all basques and suspenders and stockings and petticoats and stuff — and you don't mind that, do you?"

"That's different."

Well, it was, Sukie thought as she marched upstairs clutching the Big Sava bag. As they had so far can-canned only to various audiences in care homes or at school fêtes, Ronnie's interpretation of the Moulin Rouge costume seemed glamorous and exciting and well, appropriate. Sukie had never thought of it as arousing in any way. Whereas this skimpy fairy stuff — she shook the Big Sava bag — was downright inflammatory.

Still, she thought as she grabbed her can of glitter spray, as Chelsea had pointed out, at least the Weasel and Bucket would be a man-free zone tonight. It would be full of Fern's Fairies. No one would be even slightly interested in her curves spilling out of a costume that really belonged in the Mixed Infants Christmas play, would they?

The Weasel and Bucket was everything the Barmy Cow wasn't, Joss thought, looking round in delight at the highly polished surfaces, the twinkling brasses, the original low black beams, the crackling log fire. A real country pub. Cosy, friendly, warm — and, for a Saturday evening, surprisingly empty.

"Oh, isn't it lovely?" Joss turned to Marvin in delight. "Why on earth have we never been here before?"

"You know my feelings on local pubs." Marvin was already powering his way to the far end of the Weasel and Bucket's long bar. "Although this one appears passable at least — but I'm always wary of this village — you know what goes on here, don't you?"

Joss did. Fiddlesticks believed in astral magic. They had the wildest outdoor parties because the villagers believed that the moon and the stars controlled their destiny. Well, they probably didn't believe that these days, of course, but they still held the parties.

Joss thought it was wonderful. Marvin, naturally, didn't.

"Look — old Simon and Sonia have beaten us to it — trust them to have bagged a table by the fire." Marvin was rubbing his hands together. It was really irritating. Joss always longed to add superglue to his Atrixo. "You'd better get the drinks in, then."

Joss stared at his retreating tweed-jacketed back. Drinks for all of them? What on earth did Simon and Sonia drink? Could she remember? Did it matter? Did she care?

"Um — a large glass of dry white, please." She smiled at the elderly woman behind the bar. "And a large spritzer for me, please. And refills of whatever they . . ." Joss motioned towards Sonia and Simon at the fireside table, "are having? Thank you."

"They're having the same as you," the woman told her. "Except they didn't say please and thank you."

Joss smiled in sympathy. They wouldn't. "It's very quiet in here tonight."

The woman paused in pouring the wine. "Lull before the storm. There's a hen-night booked. We're just relief bar staff for the evening because the landlord and his girlfriend are getting married. He's gone off to Blackpool with the lads but she's having her do here — pink fairies is the theme, apparently. She's a lovely girl, young Fern, but fairy-like she ain't. It'll be bedlam later, you mark my words."

Joss smiled in delight. A hen-night! Not only would that drive Marvin completely insane, it would liven up her Saturday evening no end.

"Maybe I'd better take a few bottles of wine and some soda then — if it's going to be crowded later on."

"Good thinking. I'll get you a big bucket," the barmaid chuckled. "Not to drink out of, mind, dear. Just to keep your Chardonnay cool."

Joss chuckled back, pushing away the superb mental picture of Marvin slurping from a bucket, took the wine and the ice bucket, arranged the glasses on a tray and paid.

"Lovely. Thanks. Oh, we're planning on eating here tonight, too. So did the other couple ask for a menu?"

"No — but it wouldn't have mattered if they had. Timmy Pluckrose does a super spread usually, but like I said, we're only relief for the weekend. And I only do the basics. So, if you want to eat, dear, you'll have to order early because of the party — and it's steak and kidney pie or my special stew — either beef or veggie — with herb dumplings. And there's just spotted dick and custard for pud."

Joss could have capered on the spot. This was getting better and better.

"That sounds perfect. I'll go and let the others know and be back in a second . . ."

Carefully carrying the loaded tray, Joss made her way to the fireside table. Marvin didn't even look up.

Simon and Sonia, gym-honed and Next-dressed, skimmed vague smiles in her direction and didn't say thank you for their drinks. They were clearly deep in

89

conversation with Marvin about the delights on the extensive menu arrayed on blackboards around the pub's nubbly walls.

"Er —" Joss sat down, "— there's no point in choosing from there. The landlord isn't —"

They all stopped talking for a moment, looked at her as if she were some irritating insect, and then continued.

"Marv . . ."

Sonia tittered. "Marv? *Marv?* She makes you sound like some ancient soul singer! Goodness, Simon would want an instant divorce if I called him Si . . ."

If only it were that simple, Joss thought viciously.

"Jocelyn knows that I loathe being called Marv," Marvin growled. "She must have forgotten."

Joss took a deep breath, ignoring Marvin's thunderous expression. It was his purple one with the little pulsing neck veins. "The lady behind the bar has just said that she only has a reduced menu tonight . . ." and she reeled off the delights.

"Damn typical! School dinner stodge!" Marvin sniffed. "Well, I don't know about you two but I vote we go somewhere else."

Sonia and Simon exchanged a long look. Joss was pretty sure she'd kill all of them if they wanted to make a move to some faux-rustic eatery.

"I don't know — it might be fun in a retro sort of way," Simon said with an air of desperate jollity. "It's years since I had a decent steak and kidney pie. Old Sonia is a bit of a demon on the low-fat malarkey."

Sonia winced and looked as if she was just about to list the amount of saturated fats and cholesterol-inducers in pastry, not to mention the statistical likelihood of heart attacks caused by the trans-fat in dumplings.

"Whatever you think, Simon," she said, inverting her lips. "But don't come to me for sympathy if you're up all night with raging indigestion."

Marvin, still looking mauve, nodded slowly. "Probably inedible — after all, who eats that sort of stuff these days? Pastry, for heaven's sake! But still, if you're willing to take the risk . . ."

They were staying! Yessss! Joss had a little moment of mental elation. Then, taking a gulp of her spritzer, she stood up. "So? Everyone for steak and kidney? And four spotted dicks? Lovely — I'll go and order."

"Steady on. What's the rush?" Marvin frowned. "You're being very bossy tonight, old girl."

"I'm starving," Joss said happily, knowing they had to have their food on the table before the hen-night started. Marvin was far too tight to leave food untouched when it had been paid for, but she knew he'd be out of the Weasel and Bucket like a greased gannet if he got wind of the upcoming party.

She could, she thought as she hurried back to the bar, even forgive him for calling her "old girl". It was worth it to be able to watch him become apoplectic later.

The food, huge heaped platters and various tureens of fresh vegetables which looked as if they really had come from someone's garden rather than the local cash-and-carry, arrived remarkably swiftly. Joss, piling her plate with carrots and purple sprouting, noticed that Simon was already wolfing back his pie crust like a man desperate for a carb fix.

"I say. What's going on over there?" Sonia piped up through a chunky mouthful. "What are all those old ladies doing?"

Joss kept her eyes on her plate. She'd seen the twinkly banners and dozens of pink balloons and sparkly tinsel streamers stacked behind the bar when she'd ordered the food.

Everyone else stared across the pub to where a clutch of less-than-young ladies were scrambling on to chairs and small step ladders, fixing the decorations.

"Oh, Simon — look! Isn't that Gwyneth Wilkins and that huge woman she's friends with?" Sonia's voice was still muffled by a mouth filled with forbidden delights. "Ida Something? It is! We've seen them at our Slim'n'Slender Salsa class in Winterbrook, haven't we? Fit for their age of course, but both very strange old ladies. They dance in panne velvet catsuits and plimsolls."

"And there're those Motion women — the undertakers! Thank the lord they haven't brought their weird brother. And that cantankerous old Mona Jupp from the village shop here," Simon added, taking the opportunity to reach across for more gravy-mopping bread. "What on earth are they doing? And why are they all dressed up like Barbara Cartland?"

Joss dared to look then. And tried not to hoot with laughter. The more senior hen-nighters had chosen varying degrees of floor-length pink tulle, feather boas and glittery pink headgear.

They looked like the Billy and Freda Watkins Formation Ballroom Team gone mad.

"What on earth is going on here?" Marvin asked.

Joss was delighted to notice he had purple sprouting broccoli caught in his teeth.

"I think it must be some sort of party," Sonia, clearly forgetting that she never touched steak and kidney pie, had cleared her plate and was squinting across the pub. "What do the banners say? Happy Hen-Night? Congratulations to Fern and Timmy? Goodness me — I think we may have clashed with a bit of a do."

"In that case we're definitely leaving," Marvin snorted. "We certainly don't want to get involved with any village goings-on, do we?"

"But we haven't had our spotted dicks yet," Simon said plaintively.

"And the barmaid is just bringing them over — and you've paid for them — and all these drinks," Joss added, saying thank you for all of them as four huge steaming bowls were placed on the table. "Er — is the party about to start?"

"Yep. Young Fern's just come downstairs in her regalia so the countdown's started," the woman beamed. "That's why I thought I'd better get your puds dished up. You won't be able to move in a minute. Ah — here we go!"

Like the first day of the Harrods' sale, the Weasel and Bucket's door flew open and a tidal wave torrent of pink-and-sparkly women poured in, filling the pub with wands and wings. The noise was incredible.

With a further huge roar and a blast of the Dixie Cups "Going To The Chapel" from the jukebox, which clearly had nothing much prior to 1985 in its musical selection, Fern — the bride-to-be if the skin-tight skimpy pink bridal outfit and adorning L plates was anything to go by — shimmied out from behind the bar on stilt-heels.

"Bugger me," Simon spluttered through a mouthful of spotted dick and custard. "Look at the tits on that."

CHAPTER
EIGHT

Pushing into the Weasel and Bucket behind Chelsea, Sukie immediately felt better. The pub was heaving with pink fairies of varying ages all wearing similar revealing outfits. She'd had an awful feeling, in the back of Chelsea's dad's car, that Chelsea might have got the dressing up bit very wrong indeed.

And true, her fairy costume was skimpy, but some of the others were positively indecent. And she needn't have worried about not knowing Fern very well; clearly every female from the surrounding villages had been invited tonight. It was going to be okay.

"Hiya!" Fern shrieked from the bar. "I'm the Sugar Plump Fairy!"

And with every inch of her curves on display and a snazzy little veil pinned on to her curls, she bounced over to them in time to the strains of Chas and Dave belting out "I'm Getting Married In The Morning".

There was a sparkly moment of hugging and kissing and shared body-glitter. Followed by an almost identical twinkly moment of hugging and kissing and thank yous as Chelsea handed over the bag of presents.

"Great to see you both!" Fern yelled. "Drinks are all free. We've put bottles on the tables but just go to the bar for refills when they run out — I think there's some nibbles to soak up the alcohol somewhere — and there's a space for dancing over by the loos. We're having pink champagne later! Don't you both look lovely? I'm sure you know everyone — just mingle and find a table — if you can!"

"Thanks," Sukie roared back. "And congratulations. When's the wedding?"

"End of April! In the Maldives! Just me and Timmy! We're doing the parties before and after, and having the wedding — and the honeymoon — to ourselves!"

"We're doing some of the entertainment for the after-party," Chelsea screamed. "Cancanning? Remember?"

Sukie nodded. Fern hugged them again, and leaving a shower of multi-coloured dust shimmering behind her, powered off to greet another group.

"Look there's Phoebe and Clemmie!" Chelsea tugged at Sukie's wings. "They're waving! They must have saved us a space!"

Phoebe and Clemmie, girls they'd been to school with, were indicating with flashing wands that there was room at their table. Sukie, feeling her spirits soar — there was nothing like a girls' night out to make you forget all the gloom and doom — clutched her flashing tiara and waved her wand back in reply. It was like silver semaphore.

All talking at once, they crammed round the table, pouring wine, shrieking over the costumes, catching up on gossip. Sukie took a slug of Chardonnay and felt the tension ebb miraculously away.

The sadness and anger she'd felt after Topsy's revelations were no more than a twinge now. And whatever Cora had or hadn't concocted in Pixies Laughter, and her reasons for doing so, were best left as ancient history. Although, looking around her now, at all these women having a good time, she couldn't help feeling a little pang for the other women who must have sat in the Weasel and Bucket, generations before, in far less happy circumstances.

She had toyed with the idea of telling Chelsea about Topsy and Cora, but decided against it. Chelsea was lovely, but had little imagination and lived happily in the present. Chelsea probably would never understand how the women of Cora and Topsy's generation had suffered; would never be able to picture them as young girls, madly in love, grieving for the boys who never came home.

No, it was all best left well alone. As was her search for the love potions. Maybe they existed, probably they didn't. It was all in the past. And that was where it must stay.

". . . and what he sees in her is anyone's guess . . ."

". . . she's such a miserable cow . . ."

"Her dad owns a Porsche dealership."

"Ah . . ."

Sukie, relaxing, easily slipped back into the current girlie-chat.

Chelsea suddenly grabbed her arm. "Blimey! Look at them! Just come in . . . Look! Who are they?"

Obediently, Sukie looked at the newcomers: four stunning girls straight out of *Footballers' Wives*, all tall, slim, glossy and slinky, their micro-skirted pink fairy dresses showing acres of sun-tanned legs, and diamanté tiaras reflecting in their super-shiny hair.

"Blimey! Who are *they*?"

"They're with Amber," Clemmie hissed. "Her mates from Oop North. They're down here to stay with her especially for this. They were in here last night — er — Emma and Jemma, Kelly and Bex, I think — and they're really, really nice too. Like Amber. Beautiful and lovely. Not fair. It's so annoying, you'd really like to hate them for being so foxy, wouldn't you?"

Sukie grinned. She'd really wanted to dislike Amber when they'd first met, but found it impossible. No one could ever hate Amber. And, apart from their friendship, she and Amber had a lot in common as they both worked for a Mrs Blessing: Amber as Mitzi's assistant in her catering business, Hubble Bubble, and Sukie, of course, with Jennifer. The rivalry between the past and present title holders had made Sukie and Amber close allies.

Clemmie refilled the glasses again. "Talk of the devil — here's Amber now. Oh, doesn't she look gorgeous in that little pink fairy dress? And so happy."

She did, Sukie had to admit. And so she should. She'd been living with Lewis Flanagan for the last six months. That was enough to put a smile on anyone's face.

"Didn't you have a thing with her Lewis, Sukie, before she did?" Phoebe asked.

"Oh, it was only a one-night stand," Chelsea said. "Poor old Sukes — there was never any contest there, was there?"

Sukie shook her head amiably. "They were made for each other. My turn will come — but not with Lewis. That was a non-starter. Oh, hi . . ."

Amber and her girlfriends had stopped at their table. There was another round of introductions and squeals of excitement over the outfits, and speculation about what Timmy and his stags were getting up to in Blackpool.

"Has Jem gone to Blackpool too?" Sukie asked.

"Too right," Amber chuckled. "He wouldn't have missed out on a weekend of big dippers and casinos — although he was a bit miffed that the boys weren't dressing up too. You know what a show-off he is?"

Sukie laughed. Jem was Lewis's best friend and very special. A young-old man with cerebral palsy, a vibrant personality and a wicked sense of humour, he lived on a one-to-one basis with Lewis as his carer. Sukie had always found it hard to believe that the rock-star-looking Lewis was really a social worker — but he and Jem were inseparable. It also said a lot about Amber that she had fitted so happily into the set-up.

"And," Amber moved a bit closer, "I've heard on the Mona Jupp gossip grapevine that you've been entertaining our Jem's boss at your cottage. Lucky you. He's pretty bloody gorgeous, isn't he?"

"What?" Sukie was relieved that Chelsea, Clemmie and Phoebe were more interested in discussing the joys of celeb-spotting in Manchester with Amber's friends than listening-in. "I think you've got the wrong end of the stick. I haven't been out with anyone for ages. Who the heck is Jem's boss anyway?"

"Derry Kavanagh," Amber sighed the words. "Not as beautiful as Lewis of course, in my opinion, but pretty damn close."

"Derry Kavanagh . . ." Sukie shook her head. "Oh yes, he's sensational, but I'm not going out with him — more's the pity. He's seeing Milla . . . you know? She shares my cottage? And I didn't know he was Jem's boss."

"Jem does a couple of days' work placement every week at Winterbrook Joinery. Derry runs it."

Ah, Sukie thought. So that explained a lot. Derry was a carpenter; one of those superbly-toned young men you saw on summer building sites, stripped to the waist and all muscles and suntan. It would certainly explain the body — but why on earth would Milla be going out with a labourer?

"He's brilliant with wood — Derry, I mean. He's a bespoke joiner — designs and makes fabulous one-off pieces of furniture and spiral staircases and all sorts of amazingly clever things — all for the disgustingly wealthy, of course."

Sukie nodded. That made even more sense. Derry wasn't strictly a labourer, then. He was not only a talented craftsman but also the owner of a clearly expensive business — Milla would certainly love all that.

"I really don't see much of him," she said, deciding not to say that she'd seen practically all of him fairly recently and still remembered every glorious inch. "Milla seems to keep him out of the way. Mind you, he'll probably soon be history. They only met last week but Milla dumps blokes like other people dump used chewing gum."

"No one would dump Derry though," Amber's eyes were huge. "They'd have to be crazy. Maybe Derry'll turn out to be her Mr Right and we'll have another wedding on our hands."

Sukie really, really hoped not.

"Amber! Oh, you look so cool! Isn't this the greatest hen-night ever?" Fern, who everyone knew was Amber's best friend in Fiddlesticks, suddenly swooped down on her and they disappeared in a massive squealing hug, tiaras and wings entangled. "Come and dance over here — they're going to play 'Crying in the Chapel'!"

"See you later," Amber giggled as Fern dragged her away from the table. "And don't forget to say hi to Derry for me next time you see him."

Across at the fireside table the silence was cutting. After Simon's outburst, Sonia had rapped him smartly across the knuckles with her pudding spoon. The custard had landed on Marvin. Joss, having the best Saturday night she could ever remember, hadn't helped to scrape it off.

The landlady had been right. The whole pub was in uproar. It was fantastic. There were women of every age, shape and size, cavorting around in the most amazing interpretations of fairy costumes. And loud music. And laughter.

"Looks like we're here for the duration," Joss yelled cheerfully to no one in particular. "We'll never get out through that lot. Still, it's like a floorshow, isn't it? And all for free. Shall I pour more drinks?"

Still no one spoke. Marvin was thunder-faced. Sonia simply looked prim and pious. Simon's eyes were out on stalks, leering at so much female flesh. Joss took this general silence as an acceptance and happily refilled the glasses. She simply couldn't wait to tell Valerie all about it.

Settling back in her chair, her knees nicely warmed by the fire glow, her toes tapping out of sight under the table, Joss scanned the riotous crowd. Despite the disguise of the pink and sparkling costumes, she thought she recognised most of the partygoers. Oh, how she longed to be part of that colourful, noisy bunch. If only she could get up and join in and shimmy across the floor clutching her glass above her head, giggling as her wings became entangled with someone else's tiara.

Still, she thought contentedly, simply being an observer was a million times better than her usual Saturday night boredom, and even more so as Marvin had chosen the Weasel and Bucket and therefore couldn't blame her for this fiasco later.

And people-watching was such fun. All the old ladies from Fiddlesticks were doing the hokey-cokey and Fern was dancing on top of the bar with one of her friends

— oh, and wasn't that Sukie with that laughing crowd round the table by the door?

Such a pretty girl with that lovely curvy figure and her dark hair and blue eyed Irish colouring, Joss always thought, and probably more so because she always seemed totally unaware of it. And so clever, with her aromatherapy. Had Valerie arranged the illicit massage session with her yet? Joss was really looking forward to being pampered in secret. If only there was some way of having a quick word with Sukie, just to make sure she'd got them pencilled in . . .

"Sorry." She leaned towards Marvin who was glaring at the fire. "I'm going to have to make a dash for the loo. Far too much soda in my spritzer."

Marvin tutted and frowned a bit more. He prided himself on never needing to use public conveniences and always became quite critical of Joss's need to find a ladies wherever they went.

Sonia raised skinny eyebrows. "You need to practise bladder control at your age, Jocelyn, or you'll be a martyr to Tena Lady. I personally never go a day without exercising my pelvic floor."

Joss felt there was no suitable response to this, so she pushed her chair back, stood up and without meeting Marvin's eyes dived across the pub into the fairy fray.

It was like being swallowed up by a twinkling cloud of sensuous scents. Joss felt she was already getting high on the heady mix of Chanel and Jean-Paul Gaultier and J-Lo's finest.

Having "sorry'd" and "excuse me'd" her way into the lavatory, and waited for a while listening to some

103

frankly wonderful scurrilous gossip in the queue, she emerged again into the mêlée.

Elbowing her way through acres of net and tulle and diaphanous dresses, she reached Sukie's table.

Clemmie Coddle from the Bagley-cum-Russet Post Office Stores was holding court.

". . . and then he said his other one was yellow and he'd bring it with him next time!"

Everyone exploded with laughter. Joss, not having a clue what was going on, joined in.

Sukie, wiping mascara from under her eyes, looked up. "Oh, hello . . . Er — Mrs Benson?"

"Jocelyn, Joss, please . . . Sorry to interrupt you, and I'm sure you don't want to talk about work, but I just wondered if Valerie — Mrs Pridmore — had mentioned to you about booking us in for a massage at her place?"

"Valerie? Oh, can-can Val? Yes, she did — and I think we arranged it for two-ish on Friday afternoon, but I was going to ring her anyway because I'm going to set up a room at home and I wondered if you'd prefer that?"

"Oh, yes — definitely," Joss said quickly. It was far, far better for her to have her massage as far away from The Close as possible. "I'll tell her shall I? Friday . . . lovely . . . thank you."

Feeling deliciously wicked at her planned deception, she turned away, hoping that Marvin hadn't spotted her detour, and found herself grabbed round the waist and dragged back towards the loos.

"C'mon!" A large woman in what looked like a fluorescent nightie yelled in her ear. "Fern's pouring

104

the pink plonk! And we're all dancing! Mind, you haven't made much effort with yer outfit, have you, duck?"

"I'm not with the hen-night —" Joss started to pull away. "I was just . . ."

But the scrum simply surrounded her and swept her along. She could see Sukie and several other familiar faces, all giggling, all being manhandled on to the minuscule dance floor.

Oh, what the heck, Joss thought, refusing the champagne because she was driving and still had some sense of responsibility, I might as well be hung for a sheep as a lamb.

And with a sense of giddy excitement, she whooped her way through Dave Edmunds claiming that he Knew The Bride When She Used To Rock'n'Roll, Sir Elton's suggesting that everyone should Kiss the Bride, and even something sassy about a teenage wedding by Chuck Berry. On and on she danced, pinned in on all sides by pink fairies.

It was just fantastic.

But as with all good things, it had to come to an end. Fern and Amber, whirling dizzily, collapsed in a heap. Several other fairies had lost their wings and looked rather green. Joss, still laughing and very out of breath, panted her way out of the madness.

The fireside table was empty.

"Jocelyn!" Marvin's voice bellowed from the inglenook's dark recess. "I've got your coat! We're going home!"

"Sonia and Simon already gone, have they?" Joss grabbed her coat, avoiding looking at Marvin. She knew that his expression would be the puce one with the petulant lower lip and the tom-tom pulse in the temples. "I must have missed them."

"They escaped as soon as there was a gap in that — that moronic rabble. I was ready to go too. In fact I've been waiting for ages. Where the hell have you been?"

"There was a queue for the ladies." Well, that was true. "Anyway, I'm here now so shall we go? And —" she smiled happily up as Marvin as they picked their way through the Weasel and Bucket's debris, "— hasn't this been a simply wonderful night?"

Marvin shuddered his way out of the door. "Are you insane, woman? It's been bloody hell on earth."

Sukie, still reeling giddily from the frantic dancing, flopped down at her table again. Wow! What a fantastic night! And to think she hadn't been looking forward to this! She grinned at Chelsea, Phoebe and Clemmie who had now been joined by Amber's girlfriends. They looked, as she did, distinctly dishevelled and dishabilled. There was probably more flesh on display at their table than on an average night in the Spearmint Rhino.

Sukie, relaxed and happy, pushed her chair away from the table, and slumped inelegantly amidst the froth of her skimpy skirt.

The door flew open, allowing a blast of welcome cold damp air to waft over the acres of hot bodies.

"Jesus!" Milla, looking superb in a little black something which definitely hadn't come from Primark, stared around her in amazement. "What the hell is going on in here?"

Sukie tried to sink beneath the table.

"You can't hide, Sukes!" Milla gurgled. "You never said you were coming here tonight. Are you the entertainment? I mean, I knew you danced the can-can — but that outfit must be strictly for poles."

"Oh, ha-ha-ha," Sukie said, still feeling slightly squiffy and trying to tug her bodice up over her escaping chest and her tutu down over her knickers. "And why are you here anyway? You're a bit late for the hen-night."

"Is that what this is? *Really*? How fascinating." Milla surveyed the scene with some amusement. "Must say it's not like any hen-night I've ever known."

Well it wouldn't be, would it, Sukie thought. This is hardly Barcelona or Rome.

Milla flicked back her hair. "Actually, we're on our way to a club in town. I thought we should pop in for a quiet rural drink first, somewhere we could be alone, but clearly that wasn't the best idea I've ever had. I guess we'll just have to head for somewhere a little more secluded, won't we?"

We, Sukie thought. The dreaded *we*.

On cue, Derry appeared behind Milla in the doorway. "Couldn't get the jeep into the car park, so I've left it out on the road. Oh, hi . . ."

"Hi . . ." Sukie said shortly, still disliking him for laughing before and knowing she'd dislike him even more now if he as much as sniggered.

He didn't. Well, not quite. True, his mouth wasn't even slightly grinning, but his eyes were. A lot.

"We're not stopping." Milla had already turned round and was trying to shove Derry out through the door.

Too late. Amber's friends had spotted him and were whooping and wolf-whistling with gusto. Chelsea, preening madly, flapped her wand at him in excitement. Clemmie and Phoebe joined in.

Derry grinned in delight. Sukie's stomach did somer-saults. God — he had a gorgeous smile . . .

"Down boy," Milla said, turning on her designer heels. "We'll find somewhere else to drink. Somewhere you won't get eaten alive."

"Shame," Derry said cheerfully. Then looked at Sukie, his lips not quite steady. "Bye, then. See you again, no doubt?"

"No doubt. Have a nice time."

Pig! Sukie thought as the door closed behind them. He was probably rolling around the crowded car park right now in paroxysms of hysteria. Why, oh why, did he always catch her at the worst possible moments?

"C'mon, Sukes!" Chelsea yelled in her ear. "The love-god's gone and I've just poured out the antidote. Drown your sorrows with the rest of us! What you need is one of these."

Sukie squinted down at the masses of tiny shot glasses, all brimful with brightly coloured liquid, on the table. Vodka Shots always gave her a mega-hangover. Oh, what the hell . . .

They all picked up their first glass and started the count-down.

"One-two-three," Phoebe laughed. "Now!"

Sukie swallowed and pulled a face. It was very strong.

"No wimping out!" Clemmie spluttered. "Next one! One-two-three . . ."

By the time the glasses were empty, Sukie felt pretty inebriated. Everyone was shrieking with unnecessary laughter.

Fern, her eyes crossed, wobbled from the throng and threw her arms round Sukie's neck. "Thanks so much for the fab present, Sukie. I don't know what to say — it was the loveliest thing I've ever had."

Was it? Sukie wondered just how much Fern had had to drink. True, the sun-blocking skin cream and moisturising lotion were certainly from Beauty's Blessings' top range, but they weren't anything that special.

"I'm so pleased you like them. I thought you'd be able to use them on honeymoon."

"Oh, I will," Fern gurgled sexily as she undulated away from their table. "Believe me — me and Timmy will make full use of them . . ."

"Fern must be well gone —" Sukie squinted at Chelsea, "— to get that excited about a couple of pots of nourishing cream."

"Crikey," Chelsea slurred. "And you must be more drunk than she is if you can't remember what present you gave her. I put those all those little bottles in my bag while you were getting dressed, remember?"

"All what little bottles? I bought her skin cream. What are you talking about?"

"Skin cream? Nah — you gave her all those little bottles of exotic massage oils. Loads of them. Nice present, Sukes — no wonder she was so excited. They'll spice her and Timmy up no end."

Holy shit!

"Chelsea! You didn't take them out of my aromatherapy case? Tell me you didn't."

"Well, yes. Grab the present, you said. On the hall table, you said. So I did — all those little bottles of — er — geranium and jasmine and lavender and rose . . . Oh, bugger . . ."

Oh bugger, indeed. She'd just given away her entire exclusive and highly expensive aromatherapy stock.

"You can't ask for them back can you?" Chelsea whimpered. "It's a present and she was so excited. Sorry, Sukes. Are you going to kill me?"

"Not me," Sukie said, thinking of the almighty wrath of Jennifer Blessing. "But I know someone who will . . ."

CHAPTER
NINE

The following morning, there was a series of increasingly apologetic texts from Chelsea, but Sukie, nursing a thumping hangover, curled in Cora's favourite chair in front of the fire, clutching her umpteenth mug of black coffee, with the rain lashing down outside, wasn't mollified.

The peach leather cases were sadly depleted. It was fortunate that Chelsea hadn't taken any of the base oils or the tiny empty replacement bottles with their flowery labels and gemstone stoppers, but even so most of the essential oils, the essences, the tools of her trade, had gone.

She only hoped Fern and Timmy would put them to good use on their Seychelles honeymoon.

But what on earth was she going to do? These were no ordinary massage oils: these had been special blends, organically nurtured, wildly expensive. Sukie knew she couldn't just nip off to the nearest Holland and Barrett for replacements, she had no reserve stocks of her own, and purloining refills from Beauty's Blessings was out of the question. One, Jennifer would notice before she'd even started decanting, and two, the supplies at the salon were only very, very basic —

certainly not comprehensive enough to replace the dozens of specially ordered, probably-made-by-monks-in-a-dew-soaked-meadow, eye-wateringly costly, missing essences.

Oh, bugger with bells on.

Dreary grey Sunday mornings in March were probably a prime time for suicides, Sukie thought. Add Jennifer Blessing's incandescent fury at the loss of what was probably hundreds and hundreds of pounds worth of stock before the mobile massages had even started, and Sukie could see the appeal of taking the easy way out.

"Is the kettle hot, Sukes?" Milla breezed into the living room, tucking a lemon silk scarf into perfect loops in that irritating way people who knew exactly what to do with scarves always did. "I'm running late so I can't wait to boil it up again but I'm dying for a shot of caffeine. Sweetheart — you do look rough. Mind you, having seen you in action last night I'm not surprised."

Sukie, wearing comfort clothes — her scruffiest jeans and an ancient baggy sweater washed second-skin-soft — glared at Milla who was naturally all band-box-fresh in designer jeans and tan leather jacket and boots and of course the perfectly looped scarf.

"You could always make the trek to the kitchen and check the kettle for yourself," Sukie grumbled, uncurling herself from the chair. "I know you're probably used to having people dance to your every whim but —"

She headed for the kitchen anyway. It was easier to bury her head in coffee-making than face Derry emerging any minute from the twisty staircase looking all gorgeously tousled and sexually fulfilled.

"There." She pushed the mug into Milla's hands. "I didn't bother making one for Derry. He can get his own when he gets up. I'm not everyone's slave."

"Clearly a bad, bad hangover." Milla smiled. "And coffee would have been wasted on Derry anyway. He's not here."

Despite feeling awful, Sukie brightened a bit as she scuttled back to Cora's chair. "Oh, right . . . Did you have a row?"

"Derry and I don't do rows." Milla flicked at her already perfect hair in the mirror. "No, the club was pretty disappointing, so we called it a day — anyway, I'm off for Sunday lunch at the parental pile, so I needed an early night. Alone." She perched on the arm of Cora's chair. "You know how Mummy and Daddy always look for signs of debauchery."

Sukie's momentary uplifted spirits plunged again. Milla was taking Derry Home To Meet The Parents. Already. It must be serious.

"And will they approve? I mean, I know Derry is — er — very attractive, but he's not your usual type, is he?"

"After my broken engagement, I no longer have a type, as you well know." Milla sipped her coffee. "And why shouldn't Derry be the Right One? Okay, he might not be a trader or an analyst or my usual city slicker as you so sharply pointed out, but look at us, Sukes. Chalk

113

and cheese — but we get on well living together, don't we?"

Sukie nodded. They did.

"I mean, when you needed a lodger, everyone thought you'd share Pixies Laughter with Chelsea, didn't they? You've been friends since infants' school. It would have made sense."

Sukie shuddered. "Chelsea couldn't have afforded the rent I needed to keep this place going. Big Sava only pays the minimum wage. And although we're lifelong best friends, we'd have probably killed one another before the first month was up."

But it was true. Bagley-cum-Russet simply couldn't understand why city-girl Milla had become Sukie's lodger rather than Chelsea. Sukie had let them wonder. She knew from Milla that her advert in the lettings papers had been exactly what Metro Milla had been looking for when she needed to escape from city living after the sudden and painful break-up of a long engagement with someone implausibly called Bo-Bo.

Bo-Bo, it transpired, had been some sort of embryo Sir Alan Sugar figure, and if the much-kissed and cried-over photo in Milla's bedroom was anything to go by, resembled an early Bryan Ferry: all gorgeously dark and dangerous and lounge lizardy. Bo-Bo had suddenly got cold feet, merely weeks before the wedding of the century. It had broken Milla's heart.

Post-Bo-Bo, Milla had embarked on a series of mad one-night stands with posh blokes in a futile attempt to heal the pain — and then she'd met Derry . . .

114

"So, if you and I can happily make a go of house-sharing, I don't see why Derry should be any different. Right," Milla stood up, "now I must fly. Mummy will have probably invited the neighbours in for pre-lunch drinks and she hates anyone being late. Thanks for the coffee, Sukes. I may stay overnight with the parents so don't worry if I don't come home. Bye, then . . ."

After the front door had slammed, Sukie stared into the gas flames again. Alone on a wet Sunday. Super . . .

"Get a grip," she muttered to herself. "You've got less than twenty-four hours to salvage the massage oil situation — sitting around here feeling sorry for yourself isn't going to solve anything."

So, what were the options?

Well, she could be honest with Jennifer. No — Jennifer would probably scream and yell and then sack her and replace her with a trainee from the FE college who'd work for pocket money and wouldn't allow her chums to give away the essences.

She could possibly fill the bottles with a few drops of synthetic fragrances from the basic oils she kept in the bathroom, top them up with water and cheat. No — absolutely not — she was very proud of her aromatherapy skills and her reputation as a masseuse and her integrity.

Or she could raid her overdraft and drive to Reading and see if she could find an organic, exclusive aromatherapy supplier open and ready to replace her stocks. No — definitely not — even if such a shop existed and was open on a Sunday, her overdraft was already a no-go area.

"Oh Cora." Sukie uncurled herself and wandered to the window, wincing as the headache thumped again. "Why aren't you here to give me advice like you used to? What on earth am I going to do?"

Staring bleary-eyed out over the rain-washed garden, at the weeds all bowed and tangled and dripping, something penetrated the buzzing fuzz in her brain. Something half-remembered. Something she'd laughed about.

Topsy's words . . .

". . . the garden is a veritable storehouse of natural energy . . . out there you have all the raw materials for your craft . . . Cora knew the power of the garden plants . . ."

Sukie bit her lip. What if? Just what if? What if Topsy had been telling the truth — what if Cora had made potions from garden flowers? What if Pixies Laughter really could give her what she needed? She'd be able to replace everything and save money at the same time. The perfect solution.

Then she sighed. Okay, so she might just have the right flowers and herbs growing out there in the back garden's soggy wilderness, but how was she supposed to turn them into the essences she needed? It wasn't something they'd covered on her course in Newcastle. They hadn't even touched on going down the Grow Your Own route.

Oh, sod it! If only there was someone who could give her some sort of instructions on what to look for and what to do with it when she found it.

116

If only she could find Cora's flowery recipe book — not that she believed it actually existed, of course — but hey, what else did she have to do with a long, wet, lonely Sunday?

Two hours later the cottage was in a state of chaos. Sukie had turned out boxes and suitcases, and drawers and cupboards. She'd even — remembering what Doll and Lulu Blessing had told her about Mitzi's discovery of the herbal cookery book — ventured into the attic.

She'd found hundreds of old photographs, and had cried fat tears over pictures of a very much younger Cora in the arms of a handsome young man who must have been the one who died in the war; and old address books and strange shopping lists and embroidery and knitting patterns — but nothing at all that resembled How To Turn Weeds Into Essences In Time To Save Sukie's Life.

She was sitting amidst a heap of papers on the living-room floor when someone knocked on the front door.

No doubt it was Chelsea escaping Sunday with her huge, boisterous family. Sukie wasn't sure she wanted to spend the rest of Sunday with Chelsea, but neither did she really want to be alone. Sighing, scrubbing the worst of the dust and cobwebs from her face and clothes, she padded to open the door.

A huge bunch of flowers greeted her.

"Hi." Derry Kavanagh grinned from behind the flowers.

Sukie groaned. Par for the course. She must look like some sort of filthy dirty, wild-haired vagrant. No doubt the remnant of last night's mascara was still clogging her eyelashes and she'd probably got congealed egg-yolk on her sweater. He'd laugh at her at any minute.

"Lovely flowers, but Milla isn't in," she said round the bouquet. "She left ages ago. Was she supposed to meet you here?"

"No." Derry shook his head. "She's gone to see her parents, I know. I wasn't invited. The flowers are for you."

"Me? Why?"

"To say a very belated thank you for letting me use your bed — and for not kicking me out of it when you must have been exhausted. It was very generous of you — and I really should have said thanks before . . . Oh, have I interrupted a spring clean?"

Sukie shook her head. She couldn't remember the last time a man had bought her flowers. And Derry still hadn't laughed at her. "Er — well, thank you. They're lovely. Um — do you want to come in? Have a coffee?"

Derry Kavanagh was bound to say thanks but no thanks.

"Great — yes, thanks — if you're sure I'm not interrupting anything." Derry stepped into the hall and glanced into the living-room. "Good God! Have you been burgled?"

"No." Sukie smiled. "I was — um — looking for something. Shall I take the flowers?"

The bouquet was huge, and not a petrol station or supermarket special. She smiled at him again through the profusion of pastel blooms. "These are wonderful — but there was no need . . ."

"Yes, there was. I should have done this straight away. And I certainly should have said how grateful I was sooner — not that I've seen you for more than a split second. If Milla had decided to stop in the pub last night I could have spoken to you then. I'd have liked that — it looked like a lot of fun."

"It was. But strictly girls only. Anyway, it was as well Milla had somewhere else in mind. You'd have probably been torn limb from limb."

"A bloke lives in hope. You all looked very — um — fairy-dollish."

"We probably looked terrible, but we had a great time . . ." Sukie hid her embarrassment by inhaling the glorious spring fragrances. "These really are gorgeous. Thank you so much. Look, sit down if you can — I'll put these in water. Oh, just chuck that lot on to the floor . . ."

Grinning to herself, Sukie managed to find the flowers a suitable home, make coffee, spike up her hair and scrape the worst of the grime off her face in less time than it took Milla to apply lip gloss.

Walking back into the living room with the coffee, she allowed herself a moment of sheer pleasure, staring at Derry, in his faded jeans and navy sweater, sprawled in Cora's favourite chair. The ice-blond hair was in the sort of textured layers you ached to touch, and his profile, as he stared into the gas flames, was almost sculpted.

She exhaled. He truly was sensational. And, of course, off limits and not even slightly interested in her.

Ah, well . . .

"Coffee up. I'll just clear a space . . . er — well if there's anywhere left to clear a space to."

"Thanks." Derry took the mug. "What exactly are you looking for?"

Sukie perched on the edge of the opposite chair. Should she tell him? No, of course she shouldn't. He'd laughed at her before — he'd probably choke himself if she told him the truth. And she reminded herself, she might fancy him like mad, but she didn't *like* him, did she? Because of the laughing.

"Nothing much."

"Really?" Derry raised his eyebrows.

God he was gorgeous, Sukie thought as she drooled over his blue, blue eyes. "No, nothing — well, actually, yes — something vitally important . . ."

And she told him. All of it. And she'd kill him if he laughed.

He didn't. Well, only at the amusing bits where it was okay to. And he was very quiet and turned away to stare into the fire when she told him about Cora and Topsy and the boys they'd loved and lost. Derry Kavanagh earned himself quite a few brownie points on that score.

"So —" she finished, "— that's it really. I was looking for something that probably doesn't exist to make something that probably won't work."

120

"Quite a challenge. Want some help?"

"No! I mean — well, no thanks — I mean — you must have far more interesting things to do with your Sunday."

"I live alone. Milla is in her stockbroker belt homeland. My mates are all playing happy families. There's no football on the telly."

"Well, if you put it like that . . ."

They grinned at one another.

"So — where do we start?" Derry drained his coffee. "Shall we look for the — um — recipes first? Or the plants?"

"That's the dilemma," Sukie sighed. "Chicken or the egg?"

"Maybe if we cleared some of this stuff up first? Make a bit of space? Get organised?"

Sukie, who rarely did organised, was impressed. A man who could tidy up. Of course, he probably had to be organised in his job, and he lived alone so didn't have anyone to come along behind him picking up debris.

She nodded. "Okay. We'll just put stuff into piles for now."

After a further half an hour and more coffee and an unhealthy but hangover-curing lunch of crisps and a whole packet of chocolate digestives, the living-room looked less of a disaster area.

"What about these?" Derry held up a pile of age-bleached squares of canvas. "Are they yours? Which heap do they go in?"

121

Sukie looked up from the sideboard. "Oh, no — they belong in Cora's needlework-basket. That big wicker thing behind the sofa. They're Cora's tapestries. Well, I think people call them cross-stitches these days. She always did them while she listened to *The Archers*. I kept them because they were so much part of her."

"They're very intricate." Derry shook out the first square. "Oh, yes — my nan had loads of these, too. Little embroidered pictures with quotations under them. Home is where the heart is and all that. She used to frame hers." He gently unfolded several others. "Your Cora was very clever — look at all these tiny flowers . . . really intricate work — and they all seem to have little poems underneath them."

Sukie nodded. "They were a huge part of my childhood. I used to play with them. Make up stories round them, use them for my dolls' dresses . . ."

She stopped and turned her head away. A nasty lump of tearful nostalgia had lodged in her throat.

"Sukie? Are you okay?"

"Fine — look, just put them in the work-basket for now."

Derry said nothing. Sukie, wiping the tears away before they fell, prayed that he wasn't laughing at her. She took a deep breath and looked across the room. He was smiling. Damn him.

"Sukie . . .?"

"I said I'm okay."

"Yes, but — look. Have you ever read the poems on these tapestries?"

"As a child I knew them off by heart. They were like my nursery rhymes. There was one about roses and honeysuckle. And one about herbs . . . oh, yes, basil and coriander because I used to think they were people — and something about cowslips and daisies . . . and — holy shit!"

"Couldn't have put it better myself." Derry grinned at her. "First part of the puzzle solved. We've found Cora's recipes."

CHAPTER
TEN

"You think I'm crazy, don't you?" Sukie, muffled unflatteringly in her mac, peered at Derry through the slanting rain. "You think all this is a load of hokum, don't you? Be honest — you're only humouring me."

The wind whipped through the slate-grey gloom of Pixies Laughter garden, slapping wet brambles and nettles and fat fleshy dock leaves against their legs.

Derry, wearing Cora's ancient gardening coat and still managing to look sexy, grinned through the raindrops. "No, I don't think you're crazy — if I did I wouldn't be humouring you; I'd be running a mile and be sitting somewhere warm and dry with a pint. No, honestly, I'm intrigued. I'm always open to new ideas. I'd never discount anything simply because it seemed a bit — well — odd. And let's face it, you don't get much odder than this. So — now, what are we looking for?"

They'd copied out the rhymes from Cora's tapestries although Sukie, once reminded, could probably recite them all off by heart. She'd never thought of them as anything other than Cora's poems. Never thought they were strange in any way. Never thought about the meaning behind the familiar and oft-repeated words. And certainly never connected her childhood playthings, always to hand in Cora's work-basket, with the elusive recipes she'd been searching for.

"Do we need myrtle?" Derry crouched down over a particularly nasty heap of vegetation. "Because if we do, I think this might be it."

"Honestly? Fantastic. Yes . . . yes, I know myrtle is mentioned in one of the rhymes," Sukie squinted at the damp pieces of paper in her hand. "Something to do with bridal bunches — along with rosemary. I remember not understanding the rhyme because I thought they must both be bridesmaids at a wedding so I asked Cora about them . . ." She stopped, instantly whisked back to her happy childhood, remembering Cora's sweet smile and hearing her gentle Berkshire voice. She swallowed. "Er — but Cora pointed out that myrtle was linked with fertile in the poem which meant she was the bride."

"Myrtle and fertile? Jesus! We're not talking Wordsworth here, are we?" Derry laughed. "Okay, so we've got poor old myrtle and I'm sure I can find rosemary the bridesmaid, so who else are we looking for? A whole churchful of guests?"

"Are you mocking me?" She looked at him quickly. "Because if you are —"

"No, honestly." He shook more raindrops from his hair which was now streaked dark-blond. "My nan taught me all sorts of nursery rhymes and things, too. I could probably do all the actions if pressed — and no I'm not going to, so don't look at me like that. So — what else do we need?"

"Um — in no particular order, violas . . . sweet briar . . . hawthorn . . . nettles . . . wild rocket . . . borage . . . cowslips . . . daises . . . wild thyme . . . basil . . . oh, there are so many." She sighed. "Even if they exist in this wilderness how on earth do we recognise them?"

"Well, I'm no Alan Titchmarsh, but my nan was a keen cottage gardener and she did teach me a bit about wild flowers and herbs and things like that. She always had a patch of wilderness garden long before it was trendy. I knew most of the plants that grew there."

Sukie looked at him in surprise. A man of many talents. And who had clearly adored his grandmother as she'd adored Cora. And, of course, firmly attached to Milla. Sod it. "Really? Okay — so are we likely to find any of these in March?"

"Possibly. Probably in some cases. I guess that Cora wrote different verses and made different potions for each season depending on what was available out here. We'll just have to go with the late winter and early spring ones for now. If this works you'll be spoilt for choice in a few months. Hey — look, this is definitely rocket. And under this lot —" Derry heaved at an upturned wheelbarrow and several chunks of stone which squelched unpleasantly in the mud, "— I reckon this could be borage. And these —" he squatted down in the soggy, cold mass of weeds, "— are definitely violas."

Sukie beamed at him in sheer admiration. And quite a lot of lust. What a man!

"Don't just stand there, woman." He grinned at her. "Grab your trowel and start digging."

★ ★ ★

A soggy hour later, having sluiced the mud from their hands and taken turns with the hair dryer, they surveyed their harvest in Pixies Laughter kitchen. Having washed the heap of plants, Derry had sorted them into relevant clumps to match Cora's verses.

"The next problem," Derry said, flicking his dampish hair away from his face, "is how we change them from their raw state into what you need."

Sukie, making restorative coffee, frowned. "When I was taking my first aromatherapy courses we did touch briefly on the history of the science. I didn't take a lot of notice, I'm afraid. It didn't seem relevant. So my methods may not be accurate, but we know we need to extract the essences, and get them into the bottles — sort of like cooking really. Er — I don't suppose you're a secret Jamie Oliver, too, are you?"

"Nah, strictly a pierce-and-ping man I'm afraid."

"Me too," Sukie shrugged. "So — we'll need something to grind them with. Then something to mix them with. And in. And something to strain them through, and then something to get them into the little bottles . . ."

"No problem there, then." Derry leaned against the kitchen table. "Any chance of finding anything useful in these cupboards? Cora's stuff? My nan keeps all sorts of ancient things that looked like they belonged in an operating theatre in her kitchen cupboards. Lovely old bits and pieces. Have you still got Cora's things here?"

Sukie nodded. Good thinking. Cora had also hoarded enamel dishes and stoneware crockery bowls and battered spoons and masses of other weird paraphernalia in the cupboards under the sink. They should still be there unless her parents had junked them in the early days of their inheritance blitz.

She knelt down and peered into the musty darkness, then pushed her hand into the recesses. Yes! Her fingers clanged against enamel and earthenware. Fantastic! Noisily, she turfed out enough late nineteenth and early twentieth century kitchen utensils to have the entire *Antiques Roadshow* team salivating.

"I reckon ladies of your Cora and my nan's generation all read the same How To Be Domestic Goddesses manual." Derry knelt beside her on the uneven quarry tiles, sorting the spoils. "This is wonderful — here's a pestle and mortar . . . and a big cake mixing bowl . . . and loads of little funnels . . . and what's this funny stuff? I don't recognise this?"

Sukie emerged backwards from the cupboard. Derry was very, very close.

"Er . . ." She shuffled away slightly and hoped he wouldn't realise she was blushing. "I've no idea — it looks like dress material . . . oh, yes I know what it is! It's buttermuslin! Cora used it to strain her ginger beer and all sorts of things — that's brilliant — I think we've got everything we need. Right — let's get cracking."

They stood up at the same time, almost colliding, both moving away at the last minute. Sukie sighed. Damn.

Clearing the table and the work surfaces, they organised themselves into a kitchen production line.

"Do you think we need to say incantations or something?" Derry looked up from squidging a massive handful of basil and coriander into the mortar. "After all, Topsy Turvey said your Cora's lotions and potions were magical."

Sukie paused in checking a heap of pastel violas — their pink, white, pale mauve petals looking like confetti strewn across the table — for livestock. "Yes, but — we've decided that's all rubbish, haven't we?"

"Have we? I don't think you have and I'm not so sure. Like I said, I always keep an open mind on everything until I'm convinced differently. Still, we'll leave that for the moment. Pass the pestle, please."

"There you are — and no incantations," Sukie said firmly, trying not to look at his muscles moving sensuously under the thin sweater as he got to work with the pestle. "Whatever Cora did or didn't do with her potions doesn't concern us right now. This performance is simply to refill the bottles to save my skin and my money and my whole career. Ooooh — that one smells lovely . . ."

In fact, by the time they'd finished pulverising and filtering and mixing and decanting, the whole cottage wafted with glorious scents. A heady, sensuous mixture of herbs and flowers and the fresh tang of rainwater drifted beneath the beams.

In fact, Sukie thought dreamily, if she closed her eyes she could imagine the kitchen being filled with tiny floating multi-coloured stars and flowers and butterflies . . .

"Don't think we need any magic," Derry grinned, sprawled on one of the mis-matched kitchen chairs. "I'm as high as a kite simply inhaling the fumes . . . and they —" he nodded towards Jennifer Blessing's little gemstone-stoppered bottles once more filled to the brim, and neatly relabelled, standing in rows on the table, "— look the business."

Sukie, tired, dishevelled, but triumphant, grinned back at him. "They do, don't they? Thank you so much. I'd never have managed this without you. Literally."

"My pleasure. This was far more fun than doing the joinery accounts or waiting for one of my mates to get fed up with playing happy Sunday families and need to make a dash for the pub." Derry stretched. It was almost unbearably exciting. "Shall we start to clear up, then?"

"Oh, we'll just shove all the mess into the bin and the crocks into the dishwasher . . ." Sukie dragged her eyes away from his body. "And I'll whizz a cloth over everything else. It'll only take five minutes."

"And the rest of the cottage?"

"I'll sort that out later — before Milla gets back. The whole place needed a spring clean anyway — and I need to clear out the dining-room because I'm setting up a massage table in there so that I can start working from home this week."

"With these?" Derry indicated the fruits of their labours.

"Yes. Why?"

"Because I think you might have missed something."

130

Sukie, who'd been wondering if inviting Derry to share a pierce-and-ping microwaved supper would be a step too far, peered at him from beneath her spiky fringe. "What? We've finished haven't we? What have we left out?"

"Nothing from the bottles — but how do you know they'll work? We need a guinea pig."

Trying really, really hard not to think lustful thoughts of pinning Derry down on the kitchen table and massaging that gorgeously tanned, muscled body with one of the new unguents, Sukie attempted to look intelligently alert. Sadly, an even more treacherously delicious fantasy — him massaging her with those beautiful long, strong fingers — rapidly overtook the first one.

Sukie made a valiant effort to rein-in the mental pictures, knowing she was failing miserably.

"Guinea pigs?" Her voice came out all squeaky, so she coughed and tried again. "Um — surely you're not suggesting that we should test drive these on each other?"

"Not a chance!" Derry laughed.

Oh, bugger. The death of two fantasies in a single stroke. And he'd laughed . . . Again.

Derry stretched. "I just think it might be an idea to find someone who knows you well, who needs a massage and who isn't likely to sue you — or Jennifer Blessing — should it go wrong."

"Er — were you thinking of Milla?"

"No way! I may not know that much about Milla, but I'd guess she goes to discreet little beauty salons in

London where she pays a fortune to someone called Camilla or Sophie to sort out her executive stresses. I also have a feeling she wouldn't take kindly to being rubbed up the wrong way with a few weeds from the garden. Especially by you — er — us."

He was right, of course. So — who? Well, of course Chelsea would be the ideal choice, but Sukie definitely, definitely, definitely didn't want Chelsea muscling in on the rest of the afternoon and the pierce-and-ping supper.

Then again, there was Valerie Pridmore who was already booked in for a massage — but Valerie Pridmore was such a terrible gossip, and if she got even a whiff of an idea that this test-drive wasn't exactly kosher it'd be all over the village in no time.

"Topsy!"

Topsy would be perfect. Topsy who was fanatic about all things medical. Topsy who must never, ever know that the massage oil she was testing was created from Cora's recipes.

"Topsy Turvey?" Derry looked perplexed. "Are you sure?"

"Positive. I'll just blend one of these new essences with my base oil and we'll —" Sukie stopped. She was presuming an awful lot here. "Er — sorry. I mean, I'm sure you've had enough of all this by now and want to go home."

"I'm not going anywhere — I'm pretty curious to see what happens — but *Topsy*? Won't she wonder why we've suddenly barged into her living room on a Sunday afternoon brandishing massage oils?"

Sukie was carefully measuring almond oil into one of the tiny bottles. "Oh, she won't be in her living room. She'll be in the pub. She always is on a Sunday afternoon — like all us singletons of any age, sometimes any company is better than being alone."

"So you're going to massage some poor unsuspecting old lady in the middle of a busy pub on a Sunday afternoon?"

"Yep. That's about it. Are you up for it?"

"Wouldn't miss it for the world."

CHAPTER
ELEVEN

The lopsided pebble-dash and corrugated iron exterior of the Barmy Cow looked even more disreputable than usual in the chilly grey murk of early evening.

Sukie scrambled inelegantly from the passenger seat of Derry's scruffy jeep. She'd offered to drive the short distance — after they'd both agreed walking was out of the question because they couldn't stand getting wet again — but Derry wouldn't hear of it. This had delighted her because it meant, hopefully, that he'd drive her back to Pixies Laughter afterwards, so the pierce-and-ping could still be a possibility.

She looked at the grime-streaked, run-down, ramshackle pub with severe misgivings. "Are you quite sure you want to do this? Have you ever been in here before?"

Derry shook his head. "No, but the other night, when I saw you outside here I thought it looked — er — rather more interesting than Milla's choice of the wine bar in Winterbrook."

"Oh, yes," Sukie said coldly. "Of course. The other night. When you were laughing at me."

"I wasn't!" Derry tried not to smile.

"You were," Sukie said crossly. "You were sitting in Milla's flashy car, laughing at me."

"Laughing, yes. But not *at* you. Absolutely not at you. Oh, God — is that what you thought?"

"Thought? No. Knew? Yes." Clutching her handbag containing the massage oil against her chest, Sukie marched towards the Barmy Cow's battered door. "I know what I saw — and you were laughing! Don't try to deny it — and anyway, it's too cold to stand out here arguing."

Derry moved in front of her. "I'm not denying it and I'm certainly not arguing. Goodness, you're prickly sometimes, aren't you? Do you want to know the truth? I saw you and your friend messing around out here, acting like kids — and I thought you looked like an uninhibited, happy girl who knew how to enjoy herself. I laughed *with* you, because whatever you were doing looked fun. I had no idea that you'd seen me — and even less that it would offend you if you had. Weren't you just messing around? Wasn't it some sort of game?"

"I'd got a very ancient glacé cherry stuck in my throat. Chelsea was getting it out."

Derry laughed. "Oh — sorry . . . no, really . . . I'm sorry — but why the hell did you swallow a whole cherry? No — okay . . . Maybe I shouldn't have laughed. Oh, sod it — yes, I should."

"Pig!" Sukie shook her head, trying to hide her smile. "Just one word of warning — don't drink anything in here that contains a cocktail stick, okay?"

"You ate a cocktail stick as *well*?"

"Forget it." Sukie grinned, skipping inside the pub.

He hadn't laughed at her. He wasn't the nasty mean-minded bastard she'd thought he was. He wasn't such a bad bloke after all. In fact . . . No — whoa, girl. Remember Milla.

She took a deep breath. "And I hope you're prepared for this . . ."

Sadly, no one could really be prepared for a Sunday in the Barmy Cow.

Dim, damp, smoky from the grey ash of the fire, and smelling strangely of brilliantine and mould, it was filled with morose customers hunched over cloudy drinks.

The Berkeley Boys were, as always, arrayed neatly behind the bar. Their Sunday Best involved once-white dress shirts with unironed frills and doubtful stains, drooping polka dot bow ties and lovat cardigans with most of the buttons missing. It wasn't a good look.

"Sukie!" Valerie Pridmore, surrounded by her huge family, waved enthusiastically from the dartboard side of the pub. "Hiya!"

Sukie waved back. So did Derry. Val blew him a kiss.

"Do you know Val?" Sukie asked as they reached the bar.

"No. Never seen her before in my life. Just being friendly." Derry gazed round the pub with something like disbelief in his eyes. "Well — this is — um — unusual . . . And —" he caught his first glimpse of the ancient Boys, "— bloody hell!"

Smothering her giggles, Sukie beamed at Dorchester Berkeley. "Hello, you look really smart. Can we have a pint and a half of whichever beer you recommend today, please?"

Derry looked impressed. "That was extremely AA Gill of you. How did you know I was a beer drinker?"

"What? Oh, there's no choice here. It's just whichever beer hasn't gone rancid in the cask on the day. They've never heard of lager or anything brewed much after nineteen fifty-five." Sukie peered through the gloomy fug at the hunched punters, trying to spot Topsy. "Ah — there she is. Over there. She hasn't seen us yet."

Savoy and Hilton, jostling to pour a pint each, smiled beatifically at Derry. To give him credit he smiled bravely back.

"Haven't seen you here before, have we?" Claridge leaned across the bar. "Are you Sukie's young man?"

"No, he's not," Sukie said quickly, pushing the money across the counter before Derry could pay. "He's just a friend."

"Am I?" Derry took his pint. "Oh, good. Thanks, Sukie. And this," he grinned at Hilton, "looks like a great pint."

"It is, young man," Hilton wheezed joyously. "A perfect mix of hops, yeast and downland water. Nice to see someone of the younger age group who knows what's what."

"Smoothie," Sukie hissed as they made their way towards an empty table. "It looks like sludge. And it'll taste like nothing on earth."

"Heavenly?"

"Whatever."

If you could ignore the aura of dust and grime, the Barmy Cow wasn't too awful, Sukie thought. At least clearly not for the various lonely Bagleyites who sought refuge there. Topsy, sitting with several other elderly people, was playing cards with deft animation. She still hadn't seen them, and Sukie decided to leave her in happy ignorance for a little longer.

How awful it would be, Sukie suddenly realised, to be that old and for all the people you knew and loved to be dead and to have to make do with whoever was left for company.

"Are you okay?" Derry leaned towards her.

"Yes . . . yes, fine, thanks. I was just thinking about growing old and being alone."

"Well, there's nice and cheerful for a Sunday." Derry sipped his pint and swallowed bravely. "Um — you're right about the beer. It's probably an acquired taste. So, are you going to march straight over to Topsy and demand she allows you to massage her, or what? We didn't really discuss the plan of action, did we?"

"There was no need." Sukie watched the tiny head on her beer disappear in little pools of grease. "Topsy will be up for anything medical — you'll see. I thought we ought to let her finish her card game first though. She looks really happy."

Derry nodded. "She probably is. Is that what bothered you? Topsy being alone?"

"Yes . . . and the fact that because we're young, we're so sure we're immortal, aren't we? I mean to us they're just old people who have always been old people. We don't think we'll be like that — but we will."

"Yes, we will. But inside we'll still be young, like they are. We'll still be us, like they are. The only difference will be that we'll have a lifetime of memories and experience to draw on — like they have. And there will still be new things to look forward to. Different things, but there will still be a point to being alive even when we're very old." Derry swirled the beer in his glass. It stuck to the sides. "Finding Cora's stuff has really affected you, hasn't it?"

"Sort of. It's made me realise how many things I didn't know about her and now it's too late to ask. And that she had a life — apart from just being Cora and being old and being the person I loved most in the whole world."

Derry pushed his hair away from his eyes. "You're nothing like I thought you were. You're not at all like Milla, are you? I thought —"

But whatever Derry thought — be it good or bad — Sukie wasn't destined to discover as Valerie Pridmore chose that moment to hobble nosily up to their table.

"Sorry to interrupt," she gurgled throatily, looking anything but and staring at Derry with lust-filled eyes. "I just wanted to make sure we're still on for Friday. Me and Joss. The massages at Pixies Laughter? Only I won't be at rehearsals on Tuesday, will I? So I might not see you before, and I thought . . ."

Sukie sighed. "Yes, everything's lined up. I told Joss last night. She was dancing with us in the Weasel and

139

Bucket. She was brilliant — we might have to persuade her to take your place in the troupe."

"Her old man won't allow it," Val laughed. "Topsy's already asked her, remember — and she said she couldn't dance."

"Well she can," Sukie said. "Very well indeed. And surely no one is ruled by their partner these days, are they? I'll talk to her on Friday. She might change her mind."

"You can try." Val raised her eyebrows. "But you'll be wasting your time. Her Marvin's a complete bastard. He stops her doing anything he doesn't approve of. And he sure as hell won't approve of his Jocelyn kicking and screaming and showing her knickers. Anyway, sweeties, I'm clearly interrupting — so I'll love yer and leave yer and see you on Friday for me rub-a-dub-dub." She chortled lasciviously in Derry's ear before limping away. "While the posh cat's away, eh, duck? Don't blame yer! Young Sukie's got magic fingers."

Ooooh! Sukie wanted to sink her head onto the grubby tabletop and scream.

"If I wasn't pretty sure that this was Bagley-cum-Russet, on a Sunday in March, in the twenty-first century," Derry grinned, "I'd be convinced I was in some parallel universe. I didn't understand one word of that conversation."

"Good," Sukie said shortly. "Oh — look! Topsy's just finished her card game! Shall we —?"

"Well, that was the object of this exercise, but —" Derry was still grinning, "— just explain some of that stuff. Rehearsals? Troupe? Dancing? Are you — do you —?"

"Dance? Yes — and not round poles or on laps before you start heading down that route. We — me and Valerie and Chelsea and a few others — are the Bagley-cum-Russet can-can troupe. And," she glared at him, "if you as much as snigger I will empty that beer glass over your head."

"God forbid," Derry said straight-faced. "It'd probably skin me alive. But — I'm impressed. Do you mean you do high-kicks and the splits and all that Nicole Kidman Moulin Rouge stuff?"

"Well, we're hardly that standard and we mainly wear more clothes, but we try — and stop leering."

"I never leer."

"Good. Are you ready for this?"

"Pouncing on an old lady and massaging her with — what? Which oil did you choose, by the way?"

"Viola . . . it seemed the most gentle and the least likely to cause any problems."

"Okay, yes then, I'm up for mugging some poor unsuspecting soul and turning her into a lab rat in the weirdest pub I've ever been in. It's always my occupation of choice on a wet Sunday."

"Sarcasm is not allowed." Gathering up her bag but leaving her beer, Sukie headed across the Barmy Cow towards Topsy. "Neither is laughing or wincing or feeling obliged to tell anyone what we're really doing. Okay?"

"Okay." Derry laughed anyway. "Lead on."

Having introduced Derry, Sukie hoped her acting skills would be good enough not to let Topsy know that, despite the denials, she now knew Cora's recipes not only existed but had also been discovered and resurrected.

Topsy beamed at them, as did the half a dozen elderly members of the card school who, clearly tired of blackjack, sat back in their chairs waiting for further entertainment.

"I'm so pleased to see you, dear," Topsy smiled. "I hoped we hadn't parted on bad terms."

"No of course not. Er — did you get home in time to watch *Casualty*?"

"I did, dear, thank you. It was a lovely episode. Someone was impaled on a spiked fence. They had to carry out a roadside operation by torch light. They had to cut through the spike without damaging the vital organs. Mind you, I wouldn't have given the tracheotomy so early on and as for the sloppy use of the intravenous fluids —"

"Mmm, fascinating . . . oh, er — that medical stuff reminds me — you know how, during our can-can warm-ups, you're always stressing that if we look after our leg muscles they'll never let us down and how yours are as strong as pistons but that you sometimes get twinges in your fingers and —"

"Cut to the chase, dear, please. We've got a few hands of whist planned before closing time or death whichever comes first."

"Sorry — okay, well as you know, I'm starting up the at-home massages this week, and I wondered if you'd be interested in being a bit of a guinea pig for me. I just want to make sure I'm doing things right."

Topsy cocked her thin grey head to one side. "You've been giving massages for years. Why would you need to practice?"

Sukie groaned inwardly. Bugger Topsy for being as sharp as a tack.

"Oh — er — these new oils that Jennifer Blessing has supplied — they might not be the same as the old ones and — um . . ."

Oh, lordy! Even to her, it sounded really, really feeble.

Topsy patted Sukie's hand. "Look, if it's some sort of *medical* thing then I'm definitely your woman. Look no further. Do you want me to call into the cottage sometime?"

"No need!" Sukie exclaimed brightly, delving into her bag. "Just by chance I happen to have one of the new massage oils here! If you'd like to put your hands on the table, I'll just . . ."

There was a bit of a delay while the card school spat on hankies and scrubbed the muck from the table top and then polished the result with their sleeves.

Sukie, not daring to look at Derry, unstoppered the bottle.

The aroma from the violas was certainly wonderful: the heady, garden-fresh scent of the oil wreathed and wafted into the Barmy Cow's fug. The release of the fragrance was almost a physical thing — like the genie escaping from the lamp in Aladdin — deliciously swirling and growing and engulfing.

The smoky, mildewy atmosphere was suddenly transformed into a summer meadow with sunshine and butterflies and vibrant flowers and birdsong.

Topsy sniffed. "That smells very — oh . . . I don't know — sort of familiar . . . lovely scent, dear. So clever, these synthetic perfumes — it's almost like being outside in the garden — like being young again. Synthetic, did you say? Hmmm — they smell real enough to me . . ."

"Yes, they do," Sukie said quickly. "Amazing what they can do in the lab, isn't it? Right . . ."

Warming her hands, Sukie then applied the oil in smooth practised movements across Topsy's skinny, gnarled hand and fingers, gently stroking in the direction of the heart, rhythmically massaging the joints and pulse points, feeling the energy flow.

A sizeable crowd, including Valerie Pridmore and her entire family, had gathered, watching intently. Even the Berkeley Boys had emerged from behind the bar and were leaning over the table in a matching row.

"We've got some terrible aches and pains, young Sukie," Claridge said gruffly. "Specially in our feet. What with all that standing behind the bar. If this works on Topsy here, maybe we could all come along to Pixies Laughter for a bit of treatment?"

"Well — yes, of course," Sukie said bravely, trying not to think of the collective disgusting state of the Berkeley feet. "I'll leave you my card."

"That's lovely, Sukie," Topsy smiled sleepily. "Really lovely. I've got a pre-med sensation of floating and my hands feel like they've been amputated."

144

Phew — Sukie thought. High praise indeed. It was going to be okay . . .

Topsy gave a little sigh. "These oils of Mrs Blessing's are wonderful. You must tell her. Oooh my heart's fluttering like a defibrillator."

Oh, God, please don't let her be going to have a heart attack, Sukie thought, wondering if she should stop. "Topsy? Are you feeling okay?"

"Wonderful, dear. I can feel the tension and the knots just sliding away. My fingers are unfurling like little flowers. It's better than being on steroids. What's this one got in it?"

"Violas."

Topsy's head jerked up. Her beady eyes glittered into Sukie's. "Violas?"

"Yes," Sukie continued massaging, frantically improvising. "It's — um — one of the new wildflower aromatherapy range."

"Violas?" Topsy gave Sukie a calculating look. "You know the stories behind violas, don't you?"

Still stroking and circling, Sukie shook her head. She didn't — but she had a horrible feeling she soon would. However, what she did know was Cora's cross-stitched verse, which had just popped unbidden into her head.

Ooooh nooooo . . .

Pretty violas so sweet and shy
Can cure a maiden's lonely cry
Can soothe and smooth an aching heart
Can make a lovers' meeting start

Oh dear, oh dear . . .

Topsy stared at her. "According to legend, they were the flowers created by Zeus to seduce his bride. And they're also known colloquially as Loving Idols or Kiss Me At The Garden Gate — with very good reason. They're used in love potions."

"Really?"

"Yes, really."

"But that would only be the *real* flowers, wouldn't it?" Sukie said, her heart sinking. "Not these synthetic fragrances?"

"Oh yes — the real plants are very powerful indeed. No one should mess around with the real ones. Oh . . ."

Topsy suddenly seemed to have lost all interest in the ins and outs of violas. She was gazing dreamily across Sukie's shoulder.

Sukie turned her head. "Oh, sorry Dorchester — were you wanting to clear this table — we won't be a moment. Nearly finished."

Dorchester Berkeley had moved in really close. He simpered — there really was no other word for it — at Sukie. "No, no my dear. I just wondered if I could touch Topsy's hand. It looks like silk."

He stretched out his knobbly brown fingers and slowly caressed Topsy's hand.

Fully expecting Topsy to shriek like a banshee and wallop him smartly, Sukie held her breath.

Topsy, however, just smiled sweetly and allowed her fingers to be linked with Dorchester's.

146

"All we need now," Derry whispered, "is a crescendo of violins and an angelic choir."

Sukie swallowed. "Quick — grab the stuff and let's get out of here. Er — Topsy — if that feels okay, I'll leave you now. Thank you very much for —"

"No, thank *you*." Topsy was still staring soppily at Dorchester. "I feel wonderful. Simply wonderful. In fact I haven't felt like this since my Eddie left Bagley in nineteen thirty-nine . . ."

CHAPTER
TWELVE

Without doubt, it had been one of the most wonderful weeks she could ever remember, Joss thought on Friday, as she sang her way, accompanied by Radio 2, through the last of the ironing.

It was certainly one of the best weeks she'd had since being married long enough to realise she and Marvin were never going to be happy-ever-after; and one of the best since finally accepting that the children she'd conceived, carried, delivered and nurtured, weren't anything like she'd imagined they'd be.

Ever since the fabulous Saturday evening in the Weasel and Bucket, Marvin had been in a foul mood and hardly spoken. He'd been up and down all Saturday night, knocking back Andrews Liver Salts and groaning. Joss, knowing the indigestion was due to Marvin's temper rather than the Weasel and Bucket's superb food, had snuggled under her single duvet and smiled to herself. As Marvin's internal explosions reached a crescendo to rival the Trumpet Voluntary, Joss had closed her eyes and ears, running through the dancing and the laughter and the sheer giddy happiness of the night out in her head.

148

And on Sunday, Simon had phoned and Marvin had sunk even deeper into growling sulkiness. Apparently Simon and Sonia were sleeping in separate rooms; Sonia had banned Simon from playing golf with Marvin ever again; they'd resigned from the Saturday evening supper circuit clique; and they were both blaming Marvin, loudly and publicly, for such an appallingly *common* choice of venue.

Marvin had thrown all of the *Sunday Telegraph* across the dinette in a fit of pique and locked himself in the bathroom.

Marvin's week-long foul-tempered grouchiness had given Joss loads of time to get on quietly with her own life. She'd gone through the ritual routines with Marvin, of course. They'd just been carried out in relative silence, and the lack of grizzles and censure which could in no way be directed at her for once, had been blissful.

The housework had been a breeze, and Marvin didn't even want to talk enough to complain about burned toast, overdone eggs or anything at all she'd cooked for supper. She'd typed the Neighbourhood Watch notes with an unusual flourish, and had even taken the opportunity to write an article for the *Bagley Bugle* about the possibility of resurrecting the Russet Revels on August Bank Holiday Monday, using the nom-de-plume Maggie Mettle. And Marvin hadn't even glanced at it, but carried it off with the rest of the copy for the secretarial Anneka to print and bind.

Not that Joss had any interest at all in reviving the Russet Revels, but she loved writing these anonymous bits and pieces for the *Bugle* to liven up the rather dull content, and was really, really looking forward to interviewing young Sukie Ambrose later on about the can-can troupe, and maybe even about the link with the at-home aromatherapy sessions. She'd probably choose an exotic French-sounding pseudonym for that one — something outrageous like Fi-Fi Lamour? She giggled to herself.

Even more, she thought happily as she placed Marvin's white shirts on hangers, and folded his Y-fronts and socks — Marvin always insisted on having his smalls ironed — into their respective drawers, she was looking forward to having a massage. Today's appointment had been another deliciously thrilling secret to spice up her week.

And Valerie had said, during one of their illicit coffee morning chats, that Sukie had massaged Topsy Turvey in the Barmy Cow last Sunday and that it had been *wonderful*. Valerie had actually claimed that something rather strange and magical had happened between Topsy and the equally elderly Dorchester Berkeley — but Joss put that down to Val having supped far too much of the Barmy Cow's doubtful beverages.

Right — Joss looked round the bungalow's neat and pristine sterility — everything was done. All that she needed to do now was grab the car keys, as Valerie's can-can injury meant they couldn't walk through the village to Pixies Laughter, and go.

"Ready for this, are you?" Val puffed as she eased herself into the passenger seat. "Prepared to bare all?"

"Absolutely," Joss said happily as they swung out of the neatly-manicured Close and into the tangled, tree-lined village streets. "I can't remember when I last had any of what the magazines call 'me-time'."

"You poor cow," Valerie said kindly. "And it's a lovely day for it, innit?"

Joss nodded. It was. It was as if the weather had been arranged specially to match her mood. The gloom and darkness and rain and biting winds had suddenly disappeared this week and Springtime had arrived in Bagley-cum-Russet.

Today the sun shone in a pellucid sky, drying out the soggy ground, wreathing the village in a warm, milky, earthy haze. Flowers had appeared, as if by magic, from the ground's grim grey morass and tiny green shoots unfurled everywhere.

Spring was bringing new life, Joss thought cheerfully as they approached the Bagley and Russet junction and stopped at the Celtic cross; bringing new experiences, new opportunities. Spring never failed to make her optimism soar, and she always thought the Pagans had it right — celebrating Springtime as their new year. It made sense.

Valerie wriggled down in her seat, waving regally to any Bagleyites they passed. "I'm looking forward to this massage too — not only to get me back on me feet, but there's loads of gossip to catch up on. Not only old Topsy and Dorchester acting like Charles and Camilla on Sunday, but young Sukie turned up with Derry Kavanagh. You know Derry? Runs Winterbrook Joinery? Sex on legs?"

"Mmm, yes . . ." Joss nodded, trying to recall what Val had told her about Derry Kavanagh during their coffee morning chats. "Oh, yes — didn't you say he was going out with Sukie's house-sharer?"

"Exactly!" Val said triumphantly, sketching a royal acknowledgement to the knot of gossiping villagers dawdling in the sunshine outside Coddles Post Office Stores. "So if he's dating that swanky Milla, why was he with Sukie then? That's what I want to know."

Joss slowed down to concentrate as they approached the narrow lane leading to Pixies Laughter. She really didn't care about why Derry and Sukie were seen together, but it was simply lovely to indulge in mindless tittle-tattle.

"Watch out!" Valerie shrieked suddenly, grabbing Joss's arm. "That car's not going to stop!"

Joss stood on the brakes as the car roared towards them head-on then swept past them, missing them by a hair's-breadth.

"Stupid sod!" Joss's heart was pounding, her mouth dry as the fight-or-flight adrenaline pulsed through her body. "He must have come straight off the Hassocks road and been doing well over seventy! Are you okay, Val?"

Valerie nodded, wriggling round in her seat belt, peering over her shoulder. "Yeah — but . . . did you get a look at the driver? I could've sworn it was your Marv . . ."

"No, it couldn't possibly have been," Joss drove on carefully, still feeling incredibly shaky from the very near miss. "He's in London. At work. And there are millions of cars like his — and Marvin never, never breaks the speed limits. Oh, I really need that massage now — my heart's going mad. Are you sure you're all right?"

"Yes, yes I'm fine, love. But —" Valerie settled back in her seat, frowning, "— you know, I still think that was Marv."

"Definitely not." Joss managed a shaky smile at the very idea. "Believe me, Marvin never does anything out of character or out of routine. Marvin would never be home at this time on a Friday. Marvin's miles away, thank goodness. Ah — here we are . . ."

Sukie, preparing for her first ever at-home massage session, gazed round the dining room with a feeling of pride. With flickering banks of little rose-scented candles, the rows of essence bottles, base oils and copper blending bowls on the shelves, and all her aromatherapy and massage certificates framed on the walls, it looked every inch the exclusive private beauty salon. Cora's green and gold flocked wallpaper and bottle green velvet curtains had scrubbed up well and gave it a dark, sumptuous air, and the massage table supplied by Beauty's Blessings fitted in perfectly.

Jennifer had been wonderful this week, supplying piles of big white fluffy bath sheets and matching robes as well as the table, and moving mountains to make sure Sukie had all the right health and safety checks, and employment law and insurance paperwork in place to work from home.

Of course the fact that Sukie had been frantically busy since Monday with the mobile massages had delighted Jennifer, too. They'd quickly organised a routine, Sukie calling into the Hazy Hassocks' salon each morning to collect her appointments, and popping back there in between to help Jennifer out with nail extensions and facials.

"We're really going to have to get some help from the students at the FE college," Jennifer had said excitedly, trying to chip away a face mask from the worst crevasses of an elderly sun-worshipper from Fritton Magna. "The bookings for mobile massages are coming in thick and fast. I can see you're going to be out of Beauty's Blessings more than you're going to be in it and I can't keep up with it all on my own. It'll be like running two businesses in one. Think of all that lovely money rolling in, Sukie."

And Sukie had smiled and nodded and thanked her lucky stars that, thanks to Cora's cross-stitch tapestries and Pixies Laughter garden and, of course, Derry Kavanagh, Jennifer would never, ever need to know about the depletion of the essential oils, then set off again to ease and pamper.

Being busy with the massages each day and de-cluttering the dining room every evening had had other advantages too: it had prevented Sukie having to think about things. Things like Topsy and Dorchester. Things like Cora's concoctions. Things like love potions.

And especially things like Derry.

The hoped-for pierce-and-ping hadn't come to fruition. They'd arrived back at Pixies Laughter from the Barmy Cow, chuckling like children, still stunned by Dorchester and Topsy's inexplicable flirtatious behaviour after the massage — and both trying really hard not to think of the implications — to find Milla's car outside, and Milla pacing around the cottage in a tearing rage.

"My bloody mother!" Milla had screamed at them. "My bloody mother had invited A Man to lunch! A Man who is supposed to be Suitable Husband Material! A Man who is not only three hundred years old with four wives already under his belt, but a man who doesn't even have his own teeth or hair! But of course, he's a baronet, so that's okay according to my bloody mother! And she was sooo unsubtle! Mrs Bennet could take lessons from my bloody mother!"

Trying not to laugh, Sukie had rushed to the kitchen to make coffee, leaving Derry to placate the enraged Milla. Then there'd been a bit of fudging over the messed-up state of the cottage and where the bouquet of flowers had come from, and why Derry and Sukie had been out together.

Fortunately, Milla was far too obsessed with her bloody mother's attempts to replace Bo-Bo in her daughter's life, to dwell too long on anything else.

Derry had left soon after the coffee, kissing Milla and grinning at Sukie, and as she'd been so frantically busy she hadn't seen him since.

Ah well . . . Dragging herself back to the here and now, Sukie took a last look out of the dining-room window before pulling the velvet curtains to ensure total privacy and the right intimate and relaxing ambience. She leaned her hands flat on the sill, drinking it in. The garden looked so different in the sunshine. Nature was truly amazing. All those dreary, dripping, sinister heaps of plants had somehow dried out and disentangled themselves and were forming riotous tumbled clumps of glossy leaves with dozens of little flowers, making it look like a real cottage garden again.

If she was going to continue the pick-your-own aromatherapy system, she'd have to ask Derry to identify the burgeoning blooms for her, wouldn't she? Just so she didn't make any mistakes, of course. It would be the death knell of the business if she garnered the wrong plants and gave all her clients galloping urticaria, wouldn't it? Any excuse to keep in touch, really.

"Oh, face it," she said to herself, closing the curtains, "you just want to recreate last Sunday, don't you? And you can't and mustn't because he-belongs-to-Milla-and-isn't-remotely-interested-in-you — okay?"

Not waiting for an answer — because she knew what it would be — she padded out of the dining room to welcome her first paying customers.

Val and Joss, talking excitedly at the same time about their near-miss with the maniac driver, oohed and aahed over the interior of Pixies Laughter, and even more over the rejuvenated dining room.

"If you'd like to undress through there —" Sukie said, indicating a tiny dark green curtained-off area,

"— and wrap yourself in one of those towels — they're warm enough, I hope — then we can decide how to do this. Do you each want to have your massage privately? Or are you okay with being in together and being an audience for each other?"

"Together!" Joss and Val chorused, already unbuttoning and unzipping and giggling.

Once Val had stretched out face down on the table and Joss had snuggled in her robe on a chair, Sukie's professionalism kicked in. This was something she knew she excelled at. And she enjoyed it. Nothing else mattered while she was working. Not even Derry Kavanagh. Not really.

"I'll do your leg first, Val, before I do the full body massage, if that's okay? Just hitch the towel up a bit. Lovely. Thanks. So — toes to knee, is it?"

"Mmm, please love. And especially round the ankle. The doctor checked it out and said it was just a bit of muscle strain — but it's still giving me gyp when I put any weight on it."

"Not for much longer . . ." Sukie unstoppered one of the little gemstone bottles, carefully measuring six drops from the pipette into the almond base oil. She'd selected the home-made rosemary and lavender blend as both had wonderful healing properties.

"Oh, that smells lovely, Sukie, love." Valerie wriggled in anticipation. "It's like the garden has suddenly come indoors, innit?"

"Beautiful," Joss mumbled sleepily, inhaling deeply from her chair. "I can almost reach out and touch the flowers . . . Oh, I could get used to this . . ."

The scent escaping from the bottle was, Sukie had to admit, far more powerful than any synthetic oil she'd ever used. She'd noticed this phenomenon all week while doing her mobile massages. All her clients had commented on the "bringing the outdoors indoors" effect the moment the bottles were uncorked. Sukie'd agreed that the fragrances magically melted away the surroundings, conjuring up almost tangible images of perfect cottage gardens, gravelled pathways, hidden arbours, cascading roses, warm sunshine, butterflies and birdsong.

Having convinced herself that the Topsy — Dorchester thing was nothing more than a coincidence, Sukie had chosen not to dwell on Cora's recipes being aphrodisiacs or on the meaning behind the poems or the likelihood of her massages being the cause of unsuitable pairings across Berkshire. She was simply grateful that she now had an entire garden of raw materials to work with, and her natural ingredients were clearly far, far superior to anything concocted in a laboratory.

"Oooooh — that's bloody wonderful," Val groaned with pleasure as Sukie gently kneaded and stroked and circled. "I can feel the tension just dissolving — and that's the first time for ages that my muscles haven't been knotted up. I can feel the pain melting away. You've definitely got the gift, my love, I'll give you that."

Joss, who'd been watching avidly, looked at Sukie. "Is it okay if I write something about the can-can dancing and about your massages for the *Bagley Bugle*? I know

Topsy's looking for a replacement for Val in the troupe, and it seemed like a good idea to write a story combining the two — it'll make a nice change from the usual tripe we have in there."

"Yeah — it's mostly what do to with leftover lemon curd and how to make a montage of the Hanging Gardens of Babylon with grains and pulses, isn't it?" Sukie concentrated on Valerie's ankle tendons. "I'd be delighted. So, do you want to do a proper interview, or what?"

"I've got a really good memory." Joss smiled. "So if you just chat, I'll remember most of it — and I can ask you about the specific massage oils and things like that later — then I'll show you the copy before Marvin whisks it off to be printed so that you can make sure there are no mistakes."

"Sounds great." Sukie nodded. "And I still don't know why you don't join the can-can troupe yourself. You danced wonderfully last Saturday and you obviously love it."

"Oh, I just couldn't . . ." Joss sighed. "No, don't even bother to try to persuade me — but I'm sure you'll get loads of applicants once the article is in."

"Speaking of which," Val opened one eye. "When you went to rehearsals on Tuesday, did Topsy say anything more to you about the how-you-do in the pub with old Dorchester?"

Sukie felt herself blushing, and quickly concentrated on the long sweeping strokes along Val's plump calf. She'd had a brief conversation with Topsy as they'd all been leaving the village hall, but she certainly wasn't going to share it with Valerie — or anyone else for that matter.

"Hang fire, young Sukie," Topsy had nabbed her in the vestibule. "Before you go belting off — I'd like a word about last Sunday. My massage. You used viola oil just by happenstance, did you?"

"Er — yes," Sukie had nodded. "It's a light, floral oil and beneficial for the skin as well as unknotting muscles and relaxing joints and —"

"Poppycock! Don't try to fob me off with all that promotional gobbledegook! It might all be true, but violas aren't commonly used in aromatherapy circles, I'll be bound." Topsy's beady eyes had glittered in the darkness. "Being more of a *natural* remedy."

"Yes, well — maybe . . ."

"No maybe about it. Just remember — I *know*. And now the card school — all being in their September years — were very impressed with the demonstration and my renewed flexibility and wondered if you could pop in some other Sunday and do them all — to help with their shuffling and dealing."

"I'd be delighted," Sukie had said, relieved that this was the point of the conversation and making a move towards her car. "Anytime, you know that."

"Not so fast, young lady." Topsy had fastened her now-supple fingers round Sukie's wrist. "I'll tell the others that you'll come along to the Barmy Cow and sort 'em out — but no more violas though. Not even *synthetic* ones. Understood?"

"Yes, okay. But the viola oil worked, didn't it? On your hands and fingers I mean?"

"Oh, it worked all right my girl." Topsy had released her grip and tied her headscarf tightly beneath her wrinkled chin. "As you well know."

And Sukie had said good, and there you are then, and made her excuses and left.

Now she realised Valerie was still waiting for some sort of reply.

She shrugged. "No — not really. Er — Topsy said the massage worked well and her fingers were still really flexible and that she'd have to make it a regular thing for the card players. Chelsea had got wind of the gossip, of course, and was sort of teasing her about Dorchester. But Topsy said she and all the Berkeley Boys had been friends for ever — and changed the subject to some new heart by-pass system she'd seen on *Holby*."

"Hmmm," Val chuckled. "The pub was a right den of iniquity Sunday, wasn't it? Topsy and Dorchester — and you being out with Derry."

"There!" Sukie said brightly, "that's you done! Now I'll just sprinkle some more lavender and rosemary on this warm towel and wrap it loosely round your leg, and if you'd like to slip the robe on to make sure you don't get cold, I'll start on Joss."

As they swapped places and Sukie decanted the relaxing camomile and winter jasmine into the base oil, Joss watched with interest and asked various questions, both about the aromatherapy and can-canning.

"Oh, that's superb." Joss broke off from her investigative journalism and sighed pleasurably as Sukie's fingers kneaded the tightly-knotted shoulder muscles and circled on her rigid spine. "I can feel all my angst sort of floating away. And I don't even feel guilty about enjoying this. And I know you'll think this is completely insane, but I can practically see little jasmine flowers tumbling out of the wallpaper and the floor turning into a camomile carpet — and the scent is simply delicious. Oh, I'm going to give you a sensational write-up and tell everyone I know that you are absolutely brilliant."

Sukie smiled happily and said a silent thank-you to Cora.

Half an hour later, with Joss and Val both glowing, and relaxing sleepily in their warmed robes and sipping tea and chatting idly, Sukie washed her hands then skipped upstairs to her bedroom.

"There!" She grinned at Joss on her return, hauling armfuls of vibrantly coloured frou-frou satin and net behind her. "I thought you might like to see this. My can-can dress — I didn't know if you'd seen one close up. I thought it might help with your article. Give it a bit more colour so to speak."

Joss simply stared, saying nothing.

"Sorry." Sukie frowned. "Is there something wrong?"

Joss shook her head, sensuously stroking the satin of the black and scarlet basque and circular multi-frilled skirt, running her fingers greedily through the miles and miles of hot pink, purple, orange and crimson net petticoats.

"It's the most glorious thing I've ever seen . . . Incredible . . . oh, these colours! Like — like a fallen rainbow. Oh, I've always longed to wear something as sumptuous and wanton as this . . ."

"You could wear mine," Val chuckled from the depths of her robe. "If you'd join the troupe. Old Ronnie'd take it in a couple of hundred yards to fit you."

"Don't!" Joss's voice was anguished. "I *can't*, Val! You know I just can't! But —" she looked at Sukie, "— thank you so much for letting me see this. It's put the icing on my cake today. I'll probably dream about it . . ."

Valerie and Sukie exchanged disbelieving glances.

It wasn't until about twenty minutes later, after a very happy Joss and Valerie had left, while Sukie was clearing away the remnants of the massages and replacing the essence bottles back on the shelf, that it hit her.

Rosemary and lavender!

Sukie didn't even need to look at Cora's cross-stitch rhymes . . .

Lavender and rosemary, pretty in the sun
But beware the perfume when they become one
Apart, so innocent like a child
Joined, make passion's fires burn wild.

Oh — lordy! And she'd smothered Val with it! Mind you, Valerie and her large scruffy husband were always very touchy-feely, so maybe no one would notice.

Oh, and blimey — she looked at the second gemstone bottle; the one she'd used on Joss.

Camomile and jasmine . . .

Camomile the perfume for a lost sweetheart
Jasmine the scent for lovers torn apart
Infused together make a magic blend
And broken hearts will forever mend

Eeek! Sukie winced. Still, hopefully Joss didn't have a broken heart and surely, after what Val had told her, the ghastly Marvin couldn't possibly be anyone's lost sweetheart, could he? Hopefully, this one wouldn't be applicable either. No, of course not. Neither of them had any bearing on Val and Joss, did they? It was all hokum, wasn't it? Wasn't it . . . ?

"Well!" Val said as they approached The Close, "I don't know about you, but I feel right peculiar . . ."

"Me too." Joss wriggled under the seat belt. "Lovely, though — sort of floating and a bit — well, squiffy, I suppose."

"That's it exactly," Val giggled. "Like I've had just that bit too much to drink and feel frisky and ready for a bit of slap and tickle, know what I mean?"

"Yes," said Joss, who didn't, but could imagine.

"I hope me old man's in when I get home. I'll treat him to a bit of afternoon delight!"

"Oh, yes," Joss said wistfully. "That would be lovely. I mean — not for me with your husband, of course."

"Or with yours!" Valerie snorted. "Wouldn't touch yours with the proverbial barge pole!"

"Marvin used to be — different . . ." Joss said wistfully, still not quite recognising the strange feelings inside her. The massage had been a revelation. Her body felt young and supple for the first time in years; all her stresses had simply melted away. It had been a truly magical experience — unlike anything she'd ever experienced. And she felt — well, *frisky*? She sighed. "When we were young, when we first met — Marvin was rather dashing."

"Dashing?" Val snorted as they pulled up outside the Pridmores' bungalow. "Can't imagine it meself — and who wants bloody dashing? What you wants is downright bloody sexy! Ooooh — I feel proper perky if you get my drift." She scrambled from the car, her leg now bearing its not-inconsiderable load with ease. "Thanks, Joss — see you for coffee. Now let me get me hands on that hubby of mine!"

Valerie darted through her front door, and Joss laughed to herself as she reversed into her own drive. She felt a bit "proper perky" too. She hadn't felt like this for — oh for goodness knows how many years — if ever. Maybe, she thought, she'd *never* felt quite like this.

It took her several seconds to realise that there was another car in the drive. A beige car. Marvin's car. But, why on earth would Marvin be home so early on a Friday afternoon?

Joss was still frowning as she unlocked the front door. Was that Marvin who had almost driven into them as Valerie had thought? No, surely not . . . Although, she grinned to herself, if it was, perhaps the Pridmores wouldn't be the only ones indulging in a little afternoon delight . . .?

165

For some unknown reason she felt wickedly daring and crept into the living room. Marvin was standing, his back to her, gazing out of the window. Just for a second, Joss remembered how it had been once upon a time in another lifetime, when she and Marvin had first met.

He'd been her first, her only, boyfriend, and occasionally she'd felt ripples of what she'd imagined was lust when he kissed her, a wild desire for something more when he held her.

Oh, how she wanted that now . . .

Tiptoeing up behind him, she slid her arms round his waist.

"What the hell are you doing?" Marvin swung round, managing to shake her off at the same time. "Have you gone mad, woman?"

Joss, still feeling the ripples of something exciting and unknown, smiled at him. "Sorry to make you jump. It's lovely to have you home so early."

"*Lovely*? Buggering *lovely*?" Marvin roared. "Are you buggering *insane*?"

Aware that her lusty ripples were definitely not being reciprocated, Joss backed away from his rage. "Marvin — dear, what on earth is wrong?"

"Wrong? I'll tell you what's buggering wrong! I've been buggering sacked — that's what's buggering wrong!"

CHAPTER
THIRTEEN

You can keep April in Paris, Sukie thought, driving cheerfully through the bosky lanes on Tuesday morning; springtime in Bagley-cum-Russet is as near to perfect as it gets.

The sunshine bounced from the whitewashed walls of the pretty cottages, gardens flounced with daffodils and crocuses, and the shaggy verges were studded with cowslips, celandines and early daisies. Funny, she thought, how she was suddenly noticing flowers more; actually looking at them, recognising some, wondering about others. Strange, in fact, how many things had changed since she'd discovered Cora's recipes.

Halting for a moment at the Celtic cross, squinting into the sun, Sukie then headed towards the Hassocks road and sang along with some la-la-la-la-la 70s hit on the radio. Her mood, her energy levels, her optimism, had soared with the lighter evenings and warmer days. March had given way to a balmy April, and all round her life was emerging from the winter doldrums, sap was rising and love was in the air.

Hah! Sukie thought, hold that last bit — well on a personal level at least. Maybe it was true that this was the season for young men's fancy to lightly turn to thoughts of love — or whatever that quotation was that had made her and Chelsea giggle in Eng Lit lessons at school — but no man, young or otherwise, seemed to have any sort of romantic thoughts about her at all.

Then, of course, there was only one man who she'd really want to have flighty springtime daydreams about her, wasn't there?

Oh, sod it!

Maybe she'd just concentrate on becoming a career woman and climbing the highly-scented aromatherapy ladder and retire in a million years time and grow roses and keep hens and lots of cats. Yep, she nodded as she reached Hazy Hassocks High Street and negotiated the bottleneck by the library and Mitzi's Hubble Bubble outlet, far better to think about work.

Work, in the ten days since she'd massaged Valerie Pridmore and Jocelyn Benson, had been incredibly busy with bookings and the coming weeks were no exception. Maybe, if things continued the way they were going, she'd one day be able to make a break away from Jennifer and become self-employed. Hmmm, she smiled to herself. Now, there was something to really think about . . .

She was still smiling as she parked behind the dental surgery and scurried into Beauty's Blessings, determined to hurl herself body and soul into work and empire-building and be far, far too exhausted to entertain non-reciprocated thoughts about Derry Kavanagh.

"Sukie! Sweetheart!" Jennifer emerged from a peaches and cream cubicle followed closely by a dowdy woman who had either just had a lip-fill or who'd been in a brawl the previous evening. "It's so exciting! You're going to be so busy! I've had loads of bookings — nearly all for massages at Pixies Laughter. Is that okay with you?"

"Wonderful, thanks Jennifer — you've helped so much. I really do appreciate it."

"No probs." Jennifer whizzed the trout-pout's chip and pin through the machine and beamed her farewells as she thudded out of Beauty's Blessings' peach-shaded door. "Sad case. Discovered her husband's got a blow-up doll in the wardrobe. Wants to compete. Right — to business. How are the oil and essence stocks going? Will you need me to order any replacements this week?"

"Er — no." Sukie didn't quite meet Jennifer's eyes. "I've — um — found them really economical. In fact, I think they'll last for ages."

"Good," Jennifer beamed. "Because they were awfully expensive. Still, you're potentially earning so much money for the company now, you mustn't skimp on them."

"I won't be doing that," Sukie smiled, delving into her bag and withdrawing a folder. "And before I forget — here're the cheques and cash from last week's at-homers. And the invoices and copy receipts."

"Thank you. Oh — lovely." Jennifer's eyes sparkled as her fingers rifled through the paperwork and her brain worked out the profits for Beauty's Blessings. "Do you know, Lance, silly boy, has suggested that you should take a bigger cut of the massage money as it's

169

exceeded all expectations. I said you probably wouldn't want to, but —"

"Yes I would, actually. Thank you," Sukie interrupted. "All contributions gratefully received. I'll just collect this week's appointments then — oh, what's going on in there?"

"Ah!" Jennifer seemed to have recovered reasonably well from the fiscal blow. "I've set our new girls an easy little lower leg wax. You haven't met them yet, have you?"

Sukie hadn't. She'd heard that Jennifer's sorties into Winterbrook FE college had come up with a couple of likely students to help out in Beauty's Blessings, but she didn't know they'd actually started.

"They had their first day yesterday, a sort of induction, learning the ropes, finding their way round, that sort of thing," Jennifer said, whispering silkily towards the cubicle. "I didn't let them touch anyone, of course, but they're nice girls. Recommended by their tutors. Keen to learn. Sadly, they're both called Kylie," she swished back the curtain, "but they're very good at — oh, my God!"

Peering over Jennifer's shoulder, Sukie giggled.

The two Kylies seemed to have made one of the basic errors of waxing: never allow the bodies of the waxer and the waxee to come into close proximity whilst the latter is still sticky.

The Kylies were both welded by the overall to the chunky calves of a hockey player from Winterbrook.

Moving quickly into damage limitation mode, Jennifer grabbed the larger Kylie round the waist, easing her gently to one side, and indicated that Sukie should do the same with the smaller version, all the while murmuring professional and soothing remarks to the unfortunate victim.

"Grab a spatula," Jennifer hissed at Sukie. "Pull your Kylie's overall taut, slide the spatula under and — oooh, sorry Beryl — no, no — nothing wrong at all. Four of us? Um, yes — we do encourage a sort of *en masse* approach for our very special clients . . . right, and ease away!"

Still trying really, really hard not to laugh, Sukie wriggled the spatula between her Kylie's overall and Beryl's calf. Fortunately the wax was still pliable, and Beryl's skin appeared to be more or less intact.

"Don't say anything," Sukie hissed in the skinny Kylie's much-ringed ear. "Whatever you say now will be wrong, believe me. Just smile and look like this is meant to happen. Now brace yourself."

Kylie braced, Sukie eased, and Beryl winced.

After a bit more gentle manoeuvring and a sort of unpleasant sucking noise, Beryl's calf and the smaller Kylie parted company.

Jennifer was having a slightly tougher job with the larger version and was audibly panting. With her tongue protruding from the corner of her mouth, she sounded a bit like a Sumo wrestler as she eased and tugged.

"Ah! Gotcha!"

Jennifer and the larger Kylie shot backwards.

Both Kylies gave a little whimper and disappeared through the curtains.

"There!" Jennifer said brightly. "A superb wax, Beryl. Not a follicle left standing. Now, I'll leave you with Sukie, our senior beautician, and she'll finish you off with our special vitamin-enriched emollients and moisturisers — what? Oh — sorry, no, Beryl. No! When I say finish you off, I'm speaking professionally of course . . ."

Sukie, chewing the inside of her cheeks to prevent herself from sniggering in a most unprofessional manner, reached for the jars of scented soothers and soakers and set to work.

By the time Beryl had left Beauty's Blessings — with Sukie agreeing that the leg wax should be free of charge, much to Jennifer's chagrin — and been further placated with the promise of a free facial, Jennifer had clearly finished her dressing down of the Kylies.

Now both out of their waxy peach overalls and with identical Croydon-face-lifts scraped-back pony tails, belly-flaunting T-shirts and cargo pants, they cowered in a corner, looking tearful and absolutely terrified.

"No harm done," Sukie said kindly. "We all make mistakes when we're learning — and that's one you won't make again. Jennifer is a very kind boss, really. Oh, I do like your tattoos — er — big, aren't they?"

The Kylies nodded. Some sort of wishy-washy denim-blue Eastern hieroglyphics stretched licking tongues round their protruding stomachs from, presumably, the small of their backs.

"Tatty Spry did them, in Steeple Fritton," the smaller Kylie confided proudly. "She's ever so good.

172

They mean good luck and health and happiness in something foreign."

What they also meant, Sukie thought, was that in about fifty years' time there'd be an entire generation of OAPs queuing for their pensions and shuffling on their zimmers with wrinkly, indecipherable tattoos sagging beneath their Damarts.

"Mmmm, lovely." She smiled at them both. "My friend Chelsea has had tattoos done by Tatty Spry, too. She tried to persuade me to have one but I'm too much of a wimp. Now — I've got to fly, but if you just do exactly what Jennifer says and ask if you don't understand, you'll be fine. Trust me."

The Kylies gave her tremulous smiles and said thank you. She suddenly felt quite grown-up.

Jennifer, perched behind the reception desk watching, beamed at her. "You're a very sweet girl, Sukie. Very kind. And patient. I'm not a kiddie-person, as you know. Never been maternal. But you'll make a lovely mother one day."

"Oh, pul-lease!" Sukie pulled a face. "Let me find The Man and have the Big Romance first. Followed by the Big Wedding. Followed by a bit of a life."

"Well, you want to get a move on," Jennifer said. "You haven't got that many decent baby-making years left, have you, and you're not even seeing anyone, are you?"

Sukie now not only felt grown-up, but positively past-it. Wasn't that exactly what Valerie Pridmore had told her, too?

"I'm in my prime, if you don't mind, and happy being single — and certainly not quite ready to slap a 'desperate — apply within' sign on my forehead." She decided muttering that she also wasn't ready to stoop to Jennifer's remedy for manlessness by nicking someone else's husband to fill the gap, might not be a good move career-wise. "Anyway, if you could just let me have a list of the appointments for the rest of this week, I'll have to dash."

Jennifer printed off two closely typed sheets of paper. It would, Sukie knew, be just as easy for Jennifer to e-mail her the list of massage appointments that came in via the salon, but she also knew that Jennifer always wanted to be in control and continue to have a manicured fingernail in the pie, so to speak. One day soon, though, Sukie thought, she'd sound out Jennifer on the possibility of setting up her own business — but not just yet.

"Thanks." She skimmed the lists. "Oh, we've got several repeats here, that's good — and several 'recommended by a friend' ones." She pushed the papers into her bag. "It's going well, isn't it?"

"Very," Jennifer whispered from behind the desk to attend to a couple of pedicures. "Oh, and I knew there was something I had to tell you! You know how everyone gossips while they're having treatments? How they confide in you because you're sort of anonymous? Well, it's rather curious, but some of the people who've asked for second massages have made really funny remarks."

"Have they? What, like stand-up comedians?"

"No," Jennifer, who was a very literal person without a fully developed sense of humour, looked momentarily irritated. "I was going to tell you this straight away, but then we had the Kylie problem which put it right out of my head . . . Anyway, they've said that after they've had their massages at Pixies Laughter, they've gone home and felt — well — a bit frisky, I suppose."

Sukie held her breath.

Jennifer smiled. "Ever so enthusiastic, they were. Several of them have hinted that the massages have spiced up their love life no end. And, more than that, some of them said that afterwards they felt tempted to make *improper suggestions* to complete strangers!"

"You're kidding?" Sukie asked hopefully. "Aren't you?"

"No, I'm not. They said they felt so — well — full of oomph, that it was like being a teenager again! And that miserable old Mrs Dowding — the one who always says we don't do her corns justice when she has her nails clipped and polished — she said she went straight home and fancied the pants off the insurance man."

"Really?" Sukie reverted to the cheek-chewing. "She said *that*?"

"Well, not in so many words, no, but that was the gist. You don't think those new essences I bought could possibly have *aphrodisiac* properties, do you?"

"No, definitely not," Sukie said truthfully, concentrating fiercely on the floor of the salon. "Absolutely not. No way. Your new essences were — um — are as pure as the driven snow. It's — er — probably just the relaxing effect of the massage in the privacy of the

175

cottage that makes them feel more — um — responsive, don't you think?"

"Maybe . . ." Jennifer paused for a moment, then nodded. "Yes, you're probably right. Good — I wouldn't have wanted us to get a *reputation* for anything smutty, if you get my drift, even if it does bring in the punters. But if it's just the general ambience of the surroundings, that's fine."

"And they weren't angry about — about feeling — um — frisky?"

"Oh no, far from it. They all sounded delighted. So whatever you're doing, you carry on. They'll tell their friends, and it all means more money coming in, doesn't it?"

Sukie nodded. Did that make it okay? She could be turning the entire area into Sodom and Gomorrah and Jennifer wouldn't care as long as the shekels kept rolling in? Yeah, knowing Jennifer, it probably did.

"Right, then," Jennifer switched into pedicure mode. "You'd better scoot. You've got your first massage booked in an hour."

Waving goodbye to the Kylies, Sukie scooted out of Beauty's Blessings and into her car.

Blimey . . . Who had she massaged at Pixies Laughter during the last week? Several elderly ladies from Hazy Hassocks including the miserable Mrs Dowding and her corns, a couple from Fiddlesticks and two or three from Winterbrook — all on the pensioners' special. None of them had been under seventy, had they? None of them, surely, could have been affected by her potions? But as none of them were from Bagley-cum-Russet, she wouldn't have heard any gossip even if they had, would she?

She started the car. She'd been so careful, using a basic herbal mix for all of them — a blend for relaxing muscles and energising the spirits — basil and coriander with a dash of dill. A mixture of herbs sorted from the handfuls she and Derry had rescued from Cora's overgrown kitchen garden.

What on earth was Cora's herby rhyme? The one with basil in it . . .? Sukie furrowed her brow, trying to remember the exact cross-stitched words.

"Ooooh — noooo!" The poem filtered through just as the lights turned red at the Winterbook junction. She stood on the brakes and thumped the steering wheel. A youth in a back-to-front baseball cap in the white van alongside her leered. She ignored him. "Oh, bloody, bloody hell!"

When Basil and Coriander meet
A meal can be a tasty treat
But add to Dill and there's a danger
Even the faithful will kiss a stranger

"Damn!" Sukie groaned, roaring away as soon as the lights turned green, leaving the white van standing. "Damn and blast it!"

That evening, in the chill, dim mustiness of Hazy Hassocks village hall, the can-canners were halfway through their rehearsal. Topsy was Not Happy.

"That, girls," she snapped, "was bloody awful! I've seen patients on trolleys on *ER* with more animation than you lot!"

"Give us a break," Chelsea groaned, sitting on the stage and rubbing her ankles. "We're still trying to do the same routines with one less person. We get confused."

"Confused?" Topsy's little eyes glittered beneath her headscarf. "Confused? You have a senility problem, do you? How difficult can it be?"

Bet, Roo and Trace, the other dancers, huddled together, muttering mutinously.

"There being five of you instead of six only becomes awkward in the set pieces! And surely you've got enough intelligence to work things out between you? The crossovers, and the lines and circles should present no problems whatsoever! And there's no excuse at all for you to lumber about like hippos! I'm surprised the stage is still intact!" Topsy shook her head. "It doesn't matter how many of you there are! The lack of numbers doesn't make any difference to your suppleness and agility for heaven's sake!"

Sukie, still out breath, sat on the edge of the stage with Chelsea and puffed out her cheeks.

"You're a disgrace!" Topsy, despite her long mac, executed a perfect high-kick from a standing start. "There! I'm old enough to be your mother — and grandmother in some cases — and I can out-dance the lot of you! Anyway — what's happening with the replacement? Or are we getting Valerie Pridmore back again?"

"Val's back at work," Sukie said, brushing dust from her leggings, "but she won't be able to dance for ages. She says her leg is okay for standing and walking for little bursts, but she can't dance."

"She never could," Topsy spat. "So, have we advertised — or is that being left to me, too?"

Sukie sighed, and explained about Joss Benson and her piece about the aromatherapy and can-canning for the *Bagley Bugle*, in which she'd mention they were looking for a new dancer, and which should appear at the end of the week.

"Hmmm," Topsy pursed the thin lips, "that's still on, is it? Well, let's hope someone with a bit of verve reads the damn thing and gets in touch soon as. Mind you, most of the *Bugles* just get dumped in the bin, so I ain't holding out a lot of hope. Right," she clapped her hands. "One more time!"

There was a universal groan, but everyone hauled themselves to their feet.

Sukie, who had been massaging elderly backs and legs and shoulders all day having abandoned the old herby mixture for a new one with juniper and sage which only had a poem linked to happiness and age so it must be okay, helped Chelsea to her feet.

"Jesus! You smell like an old person!" Chelsea wrinkled her nose. "You know, when you stand behind them in the chemist and they reek of TCP? Why do they do that? Where do they put it? Is that what you've used?"

"No." Sukie grinned. "It's one of my new oils. It lingers."

"You can say that again," Chelsea held her nose. "No wonder Derry Kavanagh has vanished into the ether. Even if he wasn't gooey-eyed over Milla, he'd run a mile from you ponging like that. You're hardly alluring, are you? Is that why we haven't seen him or heard about him all week? Or has Milla eaten him?"

"Derry has apparently had an urgent commission from one of his best clients," Sukie said, reporting Milla, and trying to sound disinterested as they shuffled into some sort of order. "From some theatrical couple who own a manor house on the outskirts of Winterbrook. Derry's already rebuilt their kitchen and drawing room and they pay a fortune for craftsmanship and won't have anyone else to work on their house — so he's been there all hours, building a spiral staircase for one of the upper storeys."

"A likely story," Chelsea chuckled, straightening her T-shirt. "Oh, bugger, Topsy's cranking up the stereo and counting us in . . . Is this the bit where we go in on the skip or the run?"

". . . and two and three and . . ." Topsy stopped, looking furious. "Stop! Is that someone's phone ringing?"

Sukie groaned and broke formation. "Sorry, Topsy. Mine. I'll have to answer it — it's not on message service and it might be work." She scrabbled in her bag at the side of the stage. "Hello?"

"Sukes!" Milla's voice screamed happily in her ear. "Where are you?"

"Hassocks village hall. Cancan rehearsals. Milla, I can't chat . . ."

"I'm not calling for a chat, Sukes. Look at the phone! You've got the wrong one. You've picked up mine. Yours is here and I've spent all evening taking weirdo messages about things that I don't understand from people who sound like they think they're calling a massage parlour. And now I need mine because I'm going out and not coming home tonight and I'll go straight to work tomorrow and —"

"Sukie!" Topsy howled. "Put that bloody thing down! Now!"

"Crikey," Milla sounded shocked. "I heard that. She's in a temper, isn't she? Okay, Sukes — look, I'm on my way now — I'll just pop in with your phone and we'll do a swap, okay?"

"Okay. See you in a minute." Sukie clicked the mobile off and pulled a face at Topsy. "Sorry. I've picked up Milla's phone — we've got the same ones. She needs hers and —"

"I'm not interested!" Topsy snapped. "Now — ladies, let's get ourselves back into the Miss Bluebell mindset. Listen to the music . . . Listen . . . Let the music seep into you, fire you, inspire you. Let the music carry you away to gay Paree . . . And one and two and — go!"

Off they went again with the roar of Offenbach filling the village hall. The Bagley-cum-Russet dancers whooped and linked and ran and slid and kicked like billy-oh.

"Better, gels!" Topsy shrieked, doing an impromptu floor-to-knee-to-shoulder kick in her excitement. "Much better! And one more time — right — off we go!"

And off they went.

Sukie, who really loved the music and the routines, and the sheer sexy glamour of the dance, hurled herself into it with renewed vigour. It was a shame, she thought giddily, as she and Chelsea linked arms, circled wildly, grabbed their right ankles and hauled their legs up alongside their ears, that Joss Benson couldn't join the troupe. Poor woman. She'd have so much fun. And she obviously loved the costume and the idea of exotic dressing-up too, not to mention her being a great dancer. She'd be perfect.

The troupe separated, screaming, high-kicking. Chelsea and Sukie pranced to opposite sides of the stage, then flouncing imaginary skirts, hurled themselves into whooping diagonal cartwheels. Perfect, Sukie thought, dizzily, it's going really well. Back into line — one more set of high-kicks — then leap and scream and into the splits and finish . . .

"Superb!" Topsy shouted as Orpheus's seduction faded. "Superb! Just like the Moulin Rouge, gels!"

"Couldn't have put it better myself." Derry Kavanagh, grinning, the ice blond hair looking divine against the softness of his ancient leather jacket, appeared from the hall's dark recesses. "Er — sorry to interrupt but I just have to collect a mobile phone."

Topsy beamed at him. "Yes, yes, of course. We've finished now. Did you enjoy that?"

Derry's eyebrows rose. "You could say . . . Um — Sukie, did Milla ring?"

Sweating, out of breath, desperately embarrassed, Sukie nodded and staggered to the corner of the stage.

Chelsea, damn her, was laughing. Everyone else, including Topsy, was staring at Derry with lascivious eyes.

She grabbed Milla's phone from her bag, and held it out to Derry. "She said she'd come and get it. I wasn't expecting to see you."

"No — I think she was scared she'd be roped in if she set foot in here." Derry's gorgeous eyes crinkled. "That was very — um — impressive."

God! Sukie sighed heavily. Now he'd seen her lumbering about like a baby elephant in her truly, truly unflattering practice clothes and reeking of the residue of the massage oil which probably smelled like disinfectant and second-hand gin by now.

"Glad you liked it," she said shortly, still holding out Milla's phone. "Er — how long were you watching for?"

Derry's fingers briefly brushed hers during the handover. It was like a fizz of electricity. He moved away. "Oh, long enough to know you can touch your ear with your foot, and do perfect cartwheels, and do things with your legs a bloke can only dream about — oh, and do the splits from a run and jump."

Bugger. Bugger. Bugger.

"Far too much then," Sukie tried joking to cover her embarrassment. "It'll probably give you nightmares. Er — thanks for the phone. Um — how's the staircase going?"

"Great, thank you. Milla's coming to see the progress tonight and meet my clients. You know what she's like about celebs — even minor ones. What about the aromatherapy? Do the new oils work well?"

"Yes, fantastically. I'm busy all the time, like you."

They stared at one another for a second.

"Yes, I suppose I shouldn't keep Milla or my clients waiting," Derry said softly. "Lovely to see you again. We never seem to meet under normal circumstances, do we?"

"What's normal?" Sukie asked, knowing that her mascara was smudged under her eyes and her face was shiny and her hair probably looked like Don King's best.

"Not you." Derry grinned at her. "Thank goodness. Bye then . . ."

"Whooo!" Chelsea sighed as Derry disappeared. "He is *divine* . . . Sukes? Sukie? Ohmigod! Look at you . . . You are sooo smitten, aren't you? It's written all over your face. Oh, dear — it can-can only end in tears."

CHAPTER
FOURTEEN

"Joss!" Valerie Pridmore yelled delightedly. "Hiya, stranger! I'm so glad I've caught you. I was getting really worried, love. I haven't seen you for — what — it must be a couple of weeks? What the hell is going on? Are you avoiding me? Have we fallen out or summat?"

Joss, trying to make the early-morning back garden sorting of the recycling last forever, looked across the fence at Val and lowered her voice. "Oh, Val — I've been meaning to come round and ask about your leg and catch up with things, but —" she cast an anguished look over her shoulder towards the bungalow, "— Marvin's been here all day every day. It's difficult."

"Is he off sick?" Valerie laughed. "Nothing trivial, I trust? I'd noticed his car was in the drive — thought he might be having a bit of a holiday. And my leg's hunky-dory, thanks to young Sukie. I'm not up to dancing the can-can, but I can stand on it for hours at work now without a twinge."

"Good. I'm really pleased you're better."

"So am I — but — look at you . . . you look terrible, if you don't mind me saying. Are you okay?"

"No." Joss shook her head, knowing she was probably going to cry. "I don't think I'll ever be okay again."

"Jocelyn!" Marvin's voice roared from inside the bungalow. "What are you doing out there? You've been ages with that rubbish!"

Valerie chuckled. "He must have seen me, bless him. Look, love, I know you can't come round if he's got you under lock and key, but surely he couldn't stop you taking a little walk down to Coddles? To post a letter or buy some sugar or something? In about ten minutes or so? Okay?"

"Okay." Joss nodded. "Ten minutes. Thanks."

She trudged wearily back into the bungalow.

She'd probably end up in prison, Joss thought, if she had to spend one more day — all day — in the house with Marvin. His ongoing anger was only now surpassed by his sense of injustice and self-pity. It seemed a lifetime since she'd come home from her massage feeling renewed and energised, her body tingling — was it really only two weeks ago? It might as well have been two years.

"Now what are you doing?" Marvin looked up from his chair in front of the television. "It's nearly ten o'clock. You haven't cleared away the breakfast things."

"You could do that."

"What?" Marvin's teeth clenched. "Women's work? I don't think so. I do have my standards. Why are you changing your shoes? You're not going out?"

"Just down to Coddles. We're running low on — er — tea."

"I don't like their tea. Cheap rubbish."

"They do have named brands, too."

"Which we can't afford." Marvin dragged his eyes from the television again. "It's all spend, spend, spend with you isn't it? Are you too stupid to understand that we're having to count every penny now?"

Ignoring him, Joss flicked at her hair in the mirror and groaned inwardly. Valerie was right, she did look terrible: washed-out, wrinkled, defeated, old. She picked up her handbag. "I won't be long. Is there anything else you want?"

"Nothing we can afford," Marvin hissed, tapping his fingers on the arm of his chair. "And don't forget there's no more monthly allowance for you, so don't buy yourself some silly little frippery like shampoo or bath foam. You can use washing up liquid."

Joss took a deep breath and had a silent scream.

Marvin continued the irritating tapping. "Don't be gone long — and bring a receipt back for the tea. I don't want you overspending. And don't take the car."

"I wasn't going to. See you later."

Marvin grunted, his eyes already back on some programme about the erosion of the coastline of some third world country.

Joss stepped out into The Close, her eyes dazzled by the glorious sunlight, which failed to warm her body or lift her spirits. She had a permanent headache and a tight knot of dread deeply embedded in her stomach. Oh, what had she done so very wrong in a previous life to deserve this? Still, it'd be wonderful to unburden herself on Valerie. She'd never needed a friend more than she did right now.

Every step through the high-banked, sweet-smelling lanes towards Coddles Post Office Stores and away from the bungalow was like a glorious step to freedom. Joss felt as though she was on autopilot. If only she could go on walking away for ever . . .

Val was waiting outside Coddles, sitting on the rustic bench in the sun. "I bought us a sticky bun each," she grinned up at Joss. "You looked like you could do with a sugar rush. Oh, blimey love, it's only a cake . . . don't cry . . ."

Joss sniffed back her tears, said thank you as she squeezed alongside Val on the bench, and finally exhaled.

"Talk if you want to," Val said comfortably, "and don't if you don't."

Joss sat in silence for a while, eating the sticky bun without really tasting it, only vaguely thinking that Marvin would have a purple fit if he knew she was eating in public. She watched the Bagleyites drifting in and out of the shop as if she were watching a film. It was all unreal. But the sun was beginning to warm her, and the colours — the acid green shoots unfurling on the overhanging lime trees, and the mauves and yellows and reds of the spring flowers in tubs outside the shop — began to filter slowly through her permanently-sepia-hued brain.

"Marvin's lost his job." Wiping sugar and crumbs from her lips, she finally looked at Val. "He's not taking it well."

"Oh, love." Valerie patted Joss's hand. "What a bugger. I know what it's like — my old man is in and out of work like a yo-yo. But, I thought your Marv was one of the high-ups? Untouchable? And surely he can get another job? He's not that old . . . So — what happened?"

Joss, lifting her face to the sun, took a deep breath. "Are you sure you want to hear it?"

"What I want ain't important," Val shifted her bulk more comfortably on the bench. "But I think you need to talk about it, love, so I'm all ears. Ain't got to be at work for an hour or so, so I'm listening."

"Well," Joss sighed, "it was the day we had our massage. You were right — it was Marvin's car that nearly hit us, and when I got home . . ."

Leaving out the cringingly humiliating bit about her half-hearted attempt to seduce Marvin, Joss started to tell the whole sorry story. It was like being there all over again. Like some horrific *Groundhog Day*.

Despite Marvin's initial outburst that he'd been sacked, the reality was very different.

"I'm redundant! No longer needed! Buggering useless! The place has been taken over!" he'd stormed. "The whole company, all the divisions, all the outlets! Taken over. A boardroom coup! There'd been rumours of foreign interest and whispers of possible outside corporate investment for ages, but we'd been told they'd be putting money in and expanding us maybe overseas — not buggering this!"

It transpired the take-over had been from an Asian-based conglomerate. Marvin had sworn to never, ever eat at another curry house. Joss had been secretly relieved at that point that the taking-over company hadn't been Scandinavian; Marvin would have probably stripped the whole bungalow of the Ikea furniture and set fire to it in The Close.

"But surely," Joss had said, trying to grasp the implications, "surely you must have had some inkling?"

"If I'd had a buggering inkling," Marvin had snarled, "I'd have buggering done something about it, wouldn't I, woman? All I got this morning was a 'you're surplus to requirements, thanks for your years and years and years of work but we don't need you any more, buggering clear your desk, and buggering bugger off'!"

Joss, shell-shocked, had clasped her hands together and walked to the window. She'd wished she could comfort Marvin, say something useful and positive, but all she could think of was that he'd be at home. Always. Those awful Saturdays and Sundays would be seven days long.

"Okay, but once you've got over this initial shock," she'd said encouragingly, "you can look for something else, can't you? You'll be snapped up. And they must have given you a nice golden handshake so we'll be okay . . ."

Marvin had gone into his white-lipped, temple-pulsing mode. "Are you mad, woman? Listen to me! I've been in the same job, man and boy, all my buggering life! I'm clearly considered a buggering dinosaur! I'm ten years off retiring — and thanks to the general mismanagement of funds in this country there'll be no early pension for me! And we were given statutory redundancy payments! Peanuts! Buggering peanuts! We're on the breadline, Jocelyn! Paupers!"

190

Joss had thought this probably wasn't quite true. And the bungalow was paid for. But she could see that without Marvin's more than generous salary there'd have to be some drastic tightening of belts.

"So what's happening to everyone else?" She'd turned from the window. "Has the company suggested anything? Courses for retraining? Help to find other posts? Relocation?"

Marvin had turned magenta. His cheeks had gone shiny. "You know nothing about the business world, Jocelyn, so stop making ridiculously feeble remarks! The company doesn't give a buggering toss! The company has shed those posts the new bastards feel unnecessary. The company forgot about me the minute I walked through the buggering revolving doors!"

Joss had turned to the window again and read between the lines. So it hadn't been a full-on coup, then. Not everyone had been "surplus to require-ments". Just Marvin and possibly several others who had been there from school, who thought the company owed them a cradle-to-grave living; Marvin and the others who turned up at the office each day but who probably didn't do an awful lot of productive work; who, by dint of their length of service, now probably cost more than they earned; who could be replaced by bright young things willing to start on a basic salary and work their way up the corporate ladder.

It was the way of the business world.

"I know this has come as a blow to you," Joss had said, trying to stop the panic rising, "but you could look on it as a brand new start. You've got years yet to share

191

your — um — expertise with another company. Maybe not in London, but there are masses of firms in Reading and other places all around here that would surely be glad to give you a job."

"I don't want another buggering job!" Marvin had roared. "I had a buggering *career*! The only buggering career I've ever wanted or ever needed! I don't want to work anywhere else. No, this is the end of my life! The buggering end!"

And then it had got even worse.

Marvin had phoned Tilly and Ossie, blustering and exploding down the phone, slandering his old company and the new owners with every expletive-laden breath. And the children had turned up for the first time in — oh, it seemed like years, with their snooty corporate-minded partners and they'd all treated Joss like a skivvy and had closeted themselves in the dinette with Marvin while she'd fetched and carried.

Joss had stood in the doorway, staring at the husband she really couldn't even feel sorry for, and her son and daughter who barely acknowledged her, and wondered if her spirits had ever been at a lower ebb.

Then Tilly and Ossie and their partners had left, briefly kissing Joss's cheek as an afterthought, with vague promises to "be down again soon", and as they'd been unable to suggest any even remotely suitable employment for Marvin within their own companies, he'd sunk ever deeper into smouldering gloom.

Joss took a deep breath, back again in the present, outside Coddles, with the village coming and going around her on a glorious spring morning. Oh, how she wished she'd never have to go home.

". . . and that's it really." Joss looked at Valerie. "The whole sorry story."

Val reached out a pudgy hand and closed it round Joss's. "Poor, poor you. So, doesn't he ever leave the house? Play golf? See his cronies?"

"He says he can't afford golf any more." Joss shook her head. "And his so-called friends haven't even phoned. They don't care, Val. I doubt if they even liked him. They probably just think 'there but for the grace of God . . .' and thank their lucky stars they're still working."

"And money?" Val asked. "Look, tell me to mind my own business, but I know when my old man's been unemployed, my money's been vital. Are you really broke? I haven't got much, but if you're short . . . oh, blimey, don't cry again."

Joss squeezed the pudgy hand. "You're such a good friend. Thank you . . . it's so kind of you, but I wouldn't dream of borrowing money."

"Borrowing? It'd be a gift, love. For you, mind. Not him."

"Oh, Val — thanks. You're brilliant, but we're not quite bankrupt. We've got some savings, and we've cashed in a couple of insurances and we've got our investment income — but, unless Marvin finds another job, it means we'll be living in reduced circumstances until we reach pension age, that's for sure."

"Well, if he won't get up off his silly self-centred lazy arse and look for work, then you can, can't you?" Val grinned. "It'd be the making of you, Joss, love. You'd be out of the sodding bungalow and have a bit of independence to boot."

"But I can't do anything!" Joss shook her head. "We've already discussed this, haven't we? I can only do touch typing and shorthand — and no one needs those skills nowadays, do they?"

"I'm not suggesting you try for something highfalutin'. But there's loads of stuff you could do. Work in a shop, a pub, a café, cleaning . . ."

"Marvin wouldn't let me do anything menial —"

"Now you listen to yourself!" Valerie looked stern. "One, this isn't anything to do with Marv, and two, there's nothing menial about jobs what don't need a string of letters after your name just to walk through the door. And you need a regular income, don't you? A bit of money of your own?"

"Yes, but — oh God, Val — I can't go out to work! I wouldn't know where to start! I've got no confidence at all. I haven't worked outside the home for decades . . ."

"Neither have a lot of women, but they gets themselves little jobs easy enough."

Joss traced a pattern in the gravel with the toe of her shoe. The sun glinted on the millions of tiny fragments, making them glitter like a scatter of precious stones. "Actually, if you promise not to laugh, I've been thinking of starting a bit of a career in freelance journalism."

Valerie shook her head. "What? On the strength of a few things in the *Bagley Bugle*? Look, I'm the last person to piddle on your parade, love, and I don't know a lot about the media world, but I can't see any of the tabloids beating a path to your door because you've written a couple of articles about the Russet Revels for a local freesheet."

Of course, the *Bagley Bugle* had now also bitten the dust — or at least, Marvin's involvement in it had. Joss had rather foolishly, with hindsight, suggested that he'd have far more time to concentrate on the *Bugle* and the Neighbourhood Watch now. He'd hurled the files and folders and templates across the dinette and snarled that some other soft sod could take over the buggering thankless tasks. Joss had assumed this must have a lot to do with the secretarial Anneka no longer being available to do the *Bugle's* scanning and printing and binding.

"I sent the article about Sukie's aromatherapy and the can-can dancers to the *Winterbrook Advertiser.*"

"Did you?" Val said admiringly. "That was a bit daring. I thought it was for the *Bugle*?"

Joss explained about the Bugle's demise. "So, I thought the *Advertiser* might be interested in the article anyway, and any other little bits I could write for them. It's a start . . ."

Val nodded. "If you say so, love. It's not the *Daily Mail* though, is it? Personally, I'd be looking for something in Big Sava. Has the *Advertiser* got back to you?"

"Not yet."

Val patted her hand. "Never mind, love. Maybe they'll be on the phone when you get home offering you a regular slot or whatever they call it — but I wouldn't hold yer breath. In the meantime, do you want me to pick up an application form from Big Sava when I'm next in Hazy Hassocks?"

Joss smiled as she stood up. "Maybe that'd be a good idea, just in case I don't turn into an investigative journalist overnight. Yes, please do. I mean, surely even I could stack shelves — even if I couldn't work those computerised cash register machine till things."

"Blimey, love." Valerie puffed to her feet too. "If a scatterbrain like young Chelsea can cope with them, then you'll be able to do it with yer eyes shut. Look, until things sort themselves out, we'd better meet here for our chats. Ten tomorrow okay?"

"Yes, lovely." Joss smiled. "Thanks, Val."

They walked back through the village together, but Joss went on ahead when they reached The Close. She knew it was feeble, but she really, really didn't want to antagonise Marvin any further.

He didn't look up from the television. The third world country's coastal erosion had been succeeded by something about the development of the jet engine. It was very noisy.

"You had a phone call," he said. "And where's the receipt?"

Bugger, Joss thought, she'd make a lousy secret agent. "Oh, er — I didn't buy any tea after all. There was only the expensive loose sort. We'll have to make do . . . Who was the phone call from?"

"No idea," Marvin yawned. "I'm not your secretary, Jocelyn. I said you weren't in and hung up."

196

Thanks, Joss thought, kicking off her outdoor shoes and sliding her feet into her slippers. In the dinette, the breakfast things were untouched. She sighed, grabbed a tray and started another day of tedium.

The phone rang as she was scraping eggshells into the bin. Marvin didn't move.

"Hello?" She said tentatively. It was probably someone selling something. They didn't get many personal calls. "Yes, this is Jocelyn Benson . . . oh, hello . . . yes, oh you liked it? Wonderful! You're running it? In this week's edition? Out tomorrow. Fantastic! What? Oh, yes — the invoice . . . Yes, I included it because — what? What do you mean you don't *pay*? You mean you expect people to write for you for nothing? What? What's a by-line? Oh — is it? Well a by-line won't pay the bills, will it? Yes, of course I'm pleased that you liked it enough to use it but — no, I don't think there'll be more of the same without remuneration. Yes, I'm sorry too . . ."

She replaced the receiver with a sigh and a feeling of ever-deepening gloom. That was the end of the brief sortie into journalism, then. It looked like Big Sava was her only salvation.

"Jocelyn!" Marvin shouted. "Have you made my coffee yet?"

On the other hand, Joss thought, kicking viciously at the dinette's door and heading for the kettle, ten hours a day on a supermarket checkout was beginning to look pretty alluring.

"Coming, Marvin," she muttered under her breath. "Coffee and cyanide coming up . . ."

CHAPTER
FIFTEEN

There was quite a queue in Pixies Laughter's living room the following morning — and it wasn't yet eight o'clock.

"Bloody hell," Milla grumbled through her cigarette while making coffee in the kitchen, "it's like a doctor's waiting-room out there. I keep being ogled by geriatrics."

"Get dressed then." Sukie grinned. "Those old boys probably haven't seen so much flesh on display since the days of Jayne Mansfield."

Milla yawned, pushing her blonde hair away from her eyes. It fell straight back down again. Silkily. Just like Derry's, Sukie thought. They really were an impossibly glamorous match. Damn it.

"Who?"

"Jayne Mansfield — old-time film star, beautiful, bosomy, great legs. Hot pin-up babe of a couple of generations ago. Actually, Cora loved her films — she used to take me to see them when they were on in Winterbrook." Sukie continued decanting the almond and apricot base oils from their containers into smaller plastic bottles which were easier to deal with in the dining-room-cum-massage parlour. "And sorry if I'm in your way. When I booked the early morning sessions, I thought you either would be already at work or staying at Derry's."

"I'm on flexitime — going in this afternoon — and Derry's too knackered from working on his spiralling staircase deadline to be much fun at the moment." Milla grabbed her mug of coffee. "Is the bathroom safe? You haven't got eighteen people waiting in there, too, have you?"

Sukie laughed. "Nope. Just that lot out there — Topsy's card school. I couldn't do them all at the Barmy Cow, which was their venue of choice, so I arranged for them to pop in *en masse* this morning. They only want hand and finger massages so it shouldn't take long."

"No sweat." Milla sniffed at the base oil. "Ooh, that smells nice . . . you know, I do envy you this — and everything else, really. You've got this lovely rounded rooted life here in the village, with the aromatherapy business and your friends — not to mention the can-can dancing."

Sukie smiled. "It's okay as lives go, I suppose. It could be a hell of lot worse." Well, it could. It could be like Jocelyn Benson's. "Er — did Derry say anything about the other night, by the way? About the dancing, I mean? He looked a bit shocked . . ."

Hopefully, Sukie prayed silently, he'd simply been shocked at the sight of women of various sizes doing acrobatic things and yelping rather than being shocked rigid by realising, as Chelsea had, that she'd got a mega-sized stupid school-girly crush on him — and it showed.

"Shocked? I'll say he was shocked! He couldn't get over it! I've no idea what he thought dancing the can-can actually entailed — but it certainly opened his eyes. But blimey, Sukes, even I didn't know you could do the splits. How amazing!"

Sukie exhaled. "Oh, it's easy when you get the hang of it. Anyone can do it with the right exercises and a bit of practice. Although I did gymnastics at school which helps. And — um — that's all he said about it, was it?"

"No — believe me, it was the main topic of conversation until we met up with his clients — oh, and they were a major disappointment, let me tell you. Took themselves sooo seriously. Proper Ac-Tors, don't you know, luvvie?" Milla giggled. "Anyway, once we arrived we had to talk a boring mix of woodwork and repertory theatre for the rest of the evening — but on the way home he kept saying I should have a go — oh, not just at doing the splits, God forbid, but at joining the can-can troupe."

Sukie thanked her lucky stars that Derry clearly hadn't read the give-away signs. Phew! And she could just see Milla in the gorgeous frou-frou costume, prancing and high-kicking with those endless legs — sod her. "Well, why don't you come along? We still need someone to replace Val — you'd look ace in the frock, and you've been living here for some time without really joining in on the villagey stuff. You're always saying you need a new hobby."

200

Milla shook her head. "No way! That's *not* my idea of fun! And while playing at being a rustic suits me at the moment, I'm a city girl at heart and always will be. My hobbies involve buying shoes and handbags and lunching in European capitals — not thundering around in some draughty village hall being barracked by an ancient madwoman who thinks she's the love-child of Anna Pavlova and Christiaan Barnard."

"Yeah, well, put like that I can see it possibly wouldn't have a lot of allure." Feeling guilty about the wave of relief that immediately swamped her, Sukie concentrated on wiping down the oily work surfaces. "I seem to have made one heck of a mess in here — hope you weren't wanting breakfast any time soon. Still, once I've done the card players I've got an appointment with one of my regulars in Winterbrook at eleven, so I'll be out of your way."

"Fine by me." Milla hugged her coffee mug. "Take as long as you like. This is your home. Your business. I've got no rights to grizzle about what goes on here. What? Don't look at me like that. I can be a nice person when I want to. I'm not always a Princess Mi-Mi-Mi, you know."

"I know," Sukie grinned, tightly stoppering the bottles. "You're okay, really. Derry thinks so, obviously."

Milla smiled. "Ummm. We do get on well. He's such a lovely straight bloke. Gorgeous. Funny. Decent. Honest. And amazingly bloody sexy. But —"

"But?" Sukie paused in deciding which essence would be safe to use on Topsy's card-players without causing an OAP orgy. "There's a 'but' after that roll call of perfection?"

"Oh, not a huge but . . . But a but, yes . . ."

Sukie held her breath. "Milla, you're not thinking of dumping him are you?"

"Goodness, no! Do you think I'm mad?"

Sukie hoped that her groan wasn't audible. "So — what's the problem? Is it because he's not a wheeler-dealer with a seven-figure bank balance, a Coutts cheque book and his own island somewhere in the Indian ocean?"

Milla perched on the edge of the table, sipping her coffee. "No, of course not. I've put all that shallowness behind me, I hope, and as well as all his previously listed attributes, Derry's also supremely talented. God, Sukes, you don't think I'm that much of a materialistic snob, do you?"

Sukie nudged round Milla's long bare legs, trying and failing to shut the kitchen door with her elbow to prevent the elderly poker players from having a joint apoplexy.

"I thought you were a rich, very beautiful, scarily efficient business woman when you came here to look at the cottage. I still do, because you are. But no, I don't think you're a gold-digger or a complete snob."

"Thanks."

"You're welcome. So, if Derry being a joiner isn't the problem, what on earth is?"

Milla shrugged. Her T-shirt slipped from her shoulder. There was a mass intake of breath from the living room. "It's just — I feel we kind of drifted into this relationship. Both of us. The way we met, the way we were thrown together — it was just so easy to carry on seeing one another. But if we'd met at a party or in a club or at work, we'd have probably found each other attractive and enjoyed one another's company for a little while — but that's as far as it would have gone. For him as well as me. I just get the feeling that we're only going through the motions because neither of us can find a really good reason not to. Does that make sense?"

"Sort of." Sukie decanted her essences, trying to look non-committal. "Yes, I suppose so. So, you're not in love with him?"

"God! I don't know! I don't think so. But I'm so useless with men. There've been so many since Bo-Bo, and they've all been lovely but they haven't been —"

"Bo-Bo?"

"Exactly."

"And you know you're in love with him? Still?"

Milla shrugged. The T-shirt slipped further. "Yes, still. Sad cow that I am. I know I'll always love him — but I also know I'll never get him back. He made that perfectly clear by jilting me — and my parents will never, never forgive him for ducking out just before the wedding. It almost ruined them socially."

Sukie gathered up her bottles. "Whoever you end up with though, it's got to be your choice, Milla. Not your parents'. Wouldn't they approve of Derry?"

"Probably not. Oh, they'd probably love him to craft them some bespoke furniture — and they'd boast about it and tell their chums that they've got this 'brilliant little man in' — but not as son-in-law material. The bloody balding toothless baronet was definitely what they think I should be aiming for."

"Shouldn't every girl?" Sukie teased, wondering if the healing properties of the buttercups she'd picked from the garden at the weekend would mingle with those of the daises already in the essence bottle for the cardsharps' shuffling fingers.

"You wouldn't, would you? Marry for money?"

"Not unless there was a lot of reciprocal love involved too, no."

"Ah, love and money . . ." Milla stubbed out her cigarette, slid from the table and decorously rearranged her T-shirt. There was a universal groan from the living room. "I had both with Bo-Bo. We had the same backgrounds, same income bracket families, same lifestyles, same social circle . . . We understood and enjoyed all the same things. It would have been perfect."

"If only he hadn't buggered off at the eleventh hour," Sukie said, feeling brutality was needed here to defend Derry's social, professional and financial standing. "I can't imagine Derry doing that."

"Neither can I." Milla stretched. "He's possibly far too good for me. Why on earth can't this lurve thing be more simple? Why does everyone always seem to fancy the wrong person?"

Sukie shrugged. It was something she and Chelsea had discussed over many a bottle of WKD Blue. "Life, I guess?"

Milla swept her hair behind her ears. "Did you do *A Midsummer Night's Dream* at school? Hermia and Lysander? Helena and Demetrius? Everyone fancying the person who fancied someone else? All in love with the wrong partner? That's what my love life seems to have been. A compete mix-up and a huge mistake. If only there was some sort of magic pill you could get on the NHS to sort it all out . . . Oh, this is all too much for me. I think I'm going back to bed for a couple of hours."

The living room fell into an awed silence as Milla undulated through and disappeared up the twisty staircase.

Sukie exhaled, a dozen possibilities whirring round her brain.

What if? Just, what if?

Is this how Cora had felt, knowing as she did, that her herbal potions could work romantic magic? That by the judicious use of a few garden plants and oils she could match suitable couples, bring happiness to people who deserved not to be lost and lonely? Where was the harm in it, really?

Sukie sighed heavily. It was pretty tempting to try a little love potion experiment on Milla. Without her knowledge, of course. The absence of Bo-Bo the runaway bridegroom might throw a bit of a spanner in the works, and then, even if by some miracle she did reunite Milla and Bo-Bo, who was to say that a dumped Derry would immediately fall in love with her anyway? The chances of that happening were slim to not-at-all, weren't they?

It was always so different in fiction, wasn't it? Shakespeare managed to handle his star-crossed lovers and his love potions with remarkable confidence. And Puck, with his fairy magic, had been the troublemaker, hadn't he? Maybe she should have concentrated more on the ins and outs of *A Midsummer Night's Dream* at school. She and Chelsea had nodded wisely at the "course of true love never runs smooth" bit — and scoffed at the gullibility of the star-crossed lovers and laughed at the Happy Ever After ending which they'd felt was pretty contrived. Real Love, they'd declared with all the arrogance of youth, couldn't possibly be that easy — could it?

No, she thought now as she had then, it couldn't. Not even with Cora's elixirs. And this was Real Life, too, not fiction. And she couldn't possibly play Puck and *dabble* in Milla's love life, could she? It wouldn't be fair or moral or ethical or . . .

"Are you ready for us yet, Sukie, duck?" Tom, one of the card players, called through from the living-room. "Only some of us is taking root here."

"Yes, sorry." Sukie dragged herself back from mulling over love potions and half-remembered Shakespearean text and gathered her bottles together on a tray. "If you'd like to follow me."

The card school, groaning and stretching, creaked after her into the dining-room. She'd dragged half a dozen odd chairs from all over the cottage so they could all sit round the massage table for the joint session.

"Eeeh, it looks like we're going to be dealing blackjack," Edie chuckled, squeezing her chair a bit closer to Tom's. "Are you licensed for gambling, Sukie?"

"Never mind the gambling," Bert snuffled, "I liked the floor show. That young lady in the T-shirt can come and shuffle my pack any time she likes."

Tom and Ken snorted with wheezy laughter. Edie and Rita didn't.

As she worked the buttercups and daisies into the gnarled and knotty fingers, the card school chattered happily about village gossip and rumours and supposed scandals.

"That's a nice smell, young Sukie," Ken interrupted, sniffing noisily. "Reminds me of summer meadows when I was a lad. Buttercups and daisies, is it? Smells like being a kiddie again — off across the fields on a hot July day with a bottle of pop and a bit of bread and cheese. Happy as larks we was then."

"Ah." Rita nodded. "Playing out from dawn 'til dusk. No worries in them days. Funny, I can almost see the flowers growing in here. Feel the sun. Hear the birds. It's like being in a dream. I'm not sure what's real and what isn't — but I could swear there's grass growing under this table. Proper makes you want to take your shoes and socks off and run barefoot it does."

The others muttered rather stunned agreement. Sukie, also aware of the swirling lush bosky ambience but no longer surprised by it, smiled happily to herself.

"We used to hold buttercups under our chin to see if they reflected golden — and if they did it meant you liked butter." Edie's voice was decades away. "Course, they reflected gold on everyone, every time, but we still did it."

"And daisy chains?" Ken said. "Remember making daisy chains? No one thought it was sissy, did they? Kept us quiet for hours."

The card school started reminiscing about long-ago hot summer childhood days.

Sukie, concentrating on the massages, didn't really listen, merely continued to smile her professional smile and nodded and murmured in what she hoped were the right places.

". . . mind you, I've heard the gossip, but I reckons Topsy's had her eye on old Dorchester for some time. I don't hold with none of that old love potion nonsense, whatever she says."

"Ooooh — sorry, Edie. Did I slip there?" Sukie pulled an apologetic face. When had the conversation shifted from summer flower nostalgia to Topsy and Dorchester? "Sorry, look I'll just work this a bit deeper into the knuckles . . . Are — um — Topsy and Dorchester — er — seeing one another, then?"

The card school chuckled.

"Oh, you know the Berkeley Boys! They don't never *see* anyone as such. Their old mum put 'em off getting involved — and who could blame 'em? But —" Bert nodded, "— strange as it seems, I reckon Topsy and Dorchester might be courting on the quiet."

"Really?" Sukie moved on to Ken's hands, hoping no one could hear her heart thundering. "Courting?"

"Ah," Tom nodded, "she reckons — after she'd had a fair few of what the Berkeleys pass off as milk stout, mind you — it's because she'd been dabbling with love potions. I reckon that was just to throw us off the scent."

"More like to put us off who's holding all the trumps . . ." Ken inhaled the buttercups and daisies infusion. "All the old Bagley love potion nonsense died out years ago — after the war — didn't it? Cora used to be the queen of the funny mixtures, or so the story goes. Don't hold with it meself, but my sister swore by 'er — Cora got our Freda out of a proper pickle with a Yank, so she reckons. Hope you don't take after her, young Sukie?"

They all laughed.

Sukie tried hard to remember the exact wording of Cora's buttercups and daises rhyme. What on earth was it? Ah, yes . . .

Buttercups with golden glow
Hearts desires and needs do know
Mix with daisies white and pure
And love forever will endure

Hmmm, fairly safe as Cora's potions went. Possibly room for misinterpretation there, but surely nothing too risky?

It was only slightly worrying, Sukie thought, that Tom and Ken, having inhaled deeply and somehow accidentally touched one another across the table's close environs, were now eyeing one another in a slightly speculative manner.

"There!" she said brightly, pushing the verse to the back of her mind. "That should have you all as nifty as a set of Las Vegas croupiers."

They all happily flexed their fingers in unison and proclaimed they'd been rejuvenated.

"Well, if this buttercups and daisies stuff is one of Cora's love potions I reckon I'll go and set me cap at Savoy, then," Rita chortled. "And Edie here's had her eye on Claridge since nineteen fifty-four . . ."

"What about poor old Hilton?" Sukie asked, joining in the gaiety. "Doesn't anyone fancy him?"

"Ah, Hilton's a different kettle of fish altogether," Bert said. "We all reckons Hilton's carried a torch for someone in Bagley-cum-Russet since he was a nipper. We don't know who, mind. But he wears a little locket under his singlet. Says it was an heirloom from his old mum, but I don't believe it. I think his heart was broke many moons since."

"Oh, how sad." Sukie collected the money from the still-flexing card school. "Poor Hilton."

And how weird, she thought. How odd to think someone as ancient as Hilton could be in love. And even more weird, that Topsy and Dorchester were an item. Not to mention pretty scary that Topsy had obviously mentioned *love potions* in the Barmy Cow.

Deciding to tidy up the massage table later, she waited patiently until the card school had gathered together various bags and coats and sticks, then waved them goodbye from the front door of Pixies Laughter.

210

"Have they gone?" Milla peered down from the twisty staircase. "Is it safe to come down again for a coffee refill?"

"Perfectly," Sukie laughed. "Although Bert will have been bitterly disappointed to have missed you."

"Which one was Bert? Not the one with the comb-over and the layers of clashing jumpers?"

"Yep."

"Definitely the man of my dreams . . . Oh, the papers came while you were in there massaging the wrinklies. I took them up to bed —" Milla giggled, "— the papers, that is, not the wrinklies. Hope you don't mind?"

"Course not." Sukie bustled round, collecting a clean overall and making sure the peach leather cases were fully stocked and reaching for her car keys. "I've got to dash off for my eleven o'clock appointment now. I won't have time to read the papers until tonight at least."

Milla headed towards the kitchen. "Whatever — but you really ought to see the *Winterbrook Advertiser* . . ."

CHAPTER
SIXTEEN

"Jocelyn!" Marvin's voice rang irritably over the drone of *Model Maniacs*, his latest morning must-view television programme. "Have you seen the *Winterbrook Advertiser*?"

In the kitchen where she was chewing the end of her pen and wondering if RSA touch typing stages I, II and III and first-class Pitman's shorthand counted as suitable qualifications for checkout work, Joss frowned and slid the half-completed Big Sava application form under a tea towel.

"Jocelyn!"

She'd taken the newspapers through and put them beside Marvin's chair an hour or so ago when they'd first arrived. Of course she knew they were on his list of "things we can do without" along with her car, and her monthly allowance, and her hair appointments, and a million other things which didn't impinge one iota on his comfort, but somehow she couldn't bring herself to make that final cancellation. How else would she have any sort of contact with the outside world?

"It's by your chair, Marvin! With the other papers."

"I know where it is! I asked you if you'd seen it!"

This is it, Joss thought, he's flipped. The last couple of weeks have finally taken their toll. He's lost his grip on reality. He's joined all those other sad and deluded people with too much time on their hands without whom the daytime-television schedules would be bereft. People who not only watched the brain-numbing stuff but also featured in Marvin's now-favourite all-day viewing; people who spent their lives worrying about crop circles, or alien invasions, or having trans-gender realignments, or their neighbours building nuclear warheads in the spare bedroom.

Making sure her application form was well hidden, Joss walked warily towards the living room.

Marvin was hunched, as always, his hands bunched into fists on his knees, slightly leaning forward towards the ever-flickering screen. He didn't look up.

The programme, as far as Joss could tell from the constantly repeated updates for those viewers with less attention span than a gnat, seemed to involve Russell, an ex-policeman, who'd spent five years painstakingly building an extremely large scale model of a Nautilus submarine from egg boxes and matchsticks in his garden shed and then discovered he couldn't get it out through the door. A crane and three fat people in fluorescent jackets were currently removing the shed's roof as the presenter kept up a bouncily unintelligent commentary, Russell supervised nervously, and a grey-faced women — presumably Russell's wife — stood looking woebegone in the background.

Marvin was riveted.

"There!" Joss said with as much false gaiety as the telly presenter. "There's the *Winterbrook Advertiser!* By your chair!"

"I know where it is," Marvin growled, still watching Russell's discomfiture with some sort of grim satisfaction, "I just wanted to know if you'd read it."

Oh, right. "No." Joss shook her head. "No time yet. What with breakfast and the washing and everything. I was going to glance at it over a cup of coffee later."

Marvin lost interest in Russell and his submarine for a moment and looked at her. His eyes were cold. "You're in it."

"Am I? What on earth have I done to be — Oh! You mean the article about the aromatherapy and the can-can dancing! Of course!"

"It's got your name on it and it's utter buggering bilge." Marvin continued to stare at her. "We'll be even more of a laughing stock than we already are. What gave you the buggering idea that you could write for the local rag? Those ridiculous bits you slipped into the *Bugle* when you thought I didn't know were bad enough but at least they weren't under your own name! Are you mad, woman?"

Probably, Joss thought, recoiling from the verbal onslaught, which hurt far more than any physical abuse. Mad to have married you, mad to have stayed, mad to still be here . . .

"I don't suppose anyone will actually look at my name," she said defensively. "I never take any notice of who's written what, do you?" She picked up the paper.

214

"And anyway, it can't be that bad otherwise they wouldn't have printed it."

"They'll print any old rubbish to fill up space in that two-bit tat." Marvin resumed gawping at Russell and his problems. "Especially if they get it for free. And while you're not doing anything, I want more coffee."

"Oh, get it yourself," Joss muttered. "I'm far too busy."

She walked into the kitchen, holding her breath, waiting for the explosion. She didn't have to wait long.

"Jocelyn! I said —"

"I know what you said!" She marched back into the living room and stared at Marvin. "And I said I was too busy. Which actually is a lie. I'm only going through the motions of the housework — but you are doing absolutely nothing — and don't —" she held up her hands, "— don't start telling me, yet again, that I don't understand how you feel or how you're suffering."

"Of course you don't understand," Marvin said coldly. "How could you possibly understand what this has done to me? You have no comprehension of my situation. You're not only unemployable but you've also been a kept woman for years. You've never had any standing or importance in the greater scheme of things. Whereas I — who had it all — have lost everything. With one stroke I've lost not only my self-respect, but my very reason for living. And has there been one word of sympathy from you? One word? No! Not one!"

Biting back tears and the bitter words which so often almost, but never quite, escaped, Joss swallowed. "That's unfair, Marvin. I've been sympathetic and I've tried to talk to you. To suggest things. This happens — it happens to lots of people. They don't simply wallow — they're shocked of course, and they reel a bit, then they shake themselves down and get on with the rest of their lives."

"What life do I have left? Eh? Answer me that?"

"Probably about another thirty or forty years — at least half of which could be spent working," Joss tried hard to keep her voice steady. "You really ought to find another job. There are plenty of opportunities out there for someone like you. But they won't come to you. You have to go and look for them."

"And you're the expert in employment matters, are you?"

"Actually," Joss said, glancing at the television screen and willing Russell's wife to run at her stupid husband with a machete in a gesture of solidarity, "no, I'm not. But I intend to be. If you won't get another job then I'm going to. I'm going to go out to work, Marvin."

He laughed. A lot. Without humour.

"And who in God's name do you think will employ you? Someone who had the minimum qualifications thirty years ago and who hasn't been employed outside the home since? The world has moved on, Jocelyn, while you've been living in your ivory tower being spoilt rotten. You won't ever find a job. No one in their right mind would want you!"

Digging her nails into her palms, Joss managed not to explode until she'd reached the sanctuary of the kitchen. Then through a blur of angry and impotent tears, she slammed doors, kicked cupboards and hurled knives into the sink.

Feeling slightly better, she poured herself a cup of coffee hoping Marvin would smell it and recognise the defiance, then she spread the *Winterbrook Advertiser* across the table and, her hands still shaking slightly, flicked through it until she reached her article.

It looked really good: a whole page, with a couple of library photographs — one of the can-canners performing energetically at a local Christmas show, and a second of Sukie with Jennifer Blessing on the day Beauty's Blessings had opened in Hazy Hassocks — and with her own name printed boldly under the rather cringe-worthy but typical title: Can-can Girl's Sweet Smell of Success.

Joss skimmed though it, reading her words, and gradually feeling inordinately proud of herself. The *Winterbrook Advertiser's* editor seemed to have left her original article pretty much as it was. There didn't seem to be too many embellishments and very few additions, corrections or errors. Sukie should be really pleased with the coverage for her aromatherapy business — and there surely would be several applications for the vacant can-can post too.

Joss glanced through the kitchen window. It was a shame Valerie had already left for work — she'd have loved to share this moment of mini-triumph with her. With someone. She shook her head quickly. It wouldn't do to dwell on the fact that she actually had no one else to share this with. No one who cared.

Still, staying positive, she'd had something published. Her name was in print. She'd achieved something, hadn't she? All on her own. She sipped her coffee and relished the thought, trying hard not let Marvin's sneering reaction take root in her brain and her heart. No, damn Marvin to hell! He wasn't the only one with a life to live. He was probably madly jealous that she'd written something worth publishing — it was more than he ever had. Ha! That was it! He was jealous! Unwittingly, she'd made Marvin jealous. It was a soul-stirring moment.

And this was just the start. The world was her oyster. The sky was the limit. And every other cliché she could think of.

Buoyed up by this small success, and because she, at this moment, loathed Marvin more than she could ever remember, she removed the Big Sava application form from beneath the tea towel and pondered on the possibilities of fictionally tweaking her entries in the "Previous Experience" section.

She'd just reached the bit about "what I hope the company can do for me" when the phone rang. And rang. As Marvin would probably sulk for the rest of the day and was no doubt far too involved with Russell and his almost-roofless shed to answer it, she pushed the application form under the paper, and padded into the hall.

"Hello? Yes, this is Jocelyn Benson . . . Sorry? Who?" Joss frowned. The name was familiar. Oh, yes, the editor of the *Winterbrook Advertiser*. "Oh, hello . . . yes, I've seen it. Lovely, yes thank you — what? Yes, even without payment . . . Sorry? For me? Are you sure? Oh, right . . . Yes, oh no . . . no — I'll come into Winterbrook and sort it out. Yes, I'm sure it's not a problem. Yes, thank you for letting me know."

She replaced the receiver with a smile.

"Who was that?" Marvin barked from the living room above something that sounded like feral screams emanating from Russell as the crane dropped the shed roof on to his submarine. "Some captain of industry offering you a six figure salary?"

"Just someone selling double glazing," Joss said, kicking off her slippers and delving into the coats cupboard for her shoes. "And I'm going out."

"Don't take the car."

"Sorry, have to. I'm going into Winterbrook."

"Catch the bus."

"No." She jangled the car keys. "I've just missed one and there won't be another for three hours."

"You'll have to wait then, won't you? And why are you going into Winterbrook?" Marvin yelled. "Jocelyn! I said why —?"

Joss slammed the front door and raising her face to the glorious April sun, practically skipped towards the car.

"How does that feel?" Sukie stood back as Ellen, her Winterbrook appointment, gingerly slid her frail legs to the floor. "Better?"

"Superb." Ellen stood upright and took a few steps. "Cheers, Sukie. That's miraculous — as always. Carry on like this and I'll be running the marathon next year."

Sukie grinned. Ellen was in her late thirties and had been diagnosed with MS a couple of years before. She swore that Sukie's weekly massages and a fair amount of cannabis worked far better than all the beta-blockers and steroids under the sun.

While she'd been massaging Ellen, they'd gossiped about Sukie's splash in the *Winterbrook Advertiser*, and Sukie had told her all about having to replace the synthetic essences and why, and the love potions thing, and the rumours that her clients had been reporting rejuvenated lust-lives and fancying mostly the wrong people ever since.

Ellen had laughed a lot and said she was okay in that department, thanks. Her bloke, a rock since her diagnosis, still had the hots for her big-time, and they had no need of any outside help from Sukie's potions.

"I'm using the ginger and sweet nettle on you anyway," Sukie had said, working the oils deeply into Ellen's disappearing muscles. "You've always had that one. It's just this is the home-made version."

"And did your Auntie Cora have a poem for it?"

"Mmmm, yes — let me think — oooh!"

Nettle sweet and ginger hot
Can reach a lover's lonely spot
Pain they'll quench with natural fire
And light the way to true desire

"Wow!" Ellen had pulled on her jogging pants. "Maybe I'd better ring my bloke right now after all. He'd be right dogged off to have wasted that."

220

They laughed together and Sukie declined the offer of a shared spliff to celebrate, and said she'd see Ellen again same time, same place, next week.

Then she packed her cases into the boot of her car, and drove away from the crescent of Victorian terraced houses and towards Winterbrook's town centre. She had no more appointments until the afternoon, and wondered idly if it was worth ringing Chelsea and meeting her for lunch in Hazy Hassocks. The Faery Glen did great bar snacks, and Patsy's Pantry literally oozed cream cakes and sticky buns.

On the other hand, if she was in Hassocks, it'd be sod's law for Jennifer to spot her, and as she really didn't want to get roped into working for a couple of hours in Beauty's Blessings while hearing about the further shortcomings of the Kylies, maybe it wasn't such a good idea.

Mind you, Jennifer would be delighted with Beauty's Blessings name-check in the *Winterbrook Advertiser*. Jennifer loved something for nothing, especially publicity. Joss Benson had done a great job. Even the photographs were okay and that, considering the varying ages, shapes and sizes of the can-canners, was nothing short of miraculous.

So, Sukie pondered at the first set of traffic lights — to lunch in Hassocks with Chelsea or not? Probably not, she decided, moving slowly through the congested market-town main roads. Not only did she not want to be cornered by Jennifer, but there was also the drawback of the fancying-Derry-thing with Chelsea.

Chelsea's texts on the subject had been more than enough; face-to-face, she'd go on and on and on about it. As best friends had a right to do really, Sukie thought. If the Mukluk was on the other foot, she knew she'd be just as dogged.

So — no to Hazy Hassocks on both counts then. She'd go home for lunch and tidy up after the card school and prepare for this afternoon's clients at Pixies Laughter and possibly pick some more flowers from the garden to replenish her stocks. She'd noticed celandines and periwinkles growing in one of the borders — and maybe arrange to meet Chelsea in the Barmy Cow tonight.

Goodness, the traffic was awful, nose to tail, crawling along . . . Sukie rolled down the window, allowing the warm air to billow into the car. The sun was really strong, and it wasn't yet Easter. Hopefully it'd be another scorching summer like last year. She inched into the right-hand lane alongside Winterbrook's municipal park where the flowering cherry trees frothed pastel pink and white, like giant sticks of candyfloss, against the eggshell blue of the sky.

It truly was turning out to be a gorgeous spring.

Oh, sod this, Sukie thought a second later, all bucolic reverie squashed flat by the sheer volume of traffic and bad-tempered drivers. There now seemed to be a massive traffic jam right into the town centre. She'd be here for ever. The diversion through the trading estate would surely be less congested than this . . . if she could just squeeze into the other lane . . . Indicating left, she infuriated an entire line of traffic by changing lanes and heading away from the town.

Winterbrook Trading Estate had grown, like a small dormitory town, over the years. From its early beginnings in the Thatcherite eighties, when a few brave entrepreneurial souls risked renting the half-a-dozen Portakabins, to the current flourishing Village of Industry as the signboards proclaimed. Much as the trading estaters hated it, the mesh of narrow roads had turned into a bit of a rat run for those locals anxious to escape Winterbrook and head for the neighbouring hamlets.

Sukie, singing along with the radio, turned a sharp bend and observing the walking-pace speed limit drove slowly through the trading estates main gates. There were masses of different businesses here, and all doing very nicely, if their brightly coloured exteriors and full car parks were anything to go by. Even the *Winterbrook Advertiser* had moved from its high street premises and now filled two single storey buildings. Slowing even more to take the bend by the newspaper's car park, Sukie came to a rapid halt.

A vibrant green van with dayglo pink lettering was practically blocking the road ahead of her. A girl with long blonde hair and a very short black skirt, and a tiny, shock-headed man were attempting to change a tyre.

Sukie sighed. So much for her short-cut.

She leaned from the window. "Do you need a hand? Is there anything I can do? Oh — Amber — and Jem! I didn't realise — hang on! What happened?"

Sukie pulled her car on to the verge and scrambled out.

Jem, young-old, bird-boned and pixie-faced, was squatting beside Amber, and fixed Sukie with a challenging stare.

Sukie, aware that the previous year when she'd had her mini fling with Lewis Flanagan that Jem, who had adored Amber from the start, had been less than friendly towards her, smiled at him. "Hi, Jem. Great to see you again. What's going on here?"

In his trademark sign language and with extremely mobile facial expressions, Jem explained about the burst tyre and the need to change the wheel.

"Blimey." Sukie shook her head. "That's a bummer."

Jem's eye's danced wickedly and he gave her a double thumbs up.

Phew, Sukie thought, I think I've been forgiven.

"Sorry if I'm in your way," Amber, dexterously removing the Hubble Bubble van's ragged tyre, pulled a face. "Bloody thing! It went with an almighty bang. Scared me to death — mind you, Jem loved it."

Jem grinned and nodded.

"Are you both okay?" Sukie asked. "Have you got a spare? Can I ring anyone?"

"We're both fine, thanks." Amber straightened up. "And I can handle this easily enough. I've surprised myself with the stuff I can do since I've lived in Fiddlesticks. I've learned all sorts of new skills — so yes, I can change a wheel. And —" she chuckled, "— I can even milk a goat."

224

Sukie frowned. "Er — can you? Why would you need to?"

"Gwyneth and Big Ida's latest rescue mission. Goats. Allegedly destined for the curry market," Amber pulled a face. "Now all named after characters in *Coronation Street* and living in luxury on Fiddlesticks village green and providing everyone with milk and cheese."

"Aaah, sweet. I'm so glad they're okay. I do love a happy ending — but are you sure you're all right here? You don't want a hand?"

"Well, actually," Amber wiped her hands down her skirt, "there is something you could do for me — if you're not in a tearing hurry, that is."

"Anything. I'm only going home — I haven't got any appointments until later this afternoon. What do you need?"

Amber, aided by Jem, gave the wheel another yank. It clattered on to the road. "I'm on my way to do a kiddies' party at the trading estate crèche — got all the food in the back — as Mitzi's tied up with a funeral wake with the Motions. And Lewis is driving Fern and Timmy to the airport for their island wedding trip and —"

Jem made rapid wind-up movements with his hands and pulled a face at Amber.

"Yeah, okay — cutting to the chase. If you could just drop Jem off at work for me while I fix this. He hates being late for his shift and —"

"Of course," Sukie said, giving Jem a wary look. "As long as it's okay with Jem?"

Jem winked and nodded.

"Oh, great." Amber straightened up and lifted the spare wheel from the back of the van. "You're a lifesaver. I'll pick him up later, of course, but —"

"Where do we have to go?" Sukie asked Jem. "Is it far?"

Jem shook his head, gave a few extravagant gestures and then jerked his head further into the depths of the trading estate.

Amber laughed and looked at Sukie, her eyes glinting. "Surely you haven't forgotten? Jem does his work placement a couple of blocks away. At Winterbrook Joinery . . ."

CHAPTER
SEVENTEEN

Joss took a deep breath and walked into the *Winterbrook Advertiser*'s chrome, glass and fleshy-plant reception area. She'd driven round and round the trading estate's narrow roads for what seemed like hours, putting off this moment, alternately feeling sick then immediately furious with herself for the feeling.

How pathetic was she? No, correction, how pathetic had Marvin made her?

Why should doing something as simple as this make her feel so inadequate? So damn ill?

She had to keep reminding herself that if she gave in to her nerves at this point, she'd have simply let herself down. No one else. There was no one else in the equation — just her and her self-worth. If she turned tail, Marvin and his years of domineering and vicious barbs would have won.

This may be the biggest wild goose chase in the world, but she'd stood up to Marvin and on her own feet at least twice already this morning — might as well go for the hat-trick. And to the majority of women, women with normal lives and confidence and a grip on reality, this would be absolutely nothing, wouldn't it? Walking into a strange office and asking to see someone? Other women did this sort of thing all the time without even thinking about it.

Well then, so could she . . . couldn't she?

Glimpsing herself in the plate glass she nodded with some small satisfaction. She didn't look cowed or bowed or some sort of sad cipher. She looked exactly what she was this morning: a middle-aged woman, neatly groomed and safely dressed, if a bit pale and rather insignificant.

The reception area was empty. Nowhere to hide. Joss swallowed.

"Good morning. Can I help you?" A woman of about her own age, wearing a light blue cardigan and a tweed skirt, smiled kindly from behind the sleek beech and silver desk. "Do you have an appointment?"

No time to turn and walk away now.

"No, not really." Joss returned the smile. This was a good sign. The receptionist wasn't intimidating or ultra-glossy or about twelve or glottal-stop-challenged. Just normal. "The editor — er, Mr Brewster — rang me earlier. I said I'd pop in and see him. My name's Jocelyn Benson. I-I wrote an article for this week's paper."

If she'd expected the receptionist to leap to her feet, grab her from across the desk and hug her with screams of adulation normally reserved for the name of the winner of the Nobel Prize for Literature, she'd have been very disappointed.

"Did you? How nice. Rang you, did he? Benson? Hmmm — can't see anything mentioned in the diary here. Just hang on and I'll give him a buzz."

Joss hung on and the receptionist buzzed.

"You're in luck. He'll be free in about five minutes. He'll buzz down. Would you like to take a seat?"

"Thank you." Joss retired to some rather strangely shaped beechwood chairs, which were surprisingly comfortable, and while awaiting the further buzzing gazed at the ranks of silver-framed photos on the wall.

She'd expected a newspaper office to be more — well — gritty and exciting. All whirring machines and constantly ringing phones and masses of people rushing about shouting a lot. Maybe all that went on somewhere else unseen. This was like being in the foyer of an anonymous well-appointed company anywhere.

The photos weren't even culled from the *Advertiser*. They seemed to be of the staff, like they were in Hazy Hassocks Health Centre, all taken at the same time, with the same lighting and the same background and the same coy smiles.

The photo of Mr Brewster, the editor, who had sounded like Jeremy Paxman on the phone, looked exactly like one of those interchangeable politicians who used to want be in charge of the Conservative party: pleasant, pale and slightly balding.

Joss thought it was all most unsatisfactory.

And now her nerves were starting to get the better of her again. Her palms were sweating and her mouth was dry. She'd never done anything like this before. Her life was so regulated — what on earth was she doing here anyway? It wouldn't matter what Mr Brewster said to her, she'd still have to go home and live her sad life with Marvin, wouldn't she? In fact, she might as well do it right now.

She made her way across to the reception desk. "Er — I'm sorry. I don't think I'll wait —"

The receptionist was on the phone and waved her fingers. "Right — yes, she's here now. I'll send her through." She put the phone down. "Mr Brewster is free for you now. Were you saying something?"

"No, not really." Joss felt sick to her stomach. "No — thank you. Where do I go?"

Following the directions, she walked slowly along a couple of cloned glass and chrome corridors, past closed doors which may or may not have housed the whirring, mad, newspaper offices she'd expected. There was certainly no sign of anyone shouting "hold the front page!" or enthusiastic cub reporters tearing off with a coffee in one hand and a notebook in the other to capture the latest local scoop.

Mr Brewster's office was, as the receptionist had said, at the end of the second corridor. He answered her knock with a Jeremy Paxman bark.

Joss walked in and almost smiled. This was more like it. Well, almost. Piles of newspapers, albeit very neat and orderly looking piles, covered every surface; cuttings bulged out of files on the shelves; two computers whirled with *Winterbrook Advertiser* screen savers, and three spiked note-holders labelled "leads: current", "possibles" and "dead" bristled with pieces of paper like miniature Christmas trees.

The pleasant, pale and balding Mr Brewster sketched a smile and indicated that she should take a chair. "Mrs Benson. Nice to meet you. Nice article. But I must say, there was absolutely no need for you to come in to see me."

"Yes there was." Joss smiled back at him. "For various reasons I didn't want to discuss whatever you wanted to talk to me about at home."

Mr Brewster raised sandy eyebrows but made no comment on her personal circumstances. "I actually didn't want to talk to you about anything."

Joss's spirits plunged.

"No," he continued, "I'm sorry if you thought I'd reconsidered giving you a regular job as a freelance — although of course I'll happily look at anything you care to send in ad hoc, but I have salaried journalists to cover everything I need on a weekly basis."

"Yes, of course." Joss fiddled with her fingers, twisting Marvin's wedding ring round and round as she always did when she was nervous. "And I didn't expect . . . but you did say . . ."

"That I had a query for you, yes." Mr Brewster flicked on one of the computers and expertly scrolled through various screens. "Ah, here we are. Now — someone rang me about your article this morning. Asked if we could put you in touch. Because of the Data Protection Act naturally I couldn't give the caller your contact details. All I am allowed to do is pass their details on to you and allow you to make the next move — or not."

Joss sighed. "Oh, right. Is that all? It's probably someone wanting to join the can-can troupe — in which case they'd have to contact Topsy — er — Mrs

231

Turvey in Bagley-cum-Russet. Or if it was to do with the aromatherapy massages then Sukie Ambrose would be able to help them. I don't think they want to contact me at all."

A phone rang somewhere. In one of the other offices someone shouted and someone laughed.

"Maybe not." Mr Brewster looked kindly at her. "They certainly didn't tell me what they wanted. Just asked if you could contact them — as the author of the article. You never know, they might run some little county magazine or something and be looking for someone to fill a local correspondent role. As I say, we could have discussed this on the phone."

"No." Joss shook her head. "Believe me, we couldn't. And I needed to come into Winterbrook anyway." Well, she had. Just to escape. "Look, if you just pass the details to me I'll ring the person and see what they want, then make sure either Topsy or Sukie gets them — and thank you anyway. This has helped me a lot."

"Has it? Really?" Mr Brewster looked a bit bewildered, but printed off the details from his screen. "There we are. Just a name and a couple of phone numbers. No e-mail address. Apparently the caller doesn't have internet communication."

"Neither do I." Joss took the piece of paper. The name — Mr F. Fabian — meant absolutely nothing to her. She'd somehow expected it to be a woman. "Oh, the first number's local and the other I presume is a mobile. I don't have one of those, either."

Mr Brewster looked as if this was inconceivable but said nothing.

232

"I wonder," Joss leaned forward slightly, "if I might make the call from here? Only — well — making it from home would pose all sorts of difficulties."

Mr Brewster sighed. "Well, yes . . ." he pushed one of the desk phones towards her. "Yes, of course."

"I'll pay, naturally." Joss punched in the local landline number with shaking fingers. She never liked ringing people's mobiles in case she was interrupting them doing something vital. It rang out continuously. "Oh . . . I don't think there's anyone there . . ."

"Try the mobile, then," Mr Brewster sighed again. "But please make it snappy."

It took Joss three attempts to get the sequence of numbers right. Then there was a silence. Should she hang up? Had she got it wrong — again? Then the ringing began. On and on and on.

She was about to put the phone down for the second time when a voice answered.

"Hello?"

"Um," Joss started, but her mouth was too dry to speak properly. She tried again. "Er — hello. Is that — um — Mr Fabian?"

"Speaking. And who are you, duck?"

Joss felt a bit better. The voice was warm and full-on Berkshire.

"Jocelyn Benson. I'm at the offices of the *Winterbrook Advertiser*. I wrote the article about the can-can dancing and the aromatherapy and —"

"Bingo!" The voice burred happily. "Thanks for ringing back so quick, duck. Lovely bit of writing by the way. Right — when can we meet?"

"Er — well, I mean . . . I don't think you want to meet me, actually. Maybe you need to talk to someone who can help you more with the details of the dancing or the massages."

"Maybe, duck. Maybe. But first I'd like to meet you to get the bigger picture. You free tomorrow? About two or thereabouts?"

"Yes, but can't we do this on the phone?"

"Not my way of doing business, duck. I likes face-to-face hands-on if you see what I mean." The Berkshire burr dissolved into throaty laughter. "So — we on for two tomorrow, then?"

"Oh . . . I don't know . . ." Joss looked down at her wedding ring, then heard Marvin's voice in her head. She swallowed. "Yes. Yes, two o'clock tomorrow will be perfect."

"Lovely, duck. You know Winterbrook okay, do you? My office is right next to the bank on the High Street. Green door. Got a name-plate. You can't miss it."

Joss hesitated for a moment. Mr Brewster was looking as if he wanted her to finish the call and leave. Quickly. And at least Mr Fabian — even if he was some sort of closet Lionel Blair or had got completely the wrong idea about the massages — hadn't suggested that she should come to his home, had he? An office meeting was surely safe, wasn't it? And Marvin would absolutely forbid it.

"Very well, yes. Tomorrow at two."

"Smashing, duck. Look forward to it. Bye."

Joss put the phone down feeling — goodness — what did she feel? Scared? Excited? Daring? Sick?

All those. And more.

She stood up and held out her hand. "Thank you. I'm very grateful to you."

"Are you?" Mr Brewster, still looking perplexed, shook her hand. "Well, good. Good. I hope everything goes well with your meeting. And glad to have helped. And don't forget what I said about sending in more articles."

"For no money?" Joss almost grinned as she reached the door. "Just a by-line — isn't that what you called it? We'll see . . . And thank you again."

And beaming at the receptionist, she walked out into the trading estate's balmy golden glow.

On the other side of the estate, Sukie pulled up outside Winterbrook Joinery and stared at the three sprawling buildings with interest. Nice. Very nice. Prosperous looking, spacious, well-kept units, several cars parked in the vast yard area outside, including Derry's mucky jeep, and a very impressively liveried name plate. The two larger units had their roller doors open and it appeared one was a workshop, while the other was a showroom of sorts. The third smaller unit must be the office.

Helping a bouncing Jem unfasten his seat belt and open the car door, Sukie grinned at him. "Do you want me to come in with you? Or are you okay on your own? Help me here, Jem — I'm not Amber. I don't want to insult you — or do the wrong thing."

He winked at her and held out his hand, cocking his head towards the workshop area.

"Okay," she took his hand. "I'll walk in with you, deliver you safely and — oh . . . hi . . ."

She blinked as Derry appeared in the workshop doorway. Oh, God — her heart went into overdrive. He was wearing age-bleached jeans and a black T-shirt with a faded logo. His blond hair was untidy and multi-streaked in the sun. He was truly the most beautiful man she had ever seen.

"Hi." He grinned at them both. "Amber just rang to say you were on your way. I'd have driven round the estate to collect Jem myself but she said you'd already left." He looked at Jem. "Lucky sod. Two gorgeous women performing escort duty today."

Jem said something in sign language and gave Derry the thumbs up.

"Yeah — right." Derry grinned. "No chance. Okay, you go in with Pauly —" he indicated a sturdy elderly man walking towards them from the workshop, "— and make a start. I'll be along in a minute. You know what you're doing today, don't you?"

Jem nodded.

"Tell Sukie."

Jem made flapping movements with his elbows, then linked his twisted fingers together.

Sukie frowned. "No, sorry Jem, I'm no good at this. Try me again, please?"

Jem repeated the performance, this time flapping his arms behind his back.

"Wings? Tails?" Sukie hazarded. "Birds? Flying?"

Jem shook his head, going through the routine more slowly. Twice. Sukie, dredging up everything she knew about woodwork, suddenly had a light-bulb moment.

"Dovetails! You're doing dovetail joints!"

Jem punched the air, capered on the spot, threw his arms round Sukie and kissed her, then holding Pauly's hand, walked slowly and carefully across the yard.

"Nice one." Derry smiled at her. "You'll have made his day."

"I'd've felt terrible if I'd got it wrong," she admitted. "And this —" she looked round the units, "— is very impressive."

"Thanks. Are you in a hurry or would you like a quick guided tour?"

Even if she'd had half the royal family and the entire England football squad waiting impatiently for massages at Pixies Laughter, Sukie knew her reply would have been the same.

"No — I'm not in any rush at all."

"Right answer." Derry said. "So, how are things going?"

"With the aromatherapy stuff? Brilliantly, thanks." She walked beside him, hotly aware of his body, the way he moved, the clean, warm, working-man smell of him. "Fully booked for weeks ahead. Or did you mean the dancing?"

"That blew me away," Derry laughed. "If that was a rehearsal — I can't wait to see it for real."

"Same as all blokes — just in it for a glimpse of stocking tops and suspenders."

"Yep. What else?"

They grinned at one another. Oh, help . . . Sukie thought. This is so, so wrong.

"And no more trouble with Aunt Cora's love potions?"

"Not what you'd call trouble, no. Although everyone has said that they've felt something has happened to them after they've had a massage. And there have been a few reported — um — unlikely liaisons."

"Really?" Derry chuckled. "Good old Cora."

They'd reached the doorway of the workshop and Sukie inhaled the gorgeous scent of sawdust and raw, fresh timber. Several men were working at massive benches with what looked like terrifying circular saws and other whining, screaming machinery, sending showers of what she imagined must be chips of oak and ash and cherry and walnut skittering into the air like a manic sweet-smelling snow-storm.

"We're really busy at the moment," Derry shouted above the noise. "Tons of orders. I'll have to take on more carpenters — and I'll need a couple of good lads as apprentices this year, too."

Sukie, suddenly wishing she'd done woodwork at school, watched the craftsmen somehow manoeuvring the great hulks of wood, checking drawings, measuring, slicing the finest sliver off, planing, sanding.

"It must be wonderful — starting with well, trees, and, through age-old skills, ending up with something handmade and beautiful — oh, not that trees aren't beautiful, of course — but —"

"You don't have to come over all environmentally friendly here," Derry said, his mouth close — too close

— to her ear. "And we only use sustainable timber. Come and have a look at the samples."

Jem, sitting at a bench with the ever-watchful Pauly, glanced up at her and blew her a kiss. She blew one back.

"I'm glad Jem's so happy here."

"He's got a natural talent," Derry said as they moved along the yard to the next unit. "He loves working with wood and he has infinite patience. And despite his coordination being not great when it comes to walking, and his hands maybe not functioning in quite the normal way, he'll sit for hours and produce the most amazingly delicate stuff — better than I ever could."

"It was kind of you to take the time to find out, though."

"Not kind at all," Derry grinned. "It wasn't an act of charity — although I hope I'm a nice enough person — but we're bloody lucky to have him. He came here initially because Lewis is a mate of mine and Jem needed a work placement, but he's on the payroll now. The blokes love him as much as I do, and we couldn't do without him."

Lucky, lucky Jem, Sukie thought.

They'd walked along to the next unit. The shingle scrunched under their feet, and the sun was increasingly warm, and the sky was a glorious pale and cloudless blue. Sukie gave a little shiver of enjoyment: it was almost like being at the seaside.

"In here," Derry said, standing back to let her into the showroom area first, "I keep all the catalogued pictures and photos of stuff we've produced, and

239

samples of wood, and some mock-up furniture and of course, the apprentice cabinets."

"The what?"

"Apprentice cabinets." He said. "No, they're not somewhere we lock away our NVQ kids at night. They're considered old-fashioned now I think, but I still like the newcomers to make them because there's no better way to learn. They're small scaled-down items of furniture and boxes and stairs — practice runs for every woodworking skill. But they also come in handy to give potential customers some idea of what we can do."

Sukie moved round the showroom, still inhaling sawdust and the fabulously natural smell of sap and fresh-cut wood, admiring the beautifully enhanced grains, and the colours and textures of the exquisitely crafted pieces.

"Wow." She looked at the catalogue of photos on the wall. "These are absolutely amazing. Did you really make all these?"

"With a little help from my friends." Derry did the standing-close thing again. "Yep. Most of these are my designs, but I'm always open to suggestions from potential clients — and most of them know more or less what they want. I'll just advise and then translate their ideas, hopefully, into something that pleases us both."

"You're brilliant." Sukie shook her head. "Do you know, I had no idea . . . I'm really sorry but I thought that you went out on to building sites and probably nailed bits of wood together to make door frames or ceiling joists or something like that."

"Oh, I'll do that too," Derry said cheerfully. "No job too big or too small. I just love working with wood and creating things."

"And I thought there'd be a plate over the workshop door saying 'established eighteen-oh-four' or something." Sukie moved a little bit away from him, afraid that he'd hear her heart thundering under her T-shirt. "But this is all yours, isn't it? Not inherited?"

"All mine. Risky to set up at first, and we flew very close to the wind to start with." Derry ran his long slender fingers lovingly across a small table with criss-crossed veneers in several different types of wood. "Of course, when I started, most people were setting up small businesses in technology and IT — the safe way forwards in the twenty-first century. My bank manager nearly had a fit when I told him I wanted to set up my own company using traditional skills from over a thousand years ago."

"But he believed in you and backed you? Eventually?"

"Eventually, yes. With a million get-out clauses for the bank, and even more millions of dire warnings of what would happen if I failed. The first couple of years we made no profit at all and only just broke even. After that, well, by word of mouth, things just grew . . . and now —" he smiled at her, "— now the bank manager sends me a Christmas card and invites me to his parties."

"Great stuff," Sukie laughed. "So, in a way, I suppose we're both working with ancient wisdoms, aren't we?"

He nodded, pushing his hair away from his eyes with the unselfconscious gesture that had started to haunt her dreams. "I'd say we've got a lot in common, yes. We're very hands-on, working closely with our customers, creating magic from nature."

They looked at each for a fraction too long.

"Er . . ." Sukie swallowed, "Milla must love all this."

"Milla's never been here. She's not really interested. This isn't her sort of thing. Any more than corporate wheeling and dealing is mine."

"Still," Sukie said, breaking her own heart, "you know what they say about opposites attracting and all that."

"Yeah." Derry nodded. "And you don't get more opposite than Milla and me. Sorry to cut this short, but I really ought to be getting back to make sure Pauly and Jem are okay . . ."

"Yes, of course — I shouldn't have kept you so long. Although I could spend ages in here."

"So could I." Derry smiled, "but we both have businesses to run, don't we?"

They walked back in the sun, across the beach-like shingle, towards the workshop.

Above the scream and whine of the machinery, Jem waved at them and winked.

"Thanks again," Sukie said, fishing her car keys from her bag. "For taking time to show me all this. I've loved it."

"Me too." Derry nodded. "Look, Sukie —"

242

"Derry!" Pauly had walked to the workshop door. "Sorry to interrupt, mate! We need your input here!"

"I'll have to go." Derry turned away from her. "See you soon?"

"No doubt. And thanks again."

She slid into her car, started the engine and turned slowly in the yard. The last view she had of Derry was through the open workshop doorway. He was sitting next to Jem at the bench, leaning close to him, explaining something, making him laugh, guiding his hands with infinite patience.

Ooooh, Sukie groaned, racheting up the plinketty-plonk radio music to teeth-vibrating levels. Oooh, damn and bloody sod it!

By the time she'd turned on to the trading estate's exit road, she still felt dazed and confused and irrationally restless. The current accompanying blast of the Bay City Rollers' "Summer Love Sensation" made her feel even worse. And now there was a bloody beige hatchback dithering in front of her, signalling to turn out of the *Winterbrook Advertiser*'s car park across her path.

Sukie, furious with herself for being silly enough to fall head-over-heels for someone who not only could never, ever love her in return but was also forbidden fruit, fought the urge to give a sharp blast of her horn. No point in taking it out on other people. Instead, she slowed and flashed her lights.

The driver of the hatchback raised her hand in acknowledgement, then to Sukie's surprise, changed the gesture to a wave, stopped her car and rolled down the window.

"Sukie!" Joss Benson called across to her. "How fortuitous! The very person! Have you got a moment?"

Sukie pulled over and switched off her engine. This must be her day for rescuing damsels in distress. "Hi, Joss. Are you okay?"

Joss looked, Sukie thought, rather flushed and flustered.

"Well, yes . . ." Joss slid from her car and walked across to Sukie. "At least I think so. I've just done something rather daring."

Sukie listened, smiling despite herself, at Joss's enthusiastic retelling of the whole story; reminding herself that for someone as browbeaten as Jocelyn this was indeed a hugely brave step to have taken.

". . . and —" Joss finished, "— I was going to ring and ask you if there was any chance of a massage to relax my stupid nerves and give me, well, maybe a bit of confidence for this meeting with Mr Fabian tomorrow? Oh, I know it must sound really silly to you, and it's probably a wild goose chase anyway, but I really need something to make me feel — well — less petrified and —"

Sukie smiled and nodded. "I understand, believe me. And I've got the very thing you need. It's not a massage as such, but some oils absolutely guaranteed to give empowerment and confidence. Hang on . . ."

Sukie climbed out of the car into the sunshine and carried her aromatherapy cases from the boot, opening them on the back seat, watched by several passing motorists who no doubt thought they were witnessing some sort of desperate housewives' drug deal.

"Here we are — these essences will do the trick, I promise you. Now, really this should be ylang-ylang — but I've got a jasmine substitute which is just as good — and this one is lavender — and the rose here is actually hawthorn which is basically the same thing only at a different stage."

"And I can use these myself?" Joss took the tiny gemstone-stoppered bottles. "Are you sure?"

"Absolutely," Sukie agreed. "They're all used in massage oils, but in this case all you need is to add them to a warm bath just before you leave for your meeting. Four drops of the jasmine, three of the lavender, and one of the hawthorn. Okay? Relax in the bath, close your eyes, inhale the fragrances as they blend in the steam, imagine yourself being confident when you meet this — er, Mr Fabian — and you will be everything you want to be. Honestly."

Joss beamed. "Fabulous! Thank you — and I'll let you know how it goes. I mean — I expect it'll be you he wants to talk to really, but I'm sure this will make me feel so much better." She slipped the tiny bottles into her bag. "Four drops of this one, then three of that, and one of this — I'll remember that. Thank you — oh, how much do I owe you?"

"Nothing at all." Sukie grinned. "Honestly, Joss I'm just delighted to be able to help. And don't forget to let me know how it goes. Good luck."

Joss hugged Sukie. "You're wonderful. Thank you. And of course I'll let you know what happens."

Sukie watched Joss practically skip back into her car and drive away with a huge smile.

Ah well, at least with her lotions and potions she'd solved poor Jocelyn Benson's problem today. And the card school's. And Ellen's. And indirectly Amber's. And Jem's.

If only she could concoct something which would deal so easily with her own . . .

CHAPTER
EIGHTEEN

Having spent the rest of the afternoon daydreaming about Derry in particular and pondering on star-crossed lovers in general, Sukie ate a late-lunch-early-tea pot noodle, cleared up the dining-room-cum-massage parlour and carried out her final at-home appointments for the day.

Given the successes of the home-grown remedies so far, Sukie was sure — absolutely positive — that Cora must have had some sort of recipe for this long-distance lonely hearts problem, given her alleged wartime matchmaking skills.

In fact, Sukie was sure she half-remembered a verse, a longer verse than the love potion ones, which Cora would sometimes unfurl and read softly, almost to herself. The poem had always made Sukie sad in childhood, even though she hadn't understood its implications. The words — involving loss and loneliness — had always made Cora stare into the far distance and stop smiling, and the young Sukie had shared her great-aunt's sorrow without knowing why.

So far, this particular piece of cross-stitch hadn't emerged with the others, probably, she decided now, because it didn't involve a massage potion. But it might be just what she was looking for and it must be somewhere . . . And she knew she wouldn't rest until she'd found it.

So, breaking off only to answer several congratulatory phone calls about Joss's article, including one from her mother who became very chatty and said they really must see one another for a meal or shopping or something soon; a mickey-taking text from Chelsea; a lengthy gush from Jennifer to say the publicity for Beauty's Blessings was fab and the Kylies were settling in and shaping up nicely; and a text from Derry — which she'd clicked through with stupidly trembling fingers — to say that the blokes in the workshop had cut out the can-can picture and pinned it on the wall alongside Jordan and Jodie Marsh, Sukie delved once more into the darkest recesses of the work-basket.

As the afternoon melted into evening, right at the bottom of the pile of faded cross-stitched embroidered verses, she found what she was looking for, wrapped in brittle-with-age tissue paper:

So many lonely people
So many broken hearts
So many lovers torn apart
So much loss and so much sorrow
Can be cured maybe tomorrow
No matter how many miles away
Love can be brought home to stay
Belief in the herbal powers
Belief in the scented flowers
Will bring true lovers back together

248

To be in love for ever and ever
With no more tears and no more pain
Together, never to part again

Sukie read and re-read the verse. Okay, it probably wouldn't pass muster with the literati, but the meaning and the emotion was surely raw enough for anyone. Now Topsy had told her about Cora's lost love, no wonder the words had made her cry. Sukie sniffed back a tear of her own, wishing she'd known then, been old enough to understand and sympathise.

Still, she thought as she folded the piece of cross-stitch and slid it carefully back into its tissue paper, the poem was one thing — but without a potion recipe it was totally useless. So near and yet so far . . . Damn it. She tried to ease the tapestry back into the tissue. For some reason it didn't quite fit . . . Sukie peered into the folds. Ah! There was another piece of paper tucked inside, yellowing and crackly. Intrigued, Sukie pulled it out, opened it and read it.

Her mouth was dry. This was it, then. This was what she had been looking for . . . Cora's familiar writing blurred in front of her:

Distance love potions are very effective but are considered powerful earth magic and should only be undertaken as a last resort to bring lovers together.

They should be used only if you are absolutely sure that the outcome is what you want because they may not be reversed.

To make: 3 drops ginger, 2 drops rosemary, 2 drops jasmine, 1 drop clove, 1 drop cinnamon, 1 pinch powdered mandrake root, mixed with almond oil. The potion should be rubbed on a pulse point, preferably the left wrist as this will take the infusion straight to the heart of one of the parted lovers while they visualise their beloved. They will, in every case, be united in everlasting love.

Sukie sat back on her heels and exhaled, then pushed the piece of paper carefully into her pocket, and put the cross-stitch back into Cora's work-basket and closed the lid. The essences were easy to find. The potion simple to concoct. She even knew that at the back of the store cupboard Cora had kept a jar of powdered mandrake root. There was nothing stopping her from making it, but would she — should she — use it?

Two hours later, she'd finally reached a decision. It was, she conceded, probably the wrong one and — as it was going to involve sharing stuff with Chelsea — it was almost bound to end in tears.

At nearly nine o'clock, the balmy faux-summer day had darkened into a typically chill April evening and Sukie, shivering slightly inside her second best jeans and third best sweater, hurried through the door of the Barmy Cow.

Seemingly untouched by the Rites of Spring, the pub remained grey, smoky, grubby, and was also practically empty.

250

"Hello, young Sukie!" Hilton Berkeley, clearly dying for someone to talk to, hailed her garrulously from behind the bar. "Lovely pic of you in the *Advertiser* today, and Mrs Benson from The Close wrote nicely about them massages, too. And Topsy was cock-a-hoop over the can-can bit. She reckons she'll have more applications for the vacancy than that Factor-X programme. I hope it does you both a power of good."

"Thank you." She leaned her elbows on the bar top, belatedly remembering the ongoing stickiness and quickly stood up straight. "It's very quiet in here tonight — and I think there's something else strange as well but I can't quite put my finger on it."

"Is there?" Hilton beamed at her. "That's nice. Mind, we're often quiet in the week these days. People seem to prefer the telly to the pub — can't think why."

Sukie could but was far too polite to say so. "Oh — I know what's odd! It's you! You're on your own! I don't think I've ever seen any of you working solo before."

"It happens occasionally." Hilton inclined his grizzled grey head kindly towards her. "Not often, I'll admit, but it does occur sometimes when one or other of us is unwell, or is invited out. What would you like, my dear?"

"Oh, two halves of shandy please." Sukie went for the safest option. "Chelsea should be here shortly. So, where are the other Boys tonight, then? Not ill, I hope?"

"No, thank the Lord." Hilton mixed two shaky half pints. "Dorchester is upstairs with young Topsy. He's bought her a boxed set of *Dr Kildare* but she don't have a DVD whatsit so they're having a pizza and film night in his room."

On a school night? Sukie thought, trying not to giggle. Without parental supervision? And clever old Dorchester — the entire set of *Dr Kildare* would make Topsy putty in his blue-veined hands. The viola massage mixture was clearly still working its magic there.

"This — um — thing with Topsy and Dorchester. Being friends, I mean. You don't mind? I know how close you and the Boys are . . ."

"Bless you, no!" Hilton beamed. "Between ourselves, I think Dorchester has had his eye on Topsy for several years. And what's the point of people being alone when they don't have to be? Especially at our age. We've all steered clear of affairs of the heart because they never did our beloved mother any good," he inclined his head towards the awful picture of Honour Berkeley above the bar. "But, tell the truth, it makes me rightly glad to see our Dorchester so happy."

Sukie offered up a silent prayer of thanks. Maybe the viola massage had done some good, then? Maybe her plans for this evening weren't so risky after all? Then again . . .

"And Claridge and Savoy?" She paid for her drink. "Are they upstairs too?"

Hilton shook his head. "That was a very funny thing, Sukie, my duck. The card players came in at six, like they always do, for their apéritifs, and Edie and Rita were behaving really oddly."

252

Sukie took a sip of her shandy. It was strangely thick and tasted neither of beer nor lemonade. She wasn't sure she wanted to hear the rest of the story. "Oddly?"

"Ah," Hilton leaned across the bar, clearly oblivious to the residue that was now clinging to his lovat sleeves, "flirty and that. You know, all coy and giggling? They were done up to the nines, the pair of 'em too, and well, they made a fair old play for Claridge and Savoy. Upshot being, as we're quiet tonight, they've all four of 'em gone off to the flicks in Winterbrook."

Oh, dear . . . Sukie thought. Oh dear . . . Less than twelve hours after the buttercups and daisies rub . . . Less than twelve hours after using the potion that Cora had sworn "*hearts desires and needs do know*" and that having used it "*love forever will endure*".

Oh, dear . . . The folded, yellowing paper and the little glass phial in her bag felt almost incendiary now. She really, really shouldn't even consider doing this, should she?

"Er — I thought they'd closed the cinema in Winterbrook? Turned it into a rabbit hutch housing estate for singletons called Alhambra Meadows or something?"

"Ah." Hilton tapped the side of his nose. "That they did, duck. But they'm showing films at the Corn Exchange now three nights a week. The boys and Edie and Rita have gorn to see *Revenge Massacre of the Zombie Flesh Eaters*."

"Oh, lovely." Sukie tried not to look too appalled. "And — um — what about the others in the card school? Tom and Bert and Ken? Did they all go home?"

Hilton unpeeled himself from the bar top and chuckled. "Well, call me a silly old duffer if you likes, but I'd stake me cellar full of best bitter that Tom and Ken went off *together* if you get my drift. Chummy as anything they were. Tom was saying that Ken ought to come back to his place and look at his curly kale."

Sukie inhaled her shandy. There was a prolonged moment of spluttering and mopping.

Oh, dear.

Still, at least Bert was untouched . . . so far.

"Bert seemed at a bit of a loss." Hilton looked sad. "All his pals gorn off like that. Said he was going home to have a cheese and chutney sandwich and watch *Men and Motors*."

Phew — well, at least she couldn't be blamed for that, could she?

Fortunately Chelsea arrived at that moment and her denim mini skirt and tight jumper seemed to take Hilton's mind off the defection of his brothers and the majority of his regulars.

There was a lot of girlie giggling over the *Winterbrook Advertiser* article as they crammed into a clean settle, and shared a bit of a catch-up generally: Sukie filled Chelsea in on an expurgated version of the events of her day, and Chelsea told a funny-in-retrospect Big Sava story about a man with a hairpiece and the faulty door on the upright chiller cabinet.

"So —" Chelsea peered at Sukie through her shandy, "— what's all this stuff you have to talk to me about? Is it to do with Derry? Now we both know that you fancy

254

him like crazy, are you going to pinch him from Milla and be labelled The Man-Stealing Bitch From Hell?"

"Nooo, of course not." Sukie hoped she wasn't blushing. "But I have got something a bit — well — tricky in mind and I'll need your help."

"Really?" Chelsea's eyes widened. "No — let me guess. Does it involve me acting as a decoy and dressing up and pretending to be seducing him while you come to the rescue and Milla sees me as the villain of the piece and —?"

"You read far too many Real Life magazines." Sukie grinned at her. "No, what I've been wondering about is whether it would be possible to reunite Milla and Bo-Bo."

"Whoa!" Chelsea slammed her glass down. "Stop right there! How the hell do you think you can do that? I was only joking about the tabloid mag stuff — but you mean it, don't you? And didn't you say he'd practically left her at the altar? He must be a right bastard. And just suppose you could get them back together, what if Derry loves Milla to bits, and his heart is broken — he'd hate you for splitting them up, wouldn't he? You'd be the last person he'd want to be with after that! Good God, Sukie — have you lost all your marbles?"

Sukie raised her eyebrows. Whatever reaction she'd expected from Chelsea, it certainly hadn't involved moral outrage. "Look, I know it all sounds devious . . ."

"Too right it does! I'm shocked. Really. There is a Girl Code, you know. Sisters together and all that."

"Yes, okay — just listen . . ."

And giving the carefully edited version, leaving out Cora's love potions and the re-uniting elixir for the moment — because Chelsea would never understand or accept any of that in her current high-ground mode, Sukie outlined her plan.

"Crap," Chelsea said at the end. "You're going to turn yourself into some sort of witch, are you? Just like that. And somehow magic — bloody *magic* — up something that will make Milla and this Bo-Bo bloke fall into each other's arms and live happily ever after?"

"That's more or less it," Sukie agreed, realising that without sharing Pixies Laughter's secrets with Chelsea, the scheme wouldn't seem at all viable. "Although I probably wouldn't have used quite such pagan language."

"Of course it's pagan! What else can you call it? And all this old hokum rampaging round the village, started by mad Topsy, about love potions has finally gone to your head, has it?" Chelsea was scathing. "Get real, Sukes. You know what happens to people who start believing in their own hype? They come crashing down in flames and look like prats."

Sukie drained her glass. There was sediment at the bottom. "Okay, but just suppose I could do it — could find something to bring Milla and Bo-Bo back together — because she really does love him you know, and she'll always be miserable without him, would that still be so wrong?"

"Of course it would! It would be meddling! And it still wouldn't mean you'd get your carefully manicured

256

Beauty's Blessings nails into Derry, would it? Or are you planning to use voodoo on him, too?"

"No, of course not. But Milla and Bo-Bo —"

"Stop! First stumbling block — how the hell would you find this Bo-Bo? None of us knows what his real name is, do we? Milla is hardly likely to tell you without wanting to know why, and I can just see Companies House, or wherever it is you'd need to go, being able to give you a life-file on someone who sounds like a cartoon rabbit."

"Yeah, I've thought about that. Now, suppose again that I didn't need to find Bo-Bo — suppose all I needed was Milla — and suppose all she needed to do was think about being with him again for ever and ever."

"You," Chelsea said, standing up and collecting the empty glasses, "are getting seriously unhinged. You scare me sometimes, Sukes, do you know that? Same again?"

"Please . . ."

Sukie sighed and slumped back in her settle. Maybe she should have considered that Chelsea wouldn't jump at this once in a lifetime opportunity to test drive a love potion. Maybe she'd have to tell her the truth about Cora and the verses and the discovery of earth magic in Pixies Laughter's cottage garden.

No — she simply couldn't. If Chelsea was sceptical now, she'd run a mile after hearing all that wouldn't she? Bugger.

"Thanks." She took her second shandy. "Oh nice — it's got crumbs in it."

"Hilton was eating crisps." Chelsea sat down. "Probably best to scoop them out with a beer mat."

"Look at this another way." Sukie tried again. "You know when we fancied boys at school and we did the Truth, Dare, Kiss, Promise thing? And we all thought it worked because we absolutely believed in it? And remember that time at Phoebe's birthday party when you got Nicky Hambly's name up three times on a promise to love for ever, and you went after him like a starving dog after a bowl of raw liver?"

"I never remember it being *quite* so romantic, but yes." Chelsea stared at her. "Go on."

"Well, what if we could do a grown-up version? What if there's a grown-up version of Nicky Hambly — the love of your life — out there, just waiting for you? What if you could meet and fall in love and be together for ever and ever?"

"What if you got a grip?"

"Oh, come on, Chelsea, join in here — you're always the first up for party games and pretend spooky stuff. You're always saying you hate being single and still being at home with your mum and dad and all your brothers and sisters, aren't you? You're the one who says they want to be married to Mr Absolutely Perfect and have kids and a semi. Wouldn't it be wonderful to be in love with this man who's — well — perfect for you, who loves you just as much in return, for always? Who would you like to be with for the rest of your life? Who's your secret heart's desire? Not some film star or footballer or anything — but a real man. Who's your grown-up Nicky Hambly?"

"Nicky Hambly."

"No, I mean . . . What? *Really*? How come I didn't know that?"

"Because." Chelsea pushed a beer mat across the table in a circular motion. It got stuck and puckered. "Because he told me to push off when we were sixteen and broke my heart. He didn't fancy me then, and he wouldn't fancy me now — even assuming he's still single, and straight, and alive."

"Didn't he join the RAF?"

"Yep. Haven't seen or heard of him for over ten years."

"And no one has come close to taking his place?"

"No."

"And when you've gone on and on about your Mr Absolutely Perfect — you've meant *Nicky Hambly*?"

"Yes, okay?" Chelsea was suddenly defensive. "And don't look at me in that 'I'm your best and oldest friend — why didn't you tell me?' way."

"No, but why didn't you?"

"Because you never had any trouble getting boyfriends, and it just seemed easier to be known as your happy-go-lucky mate who played the field, rather than the sad one who listened to heartbreaking songs and wrote Chelsea Hambly over anything that didn't move and dreamed hopelessly about our wedding and our house and our babies."

"Blimey." Sukie was genuinely shocked. "Chelsea, I never had an inkling. And you still — er — fancy him?"

"Love him. Love him truly, madly, deeply. Love him so much that any other bloke is measured on my Nicky

Hambly scale and never gets past halfway. Hopelessly unrequited love for some skinny kid who is now a grown-up stranger and probably happily married with umpteen children and wouldn't even remember my name." Chelsea stared at her. "So, what are you going to do about that, then?"

Sukie looked down into her shandy glass. The little phial was practically bubbling its way out of her handbag. "God, Chelsea — I am sorry — really. I had no idea. You should have told me."

"There was nothing to tell, was there? Stop looking so guilty, Sukes. It was my secret. How sad would it have been if you'd *known*? And, who knows, maybe one day someone else will come along and knock Nicky into second place."

Sukie gave Chelsea a quick hug across the table. They had to peel themselves off the beer mats.

"Do you know the thing I find funny about all this?" Sukie swirled the remains of her cloudy shandy. "The fact that you — the original Miss Trippy Lips — have managed to keep it a secret for years and years. I didn't think you could ever keep quiet about anything."

"Spoken like a true best friend." Chelsea grinned. "And just goes to show that you don't know everything about me, doesn't it?"

Sukie nodded. It did. It also meant that Chelsea might, just might, be able to be trusted with the secret of Pixies Laughter. "Well, look if we did a little experiment —"

"Oh!" Chelsea sighed. "You're not back on that again, are you? The witchcraft stuff."

"It's not witchcraft. It's earth magic — no, listen — please Chelsea — and don't tell anyone else what I'm going to tell you. Just listen . . ."

Chelsea listened. Occasionally she laughed; once or twice she snorted derisively; several times she shook her head in mocking disbelief; but she listened.

". . . so —" Sukie finished, "— that's why I thought you might be up for a bit of a trial run. I thought if you gave it a blast before I did it for real on Milla and Bo-Bo . . ."

"I certainly won't be telling anyone that load of trash," Chelsea shrugged. "Your secret is safe with me — the whole thing is bloody insane, you know that. Look, I'm really happy for you that Pixies Laughter's garden provides you with real essences — but you're just imagining that Cora's flower power love potions have worked, because Topsy told you they would. And don't tell me about Mitzi Blessing's herbal cookery magic — or even about Fiddlesticks and the star-wishing — I don't believe in any of that either."

"Okay, so as a total disbeliever, where's the harm in test-driving this for me? What's the worst that can happen? Nicky Hambly appears like magic and makes all your dreams come true?"

"It won't happen. You know it and I know it. And I still think it would be wrong to try it out on Milla without her knowing — just in case. And I also still reckon it's a really bad idea to think that by splitting her and Derry up you'll be in with a shout. That's still man-stealing in my book — whether it's by fairy means or foul."

Sukie was beginning to waver. Chelsea was right. "Oh, God — don't make me worry about ethics now. Okay, if I promise to sound out Milla before I do anything, will you still give this a go? And if it works can I be bridesmaid?"

"No."

"Oh, come on Chelsea — after all, this is all your fault, really. If you hadn't nicked most of Jennifer's madly-expensive synthetic floral essences and given them to Fern, then I wouldn't have had to look for replacements and I wouldn't have used the plants from the cottage garden and none of this would have happened."

"That's blackmail!"

"Yep. So — give me your left wrist and close your eyes and start thinking about Nicky Hambly."

"As I rarely stop, that won't be a hardship." Chelsea pulled up her sleeve and closed her eyes. "And I must be bloody mad to even think about doing this. Oh, and I'm really, really sorry Mrs Hambly, if you're listening, and all the little Hambly kiddies who may be out there, for even thinking that this might work and robbing you of your husband and father."

Quickly, before either of them could change their minds, Sukie scrabbled in her bag and removed the potion. She glanced round the pub, making sure no one was watching, but Hilton was busy making snowballs for an elderly couple. All three of them were spattered with yellow froth and the remaining handful of customers were watching the advocaat manoeuvres with rapt attention.

Easing the stopper from the phial, Sukie turned Chelsea's left wrist face-up on the table.

"You don't have to dance around me and chant, do you?" Chelsea muttered. "And — actually, that smells lovely . . . all herby and sweet . . . like being in Pizza Hut with flowers on the table."

"Stop talking and start visualising Nicky Hambly running towards you through a summer glade, all diffused sunlight and flowers and butterflies, his arms outstretched, ready to hold you and love you for ever and ever."

Chelsea smiled to herself, and Sukie, her hands shaking, allowed a few drops of the elixir to fall on to the pulse point. Quickly, she massaged them into Chelsea's wrist as the glorious aroma wafted into the murk of the Barmy Cow, engulfing the grey smokiness with the essence of sun-kissed gardens and honey-sweet blossoms.

"Do you know," Chelsea said dreamily, "I can almost see that summer meadow and hear the birds . . . And as for Nicky — he's still really hot . . . You know, Sukes, it might be all baloney but it's very relaxing and rather lovely. Can I open my eyes now?"

"Yes, and thanks." Sukie pushed the phial back into her bag. "Really. I'm very grateful."

"Hmmm, so you should be." Chelsea sniffed her wrist. "Well, at least it still smells nice and my skin hasn't fallen off. And I'll have what passes for a double vodka and lemonade as payment, thanks. So, what happens now?"

"Haven't got a clue." Sukie grinned, standing up to make her way to the bar. "I suppose we just sit back and wait for Nicky Hambly to come charging through the door — blimey! That was quick!"

Startled, they both stared as the Barmy Cow's door flew open. Sukie realised she was holding her breath.

"Hiya!" Valerie Pridmore bundled inside, followed by her large, untidy husband and several of her grown-up children. "Jeeze! Dead as the grave in here tonight, innit? Smells funny an' all . . . you been using a new disinfectant in the lavs, Hilton? And who's up for a game of darts?"

Chelsea snorted. "So much for bloody earth magic. Ah well, back to reality. Nice try, Sukes — and you nearly had me believing in your hocus-pocus there. You might as well go ahead and try it on Milla and Bo-Bo — we both know it'll never work, don't we?"

CHAPTER
NINETEEN

"Jocelyn!" Marvin thundered on the bathroom door. "What the hell are you doing in there?"

"Having a bath."

"It's midday! No one has a buggering bath at midday! Midday is when you get my lunch. And did you use the immersion heater? We can't afford to run the immersion heater! You know we can't afford —"

Joss turned the taps on full, the thundering roar drowning out Marvin's latest fiscal drone.

If she thought she'd been nervous yesterday braving Mr Brewster at the *Winterbrook Advertiser*, this afternoon's meeting with Mr Fabian was such a step into the unknown that her teeth were chattering.

Clutching her towelling bathrobe more tightly round her, Joss fumbled in the pocket for the little bottles of calming essences. She'd been repeating the dosage in her sleep like a mantra: four drops of jasmine; three of lavender; one of hawthorn. Opening the bottles with trembling fingers, she carefully counted them out now, dripping them slowly into the hot water.

There! She re-stoppered the bottles and returned them to her pocket, then slid off her robe and swished the water with her hand.

"Oh, glorious . . ." She inhaled the rich, evocative fragrance rising in the clouds of steam. "Wonderful . . . Oh, Sukie, you clever, clever girl . . ."

"Jocelyn!" Marvin hammered on the door again. "Come out! Now!"

"I'm in the bath," Joss fibbed happily, swooshing the water around again, feeling oddly calm. "I'll be out in a little while. I've made some sandwiches for lunch — they're in the kitchen. Save one for me. Now please go away."

She smiled. This standing up for herself was becoming quite a habit these days. Why on earth hadn't she done it years ago? Well, she knew the answer to that, of course — but things were going to be slightly different now, weren't they? In fact, ever since the day she'd had her first-ever massage at Pixies Laughter, she'd felt bolder and slightly less intimidated. Sukie had already worked miracles on her self-esteem. Who knew what might happen in the future — especially after this self-affirming aromatherapy bath?

While Joss wasn't expecting miraculous changes in the bungalow's balance of power, she was damned if Marvin's self-pity was going to drag her down even further. She still had some small sense of self-preservation, and if Sukie's magic worked again, she may even become assertive — or something very close.

Waiting until she heard Marvin stamp off back to the television via the kitchen, Joss stepped into the bath and lowered herself luxuriously into the silky scented water. What had Sukie said she should do? Ah, yes — relax, inhale the exotic steam and imagine herself facing the unknown Mr Fabian with confidence. Okay, then . . .

Leaning her head back, closing her eyes, she did just that, and could feel herself instantly floating, drifting away. It was a slightly strange out-of-body feeling — like having a pre-med — but not unpleasant. Far from it. She felt warm, weightless, carefree; and as the perfumes from the essences engulfed her, lulling her senses, she drifted drowsily into another world . . .

Joss opened her eyes. And blinked. Surely she hadn't fallen asleep? She must have done . . . But for how long? And was she still dreaming? No — she was definitely awake, but . . .

The billows of steam swirled and dipped, forming and reforming like summer morning mist, masking the harsh edges of the austere beige and chrome bathroom in a fragrant pastel haze. And the bath was no longer a bath: it was a pool, a warm sweet-scented tree-shaded woodland pool. Joss sleepily turned her head in wonderment. The utilitarian shower had become a trickling, twinkling, dancing waterfall, and vibrantly-coloured flowers twined and blossomed down the walls, cascading rainbow petals into the water.

It was, Joss thought, just like one of those highly-imaginative television adverts for organic bath foam — only a million times better because this was *real*.

Now almost sure that the dozens of radiant jewel-coloured butterflies fluttering in and out of the green fronds surrounding her were alive, Joss was surprised that it didn't seem strange at all. Not even slightly alarming. Just simply wonderful. She tipped her head back, certain that she could see the blue of a summer sky where the ceiling should be, knowing she could hear bees buzzing in and out of the outrageous blooms just beyond her reach.

She felt so calm, so happy, so relaxed. Had Sukie added something hallucinogenic to the floral essences? Possibly — that must be the only explanation. Joss simply didn't care, because now she could, she knew, face anything. Anything at all.

"Jocelyn!" Marvin's voice outside the door sounded cruelly harsh amid all this lush glory. "You've used piccalilli in the sandwiches! They're ham! You know I like chutney with ham!"

The woodland fantasy dissolved.

Joss looked around her with a feeling of acute loss. She was back in their normal cream plastic bath, the water growing cold, the decor pale and safe.

"Jocelyn!"

"Just coming." She hauled herself out of the bath, delighted that even if the gorgeous surroundings had disappeared, the feeling of calm confidence hadn't. And she still had the little bottles in her pocket, didn't she? She could sneak off to her fantasy woodland pool anytime she wanted.

Sukie had handed her bliss on a plate.

By the time she was dry and moisturised and made-up and dressed — black skirt to the knee, flesh-coloured tights, cream shirt, black jacket — it was past one o'clock and Marvin had eaten all the sandwiches despite his pickle peccadillo.

"Where are you off to?" He looked up from a television programme about getting the best from your organic allotment. "Someone's funeral?"

"An interview," Joss said, gathering bag and keys and black court shoes. "Like yesterday."

Marvin had sulked mightily when she'd returned home from the *Winterbrook Advertiser*, especially as she'd interrupted a graphic programme about Holiday Romances From Hell. And then, as she'd been very non-committal about the details of her excursion, he'd sneered a lot and repeated his homily about no one wanting to employ someone who was without even the basic skills and how she was wasting her time and that they'd have to sell the bungalow and down-size and that would put paid to her gallivanting. And Joss had said that down-sizing from the bungalow would clearly mean living in a shed, and Marvin had blustered and gone purple and said buggering every second word and thrown the *Winterbrook Advertiser* at the television.

Now Marvin looked up from "how to mulch your bean trenches with fresh animal manure", and drew his lips back from his teeth in what passed for a smile. "If you think you're going to work in that supermarket in Hassocks, you can think again, my lady. I found the application form yesterday while you were out — it's now shredded at the bottom of the recycling box."

Joss stared at him, determined not to let her anger show, wishing she'd hidden the Big Sava form more carefully. "And you think that will stop me, do you? I can get plenty of application forms. What on earth is wrong with you, Marvin? All I'm trying to do is find a little job so that we don't have to scrimp and scrape quite so much . . . something to tide us over until you find another post, something to help out."

"I don't want your buggering help! I don't want you getting a job that an imbecilic monkey could do better than you! I do not want to be kept by a woman!"

"I'd hardly be keeping you —"

"Not by stacking supermarket shelves, no! Which is all you can possibly do — and probably not even that with any degree of success! You're useless, Jocelyn! Useless!"

Joss stared at him again. The really weird thing was that although his words hurt her as much as ever, she wasn't crumbling inside. Even if she tried really hard, she failed to feel intimidated, and there was none of her usual need to immediately apologise for her stupidity.

"Right — I must be off or I'll be late. We'll talk about this later, Marvin. Maybe you'd like to wash up the lunch stuff? I've no idea how long I'll be . . . Good bye."

The feeling of calm, quiet confidence stayed with her all the way to Winterbrook. It could only be as a result of Sukie's oils, couldn't it? Joss simply didn't care — she was delighted with herself. And what on earth would Valerie make of it all when they met, as they did now twice a week, outside Coddles? She couldn't wait to share this with Val.

270

Having parked in the Corn Exchange and averted her eyes from the gory posters outside the new "cinerama" for some horror film, Joss took a deep breath and headed for the High Street.

The sun was strong, and the black jacket may have been a mistake, she thought, as she pushed her way through the shopping crowds. She really hoped she wouldn't look flustered and shiny when she arrived.

Now what had Mr. Fabian said? Next to the bank? Joss stopped outside the bank ... okay, well as it possibly wasn't the Oxfam shop because he'd have said so, it must be the other side: the rather dingy green door, firmly shut, with a bank of faded name cards and little push-buttons.

Joss squinted at the names — ah, yes, there it was — Mr F Fabian — with something else underneath it which was too faint to read. Taking a deep breath, she pushed the intercom button.

"Yup?" A voice crackled cheerfully in her ear.

Joss, who'd never used an intercom before, jumped, then put her mouth very close to it. "Mr Fabian? I'm Mrs Benson. We arranged to meet. About my piece in the *Winterbrook Advertiser*."

"Gawd blimey, duck!" The Berkshire voice chuckled. "There's no need to shout. You've all but deafened me! Come along up!"

The green door clicked open and Joss made her way gingerly up several dingy wooden staircases, past closed doors which according to their name plates housed debt collectors, private investigators, recruitment consultants and financial advisors.

Mr Fabian's office was right at the top.

Puffing slightly, Joss tapped on a strangely painted door — faded silver with stick-on gold stars — and wondered belatedly if Mr Fabian had something to do with the sex trade.

"Come in, duck!" Mr Fabian shouted. "Straight through! There ain't no one in reception!"

Joss, still feeling slightly out-of-body and more curious than nervous, closed the silver door behind her. The small and airless reception area was covered, floor to ceiling, with show-biz posters and faded photos of old-time film and music stars. Joss recognised Marilyn Monroe and John Wayne and Humphrey Bogart and Elvis and Jimi Hendrix.

"Straight through, duck!" Mr Fabian called from an archway through to the next room. "We don't stand on ceremony here!"

Now more bemused than ever, Joss crossed the tiny cluttered reception area and into a second office, decorated in a similar vein with decades-old posters from cinemas and music halls and concerts — here she could just pick out the Rolling Stones, Cliff Richard, Bill Haley and the Comets.

"Lovely to meet you, duck." Mr Fabian rose from behind a piled-high desk, knocking over several piles of correspondence and held out his hand. "Freddo Fabian. Agent to the stars."

Smiling, because she simply couldn't help it, Joss shook hands with the cheerful, fake-tanned, leathery 60s throw-back with his dyed yellow Peter Stringfellow hair and huge friendly grin.

Marvin, she knew, would insist that Mr Fabian should be locked up and the key thrown away.

"Sit down, duck. Sorry about the mess. Paperwork's never been my forte. Can I get you anything? Coffee? Tea?"

"Coffee would be lovely, thank you," Joss amazed herself by answering calmly, clearing a pile of music papers from the chair in front of his desk. "I meant to have some before leaving home but . . ." She stopped. There was a very thin line between confidence and being over-chatty. Mr Fabian really wouldn't want to know why she'd missed her lunch. "Yes, coffee, thank you."

She watched as Freddo Fabian shimmied sure-footed around his untidy office, pouring two cups of coffee from a bubbling pot. He was wearing the sort of torn and faded jeans that Marvin always went puce over on anyone — especially anyone over sixteen — and a baggy collarless pink shirt, and a lot of bling bracelets.

"There," he handed her a rather prettily delicate porcelain mug and sat down again. "Biscuit?"

Joss, who was terrified that her stomach was going to rumble at any minute nodded. "Please — thank you — oh, lovely. Chocolate digestives. My favourites."

Crikey, she thought, helping herself from the packet, where had that come from?

Chummily, they crunched through biscuits and sipped coffee while Freddo Fabian explained about his agency business — Retro Music and Theatre — and that he was fascinated by the can-can troupe.

"Lovely bit of writing, by the way." He grinned at her through chocolatey crumbs. "You've got a real talent for stringing words together, duck. You must be professional."

Blushing, Joss said no, she wasn't, but she'd always enjoyed writing — and that she was delighted that Mr Fabian had liked it.

"Freddo, duck, please. And you are — Jocelyn, did you say?"

She nodded. "I prefer Joss."

"Pretty name. Suits you. Right, Joss it'll be then, duck, seeing as we're friends."

And Joss smiled back at him and felt as though she'd known him all her life.

Freddo rocked back on two legs of his chair. "So, this dance troupe? Do they have representation? Are you connected to them at all?"

"No." Joss shook her head regretfully. "I know several of the dancers — and Topsy — Mrs Turvey who runs them, of course. I do think you'd need to speak to her. They're only local and haven't been going very long. I think they just do fêtes and galas and things like that."

"But you can introduce me to them and this — Topsy bird, can you, duck? I'd really like to see 'em in action. I could get them a lot of work — in my line of business, the retro stuff is red-hot at the moment. Like I said to you on the phone, I needed to speak to you first to see how the land laid, get a foot in with someone on the shop floor so to speak. Do you think that would be a goer?"

274

Joss nodded. She wasn't entirely sure she understood at all, but it was wonderful — simply wonderful — to be having a proper conversation with someone who treated her as an intelligent human being whose opinion not only mattered, but was crucial.

"I'm sure Topsy would be delighted to talk to you. I think they have a few bookings coming up, but she's always saying that she needed more coverage — that's why she was pleased with my article . . ." Joss stopped in case this was a toot too far on her own trumpet. "That is, I mean — not my article as such, but the coverage."

"Don't you put yourself down, duck," Freddo Fabian laughed. "You're a very clever lady with a real talent for putting words together without over-egging the puddin'. I could do with someone like you to do my press releases." He looked a bit woebegone. "Mind, anyone I've employed here for anything like that can't write for toffee, can't spell, and wants all the fol-de-rols — computers and e-mail and all that."

"And you don't have any of those things?"

"Nah, I'm retro through and through. Never got to grips with the techno stuff. I've got a fax machine — and that scares me witless, I can tell you. I've always managed with this old girl . . ."

Joss almost clapped her hands in delight as Freddo Fabian pushed a pile of papers aside to reveal a gleaming Remington typewriter.

"Oh, I used to use one of those! Years and years ago. It was lovely! I loved it! I haven't seen one since — well, not for a very long time."

Freddo's eyes twinkled. "And you can touch type, can you?"

Joss nodded. "I used to have about one hundred words a minute — and Pitman's shorthand as well, of course." She laughed. "Back in the dark ages."

Freddo leaned forward. "Mrs Benson — Jocelyn — Joss . . . You haven't been sent by the angels, have you, duck? You wouldn't, couldn't, possibly be looking for a job . . .?"

CHAPTER
TWENTY

Joss stared at Freddo across the desk. Had she misheard him? Was he really offering her a job? Was this really happening, or was it simply a figment of her imagination, as the woodland pool had surely been? A result of some strange imbalance in the fragrances she'd inhaled? As she didn't want to leap up punching the air with excited yells if this was all part of her fantasy, she kept quiet.

"No, duck — sorry," Freddo spread his hands wide. "Of course not. No sane and sensible person, let alone an intelligent and classy lady like you, would want to hole themselves up in here and work in this pigsty for an old love-and-peace hippie like me. My mistake."

"No," Joss shook her head. "No, I mean, yes — yes — I am looking for a job — but I haven't worked outside the home for years and years. I'm pretty rusty on the old procedures, let alone the new ones. And I know nothing at all about the — er — entertainment industry. I was a sort of secretary — shorthand typist, really — for a builder's merchants before my marriage."

"A shorthand-typist would suit me down to the ground." Freddo beamed. "Especially one who could create order from this chaos, sort out the filing system, get me a bit organised. And you'll easily pick up the agency stuff as you go along, clever lass like you. But," he looked at her through his tangle of yellow hair, "it would have to be a sort of partnership, duck. I'm not good at barking orders and expecting people to jump through hoops. I'd hand it all over to you and let you get on with it. You sort out the office, I'll sort out the acts. We'd have to work as a team."

Oh, Joss thought, how wonderful that would be: working here, using her old skills, creating calm from disorder, having someone as easy-going as Freddo Fabian as her boss. Feeling that she had a purpose, that she was a real person again, that her days would be both filled and fulfilling.

She took a deep breath. "That sounds perfect to me."

"You mean — you'd like to give it a try?" Freddo reached across the desk and gripped both her hands in his. "Blimey, Joss, duck! You've just made my millennium! When can you start?"

Joss returned his grin and the squeeze of his hands. Then reality kicked in. Freeing her hands, she sat back in her chair. "Before we get too carried away with this — there are some things I think you should know."

And she told him briefly about Marvin, mentioning the redundancy but leaving out his downward spiral into self-pity and daytime telly. "I know he's feeling a bit lost," she finished diplomatically, "and — er — well, I think he might make this awkward for me."

"Well, let's play it by ear, then," Freddo said, pouring more coffee, opening a second packet of biscuits and

278

suggesting an hourly rate for the secretarial post which knocked Big Sava's salary into a cocked hat. "Let's see how it goes. If you can't, or don't want to, work full-time, then we'll arrange the hours to suit. I'm flexible. Shall we say give it a month either way? If at the end of that time we decide we're not right for one another, or it's causing you more problems than you can deal with, then we'll part company with no hard feelings. Does that sound hunky-dory to you?"

"Very hunky-dory." Joss smiled, realising with some small alarm that she was, like Freddo, actually dunking her biscuit. Marvin didn't allow dunking. "Yes, thank you. Thank you so much."

"No, duck, thank *you*." Freddo chuckled through his chocolatey crumbs. "And tell you what — why don't I invite your Marvin along here to meet me, see the place, let him know that I'm not a shyster, set his mind at rest over the whole business?"

"Oh, no — I don't think so," Joss said quickly, knowing exactly how Marvin would react to the golden-haired, pink-shirted, much-blinged Freddo. "No, I'll explain it to him — he'll be fine, honestly."

"Jealous bloke, is he?" Freddo smiled warmly at her. "A bit protective?"

Joss considered this for a moment. "Protective? Do you know, I'm not sure . . . No, I don't think he is. I think he used to be, years ago, but not any longer. And jealous? Definitely not."

"Then he's barking." Freddo chuckled. "You'd make any man proud as punch, duck, so don't let your Marvin tell you different."

Joss smiled. "Thank you — I think . . . I'm not used to getting compliments. Funny, isn't it? You start out in life with someone and you just assume it'll be roses all the way . . ." she stopped. "Goodness, sorry! I didn't mean to unburden all my personal problems."

"Don't mind me," Freddo handed her another biscuit. "My wife walked out on me years ago. Ran off with one of my clients — a bleeding conjurer, can you believe that? Spends her life now on stage in seedy clubs in tights and spangles watching him pull rabbits from his hat. Says it was the excitement that did it for her. She always wanted to be on the business side of the footlights."

Joss bit her lip. "Oh, I'm sorry. Do you miss her?"

"Not any more, duck — but I miss his fifteen per cent."

They giggled together.

And after finishing the coffee and the biscuits, Joss filled in an application form, then Freddo gave Joss a quick guided tour of the business. Retro Music and Theatre, he explained, didn't actually represent any of the golden oldies displayed on his walls, they were just for show, but he did have a bulging client list and his agency was not only solvent but extremely healthy.

Joss simply hugged herself and still couldn't quite believe this had happened. Nor could she believe that she hadn't felt nervous or hadn't clammed up at any point. Was it really thanks to the aromatherapy bath that she'd sailed through this with calm competence? Whatever the reason, she'd have to buy Sukie an massive thank-you present for helping to make this possible.

"So," Freddo said when they'd finished the introductory tour, "does this all seem okay, duck? Something you'd like to get your teeth into?"

"Oh, yes, please." Joss was simply itching to sort out the filing system and tidy the two higgledy-piggledy offices and get her hands on the Remington. "Er — when would you like me to start?"

"Right now," Freddo grinned at her. "But seriously — how about a week on Monday? That'll give you ten days or so to square it with your husband, and give me a bit of time to tidy up at least some of the stuff here so it doesn't frighten you off before you've even got started."

"Lovely." Joss nodded. "And in the meantime I'll speak to Topsy about you having a look at the can-can troupe, shall I?"

"If you could, duck. Thanks. And you'd better take one of my cards with the mobile on. Then you can give me a bell and keep me up to speed can't you?"

Joss took the pink and gold Retro Music and Theatre card and slipped in her handbag. "I don't have a mobile phone but you've got all my contact details on the form there. And are you sure you'd like me to approach Topsy? Wouldn't you rather do it yourself?"

Freddo grinned. "Look on it as your first bit of work experience. No, you did a sterling job on that write up — I'll leave the contacting to you. But I'd like to come along and view them soon as. Do you know if they're doing any local gigs or anything?"

"I think," Joss said, remembering what Valerie Pridmore had told her, "that they're not appearing in public this year until the beginning of May. At a post-wedding party. In Fiddlesticks."

"Really?" Freddo pushed his hair untidily away from his face, making his bangles jangle. "Not for that couple from the pub there? Getting married out on a beach in the Seychelles or somewhere around now, and having the hoolie on the village green when they eventually come home?"

"Yes, I think so," Joss said, surprised, remembering with pleasure the sheer giddy joy of Fern's hen-night in the Weasel and Bucket. "Why? Do you know them?"

"Sort of. Indirectly." Freddo almost jigged with excitement. "But, more importantly, I've got one of my best acts booked in there, too. The JB Roadshow? Excellent soul band — they're just coming to the end of the Soul Survivors tour at the moment. This Fiddlesticks party'll be their local homecoming gig. Well, well — small world, isn't it?"

Joss nodded. "And you could kill two birds with one stone. Be there for your — um — soul band, and see the can-can troupe in action?"

"I'd like to see the dancers before that if possible," Freddo said, leafing through a diary that seemed to be filled with Post-it notes and bits of torn envelopes. "Do they have a rehearsal night?"

"Tuesdays," Joss said, knowing how much she'd always envied Val darting off to dance the can-can on Tuesday evenings. "About seven thirty. In Hazy Hassocks village hall."

"Tuesday it is, then." Freddo scribbled something on yet another Post-it note. "And you'll be there, will you?"

Joss shook her head. "Oh, no — I'm not really anything to do with them."

"I'd really like it if you could be there," Freddo said. "It'd give you some idea of what I do when I'm looking for acts, and you'd be a sort of intermediary — knowing me and knowing this Topsy bird too. Do you think that's a possible?"

Why not? Well — because Marvin would forbid it for a start.

Joss nodded. "More than that. It's a definite."

"See! You're already getting the lingo! And you'll let them know I'll be coming along, will you?"

"Yes, of course. Although I can't guarantee —"

"There's no guarantees in this business — that's something you'll find out soon enough." Freddo beamed at her. "It's what makes it so unpredictable — so exciting."

And Joss beamed back at him.

She was still beaming when she arrived home at The Close.

"Marvin?" she called through the dinette. "Marvin? Are you there? I've got some wonderful news . . ."

Well, she thought, shedding her shoes, handbag and jacket, it was wonderful to her. And even if Marvin had become sniffy over her wanting to work at Big Sava, surely he couldn't object to her working in an office, could he? He couldn't find any reason to denigrate her

283

ancient skills now, could he? Not when she told him they were exactly what Freddo needed and she'd be working in a proper secretarial environment, for a very good salary. It might even spur him on to look for another post himself.

"Marvin?"

The bungalow was empty. The television was silent. The lunch things were still on the table. Where on earth had Marvin gone? He hadn't left the bungalow for — well, since he'd been made redundant.

As she'd floated into the bungalow on a high, Joss now couldn't remember if Marvin's car had been on the drive or not. She peered out of the window — and felt the first twinge of unease.

Marvin's car had gone.

Oh, God. While she'd been laughing and dunking biscuits with Freddo, Marvin had finally snapped. The depression had taken over. He'd driven off — too fast — and . . .

Whoa! Joss tried to rein in her imagination. Maybe he'd simply decided that enough wallowing was enough and he should do as she was doing, and get on his bike — metaphorically, of course.

Going through the mechanics of clearing the kitchen, Joss's earlier euphoria had now all-but evaporated. Of course there was bound to be a simple explanation — but what if Marvin really had driven off in a tearing temper, driven to despair by her sudden new-found confidence, by her new self-assurance? Maybe she hadn't shown him enough sympathy? Enough understanding? How could she understand what the loss of his job

284

had meant to him? She, who'd — as Marvin so often reminded her — simply been a parasite all her married life.

No! She slammed the last plate into the cupboard. She'd been a good wife, mother and homemaker. She'd put up with being put down at every opportunity for years. She'd believed everything Marvin had thrown at her for far too long. Other less loyal or committed women would have left him or at least stood up to him, if they hadn't attempted to murder him, wouldn't they?

Damn it! Joss took a deep breath. She would *not*, under any circumstances, dissolve once more into a wee, timorous, cowering beastie . . .

Wishing, as always, that Val was at home next door so that she could share both the amazing events at Retro Music and Theatre and her concerns over Marvin, she paced restlessly round the bungalow, picking things up and putting them down again, flicking at non-existent dust, straightening already regimented curtains. How awful would it be if Marvin had done something stupid?

Whatever she felt — or didn't — for him, she'd never wanted him dead. But, on the other hand, if Marvin had simply decided to leave her, leave the bungalow, start afresh alone — what would she feel about that?

Shockingly, she realised she really wouldn't mind at all. In fact it would be a lovely satisfying conclusion to the awful sterility of their relationship. It would probably mean the bungalow would have to be sold, and she'd have to rent somewhere — but she could cope with that, couldn't she? It was far easier, she decided, to concentrate on imagining herself being a divorcee, living in a small flat and queuing at the launderette, than as a widow planning Marvin's funeral.

Oh, where the hell was he? And why had he chosen now to disappear — now, when she'd been on top of the world. Typical of Marvin, he'd yet again managed to ruin her happiness — without even trying.

She really should try to ring round and track him down. She knew from watching police dramas on the television that vital hours were always lost by victims' nearest and dearest because they'd always assumed the missing person wasn't one at all until it was too late.

Of course, previously she'd always been able to contact Marvin on his mobile but, as this had been a perk of the job, it had been left at the office with the rest of his life. Joss stared at the phone in the hall, wishing she knew where to start. Would he have gone to see Simon? Perhaps to take up his old golfing skills? Or any of his other friends — their dinner party circle? The ones who Marvin had said would never want to socialise with him again? Or the children? Could he possibly have decided to bare his soul to Ossie and Tilly?

Wherever he was, she was pretty sure he'd be spittingly angry that she was trying to find him, but she'd live with that. Taking a deep breath, and with the phone in one hand and their address book in the other, she started her search.

Half an hour later, having drawn a blank and exhausted all possibilities, Joss wandered into the kitchen and switched on the kettle. She wasn't really sure why. She didn't want a drink — but neither did she know what else to do. Marvin's so-called friends hadn't been much help, merely saying they hadn't seen him or heard from him, and seemed pretty off-hand — most of them suggesting he'd simply gone on a job-search and not to worry.

Worrying, Joss took the tea into the garden: the pristine patio leading to a neat oblong of lawn, pollarded rose bushes at each corner, a tub of pansies in the middle — neat and unexciting. The afternoon was turning into a sun-washed evening, the shadows of the bungalows looking like slumbering elephants on the lawn.

She didn't want to stray too far from the bungalow in case the children phoned back. She'd left messages on their answerphones. Casting a hopeful look next door in case Val had come home early — they'd gone for tea, which really meant supper Joss guessed, with their eldest daughter and family in Hazy Hassocks — but which was unlikely, because Valerie and her husband usually ended their soirées in the Barmy Cow, Joss sipped her tea and the worry deepened into quiet panic.

When the phone rang, she spilled the tea dregs over her hands and down her skirt in her haste to answer it.

"Mother?" Tilly's voice sounded disbelieving. "Are you okay?"

"Fine — well, no I'm not. As I said, I'm worried about your father."

"How long's he been gone?"

"Well, I went for a job interview at just after one —"

"You did what?" Tilly laughed. "You? A job? Why?"

"It doesn't matter," Joss snapped irritably. "That's not important now — and anyway, I got it and when I came back here your father had gone. And he hasn't left the house since —"

"You've got a job?" Tilly sounded totally incredulous. "You? What sort of job?"

"Secretarial. Look, Tilly, this isn't important —" Well, it was of course, but not right now. "What's important is that I'm worried about him. If he turns up at yours or rings you, you'll let me know won't you?"

"Yes, of course, but —" Tilly sounded as though she might be laughing, "— how can you possibly have got a secretarial job? You're not qualified —"

"I'm perfectly qualified for the job in question. I think your father might have become depressed because I was looking for work and he felt he was losing his authority and —"

"Dad'll be okay," Tilly said. "Ossie and I understand these things better than you do. If he's gone out, it's probably to network and get himself back into the melting pot. He probably felt the time was right."

"But why didn't he tell me? Leave a note?"

"Mother . . ." Tilly was reproving, "Think about this. Why would he leave you a note? There's nothing to worry about. He simply needed time to come to terms with the situation and plan his future. I expect that's what he's been doing."

What he's been doing, Joss thought wearily, has been making my life hell and watching daytime television, but she didn't say so. "So you don't think I should ring the police or the hospitals?"

"Not unless you want to be a laughing stock — and make dad mad as hell when he comes back, no. He's only been gone for a few hours. He'll be back for supper, you'll see."

And Tilly hung up. Then the phone rang again and this time it was Ossie who said practically the same thing, word for word.

Joss, who still felt she should report Marvin as a missing person, restlessly watched some television, prepared beans on toast for supper, phoned an irritatingly garrulous Topsy to arrange the meeting with Freddo for the following Tuesday, and was still staring out of the window waiting for Marvin's car to swing into the drive at eleven o'clock.

"Oh, Marvin . . ." Joss said wearily to herself, sitting at her dressing table removing her make-up and brushing her hair. "Where the hell are you? Why have you done this to me today? I don't want anything to have happened to you — and I'll never forgive myself if you're — well, if you don't come back . . . and I have to live the rest of my life knowing that the last words we ever exchanged were angry ones."

Sighing, she walked into the still-gloriously-essence-perfumed bathroom to clean her teeth.

There was something wrong here, surely? Living as she had, with the bungalow's almost-austere neatness for so long, even something slightly a millimetre out of place jarred on her subconscious. What was it? The bath was clean, the towels neat on the rails, the cabinet doors closed. Frowning, Joss squeezed toothpaste on to her brush and started the mechanics of brushing on autopilot — then stopped.

The three little gemstone-stoppered bottles on the window sill hadn't been there before.

With a foaming mouth, she stared at them. When she'd had her aromatherapy bath she'd replaced them, hadn't she? In her bathrobe pocket? Knowing that they meant she could return to the woodland pool fantasy any time she wanted? She knew she wasn't having a senior moment — she remembered exactly what she'd done.

Which could only mean that someone else had found them? Marvin? Surely not? But what other explanation was there?

Marvin had been infuriated and intrigued about her mid-day bath, hadn't he? Annoyed that she was doing something so out of routine? Cross that she wouldn't tell him what she was doing and why? He must have waited until she left for Winterbrook, then searched everywhere for — what? Some evidence that she was up to no good?

Joss groaned, seeing it all in her head.

And he'd have picked up her discarded bathrobe in the bedroom and the bottles would have rattled together in the pocket, wouldn't they? And he'd have taken them out and looked at them — and been angry because he didn't hold with all that frothy nonsense and he'd thought she'd been wasting money on frivolities . . .

Yes, Joss, nodded, she could definitely see him doing that.

And now the bottles sat there in a neat row, as if to accuse her.

Oh, God! Could it even be that Marvin had thought the mid-day bath was for the benefit of another man? Could he — horror of horrors — suspect her of having an affair?

Joss groaned.

It seemed unlikely, given Marvin's constant dismissal of her feminine charms, but as he'd deliberately placed the bottles in such a prominent display, surely there had to be some connection between them and his sudden disappearance? So, what if he'd decided to sniff them? And not knowing what they were, assumed they were some exotic seductive scent for — what? The benefit of a lover?

Did Marvin really suspect her of having another man?

Joss spat out her toothpaste. The whole notion was ludicrous — but Marvin certainly wouldn't have bathed using the essences, would he? No — that would be madness. So, he must have simply sniffed the heady, rich fragrances and then decided that Joss, whose life-long scent of choice was safe and conservative, was being unfaithful, mustn't he?

"Oh, Marvin!" Joss sighed. "You complete prat!"

So, had he left her because he thought she was committing adultery? Oh, God! And if so — Joss hurried into the bedroom and yanked open the wardrobe's Ikea doors.

"Hell!"

Marvin's side of the wardrobe, where she'd hung and folded his clothes in order and colour coded for years and years, and could do it in her sleep, had several telling gaps.

"Buggering hell!" Joss kicked the wardrobe door. "Marvin! You stupid, stupid, sod!"

CHAPTER
TWENTY-ONE

"They're really doing well," Jennifer Blessing said, smiling maternally at the two Kylies who were carrying out a double-handed nail extension. "And with you flat-out too, my little empire is flourishing wonderfully. I don't know about you, Sukie, but I think this is going to be one of our best years ever."

Sukie, trying to escape from Beauty's Blessings with a fresh supply of robes and towels and the next week's massage appointments, nodded. Businesswise, yes, she'd agree wholeheartedly; for her, on the personal front however, it seemed as fraught with pitfalls and heartache as any other year. But she wasn't going to admit it.

"It's all going very well, yes," she said, trying to edge her way through the door. "Sorry, Jennifer, must dash — I've got several bookings today, and other stuff to sort out as well and I'm running late. Bye!"

Bundling the towels and robes into the back of her car, Sukie headed off on foot a few yards along Hazy Hassocks High Street to Big Sava. Having dined on an omelette of leftover cheese and a couple of eggs that were probably past their sell-by date the night before,

293

she desperately needed to replenish the freezer with a pile of pierce-and-pings.

April had continued to be a summer rehearsal, and Big Sava was cashing in on the sunshine dreams by displaying pyramids of suntan lotion, sunglasses, and picnic fare. The tannoy blasted with "Summer Holiday" and "In the Summertime". Sukie, heaping far more than she'd intended into her trolley, almost expected to see the staff divested of their orange tabards and wearing bikinis.

"Sukes!" Chelsea waved from behind her checkout as Sukie emerged from the final aisle. "Over here!"

Weaving in and out of several chattering groups of women in cardigans and crossover sandals, and elderly people with cheap gin and fish fingers in their baskets, Sukie just beat a man in an expensive suit with two bottles of water and some dried figs to pole position.

"Well," Chelsea said, whizzing Sukie's month's supply of low-fat, additive-rich, ready meals through the scanner, "your mumbo jumbo earth magic was a big dud, wasn't it? Not a bloody sniff of Nicky Hambly. Not," she wrestled with the bar-code on something pseudo-Indonesian, "that I expected there to be. D'you know I even looked him up on Friends Reunited just to give your stuff a bit of a leg-up, but he wasn't even registered on there. So?"

"So? So what?" Sukie packed her bright orange Big Sava carriers.

The expensive suit, presumably wishing he'd gone to Waitrose as usual, rattled his figs and water together impatiently.

294

"So what happens now with your plot to get your claws into the delicious Derry? As the magic rubbish is clearly all a big waste of time, you won't be bothering to try and love potion Milla and Bo-Bo back together now, will you?"

"Don't make it sound so calculated." Sukie frowned. "I wasn't ever going to try and magic — as you call it — Derry away from Milla. You know that. I only had her best interests at heart."

"Pshaw!" Chelsea snorted. "Pull the other one, Sukes. Face it, Derry and Milla will stay together and you'll just have to join the rest of us — single, rushing towards thirty, always destined to be on other people's hen-nights, guests at other people's weddings . . ."

The expensive suit was getting increasingly restive.

"Thanks for making my future sound so irresistible." Sukie shoved her credit card into the machine and punched in her pin number. "And anyway, Nicky Hambly might turn up at any time — no one said the distance potion worked instantly."

Chelsea handed over the receipt, shaking her head. "Sorry, Sukes — but the whole thing was madness. I never bought all that guff you gave me about Cora's garden being magical anyway. Nice try. See you tomorrow night, then?"

"Can-can rehearsals?" Sukie hefted the last of her carrier bags into her trolley. "Yes — I'll pick you up as usual. Oh, have you heard from Topsy? About that agent coming to watch us?"

"Yeah — she's rung everyone. Sounds exciting, doesn't it? If he likes us we could get loads of bookings

— and we might even get paid for dancing. Imagine that. The extra money will certainly come in handy, won't it? And wasn't it all something to do with that article that Joss Benson wrote?"

"So Topsy said. Do you reckon we'll have to be in full costume?"

"Ooh, I hadn't thought of that. Yes, probably." Chelsea leaned her elbows chummily on the conveyor belt. "Mind you —"

The expensive suit screamed and hurled his water and figs on the floor.

"Mrs Allsop!" Chelsea yelled, pushing her alarm button and waving her hand in the air. "Mrs Allsop! Supervisor needed! Security alert! Code B! Checkout 12!"

Marvin had now been missing from home for a week. Joss, alternating between panic, despair, and occasional guilty joy at the bungalow being a Marvin-free zone, had ignored her children's advice and reported him missing to the police and also left his details with various hospitals. The latter had drawn a fortunate blank, and the former had gently explained to Joss that Marvin leaving home unexpectedly, but without violence and with a packed bag, was very sad but not criminal and that he couldn't be registered as a missing person.

One of the plusses had been that, without Marvin in situ, Valerie Pridmore had been able to call at the bungalow at any time, and had done, night or day, whenever Joss had needed her most. In fact, Joss wasn't sure if she'd have coped at all without Val. Val had been kind and supportive and after her initial amusement at Marvin's defection, had clearly realised how shattered and confused Joss really was and couldn't have been a better friend.

After promising not to breathe a word to anyone she'd helped Joss search for Marvin, taken over some of the daily round of phone calls, had arrived bearing fabulous comforting, carb-filled things which Marvin would have forbidden — like fish and chips and fresh cream cakes — and listened. Oh, bless her, Joss thought, how she'd listened. All through it, Val had remained cheerful and upbeat.

"Why doesn't he just get in touch?" Joss had asked for the millionth time. "Just to let me know he's all right. Just so I can tell him that I'm not having an affair. Why doesn't he tell me where he is?"

And every time Val had patted her hand and said that he'd be back, or he'd ring, but for someone as, well, powerfully controlling as Marvin had been, the loss of his job must have caused all sorts of problems; problems which had been building up over the last few weeks — and he probably just needed some time to get his head together. Joss would just have to be patient.

And as for Joss's wild conspiracy theory that Marvin had gone because he thought she was fooling around — Valerie had laughed kindly and said that was all nonsense. Marvin had simply gone off "to find hisself". Joss would just have to give him time. It'd all be all right in the end, she'd see.

And if Val really thought that Marvin buggering off was the best-ever thing that could happen to Joss — especially now that she'd found herself a lovely little job — she'd wisely said nothing.

Now Joss thought, walking slowly back from Coddles Post Office Stores in the sunshine, she was becoming surprisingly used to her solo life. She missed the presence of another living thing in the bungalow, but she didn't miss the nagging and the censure, or the rigid precision of her previous life. She actually didn't miss Marvin very much at all. And she'd turned relatively easily into a bit of a slob. Of course, it would all change when Marvin came back, but in the meantime, in the moments when she could convince herself that Marvin was still alive and well, she was rather enjoying the restfulness.

She'd phoned Freddo as soon as Topsy had confirmed that he'd be more than welcome at the can-can rehearsal, but had said nothing about her change in circumstances. One, she really didn't know him well enough; two, he probably wouldn't be interested; three, she wanted no one at all to know about Marvin's disappearance; and four, he might even decide to withdraw the job offer if he thought Joss was embroiled in some major domestic upheaval.

So, tomorrow evening, she'd meet up with Freddo at Hazy Hassocks village hall and pretend all was well, and tomorrow, maybe, Marvin might be home.

It really was a glorious morning, Joss thought, taking the long way home to The Close because she had nothing better to do and because Marvin never liked to walk through Bagley in case he had to speak to someone he considered beneath him. Lovely and warm, without a breath of wind, the air filled with birdsong, and blossoms fluttering against the blue of the sky, petals gently swirling around her as she wandered, like pastel confetti.

The lanes, overhung with willow trees heavy with catkins, were almost waist-high with sweet nettles and celandines and daisies, and the cottage gardens were exploding into their springtime best. She wondered if, when Marvin came back, she might suggest they make pretty borders in the front garden of the bungalow, too. It would give such a lift to the spirits to look out each morning on such a riot of colour.

"Joss! Mrs Benson! How are you?"

Joss, startled, peered across the lane. "Sorry? Oh, Sukie — hello. I didn't realise I'd drifted so far off course."

Sukie, who seemed to be removing a year's worth of groceries from the boot of her car, straightened up. "I thought you might be coming to see me. To book another massage?"

"No, I'm afraid not . . ." Joss shook her head, drinking in the tumbled rainbow of Pixies Laughter's traditional cottage garden. "Sorry — just out on a bit of a constitutional. I've been to Coddles — and it was such a lovely morning, I thought I'd stroll round the village."

"It is gorgeous, isn't it? I really should have phoned you to find out how your meeting went. Did the essences help?"

Not wanting to say either that the oils had produced a woodland fantasy in the bathroom in case Sukie thought she was insane, and especially not what havoc the essences had wreaked so soon afterwards in her private life, Joss simply nodded. "Wonderfully, Sukie, thank you so much. I'd really meant to come and say thank you earlier — I-I coped really well — and I got a job."

"Really?" Sukie grinned. "Fantastic. With the bloke who wanted to see you? How amazing. Well done."

Joss continued smiling and explained briefly about Freddo and Retro Music and Theatre and that he was the agent who would be coming to size up the can-canners the following evening. And they both laughed and said "small world" and laughed again.

"I'm really glad the essences were what you needed and worked so well," Sukie said, closing her boot lid. "I did worry a bit afterwards, because although I knew you'd memorised the quantities to use in the bath, I really should have warned you never to use them undiluted. They're very — um — powerful. And sniffing them isn't to be recommended either."

"Sniffing them? Why on earth not? They were gorgeous . . . the scent stayed in the bathroom for days."

"Oh, yes, diluted they're fine." Sukie said. "I just meant to tell you not to open the bottles and inhale them neat."

"Inhale them?" Joss suddenly felt slightly queasy. "Straight from the bottles? Why not?"

"Well, as long as you didn't, and don't in the future, that's fine." Sukie smiled happily. "It's just that they're very strong, natural extracts. And, as everyone knows, anything inhaled is immediately absorbed straight into the bloodstream. The effect of sniffing the scents from the bottles would be about three trillion times as powerful as anything mixed with gallons of bath water."

"You mean they're *dangerous?*"

"No, of course not! They certainly wouldn't kill you —" Sukie laughed, picking up her Big Sava carrier bags, "— this is aromatherapy we're talking about — one of the safest, gentlest, most natural therapies around. But that particular combination can have a slightly heady effect even when diluted — neat they'd probably work like some sort of fragrant tipsiness. I'd have hated for you to be too spaced out to even get to Winterbrook. Anyway, it all worked out for the best, didn't it? Ah, well, enjoy your walk — I'd better get this lot into the freezer before it all melts. I'll see you — and your new boss — tomorrow evening. Bye."

"What? Oh, yes . . . Bye Sukie . . ."

Joss didn't move. She suddenly suspected that *sniffing* the essences was exactly what Marvin had done. Of course, in his usual nosy way, he'd found the bottles and because he could never, ever leave anything alone, he'd unstoppered them, hadn't he? And inhaled them? And vanished . . .

This put a whole new bizarre slant on things. Knowing how vividly real her own fantasy had been, Joss could only imagine what a good whiff of the neat essences had done to Marvin. Oh, sweet heavens above!

301

She almost dropped her shopping basket as the realisation kicked in.

What if he hadn't gone off in a temper because he thought Joss was drenching herself in scent for a lover? What if he'd had an even stronger reaction to Sukie's potions and gone off on some happy hippy trip — high as a kite — experiencing — what? God alone knew! What if under the influence of mind-altering substances, he'd simply thrown some things in a bag, and driven off.

Joss swallowed. Jesus Christ! What on earth was she going to tell the children?

By the time she'd unpacked the groceries, Sukie had convinced herself that there was absolutely no need to have told Joss about the rhyme that went with her calming empowerment bath oils. No need at all. No harm done. And Joss hadn't used them undiluted, and clearly hadn't suffered any sort of ill-effects — she'd have said so, wouldn't she? And as for the other bit of the verse — the bit that could have caused all manner of problems — well, it would be all round the village by now if that had worked, wouldn't it?

Maybe Cora's poem was wrong on this one; maybe wish-fulfillment and love potions simply didn't function together. Unless, of course, Joss had fallen head-over-heels with the abysmal Marvin all over again after her bath? Nah! Not possible . . .

It had probably been a bad idea to make the hawthorn substitution though, given the mind-expanding effect of the perfumes when combined with

302

jasmine and lavender — and not a mistake she'd make in future.

Hmmm, Sukie thought as she slammed the freezer door shut, that could have been a very close call. It would only take one of her mixtures to go wrong for her to have to stop using the garden's plentiful storehouse, which would be an awful shame when everything was going so well, and, worse still, it would have put paid to her ongoing plans for reuniting Milla and Bo-Bo. She hadn't given up on the long distance love spell, despite Chelsea's scepticism; it may not have brought Nicky Hambly slavering to his knees in Big Sava — yet — but there was still time.

Anyway, Sukie smiled happily to herself as she wandered out into the sunlit garden, at least Cora's empowerment essence recipe had worked spectacularly well on Joss, hadn't it, with no disasters? Convinced as she was of the powerful earth magic contained in the cottage's bounty, Joss's stonking success still came as something of a surprise. It gave her quite a glow to think that something she'd concocted had given poor downtrodden Joss enough confidence to find a job — and a really interesting one at that.

Sukie, ducking beneath the arches of burgeoning honey-suckle and budding rambling roses, wondered idly what the appalling Marvin had had to say about Joss's job. She hoped he'd been lovely to Joss and congratulated her both on her new-found confidence and career and taken her out for a slap-up meal to celebrate. Sadly, somehow she doubted it. If she was in Joss's position she'd leave Marvin like a shot. Why on earth did she stay with him? Still, hopefully, the new job would give her a real chance of happiness at last. Joss was such a lovely person, she really deserved something nice to happen in her life.

Pixies Laughter's garden, abundantly overgrown and lush, smelled delightful. Sukie, now able to recognise most of the plants she needed to restock her essence cupboard, quickly forgot about Joss Benson's marital misery as she happily gathered jasmine and buttercups and daises and clover and nettles in the sun.

"Very rustic," Derry laughed from the garden gate. "No — don't let me stop you."

"Blimey!" Sukie straightened up, squinting at him over her armful of plants in the sun. "You made me jump! Er — Milla's at work — she went in early this morning."

"I know." He opened the flaking, creaky gate. "I've just been to price up a job a couple of streets away and thought I'd stop by and see if you were in — and if there was any chance of a cup of tea."

"No chance at all," Sukie said lightly, hiding her delight and confusion behind a clump of sweet nettles and wild parsley. "I'm far too busy. Didn't your customer provide one? I thought it was de rigueur."

Derry shook his head. "Not even as much as a sniff of a tea bag."

"Tough." Sukie grinned. "And if you want a cup of tea here you'll have to earn it. Do you reckon you can put your nan's passed-on expertise to work and tell me where in this lot I'm likely to find chickweed? I think

I've got everything else — but I still need chickweed flowers for a new potion."

"Can we come to some sort of arrangement, then?" Derry asked. "As I'm just about to die of dehydration I'll go and make tea for both of us, then I'll turn detective. Okay?"

"Okay."

Sukie watched him walk into the cottage, all faded denim and male beauty, the Spring sunshine spiralling from his blond hair, and exhaled. God — he was sooo gorgeous. And friendly. And why wouldn't he be? After all, he had no idea at all how she felt about him, had he? Thank goodness.

She dumped the armfuls of culled plants into a selection of Cora's ancient trugs by the back door, and stretched. Okay, so Chelsea was probably right, there was something slightly immoral about using the distance love elixir on Milla, but she was still going to do it. Or was she? Oh, damn it — what if Derry really did love Milla? What if reuniting Milla and Bo-Bo broke his heart? Could she live with herself having made him unhappy?

No, she couldn't and wouldn't. Ooooh — bugger!

"Tea, in a pot because it tastes better, milk, sugar, two cups, no saucers or biscuits that I could find . . ." Derry appeared in the doorway with a tray. "And, if you promise not to punch me, chickweed is that ground-hugging stuff which is covering most of the border over there — the one with the little white flowers."

"Is it? Really? But you could have said that straight away, couldn't you?"

"I could —" Derry set the tray down on a rickety wicker table under the tumbling rose arch and sat gingerly on an equally rickety wicker chair, "— but then you'd have said thanks and goodbye and I wouldn't have got tea, would I?"

"Definitely not." Sukie smiled, bending down and tugging up armfuls of what she'd always called sweet-hearts. "But you might still get a punch for your brass neck."

They grinned at one another.

"Goodness — this stuff clings, doesn't it? Right, that's got it — I think." Sukie despatched the sticky mass of chickweed on top of the other plants by the back door and joined Derry at the table. He'd poured the tea. "Cheers — and thanks. Oh, this is great."

"The tea, the weather, the garden or the company?"

She met his blue eyes over the rim of her cup, her stomach suddenly dissolving with a delicious mixture of lust and love. "All of them."

"Right answer." Derry smiled at her. "And do I gather from this — um — harvest, that the home-made potions are still doing the business?"

Relieved to move away from anything personal, Sukie nodded and told him she may need to pick his brains about becoming self-employed before too long, and also about Joss Benson's amazing experience after the empowerment bath.

"So that one wasn't a love potion as such?" Derry asked. "We didn't find anything in those cross-stitches other than matchmaking stuff, did we? Or was this one you discovered later?"

"Yes, and — well, it did have a bit of the sting in the tail, actually. The blend of essences was exactly what Joss needed for her meeting, but there was a rhyme that went with it — and I was rather worried that it might have caused a few — um — problems, but she didn't say anything."

"Go on then. What did this mixture promise?"

"Oh, lord," Sukie stared into her tea, "are you sure you want to hear this? Okay . . ."

Bathe in jasmine and lavender sweet
And love and power will always meet
Close your eyes and dream your dream
And float away on fragrant steam
Everything you wish will be
Granted for all eternity.
But mix with hawthorn's sharp desire
And lust will rage with burning fire
Driving false love from your life
Bringing true love to end your strife

"Not the catchiest thing I've ever heard — but pretty blatant." Derry grinned. "And the first bit worked — but not the second? This Mrs Benson didn't leave her husband and take up with the milkman who she'd loved in secret for years, straight from the tub so to speak?"

"No, thank goodness." Sukie shuddered. "Hopefully Cora got that last bit very wrong. Poor old Joss has got enough problems with her gruesome husband — although she should leave him in my opinion, but because she wants to, not simply because of the aromatherapy."

Derry finished his tea and laughed. "Pretty horny this older generation, weren't they? This village must have been a hotbed of swappers and swingers a couple of generations ago thanks to your great-auntie Cora."

Sukie giggled. "Yeah, it makes it seem rather dull now — oh . . ."

Derry leaned across the table towards her. "Sorry — hold still. You've got some chickweed stuck to your jumper. There . . ."

Neither of them moved. Neither of them spoke. The hazily warm garden, sweet-smelling and silent, seemed to enclose them in a magical suspended world. Sukie could hear the thundering of her heart, could see faint freckles smudged across the bridge of Derry's nose and the blond flecks in his long dark lashes, could smell the warm, clean male scent of him.

"Sukie . . . I know —"

"Cooo-eee! Anyone at home?"

They sprang apart as two elderly ladies shuffled in through the garden gate.

"Not too early are we, dear? For our foot rub? Only the ring-a-ride minibus picked us up sooner than we'd expected. Oooh — lovely! Tea! Come on Elsie — get a shift on. Bring yer bunions to the table and grab a cuppa."

308

"Er — I'd better be leaving." Derry stood up, his shoulders shaking with imploding laughter. "Excuse me, ladies. And Sukie, I'll see you — well, I'll see you."

"Yes, yes — you will . . ." Sukie said quickly. "And — um — thanks for the chickweed."

"My pleasure," Derry grinned, heading for the gate. "Enjoy the bunions."

CHAPTER
TWENTY-TWO

Hazy Hassocks village hall was heaving.

"Flip me." Chelsea gazed around in disbelief. "Are we on telly?"

"Not television, no —" Topsy, in her best long grey dress and best brown and cream paisley scarf, with her best Alice band scraping her grey hair back from her wizened face, tippy-tapped towards them, "— but there's someone from the local radio here and a reporter from the *Winterbrook Advertiser*."

"Er — why?" Sukie peered at the noisy throng. "Have I missed something?"

"It's all to do with Mrs Benson bringing that impresario tonight." Topsy gave a little on-the-spot pirouette. "That and the auditions."

"Well, yes I knew about that — but this is a bit over the top. Have we had loads of applications for Val's place, then?"

"Four," Topsy waved her hands theatrically, "but you know what the villages are like — they've brought all their friends and family for support. Quite a nice little crowd, as you see."

Sukie could see only too well. It was the usual rural turnout for anything free — especially for amateur entertainment, which may well end in the amusing humiliation of the participants. A twenty-first century version of lions and Christians but without quite so much blood.

"We're not doing a dress rehearsal, are we?" Sukie asked while Chelsea skipped off to join Roo, Betty and Trace on the stage. "I meant to check with you —"

"No," Topsy shook her head. "Dorchester and I thought that would be a little intimidating for the new gels."

Dorchester and I? Sukie squinted round the dimly-lit hall — ah, yes, there he was. Holding court in a corner, looking proud as punch in plum velvet and tweed and a Noel Coward cravat.

"Don't you look like that, young Sukie." Topsy's eyes flashed. "You and I are the only ones in this room who know the truth about me and Dorchester. Everyone else thinks it's a sweet romance of the third age and we've been biding our time to share our pensions in our twilight years or some such nonsense. You and me both know it was instant and magic and down to the violas, don't we?"

Sukie stared at the dusty floor. "Yes, well, maybe — but you're happy, aren't you?"

"Happier than I've been for decades." Topsy's beady eyes twinkled. "You were very naughty to use one of Cora's potions on me — and to lie about it, saying it were synthetic — but I'm so glad you did."

Sukie smiled. "So am I, then. Delighted. Hilton said Dorchester had bought you a boxed set of *Dr Kildare*."

"He's done more than that." Topsy's feet *plie*'d merrily. "He's introduced me to the internet cafe in Winterbrook. He's bought me my very own stethoscope and blood-pressure monitor off e-Bay."

And greater love hath no man, Sukie said to herself, as Topsy sashayed away to meet and greet, humming the theme tune to *Casualty*.

Among the crowd she could see Valerie Pridmore and her entire extended family, as well as several of her massage clients all holding hands with what looked like newish partners. Oh, and there were Rita and Edie from the card school accompanied by Savoy and Claridge — presumably poor old Hilton was holding a lone fort at the Barmy Cow again. Tom and Ken certainly looked cosy. Sukie wondered how Cora would have felt about her potions being used to bring out the best in elderly closet gays. She'd have probably been pleased — after all, she'd only wanted everyone's happiness, hadn't she? Oh, and Bert seemed to have found someone too — a stout lady with lilac curls and a sparkly caftan — and was steering her round the throng, making introductions.

Sukie sighed to herself. All in all, the Pixies Laughter potions had worked well — hadn't they? Even if some of the pairings had been a bit doubtful at first. She'd done Cora proud in keeping up the family traditions with no harm caused. And she still had great hopes for the distance potion working for Chelsea — even though she'd decided she couldn't now, in all fairness, use it on Milla. She couldn't break Derry's heart — not even to mend her own.

In The Close, Joss, watching from the dinette window, was as skittery as a kitten. Marvin was still missing, and her new information — that he was possibly suffering from some sort of mental delusion — had not made much impression on the police who'd perked up a bit when they thought they might be on the trail of a drugs baron, but had immediately lost interest when she'd mentioned aromatherapy. The hospitals had assured her again that no one fitting Marvin's description had been treated for anything — especially a fragrance-overdose.

She still hadn't told the children.

Tonight she'd have to put Marvin and his mind-blowing on the back burner, she knew that. Tonight, she'd have to be cool and competent and convince Freddo that he'd picked the right woman for the job. It would be difficult when she was still in a turmoil over her marriage, but when Marvin came back she'd still need to be the breadwinner, wouldn't she? She couldn't possibly let everyone down now.

And, Joss paced the bungalow, she'd had another woodland bath — to give her the resolve and calm she needed for this evening — and it had been wonderful. Just as magical as the previous one, but not so much of a shock — and, right now, swathed in a fragrant mist of jasmine and lavender, she realised while she should be worrying about Marvin, she simply couldn't wait to get started with her new job — she was even looking forward to seeing Freddo again.

It was all very odd.

Freddo had phoned and said that unless she and Marvin were planning to go to the rehearsals together, he'd be delighted to collect her from The Close if that wouldn't cause any trouble. And Joss had said — truthfully — that Marvin was away from home — so yes, thank you, she'd love Freddo to pick her up.

Now, knowing that he must be on his way, she felt giddy with anticipation like a teenager waiting for her first date.

Valerie Pridmore, who was going to be at Hazy Hassocks village hall like almost everyone else in Bagley-cum-Russet, had been really miffed that she'd miss the collection bit.

"I'd like to give him the once-over," she'd said, "just to make sure he looks okay. You're such an innocent, Joss, you really shouldn't go off with strange men in cars."

And Joss had laughed and said Val sounded like her mother, and that there was nothing remotely strange about Freddo Fabian.

Actually, she thought now, that wasn't really true, was it? Oh, she had absolutely no doubts about Freddo's decency and honesty — but his appearance was sure to raise more than a few eyebrows — probably even Val's.

Joss giggled to herself at the thought, tried to stop, and couldn't. Oh, how wicked she was! Giggling when poor Marvin could be living in a cardboard box or in a hostel for the terminally confused — or anywhere . . .

She hadn't mentioned the aromatherapy bit to Val either — just in case she laughed. Joss couldn't bear the thought of anyone laughing at Marvin. Not now. Poor Marvin — he'd truly been his own worst enemy — and the cause of his own downfall — and she was becoming scarily used to life without him. Since he'd been gone she'd got into the habit of eating cosy nursery meals in front of the television, and had discovered soaps and makeover programmes and comedy shows which in their previous life would have sent Marvin into purple-faced vein-throbbing mode.

And she'd made a bit of a sea-change in her wardrobe, too. Not wanting to touch their bank account because money was even more of an issue than ever and Marvin had always held the purse-strings, Joss had taken several of her more boring cream, beige and taupe outfits to an animal charity shop run by Biff and Hedley Pippin in Winterbrook, and had rather surprised herself by haggling a little for a few replacement items.

She'd emerged with several gypsy skirts which according to Biff were so last year, a couple of almost-new brightly coloured Marks and Spencer tops, a floppy bo-ho shoulder bag and a pair of sequinned sandals — all for practically peanuts.

Tonight, sporting this new look, and with her short fair hair more ruffled than groomed, Joss secretly thought she looked a good twenty years younger. It would all change when Marvin came home, of course, because he'd have a spluttering buggering fit, but for tonight's showbiz venue the outfit seemed absolutely perfect.

Oh, goodness! Joss's heart nearly stopped beating. She could hear a car turning into the drive. In a moment of mental infidelity she prayed and prayed that it wasn't a homeward-bound Marvin. Not tonight. She really wasn't ready for him to return tonight.

With crossed fingers and holding her breath, she peeped round the Ikea curtains and laughed out loud.

A vast, pink and chromium Cadillac convertible was purring on the drive.

Freddo, golden hair flowing, bracelets blinging, a white shirt over black trousers, leapt out of the car and almost collided with her as she hurled herself out of the front door.

"Sorry, Joss, duck — not late am I? And — my word — you look wonderful. Wonderful. Like a princess. Stunning, duck. I'll be the proudest man in Hazy Hassocks tonight."

"Thank you." Joss was fairly sure that simply accepting a compliment was the thing to do. "You look wonderful, too."

Well, he did. Different — but wonderful. And that car . . .

"I'll hold the door open for you," Freddo did so with a flourish, "but if you just want to leap in to the passenger seat over the top, that's fine by me."

Joss chuckled. "No, I'll use the conventional route, thank you. I'll save the leaping for later." She slid into the dark red leather seat. "Oh, heavens — this is fabulous. Is it yours?"

Freddo nodded, jumping into the driving seat. "A bit ostentatious some would say, and one heck of a gas-guzzler, but I love it. I bought it at auction after a boy band went bust and their management had to flog off everything right down to the paper-clips. Right — are we all set?"

Joss nodded, wondering if this was part of her fantasy too, wishing with all her heart that Val could see her now.

Freddo started the car and the feral roar convinced her that this was very, very real indeed.

"Your husband okay with this, is he?" Freddo asked as they left The Close. "It hasn't caused any problems, I hope."

"He's still away," Joss said lightly, loving the warm evening breeze on her face, and the way her hair danced and her skirts billowed. "But I'm sure he wouldn't mind at all."

She'd have to come clean about Marvin's disappearance before long, she knew, but not tonight. Nothing was going to spoil tonight.

As the Cadillac swept across the Bagley and Russet intersection, past the Celtic cross and Coddles Stores, several children stood and stared and whooped and waved at them. Feeling as though life could, never, ever get any better than this, Joss smiled and laughed and waved back.

And she was still laughing as Freddo turned up the eight-track and they sang along to Sam and Dave's "Soul Man", roaring through the Spring countryside towards Hazy Hassocks at dizzying speed.

Outside the village hall, Valerie Pridmore, having a crafty cigarette, was joined by Sukie who wasn't sneaking out for a smoke but who could no longer bear Topsy turning into Arlene Phillips.

"She's driving me mad," Sukie said, leaning against the pebble-dash with Val in the evening sun. "Because the press are here she's making us do the most ridiculous moves. I hope she'll tone them down for the auditions otherwise she'll have the hopefuls in traction before the night's over. You're well out of this."

"Tell me about it." Val blew a plume of smoke into the gentle air. "Knackering me leg was the best thing I've ever done. Topsy's got far more energy than's good for her at her age. She'll probably kill old Dorchester."

"Yeah, but he'll die with a smile in his face, won't he?"

"He will that," Val chuckled. "Oh — blimey! Look at this!"

Sukie looked.

A long, low, bright pink American open-topped car was cruising into the car park, skittering gravel from beneath its tyres.

"Smart or what? Hell's teeth, Val! It's Joss."

"Never?" Val choked on her cigarette. "Never in this world? Oh — bloody hell! Yes, it is! That must belong to the agent bloke she's going to be working for . . . Jesus! Lucky cow!"

Sukie laughed to herself. Well, well, well . . . And surely the cheerful man behind the wheel, with his flowing yellow hair and tanned skin and air of celebrity,

318

looked familiar. Had she seen him somewhere before? She was sure she had.

"Look at that!" Val breathed in awe as Freddo leapt out and opened the door for Joss. "Her Marv never did anything like that. And look at him! He's a bit of all right! Oh, wow, Joss — you've fallen right on your size fives, my love. Oh, and look at her clothes! She looks bloody brill, don't she?"

"And she's smiling like she's lit up from inside," Sukie marvelled at the transformation, hoping that at least some of it was as a result of her potions. "And so is he. I wonder if they realise . . ."

Val grinned. "If they don't then they soon will — I hope her Marv never comes back."

"What?" Sukie frowned. "Has Marvin gone away, then? She didn't say anything to me when I saw her yesterday."

"Shit!" Val looked stricken. "Forget I said anything, Sukie, please. I'm not supposed to have told anyone, and I haven't. Until now. Yes, he's done a runner — best thing that could happen."

Sukie nodded in agreement. "I won't breathe a word. No wonder she looks as if she's got a new lease of life. Oh, isn't it funny how life has a way of working things out for everyone?"

Well, life and a few plants from Pixies Laughter's garden . . .

Joss and Mr Fabian walked towards them, not quite touching, still smiling together. Joss, blushing slightly, made introductions. Sukie, still convinced she'd seen Freddo Fabian somewhere before, shook hands to a rattle of bling bracelets. Joss and Val hugged one another wordlessly — words simply not being needed between them now.

"Sukie!" Topsy appeared in the doorway. "Stop chattering and come along, dear! We're ready to start! Oh — Mrs Benson and Mr —?"

"Fabian. Freddo Fabian." Freddo pumped Topsy's hand. "You must be young Topsy. Delighted to meet you, duck. I can't wait for this gig tonight."

Topsy, preening, was almost turning herself inside out with excitement in the presence of a real show-business person as Sukie skipped back into the village hall.

The auditions were truly awful. The four applicants — Sheila, Mary, Loz and Grace — were all good-enough dancers, but Topsy simply terrified them. None of them could remember one step of the routines for more than thirty seconds. Sukie puffed to a halt, yet again, as Topsy screamed for a rerun.

The audience, packed into the body of the hall, was loving every minute. It would have spoiled their enjoyment of the entire evening if things had gone smoothly.

"Frigging hell," Chelsea muttered as Orpheus retreated into his Underworld and they reformed once more, "my legs are dropping off."

"Mine too." Sukie massaged her calves. "Topsy — give us a break, please. Let the new girls have a go on their own — just show them a couple of the moves and let them copy you. You can't expect them to know the whole routine."

Topsy frowned at her. "When you're good enough to be a choreographer, Sukie, I'll ask for your opinion. But, as we need to put this one to bed as soon as possible, it might be the only way. Gels?" She looked beadily at a quivering Sheila, Mary, Loz and Grace. "Would you be happier with a solo run? Even in front of this audience?"

Sheila, Mary, Loz and Grace nodded.

"Right," Topsy sighed, nodding to Dorchester who was in chance of the sound-system, "off we go again — Sheila first . . ."

Offenbach's rousing music swooped out into the hall, the audience tapped their feet and clapped their hands, Sukie, Chelsea, Trace, Roo and Bet sank gratefully on to the side of the stage, and Topsy put Sheila through her paces.

It was much, much better. Mary, Loz and Grace followed suit with equally vast improvements.

"They're all really good now they're not scared witless," Sukie whispered. "Wonder which one she'll choose?"

"Search me." Chelsea stretched her legs out in front of her. "Oh, bugger — here she comes again."

Topsy, almost skipping out, stood in front of the stage. "Right, ladies — now I'd like my original troupe to give our celebrity and media guests an idea of what we can do while I come to my decision."

Joss, sitting beside Freddo in the front row of chairs provided for the special guests, caught Sukie's eye and smiled. Sukie, thinking Joss had never looked happier, smiled back.

Then they were off with their proper routine, and all the aching muscles were forgotten as they swirled and circled and high-kicked and leaped and screamed and flounced and cartwheeled and finally leapt into flourishing splits.

Freddo was on his feet, whooping, applauding loudly, followed by the rest of the village hall.

Topsy climbed on to the stage and beamed at her troupe. "Super, gels. Absolutely super. Not a step wrong. And Mr Fabian is apparently delighted with us. Delighted. He's going to have us on his books — which is wonderful news. But we do have a bit of a problem — I can't choose between the new ladies. I'd take them all — but then we'd be back with the original problem — an odd number. Oh, dear me — what to do? I don't want to lose any of those new gels. What we need is one more lady to step up on stage to give us ten dancers — then we'd have a proper Moulin Rouge line-up."

Sukie said nothing for a moment, then she whispered in Topsy's ear.

"Are you sure?" Topsy looked disbelieving. "Mrs Benson? You're turning into a talent scout as well as a choreographer, are you?"

"Ask her," Sukie said, hoping the empowerment essences were still working. "She can only say no. And she is a wonderful dancer — I've seen her in action —"

Shrugging, Topsy squatted on the edge of the stage. "Mrs Benson — I wonder if you could help us out here, my dear."

Joss, looking slightly flustered, nodded, listened intently, shook her head, then smiled. Sukie watched as she whispered something to Freddo and he whispered something back.

Then to the village hall's amazement, Jocelyn Benson from Bagley — sad, frightened, shy, downtrodden Jocelyn Benson — stepped up on to the stage.

Dorchester cranked up Offenbach all over again and Joss, watched Topsy intently, then held her gypsy skirts, tapped her sequinned sandals, counted herself in on the beat and swept across the stage.

"She's a bloody natural," Chelsea whispered. "And she must be ancient!"

The village hall was on its feet again, stamping and clapping as Joss simply whirled with the music, prancing and high-kicking. Freddo, Sukie noticed, was standing on his chair, whistling his approval, his eyes fixed on Joss.

Oh, wow — Sukie thought — he's sooo keen on her . . .

The music ended. Joss, panting pulled a face at Topsy. "Er — sorry — I'm not too good on the kicks and I can't turn cartwheels and I'll never do the splits but —"

"But nothing." Topsy beamed. "And I'll let you into a little secret — only Sukie and Chelsea do the splits properly. All my other gels simply slide the front leg forward and bend the other one up behind. No one can tell — and you'll fit in right perfect, my love. So — what do you say?"

"And I'll get to wear one of those gorgeous frocks like Sukie showed me? And all those amazing petticoats?"

"Well, yes," Topsy frowned, "of course you will. So — what do you say? Would you like to join us?"

"Yes . . ." Joss said, still out of breath. "Oh, yes, yes please."

"Ladies and gentlemen!" Topsy strode to the front of the stage. "Thank you for all your support tonight — and against all my expectations I'm happy to announce that we're going to be taking all the new ladies to join the Bagley-cum-Russet can-can troupe!"

The village hall, universally as generous in their praise as they were in their condemnation, vociferously showed their appreciation of this democratic decision.

The original dancers hugged all the newcomers.

Joss, hardly able to speak, simply hugged Sukie. "Thank you — I'm not sure how you did this for me — but thank you so very, very much . . ."

And Sukie, hoping Marvin never came home to spoil this, watched misty-eyed as Joss left the stage and was hugged by a very, very proud Freddo.

It only needed tears and a bit of kissing and a back-flip or two and it'd be just like a football match.

Topsy clapped her hands again. "So — we now have our troupe — and I'm also delighted to announce that we have an agent — the famous Mr Freddo Fabian from Winterbrook . . ." Topsy indicated Freddo, who was still hugging Joss, but who managed to bow to his audience. "And I hope you'll come along and see us dance — along with all manner of other entertainments

— on Fiddlesticks village green on May Bank Holiday, when we'll be helping to celebrate the marriage of Fern and Timmy Pluckrose."

The village hall stamped further approval and then began a stampede towards the local hostelry to continue the celebrations.

Having floated through a further delightful hour in the Faery Glen in Hazy Hassocks High Street in the company of new friends and old, Joss now sat in Freddo's car outside the bungalow. The evening had darkened into a chilly night, reminding everyone that summer hadn't quite arrived, and Joss shivered.

"I shouldn't keep you, duck." Freddo grinned at her. "Not when it's getting cold — but I've had such a fab evening, I don't want it to end."

"Neither do I," Joss said honestly. "This has been one of the best nights of my life."

Freddo laughed. "And mine, duck. Great fun. And even greater company. And you — well, you blew my socks off. You were the star of the show."

Joss blushed and giggled a bit. "I surprised myself. I loved it — I've always loved dancing, but Marvin doesn't — didn't — er — well, he doesn't approve . . ."

"Silly sod," Freddo said cheerfully. "Ah, well, duck — I suppose all good things have to come to an end, and your husband wouldn't be too happy if he thought we were sitting out here like a couple of teenagers, would he?"

Joss shook her head. Well, he wouldn't. Wherever he was. But, without really understanding why, she really,

really didn't want to leave Freddo. "Yes, I suppose I ought to go. Thank you — for everything. And I'll see you on Monday — at the office."

Freddo climbed out of the car and opened the door for her. "It can't come soon enough for me, Joss, and that's the truth. We'll make a great team. Thank you so much."

And he briefly brushed his lips against her cheek.

Joss, who couldn't remember the last time she'd been kissed, caught her breath. Then with one last smile at Freddo, she fumbled for her keys and let herself into the bungalow.

Leaning against the front door in the darkness, she listened as the Cadillac roared away, then touched her cheek in wonderment. Just one little friendly kiss and she felt as though her world was tumbling upside down. Oh, what a wonderful, wonderful evening it had been . . .

The telephone rang suddenly beside her in the hall, making her jump.

She smiled. Freddo was probably ringing her on his mobile — and he couldn't have got any further than the Celtic cross could he?

Joss lifted the receiver, almost caressing it. "Hello?"

"Hello?" a woman's voice said coolly. "I've been trying to ring you all evening — don't you have an answerphone?"

"Er — yes . . . but it's not switched on." Joss, coming down to earth with a bump, thought this wasn't the best telephone manner for someone ringing to sell her something at almost midnight. "Maybe you've got the wrong number. And whatever you're selling, I'm sorry but I don't want it. And it's far too late to —"

"I'm not selling anything. You are Jocelyn? Jocelyn Benson?"

"Yes, but —"

"You don't know me, Mrs Benson, but I feel as though I know you very well. I'm Anneka Lindstrom."

Joss shook her head, momentarily unable to focus on anything except Freddo and the kiss and the laughter and the can-can. "Sorry, it's far too late for this —"

"I was your husband's secretary," the cool voice continued. "Your husband, Marvin, who in case you haven't noticed, hasn't been with you for sometime. That's because he's now here with me. And very distressed. I think we need to meet, Mrs Benson, as soon as possible, to discuss this situation, don't you?"

CHAPTER
TWENTY-THREE

Having caught the early bus to the station, Joss sat on the Paddington-bound train the following morning, listening to office workers yelling to other office workers via their mobile phones that they were just past Reading. This, she thought, must have been the sort of journey Marvin had made every day of his working life; the sort of journey she'd never asked him about and he'd never told her. A stressful journey squeezed in with hundreds of strangers, hurtling though Berkshire, everyone yawning and looking bored.

And when she arrived at Paddington, she'd . . .

She sighed. All the rainbow euphoria of the previous day disintegrated into grey mistiness. When she arrived at Paddington, she'd take a cab, as Anneka had instructed given Joss's lack of familiarity with the underground system, and make the journey across London to Battersea and then . . .

And then what?

Joss actually had no idea at all. Anneka had said nothing further in the previous night's phone call — simply made sure Joss had the address and phone number and would be there, presumably to claim her brain-fuddled husband who could no longer remember where he really belonged.

So, would Marvin still be as high as a kite? Or angry? Or just Marvin? Joss stared at the countryside flashing past outside, and felt an overwhelming sadness. How cruel it was to have had yesterday's tantalising glimpse of happiness and excitement and *life* only to see it snatched away again so very quickly.

When Marvin was back in the bungalow, he might agree to her working at Retro Music and Theatre, but he'd make it difficult, she knew he would, but she'd fight her corner on that one. She'd come this far — she wasn't prepared to give in entirely. The can-can was a different matter. Marvin certainly wouldn't allow her to dance the can-can — and she knew she wouldn't battle him on this, not even with her new-found assertiveness. They had to live together, and she knew from years and years of experience that it was easier to give in, and if he let her work with Freddo without causing too much trouble, well, one out of two, she thought — paraphrasing Meatloaf — ain't bad.

Freddo . . . Joss exhaled. Could she really work with him now anyway? On a platonic basis? Because, she knew, as she'd known last night, that her feelings for him were far from that.

She smiled sadly to herself: Marvin and Freddo — chalk and cheese.

Freddo was everything she thought a man shouldn't be, but was everything she wanted — and she'd fallen head over heels. What a funny business this love stuff was. And wasn't she far too old to have fallen madly in love for the first time in her life? And with a wild-looking man with dubious dyed hair and spiv jewellery and odd clothes, at that?

And she didn't even have to torture herself wondering if Freddo felt anything for her in return — because she knew he did. And now it would all have to come to an end.

Joss wriggled in her seat and stared momentarily out at the dash of late-Spring countryside, trying not to mind.

The two girls sitting opposite her, young, with their smart office suits and straight glossy hair and blunt French-manicured nails, avoided meeting her eyes. What did they see with the arrogance of their youth? A middle-aged nondescript woman without a life, maybe about to cry, remembering her sad nondescript dreams?

She really wanted to lean forward and wipe the superior looks from their perfect, youthful, unlined faces by telling them that last night she'd begun to fall hopelessly in love with a man whose hair was longer and yellower than hers, and she'd danced the can-can and roared through the Berkshire lanes in an open-topped pink Cadillac singing soul songs.

But if she did, they'd probably think she was mad. Because, Joss thought sadly as the outskirts of London teetered into view outside the carriage's window, if she thought this could ever have a happy ending, she was, wasn't she?

The taxi driver negotiated London with consummate skill. Joss, simply stunned by the volume of vehicles shooting at them from every direction, and the towering buildings, and the teeming mass of people, and the colour and noise, sat back, overwhelmed.

She'd rarely been to London with Marvin; and never alone. Not even on a sight-seeing tour or shopping spree. What an admission! And she'd never met Anneka. Years ago, when Marvin was first climbing his cradle-to-grave job ladder, he'd had a secretary called June — a big, cheerful woman, with big black hair and even bigger earrings. Joss had liked June when they'd met at corporate dinners and functions. Marvin, she knew, didn't. He thought June was common. Joss had always assumed it was because June wasn't afraid of him and held him in no awe whatsoever.

Since Marvin's elevation to managerial levels, he'd never attended the company's social events unless under duress, and if there had been a function he couldn't escape from he'd simply stayed up in town and Joss hadn't joined him. Anneka had been his secretary during these latter years, but she'd simply been a name — a cool, Swedish name who had produced the finished version of the *Bagley Bugle*. Goodness — how long ago it all seemed now . . . Joss had admired Anneka's resilience, working with Marvin all day, and had never questioned the relationship, knowing it was strictly business. It would have been laughable to imagine that it could be anything else — it still was.

No, whatever Joss thought she might discover in Battersea, it certainly wasn't going to be a love-nest.

She and Marvin would be making the homeward journey to The Close together.

Joss sighed as the south London area signs started to appear at the congested road junctions. She'd always supposed Anneka would be a sort of glamorous cross between the blonde one in Abba and Ulrika Jonnson and would match Marvin's current predilection for Ikea furnishings: blonde, sleek, practical, beautiful and minimalist.

Well, she thought, as the taxi driver turned into a road of elegantly refurbished three-storey houses, she'd soon know.

Feeling strangely bereft as the cab pulled away, Joss stood on the wide white steps and studied the row of glistening brass name-plates. Oh! Oh, how long ago it seemed that she'd looked for Freddo's name-plate in Winterbrook. How long ago when she'd assumed her life was over — and discovered behind that flaking green door that it wasn't.

She rang the bell for "A. Lindstrom". No one answered. There was no clipped voice telling her to push a button or let herself in or wait or anything at all. Joss stood on the doorstep, the sun beating uncomfortably on her shoulders, waiting, wondering if there was something else she should do to gain access to these imposing-looking apartments.

The white door opened suddenly.

"Oh, good morning —" Joss dredged up a smile and some of her self-confidence. "Sorry — I think I may have rung the wrong doorbell. I'm looking for Anneka — Anneka Lindstrom."

"You've found her."

Joss was momentarily lost for words. The stocky middle-aged woman holding the door open was a Mrs Doubtfire double, with her coiled pepper and salt hair and her thick-rimmed tortoiseshell glasses, no discernible make-up, and her eminently sensible skirt and two-ply oatmeal jumper.

"Ooh — er . . ." Joss took a breath. "I mean, hello — lovely to meet you. I'm Jocelyn Benson."

"Mrs Benson." Anneka held out a very clean square hand. "Very nice to meet you, too. Please come in."

After the brief, businesslike handshake, Joss, still trying to equate the real Anneka with her imaginings, followed the sturdy legs up a short flight of gleaming white stairs with gleaming brass fixtures, through a large oak door and into a small square hallway: white-painted, pale wood-floored, uncluttered. Neat — but not as austere as she'd expected.

"Through here, Mrs Benson," Anneka instructed, almost barking the order.

This was more like it, Joss thought, looking around the living-room — all black and white and starkly expensive, with nothing out of place, no cushions or fripperies of any sort, and obscure angular monochrome things lined in parallel with the edges of other obscure angular monochrome things.

Hercule Poirot would have loved it.

"Can I get you a drink, Mrs Benson? Tea? Coffee?"

"A cup of tea would be lovely, thank you. Um — is Marvin here? Is he well?"

"Very well, now. He was strange and confused when he arrived here, but now he knows what is to happen and is his old self once more. He is out on the balcony reading the morning paper," Anneka said, still not smiling. "Maybe we should talk first, Mrs Benson?"

"Joss, please — and yes, of course." Joss followed Anneka into an equally intimidating starkly ordered white, polished chrome and black granite kitchen, realising that she'd rather delay things by talking to this forbidding woman, who had probably spent more time with Marvin than she had, than face her husband.

Anneka made tea with a ruthless businesslike briskness in businesslike white porcelain cups.

They sat at what Joss considered to be an evilly ugly black and chrome table.

"Your husband," Anneka said, "is a truly wonderful man. I want you to know this, Mrs Benson. I've admired him for many, many years. He should not have been treated so badly."

"I've never treated him badly!"

"By the company, Mrs Benson. They treated him shamefully. You, I feel, simply treated him wrongly. You, sadly, appeared not to know Marvin at all."

"Sorry?" Joss, wrong-footed, sipped her tea — which was black and too hot — and quickly put the cup down again. "I've been married to him for over thirty years, given him two children, been by his side —"

"That's not what I mean." Anneka took a mouthful of the scalding tea without flinching. "What I mean is that you clearly have never known of his dreams, or his hopes, or encouraged him in any way. Marvin has the

334

mind of a genius when it comes to business. He's a talented and intelligent man who has never been fully appreciated either at work or at home."

"Excuse me?" Joss, despite everything, felt obliged to defend herself. "How can you say that? What business is it of yours? I've been a model wife — I've done exactly what Marvin wanted all our life, I've never let him down socially, never argued, never put myself first, never —"

"Never loved him?" Anneka's face twitched into what might pass for a smile. "Never listened to his heart? Never shared his dreams?"

"I'll thank you not to discuss my personal relationship with my husband! And he didn't have a heart and he certainly didn't share any dreams with me! Look, Anneka, I'm sure you know one side of Marvin very well indeed — but that's simply the work side, and whatever he's chosen to tell you about our home life. You don't know anything about the real man. And I'm very grateful to you for looking after him now while he's obviously unhappy and confused, but —"

Anneka shrugged her large shoulders. "Marvin said you were a shadow," she said. "Someone who didn't have a spark. He was wrong to say that. It isn't true. Do you love him, Mrs Benson?"

"He's my husband."

"But do you love him?"

"I'm not prepared to discuss this with you. This isn't why you asked me here, surely?" Joss pushed back the spindly chair. "Please let me speak to Marvin, now. I need to know how he is."

"Very well — the balcony doors are on the far side of the sitting room." Anneka didn't move. "I will not interfere."

"Good," Joss said, heading out of the kitchen. "Please don't."

The double glass balcony doors were open, and Marvin, looking amazingly fit and relaxed and wearing a pair of beige chinos and a dark red polo shirt, neither of which she'd ever seen before, was reclining on a very trendy chair, reading the paper in the sun. A glass, a jug of orange juice and a crumb-speckled plate was on the table beside him. The city spread mistily away as far as the eye could see.

"Hello, Marvin. How are you?"

"Jocelyn . . ." Marvin folded his paper and squinted up at her. "Anneka said she'd phoned you. I told her it was a mistake but she — good God!"

Joss, who was wearing another of her gypsy skirts and vivid tops and the sequinned sandals, smiled. "This is my new look. Second-hand bo-ho. Lovely, isn't it?"

"No." Marvin eased himself up in the recliner. "You're far too old for that sort of get-up and your hair is a mess. And I really wish Anneka hadn't contacted you, but she insisted that you should know where I was. I said you wouldn't give a damn."

"How can you possibly have thought that? I was frantic. I've been worried sick. I've phoned the police and the hospitals and all your friends and searched everywhere and — where have you been, for heaven's sake?"

"Here."

336

"What? All the time?"

Marvin nodded.

"You bastard! You've put me through hell and —"

"Sit down, Jocelyn. Now you're here, we do need to talk."

"Too right." Joss perched on an opposite chair. "I think you owe me some sort of explanation, don't you? So, talk, Marvin — I'm all ears."

Marvin, retelling the story, said he had no idea why he'd suddenly felt impelled to leave the bungalow, The Close, Bagley-cum-Russet, with such urgency.

"It was as if my mind had suddenly been cleared of all the turmoil." He looked at Joss. "As if I'd been another person, living in some sort of shrouded half-life until that moment — then suddenly, the solution was there. Crystal clear. I didn't stop to question what I was feeling, or why, I just instinctively knew what I had to do."

"Which was to leave home and come here? To Anneka?"

"Yes. Sorry. Oh, not for coming here — but I suppose for not letting you know. Although, you'd changed so much, Jocelyn, since I-I lost my job . . . I felt you'd probably not even notice I'd gone. Again, I'm sorry."

"Don't apologise," Joss said. "You've never bothered to before — and it's far too late now. But yes, I did notice and yes, I did worry — and I desperately tried to find you — of course I didn't know about this little — er — romantic hide-away, did I?"

Marvin flinched. "It was never that, Jocelyn. That wasn't why I came here. I've never been unfaithful to you."

"You mean this and — and Anneka —" Joss swept her hands round the balcony, "— are simply business?"

Marvin shook his head. "Not now, no. Now it's much, much more — but when I first came here I wasn't aware of that. I just knew that this was where I had to be, that Anneka was the one person I needed to be with, the one person who understood me and what was happening to me. That she was the only person in the world who mattered — and who would know how to make the future bearable. I'm sorry, Jocelyn, I have no further explanation — but nor do I have any regrets."

Joss stared out across the rooftops, where the sun draped itself across the slates and tiles in a shawl of yellow mistiness. How very odd was that? Marvin preferring that huge, scary, self-assured, unfeminine woman to her? Was she insulted? Hurt, even? Joss probed her feelings and realised that what she actually felt was relief.

She looked at Marvin again. "So was that why you behaved as badly as you did? Oh — I mean — worse than usual, after you'd been made redundant? With all that sniping and griping and watching awful television programmes? Because you were pining for Anneka?"

Marvin sighed. "Maybe, yes — possibly. Probably. I don't know. All I know is that since I've been here I've felt like me again. I've been happy. Truly happy."

"Well, bully for you."

"Jocelyn — I know this is hurting you, but let me try to explain this. When I lost my job I was hurt and confused and frightened. *I* was frightened. I'd always been in control of everything in my life — and suddenly it had all gone. And you — you started to answer back and stand up to me and, for pity's sake, you even wanted to become the breadwinner and suddenly, suddenly I couldn't control you, either."

They sat and stared at one another in silence for a moment.

Joss traced the pattern of the floor tiles with the toe of her sandals. The sequins danced in the sun. "The day you left — did you sniff my bath oils?"

"*What?*"

"The bath essences that you found in my bathrobe pocket. Sukie Ambrose told me afterwards they might have — um — strange effects. She didn't know that you'd inhaled them, but I guessed you had and —"

"Tommy-rot and balderdash, Jocelyn! I've never heard such nonsense!"

"But you did sniff my bath stuff? After I'd left for my interview? You nosed around because the mid-day bath was something else I'd done out of routine — and you found those little bottles and opened them and —"

"I can't remember. Maybe I did — I've no idea. Nor do I care. All I know is that until that point I was living a half-life, and you'd walked out on me — saying you were going to find a job — then — yes, I found those stupid little scent bottles . . . and immediately I felt free and knew what I wanted."

Joss stared at him, this man who she'd lived with and slept beside for nearly all her adult life. This man who she now not only didn't love but probably didn't like very much.

"That's fine, Marvin. I'm glad you've found yourself, however you did it. Most people never do. I'll put the bungalow on the market, shall I?"

"What?" Marvin jerked his head round. "You mean you haven't come here to beg me to come home?"

"No! Why on earth would I?" Joss felt the power surge through her veins. "You're not the only one to get a life, Marvin. Despite everything you've done to me over the years, I've got a job — a really good job as a PA-cum-secretary — and I'll find a cheap flat to rent or something." She leaned towards him. "And last night I drove through Bagley in a pink Cadillac with my new boss and I danced the can-can."

"Now who's hallucinating?" Marvin went into a toned-down version of the purple vein-throbbing. "Don't tell such lies, Jocelyn. It's neither becoming nor necessary."

"I don't tell lies. Last night I found out what I've been missing. And I've enjoyed every minute of being without you. It was like being released from prison after a very, very long sentence."

"Jocelyn . . ." Marvin frowned. "This isn't what I was expecting —"

"No? Why? Did you think that I'd still be your victim? Marvin, I should have said this, done this, years ago. You've bullied me all our married life — made me miserable and guilty and unhappy. Now, as long as I know you're safe and well, I'm more than happy to live — really live — the rest of my life without you."

Marvin swallowed and turned his head away from her, staring out over the rooftops.

Oh, God. He wasn't crying was he?

"Marvin . . .?"

"You —" he snapped his head round, "— have stolen my buggering thunder! How dare you do this to me, Jocelyn? It was I who was leaving you! I was intending to tell you it was all over — how dare you — what? Jocelyn? Are you buggering laughing — at me?"

"Yes, sorry," Joss giggled. "Not very appropriate is it? But beautifully-timed. My moment of glory. I wish I'd caught it on camcorder. Now, what were we saying? Ah, yes — the bungalow — and how about a divorce while we're at it?"

Three hours later, on the Reading train, rattling away from London, Joss leaned back in her seat, smiling. It had all gone so much better than she'd even dared to dream it could.

Anneka had been called out to the balcony, and presumably after years of secretarial nannying, had made fresh orange juice all round and provided warm croissants and cherry jam, and Marvin had said please and thank you in a most unfamiliar way, and they'd smiled at one another almost soppily. And Joss, watching them, had felt no jealously, just a little sadness that they'd all wasted so much time before discovering what it was they really wanted.

And then Marvin had said that she must stay in the bungalow — and he'd be down to collect the remainder of his things, and he'd already drawn up plans for an equity release scheme to give them both a lump sum: Joss's to live on and his to invest in his and Anneka's new corporate head-hunting business.

And Joss had agreed to it all because there was no reason not to, and said she'd sign any papers, deal with any solicitors, do whatever was necessary to finalise everything to do with their marriage — she'd refused to use the word closure as it was one of Marvin's favourites — as long as Marvin made it his business to inform the children.

She'd used Anneka's phone to ring Valerie and tell her briefly what had happened and ask her, if it was at all possible, to find someone to pick her up at Reading station because she didn't want to hang around for the late evening Bagley bus or pay the huge taxi fare across Berkshire. Then she'd said goodbye to Anneka and Marvin, and been brave and happy enough to find her own way back to Paddington on the tube.

And now, she thought, smiling dreamily at the two women opposite her who had clearly been on a shopping spree, she'd go home and invite Val round for the evening — and her big, untidy husband too — and they'd have fish and chips from the paper and cheap wine and play loud music to celebrate.

She was still smiling when she emerged from Reading railway station's concourse into the low, warm late sunshine. What a perfect evening to start her new life . . .

"Joss!" Valerie Pridmore bustled towards her through the throng of coming and going passengers. "Over here, love! We've found a parking space!"

Joss beamed and they hugged one another and as they chatted at the same time about the wondrous events in Battersea, Joss wondered very briefly which one of Val's offspring's possibly illegal cars she'd be travelling home in — and didn't care. Just as long as she could get home — to her home . . . When she got her first pay-packet she'd paint the bungalow's rooms in bright colours, and buy rugs and cushions and big showy plants for the garden and . . .

She stopped abruptly.

The pink Cadillac was causing something of a kerfuffle, as was Freddo in his denim and leather and bling.

Joss swallowed her tears, and shook her head at Val who was laughing.

"I didn't have to use much persuasion," she chuckled. "Believe me, when I told him what was going on, he was all for driving all the way up to the Smoke to get you. And I came along for the ride — I know three's a crowd and all that — but I ain't going to get many opportunities to ride in a motor like that now, am I?"

And Joss hugged her fiercely, and whispered thank you, and said she was the best friend in the world.

Freddo, spotting them, leapt out of the car and ran towards them through the crowds. With a whoop of glee, he picked Joss up and swirled her round, and then kissed her. And she kissed him back. And it was simply amazing.

"Welcome home, Joss, duck," he said softly, holding her tightly against him, and looking at her with unconditional love. "Welcome home."

CHAPTER
TWENTY-FOUR

"This is almost like a perfect summer evening." Milla stretched her long legs, bare beneath her neat linen shirt dress, out in front of her. "And just what I need after a week of non-stop meetings and frantic buying and selling, relaxing in a peaceful garden. And it's so gloriously warm for April. I'm definitely not a winter person."

"Nor me." Sukie, less elegantly dressed in jeans and a T-shirt, slid down in the rickety wicker chair opposite Milla and raised her glass of Chardonnay. "Here's to May Day tomorrow — and long may this weather continue."

They chinked glasses, giggling because they were already on their second bottle and the overuse of the word "may" seemed really funny.

Pixies Laughter's garden was certainly coming into its own. The overgrown jasmine and honeysuckle and clematis formed lush canopied corners, and the orange blossom and lilacs were thrusting glossy leaves into every available nook and cranny. It was a dark green perfumed oasis, away from the world.

"On May Day," Milla lit a cigarette and blew smoke across the table, "Bo-Bo and I —"

"Go on . . ."

"No, it's stupid really."

"Talk about him, Milla — if it helps."

"Nothing helps, Sukes. The bugger jilted me and vanished without a trace — nothing can help that, how can it? But I still remember every damn silly little thing that we did together."

"Like on May Day? Was that special?"

"Very." Milla nodded dreamily. "We used to go to Oxford at dawn to see the sun rise. After we'd partied all night, we'd stand on Magdalen bridge with zillions of other people, listening to the choir — which made the hairs on your neck stand on end it was so ethereal — and welcoming in May morning. And then, because it hadn't been banned by the nanny state in those days, we'd stand on the parapet of the bridge and jump into the river!" Milla laughed. "Hand-in-hand. In full evening regalia! And the police would go mad and fish us out — and then we'd get sort of dry and go to the covered market for a full English . . ."

Sukie watched Milla's face, alive, her eyes sparkling. Oh, dear . . . The Bo-Bo memories were alive and kicking tonight.

"And, hand on heart, have you seriously never tried to contact him since he — er — defected?"

"Not since the early days, no," Milla refilled the glasses. "I guess he didn't want to be found. Big wall of silence from anyone who knew him. Changed his mobile phone and all other mode of contact. Sold his shares, sold his companies, left his flat. Vanished — like he'd never existed. Except, of course, he'll always

346

exist here and here . . ." she thumped her head and her heart. "Sad cow that I am. I hate him so much for what he did to me, and yet —"

Sukie said nothing. It would be the ideal opportunity to raise the issue of the long distance love potion, but she still couldn't do it — not morally or ethically — could she?

"Bo-Bo obviously changed his way of life and forgot about me — and I really think I should be moving on too," Milla reached to help herself from the bowl of nachos on the rickety wicker table, aiming wildly for the dips. "Maybe it's time to start anew. Maybe in May?"

They giggled again.

Sukie brushed nacho crumbs from her jeans. "What — you mean — er — with Derry?"

"Yes — no — God, Sukes, I haven't a clue! I've been thinking though that before long I should bite the bullet and stop running away from everything. It's been great living here, it's done what I always wanted it to do, and you've been a star — but I know I don't belong here. I'm a metro-chick. I need my city-fix. I can't live here for ever, can I?"

"No, I suppose not. But I'd really miss you — even though I never thought it would work out, us sharing."

"It's been great fun." Milla chinked her glass against Sukie's with a slightly unsteady hand. "And of course I wouldn't leave you in the lurch — unlike some. I'd wait until you found another suitable house-mate. But yes, I think I'll have to go sooner rather than later."

Sukie felt sick — and it had nothing to do with a surfeit of wine and nibbles.

"You mean — you, and Derry, would leave here and —?"

Milla shrugged. "Derry complicates things, Sukes. We're happy together, I think. But his heart is here, in Berkshire, as is his business — and I wouldn't ask him to give that up for me because I know he couldn't and wouldn't. I suppose we could carry on seeing one another even if I moved back to London, couldn't we?"

"Yes," Sukie said brightly, stabbing herself in the heart. "Yes, of course you could. It would probably work out really well Have you told him this yet?"

"No!" Milla rocked back on her chair. "It's all such a mess, really. I know I need to move on, but even though Derry and I haven't been together for long, he's shown me that there are lovely, funny, kind, decent men around — not to mention his fabulous physical attributes — and I certainly can't imagine him jilting anyone, can you?"

Sukie shook her head. She couldn't. She hoped fervently that this wasn't leading where she thought it might be. "You mean — you've — um — actually considered marrying him . . .?"

"Why not? He might be persuaded to start a joinery business in London, which would go down a storm in all those up-and-coming reclamation areas — and it would hugely piss off my parents."

Oh, God . . . Sukie buried herself in a handful of nachos she really wasn't sure she'd be able to swallow. Oh, sod morals and ethics! This was self-preservation!

348

She stared up at the sky, fragmented by the tall bushes, a pastel blur of blue and grey and pink and lilac. "Okay — what if — just supposing — suspending all disbelief for a moment, it was possible, and you had to choose between them? One man to spend the rest of your life with, to love forever? Which would it be? Derry or Bo-Bo?"

Milla didn't answer. She swirled the Chardonnay in her glass. Sukie couldn't bear it. She'd promised Chelsea she wouldn't try the love potion on Milla without her knowledge — but she simply couldn't stand this any longer.

She balanced her glass on the uneven table and stood up. "No — don't tell me. Don't answer that question. Please don't. And wait just a minute . . ."

And leaving Milla frowning, she rushed back into Pixies Laughter.

This was the only way to sort things out, wasn't it? Well, maybe not anyone's normal way, but it was what Cora would have done, wasn't it? Cora had left Pixies Laughter and its secrets hoping that Sukie might never discover them, but she had — and she'd used them well so far, hadn't she? Would anyone blame her if she now dabbled a bit on her own behalf? Oh, God — where had she put the little phial she'd used on Chelsea? Where? Which bag was it in? Oh, why had she had so many glasses of wine? Why couldn't she think straight? She'd just have to make some more stuff . . .

What was the potion rhyme? And the recipe? Could she remember either of them — or would she have to go and raid the work-basket again? Oh, no . . . the poem was there, but without the ingredients it was useless — and the ingredients were on that scrap of paper which was — where, exactly? Oh, bugger, bugger, bugger!

Trying to remember, her brain sticking on rosemary and coriander, knowing that Milla would lose interest at any moment, or worse still trot into the kitchen and say the name Sukie knew she didn't want to hear, she resorted to desperate measures. "Cora," she muttered out loud, "if this is even remotely the right thing to do — help me — please."

And suddenly she was calm. Everything was still. And the words she needed were there, in her brain, on her tongue, as easily remembered again as all her childhood nursery rhymes:

> So many lonely people
> So many broken hearts
> So many lovers torn apart
> So much loss and so much sorrow
> Can be cured maybe tomorrow
> No matter how many miles away
> Love can be brought home to stay
> Belief in the herbal powers
> Belief in the scented flowers
> Will bring true lovers back together
> To be in love for ever and ever
> With no more tears and no more pain
> Together, never to part again

* ★ ★

Shakily, Sukie rubbed her eyes. The list of ingredients and Cora's dire warning, was also imprinted indelibly in her head now . . .

Distance love potions are very effective but are considered powerful earth magic and should only be undertaken as a last resort to bring lovers together.

They should be used only if you are absolutely sure that the outcome is what you want because they may not be reversed.

To make: 3 drops ginger, 2 drops rosemary, 2 drops jasmine, 1 drop clove, 1 drop cinnamon, 1 pinch powdered mandrake root, mixed with almond oil. The potion should be rubbed on a pulse point, preferably the left wrist as this will take the infusion straight to the heart of one of the parted lovers while they visualise their beloved. They will, in every case, be united in everlasting love.

Frantically delving into the kitchen cupboard, Sukie emerged with the essences she needed and a bottle of base oil. Slopping everything everywhere, she rapidly measured and blended and knew that what she was doing was probably wrong, and would probably break her heart for ever.

But she had to know.

Milla blinked lazily as Sukie emerged from the back door. "I thought you'd gone for good. Left me — like everyone else seems to. Oh, what's that? Something nice to drink?"

Sukie sat down and put the phial on the table between them.

"No, it's part of the game."

"Oh, fantastic." Milla leaned forward, pushing her blonde hair behind her ears. "You mean we have to balance it on our foreheads without spilling it while reciting Shakespeare or something?"

Sukie frowned. "What sort of weird parties do you go to? No — it's much easier than that. This —" she took a deep breath, "— is a love potion."

"Oh, I adore it!" Milla screamed with laughter. "This gets better and better! Go on then, Sukes — what do we have to do?"

"You have to do what you were doing earlier. Imagine just one man, the one man you honestly, truthfully love with all your heart and want to spend the rest of your life with. Don't say anything though. Don't tell me his name. Just think it in your head — and imagine being with him in the most romantic setting possible."

"Okay, that's easy now — I think — and what do you do?"

"I," Sukie said, shaking the phial and removing the stopper, "just rub a few drops of this on your left wrist and massage it in — so that the love potion travels straight to your heart, while you're having your fantasy meeting with the love of your life."

Milla obediently laid her left arm on the wobbly table, wrist up. "I must remember this for my next board meeting. It'll liven it up no end . . . oh, no — sorry — right — I'm closing my eyes and I'm dreaming of —"

"Don't say it!"

"Sorry — okay. Go on then. I'm ready . . ."

With her heart thundering, and her mouth dry, Sukie sprinkled the potion on to Milla's slender wrist, massaging it gently into the pulse point at the base of her thumb.

There. It was done. Too late now. And if things didn't work out the way she wanted them to, well, it was better to know now than carry on hoping for the impossible, wasn't it?

"Is that it?" Milla opened her eyes and sniffed her wrist. "Oh, Sukes — I've no idea what's in this but I think you could give Chanel a bit of a battle. It's absolutely scrummy. So — what happens next? This is fun!"

Sukie smiled. "Well — now we just wait and see what happens."

Which, if it was anything like Chelsea and Nicky Hambly, would be precisely nothing.

The garden gate suddenly creaked in the soft twilight, making them both turn their heads.

"Hi." Derry grinned at them. "Hope you've left some wine in that bottle. I'm dying for a drink."

Sukie, knowing that she was going to disgrace herself, managed to haul herself to her feet. "Er — I'll go and get another glass — and another bottle. Oh, and some more bits to eat. No, you two stay there — I've had more than enough anyway."

And with stupid tears blurring her eyes, she blundered into the kitchen.

Half an hour later, the Barmy Cow offered scant solace. Sukie, huddled on a high stool at the corner of the bar with an untouched pint of shandy, miserably watched the customers laughing and chatting around her, as if they were miles away. The warm evening had somehow managed to penetrate the pub's grey fug, and even the dust had a bit of a sparkle.

Unable to stay in Pixies Laughter while Milla and Derry planned their happy ever after in the garden, she'd escaped as soon as possible, almost running through the darkening village, in the hope that Chelsea, who hadn't answered her mobile, would be in the pub.

Chelsea wasn't.

Everyone else seemed to be though, and all four Berkeley Boys were working like dervishes behind the bar, with Topsy, Edie and Rita sitting together at a corner table watching them avidly like groupies at a gig.

It only took one warm evening to drag the Bagleyites out in force. And tomorrow was a bank holiday, so no one had to worry about having an early night and — Sukie wanted to weep into her shandy. The long distance love potion gamble hadn't paid off — and she only had herself to blame, didn't she?

And this was the worst-ever torture. Not only was she forced to imagine what was happening at home, but she was surrounded by most of the mismatched couples her massage love potions had inadvertently brought together.

Even Joss Benson, looking splendid and carefree and glowing with happiness, was playing darts with Val Pridmore and her family and the glizty Freddo Fabian. And they were all laughing together — not, Sukie thought, half-heartedly sipping the flat top from her shandy, that she begrudged Joss her happiness. If anyone deserved to be freed from an unsuitable partner, it was Joss — and at least the Pixies Laughter potions had played no part in that little scenario, had they?

The can-can rehearsals had been a-buzz with the news that Joss and the vile Marvin had split for good, and that Joss had not only changed her image, but also her man — and was now an item with Freddo. It was the best gossip Bagley-cum-Russet had had for years.

"You all on your own, young Sukie?" Topsy had tip-tapped her way to the bar. "Nothing amiss, I hope? Nothing medical? Nothing I can help you with?"

"No, I'm fine," Sukie said quickly, hoping Dorchester hadn't given Topsy a full set of "Make Your Own Diagnoses For Friends and Family" manuals. "I thought Chelsea might be here . . ."

"Gorn to Newbury with her family. They was all in here earlier. Some do on at the Watermill."

Sukie sighed. Everyone was doing something with someone tonight, then. Oh, goody . . .

Topsy, pausing for a quick flirtatious word with Dorchester, peered at Sukie again. "You sure you're okay? You looks a bit peaky to me? You'll be all right for tomorrow, won't you? The wedding thingy at Fiddlesticks? Only it being our first public performance this year, we don't want to let Mr Fabian down, now do we?"

"I'll be fine, honestly," Sukie said, wondering if she could really face slapping on the showbiz smile and high-kicking her way across a makeshift stage to celebrate someone else's happy event. "Looking forward to it. Loads."

"Good gel. That's the spirit. Going to be another lovely day according to the weather forecast. Should draw in a smashing crowd."

"Great — I mean — oh, that's great."

Topsy nodded happily, and carrying three small glasses of something that could be port and lemon but probably wasn't, manoeuvred her way back to Rita and Edie.

Hilton leaned across the bar. "Something wrong with your shandy, Sukie? You don't seem to have touched it."

"No, I'm sure it's lovely . . . I'm just not in the mood."

"Let me add a bit more lemonade for you," Hilton wheezed across the bar. "Give it a bit more oomph."

Too morose to stop him, Sukie sat back as he dripped some flat lemonade into her already torpid glass. Like the other Berkeley Boys, Hilton had paid homage to the warmer weather by wearing an open-necked sports shirt in an unbecoming teal green. Sukie watched with alarm as some sort of medallion escaped from his wrinkly chest and hovered over the shandy.

"Hilton . . . your — um — locket thingy — it's dangling — oh, and it's open."

"Oh," Hilton seemed momentarily fuddled. "Right. Thank you. I'll just . . ."

Sukie peered at the heart-shaped locket and then at the glimpse of the heart-shaped photo it contained and felt sicker than ever.

God alive! Surely not . . .?

"Hilton — I'm not sure I want to know this — but why the hell have you got a picture of me round your neck?"

Hilton blushed and chuckled, and put down the lemonade bottle.

"It ain't you, young Sukie. Oh — what's the harm. Look —" his elderly fingers fumbled with the locket. "See — yes, it could be you, I'll grant you, but it ain't. It's your Auntie Cora when she was about your age."

Sukie gazed at the faded sepia picture. Of course, she could see it was Cora now. She'd seen enough early photos of Cora to recognise her great-aunt — but at first glance it really could have been her: same oval face, same thick dark hair, same pale eyes, same determined expression.

Hilton stroked the locket. "Cora was a beautiful girl, just like you, and I loved her with all my heart. But she never knew — not really. Her heart was broke when her young man was killed in the war and she never got over it. She couldn't care for me or anyone else after that. She never knew I had the photograph, mind. I took that on a village picnic in nineteen thirty-seven — and she gave me the locket, oh years since, when she was clearing out some junk for a village jumble sale. I kept it, probably wrong of me, and put the photo in . . ."

357

"And you've worn it ever since? And you've never looked at anyone else? Or loved anyone else?"

Hilton nodded his elderly cropped head, tenderly closing the locket. "Ah, that's about it, Sukie. And I'd thank you not to tell anyone if you don't mind. I've kept it a secret from people — except my brothers — for most of my life, and that's the way I'd like it to stay."

"Yes . . ." Sukie patted his hand. "Yes, of course. Oh, Hilton — why is love so bloody sad?"

"It ain't always, duck. Look at old Claridge and Savoy and Dorchester — they're like puppy dogs these days. And Ken and Tom have found each other — and even Bert's taken up with that Brenda woman from Hassocks what looks like Demis Roussos. And what about Mrs Benson and that there Freddo. Smashing bloke, he is, and makes her really happy. See — it ain't all doom and gloom."

"But — you're okay? Not being with anyone. Not being in love?"

"Bless your heart, duck, course I am. I've got me health and me pub and me brothers and me friends. And it was enough just to be around Cora and be her chum for all them years."

Feeling more miserable than ever, Sukie leaned her elbows on the bar, not giving a damn about the stickiness any more, while Hilton bustled off to serve more customers. Would it be enough for her? Being around Derry as his friend? Being able to see him and speak to him and laugh with him, but never, ever being able to love him?

No, she shook her head sadly, it wouldn't.

"Sukie!" Valerie Pridmore was waving from the other end of the bar. "Sukie!"

Not wanting to make up the numbers in the darts team, Sukie waved lethargically back.

"Sukie!" Val was beckoning furiously. "Come here a moment!"

Sighing, knowing she was going to be dragged into some interminable game of darts which she hated at the best of times, Sukie slid from her stool and forced her way through the Barmy Cow's clientele.

Val grabbed her arm and dragged her into a less-crowded corner. "Is Milla at home?"

"What? Yes . . ." Sukie frowned, not wanting to even think about the subtext. "Why?"

"Because there's a gentleman over there talking to Joss and Freddo who's looking for her. Says he thinks she lives in this village — not sure where. Says he's been trying to contact her. I didn't want to give him your address just in case he wasn't kosher. What do you think?"

"Probably someone she chatted up in a club and forgot about." Sukie shrugged. "Best not to tell him anything. Does he seem like a stalker?"

"He's bloody smashing if you ask me — well, not quite as much of a sex-pot as Derry, but a bit of all right. And posh as they come."

Oh, God, Sukie thought — it was probably the bald, toothless, much-married baronet who was Milla's mother's son-in-law of choice.

Wearily, she shook her head. "Don't tell him anything. Anyway, she's with Derry tonight. She wouldn't want a threesome."

"I wouldn't say no," Val cackled. "You have a quick look at him, Sukes. What do you reckon? Kick him out of bed, would you?"

Sukie, not caring one way or the other, peered through the fug.

Jesus!

The man talking to Joss and Freddo was the dead spit of a young Bryan Ferry — all sexy smoulder, with black hair falling over his forehead, and killer cheekbones. The face she'd seen in the photo beside Milla's bed.

He looked up and saw her looking at him. And smiled.

"Er," Sukie cleared her throat. "Um — you're looking for Milla, I understand? Would you possibly be —"

"Boswell Borthington." He grinned, showing a lot of very white teeth. "Sir Boswell Borthington to my enemies — Bo-Bo to my friends."

Buggering hell! Sukie closed her eyes. Bo-Bo! At last! And far, far too bloody late!

CHAPTER
TWENTY-FIVE

Fern and Timmy's wedding party was in full swing. Since midday, Fiddlesticks' vast village green — an anglophile's dream with its criss-crossing sandy pathways, plentiful weeping willow trees, and a rustic bridge over a fat, slow-running, brown-bedded stream — had been like Mardi Gras meets Notting Hill Carnival with extras. Or at least that's how it seemed to the villagers, out in force on May Day, ready to enjoy whatever delectations were offered as long as they were offered for free.

The weather forecast had proved accurate for once, and Fiddlesticks shimmered beneath a clear azure sky and wall-to-wall sunshine. Rafts of people had arrived from Hassocks and Bagley and Winterbrook — and even as far afield as Steeple Fritton, Lesser Fritton and Fritton Magna — to party the day and night away, with free food outside the Weasel and Bucket, and free drinks inside, and Petronella Bradley's Memory Lane Fairground providing traditional rides, and Flynn and Posy Malone's showmen's traction engine adding age-old glamour and excitement to the proceedings.

Joss, who had always dreaded Bank Holidays because they meant Marvin was at home all day and even more snippy than usual, couldn't quite get used to her sense of freedom, of feeling she was somehow bunking off school. Surely, there must be something grown-up she should be doing?

Well, yes, there was: later she'd be up there — she cast another nervous glance at the very professional stage, with its banks of lights and towering speakers and writhing black cables on the far side of the green — dancing the can-can as part of the evening's entertainment, but for now she was simply enjoying every minute of the party.

She was, she admitted to herself, pretty terrified of dancing in public for the first time, although she'd practised and practised the routines, rehearsing each evening until she felt she'd drop, and Sukie and Chelsea had been amazingly patient with her and helped her no end.

She really, really hoped she wouldn't let them down tonight.

Fern and Timmy, blissfully happy, nicely bronzed from their Indian Ocean honeymoon, and wearing full wedding regalia, had been circulating the green for sometime. Joss, her hand firmly in Freddo's, had congratulated them, and wondered, as she did every day since her return from Battersea, how much better life could get.

She'd started work at Retro Music and Theatre and absolutely adored it. She and Freddo were a team in every sense of the word, and however long it took the lawyers to disentangle her previous life, Joss simply

362

didn't care. She felt fulfilled, loved, appreciated and supremely happy.

Before long, she knew, she'd ask Freddo to leave his rather chaotic Winterbrook flat, and move into the bungalow with her, and she knew he would, like a shot — but not just yet. Self-assured she might be — but she'd never be pushy or overconfident. Anyway, there was all the time in the world for that: right now she was simply revelling in her new life; in her independence and the challenge of her job, and, more than anything, being in love and being loved in return.

"I'm just going to sort out a few things for the band," Freddo said to her, as they skirted the fairground with its old fashioned maroon and gold living wagons and galloping horses circling in the sun. "They should be here shortly. Would you like to come with me — or are you okay here, duck?"

Joss nodded. "I've just seen Val and her family over there. I'm sure she'll keep me entertained." She touched his face. "It's okay, Freddo. Really. We don't have to be joined at the hip. I know you have work to do today — and I'm not going anywhere."

He grinned at her. "You'd better not. I just don't want you to think — worry — that I don't want to be with you. I do. Always. All the time."

"Me too." Joss smiled back at him. "And we will be, won't we?"

Goodness! Had she really said that? How very forward of her!

Freddo kissed her. "As soon as it's legally possible to make you Mrs Fabian, yes. Joss Fabian . . ." He pondered for a moment. "Sounds like a rock star, don't it, duck?"

"It sounds wonderful," Joss said giddily, not sure that she understood. "And is that — are you —?"

"Asking you to marry me? Yes . . ." Freddo laughed. "Bugger it, Joss — I was planning to do it all romantic like tonight, with moonlight and champagne and roses. Sorry."

"Don't ever, ever say sorry." Joss hugged him. "That's the most romantic proposal anyone could ever have."

Freddo pulled away slightly, holding her hands in his, and looked at her. "You — you are going to say yes, aren't you?"

Joss shrugged. "Oh, I don't know . . . Do I really want to marry you? Marry anyone again? The first time round wasn't that great, was it? And as I'm still married anyway, it's probably not legal, so —"

She stared at his face. The tanned leathery lines had practically puckered and his eyes were bleak. He looked totally woebegone. Freddo was absolutely useless at hiding his emotions. Deviousness had passed him by — thank goodness.

She laughed. "Of course I'm saying yes! Yes! Yes! Yes!" She practically danced on the spot. "Er — YES!"

"Jesus!" Freddo exhaled, sweeping her up into his arms and almost dancing with her, kissing her again and again. "Thank God for that. Blimey, duck — that was the worst moment of my life there. Oh, blimey! We're going to be so blooming happy, aren't we?"

Joss nodded, unable to speak, then she grabbed his hand and shoving through the crowds, hurried him towards the rustic bridge.

Delving into her bag — not the neat and safe bag matching her previous life, but the sloppy, floppy patchwork affair of sequins and glitter — she dragged out her wedding ring and sapphire and diamond engagement ring from Marvin. She'd taken them off on the train home from London, and had intended to dump them in the recycling box but had forgotten.

With an overarm throw that Freddie Flintoff would have been delighted to claim for his own, she hurled them through the air in a glittering arc. They landed several yards away in the fat brown stream with a satisfying splash, hovering on the surface for a nanosecond, before sinking forever into the peaty bed.

"There," she sighed happily. "End of an era."

"You're one heck of a woman." Freddo grinned at her. "And that little bauble was pretty sophisticated — which might make this . . ." he dragged a box from the back pocket of his tattered Levis, "look a bit tawdry in comparison. But —" he dropped down on one knee, to the delight of the watching hordes, "— I'll be the proudest man in the world if you'll accept it. Joss — I love you with all my heart — and I always will."

Joss looked at the massively ostentatious square pink bling ring and squealed with delight. "Oh! It's gorgeous! Oh, thank you! I love it! And —" she blinked away a tear, "— I love you, too."

Freddo stood up again, to rousing cheers, and slid the ring on to Joss's finger.

Then, oblivious to the noise and the crowds, they simply melted into one another's arms.

"Hurry up," Chelsea said crossly. "I want to get to Fiddlesticks and enjoy at least some of the party before we have to go on stage."

"You can't dance the can-can bladdered," Sukie said, looking up from the big theatrical boxes on the living-room floor, "so the later we are the better. And there'll be plenty of time afterwards for drinking. Now — is that the lot? Ten of dresses, petticoats, stockings, suspenders, garters, knickers, shoes, chokers, gloves, ostrich feathers — what have I forgotten?"

"A sense of humour?" Chelsea squatted beside her. "Oh, shit Sukes, look, I know how you feel, but —"

"No you don't," Sukie said quickly, fastening the cases. "You can't possibly know how I feel — but thanks for trying."

Chelsea hugged her. "And you've no idea what happened? What's happening? Where they've gone?"

"No." Sukie stood up and hauled the boxes across the floor. Ronald, who had been sewing all night like the Tailor of Gloucester's mice on the new dancers' costumes, had delivered them all only half an hour earlier. "Could you grab one of these, please? If they won't all fit in the boot we can get at least one on the back seat."

Chelsea, with a final sympathetic look, grabbed the nearest box and dragged it out into the hot May afternoon.

366

Sukie, checking her make-up in the mirror because she doubted if there'd be any facilities in Fiddlesticks apart from the loos in the pub which was bound to be chock-a-block, was amazed that she managed to look passably human. Surprising, she thought, what a bit of slap can do to hide a terminally broken heart.

Last night, after the mad excitement of discovering Bo-Bo in the Barmy Cow, and deciding that the best thing to do was to ring Milla herself and break the news, life had become a bit of a blur.

Milla, who had probably been romping with Derry, simply hadn't believed her.

Then Sukie had handed her mobile to Bo-Bo and, like the rest of the pub, had eavesdropped as he'd convinced a squawking Milla that it was indeed he, and they needed to meet.

Sukie, who really hadn't thought past the fact that Bo-Bo was there — magically, mysteriously — in Bagley-cum-Russet, had reclaimed her mobile and looked at him.

"So? Does she want to see you?"

"She does," Bo-Bo had said in his gloriously plummy voice. "Thank the lord — it's far more than I deserve. She say there's something she needs to tell me, but not, it appears, on her home ground."

Sukie could understand this. Best not entertain your old lover while your new one was probably swinging naked from the chandeliers.

"We're meeting, in a rather cloak and dagger fashion," Bo-Bo had said, "by the Celtic cross in half an hour. Milla informs me that you will give me directions."

So Sukie had, and then spent the waiting time as any normal house-mate and concerned chum would do, pumping him for every bit of information she could squeeze from him.

Bo-Bo was a good talker. He seemed more than happy to unburden himself.

The jilting, it appeared, was down to Milla's mother. Bo-Bo, already feeling pressurised by the threatened presence of eighteen million wedding guests and exclusive media coverage by *Celeb Watcher* magazine, had finally flunked it after Milla's mother had insisted he must stand up in the family chapel and sing all ninety-three verses of the family song. In Latin. Well — no, he'd admitted, it wasn't quite that bad, but that's what it seemed like.

"She's very scary," he'd confided over a pint of shandy. "I'm used to running various companies, and having people jump when I raise my eyebrows, but she absolutely terrified me. So did the wedding. Not, you understand, the marriage. I adored Milla. I always have and always will. I truly wanted to marry her. But I simply couldn't cope with the bloody three ring circus it was turning into."

"But," Sukie had had one eye on the clock, wanting to gain as much info as possible in the time, "surely you told Milla this?"

"Yes. And she understood, I think. But she was just swept along on the whole tidal wave of big, big wedding preparations and operations and military planning — and she didn't want to upset her mother."

"But — just running away . . .?" Sukie had frowned. "That was the coward's way out, surely?"

"Yes, I suppose it was. But I didn't know what else to do. And I didn't just run away from the wedding." Bo-Bo had examined several small furry things floating in his shandy with interest. "Once I knew I couldn't go through with the whole fiasco, and knew Milla simply couldn't face telling her parents that we'd like a quiet affair, I decided to run away from everything."

Sukie had kindly fished the floating things out of his shandy with the edge of a beer mat.

"No doubt Milla has told you that I sold my companies, sold my shares, sold everything — and vanished. I hated myself for hurting her, loathed myself for leaving her — and maybe I was weak — but she knew how much I wanted her. Will always want her. I just didn't want her family and all the trappings. So — I went to Greece. Not mainland Greece, a small island where no one knew me and —"

"You started working in a bar overlooking the Aegean," Sukie had sighed, "and turned into a male version of *Shirley Valentine*. And now you spend your days barefooted in shorts serving retsina to tourists and no one knows you're a Sir and a multi-millionaire."

Bo-Bo had looked askance over the top of the shandy. "Good God, no. I bought a couple of hotels, one or two apartment blocks, a restaurant, several villas — I'm a sort of Greek island package holiday king now."

"Oh." Sukie had been a bit disillusioned by this. "And you never wanted to get in touch with Milla and ask her to join you."

"Of course I did. I never stopped thinking about her, loving her, but how could I expect her to ever forgive me after what I'd done? I'd heaped the worst sort of humiliation on her head. I'd insulted her. Ruined her. I knew she'd hate me. I just tried to live my new life without her — but I couldn't."

Sukie had leaned forward crossing her fingers. "So why, after all this time — are you here tonight? How come you're in this backwater village, miles from your Greek idyll? Why?"

"Because —" Bo-Bo pushed his shandy away, "— I had urgent business in the UK for the first time since I left. I told myself I wouldn't try to find Milla because I knew she'd have married someone who really deserved her, and I knew my heart would break even more — but I couldn't let it rest. Everywhere I went I just met a brick wall of silence. No one, even if they knew anything, was prepared to tell me. And then —"

"And then?" Sukie had held her breath.

"And then tonight, I did the decent thing at last. I just had this really, really strange feeling that Milla was close. That she wanted to see me . . ."

Ooooh! Sukie had to sit on her hands to stop herself leaping up and punching the air.

"So, I called on her parents."

"Bloody hell! That was brave."

"About time I was brave," Bo-Bo said sadly. "Anyway, her mother used the worst language I've ever heard in my life. I didn't even understand some of the Anglo-Saxon epithets — but the vitriol was all too clear. Piss off you fucking bastard is much the same in any tongue, isn't it?"

"Yes, I suppose it is. But —"

"Just when I was feeling my absolute worst, and getting into my car, and thinking I'd have to go back to Greece without her and live without her for the rest of my life, her father — who is also terrified of her mother, by the way — scurried out of the orangery and whispered that Milla was living in Berkshire, in Bagley-cum-Russet — but he couldn't remember the address. Then he scuttled off again — and well, here I am . . ."

"Here you are," Sukie had said happily.

"Do you think she will ever, ever begin to forgive me?"

"She might — if you beg her to. A lot. And grovel your heart out. And if you're going to meet her by the Celtic cross you'd better be going — oh, and tell her absolutely everything that you've told me — but more than that — tell her you love her, okay?"

And Bo-Bo had said okay and thank you and kissed her cheek and left.

And Sukie, feeling on top of the world, had finished her shandy — thanked Cora with all her heart — and skipped all the way back to Pixies Laughter.

Derry, she was sure, would be devastated at Milla's defection — and would need comforting and consoling. He'd probably be sitting sadly in the garden, nursing the wine and the nachos and be in desperate need of a friendly shoulder . . .

He wasn't.

Pixies Laughter was empty. Deserted. There were items of Milla's clothing trailing from her bedroom down the twisty staircase, a suitcase, half-packed, left on the landing and a note:

Dearest Sukes,

You're magic! Thank you! I think I already knew what I was going to do — but in the end the choice was made for me, wasn't it? I'm moving out sooner rather than later — hope that's okay. I 'll miss you loads. Will be in touch — and arrange for someone to collect the rest of my stuff. Have left a cheque in my room to cover my rent and then some. Thank you again a googol times for the love potion. You've changed my life — and now I'll always be with the right man — the man I love.

Hugs and kisses
Milla xxxx

"Which one?" Sukie had howled at the dung-heap kitchen, with its mess of potions and essences and empty wine bottles and crushed nachos and curdled sour cream. "Which bloody one?"

CHAPTER
TWENTY-SIX

Topsy was on pins, driving the Bagley-cum-Russet can-can troupe mad. They were nervous enough anyway, fidgeting with their stocking tops, tucking themselves into the big white frilly modesty knickers, fastening ostrich feathers in each other's hair.

As the light faded, the JB Roadshow had already performed for a sensational soul-filled hour, and were now sitting on the edge of the stage, drinking beer, smoking, laughing and relaxing as the can-can troupe prepared for their show.

Sukie, feeling numb, had spent the afternoon scouring the crowd for Derry; had pushed in and out of the Weasel and Bucket, searching; had less-than-casually questioned all the Bagleyites, Fern and Timmy, Amber and Lewis and Jem, the Kylies, both sets of Blessing families, Gwyneth and her dog, Pike, and Big Ida and Val Pridmore and Joss and Freddo — and even Zillah Flanagan, Lewis's mother, who had been on tour with the JB Roadshow after marrying their bass player, the divine Clancy Tavistock, the previous autumn.

None of them it seemed, had set eyes on Derry all day.

And his phone was switched off. And Winterbrook Joinery, closed for the Bank Holiday, simply had his voice on the answerphone. Sukie had rung it innumerable times, just to listen to him, and cry.

Now she leaned against the side of the stage in the falling darkness, staring out at the milling sea of mostly-familiar faces, hundreds and hundreds of them, all crowding though the fairground, and picnicking by the stream, knowing that Derry and Milla must be somewhere, in some small love-nest, celebrating being together forever.

Bo-Bo must have failed in his pursuit, as she'd feared he would. He was probably flying back to his Greek island paradise right now feeling as heartbroken and awful as she did.

Of course she realised now, Milla must have written that note the minute Sukie had dashed off to the Barmy Cow; the moment Derry had arrived in answer to the love potion's magical pull; before Bo-Bo had tracked her down. Even as Bo-Bo and Milla were speaking on the phone, the decision had already been made. Milla must have known she was going to choose Derry; must have known that Bo-Bo had appeared just that bit too late; must have known what she was going to tell him at the meeting by the Celtic cross . . .

Sukie sighed.

Ah, well — she'd only got herself to blame. She'd been warned about dabbling with the love potions, hadn't she? She'd taken the risk — and would reap the heartbreaking consequences for the rest of her life.

374

"Right gels!" Topsy clapped her hands. "Let's have you backstage. Come along! Quickly! The band is ready to start. They're happy with the Offenbach — and it should be absolutely sensational with live music. Are we all ready?"

"Ready as I'll ever be." Sukie peeled herself away from the stage. "Oh, don't frown, Topsy. We'll be brilliant."

Once behind the canvas backdrop, Chelsea and Sukie exchanged secret doubtful glances. The rehearsals with the ten of them had been very curate's egg. Still, what they lacked in Moulin Rouge expertise, they made up for in whooping, screaming enthusiasm and now — all in their red and black dresses, with the masses of petticoats, and the dancing ostrich feathers in their hair — they certainly looked the part.

"Sukie . . ." Joss edged along the line and squeezed her hand. "Thank you. This is something I've longed to do for — oh, I don't know how long. My life has changed completely because of you. I've no idea what you put in your potions — or even if they really played any part in this — but whatever you did for me, I'll be forever grateful."

And Sukie had hugged Joss and then the JB Roadshow had roared into the familiar opening bars of Orpheus and the crowd had started screaming encouragement — and they were on.

Running on to the stage to tumultuous applause, they linked arms, and flounced skirts, and flashed their knickers, and kicked and skipped and circled and kicked some more. Almost able to forget her misery,

375

Sukie was swept along by the noisy, dizzying, colourful excitement. Giddily she thought the live band transformed them from some amateur troupe in a village hall into real, live Parisian Bluebell girls — glamorous and talented.

The routines were inch perfect, even with ten of them no one collided with anyone else, and no one missed a beat.

Again, almost able to forget that her heart was broken, Sukie linked with Chelsea, circled, kicked, flounced, screamed and cartwheeled.

The JB Roadshow, playing their socks off, clearly loved every minute of it, and Joss was absolutely amazing. Then they were coming towards the finale, with the final running, and the sexy shimmying of skirts and petticoats over their heads, back, then front, tantalising and teasing, then one final flourish — one last yell — and into the splits.

The applause was astounding. Shakily, out of breath, Sukie could see a blur of faces, all whistling, and calling. It had been mind-blowing. The dancers, way up in the stratosphere, scrambled to their feet and hugged one another with exhausted glee.

"Wonderful gels." Topsy wiped away a tear. "Wonderful; the band loved it — and they want to do another show in an hour or so. After the Gunpowder Plot have done their firework display. Is that okay with you all?"

And everyone, panting and beaming, nodded.

As the JB Roadshow slammed into another superb soul selection and everyone started dancing on the green, and Joss and Freddo sneaked away into the shadows, Chelsea grabbed Sukie's arm.

"I need a drink," she puffed. "Bet there's a queue a mile long in the pub. I'm going to sneak some beer from the band's cool box backstage. Coming?"

Why not? She'd scrumped apples with Chelsea as a child, pinching a can of beer wasn't so different was it?

The music thrummed into her body as she followed Chelsea round the back of the stage, amid cases and boxes and huge rolls of cables. Several couples were hidden in the longer grass and Sukie muttered her apologies as she stumbled over bits of semi-naked flesh in the search for the cool box.

"Here! Got it! Catch!" Chelsea yelled above the band.

Sukie caught.

They'd just opened ice-cold cans of beer with a delicious fizz of froth, just lifted them to their parched mouths, when someone tramped round the side of the stage.

"What are you doing?" a voice barked. "You two! Yes — you!"

They stopped. A policeman loomed out of the darkness. Shit, Sukie thought, heartbroken and arrested all in the same twenty-four hours. How much better could life get?

His eyes fastened on their jacked-up bosoms and fishnet stockings and gaudy frocks and he grinned — then stopped, looking puzzled. "Chelsea? Chelsea Hopkins? And Sukie Ambrose? Bloody hell! I'd've thought you'd have been miles away from here by now!

Bugger me — were you dancing? Was that really you up there? You were really, really hot!"

Oh, great, Sukie thought, a sex-mad policeman — and one who scarily knew their names.

She peered at him. Tall, thin, dark . . .

He didn't move. "I don't believe this . . . Chelsea, I doubt if you'll remember me, but I had such a crush on you at school. I was so scared that you'd mess me about, I always blanked you. I was such a prat! I've never found anyone to take your place . . ."

Chelsea was making a gagging noise.

"Jesus Christ!" Sukie shook her head. "Nicky Hambly! I thought you were in the RAF — still swapping one uniformed job for another must be fairly easy. Chelsea — it's —"

But Chelsea clearly didn't need any introduction. She and Nicky stared dopily at one another for a split-second, then with a whoop of laughter and holding hands, scampered giggling away into the dark shadows.

Sukie, feeling about as unnecessary as it was possible to get, picked up Chelsea's discarded drink, and wandered miserably out to the front of the stage again.

The band, strutting and swaying and belting out a Lee Dorsey classic, had everyone on their feet.

Oh, God, Sukie thought, skirting the enclosure where Amber's Corrie-named goats had been safely penned for the evening, and sitting on a rustic bench in the darkness, how was it possible to feel this lonely in the midst of all this jollity and noise and millions of happy people? How had she managed to magic up

378

romances for her best friends, several acquaintances, and a few for people who didn't even know she'd done it — and feel this bloody awful herself?

She'd just have to concentrate on her career now, immerse herself in work, not give herself time to think about the what-might-have-been with Derry. She'd definitely tell Jennifer as soon as possible that she wanted to break away from Beauty's Blessings and fly solo with the aromatherapy business and work at least twenty hours a day. Jennifer would probably be okay about it — eventually — as long as she could take some commission for any appointments made via the salon or something. Yes, it would be okay.

And whatever the rights and wrongs of the love potions, she knew she'd continue to use the storehouse of garden plants in Pixies Laughter for her massage oils. Cora's legacy would not be wasted. Sukie would carry on the tradition — making people happy in her own earth-magic fashion.

Sukie nodded sadly in the darkness. If only she could be happy, too . . .

"Shove up."

She turned her head.

Derry grinned at her. "Budge up a bit. Your petticoats should have a seat all of their own."

She swallowed, not looking at him, not wanting to see Milla, all glowing, behind him.

"Oh, and beer —" Squeezing on to the bench, Derry removed one of the cans from her fingers. "How brilliant is that. The most beautiful girl in the world, dressed up in an outfit that would stir a eunuch, and providing cold beer. Thank you God."

She smiled. He always made her smile.

"You were awesome. On stage. I was so proud of you. And aren't you speaking to me?"

She nodded. "Yes, of course. And thank you — I-I didn't know you were here."

"Got here just in time for your show. Stood there, beaming like an idiot, waiting for you to come off so I could tell you how brilliant you were, and then you and Chelsea just vanished."

She sipped her beer. "Is Milla here?"

"No, why would she be? She left you a note, didn't she?"

Sukie nodded again. "It didn't say much . . . It didn't have to."

"No, I suppose not. Sukie — why are we talking to one another as though we've only just been introduced?"

"Are we? Oh, sod it, Derry — you know why!"

"No I don't. I got here as soon as I could. I wasn't going to miss your show. I had to leave Bo-Bo's hire car at the airport, and get all Milla's junk in my jeep, and was running backwards and forwards and — what?"

"Milla and Bo-Bo have gone to the airport? Milla and *Bo-Bo*? Together?"

"Yes, that's what I've just said. Milla said she'd left you a note to explain. She wanted to leave her car at Reading station so her company's fleet manager could collect it, and Bo-Bo — bloody stupid name that is, nice bloke though — only had a little two-seater. And

380

Milla had so much stuff — so I volunteered to be an extra driver with the jeep and run everyone everywhere, and make as many journeys as was possible to get them to Heathrow in time for their flight out to Greece. So I eventually left her and Bo-Bo at the airport, which was neat really — sort of full circle — seeing as that's where we'd met. Anyway, it took all night and most of the day and I had to get a couple of hours sleep but —"

Sukie clapped her hand over his mouth. "Stop! So Milla went with Bo-Bo? Not you?"

"No." Derry gently removed her hand, but held it, stroking her fingers. "Not with me. I'm here. With you. Last night, when I came round to the cottage, I'd come to tell Milla it was all over. Which I did. I felt bad about it, but it had to be done. And she was okay about it really, and then you phoned about Bo-Bo. And where I'd been planning to rush to the Barmy Cow and join you in whatever dubious alcoholic beverage the Berkeley Boys could conjure up for the occasion, Milla said she was going to meet Bo-Bo, and she loved him, and she intended to be with him — and would I help her . . . So I did."

"Because you're a nice bloke?"

"Yes, precisely." Derry grinned. "And because she said she'd leave you a note. And because I liked her, but mainly because I wanted to get her and bloody Bo-Bo out of the way so that I really could have some space and time to be with you — which is something I've wanted for — oh, God — since the day I woke up in your bed."

Sukie grinned. "That sounds wrong, somehow."

"Sounds pretty good to me." Derry removed the beer can from her other hand and kissed her. "And if I've just made one huge mistake — please tell me and I'll go away and quietly hang myself from one of those conveniently placed willow trees."

"You've just made one huge mistake."

"What? Bugger — and I haven't got any stout rope."

They grinned at one another, then Sukie wriggled against him and kissed him again. And again, just in case the first time had been a fantasy.

"I used a love potion on Milla and Bo-Bo," she said softly. "And I so wanted to on you — but I didn't."

"Would have been a complete waste." Derry traced the outline of her lips with his forefinger. "I was already way under your spell. However —" he grinned at her, "— I did use one on you — just in case."

"What?" She stared at him. "When?"

"That afternoon when we were in the garden. When the bunion ladies arrived. I'd made the tea, remember? In a pot?"

She nodded.

"And I thought it might just help things along a bit — so I did the forget-me-not and scarlet pimpernel one — because it was quick and I could find the right essences in the cupboard and I remembered the rhyme."

Sukie punched him. "Sneaky sod! Go on then — remind me."

"*Pimpernel red and forget-me-not blue; Together make love's dreams come true.*" Derry laughed. "No, sorry — but the poetry's bloody awful, isn't it? The effect, however, hopefully, wasn't."

"The bunion ladies may have benefited —" Sukie snuggled even closer, "— but it was wasted on me, too. I was already in love."

"Oh, dear — who's the fortunate bloke? Anyone I know?"

"Nah. Just some gorgeously sexy and very talented joiner from Winterbrook who one day — soon, I hope — might just be moving into Pixies Laughter with me."

"Lucky sod." Derry kissed her slowly. "Bet he can't wait."

"I hope not." Sukie bunched her skirts together as he pulled her on to his lap. She slid her arms round his neck. "And somehow I don't think we'll be needing any of Cora's love potions to help things along, do you?"

"Absolutely, definitely not," Derry said softly, kissing her again. "We'll never need any outside influences, Sukes. I reckon we've got more than enough magic of our own . . ."

Also available in ISIS Large Print:

Welcome to the Real World

Carole Matthews

Pub singer Fern Kendal has the voice of an angel but her talent is wasted. Like millions of others, all she needs is a break, but in the real world she knows that'll never happen.

Evan David's exquisite tones have enthralled opera buffs throughout the world. People pander to his every need. But what Evan needs now is a break — from it all.

When Fern is picked to be Evan's PA their two worlds collide. Neither one is prepared for the effect they will have on each other. For something happens when they are together — and it's more than just music . . .

ISBN 978-0-7531-7794-5 (hb)
ISBN 978-0-7531-7795-2 (pb)

Flatmates

Chris Manby

Have you ever shared a flat with your so-called friends? Do you remember squabbling over phone bills, ignoring cleaning rotas and poisoning the pesto?

Welcome to 67 Artesia Road — the place where Kerry fantasises about her handsome, but homosexual, boss. Where Fiona can't bear to leave her wayward fiancé. And Linzi juggles men and work like they were disposable contact lenses.

But nothing can prepare them for the arrival of gorgeous Gaetano, Linzi's latest boyfriend. Will they manage to remain friends, let alone flatmates . . . ?

ISBN 978-0-7531-7730-3 (hb)
ISBN 978-0-7531-7731-0 (pb)